DISCARDED

Praise for

The Crimson Empire Series

"This is my favorite kind of fantasy—alternatively irreverent and brutal, with a cast of wonderfully scarred and nasty people. Any fans of Steven Erikson, Mark Lawrence, or Joe Abercrombie will love *A Crown for Cold Silver*; I've just finished it, and I'm already eager for more."
—Django Wexler

"Zosia and her Five Villains are as fun as they are twisted."
—David Dalglish

"An epic fantasy that will surprise you. When was the last time you read one of those? Marshall deftly sets up and subverts expectations at every turn. If you think you know what's coming, think again."
—Kameron Hurley

"Brimming with imagination and invention...Fabulous!"
—John Gwynne

"Exceptional writing, middle-aged warrior heroine, and organically infused gender nonconformity make this fantasy epic a first-rate trail-blazer...splendid storytelling, wry humor, and unresolved intrigue."
—*Publishers Weekly* (starred review)

"This brawny revenge fantasy feels like a Tarantino movie: a hugely entertaining mix of adventure and comedy, punctuated by moments of darkness, with clever dialogue and explosive set pieces...A pure joy to read."
—*Booklist* (starred review)

"This sweeping adventure is a first from Marshall (apparently a pseudonym of an acclaimed author) and delivers a colorful cast. It sparkles with details that make a fantasy world come alive: echoes of cultures jumbled together in new ways, drug addicts who allow poisonous insects to sting them for a high, and unusual gender roles and depictions." —*Library Journal* (starred review)

"Marshall's rich cast of characters...are driven by passion, duty, and humanizing, terrifying flaws...*A Crown for Cold Silver* drags epic fantasy through the mud—but it does so with wit, wonder and wisdom." —*NPR Books* (starred review)

"This lusty debut will have you gasping in one breath and laughing in the next with its cast of multicultural characters, gender-bending soldiers, same-sex coupled kings and warrior women of all ages who throw themselves into the fray. By the latter half of the novel, you realize Marshall is playing a long, glorious game."
—*Washington Post*

"A complex, mold-breaking fantasy protagonist."
—*B&N Sci-Fi & Fantasy Blog*

"Full of bloody battles, intimidating monsters and incledible feats, fans of thoughtful storytelling, tough-as-nails heroines, and absorbing fantasy will love this novel." —*RT Book Reviews*

"I'm looking forward to [seeing] more of this complicated and dark world." —*Philadelphia Free Press*

A
WAR
in
CRIMSON
EMBERS

By Alex Marshall

The Crimson Empire

A Crown for Cold Silver
A Blade of Black Steel
A War in Crimson Embers

A WAR

in

CRIMSON EMBERS

ALEX MARSHALL

www.orbitbooks.net

Copyright © 2017 by Alex Marshall
Excerpt from *The Two of Swords: Volume One* copyright © 2015 by K. J. Parker
Excerpt from *Soul of the World* copyright © 2017 by David Mealing

Author photograph by Molly Tanzer
Cover design by Lisa Marie Pompilio
Map design by Tim Paul
Cover copyright © 2017 by Hachette Book Group, Inc.

Orbit
Hachette Book Group
1290 Avenue of the Americas
New York, NY 10104
orbitbooks.net

Originally published in hardcover and ebook by Orbit in December 2017.

First Paperback Edition: June 2018

Orbit is an imprint of Hachette Book Group.
The Orbit name and logo are trademarks of Little, Brown Book Group Limited.

The publisher is not responsible for websites (or their content) that are not owned by the publisher.

The Hachette Speakers Bureau provides a wide range of authors for speaking events. To find out more, go to www.hachettespeakersbureau.com or call (866) 376-6591.

The epigraph on p. 1 was written by Pak Hyogwan (1781–1880). The translation is from *The Book of Korean Shijo*, by Kevin O'Rourke, published by the Harvard University Asia Center, Cambridge, Massachusetts, in 2002. Copyright © 2002 by the President and Fellows of Harvard College. Used with permission of the Harvard University Asia Center.

Library of Congress Cataloging-in-Publication Data

Names: Marshall, Alex (Novelist), author.
Title: A war in crimson embers / Alex Marshall.
Description: First edition. | New York: Orbit, 2017. | Series: Crimson empire; 3
Identifiers: LCCN 2017023271 | ISBN 9780316340724 (hardback) | ISBN 9780316340717 (trade paperback) | ISBN 9781478915348 (downloadable audio book) | ISBN 9780316340748 (ebook)
Subjects: LCSH: Warriors—Fiction. | BISAC: FICTION / Fantasy / Epic. | FICTION / Action & Adventure. | FICTION / Fantasy / Historical. | GSAFD: Fantasy fiction.
Classification: LCC PS3602.U42 W37 2017 | DDC 813/.6—dc23
LC record available at https://lccn.loc.gov/2017023271

ISBNs: 978-0-316-34071-7 (paperback), 978-0-316-34072-4 (hardcover), 978-0-316-34074-8 (ebook)

Printed in the United States of America

LSC-C

10 9 8 7 6 5 4 3 2 1

For Shandra

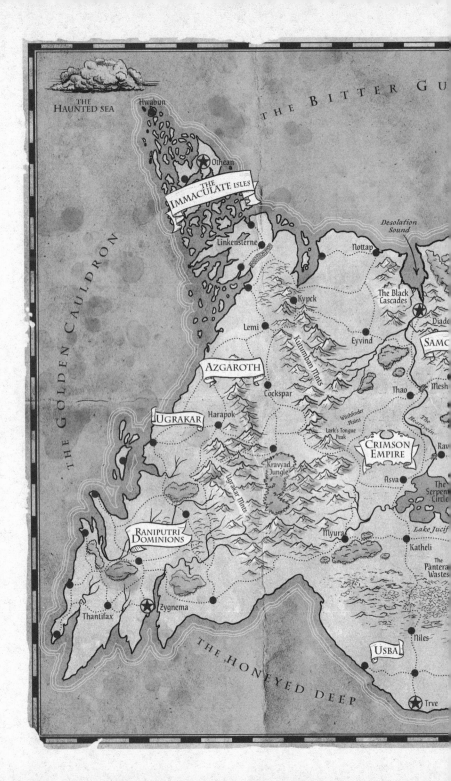

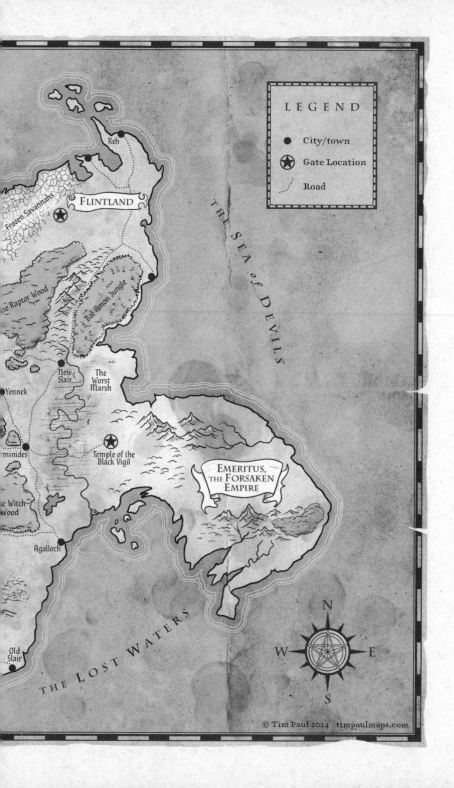

LEGEND

● City/town

✪ Gate Location

⋯ Road

THE SEA of DEVILS

Reh

Frozen Savannahs

FLINTLAND ✪

The Raptor Wood

Bal-Amon Jungle

New Slair

The Worst Marsh

Yennek

~minides ✪

Temple of the Black Vigil

EMERITUS, THE FORSAKEN EMPIRE

The Witch Wood

Agalloch

Old Slair

THE LOST WATERS

N
W   E
S

© Tim Paul 2014 timpaulmaps.com

A
WAR
in
CRIMSON
EMBERS

PART I

—✦—

MORTAL COILS

I wished to sweep away the clouds that blot the sun,
to see an age of peace ensue,
but my galloping horse stopped and aged,
   my keen sword rusted and tarnished.
White hair importunes
as time goes by; I cannot curb my indignation
                    —Pak Hyogwan (1781–1880),
      The Book of Korean Shijo, edited by Kevin O'Rourke

CHAPTER
1

Born unto a dying Star, where violence and corruption were woven into the very weft of the world, Pope Y'Homa III came of age in the darkest era of recorded history. She weathered evil upon evil, witnessed yet worse sins, and, in her sixteenth year, sacrificed that which was most precious to her so that she might save the souls of all—she renounced her station, her empire, and, if need be, her life. As her fleet of the righteous sailed from Desolation Sound, the mountaintop behind them threw a garish light up into the iron clouds, fulfilling yet another of the prophecies of the Chain Canticles. Without the Black Pope's presence to hold down the chthonic inferno that had smoldered since the Age of Wonders, the city of Diadem burned, just as foretold...but Y'Homa only learned this from the Holy See after the fact, being far too devoted to her cause to look back herself. Instead she kept her unblinking eyes on the gauzy grey horizon, beyond which lay her birthright: the Risen Kingdom of Jex Toth. Her rituals had brought it back from beneath the waves, and now it patiently awaited the coming of its keeper.

A final trial arose to thwart the Chainite pilgrims on the cusp of salvation, but Y'Homa paid the Immaculate blockade no more respect than she did the sharks that followed in the shifting shadows of her galleon. Just as a pod of sea wolves would race up from the deep to feast upon the scavenging sharks, so, too, would the Imperial fleet prey upon the Immaculate navy if they chose to force the issue. A headwind ensured that the semaphore exchange between

Y'Homa's vessel and the nearest Immaculate turtleship was brief, the Chainites calling their bluff and swiftly sweeping past the foreign boats without a shot being fired.

"They were not prepared for the strength of our ranks," said Cardinal Audhumbla as they left the blockade in their wake.

"Nor for the strength of our faith," Cardinal Messalina replied.

"They were not prepared for us at all," said Cardinal Diamond. "Thin as they are spread, I suspect their orders are to watch for any activity leaving Jex Toth, not protect against a fleet approaching it."

"Their motives are as inconsequential as the scuttling patterns of lice upon a dying ape," said Y'Homa. "Whatever the cause of their cowardice, it has bought them but a brief reprieve—soon the waves of blood shall be lapping at the shores of Othean, and every other iniquitous corner of the Star."

Cardinal Diamond cleared his throat. "With all due respect for Your Grace's certitude, in light of their naval presence so close to the coast we must consider the possibility that the Immaculates have already made landfall and—"

"They have not," said Y'Homa, ending the conversation.

While the Holy See had fretted and frowned over the possibility of the Immaculates invading the Risen Kingdom long before the Crimson ships could reach it, their Shepherdess had known the foreign heretics would be unable to set foot on those hallowed shores. The Fallen Mother had ordained Y'Homa to be the first to enter the Garden of the Star, and no mortal nor devil could prevent her from realizing her destiny. She would loose the Angelic Brood of the Allmother to cleanse the world, defeating the Deceiver once and for all, and in doing so transcend her mortal flesh to rule eternal as the Fallen Mother's avatar. From her flaming throne Y'Homa would sit in state for perpetuity, her proud virtue a beacon that would outshine and outlast both sun and moon, calling home the souls of the faithful who had been left behind upon the Star.

Oh, how ecstatically Y'Homa shivered upon first spying the holy land through the captain's hawkglass. It was just as Diadem Gate had foretold on the Day of Becoming, a luxuriously green realm set like an emerald in the shiny blue silk of the sea. She bit her lip as she scanned the mountains of the interior, beyond which lay the antediluvian cities of Jex Toth that would soon house the refugees of a diseased world. Here dwelt angels in need of a mortal mistress, an army in need of a commander.

Excited as the thought made her, when next the captain passed her his instrument with shaking hands she saw something more glorious still: the ancient harbor of Alunah coming into sight, and what a sight it was! The Burnished Chain's charts of Jex Toth were the only ones that remained from the Age of Wonders, and while the relics had steered them true to their destination no mark on a map could hint at the majesty of the place itself. Here the verdant foliage only poked out intermittently through the frozen fall of white stone that poured down from the headlands to fill the entire bowl of the cove, spreading out and across the water in a fan of ivory jetties. The buildings were in disrepair when they were not outright ruined, and Y'Homa nodded in understanding at the Fallen Mother's wisdom. The Garden of the Star was not a static realm where the idle could reap the same harvest as the industrious, but a paradise reserved for those worthy souls eager to work toward its restoration.

The black-armored angels perched on the rooftops and quays stood out against the pale stones of the city they had held fast for five hundred years awaiting the arrival of the Black Pope, and Y'Homa returned the hawkglass to the quaking captain. Well might the frail quaver before the divine, she thought, sitting up straighter in her teak throne at the prow of the ship. Pay true power the respect it deserves.

Yet even here, with the world of mortals at her back and immortal glory glinting in the sunlight ahead, the ache that had lodged in Y'Homa's heart ever since the Day of Becoming throbbed and throbbed. It was her last temptation, this sorrow in her uncle's sudden decline, and the impure hopes that hatched like maggots from that sorrow. He was demented, plain and simple, and much as she wanted him healed and sane again, that desire ran counter to everything she held most dear—her faith that the Fallen Mother would help only those who helped themselves. Shanatu was too far gone for that.

"Please, please, *please*," he said from where he cowered behind her on the deck, but Y'Homa did not turn away from the approaching harbor. She didn't want the papal guards who minded the madman to see the tears in her eyes as her once-brilliant mentor broke her heart anew with his deranged rambling. "I was wrong, we all were, don't go, turn back, back, another trick of the Deceiver, another plot... those are not angels, they are naked devils, and they will devour the Star, Jirella, please, you must stop, you must—"

"Put his gag back in," Y'Homa barked over her shoulder, Shanatu's use of her mortal name instead of her papal one a blasphemy too far, even for a condemned apostate's last words. How far he had fallen...

All through her reign he had been there for her, advising and encouraging. While the terms of the Burnished Chain's truce with Queen Indsorith had prevented Shanatu from sitting on the Holy See, his counsel meant more to Y'Homa than the rest of the church combined. Who else could understand the burdens of the papacy but her only living predecessor? He had been the voice of the Fallen Mother for longer than Y'Homa had been alive, and his abdication of the post had been entirely strategic—their savior continued to speak directly to her uncle, whereas Y'Homa only caught whispers here and there, in the midst of her most intense rites, and relied on Shanatu to interpret their meaning.

Then came the Day of Becoming, when the obedient servants of the Fallen Mother gazed through the window that had opened in Diadem Gate and beheld the Garden of the Star and its angelic guardians. All those with eyes clouded by the Deceiver fell back, demented and delirious from the vision of absolute grace. It was then that Y'Homa's true test presented itself, and Allmother protect her, she had been found wanting.

Pity was a cardinal sin, and mercy a graver one, yet when the time came she had been unable to have Shanatu crucified along with the rest of the false clerics. Surely one who had sat at the foot of the Fallen Mother could still be saved, she had told herself, surely the mere sight of Jex Toth would restore sanity to the servant who had dedicated his life to bringing about its return.

The mortal heart is capable of such hubris. Looking out over the baroquely carved bowsprit as her armada fast approached the magnificent white harbor of Jex Toth and its jet-black throngs of angels who heralded her arrival, Pope Y'Homa III gave the most difficult order of her papacy.

"Cut out my uncle's tongue and crucify him on the mast; our saviors will not find a single apostate among our number."

As soon as the words escaped her salt-cracked lips Y'Homa felt her soul lighten, and letting go of this final attachment to the deceitful world of the flesh provoked an immediate reaction from Jex Toth. Colossal ivory entities glided up through the pale blue waters of the bay to greet her navy, the leviathans trailing fronds as long as the Chainite ships, and far smaller envoys of similar cast winged down from the headland that cradled the harbor. Y'Homa wept at the sight of the Fallen Mother's children, grown monstrous by the Deceiver's seed but destined to play a role as saintly as that of the Black Pope herself. At long last the Shepherdess of the Lost had come home; she would deliver the Key to the Star to this heavenly host and they would go forth to cleanse the world of sin.

Behind Y'Homa came the sound of pounding hammers and muffled screams, but nothing could ruin the moment.

CHAPTER
2

Over the years Zosia had dreamed countless nightmares, and fought her way through nearly as many waking ones. Never before had she experienced this particular combination, however, of stirring from a bad dream to find herself exactly where the nightmare had left off: hunched over in this devildamned throne.

She shifted about in the all too familiar seat, pulling her dew-chilled furs up around her cold neck and scrunching her eyes tighter in defense against the evil sunshine that was trying to jimmy its way inside her bleary skull. This was Zosia's luck all over. The one bloody time she would have welcomed the dark clouds that usually hung like a leaden halo over the Black Cascades they went and burned off.

Choplicker gave his customary whining yawn to signal the start of the morning, but she clung to her exhaustion, desperate to pull herself back under. As her devil got up and padded around, Zosia pretended his nails were clicking on the pine boards of her old kitchen instead of the obsidian floor of the Crimson Throne Room. She was only ever truly happy in dreams and the spaces between them, now, and in this familiar drowsy fantasy if she could just fall back asleep for a little longer when she awoke it would be to Leib stroking her heavy head, whispering in her ear that she had promised him apple scones if he let her sleep in, and here the sun was already halfway up the aspens...

The dream soured. They always did. She had made him his favorite treat but he couldn't appreciate them; the monstrous young knight had placed Leib's severed head just out of reach of the plate of pastries, and try as her dead husband might to stretch out his tongue across the checked tablecloth he couldn't lick up more than a few crumbs...

No. Zosia shut that shit down, trying to replace the hot horror of her vision with cool black nothingness. Dawn had been creeping over Diadem's rim before she'd drifted off, and if she could just get comfortable on this cruelly designed hellchair before her conscience woke up enough to start needling at her she could get some much-needed rest and... and...

And it was too late to fall back asleep. The memory of finding Indsorith in the dungeons prodded at her more insistently than the sun or any nightmare. Even half-asleep Zosia now realized what a stupid, hopeless venture it had been, carrying the dying queen all the way up here to the top of the castle and then spending the night forcing juice down her throat and cleaning her wounds when she was already too far gone to ever come back. Bad as the Burnished Chain had worked over their rival for control of the Crimson Empire, it was Zosia who had inflicted the final tortures... not that Indsorith had even seemed aware of what was happening to her by that point, her moans and gasps simple animal response to the worst kinds of provocation.

And for what? To make Zosia feel a little better, to tell herself she'd done all she could, when the more humane course would have been to put Indsorith out of her misery down in her cell as soon as she'd found her. But no, Zosia had done exactly what she always did and got so hung up on hoping she could make a difference that she didn't even notice she was making matters worse until it was too late. Indsorith was just the latest victim of Zosia's sanguine streak, but by all the devils in the First Dark she would be the last—from this day forward Cold Cobalt would be as hopeless as she was, well, hopeless.

"You're sitting in my chair."

Insistent as the sun had been to get all up in Zosia's face you'd think it would cut her some slack when her eyes snapped open, but no. By the time she'd rubbed her face and properly taken in the impossible sight of Indsorith standing before her, naked save for bandages, the younger woman had begun to sway in place. Zosia barely got out of the throne in time to catch her as she fell. Her skin didn't feel as hot as it had the night before, and some of the color had come back to her ashen flesh, but it was a wonder she could even sit up in bed, let alone wander all the way out here. She shivered in Zosia's arms, slipping under again, and as Choplicker merrily trotted beside them Zosia lugged the Crimson Queen back to the royal bedchambers, marveling at the girl's tenacity. Who would even *want* to come back from that kind of a hurt?

Except Zosia knew the answer to that question already, having been there herself, or close to it. If you want vengeance badly enough you can bounce back from almost anything.

"Zosia." It was more of a sigh than a word as she tucked Indsorith back into her damask blankets. Her jade eyes were half-lidded but weren't rolling around in their orbits anymore. "You...you really came."

"Of course I did," said Zosia, and Choplicker knew better than to contradict her with one of his little chuffs. That, or he was too busy enjoying the lump in Zosia's throat as she patted Indsorith's shoulder. "Think you can stay awake a little longer? I'm going to whip you up another of my Star-famous juicy ghee drams."

Indsorith winced, and Zosia forced a smile. "If you're well enough to worry me half to death getting out of bed, you're damn sure well enough to take your medicine."

Right after that Zosia would go exploring and see if she could get some answers as to just what in the happy hells had happened to Diadem; hard to decide which was more unsettling, the riots in the streets or the shuttered, deserted castle. Hoartrap had insisted that the return of the Jex Toth signaled a mortal threat to the entire Star but hadn't been specific about how exactly that would come to pass—was whatever had happened here in the Imperial capital the beginning of the end? Then there was the question of what was taking Ji-hyeon and the rest of the Cobalt Company so long to arrive. According to the plan they should have already come through the

Gate and stormed this very castle. Zosia rather doubted they'd simply overslept, too...

But all that could wait. Zosia wasn't very well going to save the
Star all by herself, but she could take care of the wounded woman in
front of her. First, though, she had to look after herself—a sit on the
royal chamber pot, a hunt for kaldi beans in the servants' kitchen, a
hurried breakfast of hazelnuts, dates, and whatever else she scared
up, and retrieving that comfy seawolf mantle she'd forgotten back on
the Crimson Throne. That order.

Hurrying through her chores and picking up the forgotten fur
from where it lay draped over the arm of the fire glass throne, her
nose wrinkled as she noticed Choplicker had carried out his own foul
business on the nearby onyx cathedra. What a ridiculous monster he
was. No wonder they got along.

By the time she had come back in, built the fire in the hearth back
up, and made another concoction, Indsorith was dozing again. She
stirred when Zosia sat on the bed beside her. Obediently lifting her
head to sip the warm drink, she stared up over the chalice at her savior, and Zosia returned her gaze, the two women really looking each
other in the eye for the first time in over twenty years. Indsorith had
been little more than a child the last time they had met, and while
she couldn't yet be forty, the crown had aged her prematurely. That,
and being locked in a dungeon for an as-yet-undetermined amount
of time. Down all the years Indsorith had remained the same in
Zosia's mind, a spotty teenage queen with a big chip on her bony
shoulders, and now she was a full-grown woman—and a stout one at
that. But then Indsorith had surely thought of Zosia as she'd been in
the prime of her life, not as a worn-out, sad-eyed old widow.

"What happened?" Indsorith asked as she settled back into her pillow, her cracked, buttery lips shining in the firelight.

"Was planning on asking you the same thing," said Zosia as she
set the chalice back on the table and gave Choplicker a threatening
point of the finger—he was looking ready to jump up on the bed
beside them. "How long did they have you locked up down there?
And where'd everybody go?"

Indsorith shook her head, the movement so faint her long, coppery hair didn't rustle the bedding. Her eyes settled on the battered crown Zosia had left on a neighboring pillow. "I don't . . . they drugged me. There was a ritual . . . but . . ." Indsorith closed her eyes, and Zosia was about to stealthily remove herself from the room when the queen looked back up at her. "The Witchfinder Plains. Were you there? With the Cobalts?"

"Until last night," said Zosia, and in her state Indsorith didn't seem to notice the strangeness of that fact, given the distances involved.

"The Fifteenth Regiment caught you. That was when Y'Homa took me . . . and the rituals, and the Gate . . . the things beyond the Gate . . . they're coming . . . they're coming . . ."

"What's coming?" Zosia didn't scare easy, no she did not, but her hackles were good and raised now.

"The end . . . the end is here . . ." and Indsorith was fading again, eyelids fluttering, and hungry as she was to hear more, Zosia knew the woman needed rest more urgently than her liberator needed answers. She started to rise when Indsorith whimpered, as though the words hurt to say, "Don't go."

"I won't be gone long, and Chop will be here the whole time to keep you safe, so—"

"*Please.*" Indsorith's sunken eyes were still closed, and they scrunched tighter in a vain effort to dam back the wetness beginning to seep out around the edges. The utter ruin of the Star seemed to be off to a roaring start right here in her capital and the Crimson Queen expected Zosia to sit around playing nursemaid?

"Of course . . . Your Majesty," murmured Zosia, settling back onto the bed as Indsorith shuddered beside her, the relief on the woman's bruised and scabbing face so sincere Zosia found her own eyes stinging. It had been so long since somebody had relied on her to take care of them that she didn't even know what to do, her hand hovering uncertainly over the invalid. Zosia always had such steady hands, no matter how dangerous or frightening the encounter, but now her whole arm was trembling . . . and she only found her steel again when she gave in to her impulse and tenderly stroked the woman's brow.

The grimace melted from Indsorith's face and her breathing grew steady, and Zosia caught herself humming one of the Kvelertakan folk songs she would softly croon for Leib when he was sick—it was the only time he could guilt her into it, since she had never cared for the sound of her own singing.

The tune stuttered on her lips at the memory, but instead of letting the grief silence her, Zosia seized up the words to the ancient song, and in the tomblike quiet of Castle Diadem she sang to the sleeping queen of a crumbling empire, the devil at her feet keeping time with his tail as they waited for the world to end or Ji-hyeon to arrive with the Cobalt Company, whichever came first.

CHAPTER
3

It might have just been the most beautiful morning Domingo Hjortt had ever experienced. The sudden transition from ball-biting cold to blessedly balmy as they emerged from the Othean Gate got things off to a grand start, and the incandescent bouquet of dawnlit clouds resting atop the golden roofs of the Immaculate palace set a scene so precisely picturesque it resembled the watercolor backdrops of his sister-in-law's plays. It was not the combination of agreeable weather, impressive architecture, and tapestry-worthy sunrise that took Domingo's breath away, however, but what stood arrayed in the vastness between the Temple of Pentacles from whence he had appeared and the distant walls of the castle-city: an army the likes of which he had never seen outside his most exhilarating fantasies.

The legions were standing at attention on either side of the terracotta road that ran straight from the temple steps all the way to the palace, and by his dead mother's saber it was a sight to behold. He had always dismissed the patina of the Immaculate soldiers' armor as another herald of their degeneracy, the troops too lazy to take care of their equipment and their commanders too weak to enforce proper upkeep, but now he saw the green-tinted shoulder pads and breastplates for what they were—a glorious emerald uniform that would never fade in summer nor flake in winter.

And their ranks! Domingo prided himself on maintaining the most orderly regiment in the Crimson Empire, but he was honorable enough to admit when he was outmatched. From his vantage point on the back of a wagon bouncing down the stairs of the temple he could see far enough out into the malachite rows to have no doubt that every *single* line was as straight as the first. Fifteen thousand soldiers on each side of the road, at a minimum, and each one might as well have been a model cast from a single mold, that was how perfectly rigid they stood. It was beautiful.

There was also a terraced platform smack in the middle of the road with a biddy perched atop it, presumably the Empress of the Immaculate Isles, but Domingo barely spared her a glance before returning his attention to her army. Now that he was right in front of the woman he was beginning to feel a tingle of injudicious but undeniable guilt over having murdered her son at the beginning of his campaign against the new Cobalt Company... But every war has its casualties, damn it, and framing the Cobalts for the assassination of Prince Byeong-gu had been a masterstroke, even if it ended up proving redundant. Sons died, often for no good reason, and if Domingo could accept that then so could Empress Ryuki—and indeed, she must have already come to terms with the matter, to initiate a truce with General Ji-hyeon.

That was another difference between noble Azgarothians like Domingo and the ever-scheming Immaculates; even if his homeland was under threat from whatever monsters haunted Jex Toth he'd sooner fillet his own scrotum than strike a deal with the woman who had killed his son. True, he had made noises to just that effect to Zosia, but only to lull her into a false sense of security, and as soon as he saw his opportunity he would pay her back a hundredfold, yes he dearly would.

The carts were among the last units through the Lark's Tongue Gate and so Domingo was brought to a halt at the rear of the Cobalt troops, the company lined up on either side of the road in front of the surrounding Immaculates. The Cobalt brass had also been posted here, just off to one side of the big dais erected in front of the temple... which meant whenever General Ji-hyeon and her deadbeat father arrived they would see their officers standing not between them and the empress, but behind her. These Immaculates loved their formal little pissing contests, didn't they?

Ah, there was a familiar face, and not a pretty one. Fennec, close enough that Domingo could have spit on the Usban Villain's ponytail if only his mouth hadn't gone so dry just before they crossed over. Standing beside him was the horned anathema who had helped Maroto lead the giant wolves into the Imperial camp back in the Kutumbans—in other words, one of those directly responsible for Domingo being so brutalized by a beast that he was confined to the wagon bed. Indeed, it was that very assault on his person that had compromised his thinking and led to his allowing Brother Wan to carry out the ritual at the Battle of the Lark's Tongue. Forget Fennec the nothing-master, as soon as Domingo could muster the phlegm that white-haired witchborn was the one getting spat on.

Now that he was sitting up, something that had been vaguely niggling at him ever since his cart had lurched down the temple steps finally made itself clear: it no longer hurt to turn his head...or, he found, to raise his battered back, or to stretch his sliced cheek in a widening smile. He slowly flexed his splinted hand. That wrist had been as broken as his heart not five minutes ago, and while it didn't quite seem to have its old range of motion it definitely didn't hurt. Was this something Hoartrap had done to him? Domingo didn't believe in miracles, but whatever the source he was willing to make an exception for this!

Alas, his elation was short-lived: trying to move his left leg no longer blinded him with pain, but that damn hip of his still wasn't obeying any commands. It felt all stiff and lumpy, and Domingo simmered with disappointment. Being liberated from constant agony was all right, but what good did it do him if he still couldn't get up and kick some teeth in?

Ji-hyeon must have arrived while Domingo was taking stock of his sudden recovery, but while he heard the general's voice he couldn't see her. Peering around from the back of his wagon he could still spy the doors of the temple that opened into the nothingness of the Othean Gate, but the side of the tiered, brocaded stage was blocking his view of the front of the road. Ji-hyeon must be standing there at the base of the tower, and sure enough the empress atop the dais scowled downward as she replied to the unseen Cobalt General. Domingo took it as a point of personal pride that he did not speak High Immaculate, so the conversation meant nothing to him...until it took the sort of ugly tenor that is a universal cognate.

Not being able to see or properly overhear the exchange, Domingo was left to his imagination as to what had provoked the empress's snotty tone. Perhaps General Ji-hyeon hadn't bowed low enough or something? That would be just bloody typical of Immaculates, wouldn't it, to employ arcane deviltry to come together for a joint operation against an invading horde of demons from the Sunken Kingdom only to get into a row over etiquette. Domingo called over to Fennec to ask if he needed to drag himself up the empress's tower to spank some manners into her when he was cut off by a scream from the front of the dais, followed by the reverberating twang of dozens of arrows unleashed as one.

The scream abruptly stopped, as screams usually do once the arrows start flying.

"No...no!" Fennec reeled, steadying himself against Domingo's wagon. He must have had a slightly better vantage of what had just happened, and what the man did next washed away Domingo's surprise at the unexpected turn the negotiations had taken, replacing it with stomach-dropping dread: the Villain bolted toward the side of the empress's dais, drawing his sword. Anything that came after such a move could be nothing short of an unmitigated catastrophe. "No!"

The horned witchborn joined Fennec's mad charge at the empress's platform but moved so much swifter that her sword was in hand before the Villain's cleared leather...and then returned to its sheath so fast Domingo would have had to second-guess whether it had ever been out at all, if not for the obvious blow she'd struck to the back of Fennec's head.

Queen Indsorith's decree that Imperial regiments would have to begin incorporating Chainwitches had been a deciding factor in Domingo's retirement. He had preferred to quit the war game altogether rather than work with the anathemas. Yet seeing how efficiently this one took out as seasoned a veteran as Fennec, he had to admit these creatures must have their uses. The Usban Villain toppled without another peep, and that was yet another mark in his assailant's favor—knocking people out with your pommel is harder than it looks, and rarely takes a single pop. The witchborn caught him before he hit the red gravel and swung him around on her shoulder despite her smaller stature, and—

There was a commotion at the temple entrance, and Domingo glanced over just in time to see General Ji-hyeon jump through it, straight back into the Gate. *Well.* That was unexpected, and more than a little—

He started as a body crashed into the hay of the wagon bed beside him. Fennec, with the white-haired witchborn looming over them. She came down at Domingo fast as a shark in shallow water, and with the sharp teeth to match.

"Baron Domingo Hjortt of Cockspar, Colonel of the Fifteenth Regiment," she said in Crimson. "You will swear to do as I say or you will die immediately."

Before Domingo even had time to feel indignant at being threatened by an anathema she said, "I am Choi, your bodyguard. Not a Cobalt guard to keep you in chains, a Crimson guard to protect you, to serve you, to assist you, a concession Ji-hyeon allowed on account of your weakness. I am your bodyguard. Swear it."

"First I've heard of it," gulped Domingo, not appreciating the close proximity of her monstrous mouth nor the all-too-human stink of kaldi emanating from it. "Just what happ—"

"My last act will be to eat your face off your skull," growled the red-eyed fiend. "That, or to come close enough to the Empress Ryuki to avenge my people. You alone can decide which path I will walk, Baron Domingo Hjortt of Cockspar. The empress will have questions for a captured Imperial colonel. A captured Imperial colonel will need to have his bodyguard with him at all times, as a point of honor. His bodyguard shall never leave his side—she will help him move, and she will be his sole translator. A captured Imperial colonel will insist upon these things, or a captured Imperial colonel will have his face eaten off his skull. Now. Swear it."

"I—" Domingo wasn't even thinking, just speaking, when those pointy teeth yawned over him. There were a few gaps where fangs were missing, but plenty still remained, and before she could bite off his nose he said, "I swear it, damn you, I swear. You're my bodyguard, Choi my bodyguard, I swear it on my honor."

"Honor is good," said Choi, jerking upright and standing beside the wagon bed as though nothing had happened. Domingo felt barely more aware of what the hells had just transpired than the unconscious Fennec lying beside him. "We have both lost ours this day, Baron Domingo Hjortt of Cockspar, but together we may yet redeem ourselves."

There came a growing commotion from the Cobalt troops all around them, as was to be expected following their general's sudden flight through the Othean Gate, but Domingo was having a hard time tearing his attention away from the silently weeping witchborn who towered over him, her wet crimson eyes fixed upward at the Empress of the Immaculate Isles. Domingo wondered if he had looked half so righteous when he'd colluded with the Black Pope to seek justice for Efrain's murder...or half so doomed. Choi's taste in collaborators wasn't much better than his, he was sorry to say, but then bloody-handed vengeance makes for strange bedfellows, doesn't it?

CHAPTER
4

The Othean Gate took Ji-hyeon as it had once before, but this time it did not release her a moment later. She had closed her eyes during that first trip, keeping them shut until Fennec pulled her through the nauseating portal and out into the warm Raniputri sunshine. This time Ji-hyeon went into the Gate with open eyes.

There wasn't even darkness here in the First Dark, only grey. It looked as though she were floating through a thick fogbank, but she felt herself pass through chill, slick membranes, the unseen curtains sliding over her face. She worried they might stop her nose and mouth, and as soon as she had the thought she felt one do exactly that, puffing out and contracting with her breath. Or so it seemed, but she wasn't suffocating, and there was still nothing she could see... at first.

Contours began to emerge from the miasma, indistinct but shimmering, and with them came the distinct impression that instead of drifting aimlessly forward she was being drawn into a spiral, corkscrewing down, faster and faster. The slapping nudging tickling crawling sensations persisted, and even though she was sure her eyes had adjusted she still couldn't make out what enveloped her, the former formlessness replaced by the haze of motion. One moment it was like being surrounded by a school of silvery eels in the deepest depths of the sea and the next like sliding down the gullet of some titanic animal, and while these shifts made it all the more dreamlike it was somehow realer than anything Ji-hyeon had experienced in her life.

What's more, merely being here satiated something deep within her, a need keener than any she'd ever felt indulged as soon as it was comprehended. It was the sensation of comfortably drifting off to sleep wedded to the first shivery stirrings of waking, and persistent instead of fleeting. This was the enlightenment all sages sought, to dwell forever in the contented moment where the mind frees itself from the prison of the flesh, and lo, it was the same as the paradise promised by Chainite prophets, a place where the innocent spirit was at long last spared the constant doubts and worries of the ever-busy intellect. If she had not been so far beyond mortal sensation she would have wept at the perfection of it, at the knowledge that this tranquility was now the whole of her existence, that nothing could touch her ever again…

But something did touch her, then, something ugly and sharp and attached to the dead world of the senses. She tried to cast away the roiling coils of disgusting barbed gut entwined around her hand but they only tightened their grip, pain disrupting her absolute fulfill-ment. With her free hand Ji-hyeon reached to tear away the disgust-ing mass when a snake-like length of the slimy grey tissue whipped out and struck her chest. Its diamond-hard beak broke the surface not of her skin but the film of the First Dark that had settled over her.

Ji-hyeon's serenity was vaporized by a fury so extreme she forgot where she was, what was happening to her. Instead she saw her sec-ond father falling to the red road beside her, feathered with arrows. She saw the empress's cruel smirk as the lying old crone confessed to murdering the rest of their family. Ji-hyeon thought of her sisters falling through this place, beset by forces they couldn't understand, pictured her first father's prayers trailing off as his mind untethered and he bobbed insensate through this muted realm until the end of all things, and she screamed her wrath into the grey void.

And just like that, she was free. It wasn't like the first time, when she'd staggered out of the Gate in Zygnema clinging to Fennec's sud-denly furry hand and found herself in a bustling city. That had been an impossibly strange experience, yes, but it had been bookended by normalcy—she walked into one temple and came out another, albeit halfway across the Star. This, though, *this*…

It was as if she had been inside an opaque soap bubble that had suddenly popped. Her feet were on firm ground but she immediately toppled over, her head still traveling at impossible speeds, her ears roaring as though a high mountain cataract blasted through her skull, and there was a pressure in her left eye so intense it felt ready to pop. Ji-hyeon crashed into the mercifully soft ground, sending poor Fellwing rolling away through the snow. She couldn't see where the little owlbat ended up, because as soon Ji-hyeon opened her swollen left eye an onslaught of vivid yet alien colors blasted her brain. The intensity of the vision made her retch, and she lay there shivering with both eyes closed until the fiery afterimages finally faded into blackness.

Lifting her head and tentatively opening her right eye, she saw that Fellwing had settled a short distance down the gentle slope. The owlbat chirped and flapped her pale wings, sending plumes of grey powder flying as she tried to extricate herself from the drift. Ji-hyeon gulped, working up the courage to open her pulsing left eye again, but as soon as she began to crack it she knew it was a mistake. Closing them both tight she stayed where she lay until the blistering lights in her head again grew dim, the phantasms fading to nothing along with the nausea. Still she heard the distant crashing of the First Dark echoing through her skull, as though she held a seashell up to each ear.

Only when she was confident she could move without vomiting did Ji-hyeon open her right eye again. Fellwing had regained the air and flitted just overhead, clearly concerned for her mistress. As well the devil might be—this migraine or whatever it was that afflicted her left eye unnerved Ji-hyeon in a way she couldn't even comprehend. Those colors it blasted into her brain weren't just different from any she had ever seen before, they somehow felt *wrong*, as if she were witnessing something profane. Keeping her left eye squinted firmly shut, she sat up in the snow, too numb to even feel the chill.

Yet bad as this situation surely was, it could've been so much worse. Fellwing was all right, the devil finally landing on Ji-hyeon's shoulder and nuzzling her tear-streaked chin. The journey through the Gates had apparently revived the devil a little, and Ji-hyeon's ongoing discomfort would further nourish her back to health. Ji-hyeon clung to that, told herself that they still had each other, and had come through a Gate in one piece, had lived to fight again. They would avenge her fathers and her sisters and everyone else who had been executed at Othean by the honorless empress. They would find their friends. They would—

A cry overwhelmed the low rumble that still reverberated in her ears, close and keen. Ji-hyeon pressed a palm over her left eye just to make sure it stayed shut and looked up, still too dizzy to rise to her feet…and then found her footing in a trice, staggering in place as she gawped at the figure rushing up the slope toward her, and what lay beyond it.

Ji-hyeon had been too busy collapsing on the ground and fretting over her eye to get anything more than an impression of drab snow, the white world spinning all around her dizzy head, but that little bit of familiarity had made her assume they had come back through the Lark's Tongue Gate, on the wintry Witchfinder Plains.

They had not.

There was an undulating impression of slumped grey mountains as far as the eye could see, but far more pressing was the armored warrior who was almost upon her. She assumed it was armor, anyway, and not actual spiny shell that covered the charging figure, but considering the claymore it brandished in both hands she felt quite confident that it was indeed a warrior. A big one. Her hands went to her hilts, and she almost opened her left eye before remembering the paramount importance of keeping it scrunched shut.

She needed a blindfold for that side, an eye patch or something, but there was certainly no time to fashion one now. Her unexpected foe bellowed again as its thick legs churned through a snowdrift just down the slope, and Ji-hyeon took a low stance, drawing her twin swords. She hadn't anticipated trying out the black blade of sainted steel so soon, but then when was the last time Ji-hyeon had gotten what she expected?

Attuning yourself to your environment and using it to your advantage was basic fighting business—there hadn't been much that Choi and Ji-hyeon's dearly departed bodyguard Chevaleresse Sasamaso could agree on, but playing the field to your advantage would have been at the top of the list. The problem here was that Ji-hyeon's immediate surroundings barely had any more features than the space between Gates, a snowy, barren hillside... except that wasn't right, either, Ji-hyeon finally realized as her opponent closed the last dozen yards, because it wasn't snow after all. It was ash.

The warrior came for Ji-hyeon without slowing its plodding jog through the ankle-deep powder, the black plates of its bristly armor dull against the overcast sky and dingy landscape, the tips of most of its spikes broken off, its helm a long boxy cage that revealed nothing of the wearer. The only thing sharp about the charging figure was its enormous sword. The claymore must be as long as Ji-hyeon was tall, and even more unnerving than the warrior's wordless roars as it had approached was the silence with which it now swung its weapon side-armed at its quarry. The arc of the sword was too high to jump, too low to duck, and if Ji-hyeon tried to parry the enormous blade she would be either battered to the ground or bisected at the belly, depending on how well her swords held out. A perfect attack.

Or near perfect, anyway. Ji-hyeon threw herself to the other side of the charging brute, and while the ash wasn't as slick as snow it still had a satiny slipperiness that prevented her assailant from setting a heel and pivoting after her. Instead it stumbled as its heavy claymore whooshed through the air, and as it tried to turn after Ji-hyeon she attacked.

Judging the exact time to move and the exact places to strike would have been difficult even if Ji-hyeon had both eyes open in the stinging cloud of ash kicked up by the warrior's charge. Keeping the one squinted shut had made her evasion and counterattack even trickier, but Ji-hyeon had fought more than one battle half-blind from blood in her eyes. Fellwing helped, launching herself from Ji-hyeon's shoulder at the precise moment when she needed to dodge and then fluttering past the warrior's face to distract it as Ji-hyeon came in low, catching its leg between her scissoring blades.

Yet although she hit it directly in the back of the knee where there should be a gap in the plates, her right hand went numb as the sword bounced off it with a clang…but then there was a crunch and a screeching scrape as the black blade in her left hand sheared through the armor covering its shin.

Its leg buckled and it went down hard, a grey fume billowing up from the ash as it crashed into the ground. It bellowed again as it tried to right itself, but Ji-hyeon's black sword cut off its war cry along with its head. The killing blow felt so damn good she wanted to scream, her sword arm greedy for more, but the feeling fled as fast as the severed head came free of its neck, leaving her drained and depressed.

Not five feet outside a Gate with her ears still ringing from the journey and she was already killing, and someone she bore no grudge, a stranger whose entire life up until this point remained a perfect enigma. Wiping her blades off on her cape and sheathing them, she held out her arm and Fellwing lighted down on it. Ji-hyeon dusted the ash off the weak little devil, then knelt over the severed head, lifting the heavy helm to have a look at her mysterious attacker. The head was stuck inside the iron cage, and she had to give it a little shake to dislodge it, like a walnut from a poorly broken shell.

"Wildborn," she breathed as the head fell into the blood-muddied ash, but it was less an observation and more a prayer that the matter was as simple as that. She had met quite a few wildborn in her day but had never before seen someone with so much of the wild and so little of the human. The thick-furred face on the ground before her was more wolf than man, snub-snouted and jagged-toothed, with a snarled grey mane in place of mundane hair. Ji-hyeon's left eye throbbed angrily behind its lid, as if annoyed she wouldn't let it have a look at the unexpected prize.

More cries cut through the distant roar in Ji-hyeon's head, and her heavy heart became rather light of heel as it began to race around her chest—a dozen more black-armored figures came jogging up the barren slope toward her, some of them on all fours. She dropped the heavy helm of their scout as Fellwing nuzzled at her hauberk, feeding on her fear.

"Sorry, girl, but you'll have to wait on a real meal," she told the owlbat as soon as the initial jolt passed. She had no intention of sticking around to ask directions from the charging warband. Whether her second safe passage through the Othean Gate had come from holding on to her devil or dumb luck, she was ready to play double-or-nothing, given the alternative, and duck back inside whatever Gate had deposited her onto this dreary yet dangerous landscape. Anywhere she ended up had to be an improvement.

Yet there was no Gate behind her. Ji-hyeon staggered past the spot where she had assumed it must be, ignoring the mad sight that actually met her one good eye to look every which way for the Gate that *had* to be there, the one she *must* have stepped from…but there was only the narrow prominence of the barren, ash-coated hill, and beyond it an even steeper slope falling down, down, so far down, into the swirling grey sea whose dull roar Ji-hyeon now began to pick apart and compartmentalize as tens of thousands of distance-blurred warriors meeting in seething combat. Great shadowy things waded through the shallows of the clashing armies, reminding her in general aspect if not specific shape of the devil queen that Hoartrap had summoned onto the Lark's Tongue battlefield. Even after all the strange adventures Ji-hyeon had undergone of late, she was hypnotized by the sheer scale of the conflict and the strangeness of the combatants.

Without thinking of the consequences, Ji-hyeon blinked, and as her left eye opened those blazing colors and ephemeral shapes again flooded her vision. This time she didn't immediately close it, and while the sights were even more intense than before, her mind must have been getting used to the intrusion, for she didn't lose her footing, or her breakfast. Instead she swayed in place, laughing in wonder at the bizarre shimmering filaments that suffused everything, gasping in awe at how different those distant titans appeared now that she saw them with both eyes wide open.

Out of the corner of her vision she saw that something else had changed, the coiling devil on her shoulder no longer resembling an owlbat, or any other creature of the Star. As she experimentally winked her left eye, Fellwing resumed her old shape and then lost it again, and Ji-hyeon shivered as she realized what had happened. Hoartrap had warned them that using the Gates without his supervision would lead to *improvements*, as he called them, like Fennec's hands transforming to claws. Ji-hyeon's first trip had only drained the color from her hair, but this journey must have done something far more radical to her eye. She couldn't begin to imagine *what*, though, as she looked back out at where rivers of light flowed across the previously monochromatic horizon, illuminating the seething hordes of inhuman soldiers and revealing yet more that had previously been hidden from sight behind glassy vapors…

But then Fellwing reminded Ji-hyeon with another sharp tap of her beak that they were about to get another very close look at the warriors who rampaged across this expanse of ashen waste. Squinting her left eye shut again so as not to be distracted by its overwhelming sights, Ji-hyeon turned to see that the first of the warband was almost upon her, loping in on all fours with no helm to contain its long, vulpine muzzle. The black sword flew to Ji-hyeon's hand, as light as Fellwing catching an updraft, and she cleaved through the monster's skull, but only because she had to.

It fell but another took its place, and Ji-hyeon cut that one down, too, and the next, because they demanded it of her, and so did the black blade. They were many, but she was Princess Ji-hyeon Bong of Hwabun, last of her line, and she would kill anyone and anything that stood in her way, no matter how many of them there were, no matter how long it took, until she found a way back to Othean and delivered vengeance for her family upon the Empress Ryuki. Nothing could stop her, not distance nor devils, nor monsters nor mortals.

Of all these potential pitfalls, only the last never arose to slow her course—she would face countless foes and dangers untold after cutting down the final bestial warrior on that blasted mountaintop and setting forth with Fellwing to find her way home, but it would be two brutal, horrifying years before Ji-hyeon encountered anything remotely human.

CHAPTER
5

You really think we'll be back with the general within the week?" It sounded too good to be true, and considering who Sullen was talking to it almost definitely was... but given who they were talking *about*, he couldn't help but hope. Squinting across the smoky campfire they'd piled with cedar bark to keep the mosquitoes at bay, he saw that Keun-ju looked about as skeptical as he felt.

"Oh, sure," said Hoartrap, puffing his gnarled black pipe and blowing a geranium soap–scented cloud up to perfume the beards of moss swaying from oak and cypress. The evenings were so sultry here in the boggy Haunted Forest Sullen couldn't fathom how the sorcerer could bear to sit so close to the fire and blithely puff away. At least all the smoke helped cover up the Touch's sickly sweet funk.

"You've given it a lot of thought, then?" said Sullen, not at all satisfied with the blowhard warlock's switch to taciturnity.

"Not particularly, but then I could give the matter the barest minimum of my attention and still out-think the lot of you," said Hoartrap, which was at least more in character. "Provided my perfidious protégé guides us true to Maroto, I can't imagine we'll spend much time on Jex Toth one way or the other—either we see an easy opportunity to sabotage the invasion from within, or we simply swoop up everybody's favorite barbarian and creep back to join the Cobalts at Othean before we're discovered by the locals. I never linger in a place unless it's for leisure, and there are better holiday destinations than the Sunken Kingdom."

"What do you mean, *provided* your *protégé* directs us to Sullen's uncle?" asked Keun-ju, his pretty eyes narrowing above his stained veil. "We still have the bedeviled compass you gave us, why not just continue to follow it?"

"Because that was for me to find you, not for you to find Maroto," said Hoartrap, and if it had been anyone else setting them straight Sullen would've given Keun-ju an *I-told-you-so* look. As it stood he didn't want to give Hoartrap the satisfaction. "If it could actually pinpoint the bounder, don't you think I would have held on to it instead of giving it to you merry Moochers?"

"But the needle did line up with the magic post…" said Sullen thoughtfully, wondering if perhaps Hoartrap had been honest with them before but was now changing his song to some skullduggerous end.

"Because I set the compass to point toward Jex Toth," said Hoartrap, confirming that no, the devil-eating dick had been playing them all along. "I knew that's where we would find Maroto, generally speaking, and when dear Purna informed me you were mounting a search party I didn't want you wandering off in the wrong direction."

"You deceived us into going on a snipe hunt," said Keun-ju angrily.

"So you had an adventure," said Hoartrap with a shrug. "At my age you learn that most quests turn out to be a fowl chase of one feather or another, especially when you're smack in the middle of—"

"You lied to Purna, which means you lied to us." Sullen gripped the haft of the spear made from the bones of a man who never would have stood for such nonsense, planting the base of it in the dirt and leaning forward on his log seat. "You told us the compass would take us to Uncle Craven, but all it was doing was pointing us to a land beyond the Star, a place you knew we'd never reach!"

"A place where your uncle does indeed await us, my dear boy," said Hoartrap peevishly, wagging the jaundiced stem of his pipe at Sullen. "And before you get too irate over the gift I gave you not being good enough, let me remind you that that compass was the only reason I was able to find you so quickly, and save the both of you from yet another charming member of your family. And this is the thanks I get?"

Fired up as Sullen had been just now, he cooled off as soon as he glanced back at the similarly deflated Keun-ju and was reminded of how bad that night had been...and of how much worse it would have ended, if Hoartrap had never given them the compass that he'd used to track their movements. "Yeah, well...what about the magic post? You think that was for real or just some more bullshit?"

"Oh yes," began Hoartrap, "who could forget the magic post, save—"

"Up, magic post!" called Pasha Diggelby, looking over from his work cutting burs out of the thick white coat of the horned wolf that lay convalescing in the weeds a short ways off from the fire. When Hoartrap gave Diggelby one of the withering scowls that had become quite in vogue since the pasha had bested the warlock, the younger man explained, "It's what Purna used to say, when Sullen and Keun-ju knelt down to pick up the log. *Up, magic post!* Like, to be funny?"

"I'm laughing on the inside," said Hoartrap. "As I was saying, who could forget the wonderful magic post...save for you absentminded heroes who forgot it in a devil-haunted pond. I poked about back there but couldn't turn it up, otherwise we might have had something more reliable than Ilstrix's tricks to find Maroto. I've never had the pleasure of meeting this Procuress you spoke of, but any witch who's providing spooky services while also keeping herself outside my notice for however long she's been in business must be talented indeed. She may well have given you a tool that would take you straight to Maroto...if only you hadn't lost it, leaving us with only the shaky claims of a dropout apprentice."

"No matter your impression of her tricks, as you say, Nemi was able to find me from halfway across the Star and take my mom straight to us," Sullen pointed out.

"With the help of Myrkur, apparently," Diggelby added, throwing an arm around the enormous neck of the dozing horned wolf. Hoartrap had apparently put some sort of bad magic on the animal before coming to terms with Nemi, which explained its freshly bald face—a feature that made the mountainous monster even more intimidating.

To everyone but Diggelby, that was, the dotty noble now giving its thickly corded neck a serious rubdown. It flicked an ear as big as a tricorn hat at him, as if the protective pasha were a fly rustling its fur. "Between wolf and witch I have no doubt we will soon be reunited with our friend and officer. When we do discover him, though, I pray we all remember the principle I proved the other night—that neither daggers nor the dark arts are so powerful a weapon as diplomacy, what?"

"With all due respect, gentlemen!" said Keun-ju, the Immaculate expression one that Ji-hyeon had taught Sullen actually meant *with no respect whatsoever.* "Finding the missing Captain Maroto once we land on Jex Toth is hardly our most pressing concern. What I wish to know is how we can possibly travel such great distances in so little time. Are you proposing we resort to blackest deviltry?"

"It's actually as simple as braiding buttercups in our nose hair, holding hands, and having a good old-fashioned Usban sing-along," said Hoartrap, idly peeling a strip of skin from a blister on his cheek and dropping it into the bowl of his pipe, where it writhed across the hot ash like the snake that had bit him.

"Really?" Diggelby asked hopefully, but Sullen wasn't falling for the Touch's claim—Hoartrap's nose produced an overabundance of white hairs, yes, but they weren't nearly long enough to braid. Sullen wished he'd never gotten close enough to the warlock to notice such things, but like his grandfather always said, wishing was what fishes did after they were already hooked.

"No," said Hoartrap, smudging the waxy yellow skin around the edge of the wound on his face until it blended out of sight, like the pasha putting on corpsepaint. "Our Immaculate friend once more proves he is as astute as he is cute. Blackest deviltry is, as always, the best and brightest way forward."

"Yeah, that's what I thought you'd say," said Sullen, figuring Hoartrap's complimenting Keun-ju was probably some backhanded business but still too foggy-headed to figure out how. "But what exactly are we talking here? We're nowhere near a Gate to take one of your shortcuts through the First Dark, but you've obviously got other means of covering a lot of ground. You, uh, know how to fly?"

"Do I know how to *fly*?" Hoartrap cocked his head at Sullen as though the Flintlander were a walrus that had learned to parrot human speech. "That's a very personal sort of question, Sullen, and entirely irrelevant to our conversation. Don't be ridiculous."

"It is not ridiculous to ask for more details when you embroil us in your plots," said Keun-ju, using a stick to roll the roasting kudzu roots around in the coals. They actually didn't make for bad eating... definitely not *good* eating, right, but not bad.

"My plots, are they?" said Hoartrap huffily. "I take my orders from General Ji-hyeon Bong, same as the rest of you, I just happen to be the senior officer of this elite squadron. Even if you don't like the meal our chef has prepared us, it hardly seems fair to take it out on the cupbearer bringing you your plate."

"Now *that* is what I call a dodge," said Diggelby, giving Myrkur a final scritch and then brushing himself off. He'd been at it for an hour and not even cleared half of the monster's vast acreage of fur. "We already know we won't like the taste of your beans, old beast, so go ahead and spill them already. How do we go from the Haunted Forest to the De-sunken Kingdom in but a twinkling?"

"By summoning enough devils to carry us through the First Dark, and binding them according to the ancient laws to ensure their loyalty," said Hoartrap, and from the evil smile on his jacked-up face Sullen had a notion the sorcerer relished looking Diggelby in the eye as he delivered that bit of intelligence. "The actual passage ought to be swift enough, though not as easy as if we had Gates to use. What's going to take up the lion's share of our time is acquiring the sacrifices we'll need to make. You said it was a day's march back to the last town you passed through, yes?"

Keun-ju sucked through his teeth and Diggelby staggered back dramatically as though the news were a physical blow, or worse, a critique of his wardrobe, but Sullen had braced himself for something like this. The very first time he had met Hoartrap he'd watched the Touch eat an innocent devil alive, and discovered the next morning that the witch had disappeared entirely, leaving only a scorched and oily stain in the grass. That ill-looking blot on the earth had raised Sullen's hackles just like the Gates did. There was never any doubt that Hoartrap could achieve the seemingly impossible, or that the cost of doing so would involve devils.

Didn't mean Sullen had to like it, though, and Sullen felt a powerful need to be away from the smug sorcerer with his foul, flowery pipe smoke and his casual talk of rites profane to all peoples. Sullen leaned into his spear and clambered off the fallen log, waving Keun-ju back down when the Immaculate started to rise as well. Now that he was properly mended, Sullen was about done letting his sweet friend help him out—the witchwoman's eggy cures had set them both up right, but while Sullen's wounds were fast healing, Keun-ju's right arm wasn't ever coming back. "Suppose I better check on Ma again, see if she'll talk to me yet."

"Mind what I told you about running your mouth around rowan trees," said Hoartrap, and for the life of him Sullen couldn't figure out if the Touch actually believed all the ghost stories he'd been spinning or if he was just messing with a Flintland bumpkin. There hadn't been any rowans back in the Frozen Savannahs. But then even Purna seemed a little awed by the big flowering tree she called a Gate-ash, and the Ugrakari was the least superstitious person he'd ever met.

"If it's really dangerous, why'd you tell me to chain her up over there?" said Sullen crossly.

"Who said they were dangerous?" Hoartrap was all innocence. "All I said was they aren't actually trees, not really. They're tendrils of the First Dark that wormed their way through cracks in our world, stretching up and up to extinguish our sun, only to be betrayed by the magic of the moon and turned to wood. The devils inside them are trapped, perfectly harmless . . . but they are always listening, and you don't want a devil knowing your secrets, not even a bound one. Why do you think I had us move our camp away from that infernal thing?"

"Is that *true*?" Sullen felt a raven fly over his grave. This was different from the other songs Hoartrap had sung about rowan trees, but unlike those overtly horrific tales this one somehow felt real to his ear...

Hoartrap held it together for all of a moment, and then snickered at Sullen's ignorance. "Of course not, that's just an old Emeritus mudwives' tale." His puffy face turned grave again. "Or is it? Who knows what spirits walk this night, freed by the...the...*magic of the moon!*"

The Touch had a really good belly laugh at that, and Sullen offered him an obscene gesture since he didn't think he could make his face ugly enough to match his mood at being made the fool yet again. "Right, well, I'll give Ma and the devils of the rowan tree your regards."

"I can come, I can help," said Brother Rýt, reminding Sullen that his life had become exponentially more complicated.

The pudgy monk sat farther back from the fire, and these were the first words he'd managed since Nemi had marched him over from her wagon and placed him under Sullen's supervision. The witch had insisted the Samothan boy belonged to Sullen's mother and was therefore his responsibility. He had been all set to argue the point when he'd recognized the kid from back home, and as Nemi returned to the wheeled house where she had taken Purna for a music lesson Sullen felt a mix of happy excitement and utter dismay at seeing a familiar face. It wasn't like he'd ever spoken more than two words to the foreign boy, Father Turisa's novice not exactly going out of his way to hang out with the village anathema, but still, meeting him here and now was as unexpectedly moving as it was just plain unexpected. When it became apparent the missionary was as terrorstricken by Sullen's awkward but friendly greeting as if he'd been thrown at the mercy of a slavering devil king, Sullen tried to calm Rýt down by telling him he was a free person, right, and could leave without anyone hurting him, no problem.

But instead of thanking Sullen or even just booking it away from his inadvertent captors, the monk had slumped his shoulders and wept, his glittering amethyst eyes shedding flakes of gemstone instead of tears. It was about that time Sullen realized the kid's peepers must not just be fancy glass eyes that he'd taken to wearing after leaving the village for some inscrutable purpose of Crimson fashion or Chainite ritual, but something with an even stranger origin...but Sullen knew a thing or two about people looking at you askance on account of your eyes being odd, and had told Rýt he didn't have to leave if he didn't want to. That had finally chilled the boy out, but the ensuing campfire talk with Hoartrap must have gotten him all worked up again, and now he seemed desperate for any pretense for a break, just like Sullen.

That, or maybe he really just wanted to help with Sullen's mom—they must have come a long way together, Ma and this monk, and that right there was just plain strange. How had his hardarsed mother of all people found the patience to roll out with a nervous novice who was so recently blinded that he could barely walk upright without having somebody's arm to lean on?

"Nah, y'all hang back—I'd better go it alone," said Sullen, not really wanting an audience tagging along lest his mom finally do more than give him the silent stinkeye. "Those roots ready? I oughta take her some food."

"If the rabid she-wolf can open her mouth to eat she can use it to beg for clemency," Keun-ju said with a splash of justifiable venom. "She tried to murder us, she refused to speak when we gave her the opportunity to explain herself, and you're worried she's *hungry*?"

"Well...nobody's on their best behavior when an empty tum's worrying them," said Sullen, feeling like a total arsehole but unable to stop himself from wanting to look after his mom, even after what she'd done.

"Do you suppose that's why she came at us so hard, Sullen, because she skipped lunch?" Keun-ju turned to Rýt and said, "You were with her the whole time she was hunting us, Chainite, did she strike you as particularly peckish?"

"Um...no?" said the monk, looking even less happy to be addressed than he had when they were all ignoring him.

"Not as though you would have seen her snacking, though, would you?" said Hoartrap. "Joking, joking!"

"The only joke here is your manners," said Diggelby, going over to sit next to the dejected Samothan. "He has a name, you know, and he might be as treasure-eyed as a social-climbing townie but there's nothing wrong with his ears. Is there, Brother Rýt?"

"Um...no?"

"And while we're on the subject, brother dearest, wherever did you come by those fetching facets?" asked Hoartrap. "Don't tell me Nemi laid those in your sockets!"

"Here." Keun-ju spitted a twisted kudzu root on his poking stick and jutted it at Sullen as Brother Rýt hemmed and hawed under Hoartrap's unwelcome attention. "Just make sure she doesn't bite your hand off when you feed her. It's harder than it looks to get by with just one."

That good and got Sullen choked up, and the hot tuber scalded his fingers, but he took the words and the food with the same resigned sigh and turned away into the dark trees to check on his mom. He didn't know what else to do. As usual.

Except...

Except the fuck he didn't know what to do. Sullen might not be good at what Ji-hyeon called maths but he knew exactly what the score was, he just didn't like the sum and so he dithered and he fretted until his head was spinning from all the second-and-third-and-fourth-guessing. As usual. The same weak headspace that had cost Keun-ju his arm and almost cost Sullen even more, when his mom burst back into his life with the sole intention of ending it. He'd never so much as harbored an ill thought for her, had loved her so much he'd been willing to give her his own life if it meant he didn't have to do the harder thing and take hers, and if not for Hoartrap arriving when he did then both Sullen and Keun-ju would probably be dead.

And for what? The pride of the Horned Wolf Clan? Some even stupider reason, assuming there even *was* such a thing? He had no fucking idea why she'd come after him, because every time he'd come over to try to get her to talk, she just sneered and spat and stared him down until he left her alone.

It wasn't a long walk from the campfire to where his mom was restrained—before the sun had set he'd been able to see her sitting there in the bowl of the great rowan, watching him and his friends—but Sullen took his time, trying to get his rising bile under control before he engaged her again. Yet while he used to be able to calm himself down by focusing on all the ways he'd probably make a tense situation worse with his clumsiness, now Sullen's every thought just inflamed him further. His fist tightened on the spear Grandfather had gone into, the weapon he was using as a crutch...the one Ji-hyeon had commissioned in Sullen's absence and sent Hoartrap halfway across the Star to deliver to him. She had ordered the Touch to give Sullen this special gift even though it meant being without one of her most powerful captains when she led the Cobalt Company through the Lark's Tongue Gate, toward what might be the last battle she would ever fight.

Last night Keun-ju had tearfully told Sullen what he had been too upset to relate before: that while Sullen was knocked the fuck out following his family reunion, Hoartrap had informed everyone that Hwabun had been the first isle to fall to the armies of Jex Toth. Ji-hyeon's family and Keun-ju's fellow servants and all of their mutual friends and neighbors were gone. They no longer had a home to fight for, but still Ji-hyeon had answered Empress Ryuki's call for help in the defense of the Immaculate Isles. Their woman was standing fearless in the face of a devilish host the likes of which Sullen had never believed existed outside the oldest, craziest songs of his people, ready to sacrifice herself for the good of all mortals, and meanwhile Sullen almost threw his life away for...for...for fucking *nothing*.

No, for something even worse than nothing, because folk died for nothing every day, and there may not be pride in that but there wasn't shame, either...But after all he'd been through, how fucked was it that Sullen had been willing to die for the Horned Wolf Clan?

He wasn't taking his time anymore, hurling the roasted kudzu root off into the wood as hard as he could, carrying his spear like a warrior instead of an old man. The moon wasn't up yet but now that he'd moved away from the firelight the dark forest concealed no secrets from the eyes he'd been so blessed to be born with, just as Grandfather had always told him. These wildborn eyes of his had always shown him a little something more than others could see, and as he strode up to the familiar shape of his seated mother he saw her more clearly than he ever had before; not just her mortal frame, ankles and wrists manacled around an exposed elbow of the mighty rowan roots, but the true nature of the woman he had so long refused to see. She was his mother, yes, but she was a Horned Wolf first, and always had been.

She watched his approach, flashing her teeth at him in warning or cold greeting. He rolled up on her just as silent as she had run up on him and Keun-ju, the spear made from her father gripped in both hands. She didn't flinch as he thrust the weapon toward her, but her eyes grew wide, her mean smile turned generous, and that right there was the most fucked-up thing of all—she wanted him to take her life. She wanted a son who would skewer his own mother rather than keeping her as a prisoner, or worst of all, freeing her.

Which was too fucking bad for her, because Sullen wasn't ever granting another Horned Wolf's wish. The leaf-shaped spearhead easily sank to the haft in the clay-rich earth just beside his mother, but as her sick pride melted into an expression of disgust Sullen got right in her fucking face, bending down so low his overgrown heap of hair would have fallen in his eyes if it hadn't bumped into his mom's braids.

"You listen to me, Ma," Sullen growled. "Talk or keep that screw-face hushed, I don't give a fuck, but you listen."

Her lip started to curl into that devildamned sneer and Sullen knocked his forehead into hers before he even thought about it. Not hard, mind, but it must have surprised her as much as it surprised himself, the scabbing wound she'd opened up on his scalp aching from the impact. Keeping his mug right up in hers, he said it again.

"You *listen*. Now. Because this right here, Ma? This is the end of the fucking song."

"*The end of the song.*" The first words she'd spoken to him since they'd fought it out, and she was imitating him, mocking him through her split lip. "I prayed every day you'd grow out of your songs. Did you know that? Every day. To the Fallen Mother, Old Black, Silvereye, and every other mask our maker wears—all I wanted for you was to stop living in songs and start living a life."

"No, you didn't," said Sullen, her hypocrisy whetting his anger and resentment into something sharp that could cut through his clan's bullshit. "You just wanted me to believe in yours, in the Chainite Hymn of the reformed Horned Wolf Clan. But you know what, Ma? That song is *shit*. It's too small, and it's too ugly, and I grew the fuck out of it."

"Life isn't a fucking song!" He'd never heard his mother's voice break before, but instead of flinching away from the hurt he heard in her words he fed on it, the way a good Horned Wolf feasts on the pain of its foes.

"Thing is, Ma, I didn't think it was, either. Not really." He leaned forward so that their foreheads touched again, but gentler, rocking his brow against hers. "But then I went on a quest. I met witches. I fought monsters. I got mixed up in a quarrel between a forgotten god and a warrior of legend. I fell in love with a princess *and* her suitor. And even after all that, I told myself I was being stupid when I looked to our old sagas for strength or wisdom. I told myself I was a baby and a fool. And all the time I was living a song the likes of which I wouldn't have believed, not really, if I'd heard it as a pup at Witmouth's knee. And…and I want to sing it for you, Ma, and have you actually fucking listen for once. Because this song isn't just about you and me and if we ought to kill each other over some old tribal bullshit, it's about the whole world being in danger. About the First Dark flooding back into the Star, *right fucking now*, and everyone from Flintland to the Raniputri Dominions being overrun if we don't stop it. So *please*…will you let me sing to you?"

Something he'd said had caught her off guard, or more than that, struck some chord, because she swallowed heavily, and leaned back from his forehead, looking up at where Silvereye was just climbing up the trees of the Haunted Forest. And maybe it was the keenness of his eyes or perhaps the acuity of a hopeful son, but he was sure that his mother did want to hear him out, that she *wanted* him to tell her something to counteract whatever crazy Horned Wolf nonsense had set her after him. But then the softness of her features tightened, and narrowing her eyes she said, "I will listen to your song, Sullen, but if I am not convinced I will again demand you meet me in combat to determine—"

"You don't get to demand shit!" Sullen straightened back up, so fucking mad at her way of thinking he couldn't see straight. "I sing you my song, and then I fucking *leave*, Ma. I journey beyond the Star to war with an ancient evil, and you either come along to help or you get left tied to a fucking tree!"

As usual, she got caught up on the wrong detail entirely. "If you flee like your uncle a second time, my son, there will be no hole deep enough to hide you from my wrath."

"Well, when that happens you'll get fucking dealt with!" Sullen snatched his spear out of the dirt and waggled it in her face. "I'll use Fa to take away *your* ruddy legs, and I will leave you a third time, because you haven't done squat to earn a death at my hand, you crazy fucking savage! Fuck!"

In the panting pause that followed he glared at his mother, and she glared back up at him with a barely perceptible smile and nod of her chin. She'd never looked that way at him before, and Sullen realized she must be proud of him. Horned Wolves, man, what the actual *fuck*.

"Did my father die well?" she asked, looking at the spear, and though she tried to conceal her worry from him Sullen was far more acquainted to hearing that note in her voice.

"He did one better, Ma—he lived correct," said Sullen, twisting the spear in his hand so the blade could drink the moonlight. "And he went to Old Black's Meadhall with a bushel more kills to his name than if he'd died back on the Savannahs all them years ago, when you abandoned us."

His mother shook her head. "I did no such thing. The Clan does not carry those who cannot carry themselves. You knew this but you chose to stay with your grandfather. He was the one who—"

"*You* left *us*," said Sullen, the words catching in his throat. Maybe he was simple, after all, that he only now saw which way the glacier faulted. Even after he'd left the Savannahs, hells, even after he'd lost his grandfather and set out from the Cobalt camp in search of his uncle, he'd kept making excuses for her, and kept his anger focused on the wrong kinfolk. "You hate your brother for turning his tail on his people, but what about you? What about you turning your fucking back on me and Fa when we needed you most?"

"You know the difference, even if it doesn't suit your song," said his mother. "Your uncle Craven betrayed everything—"

"Fucking right he did! And so did your son, and so did your dad, and goons that we were, none of us saw we were all doing it for the same reason." It was so damn obvious Sullen had to laugh: a short, mean bark. "You know what I was doing out here in this wood when you finally caught me, Ma? Hunting down Maroto, for the same reason you were hunting down me. 'Cause we caught him once, me and Fa, and he cut out again, and we Horned Wolves can't abide someone running off 'fore we're done with 'em, can we? Drives us blood simple, someone not staying to fight and maybe die when and where we tell 'em to. I been focused so hard on putting a sun-knife in my uncle's face I didn't take the time to think if maybe I shouldn't tap his fist instead, for leading by example."

"You follow his example too much already."

"Yeah, 'cause excusing yourself from a bad scene is such a disgrace," said Sullen, and now he wasn't even mad at his mom, he just felt sorry for her crazy arse. "Took you almost doing for me the way I would've done for him to appreciate it, but now it's all I can see—refusing to fight is its own kinda battle, and a better one at that. How much less sorrow and death would there be in this sorry world if every time we disagreed with someone we left them to their business instead of coming to blows over it? My uncle didn't leave the Horned Wolves because he didn't care about us, he left because he knew that way wouldn't ever be his, and instead of making a stink he just walked away."

"Yet you tell me you and Father caught him, only for him to flee and lead you on another hunt," said his mother, trying to talk down at him the way she used to but it wasn't working now, and wouldn't ever again. "What noble purpose does his newest desertion serve, Sullen? Go on and tell me, I'm sure the Deceiver has provided all the excuses your uncle needs."

"He's gone ahead to scout out Jex Toth," said Sullen, leaving off any lingering skepticism he might harbor about Hoartrap having told them the whole truth where his uncle was concerned. "And that's exactly what I'm on about, how we always think the worst when someone goes away without our knowing why, instead of waiting till we see what's up to judge 'em. I figured he was just being a coward, running off to get himself safe, but I come to learn he's actually been in the most danger of anyone, all by himself in a perilous land, and doing it selfless-like. Being a fucking hero, you want to get right down to it, risking his life to try and help the rest of us mortals get a leg up on whatever monsters are out there preparing to invade our lands."

"Craven the Hero," said his mother, sounding like she believed that as much as Sullen did...which was to say, not nearly as much as he wanted to. "So long as you keep me snared to this tree I can't stop you from singing, but I shall never believe such a song until I see my brother prove his honor with my own eyes."

"That's fair, Ma," said Sullen, trying to meet her in the middle here. He wasn't so innocent as to think he could change his mom's mind all at once, right, but maybe, just maybe, this could be the start of some understanding. "Rakehell knows there's plenty I seen myself that I still barely believe. So that's all the more reason for you to come with us, raise your spear against the First Dark for a change, instead of your fellow mortals. Just hear me out—by the end I promise we'll meet my uncle again, and see what we make of him once we've got a chance to judge him by his deeds instead of his absence."

There was a pause as they appraised each other in the unseasonable mugginess of the winter night, the light of the crescent moon splashing off the clustered ivory flowers of the sprawling rowan and shining on the scars of his mother's cheeks. Sullen remembered Hoartrap's warning of devils in the wood overhearing his secrets, but even if there was any truth in the Touch's tale he didn't regret a word. So long as his mother actually listened to him, all the lesser evils of this world were welcome to eavesdrop, too, and quake at the coming of a hero such as Sullen...

"Sing me your song, then," she said at last, the same words in the same resigned tone he had heard a hundred times in his childhood, when he'd finally worn her down enough that she'd sit back on her grass mat in their hut and listen to the newest saga he'd learned. He just had to hope she stayed awake better now than she usually had back then...and that if he somehow convinced her, and they somehow managed to reach Jex Toth, and then *somehow* found Maroto, that his uncle would indeed prove to be fighting the good fight for a change, instead of sitting it out on his saggy old arse.

CHAPTER
6

Maroto, enchained. But not in actual chains, oh no, that would have been far too boring for his mute captors. Instead of more traditional manacles his hands had been enveloped in thick, tacky webbing. A sticky noose of the same material encircled his neck and rose from his nape up into the close air of the caverns, tethering him to the pale, bloated thing that had spun his shackles. It crawled upside down on the ceiling of the tunnels, keeping pace with the prisoner and his guards as they led him deeper and deeper into their grotesque realm of pulsing, fleshy walls and shiny outcroppings of bone.

When they first took Maroto, he thought that beneath their spiny black armor the Tothans might have been human, or something similar—wildborn, maybe. As their squid-dragon carried him away over the treetops he had even let himself indulge in fantasies where the Tothans were fun-loving freaks of comely cast who would welcome him to their revels, once he explained how he and Bang hadn't actually been spying on their army but were marooned on Jex Toth completely by accident. He gave up on that particular fancy as soon as they flew into the cave system where rock and earth gave way to gleaming musculature and soft, oozing stalactites. Nothing remotely human would choose to dwell in such a foul hell, and whatever parties went on down here he'd sooner sit out.

After the monstrosity released him from its tentacles he splashed down in a warm pool of gelatinous slime teeming with thankfully unseen creatures that ate away the net-like web they had first bound him in. As soon as he slipped free of the disintegrating lattice he was hauled out of the goo by more of the Tothans, and before he could recover from the shock of it all, fresh webbing was applied to hands and throat by the fat white arachnid that drew its silk from a grinning human mouth in the base of its furry abdomen. When it rappelled back to the ceiling of the meat-cave, tightening Maroto's noose as it did, he decided that here at last was an occasion so profoundly terrible that he had no fucking time to spare for self-doubt or self-pity or self-loathing. Up until the moment he escaped this nightmare—or bit off his own tongue to bleed to death, if all else failed—his every thought and action would be dedicated to self-preservation.

And so the Mighty Maroto marched obediently forward, trying to keep his cool and think rationally even in this hellscape that looked like the insides of a giant animal and smelled like an overfull terrarium in a low-rent bughouse. The funk to this place definitely had an insect origin, or at least that was the closest touchstone to the cloying, oily stench that made Maroto's eyes water. Not surprising, that, between the spiderbeast they had used to bind him and the beetle-like cast of their armor—now that he was able to take a good look at the Tothans' ridged, thorny black plate he was guessing it wasn't just made to look like bug shell but had actually come off some heretofore unknown species of giant insect. It was a fleet look, he had to admit, the pieces locking together so tightly he couldn't see a hint of chain or leather between the chinks, nor even an eye-slit in the blank, sharp crowned faceplates, yet the pair of guards moved twice as gracefully as Maroto would have in armor half as bulky. They carried neither weapons nor equipment—at least, none that he could see—but sharp as their clawed gauntlets looked he wasn't in a hurry to tangle with them.

Faceless soldiers armored in grotesque chitin, stinking of a rancid earwig nest. A domesticated spider-thing the size of a small dog, but Maroto was the one on the leash. He had assumed bugs would be the end of him, yet never in his wildest stingdreams had he imagined such a dramatically literal finale. Here in the bowels of this manifest nightmare he remembered something his old friend Carla Rossi had told him one night when they were both whacked out of their wigs on black centipede meat, following some long-forgotten production in some never-remembered town:

"Hell ain't going to hold no fresh horrors for the likes of us," she'd slurred through electric-blue lips, tears in her eyes from sentiment or her smeared greasepaint or some combination of the twain. "No, if the gods are cruel, as we well and fucking truly *know* they are, then hell's going to be nuthin' more than coming right back to where you started—only this time, you can't leave."

In the moment he'd figured the drag clown was referring to her shitty hometown on the Imperial frontier, but given the current insect overtones to Maroto's fate he had to wonder if Carla wouldn't have been better off reading fortunes than working the stage. He didn't know if you'd call it irony or poetic justice or what, but there was undeniably a certain dramatic *something* to Carla's sloppy mouth predicting this over-the-top twist half a lifetime ago. The worst part was Maroto had finally kicked the bugs once and for all, too, only to wind up here! Now granted, he'd thought he was clean and clear a few times before only to step back in that familiar antbed, but looking around this insectoid inferno one thing was for certain—if he managed to escape his captors he was never, ever banging another bug so long as he lived. *Never.*

The ribbed passage they escorted him down was dark as clotted blood, but where his bare feet struck the membranous floor it gave off pulses of black light that illuminated the shaft in front of them. Glancing back he saw three glowing trails of footprints on the floor, and a smaller, fainter track on the ceiling. Weird. Also worth keeping in mind—even if he somehow slipped free of both these guards and the arachnid overhead he'd leave an unmistakable trail wherever he went, so long as he was down in these caverns. The more he saw of this subterranean horror show and the more turns they took in the labyrinth of softly contracting tunnels, the more obvious it became that the only way he was getting free of this place was if they escorted him back out again.

"So, uh, real nice digs you've got here," Maroto said in Immaculate, trying one last time to engage his captors. "I know y'all didn't say you spoke Crimson or Immaculate or whatever when I asked before, but you didn't say you didn't, neither, so how about just a nod or something? Figure you've got your orders not to talk to prisoners, and I respect that, but it'd be nice to know if you hear anything I'm saying, yeah?"

If they did they still weren't giving any indication, neither of the guards so much as turning their helmets in his direction. Their continued silence had gone from rude to downright creepy, but presumably someone down here would be able to understand him, otherwise why keep a potentially hostile prisoner alive? Actually, that was a question he was happier not contemplating at present...

Then came real light up ahead at the end of the tunnel, bright and yellow and welcoming as the sun he hadn't seen in however many hours he'd been down here in the guts of Jex Toth. When they reached the mouth of the cave he no longer found the brightness so inviting, coming as it did from the roof of the eeriest chamber yet. They had emerged onto a ledge overlooking a sprawling grotto that must have been a mile wide and just as long. Far above stretched an illuminated, fan-vaulted ceiling that would have been the envy of every Chainite cathedral on the Star, if only the ribs hadn't actually been *ribs*. The great sunken hall looked even gnarlier than the rest of this place, with phosphorescent rivers crisscrossing the already moist meatscape, steam belching from obscenely winking pits, and a lumpy ziggurat rising from a glowing lake in the center of the cavern...And there, beached on the polyped shores of the luminous loch, was a piebald mass of twitching white meat and squirting black geysers that made Maroto need to take a knee.

He was not creative enough to imagine what dark fluids it might be jetting up, or from whence in the mountain of flesh these fountains might originate. Hells, he was too far away to even begin to guess just what in the unholy fuck it *was*, but he was already far closer than he ever wanted to be. The spider's noose tightened around his neck as he fell to his knees on the nauseatingly spongy floor, but then it relaxed before he could choke himself out. Was this why people knelt in prayer? Not from thoughtful deference to a higher power, but because some things were so enormous and terrible that your only recourse was to make yourself as small as possible, hoping you wouldn't be spotted?

The sticky rope around Maroto's neck tugged him insistently back to his unsteady feet, and he closed his eyes, on the verge of tears. He had never known animal terror like this before—he had been prepared for the worst when he sacrificed himself to save Bang, of course he had, but what the fuck even *was* this place? It would be his tomb, of that there seemed little question, because what mortal could hope to stand strong against such horrors as he couldn't even bring himself to look at for more than an instant?

One of the guards nudged him forward, and Maroto Devilskinner, the Barbarian Without Fear, whimpered.

Something heavy landed on Maroto's shoulder, thick whip-like limbs wrapping around him for purchase, and he gave a little scream that echoed to embarrassing proportion in the grotto. He tried to throw it off him, but even if his web-mittened hands had been able to find purchase on the hissing spider-thing that tightened its legs and the noose around his throat in equal measure the two guards seized his arms, reminding him of just how very wrong his day had gone...and after a promising start, too. At least he had saved his sweet-palmed Captain Bang from a similar fate, and clinging to that scrap of relief he allowed the monster on his back to get comfortable.

Bang was safe, and so were Dong-won and Niki-hyun. Maroto breathed in the malodorous air, told his heart to calm the fuck down. Diggelby was probably high as fuck in his plush tent right now, and maybe Bang had been right when she'd given him her pep talk, maybe Purna had survived the Battle of the Lark's Tongue after all. Maybe Choi and Din and Hassan had made it out all right, too, and they were all safe. They were all safe and alive and an ocean away from whatever hell their old friend had slipped into. Maybe—

Slack returned to the noose as the two guards dragged him forward, and then they unexpectedly released him as his bare feet found purchase on smooth steps. He opened his eyes but kept them focused on the enamel stairs set into the veiny cliff face beneath the over-look, a treacherous path that led down to the floor of the cavern. He should hurl himself over the edge, sparing himself whatever came next, because whatever it was it couldn't be good—these monstrous legions that dwelled within the heart of Jex Toth wanted him alive, and that probably meant he should be dead, for the sake of the Star.

He took a deep breath, ready to jump off of the cliff and plum-met to his death...but not ready enough, his knees nearly knocking together, and he took the first step down instead of going over the side. He remembered his father laughing in his face when he told him the clan had decided to name him Craven, and years later the look of scorn on his nephew's face when they had met in the Cobalt camp. They had all been right about him—he was a coward, and telling himself that going forward to face whatever awaited him below was braver than ending his life now didn't really wash. Here at the end of his adventures, Maroto was alone with himself, and found the company less than agreeable.

Alone was all he deserved, sure, but pity the simpleton who couldn't long for more than that.

And if he could have only one other person down here beside him, in this horrible place he couldn't even process, to go down beside him, to hold his hand as they both fell for the last time? It was still her. It would always be her. If only because she was the only one he'd ever met who would have still been able to summon a smile, even here, and ask him just what the devils he'd expected to see waiting for them at the finish, after the lives they'd lived? Heaven wasn't for the likes of them.

And real talk now, the main reason he wanted her here was because if one of them deserved this shit it damn sure wasn't him; he wouldn't even be here right now if it weren't for Cold Zosia.

Another, harder nudge to the neck from a bristly gauntlet, and he took another shaky step. Heights had never bothered him, and now at the one time he would've probably been better off slipping he found himself with bad vertigo and would have welcomed a steady hand to help him down the slick path. His captors stayed behind at the top of the overlook, however, letting him proceed on his own. Or as close to on his own as he was going to get, so long as the unpleasantly hot and disconcertingly soft arachnid clung to his back. As he descended the narrow stair a familiar burning returned to his calves, and he almost laughed to think how just a few short hours before he'd been hiking up the side of a scenic mountain with a handsome pirate keeping him company, and now he might be miles beneath that very spot.

Almost laughed, right, but not bloody quite. He paused to lean against the pulsing wall of meat until his head stopped spinning but the monster on his back immediately tightened its noose, and he felt even less like chuckling. There's a limit to everything, even a man's ability to find gallows humor in his own ill fortune. As he reached the bottom of the sweaty-stepped path and finally made himself look up from his feet, he figured things weren't getting funny anytime soon. Not that kind of funny, anyway.

A figure was walking swiftly toward him, through a field of wavering, luminescent meat fans. That the person appeared to be human would normally have put him at ease, but somehow this only made them more horrific. Maroto believed just about anything was possible in this world where devils granted miracles and monsters of every conceivable shape stalked and squawked; seriously, now, he'd just tromped through the literal bowels of a long-lost kingdom, so he was willing to accept anything that greeted his eyes... or almost anything, it turned out, because even though he was looking right at this he still couldn't believe it.

The dead stayed dead, that was one of the few truths the Star round. Nothing could make them stir, not deviltry nor witchery, not bugs nor drugs...yet as soon as Maroto saw the approaching figure lit up from the orange-shimmering field of flesh at its feet he was sure of one thing, and that was that while this stranger should have been long dead, it wasn't. Despite the brightness of the glowing, anemone-like fans the spindly person was cloaked in flowing shadows, and as it reached Maroto he realized this was due to the thousands of cockroaches that crawled over its naked form. It was so desiccated he couldn't begin to guess if it had skewed more to the masculine or feminine by birth if not by identity, translucent skin stretched taut as a cannibal's drum over its sharp skeleton.

"Fuck me," Maroto whimpered as the bug-clad mummy came to a stop spitting-distance away, its eyes bright and ageless in its bleached, cadaverous face. It cocked its head at him like a rooster sizing up a grub, the swarm of insects going still and forming an uncanny approximation of old-timey Immaculate attire. Aside from the chitinous slippers and trousers, shirt and housecoat, the monster's only trappings were rings made of bleached white vertebrae that crowded its left hand and a rather gaudy choker of yellow gold and red stones in the shape of miniature skulls.

"I, um, come in peace?" said Maroto when the creature took no immediate action, because you always had to hope for the best even when the worst was coming in for a great big sloppy kiss. In response its shriveled lips parted in a grin that revealed stunningly white teeth. It raised its hand, thick rings clattering on thin fingers, and reached out for Maroto's face.

That wasn't on, no fucking way. Normally he would've lashed out if some horrible monster was trying to get its dirty digits on him, but he was loath to touch this thing, even in self-defense...lest he provoke it. This fiend filled him with pure, concentrated dread, and rather than attacking it or batting away its outstretched hand he jumped back—and bumped into a second living corpse.

This one looked male—the tumescent prick rising like a mast from the maelstrom of insects swarming his crotch was a tell, and with a wordless cry of revulsion Maroto pushed away from him. This sunken-eyed ancient boasted a bloated gut and liver-spotted wattles that somehow rendered him even more gruesome than his emaciated peer, his hungry eyes the only sharp thing about him as a soft fat tongue ran over soft fat lips. Maroto's world got all tight and treacly the way it did in only the shittiest of shitshows, each moment passing so slow he had plenty of time to think about what to do next instead of just reacting...

Or so it usually went, anyway, but fast on his feet and his wits as Maroto was operating, these things were a good bit faster. A third came out of nowhere—as in, she appeared out of thin air, that was how fast she was—and swept his legs out from under him with a shin so thin it looked like it should've detonated on impact with his thick calf but hit harder than an iron rod.

Anyone else would have gone down, and gone down hard, but Maroto threw himself into a roll and came up running. Never, ever underestimate the value of a well-timed roll followed by a breakneck flight. He crashed through the wavering meat fans, finding them less like the soft flesh they resembled and more like jagged coral. The spider creature on his back tightened its noose around his throat, trying to choke him out. He slapped over his shoulder and put his hand through its surprisingly soft carapace, ripping the thing off him in gooey chunks even as his world went dim from lack of air.

The Hell of the Coward Dead. Old Watchers forgive him, he had always doubted his ancestors' warnings, had never believed that the ancient ways were anything more than savage superstition, but as he staggered forward he knew, yes he fucking did—he had finally ended up where his dad and sister had always warned him he was bound, and it damn sure wasn't Old Black's Meadhall. He was dead and in hell. Not the first time he'd jumped to such a morbid conclusion, but this time he reckoned he was really onto something.

A behemoth reared above him out of the living foliage, all the more ghastly for its familiarity. It was the larger cousin of the monster whose eggs he and Bang had stolen what seemed like a decade past—a huge black-shelled nightmare somewhere between a crab and a cobraroach, with a giant, sharp-fanged human face on its chest and snatching hairy arms in place of mandibles. The one he had lured down to the beach was big enough it could have eaten him in a few bites, but this mother could do the job in one, swallowing him whole if it had half a mind.

It looked like it intended to do just that, and Maroto reeled sideways, arms and legs refusing to do his bidding anymore—he had massacred the monster on his back, but its webbing continued to garrote him, and his fingers couldn't find purchase on the caustic noose...

But then the great monster was dismissed, fleeing as if in fright from the posse who waded through the broken meat-ferns to crowd Maroto's asphyxiation. Their spindly hands were all over him, unpleasantly reminding him of the gross arachnid he had torn off his back as they explored his body. The morbidly obese one squeezed and prodded Maroto's midsection, drool dangling from his split-sausage lips, and then the withered woman hooked her fingers under the noose and tore it free, allowing their quarry to again breathe the stinking fumes of their lair.

They kept giving each other knowing glances as they inspected Maroto with obvious relish, more and more of the shriveled old figures emerging from the bleeding landscape until there must have been a dozen of the things surrounding him. The close air crackled as the fiends gathered, and as he gasped like a landed trout Maroto reckoned by their rapidly changing expressions and fiercely knowing looks that his captors were communicating with one another by some silent, unknown means. They were intelligent. In some way he couldn't begin to guess, yes, and no doubt of diabolical intention, sure, but they were a pack of thinking creatures, and as an impossibly old man softly gummed Maroto's bicep and then let out an appreciative moan, he figured he'd at least piqued their interest.

"I'll help you," he gasped in Immaculate, hoping the universal trading tongue extended all the way down here to the bottom basement of the Sunken Kingdom of Jex Toth. "I'm useful. Whoever you are and whatever you want, I'm your boy. Just let me go."

The fat man delicately kneading Maroto's flattop paused, as did the rest…and then, one by one, they began to scream. At him. In his face, leaning in close, the shrill sounds so raw they made Maroto's throat ache in solidarity even as the rest of him trembled in panic. Then the original, roach-wreathed ancient reached down from where it had been standing aloof from the others, its spine-ringed fingers finally grazing Maroto's nose…and immediately triggering violent hallucinations.

Burning worlds.

The frozen blackness of the place between the stars, beyond the Gates.

A crowd of priests performing a ritual Maroto himself had once enacted, to bind devils, and horror of horrors, offering themselves in sacrifice instead of animals.

Armies marching, cities smoldering.

A garden of monsters.

Legions of the black-armored Tothans marching through Diadem, across the Isles and the Dominions, the Frozen Savannahs melting beneath the vile secretions of their titanic warbeasts and snow falling on the deserts of Usba as their sorceries ripped holes in reality, the armies of Jex Toth conquering the Star absolutely.

The world as sacrifice.

"Fuck." Maroto gagged on the word, on the hot spew ejecting from his guts as the visions faded, leaving him alert and aware in a netherworld of living muscle and meat beneath a breathing sky, held down by the high priests of Jex Toth, who had vanished along with the rest of their kingdom half a millennium past. He wasn't in the Hell of the Coward Dead after all, and figured going forward he would just have to assume he was still alive until proven otherwise... which might not be a long wait, anyway, considering the pack of fiends crowding their prone victim.

Eyes stared from black pits set in white faces, fingers stroked him with sensual menace, the creatures looking almost as amazed by Maroto's living body as he was by their mummy-like forms. They weren't screaming en masse anymore, and Maroto pulled a hand free of their groping paws and wiped the wetness from his eyes. Blood streaked the back of his hand in lieu of tears, and the ring-fingered monster elbowed its fellows away and started shrieking again, right in Maroto's face. He flinched back from the shrill death rattle, but then caught a word of antiquated High Immaculate, and then a second, and tough though it was to parse with just the one good ear, with some effort he was able to tune in to the shrill frequency.

"—you *will* help us! Indeed!" It crowed, reaching into its scuttling coat and withdrawing a crude dagger fashioned from curled black horn. "Our first sacrifice!"

Thin fingers tightened hard as steel all over Maroto, but while most of the cohort were enthusiastically laying hands on him the bloated man seemed to take nearly as much umbrage to this suggestion as the sacrifice himself. The ancient didn't scream, didn't speak at all, but it was plain from the shuddering of his pruny jowls and the shaking of his spoiled-salami fingers that he disapproved. From the crackling waves of energy Maroto felt flowing back and forth over him, he was sure the two monsters were exchanging something, if not words. More visions, perhaps?

"Kill me if you must, but kill me last!" Maroto cried in High Immaculate, or as close to the formal dialect as he could manage. "You want to sacrifice the Star? Good! I can help you do it! Kill me last and I'll do anything you want!"

The last shred of Maroto's pride left his lips along with the futile words. It was almost a relief. Ever since falling in with Purna he had been planning on dying like the hero he had never been in life, but that was the thing about plans—they had a way of getting fucked, and without the benefit of coconut oil to ease the passage.

At least his words had gotten the monsters' attention. A pair of them immediately released him, falling all over each other as they made the worst sounds imaginable...sounds he realized were rattling laughs, or as close as their withered bodies could manage. The woman who had knocked his legs out from under him began to sob as she stroked Maroto's neck, the lanky hair she dangled in his face swarming with spiders. Through his revulsion he realized her sick cries were more rasping words of High Immaculate, her sharp fingernails now lightly scratching his chin as she spoke.

"Sacrifiiiiice! Yessss! The first shall be the laaaaast!"

"It will do anything?" the one with the dagger screamed at Maroto, and intense and dreadful as this exchange was he still saw it as a definite improvement. He had them communicating in a way he could understand, and the more he understood them the better his odds at ingratiating himself. "It will let us peer inside for proof?"

"It will!" howled the fat geriatric, placing its puffy fingers around Maroto's throat. "Open its heart! Open its head!"

"Hey now, let's not get carried away with—" Maroto began, trying to wriggle free, but the original horror reached out again with its ringed hand. Which was better than the dagger but not by much... and in fact might have been substantially worse, as fingertips that felt carved of ice first massaged Maroto's sweaty brow and then began to press into the flesh. Had the pain been unbearable the experience might have been borne, but the feeling of the fingers gently pushing through skin and then into his skull barely hurt at all... and that made it even more horrible, Maroto writhing from an indescribable sensation the likes of which he had never before experienced, grinding his teeth so hard they felt primed to explode.

Then the horror of the moment fell away as Maroto was again overwhelmed by visions, but this time they came not from the ring-fingered Tothan but his own violated brainmeat. Didn't make them any better; hells, they might be worse, 'cause the carnage he saw repeated in his mind's eye wasn't some monster's prophecy but his own personal history—memories of murder and worse, as he helped Cold Zosia win the Crimson Throne. Then came the conjuring of the devils they bound in Emeritus, and for the first time since the torrent of visions washed over him Maroto was able to catch his breath, even as he sensed the Tothan catching his.

The ancient didn't fully break from the trance-like state, the interruption too mild for that, but it did give Maroto just enough time to realize the interloper in his brain must not be aware of what was coming next, that he was as much a passenger in this stream of memories as Maroto himself... and if no one was driving this runaway cart, that meant a quick-witted barbarian might grab the reins. He tried it out, thinking as hard as he could of his old theater troupe who had been so big on method acting—and it worked! When they came into sharp relief he focused on the time he and Two-eyed Jacques and Carla had set the playhouse of their rivals on fire. Right enough, the memory presented itself as clear as the night it went down, the air thick with smoke and the stench of burning wigs, the screams of the trapped patrons and the laughter of his friends, and at the edges of his now-aching skull Maroto was sure he could feel a shiver of pleasure from the Tothan peeper.

You like that, don't you? Maroto thought to himself, and to his guest. *You said you're looking for proof, yeah? I don't know if you wanted proof of how helpful I'd be, or proof of why I'd sell out the Star to you freaks, but there's plenty of both in this rotten old keg. Drink it up!*

And now that he had the hang of things, Maroto did his best to drown the mind-reading old monster under a tidal wave of his baddest behavior. Happy memories of Purna and the crew had no place here, nor did lusty thoughts of Choi or Bang, nor did he share a single reminiscence of his nigh-constant self-pity and hollow pledges of reformation. His many wasted years nursing a bug habit were excised from this version of his past, as were his good deeds, few and far between though they might have been. No, he had a job to do here, and that was convincing this deathless wizard or whatever he was that the Mighty Maroto was an asset to any war against humanity.

The fall of Khemmis, the fight for Nottap, and the executions he had carried out in Eyvind.

The taking of Wild Throne, where he had led the suicide squad in charge of leading the Imperials into a Cobalt trap.

The madness at Windhand, the first time Maroto saw Crimson soldiers go berserk and start attacking each other instead of the enemy, eating alive anyone they could lay hands on, even themselves.

Finally the Battle of the Lark's Tongue, where history repeated itself, and then his epic wrath and pledges of vengeance against his former friends, first against Zosia and then against Hoartrap. The Tothan *really* seemed to like that last bit, Maroto reliving his fury, recapturing his willingness to burn the world, if that was what it took to avenge Purna's preventable death on the battlefield. And with nothing else to offer from his long catalogue of crimes, he tried something new—instead of a memory of past violence, he conjured up a vision of his own, one where he donned a suit of sharp black beetle-mail and led the Tothan legions against the people of the Star, using all his experiences to show them how and where to attack each Arm, relishing in the slaughter, the sacrifice, knowing as he did that he, too, would be put to the blade, but only at the end…this was his reward. This was his reward. This was his reward.

"This is your reward," the spider-haired woman moaned in his face, Maroto shuddering as the memory-voyeur slipped its ghost hand out of his skull. He somehow knew that flesh and blood fingers hadn't actually penetrated him, knew he wasn't dying of a massive head wound...but it sure as fuck felt like it. "The first shall be the last! You shall volunteer your every secret, you shall volunteer your supple flesh, and so shall the first become the last!"

"Last in line, anyway," muttered Maroto as the fell creatures helped him to his feet. He should have been disgusted with himself for collaborating with these things, for selling the whole damn Star to buy himself a little time, but all he felt was relief. This was the role he'd always been destined to play, and Maroto was star material from way back. It was time to get evil. "Got some conditions before I'll pledge myself to the cause, though."

"Connnnnnnditions?" the ring-fingered Tothan screamed, turning back to Maroto with wrath writ large and clear on his white face. Some of the others resumed their deranged laughter, the bloated man bleating his incredulity. Even the moaning woman recoiled from him.

"Yeah," said Maroto, swaying in place in the oozing clearing of broken meat fans, surrounded by primordial, hostile, and obviously insane Tothan priests. He was about to find out if they were just toying with him or if they were really taking him on board. "I've got three underlings on the island. I'll tell you where they're hiding and you take them alive, then turn them over to me. That's my first condition—once I've got my squad back together we can talk about what else I need, and what we can offer in exchange."

The ancients laughed harder and a few others wandered away from the scene, but Ghosthand, Bloato, and Spidertresses seemed to be discussing it. Now that he'd had one of them reach into his skull on top of showing him all those ugly visions Maroto was getting properly attuned to their way of conversing, projected thoughts brushing past his deaf ear like whispered voices tickling his good one...and tickling his nose in the process. He hadn't noticed it before, given the overall fustiness of this place, but now that he was tuned-in he was sure that each one of these things gave off their own uniquely fetid funk that seemed to buoy their intentions back and forth. He tried to lean in to the faint sensations and their accompanying odors, wondering if he could somehow learn their nonverbal tongue, when the spider-haired crone snapped her hand in his direction, screamed something he didn't understand, and fell upon him with all her fury.

Well, so much for his brilliant plan—it had been worth a try, anyway. As she lashed out with talon-like black fingernails Maroto stepped into her assault instead of away from it, meaning to grab her wrist with one hand and knock her shriveled head off with the other. He'd take down as many of these shriveled-up Tothans as he could before their minions overwhelmed him, because now that his initial horror at their appearance and powers of headfuckery had passed, he wagered their ancient bodies were no match for his mighty mitts. He'd take them apart with his bare fucking hands, one by one until—

Spidertresses moved so fucking fast Maroto would have felt dizzy even if she hadn't backhanded him so hard in the temple he went flying, the meat reef that cushioned his landing bursting like giant blisters. He lay in the wet, warm wreckage, too stunned to move, and right around the time he realized he should be doing something she came for him again. He tried to fight her off but felt as helpless as a babe, arms that looked frail as twigs slapping down his defenses. He was too focused on trying to beat her back to even cry out, but she sobbed for him even as she mounted her quarry.

Pointy fingers closed around his throat, her eyes gleaming in her skeletal rictus, dozens of grey spiders tumbling from her hair onto his face, into his open, gasping mouth. Even as his world grew bright and fuzzy and desperate from lack of air, his end at hand, he could feel the little blighters biting his lips and tongue and the roof of his mouth, white-hot pinpricks, and he braced himself for one last attempt to save himself, to throw off the sprightly crone who straddled his gut, pinning his elbows beneath her knobby knees...

But his body wouldn't listen. It was over.

Except it wasn't?

"*They call you Devilskinner,*" said a regal voice as the woman stopped choking him. Her hand remained around his throat, but now the grip felt tender instead of cruel, fingertips stroking his bruised skin as he gasped the muggy vapors of this living fen. As everything came back into focus he saw it was still Spidertresses who spoke to him, and his flush of relief at being granted a reprieve turned to ice-cold dread as he saw the changes that had overtaken her, slight though they were. Bloodshot and wild but still human eyes had turned as black as the inside of a crypt. Swift, jerky movements had become slow and deliberate. And most unsettling of all, that voice... the shrill screams of the Tothans had been unpleasant, yes, but this deep, rich timbre was so, so much worse. "*You have trafficked with our kind before, mortal. You have not only gazed into the First Dark, you have drawn forth our gifts.*"

Unsure if he should answer this at all, or how, Maroto just gulped. It seemed a suitable response for the occasion, though he ended up swallowing a few spiders. He was so captivated and terrified by the creature atop him that he scarcely noticed.

"*Scheme away, little ape,*" it told him, grinning licentiously as the hand at his neck moved up to stroke his deaf ear...and instantly healing that irksome war wound, so that he heard its proclamation in perfect stereo. "*Serve or betray, fight or flee, first sacrifice or last in line, it matters not—you are ours, and very, very soon we will welcome you home. Countless eons after this world has gone as quiet as all the others we shall keep you pressed to our breast, your reward as endless as our love...But first we must reap our harvest, and you will bear witness to the end of mortal days upon the Star.*"

"Thank you," Maroto blubbered, believing every word this devil spoke. "Thank you. Thank you. Thank you."

CHAPTER
7

Zosia noticed the change as soon as she stepped up into the street. The frosty air still carried the tang of smoke, but unlike the night of her arrival it was mild enough to merely be the scent of a city, not necessarily a burning one. Choplicker had led her through a secret passage that opened into the rear of an alley several blocks away from the actual face of Castle Diadem, and as she followed her devil out to the main thoroughfare she saw they had been right to use a less obvious exit. At the end of the street a small mob was clustered in front of one of the castle's many gates, using a team of oxen to try to raise it. If she hadn't known how many more thick doors barred by stone and sorcery lay between them and the true interior of the castle she might have been concerned for Indsorith, alone in the great sepulcher of her palace, but as carefully as the Black Pope had locked up on her way out, it would take ages for anyone not in possession of a powerful and obliging devil to gain egress. Choplicker turned the other way out of the alley, and Zosia followed him into the city.

That first night had been far too hectic for her to appreciate being back in Diadem after all these years, but now that the riots had calmed and she was able to stroll along the quiet streets she was struck by how little the place had changed. The towering, close-packed buildings that made canyons out of every avenue looked so dilapidated that only being boxed in by their neighbors kept them from tipping over. Indeed, just about every other block there was a high, accidental arch where a teetering building had listed forward only to have its fall arrested by the structure across the street. Fire had recently gutted many of the rowhouses, and the whole city would have probably burned down if not for the perpetual drizzle of ash-stained rain that even now went to work dyeing Choplicker's coat the same color as his soul. Assuming he had one.

The labyrinthine streets were completely empty, but faces peered out from behind shutters, and conversations were carried on far overhead as folk leaned out their windows or lounged on precarious balconies to address their neighbors across the street. Occasionally an insult or challenge would be hurled down at Zosia, and once a bit of masonry that might have brained her if Choplicker hadn't diverted it with a swish of his tail, but she never caught sight of her presumably juvenile harassers. Only when she saw her wavering reflection in an oily puddle that filled one of the many claustrophobic courtyards did she realize that she might have been inviting more than the inevitable amount of unfriendly attention one attracts when venturing into rough neighborhoods: her dark hooded cloak looked a bit like a novice's cowl, the scarf she'd pulled over her mouth and nose might've been a Chainwitch's mask, and the large hammer she carried over one shoulder to discourage muggers was engraved with holy iconography. She had been worried someone might recognize her as the former queen, but really now, she looked like a Chainite. So much for low profile.

Glancing back with one of his lewd smiles, Choplicker turned into an arcade that opened onto the courtyard. The wide gallery was clogged with heaps of broken masonry, rotten timber, and stinking refuse, some of it reaching to the arched ceiling, but there was a narrow path winding through the debris. As soon as she stepped out of the rain into the arcade she heard a sharp whistle from the upper stories of one of the surrounding buildings, and a responding trill came from somewhere ahead, within the gallery. She must be getting close to something good, if instead of simply announcing her arrival the locals were trying to scare her off it.

She followed Choplicker into the close passage, the smell of a rained-out campfire now replaced with that of the black mold that bloomed throughout the garbage. It reminded her of a catacomb, only less pleasant, and she was glad they didn't travel deep into the arcade before her devil led her to a secret passage far less effectively concealed than the one they had used to quit the castle. Even if Choplicker hadn't stopped in front of the too-sturdy grandmother clock set too precisely in a too carefully stacked mountain of rubble, she would have suspected the spot simply based on all the footprints in the grime that led to and from its thick walnut waist. Zosia reached out to test the door but Choplicker warned her off with a bark, and pursing her lips, she made a big show of winding up her hammer to bash the thing in.

"None of that, now!" cried a voice from behind the heavily oxidized face of the clock.

"So you're going to open up, then?" she asked, imagining how demented she might seem to a casual observer. The old lady talks to *clocks.* "I'm here to see Boris."

"Not a Boris in the house," said the unseen bouncer. "Just a dozen heavily armed bruisers who pay me to see they're not disturbed while they take their tea. Now piss off or I'll shoot you where you stand."

"Uggggagh, you're really going to make me say it, aren't you?" Zosia was talking to herself, but Choplicker answered with a happy snort at her annoyance.

"Count of three, mum, and if you're not gone—"

"Zosia lives," she said, self-consciously glancing up and down the cramped track. What an embarrassment.

There was a pause from the clock, and then it said, "Come again?"

Clearing her throat and pointing a threatening finger at Choplicker, she leaned closer and repeated the phrase Boris had insisted was the universal password used by Diadem's rebels. "Zosia. Lives."

There was an even longer silence, and then the increasingly familiar-sounding voice said, "Still didn't catch that, I'm afraid. Speak up a bit. Really enunciate."

"Zosia lives," she growled, "but Boris won't if he keeps jerking me around."

"We got to stop meeting like this, Yer Majesty," said the frost-burned little man as the great door of the long-clock popped open and he ushered her inside his burrow with a bow. "Word gets out that your devil fancies the scent of my trail and nobody will invite me to their parties anymore."

"And here I thought you couldn't wait to introduce me to your friends," said Zosia as Choplicker stuck his nose in Boris's crotch in the way she knew he absolutely hated.

"Don't have much choice in the matter now that you've arrived," said Boris, hands hovering on either side of Choplicker's face as if he weren't sure which was more dangerous, to push the devil away or scratch behind his ears. She noticed that while he still wore the ostentatious auburn cloak of dyed gorilla skin and the lemur hair vest she had scared up back at the Lark's Tongue camp, he didn't carry the battle-ax she'd insisted he take from Ulver's smithy. "But looking on the bright side, I do stand to collect on a number of wagers as to whether or not I actually met the Stricken Queen, so let's get you inside and introduced to those who's running Diadem now that the Chain's left and the Crown's folded."

She ducked inside after Choplicker and pulled the door of the clock shut behind her until it clicked. The false trash heap housed a cramped cave, with a small table and a pair of stools lit by a stinking cod lamp—the catch of the day in Desolation Sound was so greasy that wicks were wiggled into the mouths of the fish and used to provide cheap if rancorous light. "Impressive use of space, Boris. It may be smaller than your tent back at the camp but it's every bit as smelly."

"Ho ho," said Boris, and when Choplicker left off him to go snuffle the fumes from the cod lamp he went to the rear wall and rapped his knuckles on an exposed beam. "My own rooms aren't so fancy as this foyer, alas. I figured you'd be coming for me soon enough, so put the word out that if a crone and her hound came creeping around to come and let me answer the door. Had my suspicions you weren't done with me yet."

A seam of light appeared in the wall of the cave and a more skillfully hidden door swung inward. Boris ushered her into the open floor of what looked to be a tavern abutting the arcade, where a dozen big bruisers did indeed sit around tables taking their tea. A stout pair of women rose from the bench, and after giving Zosia the hard-eye went back out to take Boris's place on guard duty in the clock-cave. None of the rest paid them much mind, and after snagging a bottle of rotgut Boris led her through yet another trapdoor in the back of the bar and down through a maze of sunken storerooms and corridors that bore a closer resemblance to mineshafts than to hallways... and every time they passed another guard that damn password got invoked, with Boris bowing to his companion as he said it just to twist the knife.

"What'd I tell you, Yob—Zosia lives, and I'll be collecting those five krones directly, please and thank you."

"Zosia lives, Alaka, and that's a tael that you owe me."

"A very fine morning to you, Miss Pnathval, and if I might trouble you for three shiny pieces of six? No no, not a loan, but you see, well...*Zosia lives.*"

Not a one of them actually produced payment, even when Zosia begrudgingly acknowledged her identity to the incredulous guards, but Boris didn't seem to mind much. "What comes around goes around, and once you're acknowledged by the powers that be they won't be able to welch. Let them think the con's long for now; we both know it's as short as your temper."

"You didn't waste much time using my name to turn a profit," Zosia observed.

"I'm not one for waste," said Boris, popping his thumbs through the drawstring of his orange cloak. "But really, anyone who wanted to call me a liar deserves to be shaken out of a silver or two, after all I been through to bring you here. They're the ones who coined the phrase, after all, so you'd think they'd be the first ones to believe that...wait for it...Zosia lives!"

"If you can call this a living," said Zosia, taking a pull on his bottle of turnipwine as they passed a final guard and entered a dank, circular stone chamber with a well in the center. "How big a cut of your winnings do I get when you finally collect?"

"Same as whatever percentage of the royal treasury you see fit to grant me, for arranging this meet between Diadem's past and its future."

"See, Boris, you never give me any credit—I'm not just the past, I'm the sort what comes back to haunt you." Seeing Choplicker's ears prick up and his tail wag as they came to the edge of the well where a spiral staircase descended into the black rock of the city's base, Zosia cocked her own ear and heard a hubbub echoing up from below, like a host of devils cavorting in the deep. "What's down there? A gladiator pit?"

"Close," said Boris. "All the different factions who think they ought to run the city come together for a moot."

"Ugh," said Zosia, who would have preferred taking on ten comers in a battle royal to a political squabble. "Adding me to that mix is just going to be tossing peat onto the pyre. I tracked you down to get some answers about what the hell happened here, not raise a bunch more for whoever's trying to pick up the pieces. Walk me back to the castle and fill me in as we go, and best of luck to whoever wants to try ruling this damn dump. I'm thick, I'll admit it, but not thick enough to stick my head in the same noose I already slipped."

"Not a chance," said Boris, pointing to the stairs. "You're going down there, Yer Majesty, so no sense dragging your slippers."

"Excuse me?" Zosia had thought she was too burnt out to feel strongly about much of anything, but being ordered about by this punk set her teeth to grinding...and not just with his lip, but also at her own foolishness. The runt had seemed such a minor threat it hadn't occurred to her to be chary as he led her deeper and deeper into an unknown force's territory, past dozens of armed guards. Choplicker finally looked his old self again, after his mysterious errand to retrieve the battered Carnelian Crown had left him weaker than she'd ever seen him...but whomever Boris answered to must know who Zosia was, and that she had Choplicker with her, and yet they had still admitted her to their sanctum. There were legends all over the Star about rituals and relics and such that could allegedly counteract a devil's power, so might they actually have some method of

overcoming her unholy protector? Had she just come trotting into a trap of her own volition?

"You're my miracle, Queen Zosia," said Boris with a sneer, and Zosia moved to shove the scheming weasel down the stairs when she was brought up short by Choplicker, of all fucking things—the devil got in her way as he ambled over to sniff an appealing stain on the dirty floor, and while it only slowed her for a moment it was enough for the oblivious Boris to finish his thought. "Or are your words so empty you don't even remember them as soon as they've fallen out your lips?"

"I...what now?" Zosia had no idea what he was talking about, but he sounded so sure of himself she bit the inside of her cheek and tried to puzzle it out.

"Back with the Cobalts, that pretty song you sung me?" He looked vulnerable, like it had been a damn fine speech but he needed to hear it again to keep his nerve up. Problem was she'd been so damn tired for so damn long she still couldn't remember a damn thing. Reading her face, he filled her in. "When you and your devil here came for me in the camp, you looked me in the eye and said you were sorry, and you were ready to listen to me."

She had said *that*? Didn't sound bloody likely...but then it seemed even less likely he'd invent such a tall tale.

"You said you were ready to work with us to fix Diadem, to fix the Empire." There was a pitiful shine of hope about the man, and it looked downright unnatural on his grubby features. "You said we had to work together to get rid of the Burnished Chain first and foremost, right, that you and me would come here to Diadem, and my people and your people would team up to take down the church. 'Cept since the Chainites went ahead and removed themselves from the song we can jump straight to the other things you promised. The ones what involve making things better?"

By the six devils she'd bound, that did sound familiar, even though she couldn't picture herself saying it. More than the specific words was the feeling behind them, though, the optimism she must have used to sugarcoat her call to arms—the promise that there would come a day when the foes of the common folk were cast down and the rebuilding could commence. No wonder she couldn't remember her pep talk; it had been hollow sentiment designed to get a heel-dragging heretic to sign on for a suicide mission. How many years had it been since she had honestly believed there would come a day when the yoke was lifted from the Imperial peasantry? How many decades?

"If you think the Chain's gone for good you people are dreaming," Zosia heard herself say, her tongue apparently toxic on reflex at this point. "Wherever they went I guarantee they'll be back, or someone worse will take their place. That's how it works."

"Maybe that's how it *worked* in your day, Zosia, but your day's done," said Boris, looking contemptuously at the former queen of the Crimson Empire. "The city's ours now, and maybe we'll hold it for a week or maybe we'll hold it for a thousand years, but I guarantee you this much—our reign will be better than yours or any crown-wearing fuck-buckler who came before or since. So come down and lend a hand or piss off back to counting the days till you can use Portolés's hammer to bust heads instead of chains, but if you go you find your own way out. I've got work to do."

Zosia looked down at her devil, and her devil looked back at her, and she asked herself if the curl of his lips had always struck her as an evil smile because that was all she was expecting to see there.

"You must have heard some good speeches in your day, Boris," she said at last, nodding faintly at the stair. Not like she had anything better to do with her day, even if she was completely fucking terrified of meeting the people who had thought her a martyr to their cause when in fact she'd sold them out for a cushy retirement package in the Kutumbans. She deserved a lot worse than anything they could give her, though, and had the consolation that she'd already lost more than they could ever take. "Let's go, then, before I do something smart like change my mind."

Boris grinned as wide as Choplicker and hurried down the stair, nattering on the whole while. "Glad you came when you did; even a day ago things were craaaazy down here. They'd been trying to quiet the riots 'fore we even arrived, if you can believe it, which I scarcely can given the state of the place. Hard to imagine all that fury was just the tail end of it all, and the worst was done a fortnight past. They said—"

"*They* being *who*, anyway, Boris?" she asked as the voices rumbling up the stair swelled to a roar. "Who are these factions squabbling over control of the city?"

"Well, my people have their board, right, but then there are the rival thieves' guilds and other gangs, and the loyal Imperial soldiers who hid out when they saw which way the tide was flowing in the castle, and the holy-minded wildies the Chain left behind, and whatever rebel clergy they saved from the crucifixion forests, and the beggars' society, and the nobles and merchants who bought off the lynch mobs, and—"

"I get the idea," said Zosia, feeling increasingly imprisoned as they descended through the oily light of the cod lamps set in the stairway's alcoves. She was practically shouting to be heard now over the cacophony from below. "Surprised they're not just murdering each other."

"Well, the day is young!" Boris *was* shouting now, as he reached the bottom of the stairs and greeted another guard. "Zosia lives!"

"What is this place!" Zosia asked as they emerged into a huge but crudely carved hall in the obsidian heart of the mountain, the guttering sea of lamps held by thousands of hands casting a low cloud that must not have come close to reaching the distant ceiling, given the acoustics of the place.

"Supposed to be a ghetto!" said Boris. "King Kaldruut ordered it! Wanted to clear out the tenements! Drive our kind down here! But you stopped it!"

"Who did?" Zosia's ears were ringing, and it sounded like he'd said—

"You did! When you became queen! Remember!"

It sounded more like an order than a question, and sure enough, it did ring a distant gong way, way back in the recesses of Zosia's memory. Kaldruut had implemented so many devildamned bad ideas that she'd put a stop to it was tough to keep track of them, really. "Why meet here?! A symbol?!"

"Only open space big enough for us all!"

"Oh!" And remembering another of her edicts that had flown in the face of Kaldruut and the rest of the corrupt politicians' ethos, she said, "I know a better place we can go!"

"Eh?" Boris looked excited, like he might have an inkling but didn't dare voice it lest his dream be spoiled.

"Got the keys to the castle, comrade!" Zosia shouted, and Choplicker barked his confirmation. How Indsorith would react to the unwashed masses crowding into Castle Diadem was a bridge she would cross when she got to it, but she figured the woman would approve. After all, Indsorith was the second-smartest queen to ever rule the Crimson Empire.

CHAPTER
8

The bastard angels had a terrible beauty to them, the grace of the Fallen Mother evident even in the forms twisted by their father's corruption. Neither the great flying seraphim nor the silent soldiers who rode them had appeared in Y'Homa's vision on the Day of Becoming, but these black-scaled angels were obviously of similar lineage to the swarming cherubs she had beheld when Diadem Gate became a flickering window to paradise. Yet even if she had glimpsed these beings during the ritual itself or the constant dreams that followed, it scarcely would have made their appearance less stupefying. How could the mortal mind prepare itself for the visage of the divine? Staring in awe at the seraph that delivered her to the beating heart of the Garden of the Star, she'd found herself at a loss as to how she might describe it in words or even thoughts; it simply *was*, in all its winged, tentacled glory.

When it had lifted her up from the prow of her ship and carried her through the air she had felt such ecstasy as her heart had never known, gazing down on her new kingdom and marveling at how it was at once familiar yet mysterious. Instead of mundane boats the ancient harbor of Alunah teemed with great barnacle-flanked leviathans that bobbed beside the white stone pylons, black-armored figures swarming the breached titans. Soon the old city fell behind them as Y'Homa's angelic guardian delivered her inland, and she basked in her certitude as she relived the visions from Diadem Gate...up to a point.

Instead of taking her directly to the Allmother's waiting brood of warrior angels who would cleanse the Star of sin, she was flown deep into the verdant mountains, directly into the dripping mouth of a cave. Any uncertainty she felt over this change in prophecy was quickly alleviated as she saw the same ivory-faced, ebon-shelled cherubs from her prophecy scuttling all along the walls of her new sanctum. Y'Homa was then delivered to a bath where unseen spirits divested her of her last mortal trappings, her mitre and scepter left in the pool as they cleansed her impure flesh and anointed her with pungent oils. It was thrilling. Finally she was gifted with gloves of gossamer and a ceremonial yoke from yet another of the Fallen Mother's angelic children, and proceeded through the glistening tunnels to claim the throne from whence she would rule the Garden of the Star.

It was a longer walk than she would have anticipated, and the tightness of the coils upon her throat made it difficult to breathe the humid air, but these were mortal concerns, and she pushed them away…or tried to, anyway. She frankly hadn't expected the houses of the holy to have such a powerful odor about them, or to be made of pulsing meat, so far as that went. She was no stranger to strangeness, being a living miracle herself, but with each step she and her silent escort took into this otherworldly realm Y'Homa felt her unease growing.

Which was the point, obviously. Obviously. She had been naïve to assume her final test was her arrival at the harbor, before she had even met her first angel. The Fallen Mother presented the Garden as such a nightmarish place to her heir so that Y'Homa could reaffirm her worthiness, striding proud and confident through these grotesque halls. She would not be afraid. She would not. This was her birthright, her destiny, and when she sat upon the Allmother's throne she would see this place for the paradise it truly was…yes, of course! That was it! How foolish of her, to think any mortal eyes could behold the true majesty of heaven—the sinner sees naught but sin, wherever she turns her gaze, and being still trapped in the world of the flesh, flesh was all she could see. The filth of the Star was a veil occluding her eyes, a mask that must be scrubbed free…but the rituals of cleansing were obviously well under way.

Let the tests continue! Y'Homa walked straighter, smiling wider as she felt the cherub's yoke scrape against her mortal neck. She had been born a sinner, like all her kind, but she had been chosen by the Fallen Mother to rise above her kind. She embodied the six sacred virtues, and every day from the time she could speak she had carried out the sixty-six devotions. And now her reward was at hand.

The Black Pope's respectfully silent attendants delivered her at last to a vast cathedral. The angel baby who had woven her yoke and gloves flitted down from the roof to embrace Y'Homa's naked back. She tried to find her breath as she surveyed what lay before her, the cherub wrapping its long legs around her bare breasts and ribs.

This place was no mere cathedral. Far out across the wondrous garden of shimmering fans there sprawled a glowing lake, and from this lake there rose a palace of bone and muscle. The top of the ziggurat was blurred by distance and the haze of vapors rising from the steaming floor of the majestic chamber, but Y'Homa knew from the Chain Canticles what must await her. It was written that the throne of the Allmother rose from a lake of fire, and lo, another prophecy was fulfilled. The Black Pope had come home.

Y'Homa only hesitated long enough for the cherub to finish getting comfortable on her back before she descended a stairway growing from the wall of the vast throne room. Eager though she was to assume her seat, she forced herself to keep a slow and stately pace as she followed a meandering path through this, the true Garden of the Star. The play of light from the living votive growths made Y'Homa feel like a happy babe again, delighted by the mobile of angels that hung over her crib.

Emerging from the forest of luminous flesh, she crossed a bridge of braided sinew that spanned the radiant lake. Huge cherubs scuttled along its spongy shores, and even greater angels churned through the thick yellow waters, but Y'Homa kept her gaze on the ziggurat before her. It rose like an island from the holy lake, and as she stepped from the end of the bridge to the bottom step of the towering edifice a glowing wave broke over her bare feet. It did not burn her. It could not burn her.

Y'Homa climbed the ziggurat, reverently keeping her eyes fixed on her own feet until she at last reached the top. Only when there were no more warm bone steps to climb did she look up from her saffron-stained feet and behold the throne room of the Allmother. And she gasped. Instead of a single throne, a semicircle of them jutted from the top of the ziggurat like the points of a crown.

Most of them were already occupied.

Jarring though it was, this was by no means the first discrepancy between Y'Homa's expectations and the true nature of paradise. A lesser mortal might have felt uncertainty in the face of a ring of ancient figures occupying the sacred space set aside for her, or even fear at their sinister appearance.

Y'Homa was not a lesser mortal. She was the greatest human being who had ever lived. As she stepped forward to demand answers from this unexpected council, she felt only righteous wrath at her uncle for failing to accurately describe what awaited her upon Jex Toth. Crucifixion had been too good for the false pope.

She silently counted thirteen thrones, all but one with a wasted occupant sprawled ignobly in the baroque organic seats. It felt like a grotesque parody of the Holy See, these hideous individuals even less appealing than the twelve cardinals who had forever been advising and lying and wheedling for influence.

Between Y'Homa and the half moon of enthroned figures was something else unexpected, here in the heart of heaven—a Gate stretched across the top of the ziggurat. It was far smaller than any of those on the Star, no more than a dozen yards across, but a Gate nonetheless. Unlike those vast pits on the continent that hungrily sucked in anything and everything that passed above them, this miniature hellmouth was crisscrossed with thin bridges of gleaming white bone.

"I am Pope Y'Homa III, Mother of Midnight, Shepherdess of the Lost," she announced when none of the figures acknowledged her arrival with more than an ugly stare. "I have returned home."

An enormous fat man swaddled in a toga of shimmering white sequins nearly toppled out of his throne with laughter. None of the others reacted as the braying guffaws of their confederate echoed out across the expanse, the vein-mapped roof emitting a pale green glow. Y'Homa's hands clenched into fists, any lingering uncertainty and the ensuing fear she might have felt at the unexpected aspect of this place banished as her heart swelled with hateful malice at this grotesque abomination who dared laugh at her, here at the end of her many ordeals.

"Silence!" she shouted at the thing, but to her dismay her voice sounded small and tinny in the great space, and the bloated man laughed all the harder. Another test. She must be virtuous, she must be proud as well as wroth. "Be still, oh interloper in my throne room, before I cast you out! Before I cast you all out!"

At this several of the gaunter figures began snickering as well, but then a long-haired woman in a sparkling ivory gown raised a bony palm and the rest quieted down. Then she slowly turned her hand, beckoning Y'Homa to approach. She took a step to walk around the edge of the Gate when the forgotten cherub on her back tightened its eight furry arms around her chest and queasy stomach, the yoke at her throat tugging her to the side…toward one of the bridges that spanned the Gate, bridges crafted of impossibly long and thick spinal columns.

The Black Pope did not balk for an instant, aborting her doubts before they could fully form. The bone ridges felt sharp and damp beneath her bare feet as she stepped onto the bridge, but it was sticky instead of slick, and wide enough for a woman of her small stature to walk without fear. She was almost halfway across when she noticed the design mapped out by the overlapping bridges, a white pentagram straddling the black Gate, and she took succor in the holy sigil.

When she looked back up she saw that five of the ancient figures had risen from their seats and were fanning out around the Gate, each taking a position at a point of the pentagram. None of the thrones they had vacated were the blazing chair Y'Homa had dreamed of occupying. Instead of divine flames, blinking eyes and winking orifices adorned the thrones that sprouted like toadstools from the meaty plateau. Frail was Y'Homa's heart, fluttering all over again as her mind struggled harder than ever to incorporate this bizarre place and the obvious ceremony she found herself in the middle of with all her preexisting beliefs.

She must have faith. When Pope Shanatu had summoned her to

Diadem she was but Jirella Martigore, a naïve girl who knew nothing of the numinous nor the true nature of the world, a fool who didn't even know that anathemas were real or that the Star was in spiritual crisis. The ordeal she had undergone to sacrifice her former self and become the Black Pope had also been an overwhelming, horrifying ritual, and in the moment it had not seemed as if she could possibly survive it…Yet she had, because the Fallen Mother willed it, just as she willed this. The Fallen Mother had called Y'Homa—

"Home," croaked the woman who had beckoned her forward, standing at the end of Y'Homa's bridge, both hair and gown dancing with white light. Could this be…Her? And if so, why in the name of the faith was she speaking High Immaculate instead of Crimson? "You are home, yes…but who are you? What claim have you to our kingdom?"

"I am the Black Pope," said Y'Homa, taking another step forward. Before she had been studiously keeping her eyes on the narrow path as she crossed but now she trusted in the Allmother, fixing her eyes on the ancient woman. "Ordained by the Fallen Mother to resurrect the Garden of the Star. To pilgrimage here and claim my throne, from whence I shall order the Angelic Brood to punish the iniquitous and call home the faithful."

"You summoned us!" shrieked a lanky white thing wearing a red-and-gold collar, shaking a thick-ringed finger at Y'Homa as it leaped from its throne and stalked over to stand beside the white-gowned woman. "You made the sacrifice! You brought us back!"

"I did," said Y'Homa, resisting the urge to take a bow. If anyone ought to be supplicating themselves it was these angelic servants of the Fallen Mother she had called back to the Star. "And now I have brought all the faithful children of the Burnished Chain here to accept our reward."

There was a pause while the heavenly host exchanged curious looks and gestures, and then the old woman rasped out a question so unexpected Y'Homa almost fell off the bridge.

"What is a Burnished Chain?"

"The church," said Y'Homa incredulously. "*Her* church."

"Whooooose church?" squealed one of the others who stood around the Gate, this one dressed in membranous grey robes that made it look like a heathen Immaculate.

"Who are you creatures?" Y'Homa demanded, done with whatever riddle or test this was supposed to be. She resumed walking down the bridge to confront the white-haired woman and her gem-collared confederate, her head held higher than ever. "Are you a council of archangels sent to aid in my reign, or devils intent on thwarting it? If you be true children of the Allmother, you shall welcome me properly, *now*. And if you be agents of the Deceiver, prepare for divine retribution."

At this the fat one's laughter returned, louder than ever, and even the old woman smiled sadly... but the figure beside her was not smiling. It strode past the woman in white, advancing onto Y'Homa's narrow bridge and blocking her path. Its antique costume of black beads shimmered like the Gate beneath their feet. It held its ring-crowded left hand up beside its face, murmuring to itself and clicking the jewelry together as it reached out for her with the naked fingers of its right.

She recoiled, and her foot slipped despite the sticky coating on the bridge of bone. Y'Homa lost her balance, and in that moment when the terror of falling into the Gate overwhelmed her conviction the creature seized her wrist, and revelations blasted her mind.

The Ritual.

The Vex Assembly of Old Jex Toth, witch priests convening atop a pyramid of white stone beneath the naked heavens, the stars overhead flowing into a maelstrom as they carried out their rites. One by one, they sacrificed each other to the First Dark... only for each to rise in turn. The living rendered deathless, the mortal made divine. The ascension of thirteen who would save the Star from itself.

The Betrayal.

A sacrifice so great its ripples were seen across the Star, the yellow sun turned black, the blue sky turned yellow, the howling winds lashing across Jex Toth... and then, nothing. No, not nothing—the Sunken Kingdom had not fallen beneath the waves of the Haunted Sea, but somewhere far, far worse. It had sunk into the First Dark.

The Years Without Light.
The Hunger.
The Despair.
The Bargains.
And then, the Return.

"*Yes, Jirella, you have come home... and so have we.*" The hated use of her birth name jarred Y'Homa back to the present—ever since she'd assumed the Onyx Pulpit, the only one who had dared address her that way was her uncle... just before she had him crucified.

The voice that used it now was warm as mulled wine and syrupy as snowmead, nothing like the shrieks and rasps of the Vex Assembly who had welcomed her. Yet blinking the blood from her eyes, Y'Homa saw it was the same ring-fingered priest who addressed her. It had caught her hand in its own, holding her in place as she swayed back over the side of the bridge, over the center of the pentagram, over the Tothan Gate. Something had changed in its ancient features, and now that she could guess what, she desperately wanted to pull away... but to do so would be to tumble into the very place from whence it had emerged. "*Do not despair, sweet child. In their quaint fashion your ancestors captured the essence of our worship, and we are not displeased.*"

"She... She waits... Beyond the First Dark..." Y'Homa's every breath was fire, powerful visions continuing to flash through her shuddering skull, aftershocks of the revelatory earthquake.

"*And we shall call her home, just as you called us home,*" said Y'Homa's savior. "*First we must anoint the sacrifice, to prepare it for the slaughter. Your fleet will carry out this sacred duty—you shall sail to the Star and warn your kind of our coming. You shall sow the terror and hatred that renders mortal flesh so sweet. You shall speak the ultimate truth you have always aspired to, and then we shall carry out our final work.*"

"No." Y'Homa couldn't manage any other words, her heart beating so fast she knew it must surely burst. It was like some horrible nightmare, some trick of the Deceiver to deprive her of her reward. "No no no."

The thing frowned, crinkling the leathery skin it had entered five centuries before... five centuries as the Star counted time, but so, so many more in the First Dark, waiting to come home. *"You summoned us, Your Grace, and now we shall grant your wish—to cleanse this vile world, to sacrifice the Star."*

"No... you mustn't..." Y'Homa finally gulped out the words. "You mustn't warn the world, mustn't give the sinners time to prepare. Take them unawares, use the army I have brought you—"

"This world died the moment you brought us back." It smiled at her, black eyes shining like the insects that swarmed all over its scrawny body in imitation of robe and raiment. *"The more your kind struggles, the better you taste, and the more you know, the more you struggle. We have no need of your feeble fleet, your soft soldiers—we have been breeding our own legions, our own vessels. You shall go forth and testify to our coming, that will be enough."*

"Let me stay!" Y'Homa wailed, her heart breaking. "Exile the others, but let me stay! I am the Shepherdess of the Lost, Mother of Midnight, and this is my home! I made the sacrifice to summon you, I sacrificed everything, and I was promised a throne! I was promised eternity! I was promised!"

"We promised you nothing," said the thing, though not unkindly.

"This is my destiny!" To come so close to the divine only to be rebuffed, banished back to her boats... it would not stand. It could not stand. In that moment Y'Homa felt her soul singing with all six of her sacred virtues in tandem, her greed and envy even stronger than her pride and wrath, hungering and lusting for what she knew awaited her, and she was no longer a teenage girl mewling for her reward—she was the most important mortal who had ever lived, demanding her due. "I summoned you, creature, and you are bound to give me what I came here for. Now."

"Thy wish be done," said the ancient devil of Jex Toth, and it released Y'Homa's hand. She hadn't even realized it was the only thing supporting her until she fell away from the bridge and into the Gate that lay at the heart of the Garden of the Star.

CHAPTER
9

Upon his arrest at the white-gloved hands of Othean's Samjok-o Guard, the Baron of Cockspar gave a formal declaration of his name, rank, and status as an active Crimson colonel taken hostage by the nefarious Cobalt Company...along with his loyal bodyguard. While that set the Immaculates to chattering among themselves, it didn't get Domingo an immediate audience with the empress or any of her advisors. It did, however, get him comfortable chambers in the heart of the sprawling Winter Palace, and a rattan wheelchair to roll there in. Such amenities were obvious improvements on drafty, moth-eaten tents and bouncing, splintery cart-beds.

There was a time not so long ago that the notion of allowing a witchborn into his private rooms would have been unthinkable to Domingo. *Anathema*, even. But after being laid out in the wagon beside Brother Wan and then cuddled up on by Hoartrap the Touch, he was just relieved he didn't have to share his bed with Captain Choi.

And what ridiculous beds they were, too! Their gilded cage had what looked to be two polished topaz kaldi tables instead of cots, though Domingo's estimation of the Immaculate beds improved dramatically once he learned hot coals were placed beneath them to keep the stone mattress warm throughout the night. Choi seemed to think the climate unnaturally clement for the season, but to Domingo's hot southern blood it was still damned chilly after dark, and the combination of heat and firmness against his lame hip made the Lion of Cockspar as comfy as an old tom snoring on a sunny windowsill.

Yet comfort wasn't always enough to make one comfortable. When he woke one night to use his bedpan and saw the horned silhouette of the moonlit witchborn sitting up in a meditative posture on the other side of the paper screen that divided their room, for example, he found it difficult to relax again. Too close for comfort, too close by far.

Back home in Azgaroth there had been plenty of the freaks—too many, most citizens would agree—but while they weren't persecuted the way they were in less enlightened parts of the Empire where the Chain was stronger, that didn't mean the baron invited them into his house. No it did not. Their kind had always been mistrusted if not shunned by the good people of Cockspar for the quite reasonable reason that the things were bloody monsters, albeit ones that played at being pureborn, as he had so keenly put it to Lupitera as they returned from a drama she had dragged him to that was little more than a simpering apologia for the witchborn. His sister-in-law had offered some snide rejoinder about what higher form of life Domingo might be impersonating, though he couldn't for the life of him recall if she'd compared him to a shrew or a shrike. She'd always had a flair for the one-liners, had Lupitera, having no doubt memorized a catalogue's worth of them during her misspent youth on the other side of the playhouse stage.

Forcing his insubordinate bladder to produce a weak trickle into the porcelain bedpan, he wondered what his sister-in-law might make of him now, a man risking his life to help a witchborn, and an Immaculate one at that? Not that he'd had much choice in the matter, he told himself... but then another part of Domingo piped in, the one that only ever seemed to find its voice in the wee hours. Of course he'd had a choice. He could have told the anathema to take a long march off a short parapet. And if he'd had the courage of his convictions he would have—he'd always firmly believed death was the end of one's troubles, not the start of fresh ones, and he'd rarely thought twice about ordering countless soldiers to sacrifice themselves, if the cause demanded it. Surely dying with his pride intact would be preferable to entering into a murderous pact with a monster...

And yet when the time had come he hadn't even hesitated, capitulating as fast as humanly possible when it seemed like the witchborn was going to make good on her threat. Here at the end of life's long campaign Baron Domingo Hjortt, the Lion of Cockspar, shied away from an honorable death like a spooked gelding from a Gate, despite the fact that he had absolutely nothing left to live for, and hadn't for quite some time. No spouse nor heir, no regiment nor friends, no queen nor empire, not even the ability to stand upright despite the miraculous recovery of his other wounds, and for all the shit he'd ever talked about the cowardice of every single other person he'd ever met, Domingo had done exactly what his craven son would have: he bought his worthless life at the expense of his last scrap of self-respect.

"That is *enough*," he told himself, the warm topaz beneath the bedding now oppressively hot despite the wind coming in from the sea, rattling against the thin outer screens of their room like a hungry animal eager to be let inside. "That's an order, Colonel."

His seditious heart seemed poised to ignore his command and press its attack when there came a grunt from the other side of the screen that partitioned his half of the room from that of his ostensible bodyguard. His injured neck had recovered along with the rest of him following the trip through the Gate, but he snapped his head around so quickly he nearly strained it anew. Those needly shivers were instantly forgotten as he saw the horned silhouette of Choi slowly topple from her seated posture, falling without another sound into her bedding. Was their plot discovered, had a silent, unseen assassin just cut her down in her midnight prayers? After forfeiting his honor was Domingo about to lose his life anyway, at the hands of a—

The witchborn grunted again, twisting around in her sheets, but it wasn't an unhappy grunt, and Domingo's panic turned to embarrassment at overhearing what sounded an awful lot like carnal bliss. Whether she assumed her roommate was asleep and was pleasuring herself or had dozed off in her meditations and was enjoying a wet dream was a question Domingo regretted asking himself as soon as he did, and he promptly buried his head under a pillow. It was just like being back at the Academy in Lemi, right down to the awkward erection the muffled sounds aroused. He hadn't been troubled by that old pest in quite some time, but taking the matter in hand would offer some comfort, and after his disgraceful behavior comfort was the last thing he deserved.

The last thing either of them deserved, for that matter, and first thing in the morning he'd have a word with the witchborn about making such a racket—biting a pillow was just good practice, damn it, and if randy teenagers in a military school dormitory could learn that, then so could a grown woman, even a monster.

———

"I . . . *what*?" The witchborn set down her bowl of adzuki porridge as if Domingo had casually spit in it.

"You heard me, Captain, do you really want to make this more uncomfortable by having me repeat myself?" Domingo plopped more of the coconut cream into his porridge and stirred it up with his spoon, raising a mouthful and watching it steam. The witchborn had gotten him into his chair and wheeled him over to the room's single window so they could look out at the sea as they ate breakfast, the salty breeze as bracing as kaldi would have been, if only they'd been brought that instead of thick, nutty tea. "I'm not even asking you to desist, just show a little respect for your neighbor and keep it to a low roar."

"I was unaware," said Choi, looking more mystified than mortified. "I kept my own tent at the Lark's Tongue camp, so I did not know."

"Didn't know you make more of a ruckus than a cadet showing off at his first brothel, or didn't know that parchment-thin scroll they put up between our beds wasn't enough to mute your racket?" Domingo spooned porridge into his mouth. Back in the Cobalt camp he'd lived off soft foods, the wound Brother Wan had opened in his face making it agonizing to eat anything else, and he had sworn that if he lived long enough to recover he would never touch another bowl of gruel . . . yet even with a shiny new scar on his mouth instead of a braid of stitches he kept coming back to this delicately sweet slop. At first he'd been skeptical of the dish, as it bore a striking resemblance to refried beans—that always pasty and often rancid staple of Azgarothian camp cooks—but he had warmed surprisingly quickly to Immaculate cuisine. Even if breakfast bore an uncanny resemblance to dinner, both meals came with a wide array of options, so that on mornings when he didn't feel up to a platter of pork belly with lettuce cups or a piping hot bowl of oxblood soup he could always fall back on a porridge or three.

His growing fondness for the foreign fare was a development as unexpected as Choi choosing to press the issue of her night songs. At least he'd cleared the air, and while nobody likes hearing that their solo sessions have been overheard, he assumed anyone in her position would prefer to be informed.

"Did I say anything?" Her bloodred eyes were intently fixed on him, as though he had a spider hanging from his forehead and she was a sting-junkie trying to ascertain the breed. "Anything at all? What did you hear, precisely?"

"What did I hear?" Now Domingo was the flustered one, his cheeks going the color of the chilies in the kimchi as he recalled his unintended excitement of the night before. "Captain, I will have you know I was doing my best *not* to listen! You didn't make it very easy, with all the grunting and—"

"Tonight you'll watch over me and listen," she said, and before his dangling chin could reach his porridge she made a face as though he were the kinky one. "Not to... *that*. I was dreaming, and tonight when I dream I will try to speak to you. You will give your word to repeat what I have said to you when I awake. If I can even make myself heard..."

"I will, will I?" Domingo set down his breakfast and wiped off his chin with a blue silk napkin. He was getting far too stubbly. Even here in captivity the Immaculates had let both him and Choi keep their swords so he didn't think he'd have trouble getting a razor; the question was whether he could keep a blade steady enough not to cut his own throat, considering he had yet to make it through a meal without his age-traitorous hand making a mess of him. "I swore to help you... well, I swore what I swore, and that's the last we need speak of it, really, especially so long as we are guests of the empress. But I did not swear an oath to be your trained poodle, sitting or fetching or staying up all hours with a quill to write down anything you might say in your sleep."

"I do not think dogs can actually—"

"You know what I mean!"

"This is important," she said, as though that settled the matter. The dainty celadon teacup she lifted to her lips looked even more out of place in her scraped and callused fingers than it did in Domingo's liver-spotted hands. This woman must have seen her share of action, and more, or Domingo was no judge at all.

"Oh, well, if it's important then…" said Domingo, but when she didn't pick up on his obvious sarcasm he spelled it out for her. "If it's that important then you'll really want to do a better job of explaining yourself, is my meaning, because I don't intend to waste my nights waiting to see if you're a sleep talker. So you have a good long think on the tone with which you address me from now on, Captain Choi, because Colonel Hjortt does not respond well to nonsense."

The moony witchborn stared past Domingo as if he weren't even there. As she gazed off into space she opened her mouth a little but didn't drink the tea or speak, running her tongue back and forth behind her fangs—he could tell that was what she was doing from all the missing teeth providing him windows to the interior. Wait…was she actually having a good long think?

"Very well," she said, her eyes back on him, and she set the teacup down without taking a sip. "You will be the first I trust with this information, Domingo Hjortt. You will swear to keep my secret?"

"Who would I tell, exactly?" said Domingo, gesturing around the pink papered walls and richly painted screens of their spacious cell. A week of internment with Choi and they hadn't seen a single other member of the Cobalt Company. Nor an Immaculate, for that matter, save the servants who delivered their meals and escorted them through the warren of empty wooden corridors to the massive bathing complex each evening. Half a regiment could have scrubbed up at the same time in that partially open-air arena of terraced pools, steaming grottos, and warm waterfalls, but the only other bather he ever saw was Choi.

There was something disquieting about being held captive in the biggest metropolis in the Star but hardly seeing another soul. But then they weren't in Othean proper, were they, but one of the four palaces that occupied the corners of the capital city. Domingo seemed to remember hearing that the Immaculate court moved around between these cardinal castles, so perhaps the empress and her ministers were currently somewhere else and the Winter Palace was empty save for a handful of important prisoners. When he'd asked Choi why there weren't guards posted in the long, screened-in hallway outside their quarters, she'd told him some ominous riddle about one viper being worth a dozen snarling hounds.

Seeing that the rhetorical nature of his question had flown right past her beastly head and she again seemed to be waiting on a literal declaration of intention, he said, "I've already sworn away my life to you, Captain Choi, so go ahead and have my word while you're at it. I'll keep your secrets. We're in thick with each other now, even though it likely means we both go down together."

As soon as he said it he realized it was what Zosia had told him when she'd called on him in the Cobalt camp, that or something like it, and he shivered at the inadvertent invocation of her words. Of all his phantoms, hers was the least welcome in his head.

"Have you heard the old songs that some wildborn may melt... ah, enter, may enter into the mind of another mortal?" Choi asked, reminding Domingo that there were actually worse ghosts haunting him of late.

"Old songs, as you say, nothing more," he said, his scarred cheek itching as he remembered Brother Wan's wagon-bed confession just before he'd tried to murder Domingo. "The witchborn...that is, the, uh, you weirdborn—"

"*Wildborn.*" It was the first time she'd corrected him on the matter, but the look on her face told him she had better not need to remind him again.

"Yes, well...you wildborn spread a lot of rumors about being able to look into other people's minds to make yourselves appear useful, and dangerous," said Domingo, remembering how violated he'd felt back when he had actually believed Wan's ruse. "But the truth is you people are just naturally good at understanding mortals, empathizing and intuiting and such."

"Wildborn *are* mortals, the same as you," said Choi, looking at Domingo like he was the one with a black horn and a half growing out of his skull. "And *my* people, as you describe us, are not mine at all. Most of us are unique from one another, just as all people are, even those born in the same place, the same time, the same family. I may be of different blood than most of my house but I am a child of Hwabun before I am anything else."

Her pedantic tone made Domingo uncomfortable; lecturing his sister-in-law on the obvious degeneracy and otherness of the witch-born was one thing, but it just seemed too rude to engage one of the things themselves in a debate on the matter. "Yes, well, we were discussing something very specific, weren't we? About how your kind can't actually get into other people's heads like you claim, that you're essentially charlatans skilled at playing the gullible, like mummers at a faire."

"That is what you were talking about," said Choi, "though I do not know why, or where you came by that story. Perhaps you have merely proven my point that the similarities among the wildborn are ascribed by those looking at us from without. The old songs I refer to have nothing to do with confidence tricksters, but dreamtrekkers."

"Eh?" She had the infuriating quality of making less sense the more she talked. No wonder she mostly stayed silent as a scabbard despite how starved for conversation Domingo was growing, locked up with this taciturn freak. "Perhaps it would be better if you just had your say all in one go, Captain, since I can't even begin to guess what you're on about."

"To dreamtrek is to allow your spirit to take leave of your flesh and go in search of another's . . . and to melt into their mind, so that the two of you share a single dream." Choi again had that faraway look in her creepy eyes, complementing the creepy picture she was painting. "It was an art of the Age of Wonders. Like so much else it was believed lost, but lineage-keepers on the Immaculate Isles have worked for centuries to rediscover the technique. The oil of the harpyfish is one key to unlocking the dreaming spirit, though it is believed there were others, and that many wildborn required nothing more than to focus their hearts and release their minds. In doing so they were able to melt into the dreams of others, not just those who shared a bed or a house but even confederates on the far corners of the Star."

Old legends of nighthags descending on innocent sleepers and riding them until dawn flitted through Domingo's mind. For some reason this conjured the mental image of his sister-in-law Lupitera saddling him up, making him don one of her wigs, and carrying her off on his sweaty back. He winced away the hideous image as the witchborn continued.

"I had never before attempted it, for dreamtrekking is a perilous art. The flesh of the dreamer may not rouse to danger, or worse, the spirit may become stranded in the First Dark, cut off forever from the world of mortals. Yet the time came when the practice no longer seemed an unnecessary risk but a challenge to be faced with honor, and I have indeed overcome that challenge, as I have so many others. I think."

"You think?" Domingo still wasn't sure where this was going, but he was a little intrigued...even if it was all sounding rather a lot like an Immaculate variation on Brother Wan's bunkum, concocting supernatural explanations for mundane phenomena. Then again, all but his most debilitating injury had spontaneously mended themselves after the briefest exposure to the so-called First Dark, so he couldn't very well deny there was something incredible about the space beyond the Gates...but no, this was codswallop! "Forgive an old Azgarothian his skepticism, Captain, but what I'm hearing from you is that you had a dream where you what, left your body? No no, that's not even it, is it? You *think* you had a dream where you left your body. All the rest of it, if you will pardon my Crimson, sounds an awful lot like pagan pigshit."

"I pardon your Crimson and forgive your skepticism," said Choi. "It is possible you are correct, where my own experiments are concerned. I have been attempting to reach him for many, many nights, and each time I do I am sure I have succeeded. It is more vivid than any dream, it is *real*...but when I awake all the detail falls away as soon as I move to grasp it, and I am left with less than a dream, just a vague impression, like figures glimpsed retreating through a fog."

"Excuse me, you said in your dream you reach for *him*?" asked Domingo, his thoughts of nighthags now supplanted by tales of incubi, which rather seemed to fit with her performance of the night before. "Him who? What exactly are you trying to accomplish with this dreamtrekking of yours?"

"I . . ." And *now* she looked away, suddenly finding her lukewarm tea quite nice indeed. Then she smiled faintly, perhaps at the memory of her inamorato, or perhaps at her own timidity in naming her paramour to a crippled old man who already kept far more dangerous secrets of hers. "Maroto."

"Oh, *Captain*," said Domingo, utterly disgusted. "Of all the Villains, hells, of all the men!"

"You have underestimated him, too," said Choi in that same infuriatingly condescending tone she'd used when lecturing him on the witchborn. "Most do, to their peril."

"That stunt your squad pulled in the mountains didn't have anything to do with Maroto's skill, and you know it!" said Domingo, his pride smarting at the memory even if his healed wounds no longer did. "It was fool's luck, plain and simple. Unless you intend to look me in the eye and swear on your honor that you somehow timed the appearance of that horned wolf that fucking ruined me, before I could do worse to the Moldy Maroto."

"No, that was indeed what you call fool's luck," agreed Choi. "And it was you who ruined the wolf, and more *fool's luck* that in its death throes it struck you. You are as good as your reputation, Domingo Hjortt. When I spoke of your underestimating Maroto I referred to your tactics at the Battle of Willowtip, where you—"

"I know what I did at Willowtip," said Domingo, not caring to relive it with her dry summation. "But how the devils do you? Is your beefy beau still singing songs of the *one* time I played into his clumsy fingers, what, twenty-four years ago?"

"No," said Choi. "I read of it long before I left Hwabun. I have always taken an interest in military history."

"Military history," said Domingo with a sigh. "I suppose that's what I am now, aren't I? And to think I . . . as good as my reputation?"

It had taken a moment to sink in through his annoyance at being reminded of yet another of his defeats at the hands of the Cobalts, but a word of praise from a fellow veteran always attracted his notice eventually. It was the strangest thing, and no doubt a symptom of not getting enough sleep on top of all his other woes, but Domingo suddenly found himself choked up at the notion of some Immaculate monster reading about his career.

"Do you think it was coincidence that the Empress Ryuki bided until you had retired from command before launching her reclamation of Linkensterne and the construction of the accompanying wall?" Choi refilled her tea, then his, and then as if to make sure he didn't think she actually had the empress's ear, she added, "I do not think it was coincidence. You are the greatest living Crimson officer, and your province is one of the closest to the Immaculate border. Any in the Isles who are trained in the art of war learn of your deeds."

"Yes, well, we lost the one war that mattered, didn't we?" he said with a grim smile, more honest with himself than he'd been in a very long time. At least when he was fully awake.

"To only examine the victor is to learn but one set of steps, and to truly learn the dance of war you must study both partners equally," said Choi, quoting Lord Bleak's *Ironfist* as though it were the most natural thing in the world for an Immaculate to be conversant in Imperial chivalric codes. And who knew, maybe such things were common here—for all the many Azgarothian tomes, Crimson catalogues, Usban scrolls, and Raniputri histories in his library Domingo had only ever read a single Immaculate manual, and that translation of Ji-un Park's *Most Enviable Positions* was over two hundred years out of date. In retrospect he might have learned something about modern warfare from these island-dwelling fops after all, considering they hadn't lost a major conflict in his lifetime. "You may have a low opinion of Maroto, but I tell you now I have seen him in both victory and defeat, and while you may win more often, he has learned to lose better."

Domingo almost delivered a quip about just how good Maroto was at being a loser, but seeing the earnest expression of this warrior who through no fault of her own had been treating him with the utmost respect, he abandoned it at the last moment and just muttered, "Maroto is...yes, well, what about him, anyway?"

"I did not even tell my general I was attempting to contact Maroto by dreamtrekking, for her brow was already laden with worries and I did not know if I could even execute the art successfully. I chose to wait until I had results. Yet as I have told you, while I believe I have accomplished what I set out to do I cannot be certain that I am indeed dreamtrekking and not simply dreaming. When I wake I have no memory of what exactly transpired, only the sense that I have been with him, that we have communicated much to each other...but what we have said and done, exactly, is forgotten. So I keep trying, for any exercise improves with practice."

"And certain forms of exercise inspire more commitment than others," said Domingo. Her tale of nocturnal trysts reminded him of how in his dreams Concilia had never left him, that they were still husband and wife, and how every time he awoke from such dreams his mornings were bright and gay...until the moment he remembered she was long gone, and he was alone. Whether Choi was actually capable of witchy astral projection or had simply hit on the trick for ensuring happy dreams, he couldn't blame her for wanting to spend as much time there as possible. "I still don't see what you expect to gain from my keeping a vigil—even assuming you talk in your sleep, that won't prove anything."

"It may, if I remember this conversation as I am dreaming," said Choi. "I have the sense that in my dreamtreks I am far sharper and more aware than in ordinary dreams. If I find my way to Maroto again I can put questions to him that only he could answer, and if I focus hard enough perhaps I can repeat his words loud enough that they pass through my lips as I lie sleeping."

"This is sounding more and more like a carnival trick," said Domingo. "Or worse, one of those swindlers who purport to speak with the dead, bilking grieving families out of their inheritance for the promise of a word or two from the other side."

"The dead cannot speak, but sleepers often do," said Choi

decisively. "I have been attempting to do more than share pleasant dreams with him, and now we may have discovered a means. I will tell him what has befallen our general and our army, and will find out where he is and what has happened to him. I suspect we exchange this intelligence anew each time we meet, only to lose it again on waking. Perhaps the secret is not to try to carry it with us along our treks back to our flesh, but to set it sailing with our words as loudly as we can, while we are still at our sharpest in the heart of the dream. This must be why ancient oracles required a witness—to catch the wisdom they would not recall upon waking from their reveries."

"I would be lying if I said that didn't sound like utter balderdash," said Domingo, picking up his post-prandial cigar from its silver tray. It was admittedly civilized of the Immaculates to provide him with a stubby stick at every meal...and downright infuriating that these Endonian cigars they offered their prisoners of war were the equal of the very best in his humidor back home in Cockspar.

"Balderdash?" asked Choi as Domingo used the provided shears to snip off the end of his cigar and lit it on the tea candle.

"Never...mind," Domingo said around preliminary puffs. Once the woody cigar was good and going he sent a satisfied plume sailing over the ornamental waves carved into the windowsill, out to Othean Bay. "Tell you what, Choi—I'll humor you and play awestruck scribe to your midnight oracle, in exchange for a favor owed. Agreed?"

"I do not agree to terms that have not been named," said Choi. "A favor can mean many things, some which would be fair and others which would not."

"Quite so, quite so," said Domingo. "But those are my terms. You've got all day to mull it over, as I assume your nighttime sojourns are just that, but be aware I am intractable on this matter. A favor owed for my service, and nothing less."

"Then I agree," snapped Choi, more fired up than he'd seen her since the disastrous morning of their arrival at Othean. "It is that vital."

"Apparently so," said Domingo, setting down his teacup with a careless clatter on the saucer and reaching out to bump her waiting fist. "Just so I know what to do, though, what happens in the event that you aren't able to remember your mission? What if instead of interrogating Maroto's dream soul or whatever it is and passing along the word to me, you two just, well, have the same sort of encounter you did last night?"

"Then you go away," said Choi, gazing out to the windswept blue sea as she at long last seemed to feel a touch of the embarrassment Domingo would have harbored from the first, had their roles been reversed. Then she looked back at him, imperious as ever, and said, "And if my maneuver does succeed and I do pass along information, I do not expect it to take all night, and so you may wish to excuse yourself at a certain juncture regardless. I will do as you requested and attempt to be quiet, but I do not know how many more nights either of us has left, and I intend to savor each one."

"Yes, well," said Domingo, ruffled all over again. "What do you say for now we change the topic to something more pleasant, like all my military failures or the human rights of the weird, er, wildborn, or virtually anything else at all?"

"If we do, is the favor I owe you paid?" she asked, and looking at the witchborn's sharp smile he supposed she had more of a sense of humor than she'd previously let on.

"For the small matter of my eavesdropping on your dreamy rendezvous with one of my most hated enemies?" said Domingo, feeling a bit puckish himself in response to her wry smile. "Not even close, Captain, but it's a start, it's a start."

And so it was, right up until the Samjok-o Guard arrived to interrogate the captured Crimson colonel as to why the Imperial navy, while flying Chainite flags, had barged past an Immaculate blockade in the Haunted Sea only to come zipping back out again, and was now seeking asylum at Othean instead of sailing back to Diadem.

Domingo and Choi exchanged a long and meaningful look after she had translated, and clearing his throat, Domingo announced that he might have some ideas, but as a senior officer of the Crimson Empire he could only share his intelligence with the empress herself.

CHAPTER
10

Ji-hyeon's first year on the far side of the First Dark was actually worse than the second. Not because the dangers were initially greater; on the contrary, the harshness of the terrain and the frequency and ferocity of the monsters she encountered only increased the longer she wandered, and the closer she came to the black sun that hung low in the dull heavens, forever brooding over the far horizon. Or what she called the black sun, anyway; the shiny ebon disc was the only definite celestial object in the vast emptiness of the sky, and it seemed to emit both a prickling warmth and the constant purplish glare that lit this realm.

So it wasn't anything external that made the first year of Ji-hyeon's banishment to the sort of hell she had never really believed in so much harder than the second. What made the first year so exhaustingly terrible was simply that it was her first year.

A year. And a brutal one, even if she had been born to this world of perpetual twilight and snowy ash where the worst horrors walked on two legs but there was also plenty of badness stalking her on four or five or six or more. She ate some of what she killed but could only keep down a fraction of that. The rest of her diet consisted of the grey grubs and grub-shaped roots and grub-tasting lichens she excavated from the too-soft earth or pulled from the crumbling rock formations. She had no way of knowing what kept making her sick, the food she foraged or the opaque water she drank from streams and springs and lakes, which sometimes tasted of copper and other times of vinegar and still others of nothing but the ash that coated everything everything everything in this desolate place, from the low mountains she initially crossed to the ravine-fractured plains beyond to the cloud-spearing range of peaks on their far side.

Over it all presided the black sun. It never rose or set from its position, fixed in the cloud-webbed sky like a hole burned through a map. Most curious of all, instead of remaining the size of a coin it had slowly grown as big as a dinner plate over the course of Ji-hyeon's journey to the west.

Or what she called west, anyway. She had to apply some shape to this place and some direction to her quest, otherwise she would have gone mad. For all she knew the distant beacon wasn't stationary at all, and every time she awoke or it came back into sight after being obscured by the landscape it had actually moved to what would be a different point on a compass or star chart or map, in a world with compasses and star charts and maps, and people to agree on what they meant. She had asked Fellwing to lead them in the right direction, and the little owlbat always flew toward the black sun, but perhaps the devil was just as disoriented as her mistress.

Fellwing. Every day Ji-hyeon awoke with the thought that she should release the devil in exchange for passage home, and every day she balked anew. Part of her trepidation was the sad fact that the little fiend was all that Ji-hyeon had left—the empress had taken her family, her army, *everything*, and if she were to have any hope of revenge she couldn't trade away the one advantage she still retained. She would need far more than just a bound devil to take on the full might of the Immaculate Isles, obviously, but keeping Fellwing was at least a start. Returning to the Star now, without even her devil, would mean abandoning any chance of making good on her oath to destroy Empress Ryuki. Buying her miserable life in such a fashion would mean sacrificing not just her own honor but that of the entire murdered Bong family.

Try as Ji-hyeon did to convince herself this was the only reason she hesitated to wish herself home, there was another, deeper, darker motive. Even more than the shame of loosing her devil at the expense of her revenge was the fear that Fellwing wasn't actually powerful enough to transport her back to the Star, that she would finally commit herself only to have the owlbat sadly shrug her wings in defeat. Ji-hyeon had survived much, but wasn't sure if she could survive the heartbreaking confirmation that she truly had no hope of escaping this place. It made her sick to even think about it.

Sick. As if she were ever anything *but* sick. Even when her stomach wasn't punishing her for trying to stay alive against all odds she was ill, had been since her first week here. Too hot on the high mountain passes where the dirty snow was actually that instead of more drifts of ash, and too cold on the shores of the ivory ocean that lay on its far side, despite how warm the black sun's rays felt reflected off the creamy waves that rose and fell with nauseating slowness, the tides that lapped the shore coming and going as slowly as rice syrup being rolled from one side of a jar to the other. A year of sickness, marching sick, fighting sick, until like so much else she ceased to notice it, her rattling cough and perpetual fatigue as mundane a part of her existence as the thinning white hair that had grown out enough to keep getting in her right eye.

A year of keeping her left eye hidden behind an iron patch. Or her left eyes, to be strictly accurate. She had known something had changed during her final trip through the First Dark, but it wasn't until she lay panting beside the steaming corpse of a wyrm and saw her sweaty face reflected in a puddle of its silvery blood that she discovered just what had happened. Tentatively pulling aside the crude blindfold she kept over the left side of her face to block out the distracting assault of indescribable colors and phantasmal impressions, she winced and blinked the neglected orb awake...and in the mirror of metallic blood saw that a grey second iris now crowded the white of her left eye, the pupil of this new addition a horizontal black dash like the eye of a goat, or an octopus. She had blinked at her reflection, a reflection that began to take on terrible alterations as her devilish eye was again able to focus after its long banishment behind the blindfold, and then she had rushed to tie the raggedy patch back in place.

Yet as if seeing itself reflected in the lifeblood of its demonic kin had given it strength, the eye began to see through the stained cloth of the blindfold, and more disconcerting still, through her very skin when Ji-hyeon scrunched her left eyelid shut. It was as if the new eye *wanted* to see more, refusing to be shut out—and while at times it felt like it wished to warn her of things she might otherwise miss, like the spectral parasites swarming through the meat of a fresh kill, at others Ji-hyeon had the unsettling impression that it wasn't her eye at all, but that it belonged to *something else*, something that was using her to look out into this world after eons of blind darkness… But after many disconcerting days of being unable to shut out the unearthly images, she discovered that the eye's vision couldn't penetrate the rusted armor of a roving mutant. After murdering the squealing beast she wrapped a small scrap of its platemail in a rawhide pouch, and this makeshift eye patch finally darkened the devil-eye again.

It was far easier to adjust to only using one eye than it had been to try to adapt to having three, and she especially hated the way her Gate-shifted vision made her devil look like something far less cute than an owlbat. Despite all this she still found herself compelled to lift the rim of the patch when even Fellwing seemed uncertain of the path before them, or when the water source was especially questionable, or because she was so crippled by depression that without a fleeting ripple of color in the monochromatic wastes she couldn't muster the strength to get up and start moving again. The eye tempted her, encouraged her to interpret its sights, but if she looked for too long she felt her thoughts begin to quiet, her ambitions sapping away, her feet thoughtlessly carrying her off course until Fellwing ferociously flapped in front of her face enough to snap Ji-hyeon back to the moment and realize she had wandered perilously close to the bone-strewn entrance of an immense lair. Then the eye would be punished with another exile behind the iron patch.

A year of this shit! A year of keeping careful track of the days despite her exile in a land without night. She had brought very little with her through the Othean Gate, having not exactly thrown an overnight bag over her shoulder when she went to meet the empress, but many of the inhuman things she killed carried equipment, and over time she acquired an incomplete set of crude and decaying gear. Each time she awoke from fitful rest she scratched another mark in the haft of a spear she had taken from a monster she had killed within her first ten minutes of arriving here, and while the head of the weapon had long since broken off in the carapace of a dire centipede, she kept the pole as a walking stick, and more importantly, a calendar.

A year of slowly confirming that while there had once been great civilizations here, now there was little left but desecrated tombs, every city a cemetery long picked clean by the scavengers who seemed as mad as they were monstrous. The bizarrely shaped buildings were worn smooth as beach glass from the dusty wind, hollow caves with no remaining trace of door or casement, only their bleached stone sockets. She could not even find a skeleton that wasn't twisted into something bestial and wrong, Ji-hyeon the last human shape left in this forlorn world. Or the first; who could say, who could say...

A year of singing to Fellwing until her voice was hoarse. Of counting her steps and the solemn pillars of the petrified forests and the few standing columns of the ancient ruins, just to prove to herself that there was order here, even if its only name was Ji-hyeon Bong. She marked her passing by scratching a simple message in High Immaculate into whatever rock or ruin seemed most prominent when she made camp, those times when she could find something that wouldn't crumble under her writ. It read: *Ji-hyeon Was Here. She Walks To The Black Sun.*

A year of knowing that even if her first father and her sisters and the rest of their house had indeed come to this hostile land their odds of survival were far longer than even her own. Of knowing that the only eyes that would ever see her messages were not human, and if she were lucky, could not read High Immaculate.

A week of walking a blasted shore where the bones of dead things washed in by the stagnant sea crunched under her every step, and where she almost collapsed from thirst before finding a brackish stream that flowed into the ocean and following it far enough inland that she was able to drink, and every day of that week knowing her family was probably dead, that the Empress Ryuki's judgment had been far crueler than simple execution. Because the not knowing was worse, and the hope Ji-hyeon clung to was so cruel it turned Fellwing fat as a tiny pumpkin and black as a mamba before they'd even come down from the first mountain range.

A year of wondering every day where Sullen and Keun-ju were. If they were, anymore. Of hating herself for not cherishing every moment with them, and securing countless more by keeping them close, to hell with letting them leave to find Maroto, to hell with trying to save the world. Of hating herself for not forgiving Keun-ju, and of hating him all over again for forcing her to push him away... and then finally forgiving him completely, and hating herself for not doing so when it had mattered. Compared to what the Empress Ryuki had done to those who trusted her, Keun-ju's betrayal of Ji-hyeon's plan to run away from home was laughably mild. Or would have been, if Ji-hyeon ever laughed.

A year of wondering every day about the Cobalt Company, captured by a petty, vengeful empress, of Choi and Fennec and even Hoartrap. Of wondering if Chevaleresse Singh and her children were now back home in the Raniputri Dominions, their desertion on the eve of the Company's passage through the Lark's Tongue Gate the sagest military decision anyone had made all campaign. She wondered about Colonel Hjortt, though not for long. And one day, deep into her journey, she wondered about Zosia, waiting nervously in the middle of Diadem for reinforcements that would never come, and at long last Ji-hyeon laughed, laughed until muddy tears ran down her ash-dusted cheeks, kept laughing until she was sick. But really, she was going to throw up anyway.

A year of *that*, and she could survive anything. It helped that she had given up all hope for her family, for her house. No one could survive here who didn't have a devil, Ji-hyeon realized, to protect them from the toxicity of the very food and water and perhaps even the air; only Fellwing knew how much she truly shielded her mistress from. That was why no matter how debilitated Ji-hyeon might be when the horrors came for her she always found her strength in time, her fever breaking just long enough to stagger up and draw her thirsty black sword and strike down her foes...but not even her devil could fully insulate her from the poison of this realm.

Here at last, though, their relationship was completely symbiotic, for while the owlbat spent her every moment preserving her mistress, so, too, did Ji-hyeon spend her every moment feeding her devil with a never-ending torrent of the darkest emotions to ever bubble up from a mortal heart. They fed off each other, a vampiric circuit, like the clasp on one of her first father's scrolls made in the likeness of two serpents eating each other's tails. A symbol for eternity, he had told her, but if this was eternity, then all the hell scrolls she had ever scoffed at had only hinted at the true horror of existence.

Hope did not fail her completely, though, and in her second year it grew and grew, because by pulling her eye patch aside and squinting her devil-eye she had finally been able to see the black sun for what it truly was. A Gate, letting in a little feeble light and warmth from the world of mortals. From the Star. And as it slowly but surely grew on the horizon she knew that while it might take many more years to actually reach it, once she did she would crawl back up from hell and avenge herself not just on Empress Ryuki herself but on all of Othean.

Twenty thousand Immaculate soldiers had stood by and done nothing as her second father was executed for one of the few crimes he had not actually committed in a lifetime of roguery. A dozen dozen archers carrying out the murder without hesitation. And how many more evil mortals had carried her sisters and her first father and every single other member of their household up the steps of the Temple of Pentacles and cast them into this nightmare? How many more had labored to destroy her home, desecrating Hwabun just as the Black Pope's war bishops had destroyed pagan shrines in the hinterlands of the Crimson Empire, a practice all civilized people condemned?

Some members of the Immaculate court must have objected to the empress's harsh judgment, most quietly but a few loudly, but now that Ji-hyeon knew the truth of Empress Ryuki's black heart, she had no doubt that dissenters would have been silenced in just as absolute a fashion. Which meant anyone who remained on Othean when the last living Bong finally returned would be complicit, or close enough as made no difference—even if Ji-hyeon *had* killed Prince Byeong-gu, there was never any doubt the rest of her family was completely innocent, and anyone who would continue to serve an empress capable of such savagery deserved exactly what Ji-hyeon would bring them.

Dark thoughts, but they went well with the setting, and kept her going even when the memories of Sullen and Keun-ju brought frustrated tears to her eyes, and when the fantasy of being reunited with both of them felt as thin as she'd worn her boots... but without the means to steal a new pair off a dead adversary who resembled a woman covered in a diamond pattern of scaly knobs. The fallen monster's head looked like something banished from the seafloor even before Ji-hyeon hacked it apart with the black blade that howled right along with her, the rest of the creature's pack fleeing at the sound of her sainted steel. Word must be spreading among the tribes of a lone swordswoman with an enchanted blade, an all-seeing eye, and a bound devil, but while that might have discouraged some, it clearly emboldened others. The first year Ji-hyeon only defended herself, but in the second she became a ruthless huntress, ambushing anything she could take unawares, showing no mercy to her enemies... and everything that walked or crawled or slithered or flew in this place was her enemy.

For two relentless years Ji-hyeon stayed one shaky sword thrust ahead of an anonymous death, and at the end of that second year she chopped her notch-striped walking stick in two. Not because keeping the crude calendar had become too depressing, but so she could use the two ends as a brace for the arm she broke fighting a tusked monstrosity. Under Fellwing's ministrations the arm eventually healed but she didn't bother marking the days anymore. Why had she bothered in the first place? She was here until she escaped or she died, end of song.

Then, traversing the buckled ruins of a once-mighty wall that ran along the tops of the fjords that formed the northern coast of the pearlescent sea, Ji-hyeon stumbled into the very sort of trap she favored most.

She was weak and shaky from climbing up to the headland, and Fellwing was sleeping in her sling on Ji-hyeon's chest, exhausted from keeping her mistress strong and alert during the perilous ascent. Stern gusts blew in from the ocean and whistled up through sea caves in almost musical bursts. The winds kept the stone underfoot free of the slippery ash that would have made this treacherous route impassable, but they also deafened her with their near-constant trilling. She had considered moving farther inland before resuming her westward march, but beyond the sea cliffs stretched another ruined city, this wall but one edge of what must have once been a wonder to dwarf any metropolis on the Star.

To Ji-hyeon's jaded right eye it looked like nothing so much as a maze that stretched to the far horizon—if she walked into that expanse of blasted stone and teetering ruins the black sun would be obscured by uncounted miles of rubble and wreckage. Many times in her journey she had lost sight of her quarry, sometimes for weeks at a time, and there was nothing worse than cresting a ridge and finding she had been wandering off course, the black sun in a completely different direction than she had anticipated.

Flipping up her eye patch to let her devilish left eye have a gander, she saw that the dead city teemed with gossamer activity. Pastel currents swirled up out of the streets, sentient black shadows peeling themselves off the walls and roofs to swim up into the variegated air. Nothing new here, then. For the umpteenth time Ji-hyeon wondered if this realm was truly as bleak and hopeless as it seemed or if these lands actually thrived with warmth and happiness and normal life, life that she could only catch hints of with the aid of her altered eye. What if this place that appeared to be an ancient ruined city in some alien land was in fact a bustling city on the Star, and she was but a doomed ghost who could see nothing but the shadows cast by the living world?

Yes, well, as long as she was asking herself stupid questions she'd already pondered a thousand times, what if she went ahead and carved her haunted left eye out of her skull? Dropping the patch back into place, she turned away from the vastness of the city and followed the wall that ran along the coastline. Long stretches of its ancient allure still stood strong, but where the buckled wall-walk had collapsed she climbed down to wend her way through the labyrinth of scattered masonry.

It was here that the trap was sprung. A portion of the wall had pitched over the edge of the sheer cliffs into the sea, leaving a gap of mostly open ground to cross from the lonely, freestanding arch Ji-hyeon leaned against, catching her breath, to the resumption of the ruins. The wall had pulled up and away from the city here, riding a crest of land nearly as sheer on the city side as it was on that of the sea, but the ridgeline ahead wasn't too narrow and she hadn't seen sign nor spoor of anything larger than a rock squid since gaining the headland. Still, she hadn't lived this long by taking her safety for granted.

As if sensing her uncertainty her left eye itched to be let back out into the light, and she obliged it. She only let it have a quick peek, though, having learned that the longer she stared with her devilish eye the more it affected her equilibrium, her feet struggling to find purchase on illusory planes that lingered even after she put her metal patch back into place. Squinting to focus past the predictable waterfall of blushing pigments that swirled over the narrow ridge between her and the ruins on the far side, she didn't see any of the oily black smears she was looking for. She had learned that such dark smudges oftentimes limned hostile creatures lying in ambush, their cover worthless against the acuity of Ji-hyeon's witch-eye... but while the ruins ahead fluttered with countless hues and shades and ephemeral activity, none of the angry black blobs revealed themselves.

Ji-hyeon snapped her eye patch back in place, and once her feet felt steady enough to make the crossing she plowed ahead along the exposed ridge. The whistling wind rose near to a scream out here, away from the buffering ruins, and she scowled at the empty sky—a coast without birds seemed as unnatural as an ocean without water... which it might well be, since she hadn't had any interest in further investigating the slushy white tide that broke on the dismal beach.

From the corner of her eye she saw a shadow dart around the wreckage of the wall ahead of her. The only shadows in this gloomy land were made of twisted flesh and fetid blood, the black sun too weak or too weird to cast actual shade. She was already most of the way across the open path, and broke into as fast a charge as she dared. A misstep here on the rocky, uneven turf would send her either tumbling off the cliffs into the sea or bouncing all the way down the sheer slope to the ruined city far below. Her breath was short and hot and painful, her legs stumbling and twisting as the wind hit hard enough to trip her up, a crude javelin in one hand and the other keeping Fellwing from bouncing too hard on her chest even as she rubbed the devil awake.

Another shape bobbed briefly into view behind the curtain of boulder-strewn rubble. This wasn't the first time she had trusted her cursed eye to warn her of danger only to be let down, and as always the question remained if this was due to her failure to understand its bizarre visions or because the organ itself intended to deceive her into peril. A question to be revisited after she killed everything that stood in her way—there might be an army of mutants waiting beyond those first few blocks of the fallen wall, true, but if so they would immediately be on her trail and she was far too tired to lead them on a protracted chase back the way she had come. Better to press forward and push through, however many there were, until they ran screaming from her black sword. Ji-hyeon would have planned an ambush for this exact spot had their roles been reversed, but then holding a narrow path or bridge is most effective if you're trying to bottleneck a larger force, as opposed to a lone agent—as always, she had the advantage of her wits over the four armored figures who now stepped out from the cover of the stones to challenge her.

Fellwing finally woke with a frantic chirp Ji-hyeon could barely hear above the shrieking wind, the exhausted owlbat bursting out of the sling to flap around Ji-hyeon's face. While she appreciated her devil's warning she could see perfectly well what a bad idea this was as she crossed the last dozen meters of narrow trail to where it opened up at the base of the wall. None of these warriors had charged yet, waiting for her to come to them, and they had spread out enough to trap her among them. They must be smarter than most of their monstrous ilk, which meant they were more dangerous, and while they didn't wear helms and their armor wasn't as brutish as most, their blades looked every bit as keen. One of them brandished an enormous crossbow.

With Ji-hyeon's eye streaming from the wind, their faces looked almost human, their features flatter than most of the monsters here, their open mouths not displaying tusks or fangs. Ji-hyeon focused on the most intimidating, a tall female with a glaive...a glaive she thrust into the earth at her feet, raising gauntleted palms in the air just as Ji-hyeon drew back her javelin, preparing to spit this woman through her barking mouth and then draw her swords. Whatever trick this was, Ji-hyeon wasn't falling for it, what she had taken to be a deafening wind actually the howling of her black blade warning her to strike fast and now and kill kill kill these things, and just as she tried to hurl her javelin at its naked, confused face Ji-hyeon tripped.

One of the others had kicked her legs out from under her, Fellwing failing to protect her mistress, and then they fell upon her. There were four of them and Ji-hyeon felt so weak, but they were all old, she saw, old and weak, too, and she thrashed and kicked and howled, trying to headbutt a leather-skinned man in the teeth when he got too close, and snapping at a crone's hand when she tried to press something over Ji-hyeon's mouth. No, not her mouth, something wet and cold against her forehead, and the howling faded as they chanted some spell, some trick, Fellwing circling far above her attackers, again a single beacon in the empty sky above the empty sea.

"Ji-hyeon," they were saying. "General Ji-hyeon."

She was too surprised to speak, but she stopped fighting, her fevered brain finally acknowledging that these were real people, not more monsters, and they were addressing her. Her own name sounded alien on the lips of these four old-timers, three women and a man, the concern on their lined faces shifting to relief. To joy. The old man was weeping, the hands that had seized her and held her down now softly helping her sit up. It was a dream, and one Ji-hyeon had not let herself indulge in so long she had no idea where it even went from here...

"You know me," she managed, looking at the happy faces of the heavily armed and armored geriatrics. They *were* familiar, but in the way of dreams, where all mortals are cousins and known to one another. "I...I'm sorry, I don't..."

They looked taken aback for a moment but then exchanged nervous laughs. The oldest of them, the woman with the glaive whom Ji-hyeon had almost murdered, executed the unmistakably ostentatious bow of a Raniputri knight despite looking more like a Flintlander, and said, "Chevaleresse Sasamaso of the Crowned Eagle People, Captain of General Ji-hyeon Bong's Bodyguards, reporting for duty."

Ji-hyeon couldn't speak, gawping at the grinning old knight as her weathered features synchronized with the fading image of her beloved bodyguard who had died at the First Battle of the Lark's Tongue. No, not died... been consumed by the Gate that had opened up beneath the battlefield, along with so many others, like—

"Count Hassan, of the Cobalt Company, reporting for duty," said the Usban man, his voice steadier than his knocking knees as he gave as deep a bow as his old back would allow.

"Duchess Din, of the Cobalt Company, reporting as well," said the least haggard of the four, though Ji-hyeon could see that her face was just as wrinkled as the rest beneath her makeup. Looping her arm through that of the third woman, the only one Ji-hyeon didn't recognize at all, Din said, "And may I introduce Captain Meloy Shea, late of the Fifteenth Imperial Regiment, now of the Cobalt Company."

"Very, very late of that outfit," the fine-haired Azgarothian woman hastened to add, giving Ji-hyeon the Cobalt salute. "Honored to meet you, General, and serve a better cause."

"I...I don't understand," said Ji-hyeon, her head spinning as she looked around at her saviors. She was too shocked to feel anything but confusion. "I'm so sorry, I don't know what happened, to you, to me, I don't—"

"The one luxury we have here is time to discuss it all, but we can do that back at camp," said Sasamaso, easily hoisting Ji-hyeon back to her feet despite her advanced years. "And that can wait until you're rested and fed."

"Though you could tell us a little, while we walk?" said Shea nervously.

"No, she can't," said Sasamaso, smiling up at Fellwing as the devil swam laps around them here in this pocket of calm air amid the ruins, outside the raging wind. "We've waited this long, we can wait a little longer."

"You've been waiting for me?" Ji-hyeon managed, the ground seeming to float under her feet as Din and Hassan gathered up her rotting pack, rusting javelin, and everything else she'd dropped in the tussle.

"Oh, yes—this may surprise you, General, but we've been waiting a very, very long time," said the wizened chevaleresse, and together the small party limped off into the shell of a city that was ancient when the Star was young.

CHAPTER
11

Higher... higher... *there*." Nemi clicked her teeth in the eternal twilight of the mobile hut she called her *vardo*, guiding her student with gentle insistence. "That's it, back and forth, but not so fast, not so fast—slow and steady. Good girl."

Purna's fingers were aching, long as they'd been at it, but hearing Nemi call her that made her chest flutter like the witch's cockatrice had gotten inside her lungs and was flapping all around. But, like, in a good way. Keeping her hand steady and the pressure consistent, she did as Nemi commanded, and there, rising up seemingly out of nowhere, came the first quivering reward for Purna's exertions. She kept at it, a smile spreading across her face as the sweet moan of success filled the vardo. As with so much else, from playing gin to licking quim, once you figured out the basics of playing an instrument nature took care of the rest... so long as you kept an open mind and put in the hours.

"My, but you're a quick study," said Nemi, slowly letting go of Purna's elbow now that her pupil had found the right balance and amount of friction to apply with the bow to draw music out of the singing sword. It was damned hard work, though, keeping the pommel wedged between her boots and pinching the blunt point between thumb and forefinger of her off hand as she pressed down, putting just enough of an S-shaped curve in the blade that when she dragged the bow across its dull side the sword serenaded her. It sang in much the same way that rutting cats could be said to sing, a warbling wailing yowl of a song, but Purna knew from experience that strange music could prove beautiful, if you gave it a chance to win you over. "You said you played other instruments?"

"Xylobones and drums, mostly," said Purna. "Got pretty good at beatboxing, too, once I met up with those nobles I told you about, Diggelby's chums, but that's not really—balls!"

Quick as she'd found the sweet spot she lost it again, the music dying and her left hand too tired to keep the blade curved any longer. Slowly raising her arm so the sword wouldn't snap her in the thigh like before, she handed the bow back to Nemi. "Next time I'll have it for sure."

"I am already quite impressed," said the witch, slipping the bow into the smaller opening of her heavy wooden scabbard, and then sheathing the singing sword when Purna passed it over. "I could never keep it up that long when I was first learning, though my hands have grown strong from the years of playing. Yours must be sore, no?"

"Oh, it takes more than a little finger work to get these mitts miffed," said Purna, though in point of fact it felt like her digits were going to fall off and her wrists weren't far behind. If she was going to get her hands cramped up during alone time with the fit witch there were other instruments Purna would prefer to play, but you couldn't be a Maroto and rush these things. Better to let them fall naturally into place, lest you fall naturally onto your face. Of course, nothing ventured nothing gained, and if you couldn't flirt with a skirt than you probably weren't ever going to get where you wanted anyway. "My uncle always said you have to keep your hands busy or they'll get you into trouble, but in my experience trouble's the very thing that's kept these ten fingers of mine the busiest."

"I was recently accused of speaking in riddles; I wonder what my plainspoken traveling companion would have made of you, Purna Antimgran," said Nemi, brushing her mousy hair out of her bespectacled face. Her many rings and piercings glittered in the yellow light of the lantern that illuminated the narrow room, with its bench-bed, built-in bookshelves, and the hooded black-and-white cockatrice nested in its alcove. Although the music lesson had ended she remained seated next to her pupil on the bolster, and now that Purna wasn't focused so intently on playing she noticed that Nemi's thigh was flush with her own, only a witch's lacy dress and a barbarian's padded leather legging separating their skin.

"Which companion had problems parsing your words, the monk or the mook?" asked Purna. "No, let me guess—it was Sullen's mum, wasn't it? I tried talking to her, told her any sister of Maroto's was a sister of mine, but that didn't play so well."

"She would not talk to you?"

"Oh, she said plenty at first, in Flintlander. But when I made it clear I understood at least some of the spleen she was spitting she clammed right up."

"She won't speak to me at all anymore," said Nemi. "I suppose she feels I betrayed her by lending my chains to her incarceration, but when she would not take an oath of peace she left me little choice."

"Those were yours?" said Purna, shifting around to let her leg rub ever so softly against Nemi's. Nice. "Now what's a friendly witch like you need with a bunch of manacles and locks, hmmm?"

"Souvenirs from my past life as an escape artist," said Nemi, putting a long-fingered hand on Purna's knee, and stealing her breath in the process...only to use Purna as a boost to get to her unsteady feet. In the time since they had started the lesson most of Nemi's strength seemed to have fled her. She leaned forward, scanning the shelves that filled the other side of the vardo. The back that had been straight and tall when they had first sat down now had a slight but definite twist in it, and her rich auburn hair had lost its luster, looking brown and drab as dead ivy hanging against the trellised lace of her dress. Even with the mild hunch she acquired at this time of night, Nemi of the Bitter Sighs was still taller than her Ugrakari guest, and never lost that juicy rump that had so distracted Purna the night they had first met. It distracted her again now, jutting out as it did within biting distance of Purna's face. As always when she noticed the witch's evening decline or morning restoration following the ingestion of one of her special eggs, Purna burned to ask her just how the deuce she had come by such a curse—she imagined Hoartrap was to blame, because of course he was, but what a song that must be!

"Sure is cozy in here," said Purna, surreptitiously running her hand over the warm impression Nemi had left in the bedding beside her. It gave her a thrill as cheap as any Maroto would have taken, but then ever since she'd met him her luck with the ladies had been as bad as his—guilt by association, perhaps, or maybe his lack of game was actually contagious. Nemi was still leaning forward, looking for something amid the rows of boxes and jars and books on the opposite wall of the vardo, that bottom so close and yet so impossibly far... "This bed must be plenty comfy to stretch out on, after a long day riding up top."

"It is," said Nemi, and after a moment's pause, added, "You are welcome to make use of it tonight, if you so wish."

"Ah," said Purna, her mouth going dry as her palms went damp. *Don't get carried away*, she told herself. For all Nemi's creepy trappings and monstrous familiars and serious-business attitude, she was clearly still a shy nerd who wasn't nearly as world-wise as she wanted everyone to think. Purna was good and committed to the chase, no doubt about that, but she knew it couldn't be this easy. "Like a sleepover, then, just us girls? Count me in."

"No, not like a *sleepover*," said Nemi in a tone that sounded almost annoyed, looking back over her shoulder at Purna. "Unless your sleepovers usually involve fornication."

"The, uh, the best ones do?" said Purna, the fluttering in her chest back and bad as it had ever been. Was this really happening?

"Then why don't you put your hand under my dress already?" said Nemi, giving her perfect butt a little wag. This *was* really happening! "We have an early start tomorrow and the night has gotten on enough without you getting on me."

Purna's heart melted, the heat pouring down to her loins, and she reached out toward heaven on earth. She pinched the hem of Nemi's dress in fingers that didn't seem nearly so tired anymore, lifting it up so her other hand could take the witch up on her offer, when a dark and terrible thought occurred to her. "Nemi, I hope...I hope you don't feel like you owe me this, 'cause I saved you from Hoartrap? If so, let's just call it off right now, I wouldn't feel right about—"

"First, never mention that hated name in my vardo again," said Nemi, standing as straight as she was able with her crooked back and turning around to face Purna, the edge of her dress tugged out from between the girl's fingers. Looking down her sharp nose at her anxious guest, she said, "Second, the Pasha Diggelby saved both of us, after *you* prevented me from avenging myself on a terror more wicked than any devil in the First Dark. So no, I do not feel I owe you my tongue or fingers or any other part of my body...but if you wished to trade them for a spell I think you would enjoy the exchange."

"See, that's the sort of riddle I can get behind," said Purna, grinning at Nemi as her hands went to the hips of the tall girl standing in front of her. As she started hitching up the sides of the dress, she added, "Tongue-twisters are my specialty."

Cute as Nemi was, she looked even cuter when she rolled her eyes and groaned. "We had better put something in your mouth, before you improve the mood any further."

"Fuck yes we should," breathed Purna as she raised the hem of the dress to Nemi's knees, and then over the tops of her thigh-high stockings to reveal the witch's soft brown skin.

"That rough language is exactly the sort of mood improvement I refer to," said Nemi, lightly slapping the backs of Purna's hands to get her to release the dress and then shuffling to the rear of the vardo. "If your mouth is that filthy, what am I supposed to make of the rest of you?"

"My mouth is what now?" said Purna, initially wondering if her long, slobbery tongue had grossed out the witch, but that didn't make much sense; she'd also said—"Oh shit, you mean cursing? But everyone curses."

"Not so," said Nemi, opening a drawer underneath the cockatrice's alcove. She pulled out one of the black-and-gold eggs she usually only ate in the mornings, when she looked even rougher than she did in the evenings. "I find it juvenile, and am not interested in making love to adolescents."

Purna almost laughed out loud at *making love*, but then that was better than *fornication*. Whatever, to each their own, and Purna would gladly forgo talking dirty if it meant she could *get* dirty—though how dirty anyone who wouldn't even cuss was willing to get remained to be seen. Maybe because Nemi was a witch Purna had assumed once she finally loosened up she'd be as freaky as the friskiest debauched noble, but that was just an ugly stereotype, wasn't it? Besides, with Nemi being fine and primed—and hard-up as Purna was—they could have the most vanilla sport imaginable using the stodgiest barber's vocabulary and still have the time of theirs lives.

"Some of the things I like are weird," said Nemi, limping back in front of Purna. She licked her pierced lips, big, pretty eyes made even bigger and prettier through the lenses of her pince-nez. "Not bad, I hope. Just weird. So if I suggest something…it's just a suggestion."

"Girl, I can be as weird as you want, and then some," said Purna, wondering if this uptight witch's definition of weird involved cunnilingus or drifted into such mysterious, uncharted waters as tribadism or earlobe-nibbling. Why, they might even include butt stuff—Purna would try not to faint.

"That…that gets me excited," said Nemi, biting her lip ring in an incredibly sexy fashion. Eat your heart out, world, for the first time in far, far too long, Purna was about to dine on something even finer! "Open your mouth for me."

Oooh, a subtle tinge of bossiness there, even better! Purna obliged, thrilled that at long last she was in the company of someone who would appreciate the oral mutation Prince had gifted her with when Digs's devil had saved her skin…and that she'd be able to put it to the best use imaginable. She stuck out her transformed tongue as far as it would go, which was far indeed, and put a nice curl in it to show off, gazing up at Nemi with as winsome an expression as she could muster.

"Good girl," said Nemi, and there went another heatburst between Purna's legs. "Now *don't* swallow this, no matter what."

"Um..." Purna put her tongue away. "Is that safe?"

"Yes, absolutely," said Nemi, the egg she'd been holding out toward Purna now clutched to her chest as her cheeks flushed. "But is it too weird? It's too weird. Forgive me, I'll just—"

"Nah, go for it—I trust you," said Purna, sticking her tongue back out, cocking her head back, and bracing herself for something new and probably really, really gross. Maroto had warned her that best practice was keeping yourself properly sexed up, lest you get so desperate that any attention at all seemed better than none. She had airily dismissed his counsel at the time, saying there was no danger of a girl with her charms ever finding herself in such a sorry state. And now... well, at least her mentor wasn't here to see her get egg on her face. Much as he'd probably like to watch, the old wolf.

Nemi muttered something under her breath, and then with a chef's finesse she cracked the egg in one hand... directly over Purna's open mouth. The runny cargo did exactly what she didn't want it to, making a beeline for the back of her throat, but she straightened up and kept the warm mouthful where it belonged. It had the consistency but definitely not the taste of any egg she'd ever slurped, and if anything was more like an oyster fresh from the Golden Cauldron. It was also doing something weird to her tongue, something ticklish and fizzy, like she'd chased the egg with a sip of bubbly. Just as her heart jumped with concern Nemi kissed her, and kissed her hard. Mouths opened, and an exchange was made. Purna almost gagged; the sensation of the egg sliding over into Nemi's mouth was bizarrely erotic, but as soon as it passed she imagined it rolling back into her mouth, and that was a definite *no thank you*. Fortunately Nemi pulled away, looking into Purna's watering eyes as she swallowed. Which was also implausibly hot, now that Purna was good and riled up, and she pulled the witch down beside her on the bed-bench.

The next kiss still tasted a bit like Nemi's bizarre cure, but now that the egg itself was gone it wasn't so bad, and her mouth was still pleasantly tingling. It was the first time Purna had been able to try out her new equipment, and to her extreme disappointment it didn't go so well—Nemi's eyes widened and she seemed in danger of choking on Purna's tongue. But when Purna gently tried to break their kiss the witch wouldn't let her go, sucking on the long tip in a highly provocative manner.

As far as weird new experiences went this was leagues better than the egg business, and then Nemi's hands were getting Purna out of the one purely decorative article of clothing she had left, a Serpentine corset. When Maroto had made a go at it during their faux tryst back in the Panteran Wastes he had futilely fiddled with the busks on the front and made a mess of the ornamental ribbons, but Nemi went straight to the laced back. She made short work of the knot Diggelby had claimed would have to be gnawed off, after he'd helped Purna into the corset with more than one cheeky word regarding her choice in attire for a friendly music lesson.

Nemi let off slurping on Purna's tongue as she loosened the lacing and then moved her hands back to the front. She unhooked the busk studs, eyeing Purna so steamily it was a wonder her pince-nez hadn't fogged up. Then she parted the front of the corset with deliberate slowness, exposing Purna's rather plain and rather stained linen chemise. Unlike her stays, Purna could have removed this last layer by herself but nevertheless appreciated Nemi's assistance, as she did with her boots, and then her wool socks, and finally her leggings.

"Don't you feel a little overdressed?" Purna asked as she sprawled out as best she could on the bed that wasn't actually all that wide, really. Nemi still had her dress and jewelry on, and eagerly agreeing it wouldn't do to make her guest feel outclassed, she sat up on her knees and pulled the dress over her head. Sexy as she'd looked before, she was looking fresher by the moment, the russet tinge returning to her hair and the ashen hue melting away from her skin, and as she rolled over to deposit a pound or two of iron rings on a shelf at the end of the bed Purna saw that her spine was again straight and supple. Before she could roll all the way back over the Ugrakari pounced, a hand on each wonderfully fuzzy calf, and Purna kissed her way up the fine pelt that was making her drool like a wild dog. And upon reaching her lovely destination, which bawdy poets would sell short by comparing to any number of mundane flowers and geological phenomena, Purna discovered to their mutual excitement that while her monstrous tongue might be a bit much for a partner's mouth it was just right for other regions.

In the course of the night she made a careful survey of any and all of these provinces, double- and triple-checking as necessary, and discovering a few more piercings for good measure. And while Nemi's tongue was strictly human both her skill and her appetites were downright devilish.

All right, so Purna hadn't had *that* much personal experience in matters carnal, but she'd had enough to know that Nemi was right: the witch was into some weird stuff. Not bad. Not bad at all. But weird. Really weird.

It was the most fun Purna could remember. For a few blissful hours she actually forgot she was a wanted woman who had betrayed her family, had lost her friends, and was about to embark on an obscenely risky quest to save her mentor, who might not want to be saved in the first place…

The hooded cockatrice woke them in the early hours with a hideous hissing screech. Nemi hushed it, curling back into the smaller woman's embrace and immediately falling back asleep, but Purna lay awake in the dark wagon, remembering each and every thing she wished she could forget, big or small. Her quick crush on Nemi had let her focus on something other than her troubles, but now that she'd had the best bally scromp of her life it felt like her stupid brain was paying her back with interest.

What if she'd been recognized back in Black Moth or Thao from the wanted posters her aunt and uncle had apparently distributed far and wide, and even now assassins were creeping up on their sleeping camp? She hadn't told anybody but Diggelby the truth about her past and the price on her head, thinking it pretty small tubers next to Hoartrap's warning of monstrous hordes assaulting the Immaculate Isles and the rest of the Star next in line for the guillotine, but that was just an excuse for her cowardice, wasn't it? While everybody else was sleeping out in the open where any cutthroat skiptracer could take them unawares, she had pranced off to enjoy a nice piece of strange behind the only locked door around without so much as warning her friends of the danger they were in. No wonder she had done a better job pretending to be a fickle fop than she had at aspiring to be a hero—being a selfish brat came naturally to Purna.

Case in fucking point. Sullen had his murder-happy mother in chains and didn't know what to do with her, Keun-ju had lost his whole damn arm, and according to Hoartrap the entire Cobalt Company was in immediate mortal danger, on account of an army of monsters popping out of the ocean with the sole intention of slaughtering the Star... But instead of worrying about any of *that* Purna was giving herself the sweats with far-fetched fantasies of bounty hunters who only cared about her. Why not worry about someone other than herself for a change? Sometimes it felt like the only habit she'd actually picked up from Maroto was his narcissism.

Well, maybe that was a bit out of order. Maybe instead of viewing her former mentor's tendency to blame himself for whatever problems they were experiencing as mere self-absorption, she could chalk it up to something else that had never before plagued Purna: a willingness to take personal responsibility for a bad situation. Maybe the fact that Purna didn't sleep so easily showed a change for the better instead of the worse. Maybe she should start cutting herself the kind of slack she had always cut him.

Where was her old friend just now? Was he safe for the moment, or in dire peril? Was he even alive? Hoartrap had confided that he'd sent Maroto ahead to do reconnaissance of Jex Toth and that they would soon join him, but for all she knew the warlock was still lying and Maroto was as lost to her as Duchess Din and Count Hassan and every other friend who had fallen along the way. If Maroto were here to give her one piece of advice, she suspected it would be to not believe a word Hoartrap said.

Nemi smacked her lips in her sleep and wiggled backward into her partner, and feeling the witch's warm skin against her own Purna reckoned Maroto might give her a different slice of wisdom: why lie awake worrying about a grotesque like Hoartrap when she had his comely apprentice to snooze against? Maybe tonight would prove to be nothing but a onetime thing, but if that was true then all the more reason to enjoy it while it lasted. If Purna must stay awake with her thoughts, better to turn them to appreciating the comforting press of Nemi's back against her bosom, that delightful rump molded against her stomach...

Purna sighed, but unlike Nemi's moniker it was anything but bitter. She dearly hoped they would have many more nights like this, and not just for the carnal fireworks Nemi had ignited inside her lover. Now that Purna had finally unhitched her attention from the runaway cart of regrets and worries, her mind began to sleepily orbit around the naked girl in her arms, as it should have from the first. Nemi wasn't just enigmatic, she was as delightful a puzzle as was ever crafted. What was her song, and would Purna one day coax it from her just as she'd lured music from the witch's sword? From the barbs Nemi and Hoartrap had exchanged that first night and the few asides Purna had picked up afterward, she'd deduced that Nemi had faked her death to escape her apprenticeship, but beyond that the witch's relationship to Hoartrap was as mysterious as the curse that twisted her body each night, the horned wolf that hauled her vardo, and hells, everything else about her...

But then pity the boring sod who didn't love a good mystery, and suffice to say for now this one had an intriguing opening. Purna smiled to herself at that, breathing in the bouquet of stale smoke and tangy sweat and bitter herbs and earthy roots in her lover's hair. She soon drifted off again, knowing if she dreamed it couldn't be as sweet as this waking one a witch had conjured for her in the Haunted Forest.

CHAPTER
12

Everybody knows that when something sounds too good to be real it probably isn't, but in Maroto's extensive experience the reverse rarely held true—just because a thing seemed too fucking terrible to be real didn't preclude that possibility. On the contrary, it was usually much worse than first anticipated...which was why it came as a bit of a shock that daily life under the diabolical thumb of the Vex Assembly wasn't actually so bad.

His three Immaculate friends might disagree on that call, but that was piratical gratitude for you: no sense of perspective. The organic kingdom of Jex Toth didn't get any less sinister—or disgusting—the more time you spent there, but being guests in a sprawling living nightmare beat being prisoners in a mundane cell. Came a time when you didn't even notice all the rancid smells anymore, and as for the food...well, the food almost seemed like food after a while. Almost.

Dong-won and Niki-hyun seemed determined to starve to death rather than ingest the slimes and jellies excreted from the walls of their new home, but Bang took after Maroto and made the most of their sticky accommodations. They both claimed to have eaten worse, but since Maroto was lying on that count he figured Bang must be, too. The water also had a taste, pallor, and viscosity they all found disagreeable, to put it mildly, but even the picky Immaculates were too parched to turn their noses up at the burbling flesh fountains.

The three pirates had been turned over to Maroto shortly after their capture, the ancient priests not taking more than a cursory interest in the new arrivals. They were too busy plotting against the whole of humanity to pay much attention to a few specimens of that doomed race, releasing them to Maroto's custody.

As for the man himself, he was frequently called to the towering throne room of the Vex Assembly to assist in their strategizing... and to his shame, he helped them as much as he was able. He brought the long-gone Tothans up to speed on modern Star politics, told them everything he knew about the sundry governments and their militaries, drew up regional maps and palace blueprints from memory right down to the secret passages and ambush spots he and the Cobalts had exploited a quarter century past. A nobler prisoner of war might have tried to lead these enemies of mortalkind astray, feeding them false information in hope of weakening their campaign, but not Maroto. Only a fool would try to deceive a council who could peek into your brain at a moment's notice, and of all the four-letter appellations that folk had applied to Maroto, that particular F-word wasn't even in the top five.

The first time the roach-clad priest had stuck his ghost-hand into Maroto's skull and rummaged around, he had tried to control what the wizened warlock found there, and in the moment had assumed his deception had worked. And who knew, maybe it had, but even if Maroto could mislead the deathless priests he couldn't hide anything from the ancient devils that dwelled within them. His first day down here in hell he swore he'd kill himself before he would reveal a single thought or emotion regarding the people he cared about back on the Star, because whether Purna and Digs or Sullen and Da or Din and Hassan were still alive he didn't want these monsters even knowing they existed... but the first time the Vex Assembly pressed him on his past he betrayed his friends and family, giving every detail right down to the skunky smell of his dad's breath. He gave the monsters all they asked for, and frequently more, volunteering any and all intelligence he suspected they might find useful, running his mouth like a strung-out bard trying to talk his way back into a pawned lute. He sold out the Crimson Empire and every Arm of the Star besides, anything and everything to make himself appear valuable to the withered and decidedly insane council of undying priests who called the shots on this living island, and whatever fell spirits possessed them.

For a little while there it seemed like it might last, too, that he might have indeed bought himself and his friends a stay of execution here in Jex Toth. Neither Bang nor Niki-hyun seemed to judge Maroto for collaborating with their captors, and while Dong-won hadn't said a single word since arriving, that might not have anything to do with resentment and everything to do with the perpetual state of wide-eyed shock they all learned to live in. You never really got used to a place like this, but then why would you want to? Better to focus on the immediate tasks, on getting through one horrified minute to the next until you earned a few precious hours of uneasy sleep.

So in a way the endless labor was a blessing, as it gave them something specific to fix their minds on until it almost seemed mundane. Since their human fingers were far more slender and nimble than the clawed gauntlets of the silent black-armored soldiers who swarmed the place, the four refugees were put to work assisting in the birthing ponds of the living war machines, and the subterranean docks where the leviathans were housed until they reached maturity. The indentured mortals removed corrosive placenta from the hard-to-reach places in the seabeast larvae's optic clusters, difficult work that required swimming out into the lagoons and treading water beside the enormous newborns as they picked out the acidic goo.

While this was the worst of their jobs, it was far from their only duty. Dong-won was strong enough that he also picked up shifts installing plates of chitin armor into the sprawling flanks of the adults, while Bang, Niki-hyun, and Maroto were relegated to bug-hunting the vents of the juveniles—a nasty job, which involved reaching into the frigate-sized monsters' gills and rooting out the spiny, salamander-like parasites that thrived in the warm waters of the flooded caverns where the seabeasts were stabled.

Maroto had just dislodged a particularly big and bitey specimen and tossed the sludge puppy into his woven-bone basket when three members of the Vex Assembly appeared at the end of the veiny causeway, motioning for him to approach. An ominous, um, omen, their calling on him here instead of summoning him when his work was done. Still, he didn't get really worried until he started walking their way and they gave further gesture that he should bring along Bang and Niki-hyun, both of whom were working on the upper gills of the leviathan. It was the first time the Tothan bosses had expressly wanted Maroto's crew to attend one of their summits, and in the absence of an order to the contrary the pirates had been more than happy to sit out all of Maroto's meetings.

"What do they want, Useless?" Bang asked after he'd tapped the two women to join him and they all began dragging their feet down the soft dock to greet the trio of Tothans.

"They probably just stopped by to, you know, compliment us on all the hard work," said Maroto, trying to sound nonchalant despite how hard his heart was beating. A minor miracle the old muscle hadn't given out on him entirely, fierce as he'd been working it since falling in with this evil army of monsters from beyond space and time.

"Shit," said Niki-hyun glumly. "You'd fed us any other song I might have believed it, but we all know that ain't the case. I don't think you and hard work have ever been acquainted."

"Oh, he works hard enough, but only after hours," said Bang, giving Maroto what he dearly hoped wasn't to be his last hard smack on the arse. "You say they got in your head, Useless, and you got in theirs, so that implies a certain degree of familiarity. You got the feeling they're here to do us harm?"

"They can try," said Niki-hyun, flexing her fists. "One of them tries touching me or my brains I'm going to scramble theirs."

Bold words for a woman who'd been near-catatonic with fear when Maroto had come to release her, Bang, and Dong-won from their holding pit upon first being captured, but then even after the life of broad experience Maroto had lived prior to his arrival on Jex Toth he supposed these unorthodox environs had initially thrown him for a loop, too. That she had adjusted enough to their surroundings to talk a little shit boded well for her mental recuperation... just so long as she didn't talk too much shit, or to the wrong people. As they approached the enormous fat man, the woman with spiders in her hair, and a third figure Maroto hadn't met before, he dearly hoped the two Immaculates would let him do the talking, or more accurately, groveling.

"Hellllllo!" trilled the morbidly obese priest, the wrinkles of age and the wattles of fat collaborating to make him resemble a golem made from a mountain of greasy griddlecakes. One that had been left unattended at a picnic, given the colonies of giant white ants that dwelt in his folds and swarmed over his bulk like a living toga. As Maroto and his equally hangdog companions reached the waiting Tothans on the soggy causeway of the underdock beneath the flickering meat canopy overhead, the bloated old priest said, "Hellllo, and farewelllll!"

That did not bode well.

"You have served us sweetly!" shrieked the spider crone, looking exceptionally fucking sinister in her heaving gown of crowded cobwebs. "But now the time has come to reward your obedience!"

Like all the Vex Assembly, Spidertresses's vocal cords still hadn't recuperated from their long epoch in the abyss when the undying council had communicated solely in their wordless ways. Maroto was almost positive Jex Toth had been missing for only—only!—five centuries, but the Vex Assembly casually alluded to the many dusty millennia of their exile and who was he to argue with deranged monsters? However long they had gone without speaking, now that they were back in the world of ear-bearing mortals the lot of them overcompensated for their raw voices by screaming every damn thing. "We shall set you freeeee!"

"You said you'd kill me last," said Maroto, ignoring the raised eyebrows of Bang and Niki-hyun at this admission of the exact terms he had struck with the Vex Assembly. He may have neglected to volunteer all the particulars of his negotiations, sure, but what did they expect? "That was the deal!"

"Yessssss?" said Bloato, a troop of ants marching into his nostril as he beetled his hairless eyes at Maroto. "That is why you shallllll depart! With the Chainite fleeeeet!"

"Yesss! Spread the gospel!" yowled the spider-wrapped woman, and both she and the fat priest began shuddering with the horrible laughter that accompanied most of Maroto's interactions with the demented Vex Assembly. Their companion wasn't laughing, how-ever, and taking a closer look at the cockroach-enveloped woman he was taken aback by the smoothness of her skin, at the blackness of her hair beneath the mound of insects that took the shape of a coni-cal hat—she definitely hadn't been present at any of the meetings he had attended, with the council who looked every day of their sup-posed thousands of years. This new recruit was gritting her teeth so hard his own jaw winced in sympathy, and he saw that her swarming suit had parted on her stomach so that her right hand could dig its pointed fingernails into her milk-white flesh, bright red blood well-ing out as he watched in disgust...and worse still, she gave a lusty moan as she wriggled her digits in deeper, pupils that shifted from brown to black and back again rolling in their orbits.

"Chainite fleet?" asked Bang, and the horror Maroto felt at watch-ing this girl clawing her own belly open paled to that of his fearless captain courting the notice of these ancient freaks. "You saying the Burnished Chain sent boats up to Jex Toth?"

At the invocation of the church's name the roach-cloaked girl's fluctuating eyes latched onto Bang, gurgling growls bubbling out of her throat as she viciously tore at her stomach. A fungal reek began rolling off her in waves, the particular sort of stink that Maroto suspected was a byproduct of the Vex Assembly projecting their thoughts to one another, and the other two cadaverous captains also turned their attention to Bang.

"Your underlings will not address the Vex Assembly again!" screamed Spidertresses.

"Or they shall be confiscated!" yowled Bloato.

"They won't! They won't!" shouted Maroto. It was a habit these monsters invoked in him, bellowing out every word. "But that's what you're telling us, the Chain has some ships up here, yeah? And we can…we can just get on them and sail away? Like, soon?"

"Now!" Roach-girl wormed her entire hand under the skin of her stomach as she screamed, and whatever else she said was unintelligible even by Tothan standards, a rattle of grotesque exultations that made Maroto's hackles rise along with his gorge.

"Imm-ed-iat-ely!" howled the fat man. "Tell the Star what you witnessed here!"

"Tell the Star who is coming!" howled the spider-haired woman.

The girl just howled, then yanked her fingers out of her guts and shoved them all into her mouth, sucking noisily at their wetness. That was bad. Watching the gory wound on her stomach heal up like the skin on a soup re-forming after a chunk of meat fell back into the pot was almost worse. But not quite.

"I'll just grab my other lackey off the beast he's tuning up and we're out of here, just point the way to the Chainites," said Maroto, still mostly expecting this to end in a double-cross. This was just standard smug villain cat-and-mouse shit, wasn't it? When the big bads showed up unannounced and started talking about giving you your reward and setting you free you had to expect the ground to open underneath your feet, and never the more so than when said ground already had plenty of teeth to gobble you up with.

"Your third underling has completed work on your transport to the outer harbor!" The priest shook his chins toward the adult leviathan that filled the lower lagoon, and Maroto nodded knowingly. This was it, then, as brutal a method of execution as he could imagine—fed to one of the very monsters he and his crew had helped the Tothans ready for war against the Star. About what he deserved.

"Safe roads guide you to her breast!" screamed Roach-girl, her red-smeared mouth twisting into an ugly grin as she daubed a bloody inverted cross onto her forehead. Her eyes went black again and she dropped to all fours, scampering away with inhuman swiftness.

The spider-haired woman dashed after her, a fresh stench fouling the air in her wake, and the fat man turned to follow as well when his own eyes flooded with inky darkness, and he turned back to Maroto and the Immaculates with a hungry leer. His voice as cool and hon-eyed as the sting of an icebee, he said, "*Her Grace had intended to accompany you to the harbor to see her flock off, but clearly her ascension to divinity is preoccupying her at the moment. The transition can be try-ing for the mortal mind.*"

"Um, Her Grace?" said Maroto, the wheels turning slowly, but turning nonetheless. "You saying that girl's the Black Pope?"

Made some kind of sense, Pope Y'Homa being here, if there was a Chainite fleet parked outside...

"*What she was before means nothing to us,*" said the thing inside the priest. "*What she has become is what you might have been, Devilskin-ner, had you played a smarter strategy—the first sacrifice of the Star, and the last chalice to be filled. The final member of the Vex Assembly.*"

"Yeah, well, more fool me, huh?" gulped Maroto, not wanting to keep staring into those warm black eyes but unable to break their gaze. He was sure it saw right through his bluster, into his pounding chicken heart...and it offered a genial smile that was all the more humiliating for how genuine it felt.

"*We are not like your kind, mortal—this is no trick or trap. You are free to flee...for now.*"

"Thank you for your mercy," Maroto heard himself saying, bow-ing before the ancient man who housed something far more prime-val in his corpulent flesh. He felt a feeble flare of resentment as he did, realizing they were only letting him go because they believed he couldn't possibly pose even a minor threat to their campaign, but that flash dampened as he bowed lower; it was the death throes of his suffocating pride, was all, and he'd keep the pillow over its face until it went still. "I'm your boy, like I said, and wouldn't dream of going against your—"

"Come on," hissed Bang, grabbing Maroto's elbow and pulling him forward. He looked up to see that the fat priest hadn't even stuck around to witness Maroto's kowtowing, instead turning his back on the mortals and waddling away up the causeway after his fellows. "Good work polishing his toenails, Useful, you definitely bought us a chance out of here."

"Aye, very convincing performance," said Niki-hyun as they booked it down the flesh docks to where the titanic squid-dragon-thing was moored, a thousand busy figures sanding down the bony plates that covered a hundred yards of heaving flank. Once they grew to maturity and their armor was installed, the seabeasts swam down into the flooded caves beneath them, and wherever they emerged it wasn't any place Maroto had ever seen.

"Sorry in advance if hitching a ride with this thing is anywhere near as bad as I expect it to be," said Maroto, his stomach turning over as he saw a pair of Tothans unhinge one of the smaller sheets of jagged chitin, opening a glistening portal in the leviathan's side.

"Tell you one thing right now," said Niki-hyun as they wove through the throng of armored Tothans crowding the quay. "I'm not drawing a straw for who has to explain to Dong-won why we're crawling inside this thing—that's on you two."

"Since we're leaving Jex Toth that also means old Useful here is relinquishing his proxy command of our crew, so I'd say you're back to drawing any straws I tell you to, Niki-hyun," said Bang, giving a Tothan she bumped into a friendly wave. It didn't wave back.

"With all due respect, Captain," said Niki-hyun as they caught sight of Dong-won polishing a dripping arch of bone, "we haven't left yet."

CHAPTER
13

A warm wind blew through the cypress wood, the muggy gasp of a dying world. Even walking as slowly as Best did, each step was agony, her cracked ribs a long way from well, but she refused to ride inside Nemi's wagon or take more of her medicine. That would only prove to her son that she was a hypocrite, and besides, the Witch of the Bitter Sighs had betrayed her, and never again would Best trust a sorcerer, nor accept her aid.

She could feel the rest of the motley party keeping track of her at all times, like a herd of wary oryx watching the distant movements of a wolf. Well they might be anxious to see her walking free with her horned helm and spear, her great-grandmother's sun-knife in its sheath on her hip. The only reason any of these Chainless heathens still drew breath was the oath she had offered her son in exchange for her freedom, a pledge he had insisted she swear on the Fallen Mother to put aside their differences until the Star could be defended from this alleged invasion of devils.

The horned wolf–drawn hut guided them, Nemi steering from the riding board beside Purna. This smaller girl was the only one who might be worthy of Best's respect. Sullen claimed she had indeed killed the horned wolf whose hood she wore, and, if the song was to be believed, had done so fighting alongside both Best's missing brother and the strange man who dressed as a restless spirit. The ghost-faced, big-wigged Outlander had taken Best's place riding inside the hut with the faithless Brother Rýt, who hadn't dared speak to her after defecting to the side of their captors.

Her son walked along behind the wagon, shamelessly holding hands with the Immaculate he had been kissing as though they were already married. Perhaps they were, Sullen had not sung of his courtship to the foreign boy. As Best watched her battered, weak son stroll along with his one-armed love, a part of her begrudgingly acknowledged that as far as Outlanders went Keun-ju had proved both swift and brave when she had attacked, risking his life and losing his right arm to protect Sullen. But as soon as the sinful thought intruded she caught herself, recognizing it as the wiles of the Deceiver tempting her away from the righteous fury she must preserve. Besides, even if the Immaculate had been a great warrior before her coming, he was now without a weapon or the arm to wield it, and as soon as her oath was fulfilled she would deal with both her son and his crippled partner.

If this war against the devils ever came to pass. It was her son who sang of it, after all, and while he certainly believed it that didn't mean much, since Sullen's head was forever full of fancies. If he did not present her with all the magical wonders and devilish horrors he had promised, and soon, she would consider her pledge more than paid and get on with carrying out the judgment passed down by the Horned Wolf Council.

Looking down at the fading marks on her wrists that had never before known bondage, Best knew and acknowledged her soul was already in danger. She was succumbing to temptation, because she *wanted* to believe her son's song, wanted the Council to be wrong and her boy to be right. Absurd as his many claims surely were, if even a few of them were true Sullen was actually stronger and wiser than she had ever let herself believe, a credit to his ancestors instead of a disgrace. And if he did indeed lead them to an epic battle with an ancient evil, well then, perhaps his spirit would not need rescuing from the Hell of the Coward Dead but could proceed directly to the Fallen Mother's Meadhall. Perhaps he would even earn a virtuous death in combat, sparing Best from giving him one herself.

"They make quite the pair—you must be *so* proud."

Best didn't give the warlock the satisfaction of acknowledging he had again snuck up behind her. The first time had almost been her undoing, but now she knew he posed no immediate danger, and so as fast as her heart had leaped she calmed it back down. She didn't answer his harassment, either, having learned that no good could come of speaking to witches, and according to her former ally Nemi of the Bitter Sighs this Hoartrap the Touch was the most danger-ous sorcerer of them all. As the swollen, pale giant sidled up beside her she saw that in addition to his enormous wicker pack he carried a smoldering black pipe in one hand, and his other steadied a long white log balanced over his shoulder. Its smooth surface appeared to be meticulously carved with—

Best growled at the unmistakable markings of the Jackal People and tried to speed away from the hated symbol and the man who carried it, but the sudden movement made her ribs feel like they were breaking anew. She steadied herself against a cypress.

"Oh my, need a hand?" said Hoartrap, scratching his forehead with the yellow stem of his pipe. "Since mine are full we could always ask Keun-ju if he . . . no, wait, *that* won't work."

"You seek to quarrel with me, witch?" she spat, forgetting her pledge to herself not to engage him. "How strong and sure you must be, to attack me from behind and then provoke me before I am recovered."

"Best of the Horned Wolf Clan, Mother of Sullen, Daughter of Ruthless, and Sister of Maroto, I swear on the Fallen Biddy you love so much that I haven't *begun* to provoke you yet," said Hoartrap, and jovial as he sounded he made Best's hairs stand up in a way that hadn't happened since she had thrown down on the horned wolf she had hunted as a girl. Nodding his ugly head at his uglier cargo, he said, "I see you're admiring the log. I'd offer to let you hold it but it's got some decent work on it and I'm worried it would pull you right off your feet . . . and besides, it's not mine to pass around, it's Sullen's. I only just recovered it for him, since he misplaced it, and I had a real toot of a time finding it, I tell you what. Once you've splashed around the swamp as much as I have, one soggy bog looks the same as the next, if you catch—"

"That belongs to Sullen?" she demanded, his song of the night before certainly not mentioning his owning any relics belonging to the Horned Wolf Clan's most hated enemies.

"I believe they all pitched in on it, but yes, he commissioned it from a Jackal Witch to help locate your missing brother—you know, I'm sure Sullen wouldn't mind you touching it," said Hoartrap, clenching his pipe in his teeth and swinging the post down from his shoulder to hold it out in both hands. "Here, just feel the grain on this tamarind, it—"

"Be gone," hissed Best. "You may frighten all the others, but you do not frighten me. I have no fear of scavengers who stoop to deviltry, who sneak instead of strutting. And you may not fear me yet, but you shall, Hoartrap the Touch, just before I send you to the Hell of the Coward Dead."

"So that's a no to holding the magic log?" Hoartrap spoke around the pipe in the corner of his mouth, and then with a shrug he slung it back over his shoulder and gestured to the figures diminishing through the forest. "The others seem to be getting ahead so we better shake a leg, old girl... But while I have you alone just let me say that if you interfere in my plans again I will beat you to death with this very post."

"I will not be cowed by such as you," said Best.

"Well, moo to you, too," said Hoartrap, giving the butt of the post a pat with his free hand and then taking his pipe back out of his mouth. A thread of saliva hung from the stem and then broke, swinging from his chin into the charms embossing his yellowing leather robe as he pocketed the still-smoldering bowl. "And in case I am speaking over your bullish head, be assured my plans very much involve your son. No touching him or I touch you, and unfair though I find it, ain't nobody wants to get touched by the Touch."

"That... boy is not my son," snarled Best. "No son of mine would rely on a witch to protect him."

"No? Well, that makes things much simpler for me! I would have felt a twinge of regret over beating Sullen's mother to death, but seeing as you're not related I shan't shed a tear," said Hoartrap, and then he sprang at her, seizing the post in both hands and swinging it like a massive club. Best darted backward, putting the tree she'd been leaning against between them as she raised her spear . . . or tried to, but the sudden jerking motion aggravated her ribs so badly that she staggered in place for a moment, paralyzed with anguish. But instead of bludgeoning her with his post he had already pivoted on his heel and marched away with it, cackling to himself as he went. He could have killed her where she stood, but instead he just toyed with her . . . and now showed her his back.

If she had been able to draw her sun-knife she would have, such was her rage at his disrespect, but by the time her pain had passed enough to try it she had overpowered the impulse. Best of the Horned Wolf Clan was better than a backstabbing witch, and she would wait until she could make him look her in the eyes when she killed him. She would do it in front of Sullen, to show him how little the warlock's protection meant in the face of a true predator. Then she would teach the boy what came of trafficking with sorcerers and worse, Jackal People. She would wait until her oath was paid or void, for she was a woman of her word, but there was nothing in what she had sworn to prevent her from slaying the lot of these degenerates as soon as she was free of her bond. Best knew her limits, acknowledged she did not possess all the answers, and as a mortal could be flawed in her judgment of good and evil, right and wrong—which was why she would deliver them all to someone who could. Not that she thought the Fallen Mother would have too high an opinion of Hoartrap the Touch, or his familiar, Sullen.

Before that, though, she would let them lead her to the start of all their woes: her brother. Then all of these heretics would bear witness to the will of the Allmother, and Best would finally purchase peace with the righteous coin of her blazing wrath. Any who stood before her would burn. Any who turned their back on her would burn. The whole fucking Star would burn, if that was what it took to save it.

CHAPTER
14

A crackling fire casting merry shadows on the wall. A dog dozing in front of the hearth. A bellyful of shredded potato cakes and applesauce, and a mug of boozy hunter's tea warming her hands. The piquant tickle of exotic pipe smoke, and the homey scent of braided cinnamon bread wafting from a nearby oven. In all her years as Crimson Queen, Indsorith had never known such a peaceful night, not in Serpentine Keep where she had spent most of her rule nor her shorter tenure here in Castle Diadem nor any of the other palaces and lodges she had brought her court.

"If I'd known how cozy my kitchens were I would have come down ages ago," she told her nursemaid, huffing the hot herbal fumes of her tea and squirming around on the plush chairs they had dragged in from halfway across the castle.

"I don't reckon it was very cozy when things were going all guns down here," said Zosia, tapping the ash from her corncob pipe as her warm blue eyes glided over the deep shadows that surrounded their island of firelight in the vast and dark kitchen complex. Not for the first time Indsorith felt like a ghost haunting her old life. Not for the first time she found she enjoyed the sensation. And not for the first time she immediately felt guilty at taking relief in her relinquishment of duty, involuntarily or not.

"I should have made time to come here, to meet and thank the army of chefs and dogsbodies and turnip peelers who made sure I always ate so well..." Indsorith thought out loud. She must have fallen into the habit during the long agony of her solitary imprisonment, but instead of being embarrassed to have a witness to her doubts and regrets she found Zosia the ideal listener. Who else could have understood the petty pains of one so privileged but a fellow queen?

"It's good to get down in the scrum with your people whenever you can," agreed Zosia, which just proved that spending time with your big-booted predecessor could also be a touch annoying. Indsorith didn't think Zosia intended to sound judgmental, and after all the years of near-universal toadying there was something refreshing about talking to someone who didn't coach her every word to avoid giving offense, but all the same the older woman sometimes came off as condescending.

"I suppose her highness Queen Cobalt not only visited her kitchens on a daily basis but also took her turn stirring the stew?" said Indsorith.

"Even with a devil to mind her, Queen Cobalt was too paranoid of being poisoned to touch anything that came out of these kitchens, to say fuck-all of walking my butt down here." Zosia smirked. As usual the expression seemed both genuine and pained, as if she were so long out of the habit that the muscles in her face cried out whenever she smiled. "I installed my old camp cook in that servant's station just down the hall from the royal chambers and lived off his rations, same as I did before we captured the castle."

"Ugh, always with the poisoning!" Indsorith took a gulp of tea, her every slow-healing wound flaring at the memory of the salted wine Y'Homa had drugged her with. "Even with all the precautions and preventatives and mystic alarms and miracle cures and potions and poison tasters I doubt I ever made it more than a year without something slipping through and making me sick as seven devils. That I lasted as long as I did without something taking me out for good just proves that I had a lot of people watching my back—for all their grief the nobles and colonels were sane enough to know I was the better alternative to a Chainite coup or Imperial infighting over the Crimson Throne." Zosia was watching her over her mug, and rather than giving the older woman the pleasure of pointing out the obvious Indsorith added, "Or the Burnished Chain and their collaborators could have actually poisoned me any time they wished but chose to bide until now, as I unwittingly played into their hands for year after year."

"Perhaps, but I rather doubt it," said Zosia. "I'm sure someone would have assassinated you years ago, if you weren't relentlessly hard to kill. Don't forget you almost bested the greatest swordswoman the Star has ever known."

"Almost," said Indsorith, smiling as she admired the white slash she had etched into Zosia's chin. The aging legend boasted quite a few scars, but that was the most pronounced. "Bad as you wanted to lose that duel, I should have given you a much bigger beauty mark."

"Implying I went easy on you is an insult to both my honor and your skill," said Zosia, jutting her chin at Indsorith. "Besides, I happened to like my face just fine the way it was."

"Hmmm," said Indsorith, giving the woman's hard features a mock-serious inspection. It probably had a lot to do with the fact that she no longer looked upon Zosia with furious hatred, but she spoke truthfully when she said, "No, you look much better now, trust me."

"That so? Maybe like a fine cheese, the spreading cracks in my rind hint at an inner improvement." Perhaps second-guessing this tipsy pronouncement, Zosia pursed her lips as the shadow of a blush spread between the finer scars on her cheeks. "In all seriousness, it was one of the hardest fights of my life."

"It should have been harder," said Indsorith. "But I didn't figure out why until your lover stormed the castle and tried to smear me all over the throne room."

"Eh?" Zosia frowned. "My...oh hells no! Maroto told me he dueled you after he thought you killed me, but he is not now nor has he ever been more than a friend. And a fair-weather one at that."

"But he did find out you're still alive, then? You were reunited?" Indsorith remembered how heartbroken the man had seemed after she had bested him, as ruined as her father had been after her mother's death in the work farm, and felt a pleasant hum in her chest. Here at long last was a story with a happy ending.

"That we were, that we were," said Zosia, but from the way she stared down into her mug it didn't look as though this story had such a cheerful conclusion after all. Maybe no tale truly does, if you keep following it past the point where a savvy storyteller knows to trail off… "So what did he say that's stuck with you after all these years?"

"It wasn't what he said, it was how he fought," said Indsorith. "He was too angry, just like I was when I came for you. I thought my fury would make me unstoppable, but fighting him I realized anger just makes us sloppy. If I had learned to control my wrath before we fought I would have beaten you."

"Hmmm," said Zosia, nodding a little as she considered this. "First off, you need a little anger or your heart won't be in the fight. That's even worse than being too pissed at your opponent. Second, if you hadn't been so furious you might have done *better*, sure, but no way in all the forgotten war gods of Emeritus would you have actually taken me out. Sorry, kid, you may be good but I'm the best."

"Maybe once upon a time," said Indsorith, unable to resist. "But that was a long, long, looong time ago."

"Not so long as all that!"

"Then I challenge you to a rematch," said Indsorith, leaning as far forward in her chair as her aching back would allow and extending a bandaged hand. "As soon as I'm fit enough to lift Moonspell we go again, you and I."

"And for what stakes will we duel this time, Your Majesty?" To Zosia's credit she didn't wait for an answer before shaking her challenger's hand.

"The only stakes that matter to women who have tasted every luxury life affords, and lost more than most people will ever win."

"Look, you're an attractive young lady," said Zosia, raising a deferential palm, "but as a matter of principle I refuse to assign sexual favors as a prize in any contest. Much to Maroto's chagrin, the old—"

"Bragging rights," said Indsorith, rolling her eyes. It was lonely being queen, but not *that* lonely. "I'm talking about bragging rights."

"Of course, of course…" Another of those pained smiles. "So if you think you stand a chance, that must mean you're no longer mad at me?"

"Why didn't you tell me it wasn't your fault?" Indsorith said quietly, figuring she knew the answer but needing to hear it from Zosia all the same. "When I came for your head, and told you who I was and why I was there, why the fuck didn't you tell me what happened to my people wasn't your fault?"

"Because it was," said Zosia, slumping back in her chair and draining her tea. "You were right to blame me for the fall of Junius, and everything that came after."

"But those farms weren't what you wanted," Indsorith protested. "After I took the crown I found the reports about Karilemin, and the other work camps—I know that wasn't what you wanted. I know you put a stop to them as soon as you found out."

"Too late to save your family," murmured Zosia, and though their voices were low and Choplicker looked asleep, his tail began softly drumming on the hearthstones. "Too late to save a lot of families."

"You didn't tell me because you thought as queen you should have somehow known what people halfway across the Empire were doing in your name," said Indsorith, knowing that feeling herself.

"What sort of a queen would I have been if I answered your challenge by blaming somebody else?" asked Zosia.

"A good one," snapped Indsorith. "The kind of queen I've tried to be. One who holds herself accountable to her subjects, but isn't so crushed under the enormity of her responsibility that she accepts more than her fair share of blame. You don't help yourself or your people by playing the martyr—letting the guilt of not doing more distract you from doing anything at all leaves the whole fucking Star worse off than it was before."

"And would you have listened if I'd told you?" Zosia said wearily. "If I'd tried to explain what I actually wanted my soldiers to do in Junius, and how far from the mark those farms fell? That by the time you stormed this castle I'd already gone to Karilemin and tried to set things right? Would you have believed me, and kept your sword in your sheath?"

"Not in a thousand fucking years," said Indsorith, raising her mug in salute. "But that's missing the point entirely. It's easy to do the right thing when you know it'll help a situation. But even knowing it wouldn't, you still should have done right by me. You owed me the truth, even if it was all you could offer. Especially then."

"I gave you the Crimson Throne, and the Carnelian Crown to wear while you sat in it—how's that doing right for you?" said Zosia, getting up with that sprightly ease Indsorith so envied. Even if she wasn't recuperating from her many ordeals she doubted she was as fit as this woman some twenty years her senior. Then again, she didn't have a devil keeping her strong like some fairybook witch.

"We're alone at what feels remarkably like the end of civilization, so spare me the bullshit," said Indsorith as she watched Zosia bend over to get the cinnamon bread out of the oven with an appreciative eye. There was certainly no harm in admiring the cut of another woman's peasant dress... nor the cut of her figure, while your eye was in the neighborhood. "I learned soon enough why you were so quick to let me take your place—being the queen is the fucking pits. You weren't doing me a good turn at all, you were doing yourself one."

"I won your life when I won the duel," said Zosia, batting the twisted loaf out of the oven with her bare hand and juggling it onto a cooling rack. "That I made you queen instead of a corpse I consider a *very* good turn, however selfish my motivations. Which... well, yeah, were entirely selfish, but then I'm a very selfish person in general so you shouldn't take it personally."

"And that's why you've returned in the Empire's darkest hour, ready to once more rally the people to the common good? Because you're such a selfish jerk?" Indsorith wasn't crazy about Zosia's plan to turn over her castle to a confederation of rabble and their rousers whose only common ideology was their antipathy to the Crown, but her reservations came from simple self-preservation—Indsorith was more than happy to quit her former station, so long as she left it on her own two feet instead of with her head on a pike. Zosia put a lot more faith in Indsorith's subjects than she did, but then Zosia hadn't been the one trying to govern them for the past two decades.

"Yup. When they sing this song maybe they'll keep me on as the hero, but it was naught but pure egotism that brought me back." Zosia licked melted sugar off her fingers. "Vengeance put me on the path that led me here, same as it first carried you to this castle all those years ago. For as much as history repeats its sad dirge over and over down the years you'd think someone would bother learning the lyrics, keep us from falling into the same snares of fate and fortune."

"Hunger for revenge may have set you on your way, but I don't believe it's still what drives you," said Indsorith, clambering out of her chair to top off their mugs with the overproof Insomnium rhum that had elevated their tea from humble cuppa to pure ambrosia.

"Something else we have in common, huh?" said Zosia. "By the time you storm the castle you find you don't want to burn it down anymore."

"Only a fanatic would rather burn than build, when given the choice," said Indsorith, her hand shaking as she poured despite how much they had lightened the jug. All this heavy talk with a veteran warrior queen brought her back to the ramparts of her childhood castle, the flickering fireplace standing in for the fields that Lady Shels had burned to prevent the Cobalts-cum-Imperials from reaping Junius's fair harvest. What an impression that spectacle had made on her young, confused mind—which had been its whole purpose, of course, and which had succeeded in making Indsorith into a dogmatic doppelgänger of her mother right up until her investigation into the Imperial records proved beyond a shadow of a doubt that Lady Shels had been the instigator of the bloody showdown, that all the horrors that came after could have been prevented if only the Lady of Junius had been willing to compromise a *fucking little* with the new queen.

Not that change had occurred overnight. No, it had taken years for Indsorith to accept the full truth, slowly growing from the rich manure of her mother's warped philosophy into something that might resemble a fair and gracious regent. That transition had been nurtured by her meticulous studying of Zosia's failed policies, until it occurred to Indsorith one rainy midsummer eve that the woman she had once blamed for every evil in all the Star had become even more of an influence on her life than her own mother. She had never shared this epiphany with anyone, and watching Zosia break apart the steaming braids of cinnamon bread she stifled the impulse to blurt it out now. It had been a very, very long time since Indsorith had cared a jot about impressing anybody, but then it had been a very, very long time since she had been around anyone she genuinely respected.

"Speaking of burning things, I really did a number on this bread," said Zosia as she brought the platter over. The sticky braids looked perfectly baked.

"I don't know what's more annoying, your ability to do absolutely everything or your false modesty," said Indsorith as she sat back down and reached for the treat.

"I can't do absolutely everything, only most everything," said Zosia with a wink, then speared one of the braids with a fork and turned it over to display the blackened bottom. "See? This loaf is me all over—looks good enough at a glance, but is actually a total disaster."

"I'm sure I've had worse things in my mouth," said Indsorith, peeling a morsel of soft, steaming bread from the top of a braid. Before Zosia could seize the opportunity she added, "I wouldn't trust myself to successfully make toast, let alone bake bread, or curries or soups or any of the other things you've made. Did you work in a kitchen before leading the revolution?"

"I wore many hats before I formed the Cobalt Company, but a toque wasn't one of them," said Zosia, and just for a moment her smile was sweeter than the buttery cinnamon bread melting in Indsorith's mouth. "I learned to cook after I left you the Empire. My husband, Leib, was good at many things, but was even worse in the kitchen than I was. Our first year in the village we took turns suffering each other's atrocities, and after that I was so desperate for a decent vindaloo or barbecue I begged a neighbor with a culinary reputation to take me under his wing. Just goes to show one day you can be queen, and the next you're taking all kind of abuse apprenticing yourself to a cranky old bastard just to learn how to caramelize onions."

"We find teachers in unexpected places," Indsorith said through another mouthful of the wonderful spiced dessert.

"That we do," agreed Zosia. Indsorith couldn't tell if she was staring at her dozing devil or into the fire. "In time I was able to get a few cookbooks and the stale spices to go with them from a passing peddler, but nothing I taught myself was the equal of that old bastard's recipes. Nothing sounds simpler than venison medallions and mushrooms or an apple scone, but the way he cooked them... gods, the way Leib's face would light up when he came in from the cold hike up to our cabin and smelled those scones."

Zosia was smiling wider than ever at the memory, yet at the same time Indsorith had never seen her closer to tears. She knew that pain, and felt it again now as she remembered the grubby, cherubic faces of her brothers just before they'd succumbed to their fate at the work farm. Nothing the Burnished Chain had done to Indsorith had hurt as much as those memories, and all through the many ordeals they had subjected her to she undercut their efforts by hiding in her past. It gave a justification to her tortures, her conscience almost welcoming this long-belated punishment for her failure to save her family... and to save her Empire.

"I know Sister Portolés must have told you or we wouldn't be here, but I still need to tell you myself," Indsorith said, recognizing the time had come at last. There wasn't a whole lot to even say, but what little there was carried such weight she hadn't felt strong enough to hoist it until now. "I'm sorry for what happened to your husband, to your village. I don't know for sure who ordered Sir Hjortt to do what he did, but I've come to suspect it was his father, the former colonel of the same regiment. Of all the old guard Domingo Hjortt is the last officer I would have accused of being a double agent for the Chain, but while Y'Homa was gloating over me during one of her interrogations she claimed he defected to the church. That he helped make some sacrifice at the Lark's Tongue that brought back Jex Toth. I know he was your nemesis from before you even took the throne, so who knows, maybe the Chain bought old man Hjortt's loyalty in exchange for telling him where you were hiding out, so he could send his son after you. But the truth is I just don't know how it happened, or why—on my life, Zosia, I didn't even know if you were still alive after all this time, let alone where you were."

The older woman sighed, pushing a loose braid of bread around the platter. "Yeah, I figured out it probably wasn't you early on, but I appreciate hearing it said for certain. As for Portolés... well, she did her best to reach me, but you should know I didn't listen to her, not until it was too late. And as for the culprit it wasn't Domingo, either, I'm sure of that—he would have rubbed my nose in it when we met in the camp. Besides, it's not his style to send his cub after me instead of doing it himself. Which leaves the Burnished Chain as the obvious suspect, drawing me out of retirement to pit me against the Empire... but it may just as well have been Hoartrap or one of my other best friends, knowing such a tragedy was the only way to coax me back into their schemes. Or maybe it was one of a hundred thousand other enemies I made over the course of a long and shitty life, or maybe it was nothing more than the devil of ambition whispering in a green colonel's ear, telling him if he wanted to fill his daddy's spurs he had to start his command with a big show of force. Maybe it was just a fucking accident that Leib and the rest of Kypck ended up dead... maybe... but not knowing, knowing I may never know... *that's* the fucking ragged edge that keeps twisting and tearing at my fucking heart... it's what I deserve, this doubt, this chaos, but he didn't... he didn't deserve it... none of them... all they did was love me, and I couldn't save them. Me, Queen fucking Zosia, I couldn't protect a fucking *village*—I got them all killed, and I'll never even know *who* or *why* or... *fuck*."

Zosia finally looked back at Indsorith, and in the fading firelight of the neglected hearth it seemed as though a mask she had worn every day of her many years had slipped out of place, the wry, ruthless warrior queen of song revealed to be a mere mortal. Shimmering creeks escaped the cool blue depths of her eyes, slipping down the channels of wrinkle and scar, and Indsorith felt her own throat constrict in sympathy with the woman's grief. Choplicker's tail thumped in time with Indsorith's heart as she leaned forward, her scabs cracking and her stitches tugging as she stretched her arms across the laden table. There was a danger to it, like reaching out to pet a snarling feral dog, but also the exhilaration of knowing she was safe, that fierce as this creature seemed it would not harm her. Zosia balked, looking down at the proffered hands as though she didn't know what they were, and then took them in her own. Her hands were shaking, and Indsorith squeezed them.

"The first time I fell truly in love I was seventeen," Indsorith said softly. This must be how Chainites felt like when they gave confession, both scared and elated to finally be giving up their secrets. "He was a minor noble in my court, so strong and fair and kind. You were queen long enough to know how rare such traits are in those who rise to power, but Crepax...he was special. You'll think me naïve but even after all this time I know that what brought us together was love, real love, not any ambition on his part..." Indsorith smiled as she remembered his smile. "We were together less than a year before his murder, and even after all these years and all my efforts I never discovered if the Chain was behind it, or one of my own ministers. I gave up on ever finding out...well, I tried to give up, knowing it was futile, but of course I can't, not ever. You know that."

Now it was Zosia's turn to squeeze Indsorith's hands, offering her a sympathetic grimace.

"The second time was even worse," Indsorith confided, feeling weirdly powerful as she watched Zosia's devil tent one ear in her direction. "I swore I'd never love again, of course, but then Simone of the Gale joined my Dread Guard—you have passed through over the Bridge of Grails, I assume, and know those great statues that form the eastern arch? She was as hard and as beautiful as one of those titans of the Age of Wonders, only more impressive. I never had a chance. Neither did she..."

Choplicker finally turned to look at Indsorith but she closed her eyes before she could spill a drop, the taste of her lover's blood flooding her mouth.

"You never found her killer, either?" Zosia's voice was still gruff with grief.

"I see her in every mirror," said Indsorith, deciding not to tell Zosia how close she had come in that moment to letting Simone finish her, too heartbroken to fight back. Not yet, anyway. "I probably could have found out who she was working for, if I'd been willing to torture it out of her, but that was something I told myself I'd never do . . . Not to anyone, certainly not to her. She died quick. In my arms, but quick. And the worst, Zosia? The absolute worst? Even now . . . even now I must admit I loved her more than Crepax, more than any of those who came after, before I swore off taking lovers altogether, for my safety and theirs. I love her cruel shade, and believe the only reason I overcame her in the end is that she allowed it. I believe she fell for me, as I fell for her. How foolish is that?"

"To love is to give yourself over to folly," said Zosia, "but there are worse reasons to act the fool."

"Like whatever's compelling me to let you open up my safe little castle to the angry mob that somehow survived my rule and the Chain's coup?"

"Yes, like that," said Zosia, and while Indsorith kept her eyes closed she could tell by the woman's voice that her mask had fitted back into place. No, not a mask—a helm in the shape of a snarling devil dog. "Don't worry, though—there will be more than one disgraced Crimson Queen to welcome them home."

"Home," repeated Indsorith, shivering even in the heat of the kitchen as she remembered what Y'Homa had shown her in Diadem Gate after their nightmarish parade through the burning capital. The Black Pope had repeatedly referred to Jex Toth as her home, and even with all the drugs and bugs Indsorith had been on there was precious little doubt that fabled land had returned . . . or that it was infested with grotesque demons that had haunted her dreams ever since.

This was the real reason why she couldn't give a whole lot of fucks about Zosia's decision to invite the remaining riffraff into the castle, or their squabbles over control of the ruins of Diadem: because none of it mattered anymore. It was pretty simple, really; any child with an affinity for ghost stories could tell you that up until five hundred years ago Jex Toth had sat right there in the Haunted Sea, in the exact spot where it reappeared. That was what made the Burnished Chain's conviction that they were sailing to some promised land so absurd—the only ones who had come home were the devils banished to the First Dark, and now that they had returned it was only a matter of time before they reached the rest of the Star.

Looking at the friendly, prick-eared dog who had been her constant companion ever since Zosia had rescued her, Indsorith reckoned some of them were already here.

CHAPTER
15

It was almost sundown but they couldn't find any more stray cats. Diggelby said there was no such thing as a stray cat in the first place, as that implied domestication, and went on to argue that felines weren't ideal for the job anyway, since they weren't scavengers. Hoartrap responded that by letting wild beasts into their hearts and homes humans had made scavengers out of many a former hunter. As for what constituted a stray, the cranky wizard said that any owners who didn't keep their pets close to home couldn't very well complain if they ended up in a stewpot or worse. To Sullen's mind tonight's ritual definitely qualified as *or worse*.

"There was that crippled mutt back in that alley," said Purna as they reached the far edge of Black Moth for the second time in their search through the half-deserted town in the center of the Haunted Forest. "I know I promised Digs no dogs, but that old son there wasn't just on his last legs, he was down to three."

"Yeah...." Sullen couldn't think of anything else to say, staring down the muddy lane that ran east through the darkening forest.

"Putting an animal out of pain is a good thing," said Keun-ju, but he could afford to be sanguine about it, seeing as he had been the one to catch a rat instead of a pox-weakened cat. Many of the animals in this town seemed sick with something, but that just made the hunt all the more pathetic; what kind of hunters preyed on creatures too feeble to run or defend themselves? He had never seen wild animals with this sort of wasting disease, which made him wonder if the plague they suffered was their proximity to people.

"Yeah, screw this, I'll just take the dog," said Purna, sticking her hands in the cord-trimmed pockets of her doublet and turning back to town. "More of a cat person myself anyway, so Digs can suck it up or suck my butt, his choice."

"...Yeah," said Sullen, because while his keen eyes had just caught sight of a kitten peering out through the hollow window of a vacant shack that the forest was greedily gobbling with kudzu, there was an unspoken understanding among the gang that they wouldn't use anything that wasn't full grown. The old toms they'd found for Sullen and Hoartrap were already back at the abandoned temple the Touch had selected as being ideal for their purposes, and so Sullen carried the small squirming sack with Keun-ju's rat so they could hold hands. "Never thought I'd do something like this. Don't like it."

"This I can handle, it's what comes after that gives me pause," said Keun-ju. "I cannot decide if it's better or worse than just walking into a Gate. I am thinking worse."

"Yeah, no, that's what I mean," said Sullen. "Bad enough to kill an animal you ain't gonna eat and wear, it's what happens next I don't like, either."

"Binding the devils, or having them send us to Jex Toth?" asked Purna.

"Both," said Sullen and Keun-ju in unison, squeezing each other's hands.

"Eh, that's the fun part," said Purna, and in the course of their adventures together Sullen had gotten to know the tapai well enough to believe this wasn't just bluster. She really was that crazy. "What I don't like is Digs's crummy attitude, and I guarantee it's only going to get crummier. Our last fucking night together and he's being *such* a child."

"Do you think if I offered him my rat it would change his mind?" asked Keun-ju as they tromped back across town toward the alley behind the mercantile where they had provisioned that morning, the lightning bugs the only streetlamps in this lonely village.

"It's not just the sacrifice he's objecting to, it's binding them at all," said the girl. "But if he hadn't been keeping a bound devil all the time I'd known him I'd be dead already, so I really don't appreciate this sudden moral high ground he's found. It's probably 'cause he had a devil before anyone else so now it's passé. Meanwhile, the day I ditch my tired old style he snatches it out of the rubbish and dusts it off—you know what he did when I told him most other Ugrakari don't eat meat except, uh, on holidays? Became a vegetarian!"

"You know, Purna, I used to look down on those people as well, but ever since I tried Raniputri cuisine I've found all sorts of—" Keun-ju began, but Purna cut him off.

"You've made it abundantly clear how much you love chutney and achaar! And I don't look down on—ugh, so not the point!" Purna pointed at the cobalt cape Ji-hyeon had given Sullen, still wagging her big black tongue at a full gallop. "Can I borrow that for a minute? The point, Keun-ju, is Digs can do whatever he wants, but...but cutting out on us because he doesn't think binding devils is cool anymore is sauce so weak you could use it to cut water!"

"I don't think the pasha would refuse to take part in the ritual and join us in our quest unless he felt he had to," said Sullen, holding the rat sack in his teeth and trying to untie the knot in the cape with his off hand.

"I agree," said Keun-ju, letting go of Sullen's hand and reaching up to take the satchel from his mouth with a smile that said while he appreciated the gesture his other arm wasn't going to fall off the moment Sullen stopped holding it...but as soon as Sullen got the knot loose and swung the cape over to Purna he passed back the rat and took Sullen's hand, and firmer than before. He might be doing a better job than Sullen of hiding his nervousness, but even more than the summoning of devils the prospect of using them to travel through the First Dark obviously terrified the brave poet.

"Well, sometimes you have to make hard choices," said Purna, tossing the cape over one shoulder. Why she needed another layer in this heat when she was already sweating under her horned wolf cloak Sullen couldn't guess. "Does he think any of us *want* to do this? Does he think I wouldn't rather be taking a raunchy road trip to Diadem with Nemi and him and the monk? Fucking rescuing Maroto. Fucking saving the world and shit."

"Ahhhh," said Keun-ju, raising his eyebrow and the top of his veil as he gave Sullen a knowing look. "You are disappointed that Diggelby's path diverges from our own, at least for a time, but are you also perhaps a little sore to not have any more music lessons in your immediate future?"

"Definitely a little sore, but the good kind, like you want," said Purna, smacking her lips a couple of times and popping the rawhide drawstrings of her cloak. "And far as music lessons go, boys, I tell you what—I think I'm a savant. As a rule I don't practice the singing sword and tell, but if I *did*—"

"But you don't, you don't," said Keun-ju, looking a little flustered that his good-natured attempt to embarrass his friend had almost resulted in the sharing of more details than he wanted. Fortunately for his modesty they were passing through the town square with the ominous wooden ikon and gallows tree, and Purna became distracted by the nearby notice board pasted with wanted posters.

"Why won't Nemi come with us?" Sullen called after her as she abruptly double-timed it out of the square. "Even my ma's willing to do it, after I told her it's the only way to reach my uncle and she could either come with or get left behind, and she's got crazy-strong Chainite superstitions about trafficking with devils and such. So does your witch know something we don't about Hoartrap and his schemes?"

"I bet she knows plenty about the Touch, but I haven't gotten it out of her yet. One of the only things, if you want to—"

"We don't!"

"But really now, did she give any reason for not doing it?" Sullen pressed, basically every song he'd ever heard about witches and devils and the First Dark telling him he ought to find an excuse to back out of this plan, even though it seemed like the only way forward. "And you said she's going to Diadem instead?"

"She's not taking part because she doesn't bind devils, ever, under any circumstances," said Purna, pulling off the cape Sullen had lent her as if just now realizing that even in the winter twilight Black Moth was hot as balls. They rounded the corner of the dingy mercantile, it and the surprisingly rowdy tavern across the way the only half-timbered buildings on the main street with all their windows lit. "Not all witches, Sullen, not all witches."

"Her eggs aren't devil eggs?" asked Keun-ju.

"They...I..." For some reason the mention of the witch's mysterious eggs made Purna space out with a faint smile on her lips, pausing at the mouth of the alley. Then she shook it off, shaking out Sullen's cape in the process. "She's not like Hoartrap, okay? She hates his style of sorcery so much she faked her own death to get free of him, way back when. So while I can't say how she does her thing, not being a witch myself, I can confirm it's different. It doesn't involve summoning devils, and it *definitely* doesn't involve eating them. And so she's going to drive her vardo to Diadem, since that's where the closest Gate is, and use that to travel to Othean, where General Ji-hyeon is, and where we ought to be by the time she gets there."

"If the monsters of Jex Toth weren't already attacking the Isles, I'd say we'd all be better off doing that," said Sullen. "But we're already late to the ruckus as it is."

"I don't know," said Keun-ju. "I don't care how flippantly everyone is treating the practice these days, walking into a Gate...well. This way may not be better, but it can't be worse."

"Tell that to your rat," said Purna, taking a deep breath and heading into the blind alley. "All right, the sooner we're back with our sacrifices the sooner we can get stinko at that shitty tavern."

"You want a hand?" asked Sullen.

"Nah, this is on me," she called back. "If I'm going through with this the least I owe the mutt is being the one to carry him."

"She's going to get drunk before we summon devils?" Keun-ju didn't sound like he approved.

"You got the sand to do it straight?" asked Sullen. "I don't think I do. Not much to recommend about Hoartrap, but his saam is strong and he's generous with it. And everyone knows burning a little before consorting with the powers of the First Dark shows the proper amount of respect."

"Everyone knows that, do they?" said Keun-ju, and wiggling out of Sullen's grip again he took his rat back. "The least I can do is carry it. That cape Purna borrowed is the one Ji-hyeon gave you, isn't it?"

"Yeah." Seeing Purna come back out of the shadows between the buildings with a big lump wrapped in the blue wool, he sighed. "Yeah, that was it all right."

"I'd offer to wash it for you, but I've got my hand full," said Keun-ju, gesturing with his rat bag. Sullen wished he could play it cool for his friend, joke around or at least act nonchalant, but it was so ghoulish he must have made a face instead. This just made Keun-ju fall out giggling, the rare sound of his laughter over such a dark matter in such a dark place with the three of them on *real* dark business a portent, it seemed, of all the strangeness that lay ahead of them that night.

"What the hells are ya people doin'?!" The voice came from the upper window of the house behind the mercantile, on the far side of the alley. The room beyond was so dark there was no silhouette in the frame, just a black rectangle in the dirty grey wall. "I seen ya, creepin' all over town, pokin' yer nose every which way. Stealin' what don't belong to ya, s'if you owned the whole place and anythin' ya found was yers for the takin'!"

"We're not thieves!" Sullen protested, but perhaps too loudly in the quiet street, given Purna's hissing at him to shut up.

"Words all over, yer rustlin' cats! Our cats! And what ya go there, eh, s'at my devildamned *dog*?"

"This your dog, mister?" Purna called up.

"Devildamned right he is! You put 'im right back where ya—"

"Dog's dead," said Purna, and there was serious trouble in her tone. "From neglect, I'd say. Maybe abuse. So I'm gonna go out in the woods and bury this poor thing, and if I hear another fucking word from you on the matter I'm going to come straight back here and burn your fucking house down. With you in it."

It was quiet for a moment, and then came the sound of the shutters being slammed.

"If I knew for sure it was his and he wasn't just being a pain in the ass I'd torch that dump, I fucking swear it," said Purna, steering them back toward the ruined church where the rest of their friends awaited them. The sick dog in her arms gave a faint whine, its tail limply wagging as she carried it, and with hearts a lot heavier than a rat in a sack, Sullen and Keun-ju followed.

Black Moth might be an ugly, dying town in the middle of a boggy, dangerous forest, populated mostly by rough-looking hunters, rougher-looking trappers, and roughest-looking charcoal burners, but one thing in this place's defense was they evidently preferred their own ways to those of the Burnished Chain. That big ikon who shared the central square with the notice board and gibbet certainly didn't resemble the Fallen Mother or any boring saint—the fellow had eight faces on his giant head, and in each of his five outstretched hands folk had heaped bloody pelts that buzzed with flies, and the swamp flowers and gourds set at his three feet were all fresh. The Chainite temple, by contrast, was outside of town altogether, on a small hill overrun with brambles and crumbling headstones. There were no doors on the small wooden church and the tiled roof had partially collapsed, and as they came up the slope in the gloaming the light spilling from the entrance and two big holes in the eaves reminded Sullen of the glowing skull Queen Beautiful carried to light her way through the Witch Wood. That noble ancestor had faced bad things in a deep dark forest and come out ahead, too, so perhaps tonight's song would also have a happy ending.

As they stepped over the mossy lintel and saw what was in store for them, however, Sullen's buoyant mood sank but fast. At the back of the one-room church a circular symbol had been laid out in red sand, a white taper set on a monstrous avian skull in its center, and standing just inside the outermost ring of the pentagram were the animals they had previously rounded up. Unhappy as they'd been at being caught and brought into the church, now they were all so still they looked stuffed, staring transfixed at the green flame rising from the candle. There was the black cat Sullen had first brought back, and the tabby he had found for Hoartrap, and the badger his mother had scared up. She had initially returned with a scrawny opossum, but Hoartrap said he didn't work with the animals anymore. When called out for being superstitious, he'd shrugged and said that went with his job description.

"The three hunters return," said Hoartrap without looking up from his pack, rooting around in its cavernous interior. "Best is off again, but as soon as Sullen's sainted mother returns we can take this puss-and-pony show on the road. Well, and as soon as I find my—aha!"

"Where did everybody go?" asked Keun-ju, but as he addressed Hoartrap he was staring at the strange sight at the back of the church. "I did not see the witch's wolf and cart."

"They haven't left yet, have they?" Purna sounded a little frantic, face flushed from carrying the dog she still held in her arms. "Where do I put this? I need to catch them before they go!"

"They're long gone by now," said Hoartrap, smiling to himself as he removed a small bronze pyramid from his pack. Looking up at the distraught Purna, he said, "To the pub. They assumed they'd run into you on the walk. I am to understand, then, that you haven't even begun your protracted boo-hooing over the temporary sundering of your fellowship?"

"My ma's with 'em?" asked Sullen, the image of Diggelby and his mom sitting across the table from one another adding up to a bad scene or a good story in one hell of a hurry, and either way he wanted to be on hand.

"She is, and set that dog anywhere, and—*get away from there!*" Hoartrap went from an affable tone to a bellow, and following the sorcerer's angry movements Sullen saw that Keun-ju had walked right up to the sandy edge of the symbol. He swayed in place a moment, and then Hoartrap snatched the sack out of his hand and poked him in the chest. "Did I tell you to stare at the candle? No? Then don't stare at the candle!"

"I...what?" Keun-ju sounded sleepy, taking an awkward step back from the irate Touch and rubbing his eyes. "You did not tell us *not* to."

"*I didn't tell you not to,*" Hoartrap parroted. "Listen up, kiddies, for the rest of the night you just assume that I don't want you to do *anything* unless I expressly tell you to.*"

"I'm going to the tavern, have a few for the road with Digs and Nemi," said Purna, depositing the old hound on the floor. It was still wrapped in Sullen's cloak but he didn't have the heart to ask for it back now.

"Yes, yes, because what did I just say?" asked Hoartrap. "I can't remember, was it *do exactly what I tell you, as this is a very sensitive operation,* or was it *go get shit-hammered with my worthless apprentice and your cowardly friend*?"

"We are joining the pasha for a final round," said Keun-ju, following Purna out. "That is not up for debate."

"Oh, well then, excuuuuse me!" said Hoartrap, reaching into the sack and then making a lewd face. "Your little assistant is giving me a love bite. Who wants to take a wager on which of us gets sick from the exchange?"

"We won't be long," said Sullen, pausing in the doorway. "Can I bring you anything from town?"

"You can," said Hoartrap, pulling the squirming rat out of the bag and inspecting it in the candlelight as it dug its teeth into his enormous hand. "Find me some new heroes. Failing that…a sandwich."

"Safe," said Sullen, heading out and down the hill after Purna and Keun-ju, the distant buildings of Black Moth almost as dark as the surrounding forest. Come to think it, though, that was always how'd it been back home, too—you didn't waste good blubber on lighting up your nights, and the peat smoldering in the firepit didn't cast enough light to leak outside. His ma was right, he'd become an Outlander himself, accustomed to their ways, from mundane things like keeping lamps lit half the night to more exotic practices, like picking up take-away for a devil-eating witch.

Looking down at the spear in his hand, he said, "Sorry, Fa, know you wouldn't appreciate my associating with him."

The spear didn't speak back, much as he wished it would…silly a thought as that was, it seemed like something that'd happen in the sagas, if an old warrior got turned into a weapon. Even before Hoartrap had explained what the spear was made of, that Ji-hyeon had commissioned it when she found out there would be some of the sainted steel left after making her sword, Sullen had just *known* the old man was in the blade. How was that for silly?

Except there wasn't a damn thing silly about what was going to happen next. His mother had finally seemed to be thawing a little, only to go full hardarsed again after their long trek back into Black Moth, and now, this very night, Sullen was going to raise a devil and bind it to his will. Fa would be so disappointed. And more surprising than Diggelby's refusal to take part in the rite was Ma's casual agreement to the plan ... but then he supposed if she saw it as a feat of courage that her soft son was Horned Wolf enough to accept then she couldn't very well back down. That was what being a born-again Chainite got you in this day and age, pride so unwavering you could be peer-pressured into taking part in unmistakably evil rituals.

What would she do when she saw her brother, he wondered? Not so much of an *if,* anymore, now that Hoartrap had recovered the magic post from whatever swampy shore it had washed up on. Sullen had finally come around to his uncle, at least in theory, to giving him the benefit of the doubt until he could be heard out. But while Ma had given her word to wait until the armies of Jex Toth were defeated to sort things with Maroto and Sullen, what if after all that they still couldn't squash the beef and she demanded blood?

Then you kill the mad wolf. It was a forceful thought, frighteningly so, but his wounds throbbed as soon as he doubted it, and his heart throbbed worse when he looked ahead to Keun-ju's lopsided silhouette as he and Purna stepped down from the church path and onto the road. Kill the wolf.

That was putting the cart before the giant monster, though—first they had devils to summon, a trip through the First Dark clear over to the Sunken Kingdom, a rescue mission if Maroto was captured, as Hoartrap feared, and then a reunion with Ji-hyeon at Othean, all before the war against Jex Toth could begin in earnest. No sense worrying about troubles yet to arrive when he had plenty sitting around his fire already. A Flintland lad like him, taking a shortcut through the First Dark...the First Dark, where the Faceless Mistress dwelled, if Sullen had to guess her address when she wasn't manifesting in Emeritus to terrify poor mortals. Hard as it was to shake the feeling that she was always watching him here, under the plain night sky, what might happen when he dared traverse her realm?

Only one way to find out. It was a lesson Grandfather had worn his sharp tongue dull trying to impress into Sullen, but it had taken meeting Ji-hyeon and following her brave example to make it stick: sometimes you just had to ruddy well do a thing, instead of hoping you could fret it to death. Instead of putting it off and putting it off and putting it off, the way he had with figuring out the Faceless-Mistress-versus-Zosia problem, and so much else in his life, this time he had to grab the wolf by the horns. Somewhere halfway across the Star Ji-hyeon needed him, was waiting on him to come back to her, and bring Keun-ju along in the bargain...and no god nor devil nor mortal nor monster could stop him.

But first a quick drink in a local tavern on a warm winter night here in the Crimson Empire, where nobody seemed to know the world was on the very rim of ruin. After all they'd been through of late, everyone deserved one last quiet night before things got very loud indeed.

——

Their crew was posted up in the pub, all right, though Nemi must have parked her horned wolf somewhere out in the woods to avoid causing a scene. Or a bigger scene, anyway. Diggelby had dressed up even more than usual for the occasion, which was saying something indeed—his mirrored turban was firing off beams of reflected lamplight every which way, and his black-and-white dashiki matched his corpsepaint. Plant that in any Imperial small-town bar and you'd have yourself a local talking point for weeks to come, and that was without adding on a pierced-up girl with a funky-looking feathered walking stick. Or a gem-eyed Chainite monk in a town that must have been converted at some point only to come clear back around to worshipping a pagan deity what lived in their town square. And topping it all off was a big, sour-mugged Flintlander with war braids hanging down from her horned helmet...not that anyone here knew that those braids and that helm signified a Horned Wolf who was on the hunt and not particular about where her meat came from, so long as it was fresh.

"They look like the setup for some bad joke," said Purna as they stood on the porch of the tavern, taking turns peering through a hole in the parchment-paned window. She'd been nervous about going in for some reason, probably regretting hastily spoken words said in anger to the pasha...or regretting words not said at all to Nemi. Burning the beedi Sullen had copped from Hoartrap that morning had finally put her back in her usual good temper, though. "Stop me if you've heard this one—a Flintlander, a Chainite, a noble, and a witch walk into a bar."

"It's about to get...sillier," said Keun-ju, letting out the hit he'd been holding. Croak-voiced from the smoke, he said, "And then a studly wildborn, an Ugrakari tapai, and a dashing Immaculate poet all join them."

"Stud...lee?" Sullen tried to parse it through the saam haze. "Like...I got studs on me?"

"No no, like a—" Keun-ju began, but Purna interrupted, which was something of her specialty.

"Guys, I'm not a tapai," she said heavily. "You're my friends, too, and I can't lie to my squad anymore. I'm from a merchant family, not a noble one. By the peaks of my homeland, I hope this gets easier."

"Doesn't everybody know that already?" said Keun-ju. "There are only thirty-six tapais, obviously, hence the joke that you're the... wait, were you *actually* trying to deceive people? Who could possibly fall for that!"

"Um..." said Sullen, stubbing the beedi out because obviously none of them needed any more and tucking the roach into his mostly empty bandolier. "I believed it, but for real, I never even heard of a tapai until me and Fa met you, Purna. You always been princely to me, though, and that matters more than who bore you. One of the things I really liked about Ji-hyeon's cause was the idea of getting rid of all them...distinctions. No more nobles or any of that."

"Easy for a princess to say that, especially when people are still doing what she says." Seeing Keun-ju tense up, Purna hastened to add, "Not a burn on our general, just saying."

"Well, just say it inside," said Sullen. The conversation turning to Ji-hyeon reminded him that while they were all talking trash on a stoop, his beloved was stuck on the Isles with a horde of monsters breathing down her neck. Keun-ju's beloved, too. One of them, anyway. "We have a single drink, and then we're out."

"Your melon's gone sour if you think we're leaving before the barkeep," said Purna, moving to the owlbatwing doors.

"I mean it," said Sullen, the saam making him twitchy instead of relaxed, his heart pounding. "We can celebrate properly with the pasha when we're all together in Othean and the war's won. But every round we're sitting here on our arses is another hour Ji-hyeon and Maroto and the rest of the Cobalt Company are in danger, without us around to pitch in."

"It's cute you think a round takes an hour, too," said Purna, disappearing inside.

"Hey, are you all right?" asked Keun-ju, putting his hand on Sullen's bicep. It was only at the man's light touch that Sullen realized how tense he was, squeezing his spear fit to breaking. And as if by sorcery, that physical connection sapped all the worry out of Sullen, leaving him high but happy.

"Yeah, I'm good," said Sullen, and slyly added, "Be better if you let me under that veil again, if just to see what a handsome fellow I've caught."

"As a veteran Virtue Guard it takes more than pretty words to compromise my own," said Keun-ju airily, his fingers on Sullen's arm doing a light little dance. "How about you buy me a drink?"

"Ah dang," said Sullen. "Would if I could, but I keep forgetting about money."

"I'll buy you one, then, and say you owe me something in return," said Keun-ju, darting up on his tiptoes to give Sullen a peck through his veil. The feel of silk barricading Keun-ju's lips only inflamed Sullen more, especially now that he knew how sweet they really were, but the boy nodded to the door. "Coming?"

"It'll take more than that, but not much," said Sullen.

"Sullen of the Frozen Savannahs, was that a *dirty joke?*"

"Maybe?" said Sullen wolfishly. "It's been ages since I had any relief, so maybe not."

"Not a bad gag, either, all things considered," said Keun-ju. "But come along, and none of that in front of your mother."

"No, definitely not." Damn but Keun-ju knew how to quench a fire as fast as he'd kindled it.

The Pig's Ear Tavern was far busier than it had been on their first stopover in Black Moth, when there'd only been a few grizzled souls; now there must be near on a hundred, every one of the tree-trunk tables occupied and both the bar at the back and the roaring fireplace thronged. The open room was so thick with woodsmoke, tubāq smoke, and saam smoke that it stung Sullen's eyes, and threading among the coarse crowd he couldn't help but notice how pungent most of these locals were. Not everyone had time or coin to stop over at the bathhouse, true, but some of them smelled like they'd rolled in offal and rinsed off with cat piss. No longer irritated by the smoke, he kept his nose in the clouds and huffed as much as he could until he reached his friends.

"Last to arrive, first to buy!" Purna damn near screamed to be heard over the mob. Despite having come in just before them she'd managed to snag a stool and a drink, load a pipe, and plant Nemi on her lap. The witch looked all the taller for sitting on the smaller woman, puffing a long-stemmed pipe of her own. Sullen put his empty hands in the air, but Diggelby tossed him a pouch so heavy it hurt his palm.

"It was in here all along!" cried the fop, pointing at his turban. "Buy a case of something nice; whatever's left over we can drink on the road!"

"Shall I help?" asked Keun-ju, maybe not so inclined to be left alone with this crew. Nemi and Purna were ignoring the others, talking with their faces all in close, and Diggelby was blithely rambling at the stone-eyed monk and Sullen's stone-faced mother.

"Ehh, looks like a tight fit at the bar, I can manage," Sullen said in Keun-ju's ear. His delicate ear that sang out for a nibbling. Buzzed as Sullen was he almost went for it, but remembering his mother sitting just across the table, decided not to . . . lest he embarrass Keun-ju, not because he gave a damn what she thought anymore. "But hey, can you hold my spear?"

Keun-ju said something Sullen didn't hear, but when the Immaculate winked a big brown eye at Sullen he guessed the gist of it, passing the weapon over with a smile of his own. Then he headed off on a quest as arduous as any Boldstrut had endured—getting service as an Outlander at a busy local watering hole while doped to the gills on wizard saam. And just his luck, between him and the long black bartop was a gang of brutes as hatchet-faced as any Sullen had ever met, and armed to the teeth the lot of them.

"Make way, make way," bawled the biggest bruiser of them all as Sullen approached, a Raniputri with extra eyes tattooed all over his face and a braided beard so long he wore it tied around his neck like a noose. Which just went to show you never could tell, because the rest of the heavies all heaved over to one side, the tattooed man offering a warm smile and then turning back to his chums as Sullen slipped between them and the huddle of hunters on the other side.

Planting his elbows on the buffed ebon bar, Sullen kept Diggelby's pouch hidden from view in his fist, but when one of the flustered barkeeps came by he gave it a jingle. Back in Thao the pasha had insisted on teaching Sullen all the tricks, and sure enough this got the woman's attention, but instead of taking his order right away she held up a finger and moved on, only returning a few minutes later.

"What?" she demanded, eyes bloodshot and short-shorn head lathered in sweat.

"Case of something nice, please," he said in Crimson. Or hoped he said, anyway.

"A *case*?" she looked incredulous. "No."

"Uh, many bottles?" Shit, he had been sure the word was *case*. "Bottles in box? Cost much, but I pay. Please?"

She must have taken pity on him, then, because her features softened and she said a few intelligible words and then the Immaculate word for the Immaculate tongue.

"For sure!" he said in the same, always relieved when he didn't have to limp along in Crimson. "A case of your finest, uh, anything, if you please, and don't worry—I've got coin in hand."

"Oh, sweetheart, no," said the barkeep. "You might've noticed we're a little busy tonight?"

"Uhhh…yeah?"

"So I can't sell anyone more than a bottle a head. I start selling more and pretty soon the cellar's empty, and what am I supposed to do when the rest of the regiment comes through, huh? Hope they understand why the only tavern in town is dry and not make sport some other way?"

"The…the rest of the what now?" Maybe Sullen's Immaculate wasn't so good after all, because it sounded like she said…

"The Eyvindian regiment," said the barkeep, gesturing at the full house. "These rats might not look so bad just yet, but wait until the rest of the swarm arrives. They're headed south, obviously, to which I say go north if you can—nastiest army in the Empire. After what Cold Cobalt did to them back in the day I can't say I'm surprised the survivors decided that honor and fighting fair and all the rest was a fool's errand, but there's such a fucking thing as a middle ground. These are the same scumdogs who killed the priest and wrecked the church, oh, eight or nine years ago. A touch unhappy he didn't have more communion wine to share with the needy. So you can see why I'm reluctant to sell you a case, no?"

"Uh…yeah?" Sullen really, really wished he hadn't smoked that beedi. "But…but they're not wearing any red?"

"They're scouts," said the barkeep, "so they ain't very well going to call attention to that, are they? But look, you're the first person who's said *please* all night so I wanted to tip you off in case you didn't know, and now that you do let's complete our transaction so I can go back to praying these shitbirds don't raze my place."

"Sure, yeah, thanks," said Sullen woozily. "I'll just get the bottle, then, thanks."

As the exchange was made and Sullen turned around to find himself blocked in by reeking bodies, he indeed began to pick out Imperial trappings underneath the heavy furs and leather capes—an ornamental officer's dagger here, an ostentatious blackened chain there, shitty tattoos in Crimson script on many a sweaty neck. He was also stuck, surrounded by Imperial scouts he was suddenly very leery about just pushing through lest he get them riled. But just then the big Raniputri guy rescued him a second time, careening in for another drink himself and clearing a hole for Sullen to wiggle through... or so it looked, anyway, but when he went for it the crowd shifted and they were crammed chest to chest in the press.

"One bottle for your whole table?" the man observed as they did the awkward dance of shuffling in opposite directions. "That can't even be enough for Purna!"

"Yeah, well, she'll have to share for a change," muttered Sullen, floating free and clear of the Raniputri and oozing further through the mob of what he now knew to be the enemy. He was starting to freak the fuck out, but he just needed to hold it together a little longer, just get the whole crew outside before they were recognized as Cobalts...

The table came into sight, as did a path through the pack, but as he quickened his pace a git even smaller than Purna stepped backward into his path, and he nearly bowled the wee man over. Sullen caught him by the shoulder before he fell, praise the ancestors. The last thing he fucking needed was to make a scene, and as soon as he saw the apologetic smile on the kid's face he knew there'd be no trouble here... but then the boy's features twisted into a hideous grimace. He screamed, shrill and clear as a whistle, eyes bulging out. Sullen couldn't figure it out, didn't even recognize the piker until he whipped out a rusty serrated knife and jabbed it straight into Sullen's gut.

It didn't hurt so much as jog his memory, the whole tavern suddenly going quiet, the kid still screaming as he twisted the blade. That brought the pain, Sullen howling even louder than his attacker, and bad as the cramping agony was, the realization that he knew this boy hurt worse. It was the fucking weakbow kid. The Cobalt runt who had accidentally killed Grandfather and then lit out from the plateau above the camp instead of waiting for Sullen to return, the way he'd promised. And now, adding grave injury to that already serious insult, he'd apparently gone and killed Sullen, too.

CHAPTER

16

Might as well be dead," said Bang, a week out from Jex Toth and still sulking.

"Fine talk for someone who escaped a fate worse than that," said Maroto. "And from a place worse than hell to boot."

"This *is* hell."

"Well, it might not be perfect but it's leagues closer to heaven than where we've been," Maroto told her, gesturing out over the view they commanded from the crow's nest. "First thing you told me when the Tothans brought you all in was the most you'd hoped for was to share a cell with me before we got axed, and now you've got one better—a cell with a view, and your frisky first mate ready to take your mind off your woes."

"Niki-hyun's first mate now," said Bang. "Since Carrig nor none of the rest of the old crew ever turned up."

"Quartermaster?"

"Dong-won."

"But that means you need a bosun."

"Need a ship to have a bosun," said Bang.

"Yeah, what do you call this, then?" Maroto flicked the top of the mast that rose from the center of their little platform.

"I told you, it's hell," said Bang, finally clambering up to look over the railing instead of just using it as a backrest. She didn't seem to be admiring the dawnlit coastline with its gold-tiled walls and enormous pagodas, nor the fleet of Imperial and Immaculate ships all around them. Instead she leaned forward and spat toward the deck far below, but her missile just smacked in the yards. "Biggest and bestest tub I ever set foot on, and she was mine oh mine for what, an hour?"

"Tops," allowed Maroto, sharing his captain's disappointment but hardly surprised by its cause. There had been a hot minute there when it had looked like the Holy See might defer to the authority of the four humans who had returned to the Chainite fleet in place of their pope, but that charade only lasted until they had sailed clear of the Tothan harbor. Considering the horror-struck sailors and anxious cardinals had seen Maroto and his pals disgorged from the steaming interior of the living vessel that had carried them right up beside an Imperial carrack, it was a major blessing they hadn't been burned as abominations— but when had Bang ever appreciated a blessing, small or large? If not for Maroto's brilliant, believable performance as an ignorant castaway press-ganged into acting as messenger for the unholy horrors of Jex Toth, the Holy See might have done a lot more than just burn them. Last Maroto checked the Burnished Chain wasn't big on Cobalt captains, retired or otherwise, and if he'd been found out his allies would have suffered by association.

Hard to believe those old allegiances still mattered, in a world under threat from a cabal of undying priests and their inhuman army, but maybe once the monsters started their war everything would change. It would have to, if the Star had any chance of survival. Maroto had certainly found it easy to drop the old beef bones once he met the Vex Assembly. It wasn't that he had forgiven Zosia for refusing to loose Choplicker and save Purna's life, or Hoartrap for marooning him on Jex Toth, because really now, there's no pardoning the unpardonable... but after how badly Maroto had fucked the Star to save himself their crimes didn't just seem smaller, they almost seemed like preemptive justice.

Or the regular kind, in Zosia's case, considering Maroto's thoughtless wish to see her again was probably what had led to the massacre of her husband and people. He hadn't intended such horrors, of course, he'd just been a strung-out junkie speaking rash words to his devil-rat, but that was Maroto all over, wasn't it? He never meant to free Crumbsnatcher and get Zosia's loved ones killed in the bargain, just like he'd never meant to collude with the Vex Assembly, it just *happened*... just like it always did.

Yet when Zosia hadn't been able to magically stop Purna from bleeding to death Maroto had leaped to label her a murderer, swearing the gnarliest kind of vengeance if he ever caught her... just like he always did. It was always different when somebody else did something stupid or selfish, wasn't it, Craven? Maybe if Zosia had wished harder she could have saved Purna, sure, but then if Maroto had been protecting his protégé the way he was supposed to then she never would've gotten stabbed in the first place. Her blood wasn't on Zosia's hands, it was on Maroto's... along with the blood of Zosia's husband, and her village, and, well, the rest of the fucking Star, given what the Vex Assembly was unleashing upon the world.

You would think that would be the worst, wouldn't you? Knowing you'd doomed your race to extinction, and all to buy yourself a few more cheap meals, watered-down drinks, and sweaty lays before the curtain dropped. Yet almost more bitter than that global guilt was the shame he felt for not coming clean to Zosia when he'd had the chance. He should have looked her dead in the eye and fessed it as soon as he'd figured out what'd happened—he'd as good as murdered her family, the least he could give her was the truth. Instead he stayed sitting on his fat arse, watching her walk away into the night, telling himself he just needed time to process everything, that he'd sleep on it and do the right thing in the morning.

He would always do the right thing, in the morning. Craven, his people had dubbed him, because the Horned Wolf Clan had always seen him for what he was instead of what he pretended to be. Now he would probably never see Zosia again in this life, having denied her the most important gift he could have ever offered—closure on the hardest heartbreak of her life.

Unless Hoartrap had told Zosia. Maroto had let the truth slip to the warlock just before being whisked off to Jex Toth, and what if as soon as he'd got back to the camp Hoartrap had told Zosia everything? What if Zosia already knew?

That was a hard one, but in the end he hoped Hoartrap had indeed betrayed him. She had a right to know who was responsible for her loss, whoever told her. Zosia didn't want Maroto's love, she never had, but maybe by taking on her hatred he could help her heal. Most folk seemed down on hatred these days, but in his experience it at least gave you a reason to get out of bed in the morning.

Take Hoartrap, for example. *Fucking Hoartrap.* Maroto had always known the warlock was as nasty a stool to ever fall out of the First Dark's arse, but even still, you don't fuck over your friends! Being dumped on Jex Toth and then taken to the roach-riddled bosom of the Vex Assembly had been a real wake-up call for Maroto, yes in-fucking-deed. Now that he knew the naked truth about the Touch he doubted there was a worse monster walking the Star, nobody more deserving of a slow, agonizing death at Maroto's hands...

But every time he tried to get excited about the prospect of murdering the evil fucker he remembered sitting watch with Hoartrap on a dozen different battlements, a hundred different taverns, sharing drinks and pipes and songs and jokes. He remembered the time down in the catacombs of Obel where he'd slipped into a goblin-frog spawning pool, done and fucking *dusted*, only to have Hoartrap dive in and rescue him. And he remembered how nobody else would laugh at his impressions of the rest of the Villains, especially his Fennec, which even Maroto knew was weak...

Woof. It was hard work, hating your old friends, even when they deserved it. Better to look ahead than behind, anyway, and looking after your new cohort was more important than stewing over those ghosts of your past. He scooted forward on the crow's nest, trying to pick out Niki-hyun or Dong-won from the figures moving around the decks below. Would've been easy, if they'd been allowed to keep their duds, but no sooner had the Chainite crew reclaimed the ship Bang had prematurely dubbed the *Empress Thief* than Maroto and the pirates were obliged to convert on the spot. The penitent robes were less breathable than a tarshirt and itchier than a vest woven of seaweed but at least Maroto always looked good in black, and the outfits had lent a certain verisimilitude to last night's turn of *bad monk, worse nun*, a game of Captain Bang's own devising. Knowing how much she liked setting him straight, he pointed toward shore and said, "Say, that must be the Winter Palace, huh? Nice turrets."

"Yeah?" At last Bang looked up from the sorry sight below to scan Othean's coast. "No, that's the Autumn Palace—see the maples in the raised gardens?"

"I…" Maroto squinted inland, past the rocky shore and the band of forest to the epic castle complex that filled the horizon. He couldn't even see the silhouettes of gardens from this distance, let alone identify their flora. "No, Cap'n, I don't."

"Me neither," she said, "but we're coming in from the west, dummy, so you don't have to see any miserable maples to know it's the Autumn Palace. Othean's laid out in a big fat diamond, with a castle at each corner—city's a lot bleeding bigger than she looks on your foreign maps, too, so we're still a way out from the Winter Palace."

"Well, not too far," said Maroto, eyeing the shoreline. "Good tailwind like this…"

"And maybe we'll be there by noon," said Bang. "Idiot Chainites sailed us into the wrong bloody inlet before our Immaculate escort could stop them, and that tailwind of yours is going to be smacking us in the nose the whole way back out and around to Othean Bay."

"In that case we've got some time to kill," said Maroto, suggestively cocking a hip in her direction and wincing as the sandpaper-smooth robe scraped over his skin.

"Time never dies, it just gets old and annoying, like certain other things I could mention," she said, retrieving her waterskin and the shipbiscuits that were appealingly mundane after the weeks of obscene edibles they had sampled in the Sunken Kingdom. On the other hand, while they hadn't known what they were eating and drinking, and sometimes it had made sensual noises going down, the rations on Jex Toth had tasted better than bilge water and worm-castles. "You sure you got anything left after last night, tiger?"

"Let the contrite novice remind his confessor he wasn't actually granted any dispensation last night," said Maroto, trying to break off a piece of her shipbiscuit and nearly breaking a nail instead.

"I wasn't talking about me, I was talking about your succubus," said Bang. "You were doing it again last night."

"Oh!" Now that she brought it up he remembered he had been dreaming of Choi again; sweet as they were when they came upon him, they were always the slipperiest to remember. He was long past any embarrassment with Bang or she with him, after the things they'd seen and done and shared to while away their captivity in Jex Toth, but it was curious she only reported his night-moans and grunts on mornings after his mind had drifted to the wildborn cutie. He'd never made much noise in his sleep before, he didn't think, but maybe this was just another symptom of getting on in years, the brain getting funny. Then again, if vivid yet impossible-to-recall wet dreams were part of the ravages of age, he could do a lot worse. "Well, Cap'n, friendly sprites of the spray and the aether are one thing, but I know you call your crew your hearties, so your bosun will serve you better with a hearty meal of flesh and blood...among other fluids."

"Bosun my butt," said Bang, crumbs falling from her sunburned lips as she surveyed the sprawling capital of her homeland. "You'll be lucky if you make cabin boy, and there'll be no flesh or blood for you till I've supped on some myself. At least we'll get something proper to eat when we put in at the Winter Palace. Assuming they grant us a last meal once they recognize me for the fell pirate queen that I surely am."

"This is wild," said Maroto, turning slowly in place to survey their flock of galleons and carracks and the Immaculate turtleships that had escorted them all the way from the Haunted Sea. He was living through the end of days, all right, and only a pedant would point out that Maroto himself had helped usher them in. "Can't believe we're going to witness the first time in history a Crimson fleet sails into Othean Bay."

"These sails are black as a war priest's panties," Bang pointed out. "The Empire's not so red as she used to be."

"All empires are going to be red in one hell of a hurry if we aren't able to bring the Star together and mount a unified defense against Jex Toth," he said, shivering despite the hot morning. He just hoped it warmed up enough to gel his half-baked plans of saving the world from the very enemy to whom he had so recently betrayed it. "I'm just relieved that once those cardinals heard about the Vex Assembly driving their pope mad and declaring war on the Star they decided to do the sensible thing and come straight down here to form an alliance."

"If you honestly think the Holy See is *ever* going to do the sensible thing, you're having another of your sweet dreams," said Bang. "You think just because we told them the whole Star is in danger they're going to suddenly stop being selfish, evil shitstains and join hands with all their heathen neighbors? You think villains can really change as simple as that?"

"I never said it was simple, but if I didn't think people could change I would've given up on this world a long time ago," said Maroto, though he felt a cold pulse of disgrace ripple through him as soon as the hypocrisy left his lips. For all his years of trying to be a better barbarian, as soon as the Tothans got in his grill he didn't just revert to his shameless old self, he somehow managed to sink to the lowest depths of his bottom-feeder life. If he had changed at all over the many humiliating decades, it was for the worse…

Except that was all a bit melodramatic, wasn't it? Sure, he'd made a mess of things with the Vex Assembly, no sugarcoating that, but how had he fallen into their clutches in the first place? By sacrificing himself so that Bang could escape from the flying Tothan patrol that had discovered them on the ridgeline. He hadn't even thought about it, just hurled himself in harm's way to protect his friend…same as he had when a massive egg-laying monster had attacked their camp. Same as he had when that horned wolf had come stalking his squad in the Kutumbans, and same as he had when those punkarse bodyguards had tried to double-cross the nobles' caravan clear back in the Panteran Wastes. Same as he had over and over again of late, despite the fact that after years of not caring if he lived or died so long as he was high he'd finally found some real value in life.

Fool that he was, he'd long assumed that paradigm shift had come when he first heard the rumor that Zosia was still alive, but looking back on it there'd been another big change in his life right around that time: it was when he'd fallen in with Purna and Digs and the rest of his new friends. Purna especially. Late as she'd come into his song she'd sure changed the tune in one hell of a hurry! If he'd only been lucky enough to die one of those many times he'd put his life on the line to save her crazy arse then he would've gone out as the hero she believed him to be, instead of persisting long enough to land on Jex Toth and fail his final trial in epic fashion…

But he was still alive, whether he deserved to be or not, and that meant maybe, just maybe, his pathetic capitulation to the Vex Assembly hadn't been his last chance to define himself. Maybe he could still become the person his friends thought he was, the person he so desperately wanted to be. Whenever he had an audience he didn't do half-bad, after all, risking his arse left and right for his pals. It was only when he was left alone with his doubts—or a coven of horrifying immortal sorcerers—that the old devil of his baser nature tripped him up.

So now that he had shat the bed there was nothing for it but to try to clean up after himself, preferably before anyone else caught a whiff. Of course, back in Flintland such an accident would require burning your straw mat altogether and then weaving a new one, a point that made that particular turn of phrase even more ominous, but now was not the time to get bogged down in verbiage. Today must be a day of positive action, with not a word wasted.

"Maybe every cardinal on the Holy See is just as wicked as they ever were, but that doesn't mean they can't do the right thing, even if it's just from self-interest," said Maroto, trying to stay sunny in the face of Bang's spiritual storm front. "Joining arms with the Immaculates and everyone else isn't some noble sacrifice for the Chain to make, it's the only chance they have for survival. They must understand that—why else would we be going down here instead of sailing back to Diadem? You made the point yourself that these Chainites look to have the whole Samothan navy even if they aren't hoisting the Crimson, so why come here instead of home unless they were ready to work together?"

"If those hollowheads on the Holy See don't want to go home it's probably 'cause they didn't leave any reinforcements in reserve and are looking for a safer harbor," said Bang. "Or maybe that Immaculate blockade that met us on our way out of the Haunted Sea didn't give them much choice but to come down for a visit. So stow all the we're-all-in-this-together business, because I don't think for a moment the Star's going to join forces against Jex Toth. If anything it'll be a race to see who can sell out the rest, a plan that certain forward-thinking persons have already employed, albeit to disappointing result."

"Don't remind me," said Maroto, dying inside all over again at yet another reminder of just how swiftly he'd sold out the Star to save his own skin. The farther they sailed from Jex Toth the worse his guilt grew—next time he got the opportunity to play the martyr he wouldn't make such a mess of it. One of his favorite lies. Angrily shaking his head, he said, "I've got this notion of myself, Bang, that I'm a good guy. Or all right, not good, exactly, but working toward it—that I may have done a lot of bad but going forward I'm going to do better. But *every fucking time* I blow it, don't I? Every fucking time I do the worst thing possible. Which raises the question if I'm not just a selfish piece of shit at heart, just like everyone always said."

"That's not a question I've ever had to ask," said Bang, slouching against the railing and speaking in her real voice, the one free of bravado. The one he barely ever heard her use, and never when he went looking for it. "About myself, maybe, but never about you— and that's my whole point. You're not so bad, Useful, and if you knew your only play was working with those Tothan demons, then I can't see a fleet of nutty Imperials thinking any different. They might not be any better at it than you are, but they'll try to betray the rest of the Star twice as fast."

"See, you're still thinking like a pirate when you should be thinking like a zealot." Maroto scratched under his robe. "The key to any performance is to really get into the headspace, live in it, make it—"

"I prefer experiencing your entertainments to hearing about them," said Bang, draining the last few drops of her waterskin...No, his waterskin, he saw the brown stain on it now. Which meant he'd be climbing down soon, since he'd sensibly slurped the dew-catchers before she'd risen. "If only the Tothans were a little more taken with your performance as archenemy of humanity, maybe they would have ensured this fleet was securely under our nefarious command before bidding us a fond farewell."

"They bought it for a while, anyway," said Maroto sadly, reflecting on his final, tragic role as the man who sold the Star. His loopy old friend Carla was right; hell was nothing more or less than struggling every day of your damn life to play a better part only to end up right back where you'd started. "You know why those monsters believed I was the mortal enemy of humanity? Because I am. Or at least that's how I felt, back there in the tummy of the titan—method acting or just a depressive personality, you make the call."

"Well, see that this time around you don't lose yourself in the part," said Bang, planting the last of her shipbiscuit in the middle of the gull snare she'd rigged but had yet to catch anything with. "The end times already have enough Chainites to go around. In fact, I've got a different sort of character for you to play…"

"An even naughtier novice?" asked Maroto, perking up a little as a familiar lecherous smile enlivened her freckled face. "A beastly bishop?"

"A mutineer in monk's clothing," said Bang. "That Immaculate blockade would have nabbed us for sure if we'd broken away from the armada before, but now that we're long past it we can start sowing some dissent. Even if everyone who's working this ship was a true believer when they sailed from Diadem, they've got to be second-guessing things now that they've seen the shape of their so-called angels. Some are probably even looking for a new messiah, someone to show them the way to salvation."

"Now who's jumping to conclusions?" said Maroto, because according to the Holy See the return of Jex Toth was one of their main prophecies, and witnessing a manifest miracle had to solidify a Chainite's faith rather than rattle it. Might take some work to incorporate all the gooey details, sure, but religious types spent their whole lives twisting facts around to suit their faith, so they were in good practice.

"When I say jump, you say?" said Bang.

"Pants on or off, Cap'n," Maroto dutifully recited, but now he was smiling hungrily, too. When they had escaped Jex Toth he had felt compelled to try to play this one last adventure honest, to see if he could make up for his crimes by having a hand in unifying the Star against their alien enemies. But now that he'd had some time and perspective it was worth remembering that the Immaculates had never once helped the Cobalts in their campaigns to liberate the Crimson Empire, and the Burnished Chain was obviously the worst band of ball-sniffers around. Neither faction gave a hot squat about anyone else, so if getting them both on board for a united front didn't work, a smart fellow could do worse than having a backup plan that involved a fast ship to take them as far from the Haunted Sea as possible.

"But for now we play it cool, right, see if we can get in on an audience with the Holy See and the Empress of the Isles and convince them to work together... right?" asked Maroto, the withered nub of his better nature jostling his sense of self-interest out of the way. He had to try, damn it. He knew it was just the old devil of his guilt rising back up in his heart, trying to eat him alive just as so many other monsters had attempted... but there was no more sense dwelling on who or what might have eaten you than on whom or what you might have eaten.

"How do you suggest you get the ears of the most powerful people in this corner of the Star, exactly?" asked Bang. "After all the effort you went through to sell the Holy See on that simple-shipwrecked-sailors-of-a-merchant-vessel line, they haven't taken much of an interest in us. Convincing them we're as stupid as we are harmless was good for lying low, but lying low doesn't translate to an invitation to the captain's table."

"No," said Maroto, his palms damp on the railing as he looked at the fabulous, intimidating megalopolis that from here seemed to fill all of Othean Isle. "But once we put in I might just have to take on my most ambitious role yet."

"And who might that be?" asked Bang, looking up at him and shielding her eyes with her hand to protect her from the halo that must be enveloping Maroto's head as he adopted a gallant pose.

"Why, that of the man who once brought the Crimson Empire to its knees, and who returned to challenge Queen Indsorith herself. The man who cheated death a hundred times, who led mortals and monsters alike into combat against odds so long not even Pasha Diggelby would dare lay a wager. The first man captured by the armies of Jex Toth, the first to meet with their leaders, and the first to be released! The man—"

"You," said Bang, smacking her lips just as Maroto was getting good and into it, too. "You're talking about you."

"You're fucking right I am, Cap'n," said Maroto with a grin so big he knew Purna and Choi and Diggelby and Da and Sullen and Zosia and fusty old Hoartrap and everyone else would see it flashing in the distance, whatever side of the First Dark they might be on these days. "I'll admit I know more about wrecking the world than saving it, but that's what's great about the stage—one ham can get hung on many hooks, and you never know which cut is tastiest till you try them all."

CHAPTER
17

This Imperial meadhall was not so different from those in the Savannahs, except back home each clan had their own, whereas here in Black Moth the entire Crimson Empire seemed packed into the one. There were more people in this sweltering, smoky room than there were named hunters of the Horned Wolf Clan. Yet Best must give these Outlanders the little tribute they were due: most of them were clearly hardened killers, with steel at their belts and furs on their backs. Their blatant display of weaponry also gave her further cause to be annoyed with the one called Diggelby. He had goaded her into coming here but also insisted she leave her spear back at the church, lest she breach something he called a *social contract*... only to see her son arrive carrying his own.

Her annoyance grew along with the noise in the room, and when Sullen wandered off again without even offering her a word of greeting she decided she'd had enough of this place. The strong drink had dulled her aching injuries but also sharpened the barbs hooked into her troubled spirit. This plan to conjure devils and trip through the First Dark seemed bound to cost Best her soul if not her life, and she would rather spend what little time she had left roaming beneath the stars instead of sitting on her arse in a hellish meadhall. Prayer always came more naturally when she was moving.

"I am leaving, Brother Rýt," she told the monk, her lips beside his ear to be heard, and he flinched at her voice. Just as he always had, even before he went blind. "I go to carry out the order of the poison oracle and Father Turisa. They bid me bring justice to my family, but to learn what shape justice must take I shall journey to Jex Toth, to the very threshold of Old Black's Meadhall, and there I shall test my son and his claims. Either the Deceiver speaks through him and he shall be killed, or he speaks true and by joining his fight I am serving the Fallen Mother. But Nemi of the Bitter Sighs tells me you have asked to ride to Diadem with her, instead of seeing our quest through together—is this true?"

"The...the Fallen Mother has other plans for me?" squeaked the monk. "Everything happens, after all, and Father Turisa did order me to return to the Holy City..."

"Where I told you I would take you, once we had rescued the Star from the catastrophe that threatens it," said Best, hardly expecting him to grow the courage to accompany her now but as a true Chainite obliged to offer him the opportunity. "I do not think Father Turisa should wish you to run away with a witch instead of raising arms against the First Dark."

"Whatever you may *think*, Huntress Best, I *know* he would not condone the summoning of devils for any purpose." Brother Rýt suddenly sounded almost authoritative. "The Fallen Mother calls me to Diadem, and I must answer."

He had never before taken such a tone with her, and while it was not the exact sort of bravery she had sought to stir in his breast it was at least an honorable emotion. Then again, this Crimson ryefire had provoked uncommon sentimentality in her own bosom, so perhaps it had helped him find his pluck as well. She nodded her approval, and then remembering he could not see it, said, "If you return to the Clan before I do, or if I do not return at all..."

But then she trailed off, seeing his incredulous expression. She knew what that look meant. It was the same one Sullen had worn after his epic song, when she suggested that if the Star truly was beset by monsters and they drove them back together he could then return to the village with her. It was the mien of someone who was never going anywhere near the Frozen Savannahs or another Horned Wolf ever again, so long as he had any say in the matter.

"Good hunting then, Brother Rýt," she told him, for unlike her son this foreign boy was without a doubt guided by the hand of the Fallen Mother, and thus beyond reproach. "And may safe roads guide you to her breast."

"Safe havens keep you at your rest," said the monk automatically, and then gave a little bow of his tonsured head. "And… and good hunting to you, Best of the Horned Wolf Clan."

Coming from the mouth of a monk, even this one, the words carried the weight of a blessing.

Best exchanged a terse farewell with Nemi of the Bitter Sighs and was in the midst of a completely unnecessary and protracted goodbye with the Diggelby creature when over his flashing turban she saw Sullen approach. As if tripping over her gaze he clumsily bounced into a shorter figure, and then, right there in the middle of the crowd, the little person attacked her son. Sullen looked surprised, as well he might to be jabbed in the gut by someone half his size over so slight a slight as bumping into a stranger in a busy meadhall. And instead of doing something about it Sullen just stood there gawping down at his assailant, who in turn began screaming his head off as though he'd been the one to get stuck.

For as hard as these people looked everyone seemed shocked by the scream and nobody did anything except stumble back from the fight. Everybody save Best, that was, who was already moving. The Immaculate whose arm she had taken off stood holding Sullen's spear, and by the time he'd noticed what was happening to his lover, Best had snatched the weapon out of his hand. As she darted across the floor she lowered the blade to jab it into the back of Sullen's diminutive attacker, but at last her simple son did what he should have from the first and defended himself. In doing so he saved Best the journey of half a dozen steps, kneeing the little man so hard in the sternum he went flying backward. The thug nearly pulled the spear out of Best's hands as the point punched through his back and out through his ribs. He didn't weigh much, though, and sliding into a low stance Best was able to hold on to the weapon and keep him spitted, his short legs kicking in the air, until she was sure he was no longer a threat.

"No!" Over the shoulder of the speared man Best saw her son cry out and stagger toward her, a bloody hand holding his bloody stomach. "No, Ma, no!"

Well, this was just like Sullen—the one time in his whole life she had come to his defense and he was mad about it. Oh, how he had cried and cried when he was five and Oryxdoom and Yaw Thrim had worked him over. He hadn't shed a tear while they were at it, but afterward, when she was picking the pebbles out of his face, he'd blubbered the whole time, asking why she'd just stood by and watched. After what he'd ended up doing to One-arm Yaw years later she had assumed he had learned how to stand up for himself, but apparently not...At least he had grown out of wanting her help.

"Put 'im down! Put 'im down!" Sullen was crying as he reached her, and seeing that the spasming body on her spear had dropped his knife she acquiesced, flipping him down on his face and yanking the weapon free. The spear had a perfect heft to it, and while the blade scraped against a rib on its way out there was no resistance at all, and she smiled at the healthy gout of blood from the wound. Her father was in this spear all right, biting hard and deep.

"Fuuuck!" Sullen foolishly took his hand off his own wound and clapped it on the man's back, rolling him over to put his other palm on the hole in his chest. No, not a man, a boy, she saw now, his lips bubbling with crimson foam and his eyes rolled back in his small skull. There were angry mutters from the crowd and Sullen sobbed again, which didn't make any sense at all—this boy was probably twice as old as Sullen had been when he first went to war, and had drawn first blood over nothing greater than a bump in a bar.

"Somebody help!" Sullen yowled. "Nemi! Nemi, help him!"

"What the fuck you do that for?" a big woman in ringmail demanded of Best, as though she were the one in the wrong here. Not owing her any answer and insulted by the implication, Best whipped the spear down so hard that most of the blood spattered down on the floorboards at the woman's boots.

"I let you go!" Sullen was shouting in the dead boy's face. Was her son such a weak hunter he couldn't see when the life had left the dying? "I let you go! I wasn't here for you! I wasn't! I let you go!"

"You're pretty good at using that on kids, Flintlander, how about someone a little bigger?" said the armored woman, taking a step toward Best and putting her hand on the pommel of her sword. Best smiled at her stupid question. The larger the game, the easier it was to hit her target.

"It was an accident, we all saw, and the boy struck first besides," said a much darker Outlander with a tattooed face and a curious beard, stepping between the two women with a palm raised at each of them.

"We didn't see shit, Raniput, except these savages double-team a ten-year-old," said a grizzled man behind the big woman. He already had an ax in hand, and several more helmeted heads in the crowd nodded at this.

"I wasn't…after you…" Sullen's hand slipped off the boy's wounds, and sitting back on his knees, he raised his slick red hands in front of his face as though seeing them for the first time.

"Look at that and tell me he wasn't provoked," said the tattooed man, gesturing at Sullen's gut, and that seemed to diffuse some of the violence in the smoky air. The torn front of Sullen's tunic burped out blood, and Best realized the wound was far worse than she'd thought. She was about to kneel and help him when his friends pushed through the crowd and gathered around, Keun-ju crying out and Purna cursing and Nemi muttering and Diggelby flapping his arms in distress. The whole meadhall pressed inward around them, more angry voices rising up—Best's Crimson had come a long way since first being saddled with Brother Rýt, and she wasn't pleased by what she parsed of the crowd's angry voices.

"Who knows the kid?"

"What happened?"

"Was it murder?"

"Who murdered the kid?"

The tattooed Outlander who had intervened was trying hard to look nonchalant, but there was definite worry in his voice when he addressed them. "You'll want to get your friend out of here. Now."

"He shouldn't be moved," said Nemi as she stood back up from her quick examination, her hands now as bloody as Sullen's. He was still on his knees but looked on the verge of blacking out, his lips moving as if in silent prayer, his glassy eyes staring at nothing. Diggelby and Purna eased him down to the ground as Keun-ju kept his hand pressed to the wound, his pale veil spattered with red drops.

"Should or shouldn't, he *has* to go," hissed the Outlander, his voice almost eaten by the angry murmurs of the crowd. "My crew can help you carry him somewhere, anywhere but here."

"I'll fetch my vardo," said Nemi with a nod at the stranger. "Riding in the wagon will be better than being carried. Take him outside if you must but not farther. If he tears any wider he'll die."

"Hurry!" called Keun-ju as the witch wove away through the crowd, as if that weren't obvious enough.

"What happened?" Purna asked, looking up from Best's limp, ashen-faced son. "What the fuck happened?"

Best just shook her head, unsure herself, the spear vibrating in her hand like a dowsing rod. Maybe it was, of a sort, but not for water... Yet looking down she saw it wasn't the spear that was shaking, but her hand. Purna posed an important question—what *had* happened? Sullen had just lost more blood from a single blow than she had taken from him during their entire duel, and more leaked out around Keun-ju's hand, the entire room buzzing like an angry icebee hive. Her son might be about to die right here, over something she didn't even understand.

"Serves him fucking right, picking a fight with a kid," came a voice from the mob.

"That what happened?"

"Seen it! He came at the kid, kid drew on him, and that other fucker stabbed him in the back!" This last sounded like it came from the first woman to run her mouth, who had crept back into the crowd.

"And that's our cue," said Purna, wrapping her small arms around one of Sullen's beefy shoulders as Best shook off her unexpected torpor and went to his other side. "Let's get him outside, steady as we can."

Big as her boy had grown it was going to be hard, but then the helpful Outlander elbowed his way back through the increasingly ugly mob, calling over his shoulder, "Come, my leopards, work to be done!"

In a flash there were too many hands instead of not enough, but while Sullen rose into the air the crowd showed no signs of parting.

"We just gonna let them leave?"

"We owe the kid better than that!"

"Was the kid one of ours?"

"The kid was one of ours!"

At this last Best felt the mood make the final fatal shift from angry to violent.

"Put the killer back on the floor!" called an older man who had clambered onto a nearby table, swaying from simple drunkenness or the thickness of the smoke up there, Best couldn't guess which. "I'm Captain Crosstau of Eyvind's Rangers, and I'll have justice for...for the kid!"

"Annnnd you're on your own," the tattooed Outlander told them, signaling his crew to lower Sullen. "Sorry."

"Not as sorry as they're going to be," growled Best, her heart growing light as a windblown leaf floating over the Savannahs. Not even a Horned Wolf could escape a trap like this, surrounded by a hundred hostile hunters. The Fallen Mother was calling her home, and with her son at her side—she just had to earn enough valor for the both of them before they crossed over from this meadhall to that of Old Black. Seeing the bigmouthed woman in ringmail begin to draw her sword, Best didn't think she'd have any trouble on that count, and drawing back the spear of her son, the spear of her father, she—

"*Where the fuck is my sandwich?!*" Best couldn't see the door to the tavern behind the wall of the mob, but she recognized the voice.

The captain on the table slowly turned to the doorway. "Piss off, you old coot, before you get strung up along with the barbarians. You and your fucking sandwich."

There were a few laughs from the crowd as he turned back to Best and her surrounded pack...and then his short hair burst into flames, a blinding column of fire shooting up so high it blasted the ceiling beams. The heat instantly blackened his face, and then his skull exploded.

Best blinked, unable to believe what she had just seen even as hair and bone and brain pelted the crowd. The headless body fell over. Sorcery. Insane, incomprehensible sorcery.

Pandemonium. Understandable, utter pandemonium. And in that pandemonium Sullen's friends and the helpful Outlanders hustled his limp body out the front door where Hoartrap stood scowling. His lips were wet with blood and bristly with fur, Best recognizing his expression for that of a predator whose first meal had only been large enough to make his hunger more severe. The rest of the crowd stampeded toward the back of the common room, flames licking across the ceiling. Only when the small party had carried Sullen a few blocks in the direction from whence Nemi would be bringing her cart did Best remember they had forgotten something in the burning tavern, and jogged back to collect Brother Rýt.

CHAPTER
18

Thousands of candles lit the Upper Chainhouse, and through the ingenious construction of the echo chamber the soft voice of the cardinal at the Onyx Pulpit reached all the way to the velvet-padded pews in the far back. These seats must be a novelty even to those in the audience who had attended sermons in the past, for they had always done so in the Lower Chainhouse where there was only the cold obsidian floor to kneel on. That immense cathedral had ten times as many in attendance as this far smaller facility, and the Middle Chainhouse was likewise crammed to capacity. The cardinal spoke into the open mouth of the graven angel whose six blazing wings formed the lectern, and his words carried down through the pipes, amplifying along the way to the countless ears below. Even the three largest Chainhouses in the Star weren't nearly big enough to house all of Diadem's citizens who might be interested in attending the first assembly of the burgeoning parliament, but that was just the way of government, and the rest could be filled in the same as they always had: via gossip and the distribution of tracts.

Behind the cardinal the rest of the speakers sat crammed into the benches of the chancel, the rose window of smoked glass seeming to hang over their heads like a murky sun. Zosia had met with most of these representatives already, and had been more than happy when they had decided that neither she nor Indsorith should sit with them at the front of the Chainhouse. Instead the two women were to wait in the audience, sitting with the common people until called upon.

Not one for squeezing in and out of benches, Zosia had compromised by posting herself and Indsorith in one of the confessionals that ran alongside the nave, busting out the grate that divided the booth so they could see each other as they talked. It had felt pretty damn satisfying to use a war nun's sainted hammer to smash up the latticed likeness of the Fallen Mother and toss it on the floor for Choplicker to gnaw like a choice bone. Couldn't be good for his teeth…but then again, monster that he was, maybe it just made them sharper.

Indsorith had been wary of attending the meeting at all. She doubted the gesture of opening up Castle Diadem to the public would be enough to win over the very revolutionaries that agents of the Crown had apparently been torturing in her name, but Zosia eventually convinced her. Boris's dissident organization was but one of the many factions who now claimed a stake in Diadem's future rule, and there had to be countless loyal subjects who would take heart in the news that the Crimson Queen had survived Pope Y'Homa's assassination attempt. Indsorith and Zosia publicly paying the revolution the respect it was due with a little genuflection would go a long way to ameliorating any frustrations certain parties might have with the surprisingly alive Stricken Queen or her less popular successor.

This would-be senate's invitation for the former regents to take part in their inaugural summit wasn't just a smart move, it was a necessary one. The Burnished Chain had overthrown the Crown and then cleared out of Diadem so fast there was a vacuum to be filled here in Samoth's capital, yes, but there were also twenty-two other provinces in the Crimson Empire to consider. Each of these had a regiment loyal to the sovereign of the realm, in name if not in recent deed. Having a Crimson Queen or two willing to bestow legitimacy on the new government was also essential to staving off civil war and beginning the long process of freeing the Star from tyranny.

Or so the reasoning went. Zosia was rather skeptical of the revolution's long-term prospects even without little potential complications like Ji-hyeon's long-overdue ass finally leading the Cobalt Company through Diadem Gate. Yet with each passing day that possibility seemed more remote—Zosia dearly hoped the kid was all right, that there had simply been some change in plans, but if so, why hadn't Hoartrap appeared to alert her? Anytime she let her imagination loose she pictured the old sorcerer opening up the Lark's Tongue Gate with promises of leading the Cobalt Company safely to Diadem, only for the First Dark to swallow up every single one of them without so much as a burp. The image of Hoartrap overestimating his ability to lead a large force through the Gates and inadvertently dooming the entire Cobalt Company wasn't too far a stretch... but then neither was the far darker scenario of Hoartrap duping Ji-hyeon into sacrificing her entire army for some heinous ritual that required thousands of souls voluntarily entering a Gate. The sorry truth was she didn't trust the Touch any more now than she had when they'd first summoned their devils together all those years ago—as a matter of fact, she probably trusted him less, now that she'd gotten to know him better.

Anyway, fretting over the dismal possibilities only distracted her from the matter at hand, and as far as such things went the sudden arrival of General Ji-hyeon and her wannabe Cobalts would be a blessing for Diadem's new parliament compared to who else might crash their inaugural ball. What would this amateur government do if the Black Pope sailed the Imperial fleet back into Desolation Sound? Or if the resurrection of Jex Toth caused some unpredictable mayhem, as Indsorith feared? Or thinking even simpler, what if an opportunistic noble from a neighboring province joined forces with a Crimson colonel to invade Diadem and make a claim for the throne?

Yet even assuming nobody came knocking at the city's admittedly impressive gate for the next hundred years, Zosia doubted this crew could amicably rule for a hundred days before a fresh power struggle led to even worse riots than before. She had gone into the meeting fairly hopeful, but after hours of droning speeches with conflicting messages about Diadem's future she was less than convinced they could all work together... but then Choplicker seemed to have dozed off on her feet, and if he was bored that had to be a good sign, didn't it?

"I don't like this talk of martyrs," murmured Indsorith from the other side of the confessional. "Especially coming from an officer of the Burnished Chain."

"Well, at least he's winding down," said Zosia as the cardinal raised his bandaged hands in the air to punctuate his call for a newer, kinder interpretation of the Chain Canticles. "And they did crucify him, so I understand being hung up on martyrdom."

"Wouldn't he have had to *stay* hung up to actually be a martyr?" said Indsorith, and Zosia almost lost her shit. Not because it was hilarious, because really now, but just on account of how good it felt to see Indsorith well and truly on the mend, her personality coming out along with her stitches. Indsorith had lived, she had made it, and all because Zosia had done the right fucking thing for once and come here to Diadem instead of cutting out on the Cobalts the way she'd planned. One year ago Zosia had been snowed in at the back of an ice cave in the Kutumbans, obsessing over all the tortures she would inflict on Indsorith for the murder of Leib and the rest of the village, and now they were cutting up in church like a couple of kids dragged to mass. Holding up her own injured hands, Indsorith said, "At least Y'Homa is consistent in her madness—she never liked me, but nailing up her own people…"

"They say even a few of the Holy See ended up like that, and entire factions of the rank and file faith. It was like a screaming forest, one of the rebels told me, and even as quick as the wildborn moved to take them down, plenty bled out before they could be saved." Their talk of tortured cardinals and bishops and priestesses roused Choplicker enough to sleepily raise his head and look around the crowded Chainhouse.

"I'm just surprised they didn't crucify the wildborn, too," said Indsorith.

"I guess Y'Homa tried to fumigate their monasteries instead," said Zosia. "The what do they call it, the Pens? Except some of those in charge of passing out the poisoned censers refused and warned off the wildborn clergy instead, so they were able to escape."

"Say one thing for the Burnished Chain, they make us look like sane and sensible sovereigns."

"Let's not get carried away," replied Zosia, trying not to smirk, and then marveling at herself—when was the last time she had tried to stifle a smile instead of faking one? Ever since that drunken night in the kitchens when she'd found herself unexpectedly opening up to Indsorith she had felt more and more at ease with the last woman she would have ever expected to befriend. Whether you wanted to attribute it to their similar experiences, the ensuing worldviews, and cynical senses of humor, or just a natural kinship, their bond grew swift and strong. It probably didn't hurt that Indsorith was rather cute, too, but Zosia had known plenty of gorgeous people she despised, so you couldn't put too much import on that.

"I'm guessing you weren't brought up in the church?" Zosia asked her bored friend.

Indsorith shook her red tresses, taking a nip from her silver flask and offering it to Zosia. "Devils, no, my mother hated the Chain even more than she hated you and your Cobalts. Well, maybe not that much, but close, close."

"Well, there's no accounting for taste, is there?" Zosia declined the flask, knowing it only contained cold-brewed kaldi and not wanting to get any more jittery after chain-smoking her corncob pipe all through the summit. Maybe it was the smaller size of the bowls leading her to pack more of them, but she always seemed to overdo it with cobs. By the six devils she'd bound, Zosia needed to get serious about finding a block of briar to make a proper pipe…

"My turn to guess," said Indsorith. "I'm imagining you as a choir girl in a rural Chainhouse…from a devout family of farmers…a bright future in a nunnery…"

"Warmer, warmer…" Zosia grinned.

"…until an illicit tumble with an Usban missionary cost you everything."

"Ew!" Zosia couldn't help but imagine Fennec. "I'll have you know I don't raise my habit for just any—"

"Shhh!" hissed a teenage boy at the end of the closest pew, shooting daggers at the open doors of the confessional.

Zosia rolled her eyes but saw Indsorith mouth *Sorry* at the lad.

And that right there was why the girl had made a better queen than Zosia, because Zosia just couldn't be fucked. Granted, this cardinal at the Onyx Pulpit had suffered, and he'd clearly been on the right side when Pope Y'Homa announced her apocalyptic plan, and his version of Chainite theology might not be as bugnuts and violent as the old school—he was *one of the good ones*, as Leib would describe religious neighbors who didn't try to cajole them to their mossy altars in the heart of the aspen wood. Yet as hard as Zosia had tried to pay attention to this man's words she found it impossible to stomach a sermon, and that was just what this was. A humanist one, especially compared to those that must have been given in this Chainhouse before the fall, but underlying it all was the inevitable message that the Fallen Mother witnessed all mortal deeds and would judge them accordingly.

"... *This* is why faith in the Fallen Mother is not itself any measure of goodness in one's breast," said the bruised cardinal. "The Deceiver forever seeks to use our sacred virtues against us, tempting us with those sweetest of fruits. Deny him. *Blessed are the proud, for they shall seize the Star.* Familiar words to even nonbelievers, I am sure, but too often their meaning is perverted. This is no justification for tyranny nor an appeal to pettiness—on the contrary, it is a call to be as strong and resolute as our maker, to take the authority for salvation into our own hands instead of waiting for the Allmother's intervention. We *must* live our lives as though this frail world is all we have, and we must be proud enough to believe we can save it. We must deliver justice to those in need, instead of sitting by and allowing crimes to go unanswered, relying on a posthumous evening of scales. Do not wait for a god—act as one. Thank you, my friends."

And that was it, not even a *safe roads guide you to her breast* to wrap things up. Zosia wished she'd paid more attention after all as the cardinal shuffled over and sat beside the disfigured mother superior who had spoken before him on behalf of the surviving reformed anathemas, as she referred to her wildborn sisters and brothers. The use of that term had almost caused a fight to break out, the cyclopean representative of Diadem's small and previously underground population of unaltered wildborn leaping to her hooves and demanding an apology. Now the two speakers studiously ignored each other, sitting on far ends of the chancel. How many of the so-called Chainwitches who had been left behind by their pope still remained loyal to the church, albeit as the evolving institution this cardinal championed, and how many had rejected their Chainite upbringing entirely, allying themselves with those who sought to destroy the institution in all its guises? Zosia hoped in time all the poor indoctrinated wildborn came around, casting off the Chain that shackled their souls to scripture penned and interpreted by people who saw them as inferior by birth.

"Thank you, Cardinal Obedear," said Eluveitie, the ancient matron whom the rest of the representatives had unanimously voted to chair this summit. It was the only thing they had all been able to agree on. As she rested her hands on either side of the lectern's uppermost wings Zosia squinted, thinking at first it was a trick of the candlelight and the cloud-darkened clerestory windows, but no, she saw the woman was missing every single one of her fingers. "We have heard many arguments this day, and much anger. This is as it should be—if there is no debate at the start of something new and great, then somebody is muzzled. We seek to change Diadem, and in doing so, we seek to change our very world. It shall not be easy. We seek to please the many instead of the few, to hear the faintest whisper of the downtrodden, and to speak for those who have no voice at all. It shall not be easy."

Frail as she looked, the old woman's voice was strong and warm, commanding, even. She was a natural leader of mortals, and stirred by something in her tone as much as her words, Zosia wondered if this was how folk must have felt back in the day, when she'd given her own speeches in town squares and atop hay wains. The peasants must have felt something to throng to her banner the way they had.

"How many of us wished for freedom from the Crown *and* from the Chain? How many of us prayed for it, to forbidden gods or unforgotten ancestors or anything else that might listen? How many of us thought we knew *exactly* how Diadem should be, once that happened?" This drew a few self-conscious chuckles from the sea of citizenry filling the pews. "And how many of us never thought that far ahead, thinking it would be enough to be free? I tell you, my friends, I *have* wished for this day, I *have* prayed for it, and while I do not know *exactly* how our city shall best flourish in the days to come, I *have* thought far enough ahead to know this much: it shall not be easy. The yoke has been removed from our back, but how shall the fields be tilled? The prison door has been torn from its hinges, the jailers have all gone, but where shall we go, how shall we survive, when all we have is each other? I do not know, and it shall not be easy...but it is better. Aye, it is *best*."

A rumble of assent, boots and turnshoes and rag-swaddled feet stamping the floor. Zosia found herself leaning forward in her seat to better hear over the tumult.

"We come together this day to be heard, yes, but we also come to hear one another," said the chairwoman, looking almost like a mendicant friar of the Ten True Gods of Trve in her simple robe of brown homespun. "We shall leave here with more questions than answers as to our future, and I say again, that is how it should be. Beware of those who offer easy solutions to hard struggles! We have talked of rights and privileges and ownership, and we have talked of whether we should have any rights or privileges or ownership at all. We have heard why we should have a thousand new laws and a militia to enforce them, and we have heard why we need but one law, the law of mutual respect for all citizens of our city.

"We have heard why those who swore allegiance to Chain or Crown ought to be exiled, or worse, and we have heard why we should build a new Chain, and a new Crown. And we have heard why suffrage is the first step to deciding what our first step shall be, but a dozen different ideas of what suffrage might mean. A dozen different ideas of how we might administer it, and protect it from corruption, and all the rest. To be honest with you, my friends, my neighbors, what I have been telling you all along very much applies to this inaugural meeting of Diadem's concerned people: it has not been easy. But it is better. It is best. And slowly, carefully, respectfully, we shall address all matters in turn, and while it shall not be easy, it shall be *easier* than what we have lived through to reach this happy, happy day. We are *free*."

That got half the Chainhouse on their feet, stamping and cheering, but Eluveitie waved them back into their seats with her stumpy hands.

"Freedom means many things, friends! We are free, yes—free to build a beautiful shining city where all are equal, but also free to sink ourselves in a mire of competition and bickering and inaction. We have much to decide. And now that we have heard as many contradictions and dissenting opinions as any novice lawyer might be expected to soak up in a dozen lectures, let us adjourn and ponder and debate again before we *decide* anything."

The cheers and applause and foot-stamping that answered this was a little more subdued than it had been before, maybe, but at least everyone was awake again after a very long day. Eluveitie let them go on a little longer this time before silencing them again, and then cleared her throat. "As a last order of business, I have two announcements to make."

"Here it comes," grumbled Zosia, and glancing over she saw that Indsorith looked about as nervous as she felt. Eluveitie had been polite but less than awestruck when she had met the Stricken Queen in whose name she had fought the powers of Diadem for over twenty years, taking the news of Cold Cobalt feigning her own death with about as little surprise or excitement as anyone Zosia had yet told. They had made small talk, of all things, and the old rebel leader explained to Zosia how she and Indsorith would publicly be brought into the fold of the new leadership.

"First, if Indsorith of Junius could please join us," said Eluveitie, her avoidance of any of the regent's titles no accident. Setting her jaw and stiffly rising from the confessional, Indsorith walked up the side aisle with deliberate slowness as the secular congregation reacted as though a saint had descended from the heavens in their midst...or a devil had risen from the First Dark. Zosia winced on her fast friend's behalf at all the hissing, but Indsorith was a big girl and didn't flinch. Nobody threw anything, so it could've gone worse. Once she had climbed the scalloped stairs to the Onyx Pulpit and taken her place at Eluveitie's side, the chairwoman said, "Indsorith of Junius joins us not as a despot, but as a simple citizen of Diadem. Is it not so?"

Indsorith said something inaudible, and after the old woman leaned over and whispered something in her ear, she spoke into the lectern. Indsorith wasn't as good a speaker as Eluveitie, but she sounded sincere, her voice quavering with candid emotion.

"It is so. I have dedicated my life to serving my people, my city, my empire, but I have not always succeeded. At times...at times I have failed you absolutely. For any harm I have caused I humbly and sincerely apologize, and I welcome this opportunity to make amends for my errors. I will endeavor to be a better citizen than I was a queen."

Damn. That was both shorter and a hell of a lot more real than Zosia had expected. It made her like the woman even more, but from the fresh round of hissing Indsorith hadn't quite won over her public just yet. To see these people who had never had to sit on the Crimson Throne passing judgment on her rule burned Zosia's ass so bad there might as well have been a penitent's candle blazing under her bench.

"Thank you, Indsorith of Junius." Eluveitie spoke forcefully into the lectern, her booming voice silencing the malcontents. "I have one more proclamation, but it will not come as a complete surprise to some of you, for I have been saying it for years. It has been the prayer of the good and the godless, the rallying cry of those faithful to our cause, and now, I am pleased to say, it welcomes home one of Diadem's greatest daughters: Zosia lives!"

Ever since Indsorith stepped out of the open door of the confessional to take her place at the front of the cathedral, quite a few curious faces had studied Zosia from the pews, no doubt wondering at the identity of the old woman who sat so close to their former queen. Now all eyes were on Zosia as she breathed a deep sigh and took her feet, much as she would have preferred to pull the confessional shut and hide out with Choplicker until everyone had filed from of the Chainhouse. Her devil clambered up, too, and gave a whiny yawn as he looked to his mistress with lazy curiosity. He was probably just as surprised as Zosia at how scared she was to face these people she had once ruled...ruled poorly, and then abandoned.

They didn't hiss the way they had at Indsorith, or maybe she just couldn't hear them over the pounding of her heart, the thunder of her boots on the polished floor as she walked up the aisle. She tried to imitate Indsorith's effortlessly regal posture, face pointed straight ahead, keeping her back straight though she tended toward the slouchy. From the corner of her eye she saw that row after row after row of Diadem's populace had risen to their feet. She had cynically supposed only those with connections to the leaders of the various factions would be allowed entry to the actual summit in the Upper Chainhouse, but here she saw the grimy and the greasy-haired rubbing patched elbows with people of obvious means. A small child stood on the end of a pew, so riveted by the sight of Cold Cobalt's return that Choplicker strolled right over and stole the bun he'd been eating out of his limp hand. Somewhere in the thick forest of faces someone was sobbing, and other people were grinning so wide she saw their pale gums. She hadn't spotted Boris yet despite his promise to be there, but maybe he'd scored a seat near the front as reward for delivering two queens for the price of one.

"Zosia lives," Eluveitie repeated as Zosia mounted the pulpit and took her place at the left hand of the leader of the rebellion, Choplicker plopping down at her feet. "And she has come back to us in our hour of need. Our beloved hero, who rose to become a powerful general in the Cobalt Uprising..."

Who, *what now*? Zosia hadn't risen to anything *in* the uprising, Zosia *was* the uprising, period...but she tried to unclench her jaw, knowing there are worse places to be kicked than the pride.

"Our beloved general," the old woman went on, "who cut down the wicked King Kaldruut and became Crimson Queen by her own hand."

That was more like it.

"Our beloved queen, who fell from Castle Diadem at the blade of Indsorith of Junius, and whose very name we were forbidden to speak in the dark days and years that followed." Eluveitie looked back

and forth between the two increasingly uncomfortable women at her
sides. "Our beloved martyr, who swore to be the last despot of Diadem, to make all mortals free or die trying. Who we all thought *died,
trying*. Who returns in our hour of need, as I said, or perhaps just a
few minutes after…"

The fuck…?

"Who all this time has been thick as thieves with Indsorith of
Junius, the *actual* Last Queen of Samoth, the tyrant of our age, and
Zosia's conspirator," the old woman went on, not giving half a hoot
that the two ferocious queens she was slagging off were right next to
her loud mouth. "I have spoken with Cold Zosia here, and heard her
song, and—"

"I can sing my own song, Grandma!" Zosia barked, Choplicker up
on his feet and growling at Eluveitie. From the smirk on the biddy's
face Zosia guessed she'd just played right into her hands; no small
feat, considering the woman didn't have any fingers. Glancing back
at the representatives in the chancel she didn't see any friendly faces,
and turning back to really take in the Chainhouse she saw thousands
of people who had counted on her, or believed in her after the fact.
Thousands of people she had failed, and who were seeing her as she
truly was for the first time.

"Go on then, go on then," said Eluveitie, stepping back and gesturing at the pulpit. "Tell them what you told me. About giving Indsorith the throne of your own free will. About faking your death.
About… how did you put it? *Retiring to the country?*"

Zosia was so livid she couldn't speak, Choplicker snarling on her
behalf.

"I am sure I have gotten some detail wrong, so set them straight!"
said the smug matron, still projecting enough to make sure her voice
carried through the pipes and echoed along the vaulted ceilings.
"You said you would sing your own song, well, now's the time—all
of Diadem's listening!"

It took everything Zosia had not to bust this crone in the jaw, and
from the corner of her eye she saw Indsorith steady herself against
the lectern. She had come a long way from death's door but any sort

of excitement could be exhausting in her condition, and this was the worst sort of excitement imaginable. Noticing Indsorith abruptly brought into focus just how precarious their position truly was, two monarchs blithely wandering into the middle of a revolution— what had she expected these people to do, throw them a parade? The insurgency Eluveitie had been leading ever since Zosia skipped town was predicated on the Stricken Queen being a martyr to their cause, which meant she was worth a lot more to them dead than she ever could be alive. Living people have a way of making their own decisions, of complicating the message, so if Zosia couldn't be a martyr anymore she could damn sure become a scapegoat, same as Indsorith…and now she had to make sure these fuckers didn't try to pull any of the usual things peasants did to goats. She wasn't too worried about herself, because if Choplicker could keep her safe from armies and devil queens he ought to be able to handle some sassy serfs, but Indsorith wasn't looking so hot. Much as Zosia wanted to smash Eluveitie's teeth out, that wouldn't help matters now…but neither would silently accepting the woman's abuse and hoping it was all sizzle and no steak.

"Easy, boy," she told her devil, and he immediately muted his snarl, though his muzzle still curled back at Eluveitie. Giving Indsorith as wry a headshake as she could manage, she spoke into the Onyx Pulpit, addressing the people of Diadem for the first time since she had deserted them. "Yeah, I'm her. Zosia. And everything this wrinkled old asshole just said about me is true."

It was a wonder the candles didn't all go out, swift as the air left the Chainhouse.

"It's not the whole truth, right, but it's the version most convenient for her, and for this revolution of yours to work this time, so sure, let's go with that. I'll own it. I did that stuff." Making an exaggerated frown and shrugging, she said, "I'm kind of a piece of shit. I tried to save the world. Failed. Tried to be a good queen. Failed again. Did I make things worse? Absolutely. You know the one thing I did right? Got the fuck out as soon as I could."

They were all just staring at her, some slack-mouthed, some so red in the face they looked about to pop like a boil under a compress. Nobody said anything yet, but they definitely weren't going to let her keep going for long. She was losing the room, and quick. A pity, since owning up to her public after all these fucking years wasn't hard at all, now that she was doing it. It was a fucking *treat*. Her first day on the Chainite hot seat and already she'd come around to the idea of confession being good for the soul.

"There are one or two things you need to hear, though," she announced, and that was when the first boo came. They had only cupped hands and ash-coated lungs, however, and she had an acoustic system hewn into the very bones of Castle Diadem, designed to amplify her voice clear down to the Lower Chainhouse. "Eluveitie was right about most of that. About me. But one thing she got wrong: I didn't show up at the last minute to save the day, nor *a few minutes after*. I didn't show up for you at all. I came here to bust up the Chain, and that's it, really, but I was too late to catch them. So I'm an even bigger cuntsmack than you thought."

She took a deep breath, and in that gap the boos and hisses swelled even louder than what they'd offered Indsorith. As well they fucking should. Pay the queen her tribute, knaves.

"Last thing I'll say, since if you're anything like me I know you're bored as hell after all the idealistic sheepshit, and that's this: Eluveitie's got me pegged, no question, but she's wrong about Indsorith. You're *all* wrong about Indsorith. She fucking *tried*. And when the Black Pope offered her a way out, to live for herself or die for her people, she chose *death*. It's easy to blame her for the big stuff, since she's queen, and for the little stuff as well. Easy to blame her for everything that goes wrong in your life...but most of it's not her fault. Maybe a little of it is, sure, but not all of it." Zosia felt a pinch on her arm, and as the jeers and shouts rose she glanced over to see Indsorith grabbing her arm and shaking her head, eyes wide. Yanking herself free, Zosia practically yelled into the lectern, because they needed to hear this, needed to know the real truth behind the agendas. "So she fucked up some. It happens, as you'll find out when you're running things. People got tortured? Well, so did she. People died? Ask her family how they feel about—oh wait, you can't. But you know what? Indsorith *cared* about you people, and when shit got dark in Diadem she didn't dip out on you the way I did, she stayed till the end. Till the end."

"Hooooly shit," Indsorith breathed, staring agape at Zosia as the last echo of her proclamation faded and the baying for their blood took its place. Choplicker's uncharacteristically anxious whine was not a welcome note to that chorus. "Holy holy shit, Zosia, what *was* that?"

"Don't thank me till we're out of this church," said Zosia, because despite the sincerity of her words she somehow hadn't won over the crowd. There was a phrase Maroto had taught her from his days as an actor, when you went out and did your damnedest and it was nothing but crickets, or worse. That phrase was *arsehole night at the theater*. It wasn't a very good phrase, but then he wasn't a very good actor. "The good news is I think you and me are finished in local politics, so on to bigger and brighter—"

"We have taken a vote," Eluveitie announced, reminding Zosia she'd been so caught up with the front of the house she'd missed what was happening backstage.

"Oh yeah? You decide you want me to be queen again?" She turned to see what the new parliament had made of her speech, but the whole lot must have cleared out through a door in one of the chapels or something, and standing just out of reach of Zosia were a dozen heavies in light armor... pointing big crossbows at her and Indsorith. Behind the screen of thugs Eluveitie looked awfully pleased for a woman whose neck was about to match her knuckles. Zosia gave Choplicker a light kick, annoyed that the bastard hadn't tipped her off to the ambush... and her stomach lurched when her boot connected with a limp lump. Looking down she saw her dog shivering on the ground, eyes bulging and tongue hanging out, black foam bubbling from his muzzle. She'd been so absorbed in trying to talk to Indsorith over the thunderous wrath of the crowd that she hadn't noticed he'd collapsed, and now he wasn't even breathing. "Chop!"

"As I said, we have put the matter to a vote," said Eluveitie, but her voice was so remote it might have been welling up through the pipes from the Lower Chainhouse. Indsorith floated to Zosia's side as she fell to her knees, lifting her dog's drooping head and feeling his chest for a pulse. Nothing.

"...While it was a close decision, we've moved to execute the both of you, instead of just the one."

CHAPTER
19

This right here was why Purna didn't smoke saam on the reg—it made her either pass out or get paranoid, and neither one of those was conducive to a night out with your chums, nor to the bar fights that often resulted. What the deuce had even happened? To think an hour ago she'd been nervous about summoning up devils beside Sullen, and now he looked like he might be getting an even closer look at what lurked on the wrong side of the First Dark. He wouldn't be the only one, either, if the mad mob from the tavern caught up with them. Hoartrap's theatrical detonation of their leader's head had sent the baddies scurrying, but from the rising clamor back at the burning building they might just be angry enough—and drunk enough— to come after them. They had a head start and were almost out of town, both good things, but then this was the only road through Black Moth and the Haunted Forest, so they wouldn't exactly be hard to find.

"Do you have any idea what kind of trouble you're in?" Hoartrap fumed, and it was unclear whether he was lecturing Sullen's prone body, the random Raniputris who were carrying him, or all concerned. "Unbelievable. I *just* saved your skin, and this is what you do with it? Why in all the Star would you hang out in a tavern full of Crimson scouts, and Eyvindians at that! After what we did to them under Zosia's command you would be hard-pressed to find a regiment who hates the Cobalts more than they do, and let me guess, you couldn't help but mention your allegiances?"

"We didn't even know they were Imperials!" snapped Keun-ju. "This wasn't our fault."

"You chaps said the boy stabbed him?" Digs asked the crew carrying Sullen's bulk, a wildborn man to each arm, a mundane-looking woman to each leg, their leader with the face-ink and oiled beard necklace on one side and Keun-ju on the other with their hands stacked on his wound. "Whatever for?"

"They bumped each other," said the leader, "and quick as a kiss, it was over. That boy looked in fear of his soul when he pulled the knife. Might have been on ugly bugs, who knows."

"Best, did you see if—" Purna began, but then realized the woman was gone, and looking around saw her hightailing it back the way they had come. "Where's she going?!"

"A distraction to slow pursuit?" guessed the Raniputri man.

"In practice if not design," said Hoartrap, "which is better than I expected from the old girl, considering her refusal to take any first aid from Nemi or I."

"I just *knew* that batty woman was itching to stick her spear in something," moaned Digs. "I talked myself hoarse convincing her to leave it back at the church, because there's nothing more gauche than a bloody bar fight—I should have been more specific that it was her potential poking-people-with-sharp-sticks that I objected to, and not her spear in particular."

"A subtle distinction to be sure," said Hoartrap, turning his surly mug toward the helpful Raniputris. "Also, by the by, just who the happy fuck are you scoundrels and why in all the Star are you risking your necks to save those of my miscreant apprentices?"

"Innocent bystanders who have little love for the soldiers of the Crimson Empire," said the leader. "Your big friend here bought us a round just before he was shanked, so I vouched for him when the tavern looked to be turning on him…though to be frank I never anticipated matters escalating so quickly."

"They have a way of doing that when we make the scene, and your assistance in effecting our exit will be richly rewarded," said Digs, shaking the purse he had evidently recovered from Sullen's pocket.

"Doin' the right thing is its own reward," said the stockier of the two women carrying Sullen's legs, a great bear of a girl with a coat of dreads halfway down her back. "We're just happy we found ya when we—*fuck is that?!*"

She let go of Sullen's leg and went for her whipsword as a huge white shape bore down on them. The others would have dropped Sullen altogether if the great horned wolf hadn't slowed and banked so they could all see the vardo it pulled, and Nemi jumping down from her riding board. The witch must have popped another restorative egg herself, fast as she was moving, and talking even faster as she threw open the door to her wagon's interior and motioned them to bring Sullen inside.

"Lay him on the bed and I'll see to him at once but we can't stay here, so Diggelby? Can you drive Myrkur? On her own she'll trot too fast and I can't be bounced around while I'm working with Zeeta-trice to manufacture a cure."

"I can drive," said Purna, though most of her experience on riding boards had actually involved passing the reins to Maroto so she could get comfortably plastered.

"You...you're coming with us?" Nemi sounded hopeful as the strangers carried Sullen inside the vardo.

"She is not," said Hoartrap, sounding just like Purna's devildamned auntie declining an invitation to a yak race on her niece's behalf.

"I'm my own woman, creep!" she told him.

"We have unclean powers to call upon," said the Touch, his alabaster skin almost glowing in the darkness here on the edge of town. "And thanks to your 'quick round at the pub' we are running very short on time, as that light at the end of the street looks an awful lot like a burning tavern. I know from experience that burning taverns make for thirsty soldiers, and thirsty soldiers make for angry mobs. I'll already have to adjust things since Sullen can't take part, but if you or Keun-ju back out now there won't be enough of us to summon the devils we need to see this thing through. And that means the Mighty Maroto is without his necessary reinforcements in the middle of Jex Toth, all so you could take the scenic route to Othean."

"I have to stay with him," said Keun-ju, stumbling back over from the wagon in a daze. "I promised Ji-hyeon we'd come back together. I promised her."

"And *I* promised her we would strike a blow at the heart of Jex Toth and recover the missing Maroto," said Hoartrap, his fluty voice hitting some rather strained notes. "Nemi, tell Keun-ju he can't do anything to help Sullen."

"That is true—I've stanched his bleeding for now, but until I am able to explore his wound I won't know if even I can save him." Giving Purna a meaningful look over the frame of her pince-nez, she said, "But whoever is coming, they are coming with us now. Where is Brother Rýt?"

"Speak of the bedeviled," said Digs, and as he did a blur came out of the darkness, Best running full-out despite her wounds. She held Sullen's spear in both hands, the blind monk clinging to her back. She didn't even stop to address them, taking him straight to the open vardo, the gang who had carried Sullen parting to let her through. She deposited the shaky-legged Chainite on the top stair and, after a brief word and nod, handed him the black spear. The distant lights down the street looked even more ominous now; if the Eyvindian regiment hadn't guessed in which direction their quarry had fled before, Best must have straightened them out on the matter.

"Well then, it is time," said Nemi.

"Past time," said Hoartrap. "I'm going back to the church to make the necessary alterations. Assuming I can count on the two of you to put the future of the fucking world ahead of your own raging libidos?"

"That is not what this is about!" said Keun-ju.

"Speak for yourself," said Purna, giving Nemi a wink…and through the adrenaline and saam, the booze and tubāq, she found herself faced with the crystal clear reality that as soon as she'd found a cute girl she was so into that even eggplay was hot, she was about to lose her. But if the Star fell she'd lose her anyway, so better to fight for a long future instead of trying to make the most of a short one. "Shit. All right, Hoartrap, we'll be there."

"We will?" Keun-ju looked as pale as Myrkur's coat, Best coming over to join their huddle.

"Yeah, we will," said Purna, hoping she came off braver than she sounded. "Nemi and Digs will take care of him, Keun-ju, and we'll all meet up in Othean—after we've done our part to help the Cobalt Company and the Isles and the rest of the Star defeat the monsters of Jex Toth. This thing's got to get done, man, and I'll feel better if you're with us."

She knew it was a good pep talk but felt a tinge of guilt at her self-ish motivations for wanting him along; raising devils and invading the Sunken Kingdom was bad enough, but doing it with just Hoar-trap and Best would be too lame for words. From his unhappy face she saw she'd got him, and she told Hoartrap, "A little privacy? You get your devils in a row at the church and we'll be there as soon as we say our goodbyes."

"Make it snappy," he said, and as he flounced off Purna noticed Nemi had been right: unless he deigned to address his former appren-tice for some specific reason the big warlock pretended Nemi didn't even exist. He did eye Diggelby, though, and said, "I'll be seeing you soon, Pasha."

"Not if I see you first," Digs said brightly, and as soon as the hulk-ing Touch disappeared into the darkness he added, "I really, really, really hope I always see him first. Horrible man."

"Well, I guess this is it," said Purna, trying not to let herself get choked up. Mad as she'd been at Diggelby's refusal to come to Jex Toth if it meant binding devils, now it was all she could do not to bawl. They'd had each other's backs from the beginning of this damn ballad. "Keep it classy, Pasha."

"I'd tell you the same, but I know the word isn't in your ward-robe," said Digs, but then little streams began carving gullies in his corpsepaint and he threw his arms around her. In her ear he sniffled, "Safe roads guide you to her breast, Tapai."

"Here's hoping," said Purna, looking over his shoulder at Nemi. "Both of them, with any luck."

"That's not the usual Prayer of Exodus, but it'll do in a pinch," said Digs, breaking off the embrace and waving Keun-ju in for more of the same. "You go cop a quick feel while you can, girl, and give Maroto a stern word for me when you find the bounder. Running off to Jex Toth and not inviting us along!"

"You can tell him yourself, in Othean," said Purna, trying to believe that a happy reunion on a safe Isle was in their future, Maroto's Moochers back together at last. Well, those who were still among the living. Then she hurried over to Nemi, who was just finishing up with Best.

"—And if my son lives, tell him I did not believe I could be more disappointed in his behavior, until I saw him cut down by a child." Best didn't turn as Purna approached, but said, "I shall leave you to your displays, now, and await our departure at the church. Good hunting, Nemi of the Bitter Sighs."

"Good hunting, Best of the Horned Wolf Clan," said Nemi with a curtsy, and then the dour barbarian stalked off into the night after Hoartrap. "And good hunting to you, Purna."

"Thanks, Nemi, though I feel like I'm about to go the wrong way from the game I want to bag..." Purna looked at the witch's pointy boots and savored that weightless buzz Nemi conjured in her heart.

"If you think I am the prey here you haven't been paying attention," said Nemi, the taller girl putting her arms around Purna and looking down into her moonlit face. "We've tarried too long and don't have time for both words and a proper kiss goodbye, so which would you prefer?"

Purna grinned, and gave her the obvious answer...and was still giving it, fairly floating into her partner's face, when Keun-ju returned from the vardo, having checked in on Sullen a final time. Breaking the kiss, Nemi said, "Until Othean, Purna."

"Until Othean, Nemi," said Purna, and then Keun-ju put his arm around Purna as they watched Nemi climb into the vardo and shut the door behind her. From the riding board Digs gave a wave and a whistle, and then Myrkur took off down the road, pulling their friends toward Diadem. They watched them go, then slowly started in the direction of the church...when the five strangers who had helped Sullen into the vardo hailed them, still standing in the shadows at the edge of the wooded track.

"Pray join us for a drink," said their leader, "the tavern may be gone but we have the most crucial component in our jugs."

"Sorry, friends, running late as it is and—" Purna's sincerely regretful explanation died on her lips as the big, rough characters fanned out in front of them on the lonesome road. "Shit."

"Our wine isn't great, I'll admit, but it's not so bad as that," said the man, sloshing his bottle at them as he stepped closer, his teeth shining like Myrkur's horns in the light of the rising moon. "No need to make a rough night any rougher, Purna. We're taking that smug face of yours all the way back to Harapok, that is not up for negotiation—the question is how we acquire it."

"You know these people?" asked Keun-ju, leaning his hand on the pommel of his broken sword. He still carried both pieces in the scabbard, but it was as impotent a gesture as Purna resting her fingers on the grip of her unloaded pistol. Which she was also doing, because duh.

"I know their type," snarled Purna; the one fucking time saam didn't make her paranoid, this shit happened! "Bounty hunters. Sent by my family. I tried warning you back on the tavern porch something like this might happen."

"The reward's bigger if we bring you back alive," said the man, moonlight playing on the drawn blades of two of his cohort, and the gun barrels of the others. "But since I'm guessing that doesn't work for you, we can do this one of two ways."

"Which one of them involves us going our separate ways with no harm done to either party?" asked Keun-ju, the kid having either a better sense of humor than Purna gave him credit for or a very naïve understanding of what was about to go down.

"The preferable one," said the bounty hunter, taking a small box out of his long Raniputri frock coat and then setting it and the jug on the ground. "By the time we take your head clear back to Ugra-kar it'll be rotten past recognition. Which is why we'll take a death

mask as soon as we murder you, to present along with your remains."
Pointing two fingers at Purna he said, "Bang. You're dead."

Nobody said anything here in the outskirts, but back in the center
of Black Moth the lights were growing brighter and the noise was
getting louder.

"All right," said Purna, thinking she had the angles of this and
actually daring to get her hopes up. "That's a good pitch, but forgive
me if it sounds a little *too* good. Why stick your head out to protect
mine?"

"Because I have a heart of gold and hate to shed needless blood,"
said the man.

"And because you're going to give us every coin in your purse,"
added the bigger of the two women, her ringmail shimmering like
scales as she rested her sword on her shoulder.

"I thought that went without saying, Saor, but I suppose it can't
hurt to spell these things out," said their leader.

"Not that I am complaining," said Keun-ju, "but would it not be
safer for you if the head you collect on isn't still attached to its owner?
Surely it is perilous to secure payment when the object of your hunt
still walks the Star, living proof of your perfidy."

"Usually, yes," said the man, backing up from the jug and the box
he'd left in the street and sticking his thumb at the dog-eared wildborn with a harquebus trained on Purna. "But Orange Pazu here
heard enough for me to be convinced there's a better way for all of us
to get out of this thing. Seeing as you're apparently on an errand to
summon some devils and go to the Sunken fucking Kingdom I don't
think I need to worry about you coming back to Harapok anytime
soon...and if you mix up the fastmud in that box and make us a
death mask we won't have to worry about Hoartrap the Touch being
sore on us for greasing his apprentice."

Purna thought about it, but didn't have to for long—her
vengeance-minded aunt and uncle thinking she'd died could only be
good for her health. Going for the box and the jug, she said, "Make
sure you tell them I cursed their names to my last breath."

"You can't seriously trust them!" said Keun-ju as Purna squatted down and opened the box, rehydrating the pat of colorless mud with a few splashes from the jug. "What if it's poisoned!"

"That *would* make a lot more sense than just shooting us, wouldn't it?" said Purna, but just the same it took all the nerve she had to actually commit and apply the mud mask. Seeing as there was a pair of reeds in the box for her to stick in her nose and breathe through, though, she figured she wasn't the first bounty to be offered this deal. They probably turned a pretty dinar, collecting once from the victim in exchange for a new lease on life, and a second time from their employer.

Sitting in the road, she plastered it on as the leader instructed, and while she couldn't speak under the warming mud she could hear Keun-ju discussing the unusual weather with the bounty hunters… and the distant shouts from Black Moth growing louder, the scent of smoke creeping up the reeds in her nose. She hoped the fire hadn't spread from the tavern; seemed like bad form to burn down a town without meaning to, the sort of activity better suited for villains than heroes. But then again, look at who she'd studied under.

The fastmud set, well, fast, and with some help from the Raniputri man it peeled off intact. He carefully set the death mask back in the box and stowed it in his voluminous coat. Keun-ju reluctantly passed over his purse, though there seemed to be more crumbs than coins in it, and after exchanging assurances that if either party saw the other again blood must surely flow and all that, they parted. Watching the bounty hunters back away into the dark trees on the edge of the road, she gave them a wave, and the Raniputri leader waved back, and then they were gone.

"That might just be the luckiest damn break I've ever caught," Purna remarked as they headed down the road and then turned up the path through the brambles to the church. "I'd say it almost seemed too easy, except I don't believe there's any such thing."

"I suspect they must be expressing a similar sentiment," said Keun-ju. "But then they have no way of knowing you didn't bother loading your cannon before going to the pub."

"Or that your scabbard is as empty as your head! I might've run out of time to clean and prime my sidekick this afternoon, but at least I had the sense to buy powder and shot when I had the chance."

"Even snapped in twain my four-tiger is a finer weapon than anything the Black Moth mercantile had to offer."

"Snob."

"Fair. Slobby fraud."

"Fair," Purna sighed. "I guess we should thank our natures—if we'd both had weapons at the ready we might've jumped into an avoidable fight, instead of talking things through. There's a lesson there. The whole affair could've gone a lot worse."

"Not for me it couldn't have," said Keun-ju. "I am out of the last of my currency *and* I'm still burdened with your company."

"We won't need money where we're going," said Purna, too tired and heartsick from the unexpected awfulness of the night for the prospect of summoning devils and traveling through the First Dark to hold much sway over her anymore. "And hey, if you didn't like the steel they had for sale you should have gotten your sword glued back together while we were in town. Then you could've cut down all those scalp speculators by yourself instead of relying on my consummate negotiator skills."

"You cannot glue a sword back together."

"Forge it back together, then. Reforge it. Whatever."

"That is not how it works," said Keun-ju. "My four-tiger is as broken as my heart, and one could no more bring the shards back together than Nemi could put my arm back on."

"I try to be a patron of the arts, Keun-ju, I really do, but enough with the poetry," said Purna as they came up to the glowing door of the church. "I know you don't know your ass from your elbow, but confusing your heart with your sword with your arm, well, no wonder you sound so sour. Sullen's going to be okay. He's with Nemi, and if she saved him once she can do it again."

"You think so?" Keun-ju stopped and looked back the way they had come, gazing out over the thorns and the tombstones, at the angry flare of Black Moth. The town was going up just like that Eyvindian officer's head.

"I think we'd both rather be riding with our friends in that vardo so we could know for sure, but wishes are for those with devils to spare," said Purna. "So let's raise a little hell so we can raise a lot of harm on whatever it is out there in the darkness that's standing between us and a happy reunion on Othean."

And turning their backs on the firelit night, the two unlikely friends stepped through the hollow doorway of the ruined church on the overgrown hill. They never came out again.

CHAPTER
20

Domingo couldn't believe this was really working. When the administrators had come to interrogate him about the approaching Imperial navy he'd told them he would only speak to Empress Ryuki, but he hadn't counted on them actually granting him an audience, at least not right away. She was the most powerful person in the Immaculate Isles, perhaps the most powerful person alive, given the state of the Crimson Empire. And as soon as these servants were done helping Domingo shave and bathe he would be meeting her in the flesh… and bringing along her assassin. Hopefully Choi would strike as soon as they arrived, saving Domingo the awkwardness of admitting he didn't actually have the foggiest about this mysterious fleet of Crimson ships flying Chainite black sails.

Once he was out of the baths and his chin was as smooth as his rump the silent servants assisted him into a clean suit of Immaculate clothing. Not too long ago the slight would have been unforgivable and he would have refused, sending word that the empress could either return his Crimson uniform or meet with him in the nude, but why stand on ceremony when he couldn't even stand on his own two legs? What a bitter boon the First Dark had granted him, healing his wounds in the span of time it took to roll into one Gate and out the other but fusing his broken hip in such a way he doubted he would ever walk again.

The sober attendants helped thread his stiff left leg into loose trousers, then fitted him in a tunic-like jacket and overcoat, all of the garments as white as those of his helpers. He had to hand it to these Immaculates, they knew a thing or two about sending a message without saying a word—as a foreign colonel making demands to meet the empress he was shown the utmost respect, but in order to be granted an audience he had to come before her dressed as a loyal subject. All in white, Othean still in mourning for the murdered Prince Byeong-gu.

They did not return his cavalry saber as he was helped back into his rattan wheelchair, which brought a minor lump to his throat. When Hoartrap had unexpectedly returned Domingo's cherished weapon just before opening the Lark's Tongue Gate he had taken comfort in the fantasy that he would die with his blade in hand, which was all any Azgarothian officer could hope for. Now these Immaculates denied him that final fleeting honor, though they allowed him to take along something far more dangerous. Choi pushed his chair, looking just as freshly scrubbed and pressed as Domingo, even her wide-brimmed mesh hat white as porcelain, and her face no less rigid. They had never talked strategy, Choi refusing to speak of how she might strike at the empress even in the privacy of their rooms, and they certainly couldn't discuss it now that servants surrounded them.

Rolling through the labyrinth of paneled corridors and screened terraces, Domingo tried to make peace with the life that had led him to this place. There was precious little chance he would be spared if Choi actually attacked the empress, regardless of her success. Yet as resigned to an imminent and even ignoble death as he had become ever since Brother Wan's deception was revealed during the Battle of the Lark's Tongue, Domingo found himself digging his freshly pared fingernails into the armrests of his wheelchair, his heart in his throat. Maybe it was not knowing how or even if Choi intended to carry out her mission at this juncture that made him so apprehensive—what veteran doesn't get jumpy entering a hostile zone without knowing the orders of his armed escort? Or maybe it was just that as Choi pushed him out across a vast stone courtyard and through a path in the field of emerald-armored soldiers who stood at perfect attention,

Domingo felt less like an active agent in this plot for vengeance and glory and more like a helpless sacrifice.

Perhaps that was only fitting, though. As they reached the shadow of the massive triple-roofed gate at the end of the courtyard and the servants deftly slid long poles in the underside of his wheelchair to carry him up the many stairs, he supposed a reversal of roles was as common in war as it was in Lupitera's dramas. There was an unimpeachable freedom in being a pawn, a detachment from commitment no tactician could ever appreciate, so now that he was here he might as well savor it...

Yet even as he was borne up the palace-wide stairs toward the Samjok-o Throne, Domingo couldn't help but wonder if there was a way he could still get a bit of his own in against the Burnished Chain, since they were apparently trying to sail into Othean Bay and whatever Domingo told the empress might affect the reception the Immaculate Isles offered them. He would have to be both clever and quick, however, acting before Choi took her revenge against the autocrat who had executed General Ji-hyeon and all her family. Or even better than scoring a final victory over the church before losing his head, could he find a way of disentangling himself from Choi's assassination attempt altogether? Truly, what good would it do the world if he got dragged down along with her? No less an oracular luminary than Hoartrap the Touch seemed to think Domingo had some role yet to play in this grand tragedy that mortals call life, so didn't he owe it to the Star to stick around as long as possible?

Besides, the empress was dishonorable and craven and a menace, certainly, but Domingo had already taken away her son, and in doing so had proactively caused her as much pain as any parent can deal another. To live on past a child felt a crueler destiny than death, so to let Choi murder the woman now would only put an end to her suffering; hardly the stuff of high drama or poetic justice...

Not that he had mentioned this facet to Choi, thinking she would be less than impressed that her general and everyone else from her homeland had been executed because Domingo had framed Ji-hyeon for the crime he himself had taken considerable pride in committing.

Seemed such a conversation would make things needlessly tense in their already tight quarters.

Now, though, as they approached the dizzying top of the open palace steps and the candlelit interior of the hall beyond the gate, part of him regretted not volunteering the information to her sooner. Choi was an anathema, yes, but an honorable one, hard as it was to believe such a seeming oxymoron existed. Anyway, it was hard to deny she had proven more loyal to her sworn cause than Domingo had to his. The fat, pimply, bare ass of the truth was that the only reason he hadn't told her was fear of what she might do to him. Which just proved that even after he had lost everything and had nothing left to live for he still sought to prolong his wretched existence just a little bit longer. And that was why Domingo Hjortt had outlived his son and his regiment and multiple sovereigns and commanding officers and found himself here, the first Crimson colonel in living memory to meet the Empress of the Immaculate Isles: because he was a fucking *coward*.

They lowered his chair down at the top of the stairs, the smell of brine blowing in at his back, and Choi wheeled him into the throne room. Great jade pillars framed the room, with an orderly horde of perfectly silent Immaculates dressed in far nicer attire than Domingo kneeling in rows that stretched from the golden screens that composed the distant walls clear into the center of the room, where an avenue of open tile led to the waiting empress. Of the hundreds in attendance, the only members of the court not dressed in white were a dozen or so golden-masked, yellow-robed figures with matching horsehair hats who sat closest to Her Elegance, and at the very end of their row a bearded vulture perched atop a bronze statue of a harpyfish.

As the servants hung back and Choi and Domingo approached, he realized that the terraced platform the empress had erected in front of the Temple of Pentacles upon the Cobalts' arrival through the Gate must have been crowned with the actual Samjok-o Throne, for there she sat on the same impressive stage, though now it was elevated only four wide steps off the ground instead of a dozen. Behind her stood a tall white screen with a huge likeness of a three-legged raven perched above the gold leaf faces of her smiling heathen gods, and beyond this stretched a vast painting of the Immaculate Isles themselves.

There was also, incredibly, a unicorn sitting at the feet of the empress. Never having seen one before, Domingo hadn't known what to expect when Choi had claimed that the royal family of Othean was blessed with the friendship of the immortal animal; he had thought a one-horned goat, maybe, given special importance by superstitious foreigners. This was no goat, nor was it a unicorn of the equine persuasion as portrayed in Azgarothian bestiaries—this grotesque horror was closer to a lion, covered in pearlescent scales with a sharp bone rising from the end of its snout, and Domingo was loath to look at it for more than a moment. Especially since it seemed to be staring at *him*.

Only a touch less intimidating than the monster at the foot of her gold and mahogany throne was the Empress Ryuki herself. If most Immaculates' attire was so baggy it might have doubled as a bedroll, their regent's could have served as a tent, layers of starched white skirts and jackets and petticoats piled one atop another. She might have been wearing a blanket over her hands or maybe her embroidered sleeves were simply that roomy, and over this bolt of cloth dangled an enormous tasseled pendant. In lieu of a crown she wore an enormous pearlescent wig whose braids stretched out and around and coiled back in like a tangled-up devil-fish, and beneath this was the only visible part of her body: her face, which was not a kind one, and bore a close resemblance to that of her son.

Choi rolled his wheelchair past the masked, yellow-robed figures and their ugly vulture, right up to the bumper of cushions set a dozen steps from the bottom step of the elevated throne, then locked his wheels in place. He didn't get a good look at her face as she knelt on the floor beside and a little behind him, but the little he saw from the corner of his eye did not bode well for their leaving this chamber alive—she did not look angry so much as satisfied. One of the white-dressed ministers who flanked their approach to the Samjok-o Throne bawled something out in Immaculate, and the empress canted her head the tiniest bit forward.

"You are announced as the Baron of Cockspar first, a guest of Othean second, and a Crimson colonel last," Choi translated, her eyes fixed on the tiles in front of her cushion.

"Yes, well, say whatever polite greeting is expected of me," he told Choi out of the corner of his mouth.

"You will speak directly to me, Baron Hjortt," said the empress in High Azgarothian. "In your province it may be acceptable for a servant to speak on behalf of her betters, but that is not the case in Othean. Besides, close neighbors as we should have no need for intermediaries."

"You honor me and my people with the eloquence with which you speak our tongue, proving again that the souls of our nations are unmistakably entwined," said Domingo, bowing as far forward in his chair as he could manage without falling out of it altogether. Back home in his native province the Empress of the Immaculate Isles was more hated than any villain since the fall of Cobalt Zosia... and had probably surpassed even her, following recent events. The Immaculate invasion of the borderlands and conquest of independent Linkensterne was only the most recent of Ryuki's countless offenses against the Empire and all its loyal provinces, but the sheer brazenness of the crime had ignited Azgarothian wrath like nothing before. And meanwhile up here in Othean every Immaculate from the empress down to a witchborn warrior seemed fluent in Azgarothian, or at least Crimson... "While I should have wished for this day to come sooner, Your Elegance, I am overjoyed we have at long last come together."

As Domingo spoke the unicorn rose to its feet, yawned its jagged maw, and padded down the wide steps in front of the throne. It then sat on its haunches staring at him. From this close he could see its teeth looked as sharp as its horn.

"You will discover, Baron Hjortt, that I do not care for deception, even in the form of flattery," said the empress. "I know that for you Imperials deceit and treachery are so ingrained in your being that you often practice such baseness without even considering it. I have generously taken this into account, and have instructed my devil not to harm you unless you tell three lies. That was the first, but I believe any civilized person would be able to proceed without a second, and only an enemy of Othean should tell a third."

"Ah," said Domingo, and almost apologized before catching himself—that might be considered a lie, too, since he was only sorry he'd been called out for offering idle blandishments to this Immaculate warlord...and that she had a lie-detecting devil with a very big mouth pointed directly at him and Choi. "I understand, Your Elegance."

"Excellent," said the empress. "In that case you may yet prove your province's use to Othean, as I have a number of questions that perhaps you can answer."

"I hope you find my answers satisfactory," said Domingo, eyeing the so-called unicorn.

"From our interrogation of various Cobalt officers we know that they believe you led the Fifteenth Regiment during this Battle of the Lark's Tongue. We know they believe it was your collusion with the Burnished Chain and a great sacrifice of many thousands that opened a new Gate upon the battlefield. We know they also believe that this ritual sacrifice lifted the storm from the Haunted Sea and brought about the return of Jex Toth." The empress shifted slightly forward in her throne. "What I ask you now, Baron Hjortt, is if what they believe is all true."

"I...I believe so," said Domingo, and hastened to add, "save for that speculation about the Sunken Kingdom coming back. The rest of it I know for certain, and I do believe that was indeed the Chain's goal in carrying out their ritual. But the only real intelligence we received about the return of Jex Toth came from you, Your Elegance, when you wrote to...to the Cobalt Command, and spoke of monsters besieging the Isles."

"Jex Toth has indeed returned," said the empress, so offhandedly she might as well have been discussing the seasonal migration of starlings. "The presence of monsters has yet to be confirmed. Othean's lamentable but unavoidable deception to lure back the last traitor of Hwabun was predicated on a hundred prophecies from not only the Isles but all of the Star. Many believed that when the Sunken Kingdom rose it would bring with it a calamitous evil, and so our ruse capitalized on that fear. Yet now the Imperial Navy of Diadem arrives flying Chainite flags, seeking sanctuary at Othean under the very same pretext we offered the Cobalt Company—an army of demons plots to assail the Star, and we must rally together as mortals to confront the scourge."

Domingo waited, and so did the empress, and when no actual question was advanced, he said, "They do?"

"That is what I seek to find out," said the empress crossly, as though Domingo were being the difficult one here. "I know the Imperial fleet initially bypassed our blockade, and I know upon returning from Jex Toth they sought amnesty from my navy and safe passage here to Othean. What I do not know is if their claim is true, or if it is a deception of the Crimson Empire to gain access to Othean. Is this all part of your plot to destroy me?"

"*My* plot? I don't have any plot!" As soon as the words left Domingo's mouth he knew they were a mistake, the monster at the foot of the stairs standing up straight again, its pale scales shimmering as it crossed the tiles and then sat down in front of his chair. It was too late to put the rash words back in his mouth, but he could still try to outmaneuver the empress and her devil. "What I meant to say is I was never aware of the scope of the Burnished Chain's plot. I only discovered too late what they intended at the Battle of the Lark's Tongue, and ever since that day I have been stuck with the Cobalts, and even less aware of the Chain's scheming than I was before. I have heard the Crimson Queen has fallen, and the Black Pope has taken complete control of Diadem—and if the Imperial fleet is flying black flags that's further proof, isn't it? So if anyone seeks to deceive you and your nation it's likely the Burnished Chain...but you're the one with the bloody devil, so why not call this thing off me and put it on someone who knows something!"

The empress did not respond, staring down at Domingo and her monster, and then she sniffed.

"I see no purpose in allowing a single Outlander to set foot on

Othean, be they Imperial or Chainite or both," said the empress, puffing up in her nest of white finery like a spoiled cockatoo. "If they are false then we have fallen into their trap to gain access to our shores. If they speak true then we would be declaring our allegiance with them, and incurring the wrath of whatever unknown forces they have provoked upon Jex Toth. This is the law of spirits, a truth we have maintained since the Age of Wonders—do not call up that which you cannot put down, and do not come between a devil and its vengeance. I hereby deny the Imperial fleet sanctuary; exile them immediately, before whatever calamity that pursues them is visited upon us."

One of the ministers kneeling behind the yellow-robed contingent quietly rose to her feet and padded out, her muffled footfalls fading as she crossed the hall.

"I realize you're the Empress of the Isles and can do any fool thing that crawls under that wig of yours, but doesn't that seem rash?" asked Domingo, too overcome with indignation at her stupefyingly superstitious line of reasoning to remain diplomatic. "What if there *is* an army of devils or what-have-you on Jex Toth, and they don't hold to the enlightened view of only wanting revenge on the Chain for summoning them? What if they behave exactly like they do in all the legends you spoke of and wage war against us all? And even if such creatures do only come after the Imperial navy, your Isles lie squarely between Jex Toth and the rest of the Star, so you don't have much choice about coming between monsters and their meal!"

"I should not expect an Azgarothian to comprehend our traditions," said the empress, her smug expression matching that of the scaly devil that remained uncomfortably close to Domingo's crotch. "The Burnished Chain misunderstands the First Dark and its mysteries, but you ignorant people deny them altogether. There is more to existence than simply life, and more to life than simply being alive. The Immaculate Isles shall stand as we always have, apart and above the schemes of lesser lands. Our purity protects us, and should any ignoble army assault us, be they mortal or spirit, they shall be overcome, and in righteous fashion."

"Well, that certainly sounds exactly like the rot the Chain's always spouting," said Domingo, because even with a devil breathing on his fruit basket he couldn't stand to hear spiritual claptrap informing military policy. "Purity this and righteousness that in place of common sense! Your monster here knows I'm telling the truth, too, or that would've been my third offense, wouldn't it? So if you won't listen to me, why don't you listen to him?!"

The yellow-robed attendants remained as still and mute behind their masks as the statue their creepy bird sat atop, but murmurs rippled through the previously silent rows of kneeling nobles, each a monarch of one of the hundreds of Immaculate Isles that all paid homage to the Samjok-o Throne. But were some of them agreeing with Domingo and his sound argument, or were they all simply offended he'd spoken in such a fashion to their empress? He never got to find out, because without seeming the least bit perturbed by the conduct of her guest Empress Ryuki asked the last question he would have ever wanted to hear leave her wrinkly lips. Well, one of them, anyway.

"Well then, Baron Hjortt, since it is presumably separate from any designs of the Burnished Chain, what is your plot to destroy me?"

That was that, then, the unicorn's horn bobbing in the air and its scaly muzzle pulling back to show its full array of teeth as it offered Domingo a final smile. He should try to distract it with a lie, to lure it in to attack him so he could wrap his arms around its neck and pin it still long enough for Choi to charge up the steps of the throne. He could die helping the woman take her vengeance, vengeance that was more righteous than anything Empress Ryuki spoke of…but looking up past the devil at the self-satisfied face of the empress and seeing the ghost of her son looking back at him, he supposed he could do all of them one better.

"It wasn't part of my plot when I first rolled in here, I admit, but I did just hit on something choice," drawled Domingo, looking Empress Ryuki in the eye. "I murdered your son Byeong-gu, under nobody's orders but my own. I suppose I could have mentioned this to someone sooner, Your Elegance, but that's just my bad Azgarothian manners."

The empress and all her court were dumbstruck, but Choi growled low in her throat. Looking over to where she crouched beside him on her cushion, her fists tight and her gap-fanged snarl directed at him instead of the Samjok-o Throne, he gave a humble little shrug.

"No," said the empress decisively—he had momentarily rattled her with the ghastly suggestion, but he could tell she didn't believe him. "The traitor Ji-hyeon Bong of Hwabun assassinated my fourth son, the Prince Byeong-gu. They were betrothed. She sent me his—"

"Head in a box, wrapped up in a Cobalt flag, yes?" said Domingo, savoring the slow collapse of the empress's face—this must have been how Brother Wan felt when he'd finally been able to reveal his plot in the back of that damn wagon. "That is exactly what I wanted Othean to think, after I caught your runt and his bodyguards skulking around just south of that new wall you're putting up around Linkensterne. He gave me all the information he had, willingly I might add, and I murdered him. *On his knees.* This was a long time before we ever caught up with General Ji-hyeon ourselves, but I thought it might be just the thing to get the Immaculate juices flowing for a little joint offensive against the Cobalts, if it became necessary. Unlike you enlightened people who would rather lose a war than combine forces with an *ignoble army*, as you put it, we Azgarothians take a far more utilitarian perspective."

"Ji-hyeon ordered it," said the empress, climbing unsteadily to her feet on the top step of her stupid pavilion. "Ji-hyeon Bong ordered you to do it."

"You drove her back into the Othean Gate without her ever knowing it was me," said Domingo, relishing the sensation of deflating the empress in front of her entire court. The previously unflappable figures in yellow were whispering to one another behind their masks now, even their vulture ruffling its feathers at the outrage, and Domingo spoke yet louder, making sure even the minor nobles in the back rows could hear him. "Nobody knew—not Ji-hyeon nor Choi here, nor anybody else in the Cobalt Company. And you, Your Elegance, you murdered Ji-hyeon Bong, and her family, and an entire Isle's worth of your loyal subjects, all because you couldn't even wait until you had the accused general in your hands so you could question her in front of your devil. If you had just bided your time and interrogated her here instead of mounting that spectacle out by the Gate, you would have known she was innocent. Her whole family was innocent. Everyone was innocent but *me*. Isn't that right, you ugly bastard?"

And because he didn't expect to need it much longer, anyway, Domingo stuck out his sword hand and gave the unicorn's scaled head a pet. The devil seemed just as surprised by this as the empress had been by Domingo's announcement, but it quickly warmed to him. Its rumbling purr was almost as loud as the heavy footsteps charging up behind them, and he smiled to hear the clink of armor here in this throne room where the empress had thought herself invincible but now staggered from the heaviest blow of all—the comprehension that through hubris and folly one has been the death of those who trusted them most, those whom they swore to lead and protect.

"I regret I didn't tell you sooner," he told the still-kneeling Choi as the armed guards swarmed them, and he gave the purring devil a final stroke. "But I can't tell you I'm sorry I did it, not now that I've finally made a friend here in Othean!"

Domingo Hjortt was still savoring this, his final victory, as they wheeled his chair to the end of the terra-cotta road and his involuntary reunion with the Gate that lay within the Temple of Pentacles.

CHAPTER
21

It was the first time Ji-hyeon had properly slept since she had escaped into the Othean Gate. She'd begun to doubt her body even remembered how to sleep for more than a few fitful hours anymore, starting her awake at the slightest sound, but once it came upon her it was *glorious*. People of all Arms of the Star often referred to the First Dark as the wellspring of dreams, or the land where dreamers traveled in their sleep...but then most people had never spent much time on this side of a Gate, or they wouldn't have believed such nonsense for a moment. One thing that had sawed its way into Ji-hyeon's skull with grinding clarity was that this place was all too real. Everything alien and other about the landscape and its inhabitants was only in relation to her, the true outsider, and it was a world as coldly mundane as the one she had left.

Thus, when she finally slipped from a deep slumber into gentle dreams that bore no resemblance to either the dusty grey wastes or the radiant impressions that crowded her devil-eye she felt such joy as she had forgotten existed. Afterward, when she awoke and found Duchess Din and Chevaleresse Sasamaso waiting by her bedside in the hollow ruins of a temple, asking if she had suffered nightmares, for she had wept in her sleep, she shook her head and told them they must have been tears of relief, for her dreams still had all the color the world had lost.

"Not all of the realms beyond the Star are so dreary as this," said Din, looking wistfully up at the eternally drab sky through a rent in the ancient stone roof.

"As proven by your breakfast," said Sasamaso, offering Ji-hyeon a beaten copper bowl of jewel-bright seeds tossed in something clear and viscous, a tin spoon stuck in the mess. "Eat as much of this as you can, General, it will help you recover."

The two older women sat on great blocks of pale marble beside Ji-hyeon, who slowly sat up on one elbow in her lumpy bedroll. She was lying on a cushion of pine boughs, the smells of crushed needles and oozing sap sharp in her hungry nostrils. She felt like old man Ruthless, laid out on his bier back at the Lark's Tongue camp. Her heart quickened to be awake and without a weapon in hand's reach, but then she saw her gear piled in a corner of the dusty chamber, the hilts of her swords protruding from the heap. Pressing her palm into the wool bedding and feeling the bend of the branches and the prick of the needles brought a lump to her throat; it had been so long since she had found a tree that was not blasted and brittle, since she had scented something green and healthy...

"How long were you down there?" asked Chevaleresse Sasamaso, perhaps recognizing something familiar in her young general's expression.

"Two...two years," said Ji-hyeon, and now she was crying, not for herself but for the two old women who were being so kind to her, two women who had been here decades longer than her but still treated her as though she were the one who had suffered. "Only two years."

"*Only!*" Count Hassan slipped past the thin blanket that hung over the doorway to the room, carrying a weathered brass tea service that clattered in his unsteady hands. "Small wonder you look so beastly."

"Hassan," scolded Din.

"It's true," he said, setting down the steaming tray on another of the room's scattered blocks. "And I was putting it politely, wasn't I?"

"Yes, well, you don't have to say it at all," said Din, picking up the bowl Sasamaso had set on the floor when Ji-hyeon had broken down and reoffering it. "Just a few bites for now? I cannot imagine what you've been living off in such a place as this, but I doubt it was wholesome."

"I don't have to imagine," said Sasamaso. "I was the one who had to find out where the smell was coming from in her bags, remember. Our general has been eating rougher than she's been sleeping, no small feat. I'm surprised it didn't poison her, even with her devil."

"Fellwing," said Ji-hyeon, sitting up straighter in her bed and almost knocking the bowl of food out of Din's outstretched hand... but then she felt her owlbat stir under the blankets and come climbing up the clean shift they'd changed her into. The devil smacked her beak as she tasted the long-absent flavors of contentment and comfort in her mistress's breast, however mean the morsels. Looking up at the haggard but happy faces of the three Cobalts she had given up for dead after the Battle of the Lark's Tongue, Ji-hyeon asked, "But how did you all survive this hell without devils to help you? And for... for so long? How has it been so long?"

"This land is one of many, General, and some of them flirt with the hospitable," said Hassan as he poured steamy tea into little metal cups.

"As I was in the midst of explaining before the Count barged in," said Din. "We arrived somewhere very different, and only came to this eyesore for you."

"And as for how you appear before us so fresh-faced, that is not something we can explain, but it is hardly out of joint with our previous experiences," said Sasamaso, taking the hot cup Hassan had offered Ji-hyeon and holding it for her general as she ate. The juicy seeds were so tart and the syrup so sweet she felt like her teeth might crumble, but her tongue was happier than it had ever been. "Since last we saw you, General, we have lived more than half our lives, and experienced such miracles and nightmares as makes your perpetual youth a minor matter."

"That may be oversimplifying things slightly," said Din. "Meloy thinks it might mean—"

"Whatever Shea thinks it means is beside the point for now," said Hassan, blowing on his tea. "Isn't the whole point to ease her into things as gently as possible, not overwhelm her with everything at once?"

"I've spent two years fighting for my life against the worst things imaginable, and some things that I couldn't imagine at all," said Ji-hyeon through a mouthful of her heavenly breakfast. "You don't have to worry about using the baby general gloves on me. It was bad enough back home, and I'd say I'm well past the need for being coddled at this point. I don't expect *anything* to make sense out here past the Gates, so on the slim chance something does we're already coming out ahead."

The three looked around at each other but nobody seemed to know where to begin, so Ji-hyeon took charge, licking the spoon spotless and then trading her empty bowl for the tea in Sasamaso's hand. "Just start from the beginning. The Battle of the Lark's Tongue. What happened after that, how'd you end up here?"

"We don't have that kind of time right now," said Hassan, and the others nodded in agreement. "It's a very, very long story, and you know better than anyone this place is not safe. So until we have moved on to a less perilous country it would be best to focus on the immediate concerns you shall have."

"My only immediate concern is that this is real and not some fucked-up hell for sinners too stupid to realize they're dead," said Ji-hyeon, inhaling the steam from her tea. Once she might have thought it smelled weak and dirty, but now the faint grassy scent made her dizzy with excitement. "It's not that, is it? We're all still alive?"

"We are all still alive," confirmed Din. "Well, those of us who survived the transition, that is, and have lived out the many years since. Not everyone who came over during the event at the Lark's Tongue is still with us."

"A few hundred of the original soldiers, at most," said Sasamaso, stowing Ji-hyeon's dirty bowl and spoon in a sling bag. "Some started families here, so there's another generation, and now those children are having babes of their own... but there aren't many of those who have come of age, not yet. Most of our ranks at this point are recruits we've picked up on this side."

"Wait, a few hundred soldiers?" Ji-hyeon spilled her tea on her hand. It was a comforting hurt compared to all the other kinds she had endured of late, and Fellwing shivered at the novelty of it. "New generations, new recruits?"

"*Ease her into it slowly, he said,*" clucked Hassan. "As if our general ever did anything slow and easy."

"It's not just you four," said Ji-hyeon, a bloom of warmth spreading through her chest. After all she had endured, the thought that her engaging the Fifteenth Regiment that ill-fated morning hadn't automatically condemned all her missing soldiers to death made this land seem more a heaven than a hell. "The Gate opened, you fell through and landed... landed somewhere, somewhere like this, and banded together with the other survivors, some Cobalts and some Crimson, like your friend Shea. And you've found others since you've been here. I'm getting the shape of it?"

"I'm coming in?" came a voice from the other side of the dangling blanket, followed by the Azgarothian captain. "Sorry, you called?"

"If you're going to eavesdrop you ought to bring your earhorn," said Din, smiling at Shea. "The general's just getting the shape of it."

"The shape will take whatever form she gives it," said Sasamaso. "You heard her—our general doesn't need the baby general gloves, she needs gauntlets to hold the reins. She's ready."

"She's not even on her feet!" protested Hassan.

"In my experience that's not necessarily a prerequisite for strong command," said Shea.

"All right, all right, you lost me again," said Ji-hyeon, easing back down on the comfortable bed and closing her right eye even as her left itched to be let free. She was glad that while they'd dusted her off and changed her into the first clean garment she'd worn since coming here, they'd had the sense to leave her insulated eye patch in place. "Just give me a moment here. Just a moment."

"As long as you need, General!"

"But as quickly as you can?"

"Shea!"

"It's a long way back to the Cobalts and he's not been well, you know this!"

"The Cobalts," breathed Ji-hyeon, keeping her eye closed as she stroked Fellwing and listened to the lullaby of bickering captains. Exhausted as she was, she really owed it to herself to take another nap while she was on such a comfortable bed . . . and then her eye snapped open and she sat back up. "The Cobalts. She has them; Empress Ryuki captured them. I fled back through the Othean Gate but I was the only one. I think."

"Now there's a song to hear," said Shea, leaning over the foot of Ji-hyeon's bed. "How many of the Fifteenth survived the Battle of the Lark's Tongue? I know most of us tumbled through, but did—"

"Not now, Shea, can't you see she's in a state?" said Hassan, which Ji-hyeon was willing to fess to, yes she was. Elated as she'd felt before, now a panic gripped her bones and rattled her soul. Her teeth were chattering in time with Fellwing's clicking beak as she looked around in disbelief at these walking, talking phantoms or fever dreams or whatever they were. She was in hell, haunted by their spirits, it was the only explanation.

"Shea's not talking about your Cobalts, General . . . or rather, not those Cobalts," said Sasamaso. "Our Cobalts. The ones who came through with us, and the Crimson soldiers who joined us, and all the able hands we've taken on since then. Near to three thousand, all waiting for their general to return."

"It was foretold you would pass through this place, so we volunteered to wait for you," said Din, bearing more than a passing resemblance to a wild-eyed old crazy person. "And now that you have come we need to return to the rest, so he can see you, and so the others can see that he was right, that it was all true."

"Wait, *how* did you know where to wait?" asked Ji-hyeon, all these voices bouncing around this tight little room after so much solitude and silence making her head pound. "How did you know *to* wait? Who foretold this, who has to see me?"

"The oracle?" said Shea. "He prophesied your coming, and now that you have, that means the rest of it must be true, too. Doesn't it?"

"Prophecies and oracles," said Ji-hyeon, feeling sorry for whoever had given these desperate old-timers the impression she was anything but trouble for anyone who looked to her for help. "All right, Count Hassan, I'd say I'm good and eased into it now—what's the prophecy, exactly? That I accidentally push you all into a new Gate, follow along afterward, and then what?"

"Then you lead us back to the Star," said Sasamaso, and from the look on the fierce Flintlander's face she not only believed this but had for a very long time. It was the expression of a devout Chainite, or some such true believer. "We've built the Company back up in preparation for your coming. We've trained. We've armed ourselves. And now we're ready."

"As the Star falls under the shadow of the First Dark, you guide us home," said Hassan. "To defend our realm."

"But first the weapon," murmured Din. "First you must acquire the weapon we need to save the Star."

Ji-hyeon tried not to smile, and then tried not to giggle, and then tried not to lose her shit altogether, but there was nothing for it, and next thing she knew she was laughing in their demented old faces. Either she had lost her mind entirely or they had. Ji-hyeon Bong, the chosen one who would save the Star. Once upon a time she had believed that, but all along she had been nothing but a snot-nosed brat, and the last two years had taught her just how naïve she had been. She laughed and laughed, and the four codgers all looked very serious about it, talking about her as if she weren't even there, until one of them said a name that fell on her ears like a hammer to the side of a bell.

"What did you say?"

She had gone from hysterical laughter to deadly calm so quickly they kept talking right over her until she repeated herself, her voice breaking this time.

"What did you say?"

"Now you've done it," Hassan growled at Shea, who had spoken the name.

"He told us to ease you into it?" protested Shea, wrinkled hands in the air. "And that it would be a shock to hear he was here, too, and he didn't want us to worry you, so we shouldn't say—"

"The oracle you follow, the one who foretold my coming..." said Ji-hyeon, Fellwing looking up, holding her breath along with her mistress.

"Your father, King Jun-hwan," said Din, meeting Ji-hyeon's teary eye with a look of infinite pity. "I'm so sorry to be the one to tell you, General, but he was cast into the First Dark, too."

"And your sisters as well," said Sasamaso, scowling at Shea. "Would that you didn't hear in such a fashion, when you are already under such strain, but there seems little point in denying it now."

"Well, they're all still alive?" said Shea. "I mean, nobody wants to have their family tossed into a Gate, but it could be worse?"

Ji-hyeon couldn't agree more, and pushing past their weak attempts to keep her in bed a little longer, she staggered to her gear and seized up her sword belt. She'd wasted enough time already, and it didn't do to be late to your own prophecy... or a family reunion. Some things were true on both sides of the First Dark.

CHAPTER
22

Reuniting with her creator on Jex Toth had not gone quite as Y'Homa had anticipated. Instead of taking the numinous essence of the Fallen Mother into her mortal body she found herself dwelling within the eternal flesh of the Allmother, walking the lonely halls of her viscera, praying at the altars of her organs. The Chain Canticles had gotten so, so much wrong, but the one thing they had gotten right was that the Black Pope had indeed sacrificed herself for the good of the world, and in doing so drawn in that breath of the divine that would grant her wisdom above any scholar, power over every mortal creature, and life eternal. Just as she spent her undying days in the living temple of the Fallen Mother, so, too, did the angel who had saved her from the First Dark reside inside her own frame, like a second heart that had grown inside her breast. A second brain inside her heavy skull, burning bright with questions. A second soul trapped in her shivering skin, restlessly pacing through her bones.

It could not be trusted, the old clerics of Jex Toth had told her. She must become its master or be driven mad by its constant scrabbling for the ship's wheel of her mind, the endless pressure to grant it control of the body they shared.

As if they knew the first thing about it. For all their talk of having broken their angels, each and every one of the Vex Assembly slipped up at times, speaking in tongues not their own, indulging appetites that ran counter to their waking hungers. In point of fact, they were all barking mad with little connection to reality; they claimed their kingdom had been transported to a paradise beyond the First Dark for countless eons, for example, when any uneducated bumpkin in the Star could tell you Jex Toth had vanished a mere five hundred years before.

Bold and brash as these heathens had been when Y'Homa had first arrived, with the audacity to imply *she* was the one who had misunderstood the gospel, now she knew better. Even after half a millennium of cohabitation the other angeliacs warred against their divine halves, whereas Y'Homa had made peace with her own celestial passenger after only a brief if intense adjustment period. *Everything happens.* Whatever minor details the Burnished Chain had gotten wrong, that highest scriptural truth had prepared Y'Homa for her own Day of Becoming in ways the Tothans would never understand, had allowed her to accept her transformation absolutely, for indeed, everything happens. The difference between Y'Homa and her saviors was that she sought only to love that piece of the Fallen Mother that had fused with her soul, even if she could never understand it, while the rest of the Vex Assembly sought to exploit and control that which was by its very nature beyond their ken. This was why their minds had been fractured, she surmised, because their souls were unworthy—only the purest vessel could contain such intense power and not crack.

Despite her superiority over the rest of the Vex Assembly she was nevertheless bound to Sherdenn, the high priest who had sacrificed her to the Fallen Mother. By dropping her into the Tothan Gate he had transformed her from a mere window for the eyes of the divine to a living door for a higher power. For this she owed the ancient cleric far more than just her resurrected life—she owed him the very salvation of her soul, and that of the angel who had entered her. Imperfect though he and all the other Tothans were, they had been chosen by the Fallen Mother, the same as she, and together they were remaking the Star as their maker had ordained. Everything happens, and when the time came Y'Homa would supplant Sherdenn and the rest, rising to her rightful station as the Fallen Mother's sole hierophant.

For now, however, they must all proudly work together to serve the

Allmother. They were the key that would turn the lock that would open the door that would—

Come and see.

Y'Homa blinked her eyes, her breath falling out of rhythm with the pulsing walls of her chamber as she rose from her reverie to answer Sherdenn's summons. The Vex Assembly had little need for the imperfections of the spoken word, casting their very thoughts into each other's skulls across even vast distances. Each silent communication carried its own complex scent, which their soldiers could interpret more readily than word or even thought, and as her eyes watered from the oily cockroach reek Y'Homa answered her mentor with a simple affirmation. As she did she felt in the back of her mind the stirrings of another presence, one that had become so much a part of her it was increasingly indistinguishable from her own. Soon there would be no *she* and *it*, no *and* at all, just one perfect child of the Fallen Mother. In the meantime she strove to become more divine even as its angelic means of thinking became increasingly mortal... or at least comprehensible.

Dress.

She doubted she would have need of her armor anytime soon but nevertheless indulged her angel's desire to gird itself, allowing it to summon her swarm with a breath of musk. The spiny insects swept over her raw skin, grey legs slipping into the red indentations and puckered furrows in her creamy flesh as they harmoniously locked into place. Her royal armor was far more ostentatious than that of the legions in her command, and a far cry from the simple scuttling robes they had cloaked her in before she recovered from her resurrection. The queen skittered up the back of her neck, thick legs wrapping around Y'Homa's face to form her mask. The Black Pope smiled as the comforting warm weight settled atop her skull, a bloom of black quills falling luxuriously backward from her living crown as she strode though the glistening aperture that opened in the wall.

The mucus-slick passageways that had seemed so intimidating when she first arrived on Jex Toth now put her at ease, the floor shifting to help her keep her footing as the walls swayed and lurched from side to side. It felt almost like being back in the First Dark, surrounded by a vast nurturing pressure. Sherdenn was not in his chamber, and she followed the path he had mapped out in her mind, her nostrils flaring from the lingering psychic scent. From the sweet tang that now complemented his sharp fragrance Y'Homa could tell that Lagren was with him, which meant something important must indeed be afoot—the spider-frocked priestess had kept to herself of late.

Deeper and deeper they wormed into their enormous host, and finally a pulsing curtain of tissue spread itself wide for Y'Homa to join her fellows. Sherdenn had dressed for the occasion in layer upon layer of gem-bright vermin, and Lagren's gown of cobweb lace beaded with egg sacs was even more ornate that ever, but neither Y'Homa nor her angel paid them any notice, staring at what lay beyond the pair. The outer wall of the narrow chamber bulged outward, and through the translucent shell she saw that their leviathan had at long last surfaced, and their target filled the horizon.

The war begins, Sherdenn murmured in her mind as Y'Homa stepped past him, staring out at the blue waters, at the other leviathans rising like sunken kingdoms all around them, and the helpless green shore beyond.

Before she had become host to the heavenly, Y'Homa had been terrified of being sent away from Jex Toth. To be exiled from the corporeal manifestation of the Fallen Mother felt like nothing short of damnation…yet now Y'Homa understood her greater purpose. She had not been drawn to Jex Toth because it was the Garden of the Star—it wasn't. The Vex Assembly's attempt to transform their homeland into heaven had been thwarted by their jealous enemies, the ritual interrupted, the miracle compromised, and the faithful banished. Y'Homa had resurrected Jex Toth and sailed to its shores not to merely assume a place of power—she had fulfilled her destiny because the Fallen Mother needed her favorite daughter to retrieve that holiest of seeds that had survived the ages of darkness and bring it back to the world, to plant the true Garden of the Star and see that this time it took root.

The righteous did not hide in heaven. The righteous carried heaven with them, even as they sojourned down into hell. Y'Homa was not leaving the Fallen Mother behind in Jex Toth, she was bringing Her to the Star.

The enthusiasm of her angel was contagious, and when the question of who would lead the assault on the Star came to a vote Y'Homa had joyously volunteered. Now they had arrived, the living holds of their leviathans pregnant with both angelic soldiers and the malformed spawn of the Deceiver they had kept in ravenous captivity, eager to be loosed upon the wicked world, desperate to offer the final sacrifice...

And now the wait was over.

PART II

INFERNAL FREEDOM

The devil tempts us not—'tis we tempt him,
Beckoning his skill with opportunity.
—George Eliot,
Felix Holt, The Radical (1866)

CHAPTER

1

In the end it took three barbers, seven varieties of bugs, and twelve hours of surgery to save Zosia's life. All that, and the assistance of the beefiest militia thug in that quarter of the castle to remove one of the arrowheads from where it was lodged in the Stricken Queen's clavicle. The oak shaft had splintered off before either steel or bone would yield, requiring the brawny volunteer to wrench it free with pliers after none of the surgeons were able to wiggle it loose. That arrowhead, along with the rest, were reverently collected so that they could be later incorporated into the memorial statue raised to all of Zosia's countless victims; the five crossbowers she had murdered with her hammer before succumbing to her wounds in the Upper Chainhouse were the final martyrs of the revolution.

Or so the story went. Boris suspected the actual arrowheads were already on the black market, priceless relics to the right collector, or potent components to would-be witches or alchemists. Everything else she'd touched—or that had touched her—was probably long gone, too, he assumed, though even with his connections he hadn't been admitted to the royal residences of Castle Diadem, where she had left all of her things while attending that fatal first council meeting.

Ah, but he did know where her hammer was—that was going to be used during the public execution, once both queens were recovered enough to be skinned alive.

"Flayed with a hammer?" Zosia asked him and the three heavily armed guards who were her constant companions in the cell where she lay loosely shackled to a cot. "Cruel *and* unusual, and also a decent metaphor for your revolution's back-asswardness."

"Ah, no, the idea's they break your feet with Sister Portolés's maul, but you're chained upright so you can't help but have your weight on 'em, and *then* the skinning starts," Boris clarified, leaning back on the stool he'd brought along this time. "Indsorith's got some treasured sword they'll use for the flaying, make sure you're both taken apart with your own weapons."

"Subtle," said Zosia, not looking up from the lump of briar she was carving, the vise clamped to her bed frame making her whole cot shake, her lap scattered with tools and wood shavings. She'd been a little surprised they'd granted her last request, seeing as it involved pointy things, but Boris smirked at her reaction when he'd brought the pipe-making kit—as if the revolution had anything to fear from *her*. With the guards always watching her and the carefully supervised packing up of the tools and vise at the end of the day, it would have taken far more effort than it was worth to properly shank one of the bastards. And knowing how hard they were managing the story of Cold Cobalt's final hours they probably *wanted* her to try to kill herself, just so she could fail and be proven a coward. "Think once I'm done with this you can bring me a navy twist? Some folk swear by straight burly or red vergin leaf to break in a briar, but I always like my cake with a sip of rhum...or is letting me carve a pipe but denying me tubāq part of the torture?"

"I don't expect you'll live long enough to see that thing through," said Boris. "Briar's the toughest wood there is, aye? Now that you're strong enough to properly turn it I expect you're fit enough to pay for your crimes."

"Oh," said Zosia, setting her rasp down as her hands began to tremble. So that explained it.

"Don't let me stop you," he said, popping another piece of the roast chicken he'd brought her into his sore-marked mouth. He'd already eaten most of the small bird, as he usually did before leaving her with a plate of greasy bones. "I'm but the eyes of my betters, not brains nor mouth—just 'cause I think you're fit for the flensing hardly means the council will agree. They might want you able to dance before they call you out on the floor."

"No brains, but plenty of mouth in my experience," said Zosia, the words leaving her lips as easily as the shape of the briar revealed itself in her hands, despite how foggy headed she felt.

"You ever experienced my mouth you'd show me a bit more respect," said Boris, licking a dimpled piece of skin off his fingers as he turned to the guards crowding the cell. Zosia's accommodations were so dank and small she suspected it might be the same dungeon she'd rescued Indsorith from. "You know this old she-goat wanted to hit up a brothel tent just afore we came over? Tells you what kind of a person she is, the thought of blood and fire and the deviltry of the First Dark getting her randy as a spring ram."

The guards were too well disciplined to ever participate in the little man's nonsense, but as usual they looked on with a mix of amusement and embarrassment at his treatment of the prisoner who had once been the very symbol of their uprising. Zosia cocked her head at him, considering. There wasn't enough give in her shackle to actually reach Boris, but if she flicked a file at his face she might just get lucky and take out an eye.

"Yeah, I'm such an asshole, offering to buy you a lustworker before asking you to stick out your neck," she said, deciding to wait until she was definitely losing her tool privileges before going after him. "No wonder you don't like me, Heretic, all I ever did was treat you ill."

"Told you not to call me that," he said, slurping on the end of a drumstick.

"Right, only your war nun girlfriend got to use that pet name, I forgot," she said, which got the fucking stoat to drop the bone back on the plate and stand to leave.

"Always a pleasure, Yer Majesty," said Boris, offering a ridiculous bow as he rolled the chicken carcass off the plate and onto her saw-dusty bedding. "Enjoy your dinner, and we'll see if tomorrow brings breakfast or a pair of broken heels."

"I'm on pins and needles," she told him, which was true

enough—besides having painful, itchy holes sewn up in her chest and shoulder and hip and bicep, the rest of her was near-constantly tingling.

"Ah, and almost forgot," he said as the guard posted outside unlocked the barred door of the cell. "Indsorith prayed me deliver a message to you."

"Mmm?" Zosia tried to remain unreadable but the hand that had reached for the ruins of the bird was shaking worse than ever. On his first visit she'd made the mistake of asking what had happened to Indsorith and Choplicker, but when it became obvious he was only going to fuck with her she'd stopped giving him the satisfaction.

"Aye, and it sounded important, so maybe if you're nicer to your only friend the next time I call I'll remember what it was." Stepping out into the corridor, he blew her a kiss, and then was gone.

And that's why you don't help strangers. Zosia cleaned what meat and marrow he'd left her from the mess on her sheets, trying to remember just how long she'd been down here. Tried to remember what she had ever seen in Boris to make her think she could trust him, and why she had thought it was important to stick around to help fix things here in Diadem, instead of just cutting out with Indsorith as soon as they opened up the castle. Tried to remember what Kang-ho's stupid daughter was named, General Tip-of-the-tongue *still* not showing up with the Cobalt Company to liberate Diadem. Zosia tried to remember a hundred other little things, and gave up on the lot, focusing on scavenging enough flesh from a scrawny chicken carcass to keep herself going until her enemies came to kill their enfeebled old nemesis. She couldn't stop them from trying, and in the meantime she had a briar beauty to finish. She would be devildamned if her last smoke was out of a corncob fucking pipe.

CHAPTER

2

Devils and the First Dark. Two things any sane mortal sought to avoid at all costs. Even if you didn't have superstitious motivations for shunning them, simple old horse sense advised against meddling with blatantly dangerous powers you had no way of understanding. Then again, as of tonight Purna was officially a dead woman, so what did she have to fear from anything?

"Before we begin I need to make sure we all understand exactly what is going to happen," said Hoartrap as he stepped up onto the creaky pulpit of the ruined church and overlooked his meager congregation. "Once I begin the invocation the walls between worlds will grow thinner and thinner until there is nothing at all separating ours from theirs, and that is not the time for you to interrupt my focus with inanities."

"All we have to do is lay hands on the sacrifices and repeat your words, but not disturb the circle," said Keun-ju, looking down at the hypnotized rat at his feet. The animal stood just within the band of red sand that composed the outer ring of the pentagram, staring at the candle mounted on a giant bird skull in the center of the symbol. The red wax taper had turned black as it burned halfway down. Across the pentagram from Keun-ju's rat was Best's badger, the woman herself outside on a natural errand, and at the front of the star was the three-legged hound Purna had carried in here.

"Where's your cat?" Purna asked Hoartrap, nodding at the three remaining animals. "With Sullen dipping out I get why you let his go, but don't you still need a sacrifice for yourself?"

"Four is a very inauspicious number," said Hoartrap, as if everybody ought to have known that already. "And devils are bad enough luck without trying to get cute with how many you draw in at one time. No, circumstances dictate a slight change of plans but to the same end result—we call forth the devils, you bind them to mortal flesh, and then as soon as the ritual is complete you transfer their ownership to me. I use them to clear our path to Jex Toth, and that's a good night's bad magic."

"Transfer ownership?" asked Purna, the one cool part about this plot being the part where she got to loose a devil in exchange for a magical voyage to Jex Toth. "You can do that, like they were what, a thoroughbred yak you were selling with proof of pedigree?"

"Less paperwork but about the same, yes," said Hoartrap, juggling a round clay jar from hand to hand. "It's how Ji-hyeon came by her father's owlbat—Kang-ho granted the devil its freedom from his will, so long as it faithfully served his daughter instead. Strange though they seem to us, most devils are no different from any simple creature, beholden to their own laws of nature, and once you learn how to exploit their innate behavior you've come a long way toward domestication."

"Uh-huh," said Purna, looking down at the old hound that stood transfixed in the pentagram. She and her mentor had argued at length about the nature of devils, and while Hoartrap's explanation jibed more with her preconceptions of such entities than Maroto's reverential view, the Touch's casual talk of exploitation made her feel icky. She felt bad about offering up a dying dog to lure in a spirit of the First Dark, obviously, but what about whatever poor devil took the bait, only to be turned over to a warlock that would eat it alive, or worse, employing it to further ambitions it could never understand? It must just be her Ugrakari roots wiggling to the surface, but sometimes it seemed like this misery was all it meant to be mortal, a neverending cycle of abuse against every other living thing…

"And you're sure we can't use the devils to go to Othean first?" asked Keun-ju. "Just to quickly report in with the general before going on to the Sunken Kingdom?"

"If we had an actual Gate at our disposal it would certainly be feasible." Hoartrap rolled up the sleeves of his robe and started slathering on black grease from the pot he had tucked under one armpit. "We do not, however, and simple as I may make it appear, neither the conjuring of devils nor the employment of them to facilitate passage through the First Dark is an easy business. It's hard work, it's dangerous work, and it's not the sort of thing I do just so lovesick boys can rendezvous with lovesick girls."

The old Keun-ju would have jumped at the bait, but his time with Purna and Digs had apparently inured him against the warlock's insinuations. "You had anticipated making this journey to Jex Toth some time ago, before our need for recuperation delayed us. I simply think it prudent to ensure that the situation has not changed at Othean."

"You let me worry about Othean," said Hoartrap, bending down and hiking up his hem so he could liberally apply the ebon lard to his elephantine knees. "One of my little friends is keeping an eye on the place for me, and if the armies of Jex Toth drive that far south into the Isles I'll be the first to know about it. In the meantime I am not in a massive hurry to go there myself, owing to a minor disagreement between myself and the Court of the Dreaming Priests. The empress may have offered amnesty to Ji-hyeon and all who follow the Cobalt flag, but even if I trusted the Immaculate sovereign as much as our general does I'm disinclined to see how strictly her pet magicians obey her orders."

Seeing Keun-ju's bug-eyed reaction to the mysterious outfit, Purna asked, "What's the Court of the Dreaming Priests?"

"It is forbidden to even speak their name," said Keun-ju.

"Yes, well, that prohibition may have been the start of our quarrel but it's gone far beyond that now, yes it has," said Hoartrap, putting his grease pot down and going over to daub some from his fingers onto Keun-ju's forehead. "Come on over, Best, it's time to make like your ancestors and reach into the abyss for a prize."

"The soldiers are coming," said Maroto's scary-ass sister as she turned away from the doorway. "Fifty torches, at least, on the road from town."

"They might not be able to see the church from the road?" said Purna, trying to stay positive in the face of an overwhelmingly depressing night.

"Unless those bounty hunters decided it might be safest if you weren't around after all," said Keun-ju. "They have your face already, so perhaps they tipped off the mob from the tavern to hedge their bets that you never return."

"If you sold your face I hope you got a decent price for it," said Hoartrap, coming around to loom over Purna with his ooze-wet hands. Smearing a triangle on her forehead and a pair of dots on each cheek, he clucked his tongue. "No no, not a word, I see from your expression you gave away the farm. And to hoodrat bounty hunters at that! Would that you had come to me with your concerns, my runaway rug rustler, we would have taken care of all your problems long ago."

"Wait, you knew about me, too?" said Purna, her nose wrinkling at the rotten vegetal smell of the ointment.

"There's not much I don't know," said Hoartrap, turning to Best. "Except how a girl as busy as you finds the time to keep her braids so tight. Not a hair out of place."

"Your teeth shall be out of place if you continue to provoke me," said the woman, looking him in the eye as he anointed her. With her horned helm she was as tall as the Touch, though if she was a thick oak he was a trim mountain. "I tell you a warband marches upon your blood ritual and you speak of... grooming."

"I don't know why you'd think we would have time to call down devils if we don't even have time to be civil to one another," sniffed Hoartrap, finishing up Best's markings and stowing the jar back in his pack. "Fortunately I believe we have time for both, as I've gotten my deviltry down to a science, though the sooner we start the better. It will be no good for anyone if some Eyvindian with a bone to pick shoots me through the tongue as I'm trying to reseal the window I've opened into the First Dark. Can you *imagine*?"

"I would rather not," said Keun-ju, glancing nervously at the open doorway.

"Nor I," said Best, her hand going to the sun-knife on her low-slung belt as she glared down at the badger at her feet, as though it had done her some deep personal injury. "Shall I sacrifice this beast now or must you first speak your wizard-lies?"

"Yes, first the wizard-lies," said Hoartrap, returning to the far end of the pentagram on the floor; were it a map of the Star he'd be standing to the south, Best to the east and Keun-ju to the west, and Purna to the north. "No blood need be spilled, however; the act of delivering these scavengers to me was the sacrifice. That's one of the secrets of the First Dark, so obvious most people overlook it entirely—it's not death that devils want, it's life, always life."

"Maroto wouldn't tell me what happened when you did this before," gulped Purna, her face burning where Hoartrap had greased her up. It had been ages since she smoked, but she felt the saam harder than ever. Or perhaps it was just the thickness of the air in the church, the scent of burning sugar rising from the black candle on the great bird skull in the center of the pentagram... "But he said it was the worst thing he ever did."

"Maroto said that?" Hoartrap made a skeptical duckface, then shrugged. "Well, it was prettttty bad—I was a much younger Touch back then, and not knowing just how little it takes to attract a hungry devil, erred on the side of the grandiose, offering-wise. It was a different age, I tell you, we were all just making it up as we went along. Don't tell them I told you this, but in retrospect it's a wonder any of us made it out of Emeritus alive! In this world, anyway, I might have brought us all... well, it doesn't bear lingering on, especially not now. This little séance of ours will be a promenade in the park by comparison, or a stroll in the snow, if you prefer, Best. Why, you can even keep your clothes on!"

"My brother, willingly summoning devils with a witch," said Best scornfully.

"Hey, happens to the best of us," said Purna.

"I do not know if I can do this," said Keun-ju.

"Too late now!" crowed Hoartrap, and emitting an ear-piercing shriek, he tossed a small hunk of metal he'd cupped in his hand out over the pentagram. It was a bronze pyramid, and instead of flying through the pungent air it floated slow and clumsily as a coin sinking in a wishing well. Then it just stopped, hanging in place directly above the black candle, whose green flame jetted higher and higher, turning paler with each pulse...and it wasn't just the flame that lost its color with each guttering blast toward the hovering pyramid, but the candle itself, the black wax turning grey. "To your knees, to your knees! Hold on to your sacrifices, but don't disturb the border!"

"Huh?" Purna shook her head. Even more disturbing than realizing she'd slipped into a trance as she stared at the floating pyramid was coming out of the reverie now, and finding herself in the midst of a profane ritual with no fucking idea of what to do next. She'd just assumed it would all make sense once they got started, that she'd go through the motions without overthinking them...but while it had started to go that way for a hot minute now she was right back in the moment, high and anxious and also really really high?

"Kneel, Purna! Kneel!" Hoartrap's voice wobbled as it slowly crawled through the air...or voices, really, because the words seemed to split to go around the edge of the pentagram and hit her separately, one in each ear. "Hold on to your dog!"

Blinking down, Purna reeled in place at the sudden gulf that loomed beneath her. The skull and the candle were still there, as were the sandy ridges that made up the outlines of the symbol on the floor. That just made the sight even more disorienting, because everything else was gone. What should have been the dirt floor of the church was darkest nothing, a bottomless pit...Except no, it wasn't. It was a pool of black oil, the head of the dog she had brought to this unholy place breaking the still surface at her feet and issuing a scream unlike any she had ever heard in all her battles with mortals and monsters.

"Grab it, Purna!" Hoartrap sounded ecstatic, and she didn't dare look away from where her sacrifice had appeared, for as soon as it had risen it sank again. Purna dropped to her knees on the edge of the pentagram. Something churned in the First Dark, and without a thought for her own safety she thrust her hands into the cold, lightless reaches, desperate to save the poor animal from the fate she had condemned it to. She was a thoroughly modern woman and didn't believe in good and evil or any of that fairy-tale shorthand, a moral relativist through and true…but this was *wrong*. This was wrong wrong wrong, this was evil, and evil of her own making, and she was sobbing out words she didn't understand as her hands passed through nothing, and everything, and nothing…And then she felt fur. "Pull them out, pull them out!"

Purna dug in her fingers, felt wet flank and the hot skin beneath it, the dog still alive, and pulled as hard as she could. The First Dark held on, trying to wrest the hound from her grasp, but Purna would not be denied. She had made a mistake, but she was fixing it, she was fixing it, she would carry the dog out under the stars and let it die a clean death breathing the air of the world that had cradled it, she would—

She tumbled backward onto her ass as the dog came free, an oily blur of the same stinking grease Hoartrap had daubed her with. She held its heat to her chest, jubilant even as the mass of fur and bone shifted in her arms, cracking and snapping and snarling, and she ceased her frantic chanting to press her lips to its small slimy skull. Hoartrap's screams were growing louder and louder, distracting her from the prize that lapped its warm tongue against her warm cheeks, and then there was a great *whomp* like a snowbank dropping off the roof of the barn back home on a sunny winter afternoon. The light went out of the world, and with it went all the warmth, the thing squirming in Purna's arms as cold as the First Dark had been, its tongue wet dead leather, and she thrust it away from her, because whatever the fuck it was it wasn't the three-legged dog she had found in the alley.

"Purna…" A voice growled in the dizzying darkness, her own name ringing in her ears. "Purna, you fucking imbecile, what was the one thing I told you not to do?"

There was a bolt of lightning in the distance, and then another. The third time Hoartrap flicked the coalstick in his shaking, smoking hand it caught the pitch and a torch lit up the church. She didn't even realize he carried one, the Touch always making such a big deal out of how he wasn't even making a big deal of being able to light his pipe or the campfire with an easy snap of his fingers.

In the glare of the torch and the Touch she saw Hoartrap standing over the wreckage in the pentagram, the skull in the center splintered into a thousand shards. What she initially thought was the end of the candle turned out to be a melted blob of bronze that he prodded with his toe. Squinting in the gloom, she saw Keun-ju still on his knees to her left, cuddling something in his hands, and Best backed up all the way to the far wall, staring down with what might have otherwise been comic alarm at the small black badger sitting at her feet, looking up at her. Steeling herself for a peek at her own devil, telling herself it couldn't be as bad as she'd thought, Purna sat up… but instead of an animal at her feet she saw something far stranger. When she'd toppled backward with the devil in her arms her right boot had flopped out just to the edge of the pentagram, but her left had plowed through the line of sand altogether, and she belatedly dragged it back over the broken barrier.

"What…oh." Purna was about to ask what trouble this minor bit of clumsiness might have caused, but then she followed Hoartrap's gaze, looking behind her to see his torchlight shining on a heaving flank of smoldering meat that covered the doorway to the church… no, that *was* the doorway to the church. As she stared the fuming mass fizzed with bubbles of fat, and as each one burst a long-petaled white blossom spilled out, until the whole lintel of the church door was a steaming, dripping flower bed. "Um…did I…"

"Yes, you did, and no, I don't know what the fuck it is," said Hoartrap, and gave a small, joyless chuckle. "But I caught it before it escaped, so that's another favor you owe me, Purna. You and the rest of the fucking world. As if I'll ever collect from you bums."

"Make it go away," said Best, her voice low and calm but strained in a way Purna had never heard. "How do I make it go away?"

"Aren't you even going to give it a name first?" asked Hoartrap, wiping the sheen of grey sweat from his greased-up face with his still faintly smoking hand. "Not necessary, but tradition is—"

"No," breathed Best, the badger at her feet giving an unhappy huff as it looked up at its reluctant mistress. "Tell me the wizard-lies to release it, to make our debts paid."

"Poor little fellow probably knows you'd feed him better than I will," said Hoartrap, finding his good humor now that the intense conclusion of the ritual was past and he could go back to focusing on being dreadful to everyone and everything. "All you have to do is tell it you release it from its bond, on the condition it serves me as it would have served you. Using our full names, if you please."

"I release you from your bond, on the condition you serve Hoartrap the Touch as you would have served Best of the Horned Wolf Clan," said the huntress. Uptight as she already looked about the situation, Best nearly leaped out of her skin altogether when the badger responded by hissing and snapping its teeth at her... but then it turned and waddled over to Hoartrap. It looked about as displeased at being turned over to the sorcerer as Purna would have.

"Yes, you'll do nicely," said Hoartrap as he jammed the torch in the broken floorboards of the raised pulpit and scooped up the badger. It looked no bigger than a marten in his arm, and carrying the docile devil over to his pack, he removed a plain-looking burlap sack and nudged the creature inside. It gave a final ugly snarl at Best, then disappeared inside. "Come on then, Keun-ju, you next."

"I'm sorry," Keun-ju whispered to the rodent in his hands, and then, offering the same terms Best had, he placed the devil in the open sack Hoartrap jutted in his face.

"Yes, yes, we're all so very sorry," said Hoartrap, turning to Purna. "And you, gheefingers, and you—if those Eyvindians didn't know where we were before they certainly do now, and as much fun as it would be to remind them of what happens when they get on the Cobalt Company's bad side, time's a-wasting."

"And me what?" asked Purna, finally picking herself up off the ground and looking around the dim church. "I thought you said it was dead."

"What's dead?"

"My devil," said Purna, looking back at the fleshy garden sprouting from the temple doorway.

"That's not your devil," said Hoartrap, "I told you, I don't know *what* the fuck that is. Your devil took off outside as soon as I fried that weirdness. That's what comes of using dogs, the devils they attract always seem a bit smarter, which is to say, a bit more likely to misbehave. So call it back and hand it over and let's get out of here."

"How do I…" But Purna thought she had some idea before she even finished, and feeling a little jolt of some strange emotion in her chest, she whistled. It was damned hard, on account of her big fat monster tongue, but that had been one of the first things she'd relearned on the long march up here to the Haunted Forest.

And sure enough it did the trick, the devil trotting back inside on its little legs, the dead flowers drifting down overhead to land in its fur like confetti. Its four little legs, not its three long ones. Its ivory fur, nothing like the chestnut coat of the hound. It was…

"Well, I'll be a Maroto's uncle," breathed Hoartrap. "I've never even heard of one doing something like that before."

Friendly as the shuffle-stepping pup appeared, Purna couldn't help but treat it differently than she had before. Back in the Wastes she would have snatched the little bastard up in her arms, growling right back in his face when he acted all tough, but it wasn't like she could just go back to pretending he was nothing more than what he looked like. Prince was not just some spaniel, and noticing the patch of missing fur on his rear haunch and the too-human tongue lolling from his mouth she supposed he wasn't just some devil, either.

"It's not uncommon for them to warp the flesh a little this way or that, to make it more comfortable, but a whole different breed?" Hoartrap shook his head, and the open sack in Purna's direction. "Well, far be it from me to be dogscriminatory, and lapdogs spend just as well as mutts where we're going. Pass it over, Purna, and—"

"This is one devil you don't touch, Hoartrap," said Purna, seizing Prince up after all and giving him *such* a hug. Glaring at the warlock over the decidedly unique sensation of the little dog licking her chin with her own tongue, she said, "I don't care if it means you three go on ahead while I walk all the way to Othean, there is no fucking way he's going anywhere but into Diggelby's arms." Giving the devil who had saved her life another squeeze, she added, "Or mine, in the meantime."

"Ahhhhhh," said Hoartrap sagely, as if he knew half as much as he thought he did, but to her relief he didn't fight her on it. Turning back to the ruined pentagram he said, "Oh well, two are better than none, and I'd never begrudge a pal her sense of sentiment. Help me get this set back up and we can go give Maroto the shock of his life. Well, one of them, anyway, but I pride myself on being present for almost all of them."

Instead of immediately working with either the rat or the badger, Hoartrap stowed his devil-stuffed bag inside his pack and started futzing with the broken symbol on the floor. As he nudged the disturbed sand back into a solid line, Keun-ju shakily joined Purna and Prince, the Immaculate looking as blanched as Purna must. Best had taken a few steps toward the door but stopped in the middle of the empty floor, perhaps unwilling to pass under the floral horror.

"They're almost here," called the Horned Wolf, sounding more herself again now that she could focus on something wholesome, like a furious mob coming to murder them. "Firelight replaces Silvereye, they must be climbing the path."

"Bring your things, bring your things," said Hoartrap, hopping back to his feet and brushing bone dust off his hands. Tossing the last few odds and ends into his bulky wicker pack, he hoisted it onto his back and then took up the magic post under one arm. "Swiftly now, to the edge of the circle. This time we're stepping inside, but not until I say so—the door's already ajar from our first adventure and I don't want anyone falling through until I've made sure it leads where it needs to."

"Have you already freed the devils?" asked Best, shouldering her own bag and cautiously approaching the altered symbol on the floor. Or perhaps it was the floor itself that had been changed, and the pentagram remained the same. It was hard to tell since looking at it made Purna's eyes water. "Is it done?"

"Nobody's freeing anyone," said Hoartrap. "I have the means to take us all through with little more than a wave of the hand and a slip of the tongue."

"But you said we needed to free our devils to take us wherever we wanted to go," said Keun-ju. "That was the whole point of… of what you made us do."

"I didn't *make you* do anything," said Hoartrap, resuming his position at the edge of the symbol, the torch behind him throwing his grotesque shadow over everyone else. "And what I said was if you bound a devil you could then release it in exchange for safe passage through the First Dark, no Gate required. Which you could. I, however, do not need to waste good devils on such a simple trick, not with the ground so thin in front of us. So step right up, hold hands and—"

"Then why summon them at all?" demanded Best.

"To weaken the membrane between our world and theirs, thus facilitating our passage through this very spot," said Hoartrap with growing annoyance. "When they pull themselves free there is… a residual malleability in reality, to put it in layperson's terms, which we will exploit to our advantage."

"Exploit to your advantage, you mean," said Purna, holding Prince even tighter as the pieces of Hoartrap's plot slipped into joint like the proper mix of components coming together to release a devil from the First Dark. "They didn't have to give you their devils at all, did they? Even if they'd kept them you could still take us through this weak spot or whatever, isn't that what you're saying?"

"Ah, you Ugrakari and your eerie intuition," said Hoartrap. "You would make a finer apprentice than your girlfriend ever did… not that that is an invitation, mind you, I've come to the conclusion that taking on pupils is more trouble than it's worth. You give and you give and—"

"You tricked us," said Best, "to make us complicit in your crimes."

"I did not volunteer every little detail that would have flown in one ear and out the other," said Hoartrap. "I told you for a price I would take you where you need to go. I named my price. You have paid it. No tricks. No crimes."

"You are an ogre and a mage, and yet as Best points out you hide behind your wizard-lies instead of speaking boldly and nobly," said

Keun-ju, getting fired up, too. "Why have us summon devils only to pass them over to you, if it was not required?"

"Because the little shits are getting wise to me," said Hoartrap, and now his bluster was replaced with something gloomier as he scowled down at the broken bits of skull, spatters of grey wax, and melted metal in the center of the pentagram. "Eat enough devils and word gets out, I suppose, and it's getting harder and harder to draw them in... if they know it's me. It's a difficult business, practicing diabolical witchcraft without the assistance of the diabolic, but this workaround seemed to do the trick, so who knows, there's hope yet. After we find Maroto we ought to go another round, I'll certainly make it worth your while to help me refill my larder if—"

Prince barked, crossbows twanged, and half a dozen bolts banked around Purna... and then resumed course. They should have struck Hoartrap, but passing over the pentagram they became caught in the same syrupy slowness that had caused the bronze pyramid to hover during the first ritual. As the shafts swayed slowly through the air Hoartrap waved his free hand in front of his face, covering his mouth as he whispered something that made Purna's ears ache and hair stand on end. The bolts stopped moving altogether, then plummeted to the floor... and kept falling, when there was no floor to catch them.

"Our cue!" said Hoartrap, grabbing Best's elbow and hopping over the border of the pentagram, the magic post still tucked under his other arm. As Best fell into the pit Purna grabbed the horn of the woman's helm with her free hand, Prince yapping his head off now that the Eyvindians were charging into the church behind them. And as Purna was yanked down into the First Dark after them, she felt Keun-ju grab her with his free arm... which was to say his only one, though maybe if Hoartrap hadn't fleeced him of his devil he might have wished his way into having two again. This was the last thought she had before crashing into the slippery warm scratching heaving river—

Cliff. The top of a cliff, the wind buffeting her, and she would have fallen if Best hadn't continued to lurch forward, Purna dangling from her helm. Then Keun-ju was there, and his added weight pulled all three of them to the ground. But not off it, thankfully, the sheer drop Purna had glimpsed now a few yards away thanks to Best's powerful stride. Nobody tried to stand right away, the rocky earth swimming in front of Purna, but then Hoartrap's oily toes appeared in front of her, catching in the gleam of the setting sun.

"Need to work on my landings," he muttered, "but this is the spot all right. Time to see just how far the Mighty Maroto has roamed— who wants to be a dear and take the other end of this hexed piece of driftwood?"

Perhaps it was Prince licking her face with her old tongue that helped Purna get over her bends from the First Dark sooner than the others, but whatever the cause she had climbed to her feet and dusted herself off before Best and Keun-ju were even able to sit up. It was hardly the most remarkable aspect of the evening but Purna couldn't get over how dark the night had been back in Black Moth, but here the sun still slouched on the far horizon. It had felt like the magic of a moment, but had a whole day passed while they floated through the First Dark?

Really taking in her surroundings now, she saw a shimmering jungle poised to break over them like a green tidal wave, and on the other side of their narrow shelf of rock the cliffs plummeted to an ocean as vast and open as any sea she had ever glimpsed. It would have taken her breath away even if she hadn't known that she now stood on Jex Toth, the Sunken bally Kingdom from whence all Ugrakari traced their ancestry, but where none had set foot for five hundred years.

"Sightsee later, Purna, for now take the other end of this so we can determine which direction to go," said Hoartrap, bumping her hip with the magic post. "From my brief expeditions to this place in pursuit of my fellow Villain I quickly learned to stay under the cover of the canopy, especially after dark, and the sun's almost sunk. The heavens are not so pleasant as they seem, nor so vacant, for there are...there are..."

"There are what?" asked Keun-ju, but Hoartrap was as incapable of speech as Purna. She had obligingly hooked an arm around the tamarind log while still taking in the majestic vista, but as soon as she took up her end the unmistakable pull of the post captured her attention. Instead of being tugged back from the cliffs and toward the jungle interior, the wooden compass needle tried to wiggle forward in the crook of her elbow, pressing straight out toward the open sea. Oblivious to this ominous portent, Keun-ju woozily got to his feet and asked again, "There are what in the skies, Hoartrap?"

"Demons," whispered Best, her eyes wide and bright as the setting sun as she stared upward.

"Is it maybe mixed up?" asked Purna, giving the magic post a shake, as if that might sort it out. "From coming through the First Dark? Something?"

"Fuck!" Hoartrap dropped his end of the post as something popped inside his robes, smoke rising from his chest as he rooted around in the fold and then flung away a fat, glowing cockroach. Prince went right after it, but the bug was too quick for him, wiggling into a crevasse. Sucking his fingers, Hoartrap repeated himself a few more times, as if maybe they hadn't caught it. "Fuck fuck *fuck*!"

"Fuck!" yelped Purna, dropping her end of the magic post, too, as the shadow that passed overhead caught her notice. Out of the corner of her eye she saw the tamarind log roll away, right off the side of the fucking cliff, but that was hardly her biggest concern at present.

"Fuck is right!" said Hoartrap.

"What…the…fuck…" gasped Keun-ju.

"A long story with a dud ending," said Hoartrap, scowling out to sea. "Alarmlings only hatch under extremely specific circumstances. In this case, when a sword I warded for a friend comes into close proximity with a higher concentration of deviltry than has existed in this world for centuries. That friend is on Othean, and the only possible trigger would be an invasion from this very shore crashing down on—oh you meant what the fuck is *that*!"

They did, but not even Best was sticking around for an answer, everyone scattering away into the jungle like rabbits from the shadow of a hawk. Everyone except Hoartrap, anyway, who initially tried to play it cool, but over her shoulder Purna saw him hike the skirt of his robes and dash for the treeline as the colossal white thing dove down out of the blood-colored sky. He almost made it, too, but then ropey tongues exploded out from the swooping monster, enveloping its quarry, and the Touch was carried off so swiftly and silently you would have thought he had never set foot on the Sunken Kingdom at all... if not for the three shivering mortals hiding under the cover of strange, mammoth vegetation, with one small devil among them.

Before long it was fully dark.

CHAPTER
3

So, does it feel good to be the Mighty Maroto again, instead of just plain old Useful?" asked Dong-won as they strode down the gangplank to the statue-skirted jetties of Darnielle Bay, harbor city of Azgaroth. "Or let me guess, this ain't quite how you remembered it, either?"

"No, this is about how it usually went, actually," said Maroto, trying not to trip over his manacles and go into the drink. "Gonna level with you, I got clapped in irons all the damn time."

"Just not when you were trying to help people for a change?" said Niki-hyun from the front of the chain gang. Unlike certain pirates Maroto could name, Niki-hyun had taken their further decline in fortunes in good stride. Maybe it was just to rub her former captain's nose in her poor choice in cabin help, or maybe she was just pleased as rhum punch to die anywhere but on Jex Toth; didn't much matter so long as she kept taking Maroto's side.

"I can see why you'd guess that, given some of the songs they used to sing about us old Villains," said Maroto, his legs going wobbly as they reached the steady stone of the quay. "But the thing is I was always trying to help people, just so happened more often than not I was one of them what stood to benefit. Now that you mention it, though, those times I stretched out on behalf of those less fortunate than myself were the ones I was most likely to scald my fingers—you'd think I'd learn my lesson one of these years."

"Yes, you fucking would," grumbled Bang from her position right behind him. Her tone was still as black as the incense-rubbed armor of their guards, and the countless Chainite robes flooding the docks all around them…robes they had all been stripped of following Maroto's revealing himself to the Holy See back at Othean Bay. He had genuinely believed that once the Black Pope's de facto heirs heard his song they would want him to come along and meet the Empress of the Immaculate Isles, to have the famous Villain's inside scoop on Jex Toth as they engineered an alliance against the greater threat. Instead the Immaculates hadn't let any of the Imperials come ashore, the three pirates were rounded up and treated to the same shabby treatment as Maroto, and the whole fleet sailed south. "What a shitty place to die."

"Worse towns to be martyred than Darnielle Bay," Maroto opined as they were herded toward the high, spiked walls of the harbor. "You think being impaled up there is bad, but that's only because you've never seen what they do to rogues in Lemi or Cockspar. Azgaroth… Azgaroth has not been high on my list of potential retirement spots."

"Always heard the one thing this primitive province did right was they didn't let the Chain in," said Dong-won, talking good and loud so all their black-robed handlers could hear. "Everyone knows the Azgarothians would rather break off from the Empire than bow to a pope."

"Even dogs may understand the word of the divine, if it is delivered with authority," said the black-robed cardinal with the bright red hat and matching facepaint who seemed to be the gilded mouthpiece of his fellow clerics on the Holy See. "Yet many hounds shall hear an order and still disobey, until they are brought to heel. What a blessing it is for such simple beasts, to be given the gift of discipline."

That this Cardinal Triangle or whatever his name was had transferred Maroto and his cohort to the lead galleon had been worrisome, but not nearly so much as the fact that he now literally led them by a golden chain as they marched along the quays toward the harbor walls. There was a wide promenade that ran along the bay, but while an army could drop anchor and march up it toward town, wasn't nobody walking inside unless those ancient gates opened to admit them.

"Wonder how far you'd have to hike down the strand to see the edge of the Immaculate wall," said Niki-hyun.

"A lot farther than you're going," said one of the platemailed handlers who held on to the chain between the lead prisoner and the cardinal.

"If it stretches from the end of this inlet clear to the Bitter Gulf it must be the biggest miracle since the Age of Wonders," said Dongwon. "The real miracle being how this close to the construction you Imperials didn't notice our people sticking up a giant wall between you and Linkensterne."

"Probably some graft, and definitely some willful ignorance," said Bang, finally getting into the spirit of winding up their captors. "Cockspar and Lemi always took a hard line against Immaculate expansion, but Melechesh is right across the water there, so Darnielle's always had what you'd call a more progressive view of us neighbors to the north. Wouldn't be surprised if all the delays merchants are having getting into Linkensterne these days are some sort of a kickback to funnel traffic over here instead, where they've got daily barges ferrying folk back and forth between Darnielle Bay and Melechesh. No wait, either!"

"The days of such petty sins have passed. All will answer for their actions, and receive exactly what it is they have asked for," said the cardinal. Pointing toward the thickening thorns atop the harbor fortifications, he looked back at them with one of those creepy smiles you only ever saw on the faces of fundamentalist loons. "Why, when you are placed atop this wall you may well have your prayers granted, and gaze upon the fence that your infidel countryfolk constructed to cheat the Burnished Chain of its tithe."

"If you think a single money-worshipping merchant-prince of Linkensterne ever tithed anything more substantial than a dry fart to the Chain you're even stupider than the Miserable Maroto," called Bang, which led to her catching a fox-o'-nine-tails to her already raw back. Their guards must think her pretty foolish to keep needling people who carried torture implements the way most people kept pocketknives, but Maroto knew better. After all the things they'd gotten up to in Jex Toth and later, on the boat, he was convinced the captain was a bigger switch than the hickory one she liked to use on him.

"Look, Cardinal, you say we're way past petty sins and on to the big stakes, I'm right there with you," said Maroto, because while he'd thought he'd become resigned to his fate on the trip down here, now that he could actually see the human-shaped shadows spitted on those spikes he figured it really couldn't hurt to try and whittle this nut down. "So with Jex Toth risen and wroth, what good comes out of holding on to old grudges? Sure, I was with the Cobalts and you're with the Burnished Chain, but that was before the Vex Assembly declared war on the Star! We're all in this together, aren't we, mortals against monsters?"

"From the mouths of anathemas spill the gospel of the saints," said the cardinal as they reached the promenade and the sea of black they bobbed through parted to let them stand in the clearing that had formed in front of the harbor gates. "Old grudges shall indeed be put aside, and you, oh wretched architect of the apocalypse, shall assist in this healing of rifts."

"Architect of the…apocalypse?" asked Maroto, a little hurt. This cardinal had hit the nail on the noggin, all right.

"You forgot wretched," said Bang. "Wretched architect of the apocalypse, and lousy lay."

"Don't bear false witness in front of the cardinal, Cap'n," said Maroto, willing to own his past but unable to sacrifice his one point of pride just because Bang was still testy. "We both know I'm the devildamned best there is, bottom, top, or monkey in the middle."

"Muzzle their filthy mouths," said the cardinal, and once the guards had fitted Maroto's braided strap in place he looked over his shoulder at Bang to remind her how dashing he looked with a gag in place. It certainly suited him better than it did her, the pirate looking as though she might bite through the leather at any moment, or burn it off with the heat from her blazing eyes. He tried pleading with his, and perhaps she took pity on him at last, because when the call to bow went out she lowered herself down instead of forcing their captors to dole out more grief.

Turning back to the commotion ahead of them, Maroto tried to make himself comfortable kneeling in his rags on the hot flagstones because they were without a doubt going to be here all day. No matter how far in advance the Imperial fleet had exchanged messages with this Imperial city, Dong-won was right: any cooperation between Azgaroth and the Burnished Chain would not come naturally for either party. Hells, even if the two powers had been on friendly terms, marching an army of this size into any city would require plenty of pomp and ritual from the civic authorities. Add to that the Chain's flair for stretching the matter of a moment into the spectacle of an age and they would be lucky if they were admitted into Darnielle Bay before next week.

The Holy See had brought their comfy chairs all the way from Diadem, apparently, and while the rest of the blessed army knelt on the brine-dusted stones of the seafront these cardinals made their roost just ahead of the prisoners in the small open area that remained between here and the high walls. The cardinal who held their chain lifted a black glove, and a polyphonic hymn rose from the surrounding Chainites. Either they'd planted a chorus in the front rows or golden pipes were one of the Fallen Mother's blessings for all her chosen children.

Squinting at the hundred-foot gate and seeing that what he had assumed was simply bumpy white stone was actually formed from countless human skulls, Maroto supposed it didn't get much worse than being kept waiting for your own execution. When he was a younger barbarian he'd figured being obsessed with death was one of the hallmarks of old age, that it wasn't until your sand really started running out that you stopped being able to focus on life. He hated to think he'd turned into the very sort of morbid fogey he'd found so annoying, but really now, everywhere you looked were grim reminders of mortality. How could you miss them?

And here was a better question—fired up as he'd gotten at the prospect of redressing his wrongs and uniting the Star to beat back the monstrous hordes, what had he even been *thinking*? Everyone was going to die once the Tothans attacked, sure, but they were going to do that anyway, sooner or later, so why try to prolong the inevitable for strangers when all it got him was a fast track to his own end?

This right here served him right. He'd gotten so caught up with the idea of redeeming himself, in swanning back onto the stage to play the hero for the ghost of Purna and everyone else he cared about but who were also probably already dead, that he'd thrown away his life on yet another profitless gambit. If he hadn't just betrayed the whole damn Star to keep himself alive you would think Maroto didn't value his own skin, quick as he always was to volunteer it for some grand gesture. As always, it was only after his ambitions had all come to ashes that it occurred to him he really ought to have just minded his own back for a change.

And that was what pinched his pouch so bad, not fear over his current dire predicament but the self-resentment that came from knowing that even if he did somehow manage to defy the odds and slip free from yet another attempt on his life, he'd just find some other bold-hearted and hollow-headed bind to embroil himself in. Listening to the rising chorus of the Chainites and reflecting on it all, Maroto wondered if quite without his noticing he'd actually become a suicidal maniac with delusions of grandeur. Funny how those little changes slip past undetected as you age; you bemoan the fatigue and the breathlessness and the lingering aches and pains and the occasional case of jelly-bone, but somehow the spoilage of your brain-fruits escapes your notice...

Except if that were all true he would have died fighting back on Jex Toth, instead of collaborating with the enemies of mortalkind. If it were true he would have stayed with his injured father and six-year-old nephew back on a Flintland battlefield, instead of abandoning them. He would have fought Queen Indsorith to the death in their duel, instead of accepting her mercy after she disarmed him. Truth be told, he would have lived a very different life if his selfless heroism hadn't conveniently dozed off whenever the going got rough... and he could have died one of a hundred different deaths, if he'd stuck to the courage of his convictions any of those many, many times when he'd been tested and found wanting. Any one of those bloody fates would have been preferable to the one awaiting him here, and he relived them now, one by one, as he had so many times before.

Some ungodly number of paeans later bells tolled from beyond the wall of Darnielle Bay, and the spike-crowned, skull-studded gate at last creaked outward. A procession emerged from the city, some in the elegant purple Azgarothian robes of state and others in Crimson parade dress. These soldiers must be either retired or officers in strictly ceremonial uniforms, since from what Maroto had overheard in the hold of the galleon the entire Fifteenth Regiment had fallen at the Battle of the Lark's Tongue. That would explain the legion of mourners who filled out the rest of the Darnielle Bay delegation, black lace everything from their heels to their headdresses, the lot of them making a discordant caterwauling as the city's representatives greeted the Holy See.

Even with both ears working again Maroto couldn't hear everything that was being said between the two parties, but he made out enough canned phrases to read between the lines and get the gist of the Chain's pitch.

The Crimson Queen and the Black Pope have both fallen before their own ambitions. Meaning: so what do Chainites and Imperials have to fight about anymore?

Diadem is doomed. Meaning: 'cause we're sure as shit not going back there.

Jex Toth declares war upon all the Star, but the Immaculates refuse to rally to the common cause of all sane peoples. Meaning: you're not going to be like *them*, are you?

The Burnished Chain has risked everything to come warn Azgaroth. Meaning: we got booted from Othean, and Darnielle Bay is the strongest, most defensible Imperial port, so please let us in?

Imperials of all creeds bleed crimson. Meaning: we can put a cork in the religious talk and focus on good old-fashioned nationalism if that helps.

We deliver unto your justice the Villain Maroto . . . Meaning: never was that popular in Azgaroth, and everybody likes a public execution.

. . . One of the wretched architects of the apocalypse, who worked with

the rest of the Cobalt Company to summon Jex Toth back from hell.
Meaning: hey wait a tic—

Through the sacrifice of the valiant Fifteenth Regiment at the Battle of the Lark's Tongue they conspired to sell our world to the devils of the First Dark. Meaning: what the fuck, now!

The problem with them getting Maroto's dander all up with this bullshit was now he couldn't hear them over the sound of his own angry heartbeat. Yet as if they'd read his mental objections at not being able to hear just how exactly these Chainite berks were scapegoating him, several members of the Holy See and the Darnielle Bay delegation turned their heads toward him. The lead mourner was an age-shrunken old woman in a tremendous cloud of jet lace, her blocky headdress housing a clock in the shape of a coffin, and while he couldn't make out her hissing voice or clearly see her face through her black pearl veil, the accusatory finger she pointed at him didn't make Maroto think she was advising a full pardon.

"Certainly," said the cardinal who held the prisoner's chain, every syllable hitting Maroto's ears now that the rest of the wailing mourners had gone silent. "The Holy See applauds your decision to execute these war criminals immediately, and are pleased to accept your invitation to witness the justice of Azgaroth being carried out. Let the death of one who sought to tear the Crimson Empire asunder be the first act of its unification."

Everyone had a good clap about that, Chainites and Azgarothians alike, and Maroto put his own palms together. The cardinal was a miserable fucking liar, of course, but he'd given a far better performance than Maroto had expected. He'd also given the weary Villain something he'd never been able to achieve for himself: an honest-to-the-gods martyrdom. Sure, once they had him lined up for an impaling he'd probably lose his enthusiasm, but for now Maroto was just relieved that his decision to reveal his identity to the Holy See had indeed helped unify the armies of mortalkind against Jex Toth. A pity his relief was destined to be so short-lived.

CHAPTER
4

They went down into the netherworld together. The general and her four faithful captains. The princess and her four loyal handmaids. The chosen one and her four old friends. They traveled across regions unseen by mortal eyes, unimagined by waking minds, down through impossible geographies that would confound the ambitions of staid cartographers and exuberant artists alike. As befitted their fabulist descent into the catacombs of the First Dark, phantoms awaited them at the end of their arduous journey, but Ji-hyeon knew that reaching the spirit world was only ever half of the adventure, and coming back to the world of the living was a quest unto itself.

The setup was familiar from more than one of Keun-ju's tragic sonnets on doomed lovers, and given all of Sullen's invocations to Old Black's Meadhall deep beneath the earth she suspected her song would sound familiar to his ear, too. On her delirious trek through the poisoned world above she had clung as tight as she could to her memories of the two men, and her dreams for what she might have shared with them, but even so they had slipped further and further into the grey fog that numbed her mind. Like so much else, the thought of them had become a burden instead of a balm, another iron weight dragging down her skull, her heart, her feet.

But with each league her elderly Cobalt escort took Ji-hyeon away from the sickening ash of the washed-out wastes she felt... well, she *felt*. Bad things as well as good, and sometimes she woke herself up around their small campfires with her own cries, but when she did she would warm her hands over the coals, basking not only in the heat but the very idea of it. She hadn't lit a fire for two years—any wood she found either turned to stone or so rotten it crumbled beneath her fingers—yet here in the vast subterranean forests they rarely went without. Unless she pulled her eye patch to the side there was no more color in this nocturnal realm than there had been in the nightless world above, but there was life, and where there was life there was hope.

On those occasions when she did let her devil-eye look out upon these new territories, that hope faltered, as if she were peeking under a veil at something no mortal was ever meant to glimpse, and so she warred with herself to keep the eye patch in place.

They marched on through days lit by pulsing lichens that covered vegetable, mineral, and even animal outcroppings of the landscape, and rested beside burbling streams beneath the ever-burning constellations of glowing worms that punctuated the ceilings of the endless caverns. Ji-hyeon heard many songs from her companions, and they heard hers, and in the digestive silences that often fell over them they listened to the trilling cries of animals that were neither bird nor beast nor bug but something altogether different. The mortals were attacked only a few times, and never by anything beyond their ability to repel or slay. The predators that stalked the deep forests took many shapes, but none were remotely human.

They traversed bubbling bogs, climbing along the sticky grotto walls to avoid swirling vortices of quick mud, and crept through perfectly preserved palaces of ice. They hiked through putrefying fungal cities where giants once dwelt, camping amid titanic tombstones and jumping at every tiny noise. They passed through lands of shadow and lands of light, through dead worlds and worse, worlds of teeming life that ought to have never existed. Stranger than all these sprawling realms, though, were the pockets of the First Dark they used to cross from one fantastic landscape to the next. They were Gates but so small you might have missed them if you did not have a guide to direct you into this crevasse or through that hollow tree, and the transition from one place to another was so instantaneous she didn't even feel the inquisitive touch of the First Dark, let alone undergo further "improvements."

Beyond hearing the songs of what her friends knew or believed to be true about this chaotic realm beyond the Star, Ji-hyeon also heard their wildest theories, because in close to fifty years of exploring the world that had claimed them they only ever acquired more questions. Duchess Din supposed each place they explored was akin to an island in the First Dark, wholly unique and separate and never meant to mingle. Chevaleresse Sasamaso thought that everywhere from the center of the Star to the farthest reach of this place was all one single land, with curtains of the First Dark fluttering between them. Count Hassan thought that was an academic sort of quibble, and Shea confessed she wasn't convinced that they hadn't indeed fallen into some Chainite hell, while the Star persisted above and apart as the one true world. And when they at last stepped beyond a cataract of black oil that roared down an ivory cliffside and emerged in the permanent Cobalt camp in the ruins of another nameless city, Ji-hyeon discovered that her first father had some theories of his own.

———

"Hey, Papa, I…I…" said Ji-hyeon, nervously rubbing the finger stumps of her off hand with the thumb of her good one as she struggled to reconcile the shrunken, ancient figure in the net-draped bed with the hale and handsome father she remembered. Sasamaso and the others had been a shock, to say the very least, but this just seemed so fucking wrong she was crying before she'd even finished saying hello. "I…"

"I know," he said, waving her over with a hand so frail and thin it practically glowed in the lamplight. Instead of the barren, sterile tomb she had imagined when she'd looked up at the crumbling tower from outside, it was a tidy space with screens and scrolls and the nice warm rock bed he reclined on. If not for the faint, damp stink of things washed up from the sea only to bake in the sun they might have been back in his quarters on Hwabun. "Come to me, daughter, I know."

Ji-hyeon had been unable to pay any attention during the whirlwind tour of the camp the old-timers had given her on the way to see her first father, too flustered trying to imagine what she could possibly say to her family. The relief and excitement that had carried her all this way evaporated, leaving her afraid and ashamed. She wouldn't have known how to handle a reunion with her father even if her teenage scheme had actually gone off without a hitch and the worst that came of everything was a hit to his pride as she claimed Linkensterne for her own as a rogue princess. Seeing as how she had actually set into motion the events that led to him and his whole house being exiled to this alien realm where they scrabbled to survive for a literal lifetime, it was going to be an extremely awkward conversation.

Except it wasn't. After hovering at the doorway for but a moment, she flew across the chamber and crouched at his bedside, holding his hand as hard as she dared without fear of breaking it. He smiled that ever-so-faint smile of his, and while he'd lost most of his teeth and hair and every familiar feature of his face had been warped by time, that smile was eternal, and sunken though they were, the eyes above it were sharp as ever.

"You always were the troublemaker," he said, squeezing her hand so faintly she barely felt it, and then frowning at her missing fingers. "Took after your other father from the very first."

"I'm sorry," she managed, realizing that on top of everything else she had to tell him his husband was dead. "He…Kang-ho…"

"I know," he said softly. "I dreamed it, as I dreamed of your coming."

"It's my fault," said Ji-hyeon, barely able to get the words out of her grief-locked lips, tears darkening the hem of her father's nightshirt. "All of it. I made you take sides. I drove you apart."

"You are responsible for many things, daughter, but not my estrangement from my husband," he said in that matter-of-fact way of his that meant there was to be no further discussion of the subject. She was crying so hard she couldn't make out the old man naked of even his wigs, but it was really him, her first father, King Jun-hwan.

"I'm so sorry, Papa," she said, "for everything."

"An apology affects nothing," he said. "You cannot redeem yourself with *I'm sorrys*, nor can you save the Star with your regrets. Only your deeds can do this, and pure or ill, the emotions that stir you to action are less important than the consequences...But I know your heart, Ji-hyeon, as I knew Kang-ho's, and I was not surprised to see both of you act with more honor and love for your homeland than the empress herself."

"I got him killed, and you and everyone banished here, and where are Yunjin and Hyori? Are they...are they..."

"You will find your sisters," said her father, his shaky hand patting her cheeks dry with the hem of his sheets. "I have dreamed this as well. They have already begun swimming the stream you must follow. Together...together you three sisters will find the lost citadel of the Hell King, and you will take from it the weapon to win all wars, and then you shall open the road home and save the Star."

"Sasamaso and the others, they warned me about this prophecy business," Ji-hyeon sniffled. "Nothing about a Hell King, which sounds like an awfully important detail to leave out...but that you've been trapped here, waiting for me to return, and all that stuff about needing to find a mystical weapon? And the Star really being in danger from Jex Toth? That can't all be true, can it?"

"The daughter of the oracle happens to be the only one who can fulfill the prophecy?" Her father smiled. "Of course not. We have spent all our days in this place seeking to find our own way home... but it is my prerogative to interpret the dreams as I see fit. You are better at leading than being led, my daughter, and this desperate army of refugees has need of a beacon to follow. If the vision of your coming had proven as false as some of my dreamtreks, I should have revised the prophecy accordingly."

"Oh," said Ji-hyeon, the news that she wasn't actually the chosen one something of a relief. "I don't...I don't mean to second-guess you, Papa, but if some of your dreams are false how do you know we will actually find this Hell King's weapon, or even if there *is* a weapon? And everything about the Star being in peril, and us finding a way to return...how do you know any of that is real?"

"I do not," he said, "but you shall learn that the one luxury afforded us in this realm is that of ample time to find out for ourselves. And I am certain that of all the visions, the one of Jex Toth's return and the danger it poses is true."

"I thought that, too, but it was all a trick of the empress to lure us home," said Ji-hyeon. "She acknowledged that the Sunken Kingdom has indeed risen but didn't seem to think it was actually a threat."

"She is wrong. The Court of the Dreaming Priests has long suspected that the Burnished Chain sought to restore Jex Toth. Whether it was even possible or what it should mean if they succeeded was a subject of much debate. So many scrolls have been written over the centuries since the Sunken Kingdom was banished... What we all agreed was that it should usher in a new age, one where the First Dark and the Star became wedded, the spirit world and the mortal world made as one. But when this happened there should be a war unlike any the Star has ever known."

He shifted in his bedding, and Ji-hyeon's stomach heaved to see how elongated his lower half appeared beneath the blankets, curling down and around the foot of the bed. Much as she rued her devil-eye, some far more dramatic transformation had affected her father, but now was not the time to ask if it had happened when he was forced through the Othean Gate or at some point in the many years since.

"I believed, as did others, that this war would be waged between the just and the unjust, that when the Heavenly Kingdom of Jex Toth returned it would bring with it enlightenment that mortals should either embrace or lash out against. A host of supreme beings were thought to inhabit that land, and the Ugrakari and the Immaculate should be their allies from the first. We have the old blood in our veins, after all, and keep their traditions as best we may."

At the mention of maintaining Tothan traditions Ji-hyeon couldn't help but remember the many elaborate rites her first father had carried out over the years, private ceremonies she and her curious sisters had spied on...

"A few in our society were more cautious," he went on, "and warned that Jex Toth might instead be home to angry gods who crave only carnage. Who should flood our oceans with blood, sacrificing the Star to summon an even greater evil. And in the decades I have been banished to this place my every dream grows more vivid, and these visions confirm that the worst shall come to pass. I was wrong, as were most of the Court. They shall advise Empress Ryuki that the coming of Jex Toth poses no imminent threat, and this mistake shall be the undoing of not only the Immaculate Isles but all the world."

"No, it won't," said Ji-hyeon, watching Fellwing nest in one of the folds her father's twisted bulk formed in the blankets. "The empress is already responsible for the fall of one innocent Isle. I won't let her ignorance cost our people any more. I'm going to find my sisters, find this Hell King and his ultimate weapon, and then bring an army the likes of which the Star has never seen crashing down on our enemies."

"It will be a long and perilous quest," he said in the same dramatic tone he'd used when telling her bedtime stories as a girl.

"All the best ones are," she told him, giving his hand another warm squeeze. After years trapped in a seemingly endless nightmare, her first father hadn't just saved her from physical peril; he'd also rescued her from her own agonizing self-doubt. "Time passes so much slower on this side of the First Dark, I shouldn't have any trouble fulfilling your prophecies and still getting back to the Star in time to save the world, but it never hurts to get an early start. Especially when a late arrival means there's no world left to save."

"I have no doubt you shall lead our Cobalt Company home in time," he said. "No daughter of mine was ever late to a dance, and no daughter of Kang-ho's was ever late to a fight."

"I'm the only one you ever accused of being his daughter," said Ji-hyeon, the thought of their old spats on Hwabun as bittersweet as all the rest of her memories had become, now that they were outlined in loss. "But I guess it's been a while since I saw Yunjin and Hyori. I'm thinking they've changed a little over the years, huh?"

"Not as much as some," said Jun-hwan, his blankets fluttering and sending Fellwing back up into the air with a chirp as his lower half contorted. There were wide coils down there, outlined by the damp bedding as he shifted about, the smell of moldering marine life stronger than ever. "I know you think you want to see, Ji-hyeon, but you are wrong. Do you remember the harpyfish you would help me collect from the tide pools? Well...the changes I have experienced since crossing over into this realm are not without their ironies. Unlike your own transformation, it is benign enough, and has even given me a newfound appreciation for swimming."

"You dreamed about my eye, too?" It itched something fierce at being talked about, but when she reached up to rub under her eye patch her infirm father moved quickly for the first time since her arrival, grabbing her arm.

"Don't! You are wise to keep it blinded, and while you will have need of it throughout your many trials I must ask you never to let it look upon me."

"Sure, Papa, sure," said Ji-hyeon, easing him back down into his bed. "I knew it was trouble, but it's that bad?"

"Worse," he murmured, staring at the stained iron patch as if he could see through it, just as her devilish eye could see through solid walls, through solid flesh..."I cannot tell you what it means, what it has become, for to learn such secrets I would have to gaze upon it, and were I to do that it should gaze back at me, and I sense that would be calamitous. It is very potent and very dangerous, Ji-hyeon, the greatest burden you shall ever bear...but bear it you shall. This too I have seen."

"Ugh," said Ji-hyeon. "And here I thought growing an extra eyeball looked kind of fleet."

"Fleet?" Her father blinked at the Flintland expression.

"Never mind." Trying to distract herself from the goading ache in her devil-eye, she said, "So you've finally taken up swimming, huh? Me and Dad could hardly convince you to get your feet wet, but I guess you've figured out what all the fuss is about."

"More than you can even imagine," he said, his hidden lower half twitching. "Perhaps now that you have fulfilled my most important prophecy I will do as I have long dreamed of, and withdraw to one of the many seashores this place has to offer."

"Give it a little time, Papa, and we'll take you home to the waters of Othean Bay," said Ji-hyeon, rising to her aching feet and whistling

Fellwing to her shoulder as she set out to find her sisters, the weapon of the Hell King which would win all wars, and then a Gate that led back to the Star. *That order*, as her childhood hero and adult headache would've said.

Before she set out, though, she had to raise one final matter, much as she was sure they would both prefer to avoid it. "So, um, if your dreams showed you some of what happened to me back on the Star... does that mean you know about Keun-ju?"

"I have *known* about Keun-ju for some time now," said Jun-hwan with an arch smile. "Though not nearly so long as your other father— he tried to convince me to separate the two of you years ago, before anything more could grow between you, but I could not see it then. A Virtue Guard and his princess should be friendly, after all, and I had overmuch faith that the dictates of custom would keep you both firmly in your respective roles. After being swept off my feet by a scoundrel so far beneath my station you would think I would have had the sense to listen to him when it came to such matters."

"Oh." Ji-hyeon blushed at the thought of her fathers debating the subject. "Well, I'm glad you didn't. Separate us, I mean. Keun-ju is... Well, if you know what he means to me then we don't have to get into it anymore at present, but do you know if he's safe? Have you dreamed of him? Or Choi and Fennec and the rest of my Cobalts, or... or..."

Ji-hyeon was still trying to figure out how to ask her staunchly traditional father if he'd had any prophetic visions of her foreign boyfriend and his current well-being when she saw from Jun-hwan's darkening expression that he knew exactly who she was working up the moxie to ask about.

"The wildborn Flintlander," he said softly, not even trying to mask his disappointment. "Yes, I have dreamed him as well. He... he I am unsure of. The others, though, they—"

"The only thing you need to be sure of is that I love him," said Ji-hyeon, the words out before she could second-guess them. "I know he's even less conventional than Keun-ju, but Sullen is one of the greatest men I've ever met. If you just give him a chance you'll see that."

"You mistake me..." In a lifetime of discomfiting her conservative first father Ji-hyeon didn't think she had ever seen him act so awkward, and almost interrupted him again when he said, "I do not mean I am unsure of his worth. I am unsure of his fate."

"Oh." Ji-hyeon's stomach dropped, but she tried to buck herself up in the face of her father's portentous frown. "Well, whose fate is ever certain? I mean, plenty of people probably gave me up for lost, and here I am!"

"This is true," agreed her father, but before Ji-hyeon could enjoy a momentary reprieve from her fear he continued. "Yet it is also true that some fates are simply destined to be darker than others. Keun-ju had suffered a terrible loss, last I dreamed him, yet he remains strong even in mortal danger. And while your Cobalt army remains captive on Othean, the empress has not yet executed any more officers..."

"And Sullen?" She almost didn't want to hear, just as she didn't want to hear what terrible loss Keun-ju had endured since she had exiled him from her side, but she had to know. "You said you were unsure, but unsure of what?"

"I saw him fall, gravely wounded, and I have not dreamed him since," said Jun-hwan, and before that blow had fully landed on her heart he hit her with another. "Even if he recovers, I worry it shall not be for long. He has been marked by a *god*, Ji-hyeon, yet spurns her command. A brave, brave decision, or a foolish one, but whatever his motivation the result will be the same, should he persist. The fate of those who refuse the bidding of the gods is a grim one, and his time is almost up."

CHAPTER
5

Folk called it the Jewel of Samoth. It was supposed to be the most magnificent city in the Crimson Empire, maybe the whole Star. But the day they finally arrived smoke from the city smudged into the low-hanging clouds, and from the high pass overlooking Diadem's rim Sullen saw nothing but a dread prophecy poised to boil over.

All along the circuitous road from the Haunted Forest up into the Black Cascades the Faceless Mistress had kept him company, not even the comforting weight of Grandfather's spear in his hand enough to dispel her. It wasn't that he feared her wrath anymore, but that he feared she had been right. The vision she had shown him of a hollow, densely populated mountain erupting with liquid fire had been at the forefront of his thoughts ever since he had awakened in Nemi's wagon and found out where exactly they were headed.

At least the thought of a whole city burning alive with him inside it took his mind off the constant vicious cramping in his gut where the boy had stabbed him, and, almost as painful, Diggelby and Brother Rýt's theological debates. He'd asked to ride up top with Nemi but she wanted him to stay in her too-short bed as long as possible, whatever she had done to help his wound needing time and stillness to mend.

When they were still a dozen miles out from the city Nemi drove the vardo off the road, slowly winding their way deep into the forest of sky pines that blanketed the slopes. Once they were deep into the cover of the shadowy, dripping wood she ushered everyone outside. Even Sullen knew that bringing a horned wolf into a city was unthinkable, and he helped Nemi unhitch Myrkur and turn her loose. According to the witch her monstrous companion would claim a den nearby and guard the wagon until Nemi came back to collect them. The question of what the animal would do if her mistress didn't return remained unspoken; like Sullen, Nemi kept her own counsel, but also like Sullen, from her bleak mood it seemed probable she wasn't too keen about traveling through the Gates to join a war against demons from the First Dark, either.

As soon as they started hiking he realized he hadn't actually had the slightest notion of how bad his stomach really hurt—being jostled in the couch aggravated it, but each footstep was like getting stabbed all over again. Coughing and laughing alike still broke him out in a cold sweat. And laying it all out there, the worst thing in the fucking world was copping a squat; he'd come to live in fear of his own body and its mundane functions, even with the tangy eggs Nemi fed him to ease his suffering.

Before, any pilgrims they passed on the road tended to flee screaming into the underbrush from the appearance of a colossal horned wolf tugging a wheeled cottage, but once they were on foot their fellow travelers offered more coherent noises, though some of these weren't much more pleasant. Dire tidings from Diadem, said the better-to-do travelers, the whole city given over to anarchy.

Others were as wide-eyed as Chainites passing out tracts, and told not of chaos but a return to order. These mendicants had not taken to the road to flee the capital but to go and spread the good word. Diadem had been saved from itself, and all people of all creeds were welcome to take part in the revolution.

Of the many particular rumors they heard, the one that most piqued Sullen's interest was that Cobalt Zosia had attempted to retake the Carnelian Crown from the people only to be shot down in a Chainhouse, in front of thousands of witnesses. If she had died she had died, and that would presumably be the end of Sullen's obligation to the Faceless Mistress, but the whole world had thought she had fallen before and that hadn't stopped her from making a comeback.

He'd only met Zosia the couple of times, but that had been enough to convince him she was a woman who cheated death more often than Rakehell cheated at dice, and he couldn't be sure she was out of the song until he got down to Old Black's Meadhall himself and saw her standing over by the keg.

Diggelby and Brother Rýt were less concerned that one of the key players in the Cobalt Company was rumored to be dead and more upset about the news that the Burnished Chain had brutally seized control of the city only to turn right around and abandon it. Even with Diggelby wearing him down the whole wagon ride out here with tales of Chainite corruption, Brother Rýt refused to believe that the Black Pope had done half the things people said. When the consistency of the accounts seemed to confirm that most of the Burnished Chain had indeed commandeered the Imperial fleet and sailed out of Desolation Sound, the monk could not contain his amethyst tears... which Diggelby collected in a handkerchief for him, telling him that few were so blessed by the Fallen Mother that their very sorrow was profitable.

The pasha's concern over the Chain turning tail was less a spiritual crisis and more a financial one. His uncle was a cardinal here in the Holy City, and he'd intended to seek the man out for a loan before they traveled through the Diadem Gate. When Sullen had asked why on earth Diggelby would want to borrow money just before they disappeared into the First Dark, with the best-case scenario that they then emerge in Othean to join a battle that might claim all their lives, Diggelby looked at him like he was stupid.

"You'll never be rich with that attitude," said Diggelby, lighting a braided cigar off the ghostly purple flame they clustered around on the impressively cold mountain night. The closer they had come to Diadem's walls the more of these ever-burning beacons they had passed, carven tubes of stone rising from the roadside that danced with gaseous fire. Here at the base of the city's enormous gate there were hundreds of the natural lamps rising like a forest of flames all across the wide plateau where travelers were obliged to wait until the opening of the city at dawn; coming up the dark road toward the flickering field had made Sullen feel like he had found Silvereye's secret trail up into the stars.

"If one must borrow money," Diggelby went on, "I can't think of a better time. Besides, I am in *desperate* need of some new threads, and flashiness requires flash—we can't just show up in Little Heaven wearing these old rags!"

"Little Heaven?" asked Brother Rýt, talk of heavens or hells just about the only thing that provoked him into conversation.

"It's what some folk call Othean," said Sullen, his heart beating quicker at the thought of tomorrow's journey. Being real now, part of the reason he'd been obsessing so hard about the Faceless Mistress and her portents of doom might have been to keep himself from worrying the whole time about Ji-hyeon and Keun-ju. It was always there, though, the fear that something might have happened to one or the other. Or the both of them. His anxiousness to be reunited with the two Immaculates had at least taken most of the fear out of the fact that he would be entering a Gate on the morrow. Most of it.

"We go directly to the Gate," said Nemi, passing the communal sack of foraged foliage over to Sullen. His stomach gurgled and twisted, already furious with him for the day's march, and his eyes watered from the spasm. It was like his damn gut had already decided that neither the sour succulents nor the woody fungus were welcome, but he knew starving himself wouldn't help the pain, either. He had tried.

"Except for me," said Brother Rýt nervously, as though the witch had forgotten him. "Except for me."

"Yes, and it would be jolly bad form to just bid our chum here farewell as soon as we're inside the city," said Diggelby. "We have an obligation to see him safely to . . . to wherever is it you need to go, Rýt?"

"Um . . . I'm not sure?" said the monk. "Father Turisa charged me with delivering news of the strange weather in Flintland to the Holy See, but if they . . . if they are truly gone . . ."

"Chin up, chin up!" said Diggelby, taking their dinner bag from Sullen as he chewed his cud. "You heard that Usban spice-slinger, there's still a Chain in Diadem, just a better one! Less Burnished, maybe. They're working with the . . . what did he call it . . ."

"The People's Pack," said Sullen, his poor estimation of his clan making him immediately skeptical of any group who used lupine terminology to refer to themselves.

"Quite so!" said Diggelby, popping a ghost pipe in his mouth and talking on even as he chewed the white-stalked plant. "So there's been a teensy schism, which is *long* overdue in my book, and now we're all truly in this together as mortals. Better take your news straight to this People's Pack—we all ought to, really, get Diadem involved in the campaign against Jex Toth."

"I think I should just stick with talking to someone in the church," said Brother Rýt.

"Which you can do when we all go directly to the Gate," said Nemi. "No matter what land or faith, you always find priests drawn to Gates."

Sullen thought of the Jackal People hurling human sacrifices into the Flintland Gate, and that made him think of the Procuress of Thao, which gave him the creeps. It began to rain.

"Look, Nemi, I know you're late to the soiree, and not in a fashionable fashion, so let me lay it down for you," said Diggelby as he passed the weed bag back to her. "While we've been traipsing toward a reunion with the Cobalt Company, to join our friends in a righteous cause, Diadem has apparently gone ahead and accomplished what the Cobalts were trying to do in the first place! Which means we're all on the same team, and if we're all on the same team that means they can help us fight the monsters of Jex Toth. What's better for the war, if tomorrow we three pop over to Othean for breakfast, or if we wait and have brunch with the People's Pack, and then bring over a whole army by suppertime?"

"Huh," said Sullen. "That's not a bad idea."

"Good ideas are sometimes better as ideas," said Nemi, and finding a slug on the leaf she was about to eat she passed it under the blanket that covered her cockatrice's cage. "We shall be seen as curious strangers to this city, and it is common for curious strangers to be delayed when they arouse the interest of the local magistrates. What shall we do if we seek an audience with this People's Pack only to be incarcerated?"

"You *must* learn to start giving your fellow mortals the benefit of the doubt," said Diggelby. "At the absolute worst they won't help us, none of this getting-tossed-in-the-gaol-for-speaking-the-truth business."

"And if we do raise an army here you can bring them through," said Sullen, Diggelby's plan making more and more sense. "Like Hoartrap did with the Cobalt Company at the Lark's Tongue Gate, you could bring Diadem's soldiers to Little Heaven."

"No, I could not," said Nemi, fishing around in the weeds for more bugs to feed her monster. "I have never used a Gate to travel like this before, and simply getting the three of us safely to Othean shall be sufficient challenge for my maiden voyage...Although it is true if Diadem pledged their soldiers we could go ahead, find Hoartrap in Othean, and send him back here to clear the way for our reinforcements...Yes."

Nemi seemed to be coming around to the idea, but Sullen got stuck on something else. "Wait, what's this about you never using a Gate before?"

"And did I hear you say *sufficient challenge*?" asked Diggelby, relighting the three ends of his silly-looking plaited cigar—it was hard to keep it lit in the freezing drizzle. "It rather sounded like you did."

"Do you think securely navigating the First Dark is easy?" asked the witch. "I don't. But I would not be leading you through if I were not confident in my abilities. I value my life more than any of yours, and I'm going through. If you wish to actually help save the Star, you will come along."

"But first we see if we can get in with the People's Pack and warn them of the danger facing the whole great big world," said Diggelby. "Shouldn't be too hard for a pair of heroes of the resistance like Sullen and me to stir up the sentiment of the common folk."

"I'm not a hero," said Sullen, secretly delighted and trying not to blush.

"You will be to these peasants, trust me," said Diggelby. "As soon as we tell them we were very important persons in the Cobalt Company during their campaign to liberate the Star from Chain and Crown, they'll be on us like stink on bug."

Remembering the rumors of what had recently happened to Zosia in this very city, Sullen wasn't so sure that bone carried much marrow, but he couldn't debate it further because the rain was now coming down too hard to hear over. Which was okay, since he'd talked enough and wanted to be alone with his thoughts for a spell... though in his thoughts he was rarely alone. Due to the obvious need to keep Myrkur off any major roads where she might've attracted unfriendly attention from Imperial soldiers it had taken them weeks to wind their way up here from the Haunted Forest, and Sullen had spent most every hour of most every day of most every one of those weeks imagining all the bad things that might have been happening to the people he cared most about while he was stuck in the back of a bumpy wagon. Now that they'd finally arrived and the time for daydreams ran short he allowed himself the indulgence of something a little less awful.

Come daybreak he would enter one of the wonders of the Star, a city that a forgotten god had charged Sullen with saving from the deviltry of a dead woman, to rally an army and follow a witch into a Gate, and all he could think about was how badly he wanted Ji-hyeon and Keun-ju to be on either side of him, the three of them keeping each other warm on this dreary night. Not such a dramatic song, that, but as his stomach pinched him so bad he nearly doubled over Sullen reckoned he was about done with the epic shit for a good long while, and would be happy with the mushy sort of love song he used to find terminally dull.

CHAPTER
6

While Empress Ryuki had mounted quite the gala to welcome her son's supposed killer through the Othean Gate, she hadn't made much ado about tossing the prince's actual executioner back into it. It was an altogether utilitarian affair, a single squadron of the Samjok-o Guard delivering Domingo and Choi to the Temple of Pentacles. There they found no mountainous portable throne erected in the terra-cotta path, nor immaculate rows of Immaculate soldiers filling the fields, just a dull red road bordered by dull brown earth. There were a few shoots of green out there, though, the persistent heat wave prematurely drawing up last season's pumpkin seeds—Domingo wondered how long the warmth would last, before winter reasserted itself and crushed the ambitions of these sprouts.

He closed his eyes as they rolled him through the gravel toward the temple that would remove him from this world. The setting sun felt good on his face. If not for the mugginess in the air he could have been back in Cockspar, sitting out on the balcony above the piazza, overlooking the lemon groves on the distant hillsides.

Not that he had spent much time out there wasting good daylight, but still, but still. Perhaps Lupitera would make better use of it than he had; drag the bar out there and the old nag could spend the rest of her days in her own private booth, mounting amateur productions in the courtyard below. Would his sister-in-law miss him? He wasn't any more accustomed to taking her feelings into consideration than she was to respecting his, the bedrock of their relationship mutually agreed-upon antipathy, but now he found himself regretting that he hadn't said *something* to her before riding out to the south in pursuit of the Cobalts.

Well, what would he have said to the saber-tongued spinster, anyway? *Thank you, Lupitera, for all the years of bad plays and worse manners?* Well... Yes, he supposed he should have said that. He should have.

And then he chuckled, shaking his head as he fell under the shadow of the Temple of the Pentacles. Colonel Domingo Hjortt was about to die, and on his way to the gallows his last reflections on his life were not for the wife he had loved faithfully even down all the years since she had abandoned him, nor of their son whom he had failed absolutely, nor for the mother whose boots he had struggled to fill all the days of his command, nor of the soldiers he had served above or beneath or beside over the decades, and not even of all his most hated enemies, those he'd bested and those who'd gotten away... No, he'd spent his last precious thoughts on his harpy sister-in-law who referred to him as the Capon of Cockspar, a brassy cow who called him a boor for considering himself above pratfalls and toilet humor.

Well, he thought as the temple guards opened the wide opal doors to reveal the glistening Gate within, he'd certainly spent far more time thinking far worse things over the years, and nobody had to know that a career soldier's last thoughts weren't for Crown and country. This lifelong army dreamer had earned his retirement, damn it.

Just like he'd earned this execution. He felt bad for distracting Choi just long enough with his confession that she wasn't able to make an attempt on Empress Ryuki's life before the guards mobbed them. Damned unfortunate that she was now mutely led along to die beside him. The worst part of the whole affair, however, was just how good it had made him feel. Such a thrilling victory! The Azgarothian military genius, bragging to a parent how he had murdered her brash young child, and to the only result that many, many more people died senseless deaths.

It turned his stomach, how satisfied he'd felt for most of the march out here—he'd grinned from ear to ear at the expression on Empress

Ryuki's face, snuggling her disgusting unicorn as he gloated over her horror. He knew what it meant to lose a boy of her son's age, and to lose him for nothing…and Domingo had done it anyway, and then he had mocked her. *Mocked her.* Maybe the Star was truly in danger from Jex Toth, or maybe it would just carry on slowly murdering itself for another thousand years, it scarcely made much difference—how scary were monsters, now, really? Glancing over at Choi's stoic countenance, the scars and the broken horn she'd acquired fighting on behalf of pureborn armies, he thought it might be time to let the monsters have their own crack at things.

The captain of the Samjok-o squad stepped between the condemned duo and the short flight of stairs up to the Gate. In addition to the double scabbard on her belt she held a familiar Azgarothian sword out in both hands. Drawing Domingo's saber, she pointed it at the chair-bound prisoner and let fly a volley of High Immaculate.

"She says any honorable officer would be permitted to choose dying on their own tusk instead of being fed to the hungry mouth," Choi volunteered, not without a little smugness. When the Immaculate officer then cast the sword off into the empty field with another rush of words, dropping the scabbard on the ground, Choi said, "Does the Baron require further translation?"

"No, Captain Choi, my Immaculate has improved sufficiently to understand the thrust of it," said Domingo. "I'll tell you what, though: in acknowledgment of the debt I owe you for all your service, my saber is yours to keep. You just have to retrieve it."

If her sharp smile presaged a verbal riposte or was answer itself Domingo never found out, because that was when the Samjok-o Guard lowered their spear points all around them and Choi was obliged to carry Domingo up the stairs. She didn't look terribly embarrassed about it, but for the Lion of Cockspar, being lugged into a Gate in the arms of an anathema was not quite the dignified end he had imagined for himself.

The Gate began giving off a faint noise as Choi climbed the steps, almost like a distant scream. While by no means the most dramatic or strange occurrence Domingo had experienced, that faint yet climbing wail made all his remaining hairs stand at attention. Death wouldn't have been so bad. Death you could depend on for what it was, a return to the blank, silent state from which all mortals briefly emerge, but this? This was something else entirely.

Domingo had absolutely no idea what would happen once he and Choi entered a Gate without the sorceries of Hoartrap the Touch to protect them, but the best he could hope for was instant death. He had heard stories about what happened to those who vanished into Gates, after all; everyone had. Not that he had ever put stock in such ghost songs, and he still didn't believe in hell the way the Burnished Chain did, but he knew from experience that so long as you're alive you can suffer, and now that he'd traveled safely through a Gate once he knew he might again...only to emerge in some far less welcome realm, one where the devils weren't so friendly as the unicorn he had met this morning. The keening wail rose with each step they climbed, and he could make out the vermilion pentacles on the inner sides of the wide-open temple doors pulsing faster and faster in time with his heart, the Gate almost visible as Choi took another step...

"You could snap my neck," Domingo told her. "Vengeance for... vengeance's sake."

"No," said Choi, smiling at the broken old man she carried like a babe in arms. "Vengeance is letting you live with your disgrace, even if only for another...hmm?"

She stopped on the penultimate step and looked out across the barren fields to the north, and the four temple guards at the side of the door all craned their necks as well. It was damned inconvenient, because she had cradled Domingo facing the other direction, and though he squirmed he couldn't see what they were looking at. He did notice one thing, though, which was that the steadily rising scream wasn't coming from within the Temple of Pentacles, but from the far side of it, sort of to the northwest and—

Ah, Choi deftly swung him in her strong arms, and as she did he finally saw what all the fuss was about—a figure was running in from the empty fields beyond the temple, wailing all the while and waving their hands over their head. It couldn't be a stay of execution, since they were heading toward the Autumn Palace instead of away from it, so why all the hullaballoo? Standing as Choi was at the top of the temple steps, the cause wasn't immediately transparent...and then it became as clear as young grappa.

A swift grey monster loped into view and ran down the runner.

It was horse-like, but only in the way that a godguana is lizard-like. The equine shape was there but inflated to grotesque proportions, and its tall, stiff legs made it appear to be on stilts. Sharp ones, too, apparently. After galloping over the poor Immaculate, terminating their impressively sustained scream, it wheeled back around and came to a stop over the body. Its long, spiny-maned neck craned down and then its whole face split open vertically, an enormous sideways mouth stretching wide to gobble up the corpse...

Only then it paused, looking up from its prey and staring at the Samjok-o squad at the base of the steps, and then up at the temple guards, and at Choi...and, so it seemed, at Domingo. It closed its mouth, but only for a moment, before rearing back on its ten-foot-tall hind legs and emitting a shrill chittering sound that made Domingo's ears ring. They were still ringing when it dropped back down on all fours to charge, and the unpleasant cry it made was echoed dozens of times by whatever fell herd came charging from the other side of the temple.

That seemed to break the spell everyone had been under, the Samjok-o Guards keeping rank, to their credit, as they swiftly retreated down the road toward the Autumn Palace. The temple guards seemed less sure of what to do; according to Choi they'd only started posting sentries out here after Ji-hyeon's disappearing act of the previous year, and Domingo imagined babysitting a Gate was not a duty reserved for the best and brightest of the Immaculate military. This was his last thought before his perspective changed again, this time all in a rush, and Domingo only realized that Choi had been winding him up for a throw when she released him. Stark terror struck him, the likes of which he had never, ever known, because that witchborn monster had thrown him right into the fucking Gate and he—

Crashed into someone, who made no effort at all to catch Domingo, damn their eyes. He grabbed onto them, the only alternative to dashing himself on the stone stairs. It was a temple guard, the shaft of his spear pinned flat against his chest by the old man clinging to his shoulders. The lad must have stumbled back and missed a step, because fast as Domingo had been launched the first time he was falling again, but forward this time, and riding someone to break his fall. The stairs might have been more forgiving if the boy hadn't had the extra baggage weighing him down, but then a bad angle is a bad angle, and the sound the back of his skull made when it connected with the edge of a step was not a good one.

Sliding down a few more stairs atop a sled of supine, armored meat did not help Domingo recover from his dizziness, but other than being badly rattled he somehow seemed okay. Crawling off the comatose sentry took some doing, what with his bum hip, but after a bit of squirming around he was able to at last sit back on the bottom step, the slippers they'd given him in place of riding boots resting in the terra-cotta gravel. The setting sun behind the Temple of Pentacles drenched the ornate walls and terraced roofs of the Autumn Palace with a red as deep and rich as…claret, Domingo decided. And then, though it actually brought him no joy, he lowered his gaze to watch the fleeing squadron of the Samjok-o Guard be set upon by the pack of loping, lance-limbed horrors. The soldiers hadn't even made it halfway back to the palace. The light began to fail.

More of the clicking cries came from the north, and looking to those fields he saw through the gloaming that the creatures charging by had glowing green eyes. They all ignored him, so far, dozens and dozens of them charging straight toward the high walls of the Autumn Palace, but it only ever takes one overachiever breaking from formation in pursuit of glory, eh?

"Baron Domingo Hjortt of Cockspar, Colonel of the Fifteenth Regiment."

Looking away from the stampeding nightmares was surprisingly easy, because Choi had made him jump—he'd forgotten he wasn't dying alone. Looking at the witchborn, he saw she was misted in fresh blood, and craning his neck, he confirmed those green temple guards had put the color in her cheeks. More interesting than that, however, or the bloody, broken spear dangling from her left hand was the saber she held in her right. She'd retrieved it from the roadside for him, and now, of all the dramatic endings to a gallingly theatrical life, Domingo Hjortt, the pureborn colonel who had chosen retirement rather than integrate anathemas into his regiment, would die fighting side by side with one. And an Immaculate to boot! Would that Lupitera were here to see this!

"Here." She thrust it at him, and he looked at it, confused. What the devil would he do with a broken Immaculate spear? When he didn't take it right away she dropped it on the gravel at his feet and saluted him with his own saber. "I will honor your tusk, Baron."

Then she turned and walked up the steps.

"Don't you dare!" Domingo cried, realizing what she intended. When she didn't so much as acknowledge the direct order of a seasoned officer, he found himself bargaining like a spoiled child desperate for more sweets. "That favor you owe me, Choi, the one to be named later? I'm calling it due! Stay!"

"You never stood watch for one of my dreamtreks," she reminded him as she reached the top of the stairs. "I owe you nothing."

"What about honor, then?" he jeered after her. "What about a good clean death fighting for your homeland? You're a coward if you go into that Gate and we both know it—stay, for honor's sake!"

"There is no honor here, Baron," said Choi, "only the opportunity to earn it."

Then she was gone, into the First Dark, and he felt her passing, like the Gate sighing...or maybe it was just the step he sat on vibrating from the stampede. It wouldn't be long now. He knew if he looked back at the monsters he might lose his nerve, and instead he leaned down to snatch up the broken spear at his slippered feet, scanning the ground around him to see if anyone had dropped something better.

There, on the edge of the red gravel, beside his abandoned wheelchair, lay his empty scabbard. He cursed Choi's slovenliness in leaving it behind, but then he supposed she had been in an awful hurry, and it was better to have a saber without its handsome double-ringed sheath than the reverse. The engraved brass gleamed even in the twilight, and he remembered his relief when Hoartrap had returned his weapon to him just before the Cobalts crossed over to Othean. Nobody could stop death, not a witch nor an officer, but a brave warrior never went into death alone—trust your steel more than any friend or kin or fellow soldier, he had told his son, because in the end it will be all you have left.

The sun had already deserted him yet a flash of light sparked off the scabbard, and looking up Domingo met the luminous jade eyes of a great grey beast. It had spied the old man slouching on the stoop of the Gate and peeled off from its herd, charging straight down the terra-cotta path toward him. An aria should swell in this final scene, the doomed officer weighing the merits of snatching up an Immaculate spear to inflict one final wound or crawling on his belly in hopes he could reach his Azgarothian scabbard in time to hold it up as a talisman. Knowing he was dead either way, dead forever.

There was comfort in that.

But not, Domingo decided, enough to give in without a fight.

He flopped away from broken spear and empty scabbard, two strong arms and one strong leg propelling him clumsily up the stairs after Choi. He bleated like a lamb as his limp knee slammed into a step, the leg lame but not insensate, and Domingo cherished even this pain, for it meant he was alive, he still had a chance, the Gate swelling soft and black and rich before him as he scrambled up the final stair, he would live, somewhere, somehow, anything but oblivion, he would live on the other side of the First Dark, he would live forever, he would—

The demon caught Domingo just before he could slip into the Gate, and there on the edge of two worlds he died like he had lived.

Alone.

CHAPTER
7

To one who measures her life in bowls of briar, a pipe is the ideal timepiece. Not because the span of time it takes to smoke one is by any means a cold constant; quite the contrary, what makes the pipe so perfect is that it grants its owner a warmer, freer hour than they have ever known. Theirs is not the miserly unit of the hourglass, every crumb of a moment doled out with a merchant's intractable exactitude. The puffer's hour is as generous as it is forgiving, and blissfully disdainful of the mortal compulsion to treat time as a greased pig at a country faire, forever trying to seize it fast and hold it still. If time is a great invisible river that runs the course of our lives, then the pipe is a briar raft on which we bob merrily downstream, while those who put their stock in clocks wade along trying to slow the flow by catching it in their mechanical nets...but when has a net ever captured a river?

The River Enisum boasted the most colorful freshwater reefs in the Empire, and the great Tinsky built his shop upon its banks so that he might better study the coral and replicate its beguiling patterns upon his pipes. Or so the legend went, but after Zosia overcame the last of the many challenges that had weeded out every other would-be apprentice who had ever supplicated themselves at his doorstep the master artisan had told her the truth: he'd chosen this particular bend of the river because of how good the fishing was. Tinsky loved to fish. And when he'd revealed the secret technique of his glorious coral rustication it had turned out to be just as unexpectedly humble:

bang four nails through a sawn-off broom handle, grind them short and sharp, and then drag the tool all over the pipe until you like the result. Easy as that...except as with all things that sound easy to an amateur, from tying a fly to rusticating a pipe, the more time you put in the more you realize you have yet to learn.

Of course, for all its craggy beauty the coral technique was still a cover-up, something to enliven a pipe lacking in grain or pitted with sandspots. That was the riddle of briar, right there, that the most promising blocks could prove drab at heart and in need of adornment, and some that seemed dull hid incredible grain waiting to be set free. That's how this pipe had gone, the rich bird's-eye and cross grain demanding a smooth finish, deep red stain, and gold wash to really make it pop. Now it was done. She tried to show her mentor but Tinsky was out on the river, casting his line for all infinity...

They must be drugging her, Zosia decided as she turned the finished pipe this way and that in her sore hands. She was loopy as a cat's cradle, unable to really focus on anything for long...or maybe just focusing on the same thing over and over again, repeatedly forgetting she'd been thinking about it in the first place. Must be something in her water, since her guards had learned from Boris's bad example and taken to sharing most of her wine and food. Something in her water or something in the air down here, ancient miasmas leaching up from the vaults of the dead volcano, still carrying poison even after all the centuries since those fires were quenched with deviltry.

Diadem's influence had even wormed its way into the pipe, a unique shape emerging from the briar that had the swooping contours of a volcano and the flared rim of a cauldron. It was one hell of a job, but her deft hands had retained their memories better than her head, and their focus as well. Devils only knew where Boris had scared up this ornate saddle bit stem, a curve of black amber with a cobalt crystal set in the top of the saddle and a tiny silver star inlaid in its underside. It was as if it had been made just for her. All the elements came together perfectly, and while she couldn't remember how long it had taken her to carve the pipe she knew Boris had promised to bring some nice ruby vergins to inaugurate it with when last he'd visited. Zosia loved her navy flakes, but Tinsky or Cornell Reeves or Rusty Owlet or some other eminent briar philosopher insisted red vergin was the best tubāq for breaking in a bowl, the sweetness in the leaf coming through in the char, and the richness of its cake preventing the wood from developing a weak spot and burning through.

Choplicker was with her often now, the specter of her devil lying dead and cold at the foot of her bed, staring at her with wide black eyes, and no matter how many times she told the guards getting rid of him wouldn't work they still carried him off, and no matter how many times they carried him off he'd be back there again in the wee hours of the night or day, it was hard to tell which with the purple gas lamps always burning in the cavern of her cell. When she stirred in her sleep and felt him against her, under the blankets, she would smile to herself, keeping his secret until one of the screws noticed, and then she wasn't allowed to have blankets anymore. But it kept happening anyway, or maybe it just happened the once and she'd dreamed the other times. She wished she could dream of Leib, instead, but he was all the way down in Geminides plying his merry trade, and she wouldn't let him risk himself by coming here to serve as royal consort...not when everyone was trying to poison the queen.

Indsorith had had the same problem, apparently, learning in the worst way that lovers have a way of either meeting horrible accidents or revealing themselves to be undercover assassins. Usually during intimate moments. They'd had a dark laugh at that, the two queens, when Zosia said she didn't know which of those two scenarios was worse, but they hadn't laughed long, because they both knew, yes they did. As a result Indsorith hadn't taken a lover in years; she'd made the tipsy admission after Zosia complained of how long it had been since she'd done more than polish her own helm, and that just went to show there's always someone harder up than you.

Sometimes that someone is awfully fucking fit, and there's real tension there, but you don't know if it's the sexual kind or if it's because you murdered their whole family and made them the monster they see themselves as. And so even though you're fucking aching to see if those plump lips taste as good as they look you just refill her cup instead of lapping at it. And really, now that you've actually made such a great new confederate why would you want to behave like Maroto and queer everything by trying to make it more than friends?

Then again, after helping Indsorith wash herself and being unable to keep certain thoughts at bay Zosia had come to the conclusion that she'd been far too hard on Maroto. Well, maybe not *far* too hard, all things considered, but a little too hard, definitely a little too hard. Sure, he'd been relentless with his flirtations, but then he'd flirted with everyone back then, even Hoartrap. And being honest with herself now, she'd been game to flirt back on more than one occasion, when she was of a certain mood, even though she'd suspected how strongly he felt about her. They were otherwise such great friends it had seemed fun enough at times, and totally harmless—*charitable*, even—but now she realized it must have been anything but, giving him encouragement when she should have just sat his ass down and explained once and for all that she wasn't playing hard to get, she simply wasn't interested. At the time she thought it would hurt him too badly, that it would permanently damage their friendship to have such a difficult conversation, that Maroto could never *just* be pals with someone he fancied... but now that she recognized how tight his and Purna's friendship was, Zosia had to admit that she might not have been giving him enough credit. Just went to show you're never too old to learn something you should've known all along—always give your friends the truth, no matter how heavy it seems, and trust them to decide how to carry it.

Like that time when Maroto drunkenly told Zosia she should've stuck to making pipes instead of making war—she might not have been as good at it, but briar brought a lot more happiness into the world than battleaxes. A hard truth she had easily laughed off, but now she found herself drifting through fantasies of that other, quieter life... the one she didn't deserve. She floundered out of the current of her daydream before it could carry her away, clinging to the important thing: Maroto might be a goon at times but he was without a doubt the most loyal person she'd ever met, and smarter than he sometimes let on. The next time they met she'd give the old lech a great big wet kiss on the cheek, tell him she was sorry for being a hardass, and then they could get down to the long-delayed business of being best fucking friends. And since you only live once in this devil-blessed world she'd follow his example, too, tempered with a bit of her own wisdom—the next time they got a little time alone together she'd just ask Indsorith point-blank if she fancied something more than a back rub. Zosia was still pondering the age-old question of whether to fully rub out her flakes or just fold and stuff them for the pipe's all-important maiden voyage when her jailer arrived.

"And how is Yer Majesty this evening?" asked Boris. Zosia's irritation at his insistence upon calling her that despite how many times she'd told him off brought things into sharper focus. He was wearing the orange robes of the People's Pack, as Diadem's new council had dubbed themselves... to a serious fucking snort from Zosia. She would show them a wolf if they let her out of this evil bed, where every day her strength seemed to flag instead of swell. "My, that looks nice—shall we swap for a moment?"

He'd never before offered her first pass from the dinners they shared, and she eagerly exchanged her new pipe for the silver tureen piled high with fried bean curd, eels, and wild rice. She was always so hungry and there was never enough to go around, the fragrant steam making happy tears run down her face. As she emptied his bowl he filled hers, packing the pipe from a roll-up kidskin pouch, and she corrected his sloppy method through a mouthful of mush, simulating the proper technique by biting the head off an eel and then packing some rice into its neck. It didn't work out so well as she'd expected but he seemed to get the idea, doing a better job when he packed his own pipe, a cheap little clay cutty. That was Boris all over—finally made the big time and he still had to make a show of how he hadn't really left the streets.

"Our queen seems occupied with her feast, perhaps one of you could do the honors?" he said to the trio of guards who shared her cell; not a one of the thugs had ever spoken a word to her except a command, and they were all young enough and bland enough that she could scarcely tell one from the others. The real question was where they slept, when hers was the only cot in the cell and...and... Boris handed her pipe to one of those curs! Her new fucking pipe!

"I'm done," she said, wiping her mouth on the back of her increasingly spotted hand, the manacle at her wrist hanging as loose as one of those bangles Singh had given her to commemorate their first victory in the Raniputri Dominions. "Give it over, it needs to be broken in right."

"You're a master pipemaker, isn't that right, Yer Majesty?" said Boris, raising his eyebrows at the guards as he applied his coalstick to his cheap tavern pipe.

"I'm a fucking legend," she said, not with pride but as a statement of fact, glaring at the kid holding her new pipe. "That's not for you. That's for me. First pipe I ever made just for me. So don't even fucking think about—"

"This tubāq is the very last of the Crimson Queen's private reserve," said Boris, talking through the cloud of peppery smoke he blew into Zosia's face and passing over the coalstick and the tamp to the kid with her caldera, as she'd come to think of the pipe. "It's twice as old as you are, lad, and worth more than all of our lives put together, so enjoy in good health—hers!"

"Don't!" Zosia wasn't superstitious about much, but the first light of a new pipe, well, that was a ritual as sacrosanct as any practiced by the Thirty-Six Chambers of Ugrakar or the Burnished Chain...and this rough-necked ape just fucked it all up, the flame kissing the wide rim but somehow missing the tubāq entirely. When he did finally get it going she could tell at a glance he was going to smoke it too hot, his mouth breaking into a dopey grin as he tasted what must be a finer blend than most mortals ever knew. Zosia wished they'd skinned her alive instead. "Fuck, come on? Really?"

"Mmmm," said Boris, putting his feet up on the side of her bed as he savored his smoke. For such a fancy new fop he still hadn't bought new hobnails, his primordial brown boots worn through in the toes. "I almost wish I hadn't lit this. Regular leaf's ruined for me now."

The first guard groaned his assessment as he exhaled through his nose. It was somewhere between a sexual exclamation and a cow low-ing. He passed the pipe to his fellow, and then they all took turns get-ting their sloppy mouths and sharp teeth all over that pristine stem. Even the guard on the other side of the door took a hit through the bars; the gal wasn't normally a puffer, she said, but once in a lifetime, what? All the while Boris talked up the exquisite, life-altering experi-ence he was having right in front of Zosia, holding court on all the notes and flavors he kept picking up, the guards loosening up enough to join in for a change.

"Is it...chocolate?"

"*Not* chocolate. No. *Fuck no.* Cocoa. With cream. No sugar, though."

"Carob and...cherries."

"Carob is shit. Cherry is close. Cocoa is off. Semisweet chocolate. Blackcurrant."

"Leather."

"Old leather."

"An old leather strop what's just had the razor warm it."

"An old leather strop what's just had the razor warm it, with a hot bowl of soap at the ready, but instead of lye, right, the lather's been frothed up out of almond cream...almond cream, and the tears of a grieving mother whose daughter won't never be coming home from the front." Boris tried and failed to blow a smoke ring, looking around for approval. But the three guards who had sat down on the floor were all silent, as was their friend on the other side of the cell door. Still awake, it seemed, but staring off at nothing, with glassy eyes and goofy grins.

Boris stood and stretched, then spiked his pipe on the stone floor of the cell. Clay shrapnel bounced off the guards but didn't rouse them from their spell. Smacking his lips at Zosia, he said, "Notes of brushfire tinged with rancid butthole. How the devils do you people smoke this stuff?"

"Boris?" Zosia blinked, the shattering of his pipe bringing her back to the moment; she had been cods deep in visions of bloody revenge against the screws who had stolen her pipe. It took her a moment to confirm the here and now, but sure enough, the guards were all doped out of their minds and Boris was unlocking her manacles. As the chains fell from her limbs some of the haze lifted from her mind as well, the cool air on her blistered wrists and ankles as bracing as a splash of spring water. Digesting the first real meal she'd had in far too long had to help, too. "This some kind of head game, Heretic? You letting me think you're helping me escape, but it's all a trick to get my hopes up before the big finish?"

"I'm getting you out of here, Zosia, and I aim to sneak you clear out of the city," he said, looking scared enough that he might just be telling the truth. "But you've got to do exactly as I say, understand?"

"Contrary to my reputation, I've been known to follow a plan in my day," Zosia said as he helped her sit up, the aching of half a dozen bolt wounds almost as bad as her arthritis after all this time locked down in a bed. The pain was good, it was keeping her in the moment, but what a moment it turned out to be: looking down at her blood-stained shift and crusted bandages and jaundiced skin, it seemed like less of a miracle that she was still alive and more like a curse. "Just... give me a minute."

"I'm not asking you to follow a plan, I'm telling you the only way I'm taking you out of here is if you do something for me first," said Boris. "You don't promise to help me, I walk out of here and lock the door behind me."

"Ahhhh, that's more like the Boris I know," she said as he shook out his sling bag onto the foot of her bed. A blousy shirt, breeches, and belt fell onto her musty cot, along with an orange tabard to help her pass as a member of the new militia. A bundle of documents with official-looking seals. A fake beard. Basic prison-break kit. "You had me worried for a minute there, I was beginning to think you'd actually decided to practice what your revolution's been preaching. I'd rather deal with a realist than an idealist, so what's the price for my freedom?"

"You swear to go away without hurting any more people," he said, twitchy as an itchy ferret. "Your promise to leave Diadem and never come back, and not cause any mischief on your way out the back door. You do that and I'll help you escape."

"That's it?" Zosia lowered her feet to the floor. Her legs wobbled and she would have fallen if she hadn't clung to the padded vise clamped to the bed frame, her injured shoulder singing a very angry song but her arms still tough enough to hold her up. Carving briar is hard work, had kept them strong even as the rest of her was failing. "What's in it for you if this knock-kneed old crone shuffles quietly away into the darkness?"

"A good night's sleep for a change," said Boris, and now he stopped his fidgeting with the disguise and held her gaze. "We made some mistakes getting to this point. Big ones. We'll make more, I expect. But in the end it'll be worth it. It will. People will be better off."

"Would that be the royal *we*, Boris?"

"The People's Pack isn't like a queen or a pope. It's made up of people, and people make mistakes. They...I...they shouldn't have betrayed you the way they did. I didn't know that was coming, I swear I didn't. It's wrong. You helped them. You could have helped them more, and you would have, if they'd let you. And instead they're doing to you just what you did to Sister Portolés, and it's wrong. It's *wrong*. But if I set you loose and then you turn around and start murdering everyone who double-crossed you, then where does it end?"

"It doesn't," said Zosia, remembering the look on old Domingo Cavalera's face when he had told her who he was...and she'd realized that by killing his son back in Kypck she had set into motion the events that had led to the massacre of thousands and the return of Jex Toth. "It never ends, Boris, and the sooner you understand that the sooner—"

"Wrong," he snapped. "It ends here, one way or the other. Either you swear on that devil of yours to do no harm and follow me out of Diadem this night, and never come back, or you lie back down on that cot and wait to be executed. Either way Cold Zosia is done with revenge, she breaks that chain here and now."

Zosia thought about it, testing her legs again. They were steady enough to carry her. Or so she hoped. The suggestion that she should just let Eluveitie and the rest of the treacherous council go on running Diadem as if nothing had ever happened soured her stomach. She could turn the tables on Boris in a hurry, snap his scrawny neck if she had to and slip out of the cell on her own, then hunt down every member of the People's Pack...but she might not get very far at all in her state. Especially without Choplicker at her side to show her the path...and clear it when necessary.

And more than doubt over her ability to execute the sort of violence this situation demanded was the fact that Zosia was just so, so tired. Of everything. Situations don't demand anything, she reminded herself, people do, and it was long past time she took the small but oft-ignored step of taking what she wanted instead of what she felt she needed.

"Indsorith," Zosia decided, and the resolution to let go of everything else made her legs stop shaking and her back stop hurting. She stood up. "Help me spring her, too, and you have my word. We'll go away together and seek no vengeance against those who wronged us."

"Zosia...Indsorith is dead." Boris put a hand on her shoulder as she felt her throat close up, the volcanic floor of the cell shuddering beneath her. She steadied herself but was too numb to speak, staring at him in horror as he told her the rest. "I...I'm sorry. They executed her already. They took another vote and decided to do her first, instead of the two of you together. Stretch out the affair, make it more than just a day's entertainment, and—urk!"

Zosia grabbed Boris by the throat, muscles made thick from years and years of working materials harder than flesh or bone standing out as she squeezed, his eyes bulging...and then she shoved him backward. Plopped back on her cot with her head in her hands, the room spinning. What had she expected? Boris to produce a devil from his pocket and wish everything better, Zosia and Indsorith free and safe and hitting the road for fresh adventures? Fuck.

"I know you're upset," Boris eventually murmured from the world beyond Zosia's dizzy, grief-mad head, "but if we're going to go we have to go now."

Where would she go? *Why* would she go? What did she have waiting for her in this world? Why not just stay here and accept what was coming to her? Why not get it over with already?

Why?

Because giving up was what the world wanted her to do, and fuck the world.

"Let's go," she said, swaying back to her bare feet and taking a faltering step toward the blissed-out guards sitting on the floor. Figure out which of these jerks had the best boots to steal, get dressed, and a sharp exit—that order. "I'll swear to whatever you like, Boris, so long as you get me out of this fucking dump."

"Good," Boris said as she retrieved her new pipe from a slack hand, then took the guard's belt pouch so she'd have somewhere to carry it. "Good. But save your swearing for until we have your dog back. No offense, but a word's just a word, unless it's pledged on something like a devil."

"Choplicker?" Zosia turned to Boris, the candle that had almost guttered out in her breast now blazing high as a bonfire. "Choplicker's alive?"

"I didn't say that," said Boris, looking a bit queasy. "But I know where they're keeping what's left of him, and I want you carrying it out of here with you when you go. Got enough ghosts in this city as it is."

CHAPTER
8

Even from up here in the forest of spikes that ran atop Darnielle Bay's ramparts you couldn't actually see the new Immaculate wall far to the east, but the view was nonetheless stunning. The afternoon sun glittered off the blue waters of the sound, the russet islands that spotted it, and the crimson sails of the Azgarothian ships they had passed on their way into the harbor. Darnielle Bay's fleet was smaller than that of Diadem, but looking down on the black ships at the quays and the swarm of Chainites still spread across the promenade, Maroto supposed there was something to be said for quality over quantity. The Azgarothian frigates and sloops were crewed by actual marines, right, whereas there must have been some serious shake-ups in the Imperial navy right before they set sail for Jex Toth. There were more far more clerics and fat cats on board than actual sailors or soldiers, their holds light on weaponry and supplies and heavy on art, expensive wine, and other treasures. It was almost as if the Burnished Chain had been preparing to relocate to the Sunken Kingdom and not wage war on it, as the Holy See had claimed to Azgaroth's elite.

Yet even if they took out his gag before giving him the goose, Maroto wasn't inclined to waste his last few breaths pointing that out to people who wouldn't listen no matter what he said. Better to try to exonerate Bang, Niki-hyun, and Dong-won, and when that inevitably failed at least apologize for getting them dragged down with him. He should have guessed that as soon as he announced himself to the

Holy See the Chainites would take a strong interest in tracking down the other three curious castaways who had also come aboard at Jex Toth.

That was what really broke his heart now that they were all up here—that instead of going down on his own he was getting his friends killed in the bargain. The Star would be better off without Maroto around to louse it all up, presumably, but these pirates were good folk...well, okay, so they were pirates, but by piratical standards they were...no, no, actually, from the stories they'd told they were proper arseholes even by piratical standards. But they were his friends, if nothing else, and maybe with time and wisdom they would've become the sort of truly good people he didn't have much personal experience with himself.

Assuming good people even existed in this nasty world. There certainly weren't any to be found around here. The principal Azgarothian mourner with the clock sitting atop her veil was still present, but she'd left her overly dramatic coterie on a lower veranda, and so up here on the grand terrace she and the gagged prisoners chained to a stone loop in the center of the floor were the only ones bringing down the party mood. Merrily as the cardinals mingled with Darnielle Bay's officers and senators and minor royalty you never would have guessed their province had repeatedly sided with the Crown instead of the Chain during all the civil wars. There were tables laden with tapas and sangria and even some ninny with a lute working the crowd, and nobody seemed to be talking about how even with the clean sea air wafting along to stir the many myrrh braziers, the whole place reeked from the decaying corpses stuck up on points. Staring at a sun-bleached skeleton that seemed to lounge across the tops of a number of spikes like a Raniputri fakir dozing on a bed of nails, Maroto decided Jex Toth was more than welcome to end the world after all. Mortals had to die, by definition, but if they couldn't even offer a little mercy to each other, to say nothing of dignity, then why not just kill the lights and drop the curtain on the whole lousy production?

Dong-won sighed through his gag, and looking around at his

friends, Maroto nodded. Niki-hyun was staring up into the floofy clouds and humming to herself, and Dong-won joined in. Maroto didn't know the tune, wondering if it was an Immaculate shanty he'd never learned or some maritime religious thing. Bang kept shaking her head to dislodge the biting flies that had taken a premature interest in their dates for the evening, but when Maroto shuffled over to her she knocked it off. Instead of keeping with the cold shoulder she let him get close and then leaned into him, rubbing her sweaty forehead into his sweaty chest hair.

Tears began rolling down his face before he could even think about trying to hold them in, falling into the faded, dirty orange hair he had dyed a brilliant blood-coral red back when they were all castaways together. She had trusted him, and he had gotten her killed. And more than trusted him, she had come to *rescue* him, after he'd first been taken captive by the monstrous sentries on that ridge overlooking one of the ruined cities of the Sunken Kingdom. Dong-won had told him the whole story after they'd all been reunited down in the belly of Jex Toth. How Bang had declared Maroto crew, and how Captain Bang Lin would press-gang her own parents if she saw a profit in it but she never gave up on crew. Now that it was all over she forgave him, rubbing her face against his chest like a cat who doesn't know how else to tell her master how much she loves him.

"*Useless,*" she spat as the thick leather edge of the gag broke loose against Maroto's pecs. She must have been gnawing at it from clear down at the seafront. Staying perfectly still so the corded strap wouldn't fall away but remained suspended between her cheek and his chest she whispered, "You're ahead of me on the chain so they'll lead you off it first. But they'll wanna spit me before they do you, seeing as you're the main attraction. So soon as I slip off the central chain I make a break for those lower roofs, and you make a big distraction to help me. Got that?"

"Mmmm…" Even without a gag in place Maroto wouldn't have known where to begin with all that was wrong with her plan, but perhaps sensing the skepticism of his murmur she bit his tit. Hard. "Mmm!"

"You owe me, you fucking *turd,*" she hissed. "You're gonna die anyway. So you put on one hell of a show to cover my exit, I don't care how many times they stab your stupid ass. Useless fucking clot."

Bang bit him again, so hard he had to dance in place to keep from screaming through his gag, and then Niki-hyun and Dong-won informed them with their own muted noises and head bobs that maybe the captain and her cabin boy weren't being as inconspicuous as they could be. Bang let him go and caught the broken gag back between her teeth as she turned away, a fair facsimile of a helpless prisoner. Looking around the busy rooftop with all its armed guards and then down at the manacles on all of their hands and feet, he highly doubted Bang would make it halfway to the edge of the terrace even if she did slip free of the main chain…but grinning into his gag he swore that by all his ancestors' forgotten deeds he'd do what he could to help her try.

"You are the Maroto?"

That was what Dong-won and Niki-hyun had been trying to warn them about—the small woman in mourning lace with a coffin-clock crown had crept up behind him.

"Mmm-hmm." Maroto nodded down at the biddy. He had better stay on his best behavior right up until they took him off the chain gang, to give Bang any hope of escape. Even if there was no way she was getting the real deal, hope was better than nothing.

"You fought at the Lark's Tongue? Against the Azgarothian regiment?" She sounded more spry than she moved, no doubt worked up over the prospect of gory revenge for her province's soldiers. It was always the pinch-faced old prunesacks who got the most juiced up about violent tragedies.

"Mmm-hmm," said Maroto again, figuring as long as she stuck to the basics the fact that he had a salty sock tied around his mouth wouldn't fully stifle the art of conversation.

"My brother-in-law died there, along with the rest," she said flatly. "He was an officer, like you. I hate war stories, so I never asked him about what he did, but before a big battle is it anything like it is on the stage? Do the two sides send out their commanders to meet and talk and see if maybe nobody has to die after all?"

"Mmmm…" Answering that was a tall order, but then the short woman motioned him to lean over, and when he did she started untying his gag.

"Baroness, I would *strongly* advise you not to do that," called the cardinal who had brokered the arrangement, sloshing sangria onto the mosaic floor of the terrace. "From the mouths of sinners, that is, from the mouths of anathemas—"

"Thank you, Cardinal Diamond, but I have this well in hand," she said, grinding the words so hard you'd think she had to crush gemstones between her jaws to get them out. The head of the Holy See looked a bit taken aback by her curt dismissal, but he also looked a bit drunk, and was then distracted by a portly man wearing an Imperial uniform with enough medals to laminate a small dog. Tossing Maroto's gag to the sea breeze, the baroness said, "I asked if you met before the battle, you Cobalt officers and the Crimson ones."

Smacking his sore lips and wiping away as much drool as he could, Maroto said, "Nah, I'm afraid not. That does still happen, or it's supposed to, but being frank with you your Azgarothian regiment skipped that part of the protocol and charged right in."

"*Our* regiment did not keep with protocol?" The baroness sounded skeptical.

"No, ma'am, they did not," said Maroto. There was no telling what sort of thing might irritate this grieving woman, so he might as well keep it completely on the level instead of guessing what she wanted to hear. "They came sweeping down on us before dawn, and after that, well, that wasn't the only breach of the chivalric codes I witnessed, I'm sorry to report. I heard what the cardinal told you, about how it was the Cobalts' fault that the Gate opened and everything else, but I swear on my friend Purna's memory that we didn't do none of that. If anyone did, it was the Chain who—"

"I do not believe I asked you about any of that, Captain Maroto," snipped the crone, and he was guessing it was a good thing he couldn't see her face, nasty an expression as she must be wearing. "I merely sought to discover if you had met Colonel Hjortt before my idiot brother-in-law fulfilled his life's ambition to die as pointless and preventable a death as possible. Today is a sentimental one for me, and I would have liked to hear from someone who was present, who had seen him just before. To ask if Domingo appeared happy. If he *smiled*. I don't know which would disappoint me more, mind you, if that sort of thing actually did put a spring in his step, or if he was just as crabby in his element as out of it."

"Oh," said Maroto, because that just went to prove that it didn't matter if you were a barbarian from the Frozen Savannahs or a baroness from sunny Azgaroth, you couldn't escape your connection to your family, couldn't suppress the part of you that demanded closure even when you and they couldn't be more different. Besides being intent on killing each other as horribly as possible, that was another thing all peoples of the Star seemed to share, another unavoidable wart of the human condition, and... and... "Sorry, did you say your kinfolk was named Colonel Hjortt? Sharp-eyed older gent, been with the Fifteenth out of Azgaroth since back when Kaldruut was king?"

"That is he," said the featureless lace scarecrow, turning her clock up to study Maroto's features. "Or was, to be more precise, since he was not among the few prisoners the Cobalts left behind when they abandoned their camp, and to hear the reports precious few survived the initial engagement to begin with. You did know him, then?"

"Well, let me level with you, Baroness... Hjortt?"

"Lupitera is fine, Maroto."

"All right, then, Baroness Lupitera—"

"No, just Lupitera. We are both veterans with our better days behind us, Maroto, no need to squander even a moment more of those few we have left with meaningless honorifics." There was an archness to her voice that Maroto found comforting, and not just that, a realness you would never hear from a Chainite or a career politician. "You knew my brother-in-law, then, from some older campaign? You and he have been on opposite sides since the time you first swung a mace, I suppose."

"I expect we have... or were, I guess," said Maroto. Remembering the fury in the old man's eyes as he lay bleeding and broken in the sparse grass of the Imperial camp in the Kutumbans, Maroto relived

the shame of that night all over again, because he *still* could not reconcile the colonel's vaguely familiar face with his name and rank. "So
he knew me from the old days, yeah, but I honestly can't say I recall
him. But more relevant...more recently...well, shit, I don't know if
your brother-in-law ever made it to the Battle of the Lark's Tongue."

She didn't speak, the sun reflecting off the dials on her coffin-
clock, and Maroto closed his eyes to do the one thing he'd had a lot
of practice with in his storied careers as a rogue and a rascal, a prosti-
tute and a performer, a captain and klutz—he gave her the bad news:

"I was leading a Cobalt scouting party through the mountains
and we got stuck between a pack of horned wolves and an Imperial
encampment. We didn't have much choice so we booked it down
through camp, trying to throw the monsters off our scent, and...
look, I'm not telling you this 'cause I expect you to be any more
lenient with me if you don't think it was by design. I'm just telling
you how it went down."

"I'll be able to tell if you fib," said the old woman. "Pray continue."

"Not much else to it," said Maroto. "We tried to sneak through
undetected but that Colonel Hjortt, he recognized us. Recognized
me. Had us captured. Dead to rights. But then those horned wolves
we'd riled up burst onto the scene and started attacking, indiscrimi-
nate like, and your brother-in-law...well, he took down one of them,
and it took my whole team to lay out the other, but it wasn't without
cost. No it was not. I had a look at him afterward, and we exchanged
a few words. He remembered me, like I said, but I couldn't place him.
I promised I would, the next time I saw him, but rough as he looked
I didn't expect any future reunions were taking place in this world."

"I see..." said Lupitera. "I would like to think he fell fighting monsters instead of his neighbors. And if he died before the Lark's Tongue,
that would explain all those uncharacteristic breaks with protocol...
I couldn't believe he would ever turn the Burnished Chain loose like
that, but this, this makes sense...Thank you, Maroto."

"I'd say anytime, but I don't expect we'll have many more opportu-
nities," said Maroto, seeing that the cardinals clustered around the
tables looked to be about done with all this Azgarothian sunshine.

Cardinal Diamond was energetically engaging his new friends, gesturing from the naked spikes at the edge of the terrace to the huddle of prisoners, a few other members of the Holy See already recumbent in daybeds, pulling their big silly hats forward to shield their eyes.

"I understand the circumstance of your meeting was different from the scenario I initially suggested, but *do* you think he was happy?"

"Huh?" Maroto had assumed she was done with him after he'd told all there was to tell, but that was another thing about the elderly— always ready to keep jawing, so long as there was an ear to latch onto. Well, Maroto was old, too, and one last chin-wag beat being impaled by a substantial margin. "The colonel, happy? Well, no. He seemed about as unhappy a man as I've ever seen, but in his defense he was probably so smashed up inside that his parts had stopped working… well, that and he really seemed offended I didn't recognize him. That really put the sand in his shorts."

"Nobody cares to be forgotten," said Lupitera, and as simple as the words were, and the truth behind them, her regal delivery cut right to Maroto's marrow. He actually had gooseflesh, and not just from the sudden nip in the air as another gust came over the parapet, whistling through the spikes. "But anonymity has its advantages over infamy, as my aunt and her foul cohort hath discovered to gravest peril."

"Sorry, your aunt is…" Maroto blinked as Cardinal Diamond swooned, dropping his goblet to the mosaic tiles, but two Azgarothian officers caught him, easing him down onto one of the few unoccupied daybeds.

"Nobody cares to be forgotten," repeated the old woman with even more oomph, "but anonymity has its advantages over infamy, as my aunt and her foul cohort hath discovered *to gravest peril.*"

"The grave is only perilous to those whose querulous lives are naught but a frantic scamper away from its embrace," said Maroto. He enunciated every fucking syllable so the Chainite guards all the way in the nosebleeds could hear him perfectly as their Azgarothian counterparts ambushed them. The scuffle was brief but loud.

"Wha…?" asked Bang, the broken gag falling off completely as she, Niki-hyun, and Dong-won all gawked at the double-cross.

"*The Avenger's Dramedy*, Act III, line what-the-fuck-ever?" said Maroto, the long-forgotten words having been drawn from his lips like a devil from the First Dark.

"Well, I've never seen it before, but I am officially a fan," said Bang as the last armored Chainite was driven to the ground and stuck through the helm with a pike.

"Nobody has," said Maroto, his heart doing that thing hearts do when they're so flooded with joy they sort of break, but in a nice way. Looking down at the lace-veiled baroness, he said, "The author knew there was only one actor alive who could play Antonio, but he ran away on opening night, and they never saw each other again."

"Sweetheart, this play is a modern classic," said Carla, the aristocratic bearing of the proud baroness dropped along with an octave or two. Maroto wondered if she was still wearing her clown drag under that mourning veil. "You think I don't know how to fill a gaping role? Please. Your stage fright was the best thing that ever happened to that production. I kept expecting to see you in the stalls at one of the revivals, but that just proves I'm a better friend than you are."

"Never any fucking doubt of that," said Maroto, trying to give her a hug but reaching the end of his chain. "Carla, I—"

"*Lupitera*," she said. "Carla and I don't see much of one another these days, save when the moon is full, the manbane blooms, and the greasepaint is laced. The Baroness Lupitera Rossilini Hjortt. The First, the Last, the One, the Only."

"Right," gulped Maroto. "Hjortt. So, uh, small world, and really, really sorry about your brother."

"In-law, and don't be," said Lupitera, but her brassy voice scratched a little on the end there. Calling over to the servants clearing the tables and the guards clearing the bodies, she said, "Keys, please! We don't do chains in Azgaroth, burnished or otherwise."

"You...you just jumped the Holy See," said Bang. It was the first time since being brought into the company of the hyper-religious navy that she had sounded remotely reverential. "Their whole fleet and thousands of crew right outside your gate, and you just *jumped* their asses."

"And I'm just getting started," said Lupitera, shooing away the unhappy-looking Azgarothian officer who'd brought her a key ring.

"Everyone here on board with your coup?" Dong-won asked Lupitera as the woman in red parade dress went back to helping carry off the prone cardinals. "Or maybe some of them enlisted Crimson soldiers got the fidgets about going so hard at the Chain, and to help a Cobalt to boot?"

"For a man who's yet to get out of irons you ask a lot of questions," said Lupitera, turning the key in his lock.

"Sorry," said Dong-won as she stooped over to get the ones off his ankles. "And thanks."

"That's more like it," said Lupitera as she moved on to Niki-hyun. "And to answer your questions, young man, ever since word came down that Queen Indsorith fell and Jex Toth rose we've learned to stop worrying about what color flag is getting waved, so long as the hand that holds it looks human. So if some of the supporting cast are looking peaked it's because this morning was the fun part, and now comes the danger."

"For us danger *is* the fun part," said Bang, which was exactly the boneheaded sort of catchphrase Purna would've come up with. "I'm Captain Bang, and my sloop the *Empress Thief* is one of the vessels you've liberated from the Chain's criminal seizure. Can I have some of that food and drink? Or other food and drink, if that stuff's poisoned?"

"We'll put something in your belly soon enough," said Lupitera, giving Maroto a pinch on the wrist as she unlocked him. "Just making sure you're real. And who are your other rude friends?"

"Niki-hyun, ma'am," said Niki-hyun. "Sorry, ma'am."

"And I'm Dong-won, quartermaster of the *Empress Thief*," said he, stretching that sort of delicious stretch you can only really get when you've been chained up for days and days.

"You are just *convinced* if you keep telling me the name of your boat I won't steal it—it's cute," said Lupitera, unlocking Bang's wrists; the pirate shook her feet and the ankle manacles fell right off, no key required. Maybe she would've had a chance of escaping over the edge of the terrace after all . . .

"I tell you what, it is good to see you again," Maroto told the lace blur. "Such as it is."

"Keep up with the sweet talk and you'll be back in my good graces sometime never," said Lupitera, tossing the key ring over her shoulder and marching off. Maroto smiled to hear the familiar clicking of cha-cha heels under her commodious mourning gown. "Let's get something to drink, I'm dying under all this chiffon."

"So wait, you used to perform with Maroto back when he was an actor?" said Niki-hyun as they walked toward the stairs at the edge of the ramparts. "He hadn't yet told us his real name, back then, but when we was first stranded together he sang some wild songs about the playing company he used to run with."

"Except he must have had someone else in mind," said Dong-won, always looking out for Maroto's best interests. " 'Cause you're obviously good people, and the only Carla he ever talked about was a loudmouthed shipwreck with a centipede habit the size of Usba who once bit off someone's ear for talking during her performance."

"You *did* tell your friends about me!" Lupitera finally gave Maroto the warm hug he'd been jonesing for but hadn't wanted to press. "All is forgiven!"

"Where do the fucking years go, girl?" Maroto asked as they squeezed each other on the top of a wall of human skulls.

"*Blpppppppt,*" said Lupitera, blowing a raspberry that made her veil dance a moist tango. "Same place everything goes. The shitter. But we can make up for lost time on the boat."

"The boat?" asked Dong-won.

"The *Empress Thief*?" suggested Bang.

"Any boat, what do I care?" said Lupitera. "We're all going to the same place."

"The shitter?" asked Niki-hyun.

"You tell me, I ain't ever been to Othean," said Lupitera with a shrug. "But it can't be a plum holiday spot, what with the armies of monsters overrunning it, and that watered-down rotgut they call soju."

"Wait wait wait," said Maroto, swaying on top of the stairs, the sun too damn bright. "That can't be right. Othean? Capital of the

Immaculate Isles? The place we just got turned away from because they didn't have a monster problem and didn't need one, neither?"

"That's the spot," said Lupitera. "You think *you're* surprised? Forget it. I just arrived in Darnielle Bay to get away from Cockspar for a while, because have you tried living in the place you're supposed to govern? It sucks. Anyway, I blow into town, I'm meeting with the Darnielle Bay Senate, and in come two letters.

"One comes by gull, and it's from the Holy See—they're sailing down here fast, and they've captured one of the Cobalt officers who killed ten thousand Azgarothian soldiers to summon Jex Toth. The other letter comes from Othean, via scary fucking devil bird. It says the first wave of monsters has already broken on their shore, laying waste to the countryside and besieging the capital. Unless they get help the Isles are toasted turnips and the rest of the Star is next. So we heads of Azgarothian state think it over, propose some plans, put it to a vote, and that's how we ended up with *The Avenger's Dramedy* for Act I, and something completely fucking ad-libbed for whatever comes next. And you *know* my feelings on improv."

Nobody said anything, the only sound the whipping of a Crimson pennant in the sea breeze.

"And you're going because…" Maroto tried to put the pieces together according to all the usual rules of Star politics, but he knew at a glance that would never get them where they needed to be, so he tried following her off the script. "You're going because whatever your province's history with the Immaculate Isles, when it's mortals against the First Dark you know you've got to step up and help your kind."

"Fuck our kind sideways," said Lupitera, hands on her hips. "We're going because we don't have much choice but to stop this thing before it gets to us—here in Azgaroth we're all godless savages, remember? No life everlasting for me and mine. The Star's all we've got. And since we're all going to die and be dead forever, it's better to go down screaming in the face of whatever wants to deny us the nasty little lives we've worked for. What's the alternative? Pretend what's happening to our neighbors won't happen here until it's too late?"

"Damn," said Bang when not even the snapping flag at the top of a spike chimed in to break the silence. "You're going to sail your fleet, and the Chain's, right back up to Othean? To fight against hell monsters, all on the principle of the thing?"

"Well, mostly," said Lupitera, sashaying back down the long stairs to the quays. "The empress is also throwing in governorship of Linkensterne to the first party who sends substantial aid, but if that's such a cherry deal how come she keeps trying to give it away?"

CHAPTER
9

Sullen had sung of a glorious war to save the Star, and Best had wanted to believe the boy so badly she had gone along with his schemes, even when they meant conspiring with a sorcerer and summoning a devil. And now she had paid the ultimate price, for instead of being transported to the battlefield of legend she had sunk down into hell. Which hell it was exactly she could not guess, being less proficient in theology than some, but she wondered if it might be the Hell of the Coward Dead. How one as stalwart as she might have been banished to such a shameful eternity she did not know, but as they journeyed far into the trackless jungle the only denizens they met were foul demon apes who screamed her brother's Outlander name at them in challenge, before being fought back into the trees from whence they flung their excrement at the interlopers. Where else but the Hell of the Coward Dead would *Maroto* be the battle cry of shit-throwing monsters?

Rather than being disheartened by their lonely exile to this disgustingly hot hell and its equally disgusting inhabitants, Purna took heart in meeting the creatures, saying it proved Craven had come this way. Which did not preclude them both being correct, for if he had died, there was but one place her brother should have gone. True, Best did not *feel* dead—if anything she felt hale as ever, her cracked ribs and lesser injuries all miraculously healed during her journey through the First Dark—but then she did not know what being dead actually felt like, and maybe in death all mortal pains faded away...

and when she caught herself thinking such Sullen-ish thoughts she quickly tried to brush them away, as though they were the inquisitive spider crabs that infested the sea cliffs.

The small party initially stayed close to where Hoartrap had been carried off, thinking he might escape the flying monster and return. After another day and a night it was agreed that waiting could not help their cause, and that they should explore the coast in hopes of finding Tothan settlements to spy on or operations to sabotage. As with all decisions the matter was decided with a vote, and as with all votes, Keun-ju and Purna sided with one another, but unlike other decisions this one Best agreed with—better to hunt for worthy prey than to wait for a witch.

So far the hunt primarily consisted of keeping the other two alive, as they were nearly helpless in the bush. They were not, however, without their abilities in combat, as proven when the ape-things had come swinging down on them. Keun-ju fought fiercer with one arm and half a sword than some she had met with twice his blessings, and Best could tell Purna would be a strong knife-fighter even if she hadn't had the devil dog distracting her enemies with its shrill yaps. If only there had actually been a demonic army to pit their skills against they should have comported themselves well, and whenever the impossible odds overwhelmed them slipped down to Old Black's Meadhall, secure in their righteous hereafter—if this land truly was Jex Toth then it should be right beneath their feet. The only thing for it was to keep hunting and pray the Fallen Mother granted Best a foe great enough to cancel out the sins she had accrued in coming to this Deceiver-loved jungle.

"What if these monkey men *are* the dread demons of Jex Toth?" said Purna, using a leaf to pick excrement out of her devil dog's fur after their second run-in with the vulgar creatures. "Wouldn't it be a hoot if all those dire prophecies were just warning of the return of some punkass apes?"

"No," said Best, refusing to believe that the Fallen Mother would be so cruel. There *must* be something far more dangerous to this place. Best prayed nightly for a worthy foe.

Reckoning if the alleged armies of Jex Toth were attacking the Star they would need ships to reach it, the hunting party hewed as close to the coast as the difficult terrain allowed. They bore east, deciding on the direction after Purna asked her devil in which direction the enemy lay and he cocked his head to the left. That settled the matter for Purna, but since setting out Best had noticed the dog always cocked his head when his mistress addressed him, and always to that side. This was what came of dealing with devils—instead of granting you wisdom they sapped you of it, making you certain when you should be cautious.

Day and night the cacophony of the jungle set Best's teeth on edge. Even when their path led them down from the high country to gravelly black beaches they stayed in the trees as much as possible, for while the sky-devils patrolled more frequently after dark they were increasingly active during the day. One night as they all tried to sleep in makeshift hammocks of tangled vines, Best counted a dozen of them flying in formation through a chink in the canopy. She wondered how many more might be in the flock that went by unseen. The larger ones were even bigger than Nemi's horned wolf Myrkur, and in the absence of more immediate challenges Best committed herself to bringing one of them down, though what trophy their gelatinous-looking flesh might yield remained to be seen.

"That is absolutely not a good idea," Keun-ju told her when she announced her intention as they made camp the next evening on a small wooded island in the midst of a wide, shallow river that flowed out to the sea. "Dangerous, profitless sport. I vote no."

"I do not propose it for a *vote*," said Best, the word as sour as the yellow fruit they had foraged after Keun-ju excitedly declared them to be a varietal of Immaculate plum. "I offer you the opportunity to join my hunt, and you speak of votes?"

"We already have one hunt, and if you are hurt or killed then Purna and I will be in serious trouble on our own," said the Immaculate, as though confessing their weakness might somehow sway Best from pursuing personal glory. "I believe it is an issue that concerns us all, and so I put it to a vote."

"He's got a point," said Purna, draining the blood from her most recent snake—it was obvious from her grotesque tongue that the girl had the blood of devils in her, same as Sullen, so perhaps she was part mongoose. "A vote to decide whether we three postpone this thankless, blistery hike for something crazy-fun like monster hunting."

"As I said, any issue that concerns us all..." Keun-ju began, but trailed off and blew his veil out in a long sigh as Purna grinned at Best. Her devil dog barked, hopping up on his little legs to happily lick the girl's cheek. It took Best a moment to realize what had happened, and then she smiled, too. The little Ugrakari might be boastful but she was no coward, and had the hood to prove it—if the cloak had actually been cured properly it should have been as great a prize as any in the clan, but the work had been hastily done, and crudely. Still, she had taken it with her own hand, to hear Sullen sing it when she had asked how he dared associate with an Outlander who wore the mantle of their people. And now she voted with Best to seek other prey of great stature.

"How do you think we take it down?" asked Purna, pushing her face-licking devil away far more gently than Best would have been able to manage. "I mean, I've got an idea or two of my own, but one badass monster killer to another, what's your gut telling you here?"

"I have considered this all day," said Best. "It is wise to hunt birds in their nests, but I have yet to see one land. Perhaps if we capture one of the Craven-apes and stake it out in the open we may lure one to the ground, and then strike."

"Too complicated, and we haven't seen any of those chimp chumps in yonks," said Purna as she began skinning the snake. "But the principle's sound. I vote we have Keun-ju do it—wait until dark, but instead of dousing the fire have him stand out there in the stream with a torch to bring one in."

"I do not think so," he said, adding more kindling to the small fire that smoldered in the bole of a mangrove.

"I vote it as well," said Best, warming up to this democratic process after all.

"What do we hit it with, though?" said Purna. "Guess we could stick it with those bamboo spears we made, but to really get the impact we'd want it to fly right into…oh, that's it! Keun-ju, you're fired as bait, I get to do it."

"We won't need spears," said Best, patting her great-grandmother's sun-knife. "This fetish of my family never misses, and always kills."

Keun-ju cleared his throat, and it sounded an awful lot like one of those dirty two-syllable Immaculate curse words her son had picked up in his travels, and now she could guess from where. At least Purna swore in Flintlander like a civilized person. Best was about to ask the lippy boy what exactly he meant, but then her eyes caught the hollow sleeve of his coat he had tied off to prevent bugs from crawling in and she realized he was right. Best's chest tightened. She could no longer make that boast of her sun-knife, a claim that had been true all the days she had used it, and all the days of her father before her. As if he knew he had won some victory over her, Keun-ju said, "I am merely suggesting you might not want to throw Sullen's inheritance into a winged whale, lest it carry it away."

"His inheritance?" said Best, appalled at the suggestion. "My son will never wield this blade."

"Not so long as you're alive, I suppose," said Keun-ju, and Best squinted at him, trying to see if he had just threatened her or not. It was hard to tell, when he hid his mouth like a reformed anathema wearing a penitent mask.

"See, here's what I'm going to do," said Purna, skewering her snake and tossing its arrow-shaped head to her devil. "I find a nice rocky spot in the river, and take a nice long spear out there. Then I clear a little hole in the streambed, where I can brace the butt of the bamboo. Keep it lowered, inconspicuous like, until the last minute—when it zips down to nab me, I duck real low and pull up the spear. Splat."

"That is indeed the likely result," said Keun-ju. "Even if you suc-ceed in killing it in such a fashion, Purna, it will crash on top of you from such heights as I cannot begin to guess. *Splat.*"

"Oh," said Purna. "You think so?"

"A hole," said Best, inspired by the snake Purna began smoking over the fire. "Instead of the center of the river we go to the far shore.

The bank is sandy there. We dig a hole, just wide enough for you, and you wait with your spear. As it swoops you lie back in the hole. It will spit itself, and even if it strikes the earth atop you, you are safe beneath the surface."

"Hey, not bad!" said Purna, turning her snake. "How deep a hole are we talking now?"

They plotted as the sun went down, Best feeling almost herself again, the skilled huntress she had been before the Fallen Mother had seen fit to test her. Even Keun-ju's incessant mentioning of Sullen-this and Sullen-that no longer seemed intended to provoke her, for Purna sympathetically rolled her eyes at Best whenever the Immaculate made another such comment. It was not the epic song Sullen had promised her, but it was a better evening than most, and an illuminating one: when she asked Purna who had taught her to hunt such noble prey as horned wolves, the girl replied it had indeed been Best's feckless brother Craven. Sullen had told her as much, but as a rule Best distrusted second-hand hunting tales. Purna had been there, however, and watched Craven charge headlong into one of the monsters as they traveled through the mountains, and together their small pack had overwhelmed the beast, and then a second of its kind. Even the Diggelby creature had taken part in the glorious battle, which surprised Best almost as much as the thought of her brother running *at* anything, let alone a horned wolf...but one hunt does not a huntress make.

Later, after they excavated a burrow for Purna and brought her spear and torch, Best and Keun-ju retreated, along with the girl's devil dog—he had tried to stay in the depression with her but she had ordered him off and the miniature monster followed her instructions for a change. They had chosen the position of the hole carefully, and Best climbed a nearby eucalyptus, edging far enough out on a low limb that if the sky-devil landed atop Purna but was not killed outright she could leap onto its back. Keun-ju stayed in the shadows of the treeline, ready to rush in with a spear of his own.

Then they waited.

But they did not have to wait long.

Purna was singing a drinking song at the top of her lungs, waving the torch around, and then the monster was falling from the sky so swiftly Best had barely sounded the alarm when it struck. She couldn't see if Purna had dropped back in time, its great silvery bulk swooping back up into the air...and then crashing down again, skidding across the riverbank and into the current. The devil dog streaked out of the trees, running toward the fallen behemoth and yapping its head off as though they might have failed to notice where it landed.

Best dropped from the tree as Purna poked her head up with an exultant *woo*, the girl shaking all over as she crawled out of the pit. She was spattered with blood, or something like blood, it was hard to tell since the torch had gone out, but to Best's eye even in the moonlight it looked off, not dark enough.

Then they were rushing in together to confirm just how different this game truly was, wading into the water and spearing it over and over, though it was already still save for the death shivers that even strange demons in unknown lands apparently experienced. It was *huge*, its leathery opal skin translucent in places, showing organs that shimmered with phosphorescence, tentacles as thick as a mastodon trunk emerging from under one of its broken wings, swaying in the current. Strangest of all, perhaps, was a black panel on its ridged back, which almost looked like...like one of those things Outlanders used, for riding horses.

"A saddle!" said Purna, climbing up onto the seat and looking all around. "Holy fucking shit. Holy shitting fuck. Who do you think *rides* these guys?"

"I can tell you exactly who," said Keun-ju, splashing up to them from the bank. "They were thrown when it fell. And one of them is still very much alive."

CHAPTER
10

They found Choplicker in the Office of Answers, laid out on a gurney like a sacrifice on a pagan altar. It had taken them some time to navigate all the way up here from the dungeons, but at least the disguise Boris had given Zosia was cutting the mustard. That, and Castle Diadem wasn't quite the tightly guarded fortress it had been in Zosia's day, or her successor's—the few times they did encounter actual uniformed guards who asked where they were off to, Boris blathered right past them. The pair who minded the entrance to the Office of Answers hadn't even done more than glance at his papers, and the interior of the complex was deserted this late at night. Boris used his coalstick to light a pair of interrogation lamps, hanging one up to illuminate Zosia's devil as he took the other to check the adjoining torture chambers and make sure they were really alone.

"Chop," she murmured, standing over his stiff, lean form. The dog was as she'd left him in the Upper Chainhouse, when she'd turned from her fallen devil and charged the fuckers who had betrayed them. Must be his devilish blood that kept him so perfectly preserved, and running a hand through his bristly fur and feeling the coldness there her chest locked up, just as it had when Efrain Hjortt had tossed Leib's head in her lap. When she could trust herself to speak again she said, "They got you about as good as they got me, huh?"

"All clear," said Boris, splashing through the rusty puddle that had formed over a clogged drain in the volcanic glass floor; for all his talk of the new way being better than the old, this room cluttered with witch thrones, iron maidens, and lesser-known implements had seen recent use. He had found a large gunnysack and tossed it onto the rusted table beside Choplicker, reluctant to approach the devil even in death. "Don't mean to be indelicate, but stuff him in there and let's get a move on. Those guards I drugged will be stirring, if they haven't already, and once the alarm sounds getting you out of here won't be so easy."

Zosia nodded, so tired from hiking all the way up here that she didn't even know how she could carry him back out. Just thinking straight was near impossible, everything seeming like a lucid bug dream...but she would get through this. She would. She had to heal before she could figure out her next move, and she had to escape before she could heal.

"Your oath," Boris reminded her as she opened the sack to shove in his remains.

"My oath?" Zosia looked up.

"Just like we agreed in the cell," said Boris. "Before we go, swear it on your devil. You'll leave Diadem tonight and never return, nor seek vengeance nor violence on anyone here, nor cause mischief as you leave."

"Oh, right, sure," said Zosia, drowsily weaving her fingers through Choplicker's cold coat. "I swear to leave Diadem, not return, no vengeance, no violence, no mischief."

"No, say it like I said it," insisted Boris. "Like a real oath, so I know I can trust you. On pain of your devil's freedom, you'll leave Diadem tonight and never return, nor seek vengeance nor violence on anyone here, nor cause mischief as you leave."

"This is getting fucking ridiculous," said Zosia, her head aching and her fingers tightening to a fist in his fur. "You want me to swear on the freedom of my dead fucking devil? Fine, whatever. On pain of Choplicker's freedom, I'll...I'll..."

Boris started to mouth the words he thought she'd forgotten, but that was not the problem. No, it fucking was not. Relaxing her fist, she looked down at her devil, really looked at him. She let her hands roam where they would, not sure what she was seeking out, but her hackles good and raised as she leaned close, inspecting his body. It felt like there was a ravenous monster stalking through her brain fog, circling her, and if she couldn't make it out in time it would end her.

"Zosia, we have to go," said Boris, talking down to her like she was a difficult child. "*Now*. Didn't it seem a little too easy to get in here? Those guards at the door are probably checking out my story right fucking now, and when they find out it was bullshit they'll come in here and nab us both. So do as you promised and swear the oath, or I'll leave you here to be recaptured."

"You're not going anywhere," said Zosia, her heart quickening as she straightened up, tore off the itchy fake beard, and caught him in her furious gaze. She had no clue what was going on, not yet, but she was sure of one thing. "You've been lying to me, Boris."

"You're on your own," said Boris, backing away to the door, but Zosia snatched a long knife off a nearby tray, held it up by the blade.

"Come here, tell the truth, live. That order." Zosia cocked her arm back, holding in a gasp as the bolt wound in her shoulder split open from the sudden movement. Keeping the knife held up for more than another few moments would take all she had; throwing it would be impossible. Grimacing though her pain, she said, "Take another step, or tell another lie, and this knife goes into you."

He froze, considering it, and if she'd actually been able to make good on her promise she would have thrown it into his fucking leg for not immediately capitulating. As if he read this bloody intention in her eyes his shoulders slumped and he hung his head, coming back between the vacant gurneys and chairs. She dropped the knife on the table next to the sack, noticing that it already had dog fur stuck to its tacky blade. Nothing made any sense yet, but she felt a stirring at the back of her mind, like a great bulk of scaled coils twisting over one another, loosening a living knot.

"I told you true," Boris said, still sounding like he thought he could talk himself clear of whatever evil fucking mess this was. "Everything I said about there being too much killing and vengeance already, and you not deserving what the People's Pack did to you, I believe that to my bones. I swear it on Sister Portolés's soul. I want you to go free. I'm trying to help you, Zosia, and keep you from hurting other people who might yet do some good in this world!"

"Those two things don't always go together, Boris, but I played nice this time, didn't I?" said Zosia. "Gave you my word to go away and never come back? Why the lawyer routine, having me say all the proper words in the proper order, and doing so in the name of the freedom of a devil that's already dead?"

"Those were the conditions," said Boris, slumping down into an iron chair with straps instead of cushions. "I couldn't have got you out on my own, Zosia, much as I'd like. I had help. But the terms were I had to get you to swear on your devil, just to make sure this didn't come back to bite nobody. I staked my life that you'd agree to it, so my neck is as good as—"

"Who helped you, Boris, and more importantly, why?" Always the *whys* were what eluded Zosia... "Why would anyone help me, when it'd be safest for all parties just to have me killed? And why did they tell you to take me here and have me swear on Choplicker?"

"Look, tell you what..." said Boris, fiddling with one of the restraints on the arm of his chair. He reminded her of a worm that'd already been threaded onto the hook three times over but still couldn't help itself from trying to wriggle free. "I'll tell you everything, Zosia, but only after you swear the oath. That way everyone wins, nobody gets hurt, and you get all your questions answered."

"*That's* your pitch?" Zosia looked around for the most intimidating instrument she could find, and settled for a saw. She tried to brandish it at him but it was too heavy for her weak arm and she dropped it back down with a clatter. As she did she noticed more fur embedded in its teeth, her dog's fur, but there wasn't a scratch on him... She settled for picking the knife back up and pointing it at Boris. "You don't get to set the terms here. Spill, or I'll spill something else."

"All right," he said, rising back to his feet. "But pack him up and I'll tell you on the way out. I wasn't lying about time being short, neither. If we're caught it won't matter who I know or what you do, 'cause we'll all end up back here together, and—"

"No," said Zosia. "We're not leaving this room until I've heard everything there is to hear. Every word out of your lips from here until I'm done with you is something I want to hear, and the first time you disappoint me I stick you with this. Now tell me: who's helping me escape, and why, and how come they care so much about me swearing an oath of peace on a dead devil?"

"Ain't it obvious?" said Boris, looking uneasily at Choplicker. "They're not so sure he's really dead. They've tried making sure, I gather, from acid to fire to pitching him into Diadem Gate, but he keeps coming back."

"Not dead?" Zosia's heart was in her throat as she stared at the very, very dead dog in front of her. "What do you mean, he keeps coming back?"

"Like that," said Boris, nodding at the carcass. "Anytime someone doesn't have their eye on the body it goes missing, but always turns up in the same place. Down in your cell with you. They take it away and it just happens again, even happened after they threw it in the Gate. Even fucking eerier than if it rose from the dead, having the corpse vanish near daily only to turn up in your cell. Everyone's nervous about it and nobody knows what it means—they thought killing your devil would be the end of the business, but apparently it's not so easy to get rid of this one."

"Oh, Chop," she said softly, petting him but feeling none of the normal disquiet she had before at stroking something she had only ever touched in life and finding it dead. Unexpectedly choked up, she said, "Even harder to get shy of you than I thought."

Then it hit her.

"They want me swearing an oath on him in case he somehow recovers. They don't give a damn if my wrinkled old ass tries to make a big scene, they're worried about what happens if he wakes up." Seeing Boris glumly nod his assent, she said, "So who is the *they* here, huh? Let me guess—Eluveitie and the rest of your crew? She decided getting on my bad side was a mistake and is trying to protect herself on the sly?"

"Eluveitie and most of the People's Pack want you executed for your crimes," said Boris. "It's the surviving Chainites that want to get you out of the city in exchange for your oath—the wildborn clergy were the ones who reached out to me. But they assumed if they propositioned you directly instead of working through me you wouldn't trust them."

"Back to working with the Chainites, eh, Boris?" Zosia couldn't believe this shit. "They're right, I wouldn't have trusted them if they'd asked directly, and I trust them even less now that I know they orchestrated this stupid fucking plot! Why would the Chain want to help me?"

"*I* orchestrated this *brilliant* plot, just to be clear; they just provided me with certain resources," said Boris, certainly proud as a Chainite of his convoluted machinations. "And while I told the truth about my motives in wanting to free you it's possible theirs are a bit more realist than idealist, as you'd have it. They're worried if you die that might finally wake up your devil, to bad result for everyone who crossed you in life. So they want you out of here, taking it with you, and with the bond of your oath that you'll never come back down on them."

"All this fuss over one little jackal-dog," said Zosia, shaking her head at her sidekick who was more intimidating in death than she was in life. "And if I die he wakes up, huh?"

"That's obviously only a concern to some, otherwise the rest wouldn't be so keen to flay you," said Boris. "Guess nobody knows what to make of your monster for sure. Sounds like they've caught devils this way before but never had one hang on like he has, and it's making everybody nervous."

"Caught devils what way?" asked Zosia, because that right there was the most important question of the age—finding your way out of a trap was damn near impossible if you didn't know how you'd wandered into it. "What did they do to him? One minute he was fine and the next like this."

"That I couldn't tell you, on my honor as a citizen of Diadem I got no notion of how—"

"Shut up," she said, wondering if it could be that easy? Those guards down in the cell, stiff and vacant but still alive, victims of their own appetite for an illicit puff of something tasty…And what Domingo Hjortt had described happening to his regiment at the Battle of the Lark's Tongue, going crazy after being anointed with Chainite oil…Devils were all appetite, it was what defined the fiends, and if poison was the favorite trick of the church, perhaps they had fed him something? Sharper than any thought she'd had in memory, the image came to her of Choplicker snapping up some tainted morsel that caught in his craw. "Boris, spread his jaws for me."

"Do what now?" Boris looked about to mount some protest, and Zosia was ready to shut his ass down, when the double doors on the far side of the chamber rattled. There was no lock on any of the doors in the Office of Answers, for the state had insisted it had nothing to hide, but the doors opened inward to the hall and whoever was on the other side had tried to shove them open instead. "Fuck, I—"

As Boris was telling Zosia he'd told her so the doors yanked inward, a dozen orange-clad guards charging into the chamber with crossbows and polearms in hand. Boris flipped a gurney to put between himself and the guards as he made a break for the hallway leading to the adjoining rooms. Lots of shouting and crossbows twanging, her least favorite sound in all the Star these days, but Zosia didn't see if Boris made it because she was too busy wriggling her one good arm into her devil's cold, sharp mouth. Down his cold, rough throat.

Once upon a time in Kypck, a birthing cow had gotten her calf turned the wrong way around and she had watched Leib reach right inside the animal to correct the problem. This was just like that, she told herself. Except…not.

His teeth drew blood from her forearm as she reached deeper into his tight esophagus, his stiff tongue making it an even tighter fit, but then some congealed slime broke free to ease her passage, and her elbow reached his muzzle. Yet there was nothing down here, her questing fingertips finding only the inside of an animal carcass— she'd had this thought of finding something like a poisoned bit of apple caught in the throat of a fairysong princess, the image leaping so clearly to her mind it had felt like divine inspiration…or infernal, as the ballad may be.

"Take her alive!"

Glancing over from her grisly search she saw half the guards gathered around a body on the floor just in front of the hallway to the next room. The other five or six thugs were cautiously approaching her, polearms down and crossbows up.

"Stop…stop that shit!" one of them barked.

Zosia didn't stop, gagging as she felt Choplicker's jaw unhinge to accommodate her bicep. There was nothing in his gullet but she followed her desperate hunch all the way down into his stomach, thinking of all the treasures he had swallowed over the years, carrying them around in his gut and then disgorging them for his mistress no worse for the wear. He'd once coughed up a live songbird in the kitchen, which Leib had said was a nice gesture even if the tiny creature was too terrified to chirp and flew straight out the window once Zosia had wiped off its slobbery wings. Now her stretching fingertips pressed down into fermented viscera, everything soft and cold and—

Two of the guards set down their crossbows and came for her then, their nervous compatriots close enough to spear her throat or shoot her through the eye if need be. As they lunged at her Zosia's fingernails scratched something small but solid and distinct that lurked inside her devil's belly. She clutched at it, and then the guards tackled her. Still stuck in the devil, her shoulder twisted out of its socket as they took her to the ground, the gurney toppling over as Zosia screamed at the top of her lungs, her fucking arm on fucking fire, the heat of the hurt so bright it fried her brain.

By the time the conflagration of pain had cooled enough for her to think straight again she was up on one of their shoulders, being carried from the Office of Answers. Lifting her head, she saw that Boris was still alive, but probably not for long. He was crawling on his stomach, quarrels rising from his back and leg, the guards standing over him taking turns raking him with their polearms. Steeling herself, she tried to twist around and snap the neck of the guard carrying her, but only succeeded in nearly blacking out again from the exertion—her right shoulder was bleeding from the arrow wound she had reopened and her left was dislocated. As she stared down at her useless arms dangling beneath her, she noticed with detached fascination that her numb left hand was still clenched in a fist, and she tried flexing it, just to see if she still had control even though she'd lost all feeling. Her fingers opened, and a small hunk of something pliable fell from her hand—she couldn't see what.

She sensed it before she heard it, the heartbreaking keen initially so high as to be inaudible. The guards must have felt it, too, because the one carrying Zosia stopped and those who were tormenting Boris looked over toward the upended gurney in the back of the room, and through the pain Zosia followed their gaze even as the howl broke loose into the realm of mortals. There had been nothing there a moment ago but here he was, head thrown back, stretching his lungs for the first time in too long as he sat on the edge of the filthy puddle. As his howl trailed off and he lowered his muzzle Zosia saw he was grinning at her. She grinned back.

Then one of the guards said or did something, and that hungry grin was everywhere at once, a black river of mouths exploding out of her devil. The man holding Zosia dropped her but Choplicker caught her from the air in his teeth, cradling her there in his world-devouring muzzle. Through the dizzying maelstrom of molten flesh and needle-sharp fur she watched the guards be eaten alive, some consumed in staccato snaps of slavering jaws and others wolfed down whole. They continued to scream even when she couldn't see them anymore, the shrieks echoing out of his countless throats, and then a tongue as warm and wide as a blanket curled around Zosia's limp body and she joined them in the First Dark as Choplicker swallowed her alive.

It didn't hurt. She had assumed it would. But it didn't.

CHAPTER

11

One thing Sullen would say for Nemi was the witch never said *I told ya so*. Maybe it was because they all knew it went without saying, or maybe it was because she was just as down in the mouth as Sullen and Diggelby about the situation. They had really thought they could win over the People's Pack, convince 'em to lend their aid for the war against Jex Toth. And Count Raven only knew, they well might have, if they'd been able to get an audience with the council that now ruled Diadem. The rub was they hadn't got to talk to the right people, and the people they *had* talked to hadn't even known who the right people were.

The castle built into the natural walls of the city was open to the public, but they hadn't gotten very far inside before encountering long queues of folk all trying to find the right person to talk to, too. Diggelby's suggestion that they be allowed to cut in line as their business concerned the very fate of the world did not rank with those who had apparently been waiting for days. The rise of Jex Toth seemed less of an immediate concern in these parts than folks starving or plague breaking out or thugs wearing the orange livery of the new militia causing problems. Brother Rýt volunteered to wait in line on behalf of his companions. If nothing else, the queue must lead to someone who could tell him where a missionary monk home from the heathen front should go to discharge his message, his confession, and his penance.

It was agreed Rýt should be given a letter summarizing the recent global catastrophe and imminent threat, so that once he was reunited with his superiors in the church they might in turn pass it along to the People's Pack. Not that anyone had any real expectation of this yielding much benefit, even before it became apparent that the only thing they had to write on was the pasha's rolling papers. Out of options, they left the monk with verbal instructions of which highlights to hit, should he find someone receptive to hearing the biggest news since the Age of Wonders. Diggelby had repeated that phrase several times, loudly, trying to attract the attention they deserved from the guards supervising the cattle call, but it never went anywhere.

After that it was a somber trio who trudged back outside into Diadem's constant black rain, though noticing how many of the towering ancient buildings were burnt-out husks gave Sullen a brief surge of hope. Maybe Zosia had indeed tried to flood the city with burning oil or devil's fire, as the Faceless Mistress had warned, only to have someone interrupt her before it went too far, doing Sullen's job for him. Wouldn't that be nice?

Happy thoughts did not last long, however, in this dank and ashy woodpile of a metropolis. It had taken all day and well into the evening before they had finally given up on meeting the People's Pack or their representatives, exchanging the claustrophobic caves of the castle for the equally confining avenues and alleys. Sullen was usually quite good at orienting himself but was accustomed to at least being able to see the night sky, and here on the tight streets of Diadem he might as well have been lost in a giant antbed, wandering through tunnels laid out according to no order known to mortal minds. Nemi had heard that Diadem insulated its Gate behind guarded cordons and so wanted to reach it before dawn, in case they had to jump a wall to access their infernal road to Othean.

Yet the rain was coming down so hard that even with his devilish eyes Sullen could barely make out the lane in front of them. With hardly anyone out on the streets and those who were disinclined to be accosted by three weirdos in need of very detailed directions, they eventually took shelter under a bridge seemingly made of packed-together houses, waiting for the rain to let up before trying again. It had been hours since their dinner of handpies and kebabs, and Sullen immediately pulled out the extra treat Diggelby had bought him for the road, tearing into the flatfish-stuffed bread. It had gotten mushy from the rain and wasn't much like the food he'd eaten back on the Frozen Savannahs anyway, but it still had more of a Flintland taste than most anything he'd had since leaving home, and he couldn't get enough of that nutty spice. By the mysterious mug of the Faceless Mistress, if he never ate a sack of foraged weeds again it would be too soon.

"Do you think they're already there?" Diggelby asked as he squatted in the mud beside the river of rushing black runoff. Sullen leaned against the inner wall of the bridge while Nemi used her cockatrice cage as a stool. "Back in Othean, I mean, after their side trip to Jex Toth."

"With Hoartrap steering them they are definitely somewhere, let's just pray it's somewhere nice," panted Nemi, taking the handpie Sullen offered her. Her ring-striped fingers were shaking, making him suppose her slow pace hadn't just been for the benefit of her gut-stuck companion. He hadn't really gotten a feel for her yet, the witch, even though they'd been traveling together for weeks now and she'd been his barber twice over. There was definitely something up with her, though, some pox or curse that kicked in once the sun went down. She treated her affliction the same way she treated everything.

"You might want to have your egg early, before we set out," Sullen suggested as she passed the snack to Diggelby. "Seen you leaning on your stick pretty hard, and we might have to strut quick to make it before dawn."

"Is that your learned opinion as a scholar of medicine, magic, and other marvels?" asked Nemi, a little rattily. "However did I manage to take care of myself day in and day out before we met?"

"Um...pretty well, I expect?" said Sullen, realizing he'd given offense. "Sorry, was just saying is all, in case you weren't thinking 'bout it. Know my mind's been wandering all day, so..."

"Oh! I...I appreciate the concern, but it's not necessary," said Nemi, sounding as though maybe she'd misread things a little, too. "As much time as you've spent under my care since we've met you probably learned the basics of my methods, but masters rarely take kindly to their apprentices volunteering suggestions."

"Your apprentice, nice," said Sullen with a smile, because it was a smart burn—he'd definitely put in more hours getting his own pains tended to of late than he had administering aches to others. But Sullen was all right with that, his smile turning to a grimace as he remembered knocking the kid from the Cobalt camp back onto the spear his ma held. The spear he now held, and that held his grandfather. It was a beautiful weapon, but while he'd been hyped to try it out as soon as he saw it, now all he could think about was how he hoped he never stuck it in another person. Far as he could tell Nemi had yet to hurt a soul, be it mortal or devil, and used her hands to slow the flow of blood instead of hastening it.

Maybe he should ask if she would take him on as her apprentice for real. What would that be like, living a life where you didn't hurt people? Where you didn't kill kids without even trying? Sullen tried to think of an ancestor who'd done more repairing than reaping and came up dry; even the shaman Ghostbather was a hunter first and a healer second. Murder was Sullen's legacy, murder and mayhem, not medicine.

"Are you all right, old boy?" Diggelby asked gently, and Sullen realized the rain had slowed enough that they could hear him weeping. Ever since the kid in the tavern he'd been crying a lot, sometimes just out of nowhere.

"Yeah." He cleared his throat, tried to make it stick. "Yeah."

"I *am* sorry I polished off that pie. I thought you were finished. I'll buy you a whole bakery, next chance we get."

"Heh." Sullen shook his burdened brow, appreciating Diggelby's attempt to cheer him up even if he couldn't bring himself to smile. "Nah, I'm all right. Just ready to be back with our friends."

"Then off we go," said Diggelby, hopping lightly to his buckleshoed feet and then looking a little sheepish about it as Sullen and Nemi readied themselves to go back into the rain with far less celerity.

"I'm waiting to take my cure until we see if we can reach the Gate before first light, because if not I'll just sleep all day anyway," said

Nemi, making sure the oilskin cover was tight over Zeetatrice's cage. "She doesn't like being out of the vardo, and when she's nervous she's less dependable with her eggs. So I'm conserving the ones I have."

"Hey, you don't owe me an explanation," said Sullen. "You tend you and I'll tend…actually, I'll just let you tend me, too. Seems safest."

"Here, let me make sure the stitches haven't ripped," said Nemi, and was about to put the cage back down in the muck when he waved her off.

"Nah, it's fine, everything is fine." It wasn't exactly a lie, because he didn't feel *too* much worse than usual, but he also knew just pulling his wet tunic up off his belly was going to be nauseatingly bad and he could wait quite a while on that. Let him get safely back to Keun-ju and Ji-hyeon and then he could worry about his wound, and the fate of the Star, and all such other trivial matters.

"How do you think Purna's getting on with your mom?" Diggelby asked, staring off into the rain. "I couldn't have lived with myself if I subjected another poor devil to the same bondage I put Prince through, but I do find myself wishing I could have found some other way of joining them. To be a gadfly on the wall…"

"You think they're having it out?" Sullen had spent all his time imagining his mother being crazy at Keun-ju; he hadn't even stopped to think how she and Purna would clash.

"I think they've got to be tight as ticks by now," said Diggelby. "Purna lives for that barbarian buffoonery. No offense."

"None taken."

"Let's just hope Hoartrap treats them better than others who trusted him," said Nemi darkly, "and that Othean hasn't fallen in the meanwhile."

"Hope's for dopes," said Diggelby, hoisting his sequin-shedding pack and heading out into the drizzle. "That said, I've got a *great* feeling about this. Anyone care to lay a modest wager that we'll soon see our old friends?"

CHAPTER

12

Y ou know what, maybe it's a little much," said Maroto, cocking his head and watching the skull in the looking glass do the same. During the week or so of preparations they'd made before sailing from Darnielle Bay he'd helped convert the rear half of her captain's quarters into this dressing room, and it had seemed a shame to not take advantage of it, but now he was having second thoughts. "I'm way too old to rock this shit anymore."

"Some looks are timeless," said Lupitera, her own greasepaint foundation even whiter than the lead paste she'd used on him. "And if you even think of washing that off after all the time I spent putting it on I will slap the taste out your mouth."

"I should be so lucky," muttered Maroto, reaching for the jug of papaya grog on the cluttered vanity. The tropical tang reminded him of Purna's lip gloss, that nostalgic twinge in his breast the only thing that let him choke down the sugary swill. Well, that and he really needed to get his courage up for this predawn assault bullshit. "So, Carla—"

"Lupitera," she corrected, holding up a blown glass pot of candy-floss-pink rouge. "Carla doesn't come out until this goes on, and there's no way in hell I'm doing that until it's time to fight."

"Funny how when we're young we just assume we'll grow out of our demons, someday," said Maroto, frowning at his reflection. "But the older we get we're just happy if we can build little rituals to control them."

"*Funny*'s one word for it," said Lupitera, reaching over the carcass of the fried chicken they'd just housed to pop open the gilt terrarium at the back of her vanity. Using the same tongs she employed to fish pickles out of the enormous barrel next to her tufted chair, she reached into the enclosure and removed a cobraroach. With long-practiced ease she closed her eyes and held the scaly bug in front of her surprisingly smooth old face, prompting it to spit its juices onto her eyelids. "Fancy a toot?"

"Nah, it'd clash with my skullface," he said, though he knew full well he could take a hit anywhere and get the stimulating effects of the venom without the iridescent lavender swelling it triggered in thinner tissues. Used to be a time when turning down an insect hurt bad as blue balls, even after he'd been clean for ages, but ever since making the infested acquaintance of the Vex Assembly he'd come to find the creepy-crawlies utterly repulsive.

If only he'd had that moment of clarity before the Battle of the Lark's Tongue and stayed sober for the big fight, maybe he could have protected Purna from her fatal wound...*Presumably* fatal, as Bang had insisted every time he brought up his fallen friend, but then she still held out hope for the rest of her old crew and Maroto was absolutely certain the lot of them had bought it when their ship had sunk off the coast of Jex Toth.

And if even Captain Positivity thought this imminent sneak attack was an unwinnable engagement, why the devils was Maroto still going through with it?

"You look a thousand leagues away," said Lupitera, fluttering her spit-dyed eyelids as she dropped the cobraroach back into its enclosure. "Can't blame you for wishing you were, all things considered."

"At my age I've learned better than to waste time on wishes," said Maroto, daydreaming even as he said it that he'd absconded the night before with Bang, Niki-hyun, Dong-won, and all the mutineers they had enticed into crewing the *Empress Thief*, and the two other formerly Imperial ships that had defected along with them. No sense getting too down, though—assuming he lived out the war he'd most definitely see his captain again. Bang had forgotten the pipe Zosia had made her in Maroto's bunk after their final tryst, and while she might be able to do without her briar or without her cabin boy she couldn't get by missing both.

"Well, at my age I've learned that wishes sometimes come true," said Lupitera, waving an enormous candelabrum in front of her face to light a blunt and nearly setting her enormous daffodil-yellow wig on fire. After getting the cigar-wrapped saam going she passed it over and blew out an enormous purple plume. "Like I always dreamed I'd see you again, so I could call you out for being the no-account show-jumping piece of trash you are."

"And tell me what a success the show was after I left, don't forget that part," said Maroto, though there was fat chance of that happening. She'd only reminded him twice a day the whole damn trip up here to Othean.

"I'm *never* going to forget that part," she said as he took an enormous hit from the crackling blunt, the honey she'd sealed it with sticking to his white-daubed lips. "I must be demented, letting you understudy my performance as savior of the Star after all your punkassitude."

"If you'd seen the things I had on Jex Toth you wouldn't be so sure we were saving anybody," said Maroto, passing back the blunt. His smoke-tickled lungs felt warm and good, but his hands were still shaking. "And look, I oughta come clean. I told you all about how we got captured by the Vex Assembly and the Tothans, right, and how they only let us go so we'd spread the word of their coming, get everybody good and scared... but I didn't tell you everything."

Lupitera raised her bloodshot eyes as she took an enormous hit, the eggplant stain of the bug spit spreading up past her impeccably threaded eyebrows.

"Yeah, so..." Maroto gulped. Why did coming clean always feel so dirty? He'd betrayed the whole damn human race; the least he could do was own that shit. Especially since he was fixing to throw his life away to make up for the sin. "So I didn't just help birth those sea monsters of theirs while we were stuck out there...I...I kinda collaborated with the Vex Assembly?"

"*What?*" Lupitera's eyes narrowed and she took an even bigger drag.

"Those evil old priests? The ancient leaders of Jex Toth, they call themselves the Vex—"

"No, dumbass, what d'ya mean you *kinda collaborated* with them?" Lupitera darted the blunt out and tapped hot ash on Maroto's exposed knee. He jumped, belatedly pulling his dressing gown back over his leg. "What all did you collaborate on, hmmm? A new quiche recipe? A game of mash? Because I know not even Maroto Moon-fruit would be shitty enough to collaborate with monsters on their plan to take down the Star! Right?"

"Um..." said Maroto. "Can I have another hit on that?"

"Oh you're gonna get hit all right, as soon as I get these nails off!" Lupitera took another heroic drag, holding it in as she flicked the blunt at him and said, "I can't believe you, Maroto, I really can't."

"I can't, either," he said, not flinching as the burning missile bounced off his chest and landed in his lap. Picking it up before it could burn through the satin, he felt about as low as shit on a centipede's shoe. Lower, maybe. Nothing for it but to close his eyes and take the biggest hit he could, try to pass off the tears that were coming as the product of a cough.

"Say one thing for you, you're consistent," Lupitera said when Maroto was done hacking on the smoke and wiping his cheeks. She was buffing her pinwheel-painted talons instead of removing them, which was a good omen. Then she stopped and looked up, past Maroto, past the rows of gaudy gauze and chintzy chemise, past the ornate captain's chamber that had so recently housed a cardinal of the Burnished Chain, past everything...and then started buffing again, a slow smile creeping up her ghostly cheeks. "So you helped them plan their attack, is that it? Went over their tactics together?"

"I know what you're thinking, but nah, nothing that useful," he said glumly. "The Vex Assembly are definitely crazy but they ain't stupid. When I said I collaborated I meant I let them in my head, told them everything I know about the Isles, the Empire, and the rest of the Star. I even drew them maps and shit, but they definitely didn't let me in on their plans."

"Maybe not, but they would have based their plans on your intelligence...or lack thereof."

"I know." Maroto shook his head. "All I can think about is how I should've somehow found a way to misdirect them, given them bad information. But I didn't. I was too scared and too stupid and—"

"Too stupid is you all over," said Lupitera, pouring herself another brimming teacup of grog and stirring in royal jelly. "That explains why they're throwing everything they've got at the Autumn Palace."

"Because it's where the empress and her court reside, and I told them with Star politics it's best to cut the head off the scorpion straightaway," said Maroto. "Like I said, I sold out the Star without a second thought."

"One, scorpions don't have heads," said Lupitera, ranging around on the vanity for something. "And two, have you ever even been to Othean?"

"Just the once, when Kang-ho talked me into helping him steal the royal family's pet unicorn. *That* did not end well." Maroto smiled a little at the memory, disastrous though it was. Maybe his old buddy was in Othean right now, and together they'd earn noble deaths protecting the very realm they had once sought to fleece...

"And your little adventure, it was in the autumn?"

"Hells if I know," said Maroto. "That was twenty...twenty-seven years ago? Maybe?"

"It *was* the autumn, and that's exactly my point," said Lupitera, finally unearthing a sheaf of papers from beneath a pile of folios. Settling back down onto her seat with a peacock quill and pot of octopus ink she rapidly began scratching out a letter in High Immaculate.

"What's exactly your point?" Either this saam was way more potent than what they'd been smoking on the way up here or waking so early for the imminent attack had gotten him halfway to bombed before he'd even started puffing. He should make some kaldi...

"My point is you did give the Tothans disinformation, whether you meant to or not," said Lupitera. "You told them Empress Ryuki would be in the Autumn Palace, because that's where she was when you and Kang-ho tried to nab her horny horse, didn't you? Maybe you even drew them a map of where the palace is on the Isle?"

"Yeah?"

"But the empress isn't there!" Lupitera glanced up from her letter, meeting Maroto's red eyes in the looking glass. "It might just look like one giant city from outside, but there are four different palaces in Othean. They're miles and miles away from each other, and each has its own walls, its own defenses. And the royal court cycles through them according to the seasons—what season is it now?"

"Um...not autumn?" said Maroto, all the weird weather and lack of a calendar making it hard to reckon if winter was still lingering on or if they'd rounded the wheel into spring yet.

"Precisely," said Lupitera, going back to her letter. "You thought you were betraying the Star but all you were doing was giving the enemy intelligence that's a quarter century out of date, and filtered through your fat head to boot. Not only did you mislead them, but you can tell us exactly how and we can plan accordingly. You wrote their playbook, so you can read their moves."

"Yeah...yeah!" Maroto realized he'd let the blunt go out in his fingers and set it down on the vanity. His hand wasn't shaking anymore. Then he pursed his lips—was he really such a fuckup he hadn't even been able to help an army of monsters successfully ambush the Star? "I mean, there's no way of knowing how much of my intelligence they actually listened to..."

"They listened to enough," said Lupitera. "If you hadn't told them to go after the Autumn Palace first they probably would've hit the Summer Palace instead. It's at the northern tip of Othean, see, and the north shore's where the invasion is coming from. The Immaculates couldn't account for the Tothans marching so far southwest to begin their siege, and assumed it was some trick to divert forces from the Winter Palace, where the empress and her court are all holed up. But it's all thanks to you! I'm writing the Immaculate command right now to let them know we're going to amend our attack accordingly."

"Oh," said Maroto, bumming another sip on the grog jug. "But maybe leave out how you came by that information exactly, huh?"

"Me, steal your applause?" Lupitera signed the letter with a flourish. "Always."

"So we hold off on attacking for now, smart," said Maroto, hoping his words hadn't slurred as he smacked his sticky lips. Admiring his reflection in the glass as Lupitera blew on her letter, two things sprung to his bleary mind. First was that the blunt hadn't been sealed with honey but Lupitera's psychotropic royal jelly. Second was that his old friend had done a fleet job, between cleaning up his flattop and applying his skull makeup. Before they joined the war for real he'd have to get her to reapply it.

"Oh no, darling, you're still leading this morning's charge," said

Lupitera, her voice sounding as slow and drippy as the wax running down the arms of the candelabrum. She leaned in with white-blobbed fingers to fix the tear smears on his cheeks, her turquoise mouth stretching wide to swallow him whole. "The Immaculates are counting on us to send *some* reinforcements to the Autumn Palace, after all, and since you know this particular area so well I can't think of a better volunteer to lead our suicide regiment."

It took a while for all the heavy syllables to bounce down his ears, but when they did Maroto slowly nodded his assent. It said something about his recent quality of life that the only thing that really bummed him out about this plan was the fact that he was definitely going to have to bang some bugs to dispel the brain fog brought on by the royal jelly. As if sensing his need, Lupitera went straight for the buzzing jar of icebees chilling in the champagne bucket.

"Let's do this!" Maroto slapped his hands together once the stings were working their familiar magic. Now he couldn't wait to get wet, in the shallows off Othean when they landed or in rivers of monster blood, whichever flowed first. "Me leading Azgarothians on a suicide mission to save the Isles. So much for playing the Villain!"

"I never bought you in that role anyway," said Lupitera, taking a bump of candied larva off the back of her hand. "And there won't be Azgarothians in your squad."

"No?" Fast as Maroto's brain was racing now he couldn't figure out who else there might be, moored out here just off the Othean coast. "Who am I taking?"

"All those Chainites you brought into our clutches," said Lupitera, grinning even wider as a nosebleed jumped her upper lip, making her look less like a wereclown and more like a glampire. "They're in such a rush to meet their maker, I thought you could be so good as to make the introductions."

After a moment's silence they both erupted into wild cackling. It wasn't a very nice sort of laughter, but then neither of them was a very nice sort of person, really. They had shown up here at the end of the world to fight for the underdogs, though, and that was more than you could say for your average lowlife bug addict performance artist.

CHAPTER

13

He licked her face. Zosia started up onto her elbows, blinking in the harsh light of the interrogation lamp. The obsidian floor was warped beneath them into a series of ridges and valleys, twisted gurneys and chairs and tools jutting out from the frozen waves of volcanic glass. The thing that looked like an old dog wagged its tail to beat the band in the melted mess of the Office of Answers.

"Hey, buddy," she croaked, sitting up the rest of the way. "I scratch your back, you scratch mine, huh?"

He woofed, stepping over her splayed legs and then plopping down across them. She scritched behind his ears with one hand while petting him all the way down his back with the other, a technique of Leib's he had called *playing the 'Licker sitar*. Her husband had trusted the devil more than she ever had, the affable man happy to pretend the monster was just a dog. She had never been comfortable about it, but she shouldn't have begrudged the devil her husband's kindness. Leib had pretended she wasn't a monster, too. Then she realized what she was doing and her hands stopped moving.

"Yeah, I would say we are well past even," she said as she checked in with her body, marveling at how good she felt—the rest of her felt as fine and strong as her arms, and more than just her flesh, the frustrating fog that had clung to her skull having finally lifted. "How something as fucking strong as you got nabbed by me, I'll never know. But then if the Chain tricked you, too, you can't be that smart, huh?"

He playfully snapped at her, and she rubbed his head. She must be in shock.

"How'd they get you, anyway?" she wondered out loud, and he gave her a meaningful stare, and then looked at a crumbly white mess on the floor just beside them. It was whatever she'd pulled from his stomach and then dropped while the guard carried her away. It looked almost like a hunk of cake. Leaning over and prodding at the small lump with her finger she confirmed it *was* cake, or bread or something, and at its center was a shard of polished bone etched with tiny runes. Choplicker growled at it and Zosia shook her head; this was a metaphor for the whole shitty church, it was, an innocuous bit of scripture, easily swallowed. She tucked it into the pipe pouch on her belt. Never knew when a devil-paralyzing bone might come in handy.

"Zosia." The weak voice called from just over a swell in the ruined floor. "Cold Zosia, you fucker, you've murdered me."

Picking herself up off the warped ground, she saw that Boris lay on his back, half absorbed by the obsidian beneath him, a leg and a hand disappearing into the floor. His sweaty face was drained near as white as Choplicker's teeth as the devil came over and snuffled at the trapped man, smacking his jowls. He must like the heretic, since he was the only other person left in the altered Office of Answers.

"Shit, Boris, I'm sorry," said Zosia, kneeling over him. She gave a little tug on the wrist that disappeared into the floor but there was no give at all and he hissed through his teeth. Surveying the dismal situation she saw that one of the bolts he'd taken to the back had punched clean through his side and was leaking thick gore. "Fuck. I...I don't know what I can do."

"You gave me your word," he said, his teeth as red as his wounds. "You didn't swear it on your devil but you gave me your word. You did. And the Cobalt Queen's a woman of honor. Ain't she?"

"I hate to break it to you, Boris, but I was never half as righteous as they said I was," she told him, because lying to the dying was too low even for her. "You kept me drugged in a cell and plied me with lies, so I'd say I wasn't in any condition to make an informed oath."

"Never drugged you," said Boris, looking her in the eye. "Never, Yer Majesty. You started slipping all on your own, soon as your devil went down. Honest. And as for lies...I told my share, yeah. But to an end. To an end. To try and save people."

"I know, Boris," she said, and because she could see in his face he was close to losing his hold she took his free hand in hers. "You're a good man."

"The fuck I am!" Bloody spittle struck her face as he pulled his hand free. "No such thing as good."

"But that'd mean there's no such thing as evil, and we both know that's not true," she said, wanting to put him at ease as he passed over but apparently just winding him up more. "You tried to do good, Boris, and that's more than most offer the world."

"No such thing...as evil," said Boris, his dilated pupils scanning all over the room. "That would be a...comfort. I lied to you."

"I know, Boris, but it's all right, I know now, and—"

"No, you don't," he said, licking his lips and closing his eyes. "Indsorith. She wasn't dead yet. Earlier, when I said she was. A white little lie, considering, but still. Needed to just get you out, didn't want you trying to stop them."

"*What?*" Fast as she tasted relief it curdled on her tongue. "What're you saying, they're executing her tonight?"

"They probably already have," he said. "And she deserves it...Not like you...But I couldn't...I couldn't go down in the Dark...with the lie of it..."

"Where?" He was falling fast, and while Zosia tried not to jostle him too much she still jostled him a bit. "Where, Boris, where?"

"Where do they always dump the monsters...and the parts they cut off?" he said, cracking his eyes and a bloody smile. "The Gate."

"Thank you," said Zosia, meaning it like she hadn't in a long time. "And I'm sorry to leave you like this, Boris, but I've got to try to save the living, and you told me yourself you're already dead. Want me to make it official?"

"Fuck no!"

"That's the spirit."

"Safe havens guide me to her breast, then," said Boris, weakly making the sign of the Chain to ward off Choplicker as he came in for a lick. "And you...they'll catch you. Both of you. They did it once, they'll do it again. They're ready. People's Pack got their own devils, I hear, and an army of the people keyed up to kill some queens."

"Sure they do," said Zosia, as she got back to her feet and looked around for whatever weapons hadn't been incorporated into the floor. "But I've got a devil, too, and where's the fun in having one if you never get to use it?"

CHAPTER

14

Their second attempt at locating Gate Square went far better than the first, the rain finally stopping and then a group of armed, hooded figures giving them very thorough directions. These strangers happened to be headed that way themselves and offered to escort the out-of-towners, but Nemi explained she had a bit of a limp and would only slow them down. The helpful citizens bid them farewell and went on their way, which seemed to pleasantly surprise Diggelby and Nemi—perhaps Sullen had missed some nuance of the Crimson exchange.

Dark as the city had been, sputtering rushlights now danced through windows and doorways and down the street, more and more hooded folk leaving their houses and all moving in the same direction. There was a strange atmosphere to the thickening throng, at times reverential and at others carnivalesque, certain figures with large wicker masks playing pitch pipes and drums. They spilled out into a wide boulevard, where the river of hoods and bobbing lights flowed in the direction they were supposed to turn to reach Diadem's Gate. Directing Sullen and Diggelby over to an ornamental arch in the side of an arcade, Nemi kept her voice low as she expressed her doubts over their ability to slip into the Gate unnoticed on such a night as this.

"Does seem a popular destination," observed Diggelby, rubbernecking the crowd. "Some sort of harvest festival, I imagine."

"A harvest festival?" asked Nemi incredulously. "At the end of winter, in the middle of the night?"

"Apparently," said Diggelby, pointing at passersby. "Notice all the sickles and flails? Not much practical call for those in a modern city, but country gods have a long memory for how homage ought to be paid. And that drumming and piping is to warn the devils out of the fields, give the blighters notice that cold iron will soon be reaping."

"You know the weirdest stuff," said Sullen.

"I know how to party, and fluently, anywhere you care to get down." Diggelby flagged down a figure carrying a bushel of rush-lights under one arm. "Hullo hullo, how are you this fine evening?"

"Three?" said a sweaty face under a woolen cowl. "Three for three penny."

"Better make it nine," said Diggelby, rubbing thumb and forefinger at Nemi. "We're meeting friends."

"Uh-huh," said the seller, counting out nine of the fat-dipped reeds.

"Hopefully we can find them before we embarrass ourselves," Diggelby went on. "We're visiting from the sticks, and back home on the farm we ring in the harvest a mite different. Be a chum and give us the basics of your fancy metropolitan festival, so nobody mistakes us for yokels?"

"Uh?" The seller took the coins Nemi offered and handed over the rushlights. "Well, them's that want take they candle and carry it afore the queen. Then go home."

"*Afore the queen!*" said Diggelby. "And this virtuous maid chosen by the old ways to be queen of the harvest, where might we find this blessed creature?"

"Uh?" The seller seemed perplexed. "Front of the Gate? And's not no blessed maid, it's the queen."

"Quite so, quite so," agreed Diggelby.

The seller turned to reenter the scrum, but paused and said, "It's a danger, not wearing hood nor mask."

"Why is that?" asked Nemi, apparently more in line with Sullen's thinking about all this business. Unlike Diggelby, he wasn't so cavalier about jumping headfirst into other people's parties.

"People's Pack's watchin'," said the seller, pulling their own hood lower over their face at the mention of Diadem's council. "Till light of day any can pay they respect and say farewell to the queen. Call it the am-nasty. But after… you don't want any knowin' your face as one what came afore the queen. Wear a hood."

Then the seller turned back against the flow, moving upstream to peddle their rushlights as the interlopers considered these parting words.

"Well, that's sinister," said Sullen.

"Not *really*," said Diggelby. "It's just the nature of these folk traditions; they're all for show. You have to take it seriously, of course, to offer your belief as payment for the harvest, but these things aren't literal. Would that the Chain put a little more stock in actual faith and a lot less in actual black magic we'd all be happier, hmmm?"

"Diggelby, do you not recall that merchant we met on the road yesterday morning?" asked Nemi, taking a rushlight for herself and passing him the rest.

"*Ardeth Karnov*," said Diggelby in a simply terrible impression of the man's Usban accent. "Who could forget such a memorable… sorry, who were we talking about?"

"The merchant who told us he'd heard the People's Pack put Queen Indsorith on trial and intended to execute her for crimes against her citizens," said Nemi.

"No no," said Diggelby, "I remembered who Karnov was, I was just being silly because you said… *ohhhhhhh*."

"Well, Indsorith is bad, right?" said Sullen, the dull echo of drums carrying down the crumbling urban ravines to lodge right in his sore stomach. "I mean, Ji-hyeon was trying to take her down the whole time, so she's got to be a villain."

"I always thought our general had a rather elementary understanding of Imperial politics if she thought Indsorith was personally responsible for very much," said Diggelby, but he sounded like he'd lost all his enthusiasm for gatecrashing in either sense of the term. "Crimson Queen or Black Pope or People's Pack, they all just end up as symbols for whatever we want, don't they? We lose sight of who they actually are, behind the masks."

There were all quiet for a moment, and Sullen cleared his throat. "Diggelby, how high are you right now?"

"Not nearly high enough," said the pasha, popping his lace collar and pulling his tricorn hat down low over his paisley eye makeup. "But yes, all right, fairly bloody loaded. This is going to be great."

"This?" asked Nemi. "What do you mean, *this*? Tonight's ritual sacrifice of the queen is obviously a onetime event, so we will find a place to stay and wait for tomorrow night to go through the Gate. There's no flipping way I'm trying to take us tonight, the conditions would not allow me to concentrate."

"Diggelby thinks he's going to pitch our case to the People's Pack in the middle of their execution of the old queen," said Sullen, those fucking flutes making his heart pound, and when his heart pounded his guts fucking tried to dance back out of the hole in his stomach. The thought of a queen standing over a Gate conjured the image of the Faceless Mistress so fast and so hard Sullen practically saw her peer around the block, and closed his eyes to make sure she didn't actually materialize. When he'd first arrived in Diadem and noticed all the recent fire damage he had been fool enough to hope that maybe Zosia had already tried and failed to fulfill the dread vision he'd glimpsed in Emeritus, but then Nemi had explained to him just what exactly a volcano was, and how this city was supposedly built right on top of one, and that was the end of Sullen's fair-weather fantasies. Somewhere far beneath his boots an ocean of fire bubbled and crashed, and gritting his teeth, he concentrated on the cool shaft of the spear in his hand.

"If we interrupt their ceremony and they take offense we may find ourselves unable to use the Gate to reach Othean tomorrow," said Nemi, leaning on her feathered staff as she straightened the damp cover on her cockatrice's cage. "Or something yet worse might happen."

"But if we don't try we'll never know if Diadem would have helped turn the tide against the midnight armies of the First Dark," said Diggelby, and now he was playing hard to Sullen's sensibilities; *midnight armies of the First Dark* was fleet as fuck, no doubt. "I'll take charge and you two lurk about inconspicuously. That way if things go buns up you can both slip away and go to Othean tomorrow."

"And if they take you, Diggelby, what am I supposed to tell Purna?" asked Sullen, trying to make himself believe that tonight's worst-case scenario was just their reuniting with their friends sans the pasha.

"Oh tosh, I'm nobility—even if they capture me I'm worth more as a ransom than as a rug."

"I am not certain a council of revolting peasants will take good care of a nobleman," said Nemi, fiddling with the ironbound egg canisters on her belt.

"You heard her!" crowed Diggelby. "She was the one who called them revolting, not me!"

Mistaking Nemi and Sullen's silent reproach for a failure to appreciate his wit, he began to explain it when Sullen silenced him with a great big hug, badly though it pained him. If this well-intentioned ninny was willing to charge straight into a confrontation with the most powerful people in Diadem, then he would damn sure have his friend to back him up. And they'd do it without anyone getting hurt, Sullen would see to that.

Or so he hoped, looking up at the bundled head of his spear. He'd wrapped the blade in so many layers of pelts and straps that he couldn't have stuck someone with it even if he wanted to. As they stepped back into the flow of the crowd, he repeated his vow to himself to unsheathe it only when they faced a monstrous foe. He was done with shedding human blood, the boy in the bar the final victim of his savage past. He would find a better way, no matter what, and never again be forced into violence against his fellow mortals.

Why oh why oh why did Sullen ever let himself hope *anything*?

CHAPTER
15

So maybe coming to Jex Toth hadn't been the *greatest* idea. After all, just before they had lost the magic post for good it had implied the missing Maroto wasn't actually here, and then Hoartrap had informed them the Tothan attack on Othean was definitely under way just before he was gobbled up by a giant flying gross-out, leaving them stranded and directionless. In spite of all that Purna had held out hope, cheering herself up with fantasies of being reunited with Nemi in the not-too-distant future...at least initially, but these became tougher and tougher to sustain as their hours lost in the jungle stretched into days and then weeks. Still, she told herself, Hoartrap had bounced back from plenty of seemingly terminal shit before, so maybe he'd turn up again when they least expected it, talk a little trash, snap his fat fingers, and whisk them back to the Star, easy sleazy. In the meantime they could at least try to stick with the plan—even if a rescue mission for Maroto was no longer necessary, this far behind enemy lines they could certainly try to sabotage the Tothan war effort from the inside.

Now that they'd put that particular theory into practice, however, Purna was beginning to think the whole thing was a wash. Who knew that if you dropped one measly flying monster and took its surviving rider captive you'd bring the whole blooming place down on your pretty head?

They'd found the old woman lying in the soft sand of the river-bank, her spindly body dripping with smashed bugs. Something must have broken inside her, and broken bad, because despite the alertness of her black eyes she didn't seem able to sit up or use her legs at all. The other rider hadn't even been that lucky, gory smears of foul-smelling meat and crushed beetle shell strewn through the upper branches of a nearby banyan tree all that was left of it. Yet despite the gravity of her injuries the woman didn't cry out when they moved her, didn't make any noise at all—which impressed Purna and Best as much as it unnerved Keun-ju. Prince, for his part, clearly didn't like the woman one bit, keeping his angry little ass between Purna and the prisoner at all times. Given her condition they expected her to die any moment, but if anything she seemed to improve with each passing day, silently watching them with a grimace that bordered on a grin.

They were lugging the haggard old woman around because they were still Cobalts, weren't they, and Cobalts didn't execute prisoners... but the last time Purna had let a prisoner go it had been a Myuran scout she and Maroto and the gang had captured, and that bit of charity had led to their being captured themselves, soundly beaten, and locked in a closet. A thing like that will make a girl wary of the practice, and besides, you never knew when a captive could come in handy—especially an officer. This old dame must be someone important, to still be on patrol at her age.

All that notwithstanding, the crippled crone was turning out to be a real bad copper piece. Ever since they captured her the scary-armored Tothans kept rumbling them despite how deep into the jungles they retreated. At first they just assumed the enemy soldiers were expert trackers, but it soon became apparent the Tothans weren't just following their trail, they were somehow predicting the exact movements of their quarry, repeatedly cutting them off. Keun-ju suggested their mute prisoner must have something ensorcelled into her possessions that allowed them to locate her, just like the compass Hoartrap had used to find them in the Haunted Forest.

This theory led to their holding the woman down and trying to pry off the last of the armored bugs that still clung to her wrinkly flesh; most had been crushed or simply dropped off when she was thrown from her flying beastie, but a few stalwarts remained. As soon as Purna decided to try clipping their legs off with her kukri the whole patchwork crew jumped ship, scurrying off into the undergrowth as Prince went bonkers chasing them.

The woman hissed through her black teeth at the devil, which seemed to put the chill on Prince as much as it did Purna, the dog abandoning the chase and coming back to stare at the prisoner. It was the first time she'd made any noise at all, but prod her though Purna did she wouldn't make another sound. When the persistent Tothans continued to home in on them despite their captive's nakedness, Best had reluctantly thrown the strange bone blades she had claimed as trophies over a waterfall, but even still, the damn monsters found them *everywhere*.

And unlike the old prisoner, monsters they must surely be— whatever else they were underneath their living platemail, the Tothan soldiers were just a little too bally big to be strictly human. They always chose the least convenient moments to attack, too, usually when one of the heroes was taking care of a natural errand. Yet their bulky armor was not conducive to running pell-mell through the often-treacherous terrain, and so time and again Purna and her crew gave the beggars the slip. You would think with this being their homeland and all the Tothans would wear better gear, something a little sportier for jogging through mangrove swamps and bamboo groves, but Purna wasn't complaining. Plus, give the donkeys their day, that insect armor looked pretty damn righteous. Shame it didn't lend itself to looting, what with being alive and all, otherwise she might have considered facing the patrols instead of fleeing them, beat down enough to get a matching set. Probably for the best that wasn't an option, since even Best agreed they were better off outrunning the Tothans for the time being, lest they be overwhelmed by the seemingly endless numbers they had glimpsed beetling through the jungle behind them.

"I could be sharing a coach ride with Sullen right now..." Keun-ju grumbled as they clambered out of another hollow following another ambush, using the nearly horizontal trees to pull themselves up the sheer slope.

"And I'd rather be sharing a ride or two with Nemi, but you don't hear me making a stink about it," said Purna as she climbed after him, though to be fair she spent much of each waking day ruing her decision to go with Hoartrap instead of the fairer witch. And ruing her timidity at not having asked Nemi for a pair of her panties to take along as a keepsake—had she really been worried about skeeving her out, after all the things they'd done? Was such a thing even possible? Oh, how Purna missed her new friend, and for more than that, of course, of course...but seriously, that trick Nemi did with her—

"Ugh," said Keun-ju, pausing in his climb to press his veil tight to his nose and mouth. "You had to mention making a stink, didn't you?"

"Did I?" Purna had been drifting, and then something far less pleasant drifted down the steep hillside to reach her nose, too. "Woof. I know it's usually just an expression, but seriously—do you think something crawled up inside her and died?"

"Death smells more pleasant than that," said Keun-ju, and Purna had to agree. The very worst thing about their Tothan captive was her malodorous emissions, which, while infrequent, were beyond noxious when they hit. Or maybe the smell's origin was actually glandular instead of gaseous—it did have a certain sweaty funk to it—but Purna was disinclined to spend overmuch time tracking down the precise source of an old woman's reek. The smart move was just to remember not to let Best get upwind of them with the prisoner in the future.

"I'm telling you, that's how they keep finding us," said Purna as the scent mercifully dissipated into the muggy air. "All they have to do is follow their nose."

"It is almost bad enough for me to believe it," said Keun-ju. "But that would not explain how they keep heading us off, and always know the ideal time to strike."

"In-toot-ition?" suggested Purna.

"You...you are the worst person I know," said Keun-ju. "In all seriousness, she *must* be giving them some sort of signals...*other* than that."

"Impossible!" Purna pointed to the top of the rise Best had already gained despite carrying their prisoner over one shoulder. "She's naked, bound, and gagged!"

"Not that she says much," said Keun-ju, flipping his veil up to daub his forehead. This heat made even the Immaculate less of a stickler for etiquette, though it didn't stop him from reproachfully side-eyeing Purna when her long black tongue hung out of her mouth as she panted. "Not that any of them ever say anything. That's the most sinister part, I believe, how silent they remain even when you land a blow."

"Shhh!" said Purna, something rolling over in her head...and then going back to sleep. "Blast, I thought I...hmmm..."

"There's a first," said Keun-ju. Prince barked down at them from the top, and Purna barked back, which Keun-ju absolutely *hated*, apparently. "Or maybe instead of communicating with their countrywoman they simply listen out for you two yapping away without a care in the Star, as if the whole jungle was deaf to dogs."

That was it. Points to Keun-ju, though she'd never admit it. "Dog whistles."

"Dogs can't whistle," said Keun-ju, and she almost proved him wrong with her canine tongue when she realized that was probably exactly what he wanted as a setup for some burn. Or maybe that was giving him too much credit; the boy had his strengths but trash talk wasn't among them.

"Not whistling dogs, whistles for dogs," she explained, bracing her foot behind a prickly palmetto and then scrambling up to grab the trunk of a cinnamon tree. "Digs told me about them, 'cause he kept buying them to call Prince but they kept disappearing. I'm guessing the devil was the one making them go missing. Thing about them is, we can't hear 'em—you blow, but there's nothing. Except there's *something*, because dogs will come running."

"What a fascinating song," said Keun-ju, nearly slipping as they hit the really sharp climb near the top of the ridge. Catching his breath before attempting it, he looked down and said, "Surprised you didn't save that for the campfire. Oh, I forget, we cannot have fires anymore, because you and Best had to hunt that flying grotesque and now we have a new friend who makes it difficult enough to go undetected."

"My point, brightboy, is these Tothans are maybe saying things to each other, just not things we can hear," said Purna. "Like a dog whistle. Maybe she's yodeling her heart out right now but we just can't hear."

"Oh!" Keun-ju thought about it. "We gagged her, remember, just in case she decided to share her feelings at an inopportune moment?"

"Hmmm," said Purna. "Damn, forgot about that…but I mean, I could at least moan through a gag, you know? If they've got super great hearing, maybe that's enough?"

"You're stretching, Purna," said the Immaculate, doing a little of his own in preparation for the climb up the sheer hillside and then digging his toes into the loam.

"Stretching's good for every muscle, including the brain," said Purna. "And listen, I'm putting together a plan—just back me up on whatever I say. I'm going to have some words with our prisoner when we get to the top, see if I can get her to crack this time."

"Because a bizarre granny from Jex Toth who doesn't speak at all probably understands Immaculate fluently?"

"Hey, smart guy, why don't we change the topic to something you are interested in, then?" said Purna. "Like your boyfriend's hams."

That got him up the rise in a jiffy, at least, and Purna hurried up after, convinced she was onto something here…and then at the top of the rise had to put that aside for a moment as she joined Best and Keun-ju in gaping down the other side of the saddle, an even steeper slope falling away toward the cerulean sea. Stunning white ruins stretched through the jungle all the way down the hillside, and the harbor beyond teemed with…ships? Sea monsters? From up here the shapes that floated beside the docks seemed to be a mix of both. It made Purna queasy to see the long lines of Tothans disappearing inside these weird vessels—from this height the black warriors looked even smaller than the spiny bugs that made up their armor. Then Purna gave a start, because if her theory was right and the prisoner Best had set down to sit against a tree could indeed alert her people even over a decent distance and with a gag in place, well, then they were in serious trouble, given that they'd finally stumbled on an actual military base.

"Hey!" Purna snapped her fingers in the woman's pinched-up face, and she opened her sharp black eyes. She didn't like Purna, was what those expressive eyes said, that she was beneath her...but Purna was glad she could tell that at a glance, because she needed to read this lady like a scroll. Or like a book, whatever, but scrolls were just cooler, obviously. "So, Tothan, you can communicate with your friends without saying a word, huh?"

The sweat-stained stocking they'd used as a gag rose up her gaunt cheeks as the captive smiled. Prince trotted over, growling...but at Purna, not the prisoner. The little dog hated it when they tried to communicate with the old woman—being a devil and all he probably didn't approve of mercy to the captured. She shushed him, turning back to the biddy.

"And so you understand me just fine, too, huh?" she said, because Keun-ju was right: there not actually being a language barrier was a little unexpected, what with this crone being part of an invading army of monsters from this place way beyond the Star. "So the only question left is if you've been able to talk to us this whole time. You can, can't you?"

Even if it hadn't been plain from the woman's amused expression, she nodded, this time she actually nodded! Purna reached up and untied the gag, then offered the woman a hit from her waterskin. She drank, though not with the relish Purna would have expected, considering how thirsty she must be. Her slow sipping did give Purna time to figure out how best to play the hag, though, once she had her throat good and lubricated. Keun-ju came over to watch, but Best remained captivated by the bustling harbor below.

"I know it might sound funny, considering how we met, but the whole reason we've been carrying you around and seeing you're fed and watered is that we've taken a liking to you. You seem like a decent sort. Remind me of my auntie." The old woman's eyes widened along with her smile, and Purna adopted a conspiratorial tone as she put away her waterskin. "Best there, however, isn't quite as sentimental as us. She doesn't like you one bit. Isn't that right, Keun-ju?"

"I fear not," said Keun-ju.

The Tothan looked back and forth between them, clearly eating up their ruse.

"So while me and Keun-ju understand you've just been trying to save your own skin, Best isn't exactly the empathetic sort. And as soon as we tell her you've been bringing your crew down on us this whole time instead of being more friendly with the folks who rescued you from your crash, well, I don't want to think what she'll do to you."

"*I* know what she'll do," said Keun-ju, leaning in. "She'll disembowel you while you're still alive and then take cover, so that when your friends come out into the open to help you they shall die, too, and it will be all your fault."

The elderly Tothan didn't look intimidated, exactly, but her glancing at Best confirmed she understood the threat. Fortunately Purna also had a damn good mahjong face, otherwise her surprise might have given away the scheme—damn but Keun-ju went dark in a hurry! Nothing for it now but to make the offer she'd intended to slowly build to, before Keun-ju had to go all Chainite on her ass.

"We don't want that to happen, auntie, and I promise—"

Prince jumped in Purna's face, snapping and snarling, but she grabbed him out of the air and clutched him to her chest, soothing him with snugs. He was her devil now, like it or nuts, and couldn't intimidate her. Much, anyway. Holding his growling mouth shut took some effort, but the teacup tyrant was small enough she managed it after a brief but fierce struggle.

"Like I was saying, auntie, if you start cooperating I promise we'll let you go instead of letting Best show you her worst. We just want some information, so if you'll talk we'll—whoa!"

Purna had been squatting on her heels in front of the old woman but the flood of emotions and images she suddenly experienced bowled her onto her butt.

Ecstatic hatred and burning cities, shuddering pleasure and armies of monsters, the sky cracking, the earth falling into nothing…

Purna just sat there, heart pounding, mouth dry, nauseated and trying to make sense of what had just fucking happened. And then it came again, miles of wet viscera enveloping her, squeezing like a vise on her skull, a musky stench searing the inside of her nostrils, and this time she did throw up her breakfast of snake meat and taro root. As she recovered a gentler, almost friendly feeling washed over her, and looking in horror at the half-naked, bound Tothan she saw that all the unnatural blackness had left the woman's eyes, that she was now being surveyed by quite normal-looking brown irises. Purna had never been so frightened of something in her life. "If you can get into our heads, why didn't you from the first?!"

"Unlike thouuuuu I dast not speaaaaak to dogssssss," hissed the captive in High Immaculate, her screechy voice almost as grating as her mental assault. It was an odd incongruity, hearing the ancient and strictly formal tongue used to dole out a basic burn, but Purna and Keun-ju exchanged excited glances. This crone spoke a language that was five hundred years out of common usage but was the mother tongue of both her people and his. Prince wiggled out of Purna's grasp and she let him bound away, transfixed by the living enigma before her.

"Respectfully, revered elder, may we ask who art thou, from whence thou hast come, and how might we make peace between thine people and our own?" asked Keun-ju in the same dialect.

"Freeeeeedom," hissed the woman, waving her bound hands at Purna. The way she held her long-nailed fingers made it look like she was clutching invisible oranges. "Thine oooooath. Freeeeedom for my truuuuuth."

"Yeah, sure," said Purna, popping out her kukri and struggling with the archaic phrasing. "But first thine must promise we the same. We dast not come at thou, thou dast not come at us. With violence. Promise we this."

"I shalllllll *not*," said the ancient woman, positively gleeful in her refusal. "I pledge only deaaaaath. And slooooow it shall beeee."

"Well, that's hardly civil," said Purna, trying not to look as freaked-out as she felt. She figured Keun-ju looked spooked enough for both of them. Waving her long blade in the woman's face, she said, "I hate to do this but if you won't meet our pledge with one of your own I'm calling Best over. She'll get you talking or I'm—"

"No," snapped the woman. "Tooooo late. Thou hast already made the oooooath. Freedom for truuuuuth."

"Poppycock," said Purna, feeling her small hairs crawl toward heaven at the unpleasant severity of the woman's expression and belated recognition of why Prince had tried to interrupt her own carelessly spoken words. "I promised, sure, but I can't speak for my companions, who will think nothing of cutting thou down if thou displeases, uh, we."

"Besides, we hast not yet put it to a vote," said Keun-ju.

"Thou hast demanded answers threeeee," the crone snarled at the Immaculate. "Who am I? I am become a living god, one of we eternal hierophants of the First Dark. From whence hast I come? From out of time, the heavens of the deep. And how might thine creatures make peace with our legion? Thou shall not. Thou shall submit, thou shall serve, and thou shall become sacrifice to welcome She Who Comes, but not a babe of thine doomed race shall know *peace*. This is truth. Now release meeeeee, on thy word."

"I don't freakin' *think so*," said Purna, her High Immaculate slipping. "Even if what I said constituted some unbreakable contract, which it doesn't, it stipulated freedom for information, but thou hast not informed us of shit. That mystical mumbo-jumbo might wash for a Chainite, but sister, I ain't one. So if you expect me to let you go, you better tell me something worth hearing—like how many of you fuckers are out there, what's your big plan, *exactly*, and how you came to be flying a giant monster right before we wrecked your shit?"

Even having experienced it once before, Purna wasn't prepared for the blast of raw thoughts penetrating her brain. It fucking *hurt*, and it fucking *stunk*, the aroma of burning mildew locking up her chest so tight she couldn't breathe even as the blistering visions overheated her skull. She felt her scalp baking from the intensity of the transference, but that was in the background, and in the forefront was a nightmare pageant.

Flight through the First Dark, and then the naked stars burning over Jex Toth, a joyous thrill in her breast to be liberated at last and savoring the sensation of hunting mortal flesh with a vassal behind her on the saddle and the whole world her skittish quarry.

Priests of the Burnished Chain mutilating wildborn children.

Priests of Jex Toth mutilating themselves, dying as mortals to live on as gods.

Mortal armies marching under cobalt skies.

Gargantuan insects with human features roiling in their nests, spraying out cascades of wet eggs.

Fleshy kennels where lithe equine horrors were bred and broken, and bubbling pits of slime from whence crawled hulking behemoths.

Sea monsters so titanic the previous beasts were as lice upon a mammoth.

Legions of black-armored soldiers, disgorged from the leviathans to storm white sand beaches... the beaches of Othean.

Witchy generals in flight above the battlefield, surveying the field from the backs of their monstrous mounts and giving silent orders that were instantly heeded by the hordes below.

A sabbath conducted atop the beating heart of a giant, a circle of ten channeling the harvest taking place across the sea.

The earth cracking open beneath an Immaculate castle, a fissure in the First Dark that devoured flesh and steel and stone and timber to feed the living moon that swelled up out of the abyss, its brilliant whiteness taking true form only as it entered the world of mortals, a terror that would burn Purna's brain to a shriveled kernel if she beheld it in all its dread majesty but from which she could not look away as it reached up into the light of the world of mortals, uncoiling, and—

Purna's world went from ivory to crimson, awe becoming terror, the pain in her heart and her head transferring to her hand. Blinking away bloody tears, she looked down to see Prince lapping at the bite wound he had opened on her palm. The devil looked up at her with eyes as black as their prisoner's had been up until the interrogation, licking Purna with her former tongue. It was a horribly weird sensation, but like most horribly weird sensations she got used to it pretty quick. Wiping red snot from her leaky face, she petted him with bloody fingers.

"—hast thou done to her?" Keun-ju was shaking the bound devil, the knuckles of his hand covered in the same oily smear that was running from the old woman's split face. He hit her again, and would have kept at it if Best hadn't yanked him off.

"Be still," said the huntress, pivoting Keun-ju to where Purna was clambering to her feet. "She is well."

"You have to kill her!" said Keun-ju. "Purna and I swore an oath, but you can do it for us!"

"I do not attack the old and the infirm!" Best seemed actually stung by the suggestion. "For a boy who seeks to understand even monsters you know nothing of the Horned Wolf way."

"Something semantically funny about that, but I'm not touching it," said Purna, clinging to Prince as she swayed in place. That rank moldy smell lingered in her nose like cheap aromatic tubāq ghosting a pipe.

"What has befallen you?" asked Best. "Has it done this?"

"This thing…" The hot pressure in Purna's skull had eased off a little, but she still felt like a kettle just about to blow. "It can get inside your head. Talk to you, without talking to you. It talked to me, the way it's been talking to its soldiers all this time without our knowing."

"Then it is as I thought," said Best, spitting at the lame feet of their prisoner. "It has led us to this place. We have taken it home and fallen into a trap at the same time. We shall leave this anathema behind. Now."

"We can't just let it go!" said Keun-ju. "First we have to—"

"Now," repeated Best, her fist still clenched in Keun-ju's coat. "If you and Purna swore oaths not to harm it, it would be despicable of me to commit violence on your behalf. Your folly is my shame. And if it understood you then it understands us now, and we will not speak more in its hearing. Come."

"Got a point there," said Purna. Pointing an unsteady hand at the still-grinning prisoner, she said, "See? We're keeping our word. We're better than you, and by the time this war's over you'll see who—"

"Purna!"

"Anyway, go fuck thineself," she said, wishing she had time to come up with a better catchphrase. Instead she let Prince down and hobbled after her friends who were already hustling along the ridge, her devil bounding at her heels. They waited for her to catch up, eager for more answers now that the bushy kamala trees had swallowed up the prisoner at their hind, and she tried to explain what had happened as they legged it deeper into the jungle.

The dark was almost fully upon them and she was still filling them in on all the details when Prince whined in alarm just as Best held up a hand. They leaned back into the underbrush, and just when Purna didn't think she could hold her breath any longer half a dozen Tothan soldiers passed them by, moving purposefully down the ridge. After giving it ample time they hurried on, no longer contributing to the racket of the jungle with further whispered discussions on the powers and prophecy of their enemy. There was a clearing ahead and they moved to skirt it when Best gasped, no common thing, and pointed.

There were three sky-devils, as Best called the behemoths, lying down in the tall wildflowers of the dark meadow. They had never before seen them on the ground, save for the one they had brought down, and they noticed that their wide white wings were pinned back to their saddles with black straps that sparkled in the moonlight. They had no reins, but that was something Purna had gleaned through the deluge of the prisoner's impressions—the creatures themselves were simple-minded, but the saddles provided a conduit for the rider to reach their blubber-buried brains, controlling their mounts with intention alone.

"Come on," said Purna. "I don't know where we're going but I know how we're getting there."

"I know where we are bound, but…" Best licked her lips, clearly warring with herself. "But Horned Wolves do not ride. This is the law."

"This isn't riding," said Purna. "It's *flying*."

Best considered this. "All right."

Yes! Purna had just known she'd warm to the prospect! Ever since they'd captured the crippled pilot Purna had been talking the idea up, of drawing down another monster but capturing it alive so they could take to the skies with it.

"All *right*?" Keun-ju spluttered—he would be the one mortal in the whole Star who never dreamed of flying. "I don't believe this! I don't! You two really intend to mount one of those, and then what, fly back to the Star?"

"Not the two of us," said Purna, picking up Prince. "All four of us. It's a vote. I vote we go."

"As do I," said Best.

"Prince?" asked Keun-ju, hoping for a deadlock, but even if the devil's vote had counted he arfed his approval. Looking incredulously at the massive otherworldly animals, he shook his head in dismay.

"Look, even if this doesn't work you've gotta admit it's one hell of a way to go out," said Purna. "Sure beats getting chased through this jungle for the rest of our short lives. So shake a leg, before they come back. And Best, what this about knowing where we're going? You got some ideas, girl, lay 'em on me."

"We are going to save the Star." Best made it sound like the only obvious destination, which, especially coming from her, sounded really sweet and naïve... until she said, "The anathema we captured told you she was a living god. One of a cabal who dwell in this place, at the heart of this land. They are the ones who declared war on all mortals. Yes? So we fly yon beast to these living gods." Perhaps mistaking Purna and Keun-ju's stares for confusion, she added, "Such a plan is... is not unlike something in the songs Sullen would sing."

"And what do we do once we get there?" asked Keun-ju. "Once we confront this... this council of deities who control Jex Toth?"

"What else?" said Best, her eyes gleaming in the dark. "I have never hunted gods before, but if they are truly living then they can be killed."

Purna bumped Best's fist, and bumped it *hard*, but like all wet blankets Keun-ju seemed intent on spreading his damp around.

"With all due respect, Purna, you and I couldn't stand up to a handful of Raniputri bounty hunters, and now you think we can overcome a cadre of *living gods*? Even assuming we can ride those monsters, and even assuming we can somehow find the leaders of this place, what makes you think we three have any hope of stopping them?"

"I don't," Purna said with a shrug. "Like Digs always says, hope's for dopes."

"Then why press ahead with such a stupid plan?!" he demanded. "This isn't some...some absurd *song*, where everything will turn out fine no matter how reckless we behave. Your plan can only mean our lives!"

"Well, yeah, probably..." admitted Purna, "but from the way this fucking adventure has gone so far I'd say we're actually stuck in one of those songs where everybody dies."

"Those are the finest songs," opined Best.

"On that we must disagree!" said Keun-ju. "I *like* happy endings! I *want* a happy ending! Climbing on top of that...*thing*, that does not bring us to a happy ending! So why would we ever—"

"Because we're heroes, Keun-ju, and dumb shit like this is what heroes do!" Purna was disappointed that after all this time in her company she still had to explain something so basic to the kid. "We only get to die once, so we have to make the most of it. Dying back in Black Moth in some random showdown with headhunters wouldn't have helped anyone, would it? But here and now we've got one fucking chance to really do something—to swing on the band of nasties that's orchestrating the attack on Othean, an attack that's been under way for weeks but isn't lost yet, I don't think. Our friends are there, Keun-ju, or at least they should be, by now—Sullen and Nemi and Ji-hyeon and plenty of other good people. And if what that freak just showed me is true they need our help like they've never needed it before. The whole Star needs our help. And we're out of time to come up with anything better, so let's get on these gnarly sky-devils and jam them down the throats of our enemies. It's like Maroto told me this one time, when I was asking him about the secret to his success—he said, *Purna, if you want the smoke, be the fire.* So let's be a fucking inferno so big our friends can see the smoke from Othean."

It took a minute, but he got there in the end. You spent enough time around Keun-ju and you learned to tell when he was smiling under his veil. He bumped Purna's fist, not as hard as Best but hard enough. When they turned to bring the Horned Wolf in on the action they realized she and Prince were already halfway to the moored monsters. You just couldn't bring those two anywhere.

Hustling across the starlit clearing to rustle the biggest, ugliest beasties Purna had ever clapped eyes on, she caught herself wishing that the magic post had been wrong about Maroto's current whereabouts, that at the tail-end of whatever wild ride lay ahead of her this night she would somehow come face-to-face with her long-lost mentor. Not that she also wanted him to be condemned to whatever mysterious but nevertheless certain doom awaited her, duh, but by all Thirty-Six Chambers of Ugrakar she would have loved to see the look on his face as she came riding in on a giant sky-devil, her Gate-bleached hair looking just bad as hell. Since that fantasy was even less probable than this nasty thing delivering her to a tasteful-yet-sexy reunion with Nemi, however, she reminded herself that it was decidedly for the best that Maroto had already escaped Jex Toth, and hoped wherever the big bruiser had ended up he was having as much fun as she was.

CHAPTER
16

From the moment a school of aquatic abominations upended his rowboat in the shallows Maroto should have guessed he had a crap day ahead of him. At the time, though, he'd been full of foolish optimism: the quickly flooding rowboat half full, as it were. And hey, it could have been worse! The bulky, many-legged things in the water focused more on tearing up the landing craft than they did the people, and must not have sensed the interlopers' presence until they were right on top of them, seeing as how they didn't strike until the boats were almost to shore. Maroto supposed if anything the destruction of their only means of escape would light a fire under the volunteers he led—all five hundred of them.

He knew Lupitera was right about the Azgarothian navy doing more good on the northern side of the capital isle, where they could use cannon and cutlass to cut off the flow of Tothan reinforcements. Plus he'd contribute more on the ground than stuck on a galleon; for all the flotsam he talked with Bang and the crew it'd been a very long time since his sea legs had been steady. And he also knew from the final messages they'd exchanged with the Immaculate generals just before the predawn launch that the Autumn Palace was in desperate need of any able hands it could get, the outer wall breached and the inner struggling. That the empress and her court were in a different castle might prolong the inevitable, but a quick glance at a map of Othean confirmed that if one of the four palaces fell the Tothans would immediately gain the interior of the sprawling city...and once that happened the war was lost before it had even properly started, the monsters devouring the Immaculate capital from the inside out.

So Maroto knew all the reasons why his mission had to happen, but it didn't make him any happier about leading the charge, primarily because of the charges themselves: Chainites captured at Darnielle Bay. Well, not all of the prisoners, only those who'd accepted the clemency deal the Baroness of Cockspar had offered them. It wasn't a bad contract, really, fighting alongside their fellow mortals against the very demons they had summoned in exchange for a full pardon. And it wasn't that they fought poorly, for some were veteran war nuns and battle monks, and others were Imperial marines stationed at the harbor in Desolation Sound who'd converted in a hurry when it became apparent the Burnished Chain had set fire to Diadem and only the faithful were allowed on the boats escaping the blaze.

That's why it wasn't the greenness of his recruits that gave him pause, nor the size of the squad. No, the bug in Maroto's butt about this whole affair was that if word ever got out he'd led a Chainite army, even a small one, he'd never live it down. At his age pride was about all he had left, and betraying the human race was a lot less embarrassing than rolling out with Chainites.

This is what happens when you don't stay clean. The icebee stings and heaping rails of funeral moth dust Lupitera had provided to offset the sluggish effects of the laced blunt had initially been just what the barber ordered, of course, putting pep in his step... but his involuntary bath in the bay washed off most of the fluttery euphoria, leaving him twitchy and melancholic and wishing he'd either managed to stay off the bugs altogether or brought along some more to keep him good and loaded until his unavoidable death. Regret and shame and hunger for that which he regretted, that what made him ashamed.

A typical Maroto morning, in other words.

Splashing through the cold surf, he reflected on how he and Bang must have sailed past this very spot aboard the Chainite ship a few weeks back, and how she'd scoffed at the stupid Imperials for entering the wrong inlet to reach Othean Bay. He knew he'd never see her again, but he indulged a fantasy of reuniting with her on some sun-dappled deck and saucily informing her there was no such thing as a wrong inlet, if your helmsperson had a steady hand and knew his way around the tides. He could probably find a way to work in a ribald joke about inserting the Burnished Chain, too...

Time enough to worry about such things once he'd lived out the day, however, and doing a quick head count after he and his Chainites had all floundered ashore he saw they were already down two dozen troopers. Not an auspicious start, especially as the amphibious defenses began awkwardly following the invaders out of the surf. Maroto had his soggy soldiers cut a few down to get their morale back up, but when a war monk was ripped in two by one of the slow insectoid giants he decided they'd tarried long enough.

After the lumbering, soft-shelled monsters were left behind on the rocky shore, Maroto led his peanut regiment along the route laid out in the map the Immaculates had included with their final letter. Othean's four city-palaces were laid out in a diamond on the island, but over the many years their settlements had all expanded inward to create a single metropolis, around which rose two walls that were heavily patrolled even in peacetime. Now legions in spiny black armor surrounded the mighty capital and their leviathans patrolled the coast, cutting off escape from all sides. Yet even with their massive armies the Tothans were careful not to spread their siege too thin, focusing their assaults on the Autumn Palace.

In the predawn darkness Maroto led his own black-clad army in from the coast, through the carefully manicured forest stocked with wild game from all over the Star. It took far longer than it should have to cross the wood, fools bumping into trees and making a parade's worth of racket, but they were not discovered by any foot patrols, and so far there were no reports of the flying squid-dragons that were so prevalent on Jex Toth.

On the far edge of the wood they crept north for-bloody-ever, until one of the captains Maroto had appointed noticed the blue-fletched arrow jutting from a tamarack. Coalstick and mirror flashes were exchanged with the top of the wall that had come into definition through the mist, and then Maroto led his meager company huffing and puffing across the field between the forest and the southwestern edge of the Autumn Palace. Any moment he expected an inhuman horde to come charging down on them, but the only thing that struck was a rain shower, and if that's the worst you have to contend with during a monster invasion then no sense complaining.

Just as they reached the wall there came a slight creaking and then a fissure appeared in its surface, and then another, and then a massive rectangular section swung outward. Impressive as the hidden gate was, Maroto was even more impressed when they got through and found it took only a handful of Immaculates to operate. The Chainite regiment milled nervously in the narrow streets of the shantytown on the other side of the wall, looking anxiously at the dark, ramshackle buildings that edged them in. The one time Maroto had explored Othean he'd marveled at what a rare thing it was, to have a city without slums, but this low-rent neighborhood looked even older than he was. Just went to show that some things are true the Star over—the Immaculate capital had its ghettos, same as everywhere else, they just funneled them out of sight into the gap between the inner and outer walls. Prevented the peasantry from lowering the opulent tone of the place.

As the last Chainites pressed into the wet mob of their fellows that now swarmed the slum all around the secret gate, the Immaculate in charge pursed her lips, looking skeptically at Maroto. She was young but didn't look it anymore, with the sunken eyes and chafed cheeks of a cadet who'd seen far too much, far too soon.

"Where are the rest?" she asked in Crimson. "We were told to receive reinforcements, not a paltry gaggle of Chainite geese."

"Rude," said Maroto, looking down at the woman with her peacock-plumed helmet. "This flock of mine might be few in number but they're strong of talon and stout of breast."

"Loons, is more like, led by an old cuckoo," she grumbled in Immaculate. Maroto could feel her judging him—for his skull face-paint, or the cobalt lamé vest Lupitera had told him was woven from a devil worm's arse, he wasn't sure which. Quite possibly both. He was all set to respond in kind, but looking up into the rain for the Immaculate word for *ingrate* he caught sight of a wet blur overhead, on the rampart of the outer wall. It melted back behind the curtains of rain, but not before he was sure he saw water skating off shell as black as the soot-stained tiles of the roofs overhead, and the spear of shimmering white bone it held in one clawed hand.

"Time to go!" Maroto spoke in Immaculate, so as not to spook his troops. "We just got fucking made by a Tothan scout."

"Where?" The Immaculate officer and her cadre all looked around, as if that were the most vital issue here.

"On the wall there; it headed back north soon as I saw it. Just how far—" Before Maroto could finish asking how far they were from where the Tothans had broken through the outer wall, and if there were any gates or other defensive barriers cordoning off the compromised section from this particular neighborhood, the Immaculates answered by shouldering their crossbows and hauling arse into the slums, toward the inner wall. Ever the responsible leader, Maroto took off after them, calling over his shoulder in Crimson, "Move out, move out!"

On the map it was no more than a quarter mile between the inner and outer walls, but that wasn't taking into account that there wasn't a single fucking straight line in this whole fucking shantytown. Right around the time Maroto was hoping that factor might slow down the enemy, too, he heard the first screams from the rear of his regiment. Of all the lousy dick-shitting fates, to be ambushed before they'd even reached—

The inner wall reared up in front of him as they slid around the corner of the final dogleg alley. The Immaculate squad ran straight into an innocuous hut, one of countless others built up against the foot of the three-hundred-foot fortification. Trotting inside after them, he saw the soldiers swing the entire rear wall open, offering access to the Autumn Palace. Maroto stared longingly at that torchlit doorway, imagining a world where he was the first one through, and even took a step toward it when he heard another scream from back in the squalid warren.

On the boat ride over one of the Chainites had been so scared he'd wet his damn self right there, and in a rash attempt to put the kid at ease Maroto had promised him he'd do what he could to see everyone through the day. Maroto and his fucking oaths. When would he learn?

Yeah.

At least he wasn't high anymore. That counted for something, didn't it?

Fighting the current of black-robed Chainites pouring into the shack, he shouldered his way back out into the rain. There was a wider avenue here that ran parallel to the inner wall, and since pushing back into the cramped alleys would only slow everyone down he planted his boots in the mud, facing north. The street was empty for now, but as soon as it wasn't he'd be the only thing standing between the Tothans and the conscripted soldiers in his charge who came slipping out of the alleys, crossing the road and dipping into the hut.

The rain came down harder, and he hefted the flanged mace Lupitera had helped him pick out in Darnielle Bay. Wondered what had ever happened to the one Ulver Krallice had made for him a lifetime ago, the single damn piece of his history he'd managed to hold on to right up until the Battle of the Lark's Tongue. Supposed it didn't matter much; whoever scavenged it from his tent might not know the song behind the relic, but they'd improvise their own...and like all such songs, it would end in a place like this, clinging to the hope that your special weapon would see you through, right up until you stopped hoping for anything ever again.

And so the monsters. It always, always, *always* came down to monsters, didn't it? How could it come down to anything else, given that deep down, where it counts, he was the worst sort of—

Black-shelled infantry burst out of an alley just up the empty street, spoiling his tired reveries. Who said monsters were all bad, then? There were three of them and one of him, but with all the Chainites escaping into the hut at his hind surely someone would back him up. Surely.

The three Tothans ran as one, but slowly, and the rain slowed, too, everything coming into sharp relief. He could hear them even over the rain blasting the muddy street; he'd thought they were silent before, but that was only because they didn't talk. Now that he was really listening he could hear the rough scraping of their armor, insectoid plates brushing against each other as they ran, and underneath that a soft scrabbling sound, like rats in a wall. Two held bone spears in their clawed gauntlets, the third winding back a barbed net. Fuck that net in particular. Maroto sprang forward to meet them.

Some folk don't think a mace is a throwing weapon. Those people have never tried to catch one. Maroto hurled his heavy mace straight into the faceplate of the Tothan with the net, his eyes on the pair with spears as soon as the weapon left his fingers. He didn't have to hear the explosion of carapace to know his aim had been true, but he nevertheless smiled at the sound.

A slower man would have caught a spear right in his grinning teeth, and a second between his ribs. But then who wants to listen to the songs of slower men? Maroto whipped his head forward and arched his back like a cat, skating through the mud right between those two spears, between those two warriors. More Tothans were coming down the street, but they were still three blocks away. Quick as Maroto was moving, it might as well have been three miles. He turned back to the pair he'd slipped past.

They didn't turn after him, still making for the procession of Chainites crossing the street into the hut, but that just made Maroto's job easier. Wrenching his mace from the twitching wreckage of the first Tothan he had ever killed, Maroto marveled that even after all this time he still didn't know what the monsters looked like, under their insect armor. They were too big to be human—or formerly human, or whatever you wanted to call the demoniac Vex Assembly—but even when the Tothans had him bunking in titanic bowels and cleaning parasites off their sea monsters these grunts had never removed a helm in his presence, nor slipped off a single gauntlet. Now even in death this one remained a mystery—its shelled helmet had imploded from the impact of his mace, reeking grey goo covering the head of his weapon as its heavy body shuddered in the rain. There was something weird about it, though, something he only started processing as he ran after the original pair...

They were about to fall upon the fleeing Chainites when he

smashed one in the side, knocking it into the other. They both went down in the slippery mud. Maroto nearly careened into a flee-ing Chainite, caught himself. Caved in the chest of the first Tothan to rise, his mace crunching deep, ichors misting out and filling the muggy air with more of that cloying bughouse stench. It slumped forward on its knees and he was already swinging around to murder the other when the first sat back up, sticking him with its spear as if he hadn't just struck it a mortal fucking wound. The bone prong hit Maroto square in the gut, and despite not having any wind-up behind it the weapon carried so much momentum it sent Maroto skidding backward in the mud.

He crashed into the stampede of Chainites, wrapping his free arm around one to keep from falling...and only succeeding in bringing them both tumbling to earth. His belly was on fire, like the fattest cigar in Madros was being ground out against his gut. Slow as time seemed to be passing, it felt like an eternity before he could bring him-self to look down at the wound, sure he'd see a rope of his guts stretch-ing clear back to the Tothan's barbed spear. Instead he saw something almost as bad—a slight tear in the blue lamé vest Lupitera had let him borrow, with a tiny spot of blood staining the feather-light armor. If he lived long enough to return it he expected her wrath would be as bad as anything an inhuman monster could administer.

He still couldn't find his breath, let alone his feet, and looked up to see that the pair of Tothans were almost atop him. The one he'd fatally injured hadn't gotten the message that it was dead yet, lurch-ing forward despite its entire chest being a gaping wet hole of broken shell...and that was when it clicked, the crazy shit he'd seen when he'd pulled his mace from the first Tothan he dropped. It wasn't the crushed helmet that was so strange, since he knew their armor was made of insects...it was that the rest of the suit of armor was shuddering in the rain. Shuddering, and falling apart? He'd been so focused on his upright foes it hadn't even registered, but now it did, oh yes it fucking did, giant plated bugs falling away from one another to reveal...nothing.

As if sensing he'd figured out their secret, the injured Tothan made straight for Maroto, the other clearing its path through the startled Chainites. Black robes flapped in Maroto's face as his soldiers fled, and then the pair fell upon him. This was very bad, two spears coming down to spit him, the sensation returning to Maroto's stunned flesh just in time for him to experience what those jagged bone spikes felt like when they weren't rebuffed by armor, and—

The Tothans toppled back, mobbed by Chainites. The fresher of the two was hacked apart by Imperial steel, and the one he'd already injured was beheaded with a single stroke of a war nun's sword. Its black helm tumbled off in a gout of grey slime, landing six inches from Maroto's face…and uncoiling as it died, tucking its dozens of sharp legs into what remained of its ribbed belly, the end of it leaking more of the thick, foul blood. Twenty eyes stared into Maroto's as it died, the queen or brain bug or whatever the fuck it was that controlled the hollow suit of sentient armor reminding the aging addict of why he'd sworn off insects for good, following this morning's final bender with Lupitera—the things were just too fucking *creepy*.

"Up, Captain!" The last of their comrades were disappearing into the hovel beside them, and the war nun seized Maroto by the shoulder. A robed novice got under his other armpit, and together they hauled him to his numb feet…and almost let him go again, staring ahead with jaws good and dropped.

The horde of Tothans who had seemed so far away a minute ago were a lot closer now…though not so close as he would have expected, really, the whole bloody throng of them having stopped moving a good block away. Lightning crackled across the sky just overhead, and the press of Tothans in the street didn't even have to part to allow the beasts that had appeared in their midst to advance—the pointy legs of the glowing-eyed, horse-faced horrors were so long they just passed over the soldiers, stepping daintily though the crowd to reach the three mortals who stood against them.

Well, the three mortals who turned tail and booked arse toward the secret gate, if you wanted to get technical about it.

Maroto wasn't feeling so fatigued anymore, he and the two Chainites flying into the hut just in time to see the Immaculates' gate slowly swinging inward. The Chainites were ahead of him, and then they were through...and then there was a highly sketchy moment as Maroto darted around the closing aperture where he realized he'd misjudged the gap, he was about to get squished, and—

He fell safely on the other side just as the massive stone door clicked into place. It was dark in here, wherever here was. His Chainites must be climbing up an unlit stair, because high to one side of the cavernous space he saw them passing through an arch of light. Catching his breath and letting his eyes adjust to the gloom, Maroto tenderly prodded the tear in his lamé vest and the bruised and nicked belly skin beneath it until he was certain that he had indeed lived to fight another day...or at least another hour. He doubted the Tothan monsters would be busting through such a thick gate anytime soon, but mother hen that he was he addressed his concerns to the Immaculates who had cranked the hidden passage shut.

"Now that they know there's a secret entrance here they'll be working it day and night until they pop it open."

"We have destroyed the mechanism," said a barely glimpsed Immaculate as he began to head up the stairs. "This gate shall never open again, but we can pray they divert their resources to try. They have almost broken through a dozen weaker places already, and continue to harry them."

"Huh," said Maroto, following them up the slippery steps. Not for the first time that wet and miserable morning he wished he had absconded the night before with Bang and the others. Self-sacrifice always sounds better in theory than in practice, and now that he had succeeded in joining the trapped Immaculates his feet weren't just cold, they were practically frostbit. He'd made the gesture, which was the important thing, and first chance he got he'd have to cut back out of here—he was sure Bang would welcome him back to her employ, soon as he caught up with her. Easily done.

Of course, he'd spent damn near every day since Hoartrap's punkarse had dropped him on Jex Toth imagining a reunion and second chance with Choi, and just about every night doing one better in his dreams. Yet for as bad as he wanted it to come true, that wish was as impossible as any half-baked bugdream, and his ever seeing Bang again wasn't any more likely. The Star was just too damn big, and besides, it was about to end in a great big hurry, wasn't it, no matter what he did here? The Tothans had already arrived, no doubt delivered in the bellies of the same leviathans he and the pirates had helped prep for war back on Jex Toth. Just one of those things could carry thousands of troops, and in the time he'd spent there he'd seen dozens of them—how many must be beached on the northern shore of Othean right now?

But if there was one thing Maroto excelled at it was saving his own skin, and if it really had been hopeless his instincts wouldn't have led him here, would they? His very biology compelled him to cowardice, and if all were *truly* lost he'd be on a boat with Bang right now, making the most of his last days instead of hastening them along. There had to be a way to stop this...or so he told himself as they reached the first of many ornate archways, the Immaculates leading him up through Othean's inner wall—which doubled here as the outer wall of the Autumn Palace—to meet the general charged with defending it.

This place felt like Castle Diadem, the wall so thick its halls were more like roads than corridors, and always with another stair to climb. With each step the bruise blooming in his belly reminded him that while the climb was arduous the Immaculate command had positioned themselves a safe distance above the contested streets.

At last they reached the top, stepping out into the dismal dawn on the northern end of the Autumn Palace. The Immaculate officers were gathered up ahead on a covered terrace that rose from the wall-walk. Peeking over the parapet as lightning rippled through the low clouds, Maroto saw that things were even grimmer than he'd guessed.

It was as if a black sea bordered the inner wall of Othean, and the tide was coming in. Wave after wave of the inhuman army beat against the base of the fortifications only to fall back as the defenders dumped blazing oil and avalanches of masonry down on them, again and again. The Tothan army spread all the way through this quadrant of the slums, and out through a massive fissure in the low outer wall to fill the fields beyond. In the midst of all that squirming black shell Maroto glimpsed a white smudge that must be the Star-famous

Temple of Pentacles, making the whole scene look eerily as if the First Dark were seeping out of the Othean Gate to engulf the world...

In less poetic terms it was also looking an awful lot like a foregone conclusion down there, but then his Immaculate liaison delivered him to the general coordinating the defense of the Autumn Palace. When Maroto saw the old fox he burst out laughing.

"They've got you running this operation? No wonder the wall's about to fall!"

"Shoddy Immaculate construction, nothing to do with me," said Fennec, dismissing his officers with a wave of his pipe and grinning just as wide as Maroto as they embraced each other to the thunderous applause of the rain on the tiered roof of the terrace. There was that lingering pause where each man made sure there was no dagger planted in his back, and then they broke, sizing each other up. "You've put on weight, barbarian, don't tell me you've taken to eating devils on top of skinning them!"

"Was only the once, and don't remind me of Hoartrap," said Maroto, and then his pulse quickened. "Unless he's here? Is the Touch about?"

"You missed him by minutes," said Fennec, pointing his curl-toed boot at a tarry circle on the flagstones. "Blew in like this weather, and of similar mood. I brought him up to speed, and then he did the sensible thing and sodded off."

"Damn," said Maroto, scowling at the wizard's foul trace. "Did he...did he say anything before he went?"

"A few fuck words?" Fennec shrugged, puffing away. The thick billiard was the least ostentatious of the pipes Zosia had carved her Villains, but the grain was lovely. "He thinks the world's coming to an end unless he can find Zosia and asked if we'd heard any word. So I told him that as far as I knew he was the last person to see her alive, same as he was the last person to see you, and both times rather close to the Lark's Tongue Gate. *Did* he have anything to do with your disappearance?"

"About as much as I'm going to have with his, soon as I lay hands on the fickle freak," said Maroto. "Short answer is he dumped me on Jex Toth, I got free of there, tried coming here, went down to

Darnielle instead, and then bounced back up. Got five hundred reformed Chainites ready to fight for their freedom."

"Five thousand," said Fennec.

"I babysat them the whole way from the bay and there's five hundred," said Maroto, annoyed everyone had something smart to say about the size of his regiment. "Well, I'll allow there's probably fewer of them now than when we started, but you've got to expect a certain amount of shrinkage. Especially in weather like this."

"Five hundred," repeated Fennec, smiling a wry little smile that Maroto knew well, even if it didn't bode that way. "Well, what's a war without a complete intelligence failure. I never would have risked opening up the secret gates for five hundred head, and Chainites at that!"

"Reformed Chainites," corrected Maroto. "People can change, Fennec. I hope."

"Yes, well, even if it had been five thousand it wouldn't have been enough," said Fennec with a shrug. "Where are my manners, can I offer you a bowl of something?"

"A bowl of everything sounds better," said Maroto, his mouth watering as he followed Fennec to the command table. Lamps shone on moist maps and cluttered figurines, the Usban passing the Flintlander his tubāq box and then piling a jade bowl with rice porridge as Maroto packed Bang's pipe with the blend of snow burly and sweet, lightly toasted black leaves. "You really think it's that bad, huh."

"I know it's worse than bad," said Fennec, pouring them both tea as Maroto began wolfing down the cold, salty porridge. "Enjoy, because that's liable to be your last meal. When they first started chipping away at the outer wall we thought we had a chance, slow as the siege built, but now I'm thinking that was all for effect—give us plenty of time to see their army getting bigger and bigger and bigger, our morale getting lower and lower and lower. They were just camped out there for well over a fortnight, but once they went after the outer wall in earnest they broke through in less than three days. Now they've been working this one for a week. As soon as they launch their next real attack we're done for—this wall's not even standing in a couple of spots, just propped up with sticks. Sticks!"

"So why the switch?" asked Maroto, taking another big bite. Fennec looked confused, and Maroto swirled tea around his mouth to loosen up the pasty porridge, then gulped it down. It was one of those painful swallows that are so damn annoying. "If the odds are so long, why come over to working for the empress? What happened with the Cobalts after I left?"

"Ah," said Fennec, and clearly couldn't say any more for a minute, which made Maroto's heart break all over again. His worst fears for his friends must have come true. He ate faster, trying to stop up the pain in his chest with the glutinous slop. When Fennec spoke again it was a sharper, darker tone than any Maroto remembered from all their many years together. "We came here to help, but were betrayed. The Empress Ryuki trapped us, and...Kang-ho is dead. She murdered him. She murdered his whole family."

"Shit," said Maroto, tossing his bowl down to clatter on the table. He hadn't seen Kang-ho in years, and bitterly, bitterly regretted it— why hadn't he ever visited him on the Isles? Or, um, had he? Back when he got way too deep into sea scorpions he had some vague memory...but no, damn it, the point was he should have kept in real touch with his friends. Maroto had always assumed of all the Villains *he* would be the first to kick it, and careful Kang-ho would be the last to shuffle off. "I'm...I'm sorry, Fennec. I know you guys...well... I'm sure there's something in the Trve sutras we could sing for him over this offering I'm about to burn, but you'd have to take the lead on that."

Immaculate horns began sounding up and down the wall, and Fennec sighed. "Save the funerary songs for us, old wolf, and smoke fast—that's the signal. Our only hope was to hold the Autumn Palace, and it's falling. This is the end. Of the Cobalt Company, and then Othean, and then the Star."

"There's got to be something we can do!" said Maroto, nearly shouting for the words to escape the tightness in his throat. Sorrow for Kang-ho had him on the verge, but there was also the need to hear from Fennec's own lips what had happened to the rest of his friends. "Quick, man, tell me what happened after I left—you came here, Ji-hyeon and Kang-ho were killed, but what else, before and after? What happened to—"

He tried to say Purna's name but lightning blasted a rod on a nearby tower and the thunder crack deafened him, and even as it rolled away the rain was beating down so hard on the roof it was hard for Maroto to make out what Fennec was saying.

"—kept the whole company captive, but when the siege started she knew they were in trouble and offered us our freedom if we saved the Autumn Palace. The empress's representative spoke very eloquently of how all mortals are family, and while we sometimes have our differences we must put them aside to work together against the First Dark." Fennec smirked. "As soon as I took command I encouraged our soldiers to loot the castle, and sent terms to the Tothans in every language I knew, offering to unlock Othean in exchange for safe passage for the Cobalt Company. No response, alas, alas, but in the hour or two we've got left keep an eye on your Chainites, is my advice— someone who will work for you in exchange for their freedom will sooner work against you for it, if given the chance."

"My people," said Maroto, the unlit pipe he had packed shaking in his hands as Fennec stood up, outlined by another flash. Waiting until the peal of thunder had faded before repeating himself, Maroto clambered to his weary feet as well. Seemed almost a shame to hear it now, with his own doom coming in hard and fast—why not let them live in his heart until it stopped beating? Why punish himself with knowing? Because it was what he deserved, that was why. "My people, Fennec, do they live? Purna and Choi, Diggelby and Din and Hassan? My nephew and father, what of them?"

"Ah...some might still be alive?" said Fennec, which was hardly the answer Maroto wanted to hear but wasn't as bad as it could be, all things considered.

"Where might I find 'em, if they are?" said Maroto. "What part of the wall are they stationed at, or are they—"

"None of them are here, Maroto—maybe some are safe, wherever they are," said Fennec softly, putting a furry hand on Maroto's shoulder in a gesture that definitely didn't fucking bode well. "But I know your father…your father fell back at the First Battle of the Lark's Tongue."

"Oh." That was…that was not what Maroto had wanted to hear. That godsdamned son of a horned wolf had *died*? He'd been dead all this time, ever since Maroto had been marooned on Jex Toth? Before the teeth of his grief could seize hold of his tongue he said, "But the rest, you're saying they just didn't come up here with you and the Cobalts? They might be okay?"

"Only Choi…" Fennec began, but now his lip was wobbling the way Maroto's ought to, if he'd been a decent son.

"Only Choi what?" Maroto asked forlornly when Fennec closed his eyes instead of going on. "Only Choi what, Fennec?"

"Only Choi traveled here with us," said Fennec, opening his wet eyes to meet Maroto's. "She saved my life, when they executed Kang-ho. I was going to do something stupid, but she stopped me. When I woke up it was in a prison yard with the rest of the Cobalts, and…I never saw her again."

"But that doesn't mean anything for sure!" said Maroto, finally feeling the joy of Bang's philosophy as he parroted the words. "We can't give up on our friends until we know for sure they—"

"The Empress Ryuki executed her, Maroto, weeks ago," said Fennec. "Choi and old Colonel Hjortt both. I don't know about the rest of your friends, but I know she's dead."

Maroto opened his mouth…then closed it again. Nothing to say. His fists tightened up along with his chest, but the rest of him felt so limp he could barely stand. As if sensing this his old friend put his arms around him, holding him up, but beyond this meager warmth the world stretched out cold and vast and teeming with horrors.

Not that he had to gaze out at the charging armies of Jex Toth to be reminded of that. He looked down at his feet, and staring up at him out of a lamplit puddle on the flagstones was a grinning skull…

It rippled. The skull frowned, and then it wasn't just the puddle that was rippling but the terrace itself. The Tothans had broken through, and the inner wall was falling. Maroto fell with it.

CHAPTER
17

Zosia had been obliged to mess a few people up getting out of the castle, but she didn't push things further than she needed to. If she got to Gate Square and found Indsorith dead, though, she would teach this town the meaning of the word *overkill*. She jogged through the hooded mob, weaving around their crackling rushlights and following the river of sparks that flowed through the city. She didn't stop to ask anyone if the execution had already taken place—hearing she was too late would only slow her down, but it damn sure wouldn't alter her course. The treacherous representatives of the People's Pack were going to answer for what they had done to the two queens who had tried to help them.

She and her devil reached the wide plain of Gate Square, one of the few neighborhoods in Diadem open enough that you could see the sky from the street. The darkness was lifting, the heavy grey clouds tinged purple. Ahead, Zosia saw the stream of hooded citizens disappearing into the Gate, and she was so surprised she slipped in the mud and skidded to a stop. What the fuck?

Except no, they weren't actually marching into the Gate; Zosia's eyes had just been playing tricks on her. The procession passed by the rim of the Gate, into which everyone cast their rushlights, and then the darkened march took a sharp turn and filed out through one of the other four boulevards that opened onto the square. On the far side of the Gate from where the crowd quenched their candles in the First Dark was the People's Pack, sitting at a long table like nobles at a garden party. Behind them the rear of the square was filled with heavily armored militia members standing at attention, and in front of them, between Diadem's new rulers and the Gate, was Indsorith.

Zosia had imagined the worst. The girl screaming her last as the executioner removed another panel of her flesh, or already dead, crucified upside down on the edge of the Gate. Such heavy-handed symbolism seemed inevitable from the People's Pack. And while Zosia hadn't been far off on that count, she wasn't too late, either. Not quite.

Indsorith was lashed to a stake, her arms pulled up over her head. In place of a crown she wore a dunce's cap, her mouth gagged and her eyes blindfolded. An absurd array of gems sparkled at her throat and across her stomach, at her wrists and fingers, on her ankles and toes, but otherwise she wore only her skin. And as the sickliest yellow sheen bruised the low-hanging clouds overhead they prepared to deprive her of even that—the woman wearing a bear mask who knelt over a black sword to one side of the stake began to rise, as did the dog-faced man bowing over Zosia's hammer on the opposite side, and then Zosia began to move, too.

As she did, one of the hooded figures nearing the Gate broke from the procession, walking briskly around the side toward the bound queen and the seated representatives. Guards swiftly moved past the People's Pack to intercept the man as he shouted and waved his hands over its head, and Zosia hesitated. She felt fitter than she had in years, full of fighting vigor and with a powerful devil at her side, but one misstep and the militia could and definitely would execute Indsorith—slitting her throat might be less of a spectacle than the slow flaying they intended, but they would surely prefer that to letting Zosia walk away with her.

"Listen up, Chop…" From the way he was wagging his tail he must have known he was in for a treat. "We act natural, stroll up nice and easy, but as soon as they see through my disguise we rush in, grab Indsorith, and jump into the Gate. You take us through to…shit, the Usban Gate, I guess. Far from here as possible. Trve's nice this time of year."

He whined, but she didn't know if this was a criticism of her scheme on the whole or just the lack of carnage involved.

"If they kill her, though..." Zosia would want to murder everyone in this square if not the whole city, but that was hardly going to give her devil any incentive to help in the rescue. "If she dies, Chop, you and me hop into the Gate, pronto. But as long as she's alive I'm going to keep fighting to free her, which means you get to eat as much as you want. So let's go put some meat on those bones."

Choplicker barked his assent to that part of the plan, at least. Straightening the orange militia tabard Boris has provided over the ringmail shirt she'd stolen on her way out of the castle, Zosia stepped back into the procession and hurried along its side toward the Gate. Up ahead another figure detached from the throng and joined the first, the pair arguing with the guards who were preventing them from approaching either the bound queen or the People's Pack. As they carried on a member of the council rose and headed over to the commotion...

Not much of a distraction but better than none—Zosia would go around the other side, where there weren't already guards between her and Indsorith. She waited until she was at the very edge of the Gate and then hoisted the chipped buckler and shitty sword she had taken along with the armor. She started strolling around the left side of the Gate, but Choplicker, capricious monster that he was, trotted to the right, barking bloody murder as he ran to where the huddle of guards was engaging the pair who had cut from line. One of the troublemakers was a Flintlander with big white hair like Maroto's nephew, but Zosia wasn't worried about them right now, taking advantage of Choplicker's addition to the diversion to march briskly around the opposite side of the Gate.

Nothing to see here, just another member of the militia working security detail...And just like that she was rumbled, several members of the People's Pack standing up and pointing straight at her. Oh well. Zosia charged. It felt a lot like old times, rushing in with no real plan against impossible odds. Both of Indsorith's executioners were on their feet now, their weapons ready, but for the moment, at least, nothing stood between them and Cold Zosia, the Banshee with a Blade.

CHAPTER
18

Lightning struck the Temple of Pentacles, arcing down its abalone roof and webbing across the open doors so that despite the darkness of the stormy dawn, the red stars set in the peachwood panels could be seen on the far side of the Gate. Beyond the temple steps the flash illuminated the rear of the Tothan army as it crossed the fields, driving into the Autumn Palace. Ji-hyeon stepped through onto the top step, the smells of lightning and the wet earth turned up by the marching invaders making her eyes fill. Fellwing flapped back to her shoulder, perhaps to strengthen herself before the coming struggle or maybe just because she didn't like flying in such heavy rain. They were home. And even better, her sister Yunjin's scrying was proven accurate, the timing of their return as perfect as Ji-hyeon could have hoped—Jex Toth had already punched a way into Othean for her, now all she had to do was follow them through and claim the empress's head.

Tempting though it was just to let the Tothans and the Immaculates fight it out for a while, weakening each other before she swept in to dominate them both, that sort of cold calculation had no place in a hot-blooded mortal heart. Well, okay, it initially had, when Yunjin had intoned in her witch-trance that Othean had been besieged by a monstrous army, but that was over a year ago now and in the intervening months Ji-hyeon had reconsidered her initial impulse to sit back and watch them kill each other from a safe distance. She had sworn vengeance against her hated enemy, no matter the cost, but if for convenience's sake she stood by and let the innocent subjects of the Immaculate Isles perish at the hands of the Tothans, that made her no better than the empress. Besides that, her loyal Cobalts were probably still locked up in Othean.

All the same, sounding the attack now would be trouble. Better to wait until the Tothans had advanced farther across the fields toward the Autumn Palace, lest they become aware of the danger at their rear and stop the flood before it even started. Using a Gate had its advantages, but there was no escaping the fact it was one tight bottleneck— something to keep in mind once she sat on the Samjok-o Throne. If you built a barrack out here and positioned a standing force of a hundred soldiers they could defend the Gate indefinitely, no matter the size of the army attempting to cross through; you wouldn't need more than a dozen of your best, really, but eventually their arms would grow tired from all the slaying and they'd need to be swapped out.

"Ahhh!"

She jumped at the sound of Hyori's voice, and turned to scold her for coming through before Ji-hyeon gave the command—what was it with family and thinking they were exempt from following direct orders? Seeing the look of rapture on Hyori's face as she breathed in the sultry Immaculate air, though, Ji-hyeon gave her younger sister a great big hug instead of a reprimand. Her formerly younger sister, anyway—besides being one of her best captains the woman was also as old as their fathers had been, back when all this started.

"Do you think they're through the inner wall yet?" asked Hyori, a far better tactician than her sister. This was her plan, and she was more excited about seeing it go off well than hugging her general.

"Let's get up on top of the temple for a better look," said Ji-hyeon. "Choi showed me how right before we used the Gate for the first time. We crawled up and watched the sunrise over the palace. If you can reach that beam up there you pull yourself up into the eaves and—"

"You are not getting onto a roof in the middle of a thunderstorm," said Hyori, sounding exactly like their first father...and then like their second when she added a cheeky, "General."

"Oh gods, do you remember when we were climbing that droning pyramid north of Turbid and Sasamaso started in about how—"

"That's our signal," said Hyori, and following her nod Ji-hyeon saw that their appearance on the temple steps had finally been noticed, half a dozen spindly demons breaking off from the advancing army to double back and investigate. This was how it started, Ji-hyeon's three-fingered hand itching for its sword just as she knew the sword was itching for her palm. "Should you—"

"You do it," said Ji-hyeon, the inside of her chest vibrating with anticipation. She was a hardened veteran of a hundred battles, none could refute it, but this war was different, the first in a very long time to make her nervous. And if all went well, the last she'd ever fight.

"Yes, General!" Hyori ducked back inside the temple, crossing a gulf between worlds quicker than it would take Ji-hyeon to reach the bottom of the steps. Her sister loved giving orders so much Ji-hyeon would have stepped down as general and let Hyori take over long ago if she hadn't promised their first father she would lead her sisters home—he had a lot more faith in her command than she did, and you don't break oaths you swear to the dying. Would that he had held on a little longer…

Hyori came back through, leading Shagrath and Therion by the reins. Once Ji-hyeon had earned his respect Shagrath had carried her through many battles; they called their mounts dire pangolins, though they were about as close to their namesakes as the monsters cantering toward them were to horses. She petted his black-scaled head while he snuffled her, then put her boot in the stirrup and mounted up. By the time she had settled into the saddle and set her flag upright in its holster the first dozen Cobalt riders had come through, and after walking their steeds to the base of the temple steps they took off at a gallop to intercept the charging jade-eyed monsters. Before Hyori could object Ji-hyeon rode after them, not intending to plunge straight into the Tothan rear by herself but damn sure wanting any Immaculate defenders on the wall to see the Cobalt pennant flying as their salvation came charging from the very Gate through which they had banished her.

The Tothans had figured out the ambush now, the whole rear turning to face the Temple of Pentacles, but their foot soldiers had a lot of wet ground to cover. These riderless equine monsters moved fast, however, chittering herds of them galloping out of the holes the massed infantry opened for them. There were more of the demons than Ji-hyeon had anticipated, but that just meant her cavalry would have to fight twice as hard to keep the Gate clear for the rest of their army to come through. Ji-hyeon blew the horn she had carved to replace the one lost during the Second Battle of the Lark's Tongue, a trophy taken from something even bigger and meaner than a horned wolf—she couldn't wait to show Choi and sing her its song, once she rescued her captain and the rest of the Cobalts from the Immaculate stockade.

Lightning splintered the rainy heavens over Othean, and down on the ground it was pure hell as the first Cobalt riders met their spear-legged foes. These things cared nothing for the mounts, focused entirely on snatching the riders in their split-mouths, and succeeding more than once. Ji-hyeon's flanks were clear for now, but straight ahead a massive demon came barreling toward her, its flaming eyes locked on her, its sideways jaws spreading wide, and she lowered her spear... but didn't get a chance to use it.

Shagrath huffed in warning, and she held on to the saddle horn as he reared up, trotting on his hind legs with his front clearing the ground. As the Tothan monster reached them her pangolin back-handed its gaping mouth. Its entire head nearly came off, but before Ji-hyeon could cheer three more rode down on them.

She slapped Shagrath's scales but as usual he was already ahead of her, slowing to a stop as quick as he could in the wet mud and wheeling around. His thick, scaled tail was twice as long as the rest of him, and while it looked less than graceful dragging along behind him most of the time, when he put it to use it was fast as a bullwhip and sharp as a bundle of saw blades. He snapped the legs out from under two of the stampeding monsters, and Ji-hyeon punched her spear all the way down the hungry throat of the third. As it fell Shagrath looked over his shoulder to check on her and, seeing she was all right, extended his ridiculously long tongue to lick the spattered grey blood from her face. Her exploits kept him just as well fed as Fellwing, albeit on less ephemeral provender; the owlbat braved the downpour as more of the monsters rushed toward them.

Shagrath retracted his tongue and pulled toward the incoming herd but Ji-hyeon steered him back toward the temple. The Cobalts were making good time clearing the Gate, all five hundred of the cavalry on the ground and the first of their war machines wheeled over by the side of the temple. Now that it was the infantry's turn things were going to slow way the hells down, though. It would take all her cunning, and that of her captains, to see that the Tothans were held at bay long enough for the entire army to come through, and she couldn't contribute that from the front. As she glanced back to make sure they weren't pursued, lightning touched down atop the Autumn Palace, and to the accompaniment of a thunderclap she saw a huge, sagging band of the inner wall collapse.

A part of her hated to see it fall, the palace a symbol not just of Othean but all the Immaculate Isles. The larger part of her felt an ugly warmth at the sight, however, knowing that no sooner had it crumbled than word of the event had reached the empress. Ji-hyeon imagined the fear on the woman's mean, pinched face as she contemplated the end of everything she held dear... and then the confusion and shame when she was informed that none other than the exiled Bong Sisters had come to the defense of the realm.

Ji-hyeon was still smiling when another flash lit up the fields to the north, and then her confidence dropped as hard as the wall of the Autumn Palace. Another army marched down upon them, hundreds of the horselike horrors galloping at their vanguard, and larger, slower monstrosities shambling in the vast field of Tothan foot soldiers. Then they were again but a dark blur to the north as the flash failed and the rain came down harder.

Well, fuck. Even if all the Cobalts arrived before this second force, which was unlikely, they would still be pinched between the Tothan armies. While Ji-hyeon had no doubts her soldiers could overwhelm one monstrous regiment before swarming into Othean to tackle the surviving Immaculates, there's a world of difference between fighting two lesser armies in a row and fighting two at once.

"Bad luck!" Ji-hyeon called to Hyori, who sat astride Therion by the temple steps, directing the flow of soldiers as they came through the Gate. "That great plan of yours, where we trap the Tothans between us and the Immaculates? Crush one army between two?"

"I saw! I saw!" Hyori shouted over the rain and clamor of steel and shrieks of mortal beasts and chattering horrors. "Take it up with Yunjin—my strategy was based on her vision."

"What do we do?" asked Ji-hyeon, waiting for another lightning bolt to show her how close the second army was but the weather refusing to oblige.

"We fight like devils and see what unfolds," said Hyori. "Maybe the Immaculates come out from the castle to hit this first crew, keep them off our backs while we do the second."

"Maybe," said Ji-hyeon, "but they might take the opportunity to try to shore up the wall instead of running outside to fight. We Immaculates are sensible like that."

"Some of us are," said Hyori. "If something doesn't happen, though, I'd say maybe we all die out here! Wouldn't that be a laugh, after all we fucking went through to get back here?"

"I've heard better," said Ji-hyeon, her heart sinking at the prospect. "But then I've also heard worse. I guess we just have to wait and see."

CHAPTER
19

And I am telling you it can't wait!" Diggelby was shouting at the top of his lungs and bouncing on his toes, clearly hoping his voice would carry over the shoulders of the guards who had stopped him from reaching the People's Pack. "Jex Toth attacks! The Star's in danger! We have the biggest news since the Age of Wonders!"

"I told you to shut up," said the thickest woman in orange, jabbing a finger into Diggelby's chest. "I've been polite, but no more. It's time to go."

"To meet the People's Pack?" asked Sullen, seeing that one of the figures had risen from the table set back there behind the Gate and was heading their way across the square.

"To meet the inside of a cell, you fucking loonies," said the lead guard. "Hand over that baton, big boy, and come with us."

Sullen licked his lips, looking to Diggelby for direction...and then lamenting the life choices that had led him to do such an unthinkable thing. It was just as Nemi had warned, but unlike Sullen the witch hadn't broken from the hooded mob to support Diggelby, so at least one of them would make it to Othean. He felt like he might throw up as he realized what he'd just done—thrown away his one chance to get back to Ji-hyeon and Keun-ju, and for what? To back up Diggelby's brilliant plan of bum-rushing a giant state-sanctioned ritual on the rim of a Gate.

"Let's just call it a goof," Sullen told the guards. "Forget the whole thing. Me and my friend are leaving."

"Yes, you fucking are, and you're leaving with us," said another guard, holding his polearm like he was about to jab Sullen with it. Sullen's spear felt hot and hungry in his hand, and as if sensing the danger emanating from the rag-sheathed weapon, another of the half dozen guards reached out and said, "I'll just take that now, all right?"

"This is an outrage!" cried Diggelby as a pair of guards put their hands on his shoulders and began steering him away. A guard had his fist on the haft of Sullen's spear but Sullen couldn't bring himself to let go—as soon as he did, any hope of getting back to Othean died. The guard tugged but the spear didn't budge. Sullen knew from the man's expression that things were about to get very, very unpleasant but still his fingers refused to release the weapon.

"*Diggelby?*" An older man in an ostentatiously embroidered black robe with a yellow collar, a bead-brimmed orange hat, and red face-paint had come up behind the guards. "Is that really you?"

"You know these yahoos, Cardinal?" asked the lead guard.

"Unkie Obedear!" Diggelby shook off the hands on his shoulders. "You're alive! And even better, you can help us! Tell these thugs to let us talk to the People's Pack, we've got news of the utmost urgency."

"My gracious," said the old man. "We had better hear it, then. Let my nephew and his friend through, I'm sure he wouldn't make a scene if it wasn't something terribly important."

The guard let go of Sullen's spear, he and Sullen exchanging thankful smiles. What a fucking relief things had somehow uncomplicated themselves. Diggelby, man—just went to show that even without a devil of his own the fop was still lucky as one.

But then, just as everything had gone right for a change, a dog barked. Everyone turned to look behind Sullen but he didn't have to, and couldn't have even if he wanted, seeing as his blood had just frozen solid in his veins. He knew that bark, and picked up on the mocking falseness of it—what came running up behind them might look like a dog and bark like a dog but it wasn't no dog. It was Zosia's devil.

"Assassins!"

Sullen didn't see who shouted it, but as soon as the word rang out in the square it was pandemonium, pure and simple. The guards right on top of him and Diggelby went from relaxed to way past their previous level of pissed, pikes lowered back down and swords clearing sheaths all over again. Diggelby was still in the act of pushing past them toward his uncle, and right then Sullen saw the big angry woman they'd first engaged make the decision to kill the pasha. It was a queer thing; Sullen hadn't known it showed in the face like that, but there it was, a twitch of the guard's eye and a setting of the jaw, and then she thrust her polearm at Diggelby's throat.

By the time her arms were moving, though, so were Sullen's, and the day some Outlander's oversized pike was swifter than a Flintlander's spear had yet to dawn.

Sullen darted in low and swung up, batting the underside of the guard's weapon so that it popped up in the air, overshooting Diggelby completely. Sullen hadn't expected to disarm her, but as he struck all the makeshift padding somehow fell off the head of his spear and the naked blade met the middle of her pike, severing the wooden shaft... and most of the hand that held it. He couldn't fucking believe it, tight as he'd bundled up the spear, and besides that he'd been aiming for a good half foot up the haft from her fingers. But there they went, flying into the air with the broken-off head of her pike.

"Sorry!" he cried, which, as far as battle cries went, left a little something to be desired but was at least sincere...and also insufficient to placate the other guards, who did about what Sullen expected. He danced back from them but bumped into Diggelby, and then doubled over from a spasm in his stomach. Still hunched from the pain, he jabbed a charging guard through the foot and twisted his spear, hoping to just bring him down without hurting him too bad. The man shrieked as Sullen upended him, and other people were yelling, the guards surrounding them, Zosia's devil barking, and Diggelby was yelling at Sullen, demanding to know what the hells he was doing, as if this were all somehow *his* fault.

Cringing as he straightened up from the pure fucking torment in his midsection, he saw the actual cause of all this trouble dashing around the far side of the Gate—a silver-haired devil named Cold

Zosia. Sullen was supposed to stop her before she could bring hell to Diadem, but that looked to be exactly what she was doing. That they were both here, and in the middle of some shit, confirmed at least part of the prophecy he'd been dealt. Considering how very dead Zosia wasn't despite all the fresh rumors, though, Sullen wondered just what the Faceless Mistress expected him to do about it. You can't kill what won't die, that's just basic shit. But hey, Diadem wasn't flooded with fire, so things weren't as bad as they could be.

Yet.

CHAPTER
20

Things were going worse than Maroto could have predicted, and he had a pretty damn active imagination. You'd think with that creative mind of his he'd have figured a way out of this kimchi pot already, but no. As far as strategic pickles went, this was the funkiest he'd ever sampled. Not in a good way, either, but then even the best metaphors break down eventually. Point being, a bad morning in Othean was only going to get worse.

Two thousand Cobalts. Not the smartest of the bunch, either. You could tell that on account of these being the ones who'd apparently followed General Ji-hyeon straight into the Lark's Tongue Gate.

Fourteen hundred Immaculates. Better trained and equipped than the Cobalts, these, but hardly the best or brightest on the Isles. That was obvious from the fact that the empress had assigned them this bleak babysitting detail, which any sane advisor would've told her was a lost cause. With such meager numbers it was, anyway.

Ah, and five hundred Chainites. Er, four hundred and nineteen. Hard to believe he'd lost almost a fifth of his troops just getting inside the Autumn Palace. He'd expected to lose over half. That just went to show that some pickle pots are stronger than they look.

Do the sums and that added up to nearly four thousand soldiers, all tucked safe behind the walls of a legendarily impregnable fortress. Nothing to sneeze at . . . so long as that legend was true.

Which, as of about thirty seconds ago, it wasn't.

His ears were still ringing and the choking plume of dust that had enveloped the lurching terrace hadn't yet been beaten back down by the rain, so Maroto stayed where he lay a little longer. Coughing, reflecting. Choi was dead. So was Da. Even dazed from falling flat on his face, he felt as if he'd grown an extra heart at the news just so he could have two ripped apart at the same time. Granted, before he'd even stopped hugging Fennec that section of wall a quarter mile north had crumbled, sending shock waves down the line, so he'd like as not be joining his dead kith and kin before very much longer...but that just meant he had to pack in as much grief as he could, while he could.

And administer twice as much before he went. At a minimum. That was Maroto maths, elementary as the sun rising from the Sea of Devils each morn.

At last he began to feel the rain on his neck again, prickling the backs of his legs where they emerged from his battleskirt. Could breathe the burning dust instead of just hacking on it. Clear as a sign from Old Black herself, too, the fume parted before his eyes and he looked out not to the west, with its rampaging Tothan army, but to the east. It was a beautiful sight, the expanse of tiled rooftops stretching out to the horizon like the scales of a giant's armor. Othean. Why the devils weren't they already retreating into the city proper, fleeing to one of the other palaces erected at its four corners?

More importantly, why the devils was he looking for the back door when there was a good clean death knocking at the front? The Barbarian Without Fear, they'd called him in the old days, and while he'd always suspected Hoartrap had meant it sarcastically you couldn't deny as a younger man he'd fought first and worried about the consequences second. Hells, as an old man he'd done the same— he might have gotten better at avoiding trouble in general, yes, but whenever the blighter came calling he didn't pull the curtains and hide under the drysink.

Yet ever since Jex Toth it was as if he'd misplaced his guts...along with his balls, his spleen, and any other parts you could name what might give a fellow courage. Yes, the Vex Assembly were dread creepers, no doubt about that, but how much better off would Fennec and the rest of the Cobalts be right now if when the Tothans had captured

Maroto he'd taken a noble death over betraying the Star and sending the monsters straight here to Othean? He was always risking his own neck to save his people before, it was the one thing he was good at, so what fell witchery had happened to make him value his own sorry skin over those of his friends? Was it really just because since falling in with Purna and company he'd started getting more out of life, was seeing it as actually worth the bother? There was some irony for you—as soon as he started appreciating his existence he stopped leading the sort of life that was worth living.

But maybe he was getting back on track, since right about now he wished he were dead.

"Alive." Fennec wasn't asking, he was telling, and Maroto obediently let his old friend help him up. Following his gaze out over the drizzly metropolis, Fennec said, "Bad news, barbarian—I just received a final order from the empress's messenger vulture. Our last stand isn't going to be quite as heroic as I'd hoped."

"Fuck…" Maroto dissolved into coughs, and then he expelled a sticky clod from his raw throat… along with his temporary madness. "Fuck that! Last stands are for losers, Fennec, and that ain't us! We've got to fall back into the city, now, while there's still time. If we hoof it we can make one of the other palaces, and—"

"That's the very order," said Fennec, the paw that didn't rest on Maroto's shoulder crumpling a roll of parchment. "Or close enough. We're not retreating to a palace, though, but the gatehouse at the heart of Othean. We're going to try, I should say."

"What's the gatehouse?" asked Maroto, squinting into the haze. "Is it, like, some kind of secret second Gate the Immaculates have kept hidden from us Outlanders all these years?"

"Not that kind of gate, Maroto, the regular sort—over there." Fennec pointed out to the horizon, where a pale band ended the sea of buildings. "That's the wall that runs from the Summer Palace in the north all the way down to the Winter Palace at Othean Bay, bisecting the city. While we've been holding this castle for them the Immaculates have been evacuating West Othean into East Othean, behind the wall… and now we have to follow them."

"With all due respect, man, how are we not already *there*?" said Maroto, unable to believe he had to lecture Fennec of all people on when to cut a tactical retreat.

"Because that's not just a ghost town down there, it's a murder-hole. Half the capital is rigged, the biggest death trap the Star has ever seen, and we're the bait. So long as they're busy chasing a fleeing army the Tothans won't take the time to inspect their surroundings until it's too late. Her Elegance has been so good as to send us this map of the only safe route through the western city."

"Damn..." said Maroto, the quiet metropolis no longer seeming like such a welcome omen after all. "...Nobody likes to draw the short straw, granted, but you have to admit it ain't a bad plan, far as last ditches go. Gives us a chance to get across and get safe behind another wall, anyway, which is better than no chance and no wall at all."

"But not so good as if she'd shared this plan with me from the beginning, when we actually had a prayer of getting most of our soldiers out," said Fennec. "Even if we started the extraction now—"

"*Now* it is!" said Maroto, striding forward...and falling back to one knee as the world lurched again. Or at least his world did, anyway. "...Damn."

"Yes, I was waiting until I could walk in a straight line before I tried to climb down from an unstable ruin to race an army of monsters through a massive city," said Fennec, smart as ever in both the mouth and the arse. Or were those two of the same thing? "Once we start moving, Maroto, we won't have much breath for chatter, so lest I don't have another chance...thank you. For coming here, I mean, even when you had to know it was hopeless. I'm glad you came back."

"Well, shit..." said Maroto, letting Fennec help him up again, and not in such a hurry to get moving this time around. "Truth be told, Fennec, I didn't even know you were here, nor none of the other Cobalts. I just came to clean up my own mess for a change. Figure it's about time I started."

"The Mighty Maroto, a man whose ego is so grand he can take sole credit for an invasion of demons," said Fennec, shaking his head and retrieving Bang's pipe, which Maroto had dropped, and worse, forgotten he'd dropped.

"See, it's a *lengthy* song but it's not a long song…" Maroto began, but trailed off as the rain further dispelled the cloud of dust and he could see back out to the west. The beetley black swarm teemed through the slums beneath them, cascading in through the sundered outer wall and pressing toward where they'd brought down the inner. Fuck, there were a lot of them, and other things down there, too. Worse things, knowing his luck, whose blazing green eyes he could glimpse through the dreary drizzle…and at that Maroto found his balance again. "Right, maybe even if we're still at the crawling stage we get a move on, yeah?"

"Long past," agreed Fennec, coming to Maroto's side and nodding down the listing terrace to where his officers awaited their descent at a more stable stretch of the ramparts. "I hate to do anything that benefits the empress but can't very well decline a chance out for some of our loyal followers. Even if it's only postponing our final reckoning with the Ten True Gods of Trve, we've got to try."

"I thought you traded in that particular cloth ages ago," said Maroto.

"Somehow I always seem to rediscover my faith at times like these," said Fennec. "But all the same I'd rather wait a while longer before discovering just how much Korpiklani and her nine siblings appreciate the prayers of a fair-weather friar, so let's move fast."

"Faster than fast," said Maroto, pocketing the pipe Fennec had returned—a few dings in the wood, but like certain other things Zosia had graced with her touch, the lucky briar had survived another fall. It reminded him to retrieve his mace, which teetered on an edge.

"Do you see that?" Instead of squinting down from their vantage Fennec was looking up. "Am I…am I dreaming?"

Between the rain coming down and the tendrils of dust or smoke still rising from where the wall had collapsed, Maroto couldn't see at first…and when he did he wished he hadn't. Never, ever say things couldn't get any worse, was the lesson here.

"Nah, you ain't dreaming, friend, you're looking at a nightmare I've met in the flesh." Maroto scowled at the familiar flabby flapping of the squid-dragon as it rode the currents over the northern fields, shivered as he remembered being carried aloft in its sticky tendrils. It was still a ways off but those things covered ground fast, and while he could only see the one for now—

"It's her!" Fennec staggered past Maroto, lifting his fuzzy hands into the rain like a mad prophet reaching up for a handshake from the divine...and then an owlbat swooped between his claws, circled his head in a squeaking blur, and flew back out to the west. "Fellwing!"

"Kang-ho, no, Ji-hyeon's devil?" Maroto tracked the bobbing black dot through the rain, his hackles going up at the spooky image. "I heard if they outlive their master without ever being freed they've got to haunt the site of their grave, but figured that was just another myth. Poor damn thing."

"She's not dead," Fennec breathed. "She lived. She lived, and she's come back!"

"How's that? You said the empress executed her!"

"She executed Kang-ho, but Ji-hyeon fled into the Gate!" Fennec scampered over to the edge of the unstable terrace, the massive slabs beneath their feet shifting ever so slightly...and ever so queasily. "There! By the Temple of Pentacles, do you see?"

Taking a far more cautious approach, Maroto advanced a few steps and tried to follow Fennec's stare. All he could see were the countless black-shelled soldiers and their herds of warbeasts pushing into the outer wall...and of all the ill luck here came a second Tothan regiment, marching down through the northern fields. As far as the eye could see were monsters on the move, not one but three of the squid-dragons wheeling over their advancing legions. Had Fennec lost his shit entirely, to think Ji-hyeon had—

No, there they were. Blue pennants just to the west, flitting around in the narrowing gap between the Tothan force invading the Autumn Palace and the second army coming from the north. There was that speck of white behind them, the Temple of Pentacles. It rose from the fields like a tooth...or an Imperial headstone. As he stared the black flood entering the outer wall began to flow backward, the Tothans reversing course to confront the Cobalt forces harrying their rear.

"She came back," Fennec repeated breathlessly. "She came back!"

"She didn't borrow enough from Zosia, now she's got to fake her own death, too?" asked Maroto, but he was smiling wide. That kid of Kang-ho's was all right, he'd known that from the first. "How'd she do that, exactly? And how many Cobalts followed her back into that Gate after the empress double-crossed you?"

"I don't know how she fucking did it, but she did it! And nobody went in with her. Those aren't our soldiers—she's brought a brand-new army with her!"

"A brand-new army that's about to go the way of every other army that finds itself playing pastrami in a two-front sandwich," said Maroto, drawing Fennec's attention to the second Tothan regiment. "The only thing their showing up now does is buy us some much-needed time to fall back through the city."

"No . . ." Fennec's face fell and Maroto cursed himself for a tactless bastard as the inevitable sank in for his old friend. This was almost worse than if Ji-hyeon never came back at all, to return straight into the middle of a meat grinder. "We can't just turn our back on her! She's trapped out there!"

"She'd do the same if we were out there and she was in here, with one chance to make a getaway," said Maroto, hating the words even as he said them. Hating the truth in them. What a cold and terrible world they lived in, where only the ruthless could survive, where only the heartless could prosper.

"You're probably right," said Fennec. "Which is why it's so important we old-timers set a better example for the next generation."

"Yeah, I—wait, what?"

Fennec was grinning the sort of crazy grin he'd always accused Maroto and Zosia of wearing right before doing something really, really stupid. It was a good look on him.

"You see a Cobalt unit about to be crushed between two Tothan armies, but I see a Tothan unit about to be crushed between two Cobalt hordes," said Fennec, beginning to clamber down the ruined terrace toward his captains. "We smash them fast and hard with everything we've got and we can clear the way for Ji-hyeon and her soldiers to get inside Othean, before that second regiment swallows them whole. Then we all retreat together."

"That's fucking barmy!" cried Maroto. "The Tothans are already pushing into the hole they just punched in the Autumn Palace, and you told me they're ten thousand strong! We've got one golden fucking opportunity here to escape through the city and instead you want to try plowing through an army of monsters? With a second army of monsters almost on top of us? All to try to save a friend you already gave up for dead, and who's like as not going to buy it for real long before we can reach her?"

"That's your general's plan," said Fennec, the terrace wobbling even worse than before as he and Maroto picked their way down to where the officers had convened on the wall-walk below. "You don't like it, barbarian?"

"Like it?" Maroto balanced his mace on his shoulder as he swayed on a seesawing beam atop a ruined castle at the end of the world. "I fucking *love* it. Just let me pop into a washroom first—need to freshen up my makeup before we go dancing."

CHAPTER
21

*L*ove was not a word Y'Homa had been familiar with in her old life. She knew what it meant, of course, had used it many times over to describe her relationship with the Fallen Mother, and the Allmother's affection for the broken world. Yet that had all been so abstract, so speculative. Now that she had taken an angel into her flesh she not only understood love, she experienced it. Her soul was full to bursting with it, making her as giddy as a sinner reveling in the delights of the Deceiver.

She loved to bond with Sherdenn and Lagren, her fellow angeliacs. She loved the feel of Lagren's spiders crawling from their mistress onto her own flesh, and she loved Sherdenn's bombastic oration as they flew south to oversee the assault. She loved the sensation of missing Lagren, the priestess staying behind on the northern shore of Othean to supervise the stream of reinforcements swimming down from Jex Toth, and to prepare for the arrival of the Immaculate navy once the heathens realized their blockade had been useless against the deep-diving leviathans. She loved to feel the power of something greater than herself flying through her body, and more than anything else, she loved the feel of flight.

Her angelic charge had soared through the First Dark, and now they soared together over the fallow fields of Othean, and the sensation was indescribable save for that holiest of four-letter words. Their steed was also of the First Dark, which was to say, further fruit of the Fallen Mother's abyssal womb. The longer she kept counsel with her angel, the better Y'Homa came to understand that was the true nature of the First Dark, after all—the primeval paradise wrought by their maker, that eternal font from whence all good things sprung, and to where all good souls returned. That she had been raised to believe the First Dark was hell just proved how powerful the wiles of the Deceiver truly were. Hell was all too real, obviously, but it was not to be found beyond the Gates. Hell was the flesh, the world of sensation where the Deceiver held court like a mad king. To escape the snares of the Enemy one must travel beyond the veil, or better still, tear that veil asunder, so that the Allmother could cast her cleansing gaze over the clean and the unclean alike, judging all mortalkind before assuming her rightful place on the throne of the world. Everything was happening.

Still, it brought Y'Homa no pleasure to see her armies cut down the sinners who stood against them. She had thought it would, before she awoke, but now she knew better. She did not revel in the slaughter. She felt no love to see the misled mortals fall before the scythe of their savior. Their fear in her coming, *that* filled her with love, and their anguish as they realized their reckoning was at hand, certainly, but the act itself did not stir her breast. No, each death broke her heart anew, as if their failures were her own. She took no joy in her conquests, even as she knew their sacrifice on the sacred blades of the Fallen Mother's army ushered in a new age, a better age.

Yet even in the darkest hour of her pity for the wretches she exterminated there shone a light. So much had been false but there remained some deeper truth in the Chain Canticles, and that was what she saw as her armies crashed through Othean's inner wall. She was bringing salvation through sacrifice. She was lighting a candle for the First Dark. As each unworthy Immaculate perished on the bones and barbs of her righteous legions, the Fallen Mother swam ever closer through the void, and when the beacon burned bright enough she would return to this benighted world. She would save it from itself, bringing with her the host of angels who were the rightful heirs of the Star. The Deceiver had sought to claim the Star for his own, planting the evil of free will in every single mortal breast from the moment it was exiled from the womb, but soon they would be freed from that burden. Soon the Fallen Mother would return home, and her bastard offspring would know nothing but reverence, forevermore.

First, however, the sacrifices must be made. Mortal sins must be paid with mortal flesh. The world must prove itself worthy of salvation, its barren fields made rich with offerings of blood and ash. The Garden of the Star was not Jex Toth, it was what the world would become if only the faithful were strong enough to see it done. This was Y'Homa's sacred task, something only one who truly loved the world could carry out, because the truth was it agonized her to see so many die. To reap such a bitter harvest. Such was the love Y'Homa felt for her imperfect, corrupted realm, that even through her tears she would see this through to the end.

Not that it would take long now. The seed was planted deep, the earth damp and fertile. Smoke was rising from where their forces had brought down the inner wall, opening up the flank of the castle and the city beyond. The Empress of the Immaculate Isles hid within, and no matter how fiercely her guards fought they could not stand against their righteous executioners. It had taken less than ten thousand knight-queens to break through the walls, and now Y'Homa and Sherdenn brought three times as many reinforcements to overwhelm the Immaculates.

Thousands upon thousands of warriors incapable of fear or mercy, living only to serve the orders of the Vex Assembly—each blackshelled soldier consisted of dozens upon dozens of drones working in tandem to fulfill the orders of their queen, angel-ridden insects that dreamed of being human. It did not escape Y'Homa's notice that the knight-queens' very existence was a microcosm of the Tothan command, and indeed, of all life on the Star—swarms of lesser beings striving in ignorance to fulfill the obligations of their mother, to become something greater than the sum of their parts. The queens themselves even possessed souls, the same as any mortal; the only real difference was that these blessed children of the Allmother were incapable of going against the commands of their masters, which was to say, incapable of sin.

The rest of the army proved slightly less predictable, but even more powerful. Most of the holy spawn the Vex Assembly had called up from the deepest recesses of heaven loped on four legs but others lumbered on two, or eight, or didn't have legs at all, slithering their spiny bulk through the muck of this mortal realm. Banking her steed just out of arrow's reach along the outer wall, Y'Homa felt her horde's excitement at the unexpected presence of mortal fear and fury on the field ahead. She goaded her mount to fly faster through the rain, her second-soul aching with love even as she felt the twinge of remorse that they could not simply eat and eat forever, that however hard these sinners fought, their resistance must be short-lived.

Slower. Sherdenn's thought pulsed through her head, the ancient priest flying somewhere near the rear of their army. The message smelled of dust and rotten fruit. *Cautiously.*

Faster, thought Y'Homa, her angel seconding this course as she ground her flesh against the bone saddle of her steed, the thrill of reckless flight electrifying. Beneath them, the muddy fields trembled as her army picked up the hot scent of her intention and broke into a charge, struggling to keep up with their commander. Her mount began to careen from side to side through the driving rain, unable to completely satisfy her lust for speed. Despite her angel's joy in the mad flight she slowed their pace, banking again to fly back to the rear where Sherdenn waited. He wanted their legions to approach with slow and stately grace, to further amplify the fear of their damned quarry, and unless Y'Homa ceased her outriding at once the army would mistakenly follow her swift lead and the pungent trail that hung in her wake.

Just as she was about to turn back, however, she caught sight of a shred of blue banner on the distant field. She blinked through the rain running down her living helm, and though her angel didn't understand her excitement and hatred it impulsively obliged her, looking farther than any mortal eyes to confirm her suspicions.

The Cobalt Company was here, on this very field, attempting to draw the first Tothan regiment away from Othean's breached walls. Y'Homa had never felt such warring passions in her breast, primal wrath at their rebellion wrestling with enlightened gratitude at the role they had played in summoning Jex Toth back from the First Dark. Her angel reveled in her internal conflict, just as it reveled in all the raw sensations billowing up from the busy battlefield, and finding guidance in its rapture, Y'Homa smiled in thanks at yet another of the Fallen Mother's bountiful gifts.

Spurring her steed to carry her down over the vastly outnumbered mortal ranks, Y'Homa and her angel prepared to bestow their own reward upon the Cobalt Company. The only pity was it would be over so soon.

CHAPTER

22

She flew! Best flew! She flew!

Neither the wind in her eyes nor the darkness of the night could obscure the wonders before her, above her, beneath her. Best skirted the hem of Silvereye's cloak, the stars bright as wolf eyes catching firelight, and no sooner had she wondered if she might touch the very clouds than her sky-devil carried her higher and higher. This winged creature that obeyed her unspoken wishes was a prize more magical than anything in Sullen's songs, and she wished her son were here to share this reward for her bravery.

The boy's lover was clearly less appreciative of the miracle than Sullen would have been. When Purna brought her own sky-devil soaring up beside Best's, the Immaculate threw up onto the beast they shared, clinging to Purna's waist with his one arm as his spew skated off into the aether. The devil dog's head poked out of the scaly saddlebags affixed to the sky-devil's flanks and Best thought he might have barked, but any noise was lost to the whoosh of the wind. All the same she barked back, then focused on the awesome sight of the starlit jungle stretched out beneath them.

Yet more incredible than flying through the night was witnessing daybreak whilst scudding through the heavens themselves. A storm brewed far behind them in the south, but all around them the morning arrived bright and clear. Blue bled into pink in the east, where the Bright Watcher rose from Flintland to cast her baleful glare upon the world—the sun might be an aspect of the Deceiver, but watching it rise from such heights was the most beautiful thing Best had ever seen.

When they had first claimed the sky-devils and taken to the air it had been too dark for even her sharp eyes to take in the landscape far beneath them. Now, after flying inland for so long that her legs became cramped on the monster's soft-boned saddle, the panorama below commanded her full attention. There could be no denying it: just ahead the dawn-brushed mountains and the shadowed valleys formed the outline of a sleeping giant. No, a giantess—it was clearer than any picture stone, clearer even than the idol of Old Black emerging from the thorn tree back home. Were all lands built upon the barrowmounds of such titans, a secret known only to the birds and the owlbats? Or was this but further proof that Jex Toth was a realm above and beyond the world of mortals? She tried to draw the attention of the others to the awesome image but when she turned to signal them she saw they were already descending, and quickly.

Then her own sky-devil arched its wings and they began to fall as well. Dropping at such speed was even more exhilarating than climbing into the clouds, but she concentrated on going slower, reluctant to surrender her view of the anthropomorphic mountains. For the first time the creature ignored her desires, but before she lost her lofty perspective they crossed over the mighty mountains that formed the colossal bosom and she saw where they were bound. Vast white stones emerged from the jungle to form a necklace of bones around the throat of the buried giant, and flying over this sprawling wonder, they dipped ever lower even as the final mountain climbed upward into their path. At its pinnacle towered the biggest tree Best had ever glimpsed, of the same type as the one Sullen had chained her to back in the Haunted Forest but grown to divine proportion, and something about its countless white blossoms fluttering in the chill wind filled the Horned Wolf with an ecstasy so profound it was terrifying.

But this was not their destination, the lurching of her mount distracting Best from the gargantuan rowan tree. A cave yawned open in the mountainside straight ahead, and without slowing at all the two sky-devils shot straight into it...into the mouth of the Fallen Mother.

It was then that Best felt certain her glories were coming to an end, and that she must now pay the price all mortals owed after witnessing sights intended only for the gods. She had trespassed in the heavens, and for this she must now descend to hell. As the blurry stone of the surrounding cavern gave way to pulsing wet meat that shimmered with its own radiance, she reckoned she was fast on her way. Badly as Best had wanted to believe Old Black's Meadhall awaited her on Jex Toth, it was obvious this place was no paradise of the underworld but somewhere far, far worse...

Which was good. A false god was naught but a demon, and where else would a demon live but in the bowels of hell? That was how Father Turisa had always described the deepest recesses of the Deceiver's lair, and while that description had never made much sense before she now saw that it was true. That hell was found in the stinking viscera of the Fallen Mother was an unexpected development, to be sure, but then Best was neither a theologian nor a shaman. Perhaps everyone else had known all along and she had just missed this particular sermon.

The sky-devils were slowing as they zipped around spinal out-croppings and through winking apertures, and Purna's flew ahead of Best's as the cavern narrowed. A deep purple glow radiated from the heaving walls of the cave system, illuminating that which Best would have preferred never to have seen. The passage opened back up and they skimmed the surface of a lake teeming with gelatinous life. A crowd of the black-armored soldiers waited on the far shore, gleaming bone weapons raised to greet them. Best bid her beast to fly straight into them, drawing one of the bamboo javelins she carried with her proper spear in the makeshift quiver on her back, but Purna's sky-devil banked to the side to avoid them and Best's followed it.

Tempting though it was to hurl her missile into the pack, she only had a few and held on to the weapon as they soared into another tunnel. This one was almost too tight, and Best braced herself to leap backward off her beast if it crashed into one of the shiny walls. Purna shouted something back at Best but it echoed past before her ears could catch it, and then Purna and Keun-ju's sky-devil disappeared as the phantasmal flickering of the tunnel went black...

Despite her resolve to stay silent Best whooped as they burst out into the widest, brightest cavern yet and went spiraling into free-fall. The vast hall was a blur of spectral green light as they careened downward, her heart trying to leap free of her chest and almost making it. It was hard but she went to her sharp place, focused instead of fearful. The hot winds buffeting them stank of bile and carrion beetles, the enormous sky-devil whining like a puppy as the bone saddle between Best's thighs spiderwebbed with cracks, oozed burning slime. They were almost to the source of the light; Best felt it more than saw it through the dizzying drop, her sky-devil screaming now, its hide blistering off its body as though it were roasting in a clay oven. Her feet scrambled for purchase on its disintegrating back, and she kicked off, instinctually trying to leap away from it before—

It splattered into the glowing earth and Best went skipping across the sharp ground. With each bounce a piece of her battle-dress or weather-beaten skin came away, but then the brilliant earth softened, splashed, caught her instead of repelling her, and she went under the surface. They hadn't hit the ground, but a viscous, luminous lake.

The radiant ichors stung her fresh wounds, the heaviness of the liquid dragging her down…but she heaved herself up, breaching the slime and gasping the putrid air. Later she would offer prayers of thanks to her fallen father for marching her and Craven to the coast and shoving them into the icy waters, telling them Horned Wolves had been Sea Wolves once upon a time and don't they forget it, but prayers were for the living and right now Best wasn't sure she still numbered among those ignoble ranks. First she had to reach a shore, and with the light of the lake too intense keep her eyes open, she paddled blind, trying not to think about what might be underneath her…

Until it grabbed her.

By the arms, yanking her onto her feet. The bank was so soft she hadn't even realized she'd made it, had been pinwheeling her arms through foul, treacly mud. Now she struggled to stay upright, willing her porridge-soft knees to firm back up, willing her stinging, ooze-filmed eyes to focus on Purna and Keun-ju. Who else could it be, this pair of shimmering figures who had helped her up?

Except it wasn't. Best knew that even before she got the filth from her eyes and saw the wizened old witches grinning at their would-be quarry. She knew because she smelled the bad intentions coming off them like steam from a pot of jollof, felt the inquisitive push of their thoughts against her skull the way her sky-devil must have picked up on hers. Which was why she swung on the closest one before she could even see it clearly, but it bounded out of the way, chattering its teeth at her.

"Hear me, demon princes!" she said, staggering away as one disrespectfully tugged on a braid and she wiped the reeking ordure from her face. "I am Best of the Horned Wolf Clan!"

"We knoooow!" shrieked the first to come into focus, a grotesquely obese old man naked save for a crawling dashiki of ants. The second was a crone adorned in an ornate suit of snails, her bald head wreathed in slugs, and she hissed, "We are friendssssss of your brotherrrrrrr!"

Not that she had a good impression of them to begin with, but this sealed the pact as far as Best was concerned. They must have sensed the danger she posed, for they flew upon her as she reached for her great-grandmother's sun-knife. The one that never missed and always killed.

Well. Mostly.

———

Just before they crashed Purna scooped Prince out of his chitinous saddlebag and bailed from her sky-devil. It would have been a slick move, even if she hadn't done a triple backflip before landing on her heels in the inexplicably flabby earth. Her boots punched right through the skin-like surface and she sank to her knees, stinking ooze bubbling out as she wobbled in place . . . and caught herself, sticking the fucking landing!

"Woooo!" That was how you fucking *did it*, right there! Purna knew she was a badass, but she also knew that even for a badass like herself this was some next-level shit. Figuring she might have had a little help, she smooched Prince's fuzzy head—he was in for more dog treats than he could handle, just as soon as Purna figured out the devil's favorite brand. "Did you *see* that shit?"

"Impressssssive!"

Snapping her neck around, Purna saw that while she'd addressed Keun-ju he had clearly missed her display, seeing as how he was floating six feet off the ground and staring saucer-eyed at the ancient witch who seemed to be keeping him aloft. The wrinkled old woman held her claw-like hands up in front of her, Keun-ju bobbing in place as she waggled her spindly fingers. When Purna had watched Hoartrap make a keg float around a bar back in Myura she'd wondered if that trick could work on people, too, and here was her answer. Cool. Less cool was the army of earwigs swarming all over the witch; the bugs were so thick on this biddy they looked like one of Diggelby's crocheted bodysuits.

"Far as impressive goes, you're not too shabby yourself, catching my friend like that," said Purna as she clumsily extracted herself from the leaking wounds her feet had gouged in the fleshy turf. Seemed wisest to be diplomatic here, considering how powerful this buggy old Tothan must be. Now that the thrill of their flight and dramatic landing was fading she felt a deep and intense anxiety at whatever insane scene they had just blundered into, crashing into some nasty netherworld populated by insect-infested enchantresses. When she had pitched the whole heroic death angle to Keun-ju she hadn't counted on turning yellow, but here she was, shaking in her shit-filled boots—Maroto would've been so disappointed in her. "What say you put him down, gently like, so we can—"

The woman dropped her arms and Keun-ju fell from the sky like a sack of millet, splashing in the mucky shallows of the glowing lake that stretched out across the subterranean vault. A glowing lake was also cool, albeit weird...and hardly the weirdest thing about this place. Looking around, Purna saw that the floor of this cave seemed to be something like a drained tidepool, the spongy earth thick with enormous, coral-like formations...flesh coral, for lack of a better term, the giant fans ridged with veins and shining with luminescent gristle. The growths blocked her view of most of the cavern, but out in the center of the lake rose a terraced pyramid, and there, down the shore a piece, Best seemed to be dancing with two more ancient Tothans...except knowing Best that dance was anything but, and—

The earwig witch stepped in front of her, blocking her view. *Excellent work, Purna old girl, distract the obviously powerful enemy from Keun-ju and then totally ignore her to gawp at the local real estate. Smart.*

"So, uh, super nice lair you got here…" Purna said as the horrible woman took another step toward her. "I mean, I've been up in some guts in my day, but never anything this spacious."

"Wordssssss are worthlessssss," squealed the woman, and *Flintland ancestors take pity on an Ugrakari convert, there were earwigs in her mouth.* "Let us innnn, interloper, let us seeeee who sennnnnnnt you."

Maybe the long night-flight Purna had spent silently communing with her sky-devil had attuned her to this funky mental-transfer thing, because Purna could distinctly feel the witch's mind wrap around her own, like an octopus squeezing a clam. When their Tothan prisoner had injected those sinister visions into Purna's skull back on the bluff she had thought it was the nastiest violation possible, but this felt even worse—the old woman wasn't just trying to jam thoughts into her head, she was trying to take stuff *out*. A septic stench emanated from the crone, making Purna's eyes water as she tried to resist the invisible assault.

"I, um, I've got a headache?" Purna backed away from the woman, clutching the growling Prince closer to her chest and putting her free hand on the pommel of her pistol. "You seem fluent in High Immaculate, so—"

"Immmmmaculate?" Even if the witch hadn't spat bug parts as she spoke, Purna would have guessed she'd committed some linguistic faux pas. "You are not Immmmmaculate! You are mongrel spaaaawn! You are bassssstards! You are—"

Purna really, really wished she hadn't seen Keun-ju climb to his feet on the shore behind the witch and draw his broken sword, because as she did she felt the intruder break through her mental resistance, scanning Purna's thoughts like a gourmand browsing an upscale menu—and as soon as she noticed her friend, the witch stopped talking and her eyes widened. It might've been a damn fine jack move, but instead the Tothan wheeled about and slapped the air just as the Immaculate lunged forward. She didn't touch him but he flew backward into the lustrous shallows of the lake, and before Purna's pistol could clear its holster the witch was right up in her face, snatching at her throat...but Purna leaped backward. And what a leap it was; she hadn't known she could jump that far forward, let alone backward, but then you never knew what you were capable of until a dirty old bug lady tried to feel you up.

It was all instinct, though, over before she even realized she'd moved, and the witch was striding toward her even as Purna landed. Prince squirmed out of her hand, dropping to the soft ground and advancing on the Tothan with an awfully big growl for such a little guy. The ancient witch paused, staring down at the dog in her path, and then her eyes sank all the way back into her face, the sockets flooding with black ooze.

It was the opposite of what had happened with their prisoner, whose eyes had been that spooky black from the day they captured her right up until the interrogation, when they had miraculously cleared. At the time Purna had told herself their Tothan prisoner's eyes were black because they'd filled with blood as a result of the crash that had broken her body, that their suddenly becoming normal after she invaded Purna's mind was some sorcerous regeneration. Apparently not. That this switch from evil black eyes to normal peepers and back again was a trick these crusty old wizards pulled as a matter of course didn't put Purna much at ease, but other than making the witch look even freakier than before, nothing happened.

Well, not quite nothing. The fell witch and the devil dog both went completely still, staring at each other...but nothing *else* happened. Yet when Purna took a cautious step forward the air around her fairly crackled with desperate whispers and infernal aromas. She couldn't make out if they were actually saying anything she might understand, let alone what, but the intensity of the murmurs and the sulfurous scents stuck her short hairs up and kept them up. Disturbing associations were forming in Purna's frantic mind, parallels between this withered thing and the hungry corpses that had attacked them back in the swamp…and far worse, between these dead-but-not Tothans and the Living Saint of Ugrakari legend.

She took another wary step around Prince's haunch. Whatever this Tothan witch truly was, it was long past time to take her ugly head off while she was distracted. Before Purna could put the plan into action, though, the devil and the crone broke their reverie, both turning to look at her with hungry smiles. Too late, Purna realized her mistake—Maroto always told her to think before she acted, but this was just another of his lessons proved astoundingly wrong. She hoped it wouldn't be the last.

"*It has been a very, very long time since we have been surprised.*" The witch's voice was as altered as her eyes, but while those had turned black as the heart of a thunderhead her mellifluous accent was as light as cottony summer clouds. The smile of her puckered lips still looked nasty as a dead man's butthole, though, and Purna didn't much like what was coming out of them, either, even if it was in Modern Ugrakari instead of High Immaculate. "*You cannot conceive of how happy you have made us.*"

"Well, uh, that's one you owe us?" Bad as the buggy witch had looked before, these changes intimidated Purna in ways she couldn't understand; having this thing's attention on her felt like being slowly lowered into a pit full of snakes.

"*We owe you something, yes,*" agreed the crone, but the way Prince whined and nuzzled Purna's leg didn't fill her with confidence. "*Before you may be paid, however, you will help us. We summon you before the Vex Assembly, to tell us everything you know of the one who sent you assassins into our temple.*"

"Assassins?" Purna tried to fake a laugh but it just wasn't happening. "Look, you…you things came after *us*! You invaded our world! You're trying to kill everybody, and you call *us* assassins?"

"*Your world?*" The ancient thing that definitely wasn't just some super-old lady laughed. It was a jolly, tinkling, and very genuine sort of laugh. "*This was never your world, little monkey, you were but its stewards. Poor stewards at that, but for all of your other faults you have performed a single task with admirable gusto—you have been*

*fruitful. And now the time has come to lay down even that burden...
but first you will tell us of your scheming master and all the petty snares
you have set in our path.*"

"I have no master," said Purna, the strength of a good one-liner at
last giving her the courage to jut her chin out and point her pistol in
challenge. This monster might tear her apart by inches—centimeters,
even—but she wasn't spilling a single damn bean about nothing. She
had done a lot of crummy things in her day, but that day was over...
or something. Anyway, Purna wasn't a damn blabbermouth—maybe
the one decent lesson Maroto had taught her was that snitches
deserved stitches.

"*Oh, Purna—for a comrade of Maroto we expected you to be more
forthcoming,*" it said, which intrigued Purna even as it put the piss
in her porridge—had it looked into her head to know about her
relationship with the barbarian, or had he actually been here and
encountered these creatures? "*He was, and he answered every question
we asked. He answered many questions we did not think to. He told us of
all his old confederates, Purna, including yourself, told us every secret he
knew. He pledged himself to our service in exchange for a reprieve from
sacrifice, albeit temporary. Follow his example and perhaps—*"

"You lie!" It wasn't that Purna couldn't believe it, she just really,
really didn't want to.

"*We are incapable of such mortal follies, yet we can always smell them,
when your kind attempts to deceive us.*"

"You don't even have to ask," said Purna, mostly thinking out
loud. "You can just...*see* what's in our heads, so why ask at all?"

"*Because your kind is far more skilled at lying to yourselves than you
are at lying to others, and the waters grow muddy,*" said the crone, or
whatever was using her as a conduit. "*Besides, we only deign to take
that which is freely given.*"

"Then I refuse!"

"*You will answer our questions or your friends will be peeled apart
in front of your eyes,*" said the ancient. While the voice was even
sweeter than before, Purna must have struck a nerve with her defiance, because every single one of the earwigs fell from the woman's

withered body and lay dying on the sweaty, pimpled ground. Purna gulped, not daring to look and see if Best was still holding her own against the other two, or if Keun-ju had pulled himself back out of the shallows. This was so fucked. She told herself she wasn't really caving, that she had to stall for now to save her pals but when the time came she'd somehow find another way out without telling this monster a damn thing…

"So long…so long as my friends are unharmed we can talk," Purna finally managed.

"*Mortal lives are naught* but *harm,*" it said, smiling wider and stepping closer, its bare feet crunching its dying raiment, its enormous black eyes filling Purna's world. "*If it is death that concerns you, little monkey, put it from your mind. None of you assassins are escaping that easily. Not until you tell us of your master. Maroto told us much but you will tell us more. We shall hear from your lips the details of every plot and scheme, every detail you can summon down to the last rumor or legend. You will tell us of the Betrayer of Jex Toth, our renegade brother whom you mortals call Hoartrap the Touch, and only then will we speak of such mercies as death.*"

CHAPTER
23

Choplicker's barking must have provided a decent distraction, because Zosia was halfway around the Gate before anyone noticed the old woman in an orange tabard ambling toward the queen. When they did, though, the whole militia massed behind the grand table where the People's Pack presided over the square stormed forward, guards bellowing and delegates scrambling up in alarm. If she'd actually been after them she never would have gotten close, so it was a fine thing she wasn't. Ignoring the panicked parliament, she raced along the curve of the Gate, the only person standing between her and Indsorith the executioner with the hammer. Her hammer.

Zosia didn't break a sweat, even as the dog-masked man swung the sawn-off maul down to bash her head in. He might've been an ace at breaking the ankles of bound captives, but his swipe at a moving target was sloppy as hell. Under different circumstances Zosia would have felt bad cutting down someone she outmatched so hard, but all things considered it was a good feeling, slamming to a stop well out of reach of his premature swing and letting him stagger forward into her blade. She left the sword in his lung, relieving him of the hammer as the first of the charging militia crew reached her.

Sidestepping a spear, she crushed the woman's chest, then careened in between two others before they could arrest her charge. As long as she stayed on the lip of the Gate they couldn't surround her, and Indsorith was just ahead, a dozen paces away. A militiaman came between them but she bowled him over into the Gate, and then a second tried to do the same to her. The only thing for it was to grab his arm first, using her momentum to pull herself away from the Gate even as she sent him flying into it. She almost tripped over her own feet but found her balance, collapsing another guard's kneecap before she'd even reoriented herself.

The stake where Indsorith was bound was only a few steps away now, but either the guards had moved faster than she expected or she had run slower, because they had managed to surround her after all, cutting her off from helping her friend. A hole opened in the lowered polearms and women with crossbows opened up on Zosia. They were too close to miss.

Choplicker must still be somewhere nearby, though, because all the shots went wide of their easy target, hitting more militia members instead. There was no time to catch her breath or plan an attack. It was that pure sport Zosia lived for, her body not only doing what it needed to do but outperforming all others. Then, blurry and frantic as the combat was, and skillfully as she'd been maneuvering through the mob to get to Indsorith, she saw it was too late. There were still too many heavies between them, and the bear-headed executioner with the sword had just nodded in the direction of the People's Pack, bringing her ebon blade back for a swing.

Zosia bellowed at the masked killer, knowing even as she did that nothing could distract the woman from what looked to be a decapitating blow.

Except *nothing* is a foolish thing to say, for good intent or ill, because there is always *something*, as demonstrated by what did capture the executioner's attention, making her forget her victim, at least for the moment: Hoartrap the Touch.

He floated up out of the Gate and stepped onto the flagstones of the square in front of Indsorith and her executioner, who, quite reasonably, redirected her strike at the new arrival. It is best practice to kill first and ask questions never with scary-looking creeps who materialize right on top of you. And while Hoartrap's timing couldn't have been better, distraction-wise, his delivery needed some work—he seemed totally caught off guard by the battle raging right in front of him, so much so that the ursine executioner hacked deep into his shoulder before he noticed her. But when he did it did not go so well for the woman. No, it did not.

At least that was what the noises implied, both the executioner's and the aggrieved party's. Despite Choplicker's protection Zosia caught a big bash and a small gash across her shoulder as a polearm struck her, the ringmail shirt she'd borrowed from a castle guard popping a few links, and then she was back to worrying entirely about her own skin. Her shield came apart under a battle-ax, her forearm painfully shivering from the impact, and she side-armed her hammer into the thug's head. The woman had been pedaling backward, and instead of braining her the maul grazed her cheek... which took her entire face off, a grotesque wound that confirmed for Zosia that this sainted steel hammer was in better hands now than it had been in the church. She'd see it got put to its proper use, and often.

Something sharp raked through her boot and across her shin and Zosia stumbled, out of breath and getting clumsy. Her devil must have been wearing down, too, because the next volley of bolts all connected. Only the one seemed to pierce her mail, and shallowly at that, but it stuck her fucking tit. *That* was just not on. Squinting through the pain, she dodged a spear and then parried a sword by breaking the hand of the man who swung it, and followed up by kicking his legs out from under him.

A gap in the mob opened around her, nobody wanting to get too close... which showed what amateurs they were. It would mean certain death for the first few who led the charge to dogpile her, yes, but they would have taken her by now, even with Choplicker's aid. As it stood she'd dropped at least twenty of them and wasn't down yet.

Even still, too many surrounded her, and Zosia was too fucking tired. It had looked like such a short distance before, but she'd become lost in the press of orange tabards, and with her eyes stinging from her sweat and their blood she couldn't make out where Indsorith was anymore. Then a wall of them came screaming at her, which was what they should have tried from the first.

Instead of bracing for the wave that could only drown her Zosia staggered forward to meet them, hammer high...and blundered through them as she realized they posed her no threat. The lot of them were dropping their weapons and vainly trying to remove their bubbling armor, helms melting down faces as burning hair and scorching blood created an almost mechanical stench. On the other side of these poor bastards stood Hoartrap, looking good and fucking steamed himself. The right sleeve of his robe was torn and soaked as black as the Gate behind him, but of the executioner who had cut him there was no sign save for the dripping sword he held in his left hand. And just beside him, still chained to the stake, was Indsorith.

"Cut her free!" Zosia shouted, her ears ringing as she tripped over a body and staggered into the back of the stake. Now that they had merged the bubbles of space the wary militia had given them and Hoartrap was here to back her up, Zosia dropped the hammer at her feet, arm tingling. Resting her head against the wooden post, she closed her eyes as she panted, not wanting to open them again for fear of what they'd see. Indsorith had been poisoned from the first, or else caught a bolt or blade during the melee, or—

"Mmmm," came from the front of the stake. "Mmm!"

Zosia opened her eyes. Saw Hoartrap shove a squirming rat into his mouth, then wave his bloodied hand and send corpses spinning off the ground and into the archers who had come to the front of the militia. The sorcerer clenched his hand into a fist, to the sound of wet explosions and an ensuing rain of gore.

Typical Touch.

Choplicker wagged his way over from the other side of the Gate, his entire pelt slick with blood, and two other red-spattered figures stumbled after him into the small clearing the guards afforded them: so it *had* been Sullen she'd seen, and one of Maroto's fop friends.

More important than any of that, though, and just as incredible, was what she saw as she reached up with numb, shaking fingers to remove Indsorith's gag and blindfold, tearing off the conical hat. The Crimson Queen was alive. Indsorith's eyes were streaming but whether the tears were from pain or relief or just having been blinded for so long, Zosia didn't know. She did know that as Indsorith smiled at her rescuer with her full lips, she had the sudden urge to kiss the fallen queen, and might have, too, if Hoartrap hadn't spoiled the mood.

"You are *such* a treasure," said the Touch, his mouth dripping rat blood. "I come here to tell you to raze the place and you're already on it. You're a real go-getter, Zosia, always liked that about you."

"Are you all right?" Zosia asked Indsorith.

"My arms," said Indsorith, wincing as she shifted, and Zosia cursed herself for a Maroto of the first water—kissing girls who couldn't get away was the low-hanging fruit, but really now, the truth of it was not even he would be such a selfish shit as to try to suck face with a traumatized woman who was probably in a great deal of pain. But as Zosia apologized and straightened up to unclip Indsorith's shackles, she came in close enough that Indsorith could have given her a peck on the lips…which she did.

Which was…What, now? Maybe that was just how friends greeted each other in Junius, some provinces had real affectionate customs like that, but just maybe—

Indsorith almost slipped all the way to the ground as her legs buckled, but Zosia caught her. Reminding herself to stay in the moment, here, she lowered the weak queen down to the base of the stake, Indsorith wincing as she dropped her arms. The younger woman looked up at Zosia, and she felt something she hadn't in a very, very long time: she was blushing red as a Crimson Queen's cape.

"Hoartrap?" panted Sullen. "Where's Keun-ju? And Ji-hyeon?"

"And Purna?" asked the fop.

"Hold!" Hoartrap intoned in a sonorous voice, and punctuated this by making a mangled corpse go spiraling high into the air and then tumble down into the Gate behind them. "Next fucking archer I see follows him! Now! Let's talk truce! Send out a representative to parley! Or I kill you all! With *magic*!" Turning to Zosia, he said, "That ought to buy us enough time to kill them all with magic."

"Good to see you, too, Hoartrap," said Zosia, tearing off her torn-up orange tabard and slinging it around Indsorith's naked shoulders. "Let's go, sooner we're out of here the sooner I'm buying you a drink. Hell, I'm buying you the bar."

"Hoartrap, for real..." said Sullen, leaning on his spear and giving Zosia the same nervous nod he always offered her, like she was some bully he was afraid of provoking with either an actual greeting or by outright ignoring her. He was trying real hard not to notice Chop-licker sniffing around his spear, too—he better watch out or the devil might pee on it. "Where are our friends?"

"In mortal fucking danger," snapped Hoartrap. "If they're not dead already. Happy you asked?"

"*What?*" Neither Sullen nor the fop looked happy about that, and the bedraggled barbarian sounded all set to press the issue when Zosia looked up from helping Indsorith out of her ankle shackles.

"That's something we've all got in common, then, because we need to get the fuck out of here. Catch us up on the song somewhere safe, but for now tell me where we're going, and let's go." Seeing her devil exchanging a hard stare with Hoartrap, she said, "Chop, leave him alone—we're all friends again. And it's time for us to split."

"Nowhere is safe," said Hoartrap, sounding all bugged out as he spun around, his charm-and-trinket-studded yellow robes kicking up as he stepped over another body to get to Zosia. He knelt down as close as he could without brushing the bolt still sticking out of her aching chest, and in a low voice, so the others couldn't hear, he said, "The Star is done, Zosia. *Done.* We lost. Jex Toth won. And now we're all going to fucking die. Everyone in every corner of the world."

Hoartrap was a master of the half-truth and the not-quite-a-lie, as flighty with his words as he was with his friendship. So it wasn't just what he said that put the spook on Zosia but how he said it, report-ing with the same monotone directness he'd employed that night in his tent back in the Cobalt camp, when she had interrogated him at devil-point. Whether or not he was right, he was definitely telling her what he believed to be true. As her stomach sank Indsorith found Zosia's hand, squeezing it hard, and that just made her feel all the queasier. She had finally been willing to let go of everything, to forgo vengeance and move on...but now there was nowhere to move on to.

"Unless..." said Hoartrap, and she was all set to hit him for selling it to her as completely hopeless, but looking up she saw no mischievous gleam in his eye, no ironic smile at whatever suicidal scheme they had to embark on. Instead Hoartrap the Touch looked...*scared*? "It's the only way, Zosia. I knew from the first it was an option, but I prayed it wasn't the only one, and you know I'm not one for church. Alas, it is our only hope, and we are almost out of time. But it will work, if you have the courage."

Choplicker came over, smacking his lips at Hoartrap, but the warlock was too intent to be unnerved by her devil.

"Shit, Hoartrap, you know courage is all I've got in my head—lost my brains long ago," said Zosia, realizing as she said it that she was trying to sound hard to impress Indsorith. Never too late in life for such foolishness, and always at the worst times. Looking down at the younger woman, who looked back up at her, she said, "Even if it costs my life, I'm willing to try anything to save this worthless fucking world full of worthless fucking people who'd kill me and everyone I care about for a handful of cold silver. Who knows, maybe third time's the charm."

"Spoken like a true hero," said Hoartrap, but he didn't sound much relieved just yet. "It's not your life we need, though. One of the few in the house that gets a pass. But I know the guilt will be all the greater for living, and that's a burden we all must bear, even as we take heart in knowing they would have died anyway, and worse, along with the rest of the Star."

"Wait, what—ow!" Zosia began, but then Choplicker nosed at the quarrel in her chest, dislodging it with a painful pop.

"He wants you to sacrifice this city," said Sullen, looming over them with a terrified expression on his dopey face.

"Nobody likes an eavesdropper," said Hoartrap, scowling at the boy as Zosia stanched the already-slowing flow of blood from her wound.

"Oh, they're sending Uncle Obedear back over to talk!" called the fop.

"Keep 'em busy," said Zosia and Hoartrap in unison.

"That's it, isn't it?" Sullen shivered as he spoke. "You two are going to loose the fire that ends Diadem. A burnt offering."

"And what would *you* know about it?" asked Hoartrap, and now his eyes lit up with excitement. "Sullen, my boy, I always knew you were more clever than you looked, so go on and tell me, what exactly have you seen or heard, and from who?"

"Wait, are you saying the kid is right?" asked Zosia. "You want me to . . . to sacrifice all of Diadem?"

"No, *I* don't *want* you to," said Hoartrap, "the Star *needs* you to. A great sacrifice summoned Jex Toth, and only a greater sacrifice can banish them again before it's too late. And here we have the only means to such a sacrifice."

At this solemn pronouncement Choplicker did the last thing Zosia would have ever expected—the devil began licking Hoartrap's bloody hand, and when the kneeling Touch recoiled the fiend rolled over on his back, wiggling around like an excited puppy.

"I . . . I don't even know what you're asking," said Zosia, her devil's display making her heart pound so hard it hurt worse than her breast, and sinking all the while. "To murder a city . . . how could we?"

"Not we," said Hoartrap, tentatively reaching down and giving Choplicker a belly scratch. "*Him.*"

"Him?" Zosia nodded at her devil, who immediately rolled over and . . . and . . . and started fucking *begging*, his eyes big and bright and hungry.

"Nah," said Sullen.

"Hush," said the Touch. "If there is anything in the mortal realm that can awaken the sleeping volcano beneath Diadem, it is your devil. He can provide the sacrifice we need to send Jex Toth back to hell."

"That true?" she asked the friendly-faced mutt, and he barked a happy bark. "I just give the word, and you blow up the whole city?"

Choplicker held her gaze, canine lips pulling back over canine teeth, and with deliberate slowness he shook his head in a movement that wasn't the slightest bit canine. He had creeped her out plenty over the years, but never like this, and she felt Indsorith shudder against her, too.

"Devils need their freedom to work their greatest wiles," murmured Hoartrap. "All of their tenure to mortal masters is but the slow burning of their fuse, and the granting of a single wish the realization of their power. When they are set loose, in that brief moment free of bondage in this world and before they are drawn back into the First Dark, that is when they are capable of true miracles."

"Everyone knows how devils work, but Choplicker, he won't..." Zosia trailed off, remembering how eager he had been to help interrogate Hoartrap, when she had told him that if the warlock didn't volunteer his secrets the devil could force them out of him...in exchange for his freedom. Unlike when she had offered him his liberty to keep her and Leib safe, or when she had done the same to try to save Purna on the battlefield, Choplicker had made his approval of the offer known in a series of enthusiastic barks, and then had seemed ready to make good on it before Hoartrap came clean on his own. A horrible, ugly, and entirely plausible scenario unfolded in Zosia's mind, and since he seemed in a talkative mood, she looked at her devil and said, "Did I just not wish for something big enough for you? Is that really it? You were willing to stay on as long as it took for me to present something worthy of your regard, you stubborn son of a bitch?"

Choplicker threw back his head and howled, long and mournfully, and then as if that weren't answer enough, abruptly dropped his head back down and smiled all the wider at her.

"And now, Chop?" she asked, mouth dry as she stared at this alien monster she had risked her life to save but hours before. "If...*If* I offer you your freedom, could you do it? Could you wake the volcano beneath Diadem, and offer the sacrifice Hoartrap needs to banish Jex Toth?"

Worse than the head shake from before was this slow and stately nod, the devil's eyes black as Zosia's damned soul as they negotiated the terms of his release.

"Yeah, I bet you'd fuckin' like that," Zosia breathed, fury overtaking her horror at the monster's betrayal...and then ebbing as she looked at him and realized she didn't have the slightest fucking idea what she was dealing with here. The other five devils she'd helped her Villains summon during that fateful ritual in Emeritus were nothing compared to him, she'd always known that. She'd been the one to call him up out of the First Dark, not the other way around, and after a lifetime of trafficking with devils she was crying foul because he hadn't played fair? That was like toying with an asp and then complaining when it bit you. And now, at long last, she had the means not only to divest herself of the force of pure evil she'd been carrying around for almost half her life, but to do some good in the bargain. To save the fucking world . . . and at expense, sure, but given the state of Diadem's hospitality of late she could think of worse places to make the ultimate sacrifice.

"Zosia," whispered Indsorith, and looking back down at her she saw the goodhearted woman who had almost died at the hands of this toxic city on two separate occasions shaking her head. "Don't."

"Don't," agreed Sullen, and he sounded on the verge of tears. "She warned me you'd do this. Sent me to stop you. And I could have. But I didn't, 'cause it didn't seem right, doing you for something you hadn't done, 'cause I was scared of what might happen if I didn't. But you do this now, and that's what you're doing—killing people what might not deserve it, 'cause you're scared of finding another way. A better one."

"There is no better way, only a worse one, where Diadem still dies, just a slower, more painful death, and the rest of the Star dies with it," said Hoartrap, looking closely at the Flintlander. "Who warned you of all this, Sullen?"

"These folk ain't any worse than us, probably," he said, still beseeching Zosia. "You cut them down to save your friend, same as I would've, but don't you think they'd do the same for one of theirs? We're all just mortals, aren't we, lost and afraid and fighting for our friends, and how's it fair to take one life to save another, and—"

"*Sullen!* You are cracking up!" Hoartrap sounded like he had a few fissures himself. "Now focus, focus—who warned you about all this? We're your friends, and we're relying on you to be honest with us."

The boy wrestled with it for a moment, then looked Zosia in the eye. "The Faceless Mistress. In Emeritus, in the Temple of the Black Vigil."

"No shit?" Zosia hadn't thought about that broke-ass deity in decades. And after all this time she was still trying to stir the turd and send acolytes after Zosia? Unless…she looked at Hoartrap. "Do you think that's why she came at us so hard? Because even back in the day she knew I'd come to this place, make this choice?"

"Any and all philosophical discussions on destiny versus free will can wait," said Hoartrap, looking over to where the fop was talking to a cardinal, of all people. As if sensing her gaze on one of their leaders the militia tightened their ring, and Zosia wondered how long it would be until they just charged in and tried to plow the gaggle of agitators into the Gate. "Besides, our little Emeritus expedition might have rubbed her raw for all sorts of reasons. If she really was a god of those people, she can't have taken kindly to our pilfering their relics."

"You *took* stuff?" Sullen looked aghast.

"Why does a lonely god of an empty land care if I burn Diadem, anyway?" Zosia was thinking out loud. "She obviously thinks it's a bad play, so does that mean she's seen yet further into the future, and knows what happens after I detonate this place?"

"Probably!" said Hoartrap. "Call her a devil queen or a goddess or an unclean spirit, it amounts to the same—she is sentient, concentrated evil, straight from the First Dark. Of course she wants to stop you from sacrificing this city, when it's the one thing that can save our world from an invasion by her devilish kind!"

"She, uh…" Sullen's brows creased. "She didn't seem that bad when I met her."

"She is a god of devils!" shouted Hoartrap. "Nothing less!"

"Might wanna keep it down," said Zosia, noticing that the fop and the cardinal were both staring at them. Now that day had good and broken she could see it was the same cleric whose speech had impressed her during that first summit of the People's Pack, the older gent seeming downright reasonable…but then he and the rest of his reformed church couldn't be too different from the old Chain, considering they'd taken part in the betrayal of the two queens.

"In Junius we believed the Faceless Mistress devoured the people of Emeritus," said Indsorith, taking all this talk of the end of days in stride. "And we were taught that Jex Toth met the same fate—two lands who put their faith in gods, only to be betrayed, for there are no gods...only hungry devils that priests freed with the false faith that they could control them."

Choplicker chuffed at this and tried to wedge his face under Zosia's arm where it went around Indsorith's shoulders, no doubt looking to snack on what must be a very rare treat indeed in his mistress's heart, but she warned him off with a glare. She wasn't of a mood to pretend he was just an animal right now, and probably never could again. But the damage was done, Indsorith squirming away from Zosia and rising shakily to her feet to get out of range of the dog's breath. Seeing the bloody black sword Hoartrap had discarded, Indsorith somehow summoned a smile and retrieved it as the Touch pressed the urgency of the thing.

"Every moment we dawdle people are dying, *our friends* are dying, and the odds stretch longer, thinner, close to snapping once and for all. Jex Toth is launching its final push as we speak, and we must banish them back from whence they came before their psychic armies can fulfill their dread prophecy."

"Psychic armies?" That really didn't sound good. "Dread prophecy?"

"They can read our thoughts, Zosia," said Hoartrap. "Even their warbeasts are able to reach into our minds—one such monster snatched me up and it was almost my end. Fortunately for the Star my willpower was too strong and I turned the tables on it, but it left me so close to death it's taken weeks to regain my strength. Even now I'm still so damnably frail..." The Touch did look about as ragged as Zosia could remember seeing him, his once-bright tattoos now faded beneath swaths of bruises and discolored scabs. Noticing her notice, he said, "These demons are the most powerful foes we've ever faced, Zosia. They exchange thoughts like we exchange words, they have inhuman soldiers beyond count, and they have a Gate, maybe several of them...and unless we eradicate the source they will keep pumping out monsters until all mortalkind is their sacrifice!"

"Monsters and sacrifices," sighed Zosia. "Always with the monsters and sacrifices. What are they like, these psychic armies of Jex Toth? Are they anything like us at all? Are they, you know, smart?"

"If anything they're smarter than we are," said Hoartrap. "Seeing as they're on the cusp of dominating our world and our one mortal champion with the means to stop them just sits here, doing nothing!"

"Well, that went rather smashingly," said the fop, rubbing his hands together as he came back over to join them. The man looked substantially harder than the last time Zosia had seen him, his armored caftan checked with fresh stitches and fresher bloody slashes.

"Yeah?" asked Sullen, looking hopefully at Zosia like big news was coming. "They're going to listen to us? And send an army to help fight the monsters... *if nothing happens to them first?*"

Ah, so that was what the kids were doing here, trying to rally Diadem to the greater cause. You only saw that kind of optimism in the young or the stupid. Then again, hard as it would be to give the order to sacrifice a city that had recently turned against her, could she really go through with it if they joined in the fight against Jex Toth? Or would that make it easier—if they pledged to support the war effort in any way they could, that was almost permission...

"Oh no," said the fop, vigorously shaking his head. "No no no, not at all. Unkie had a rather dim prospect of the rest of the People's Pack agreeing to anything of the sort, at least right away. It's all dreadfully democratic. The bit that went smashingly was he agreed to put me up in his estate, though I gather he's sharing it with a hundred wild-born clerics since everything went tits up, private-ownership-wise. The pasha is his own plus-one, though, so I'm sure they'll find ample room to—"

"You're *staying*?" Sullen didn't sound like he could believe it, but that just proved how naïve he was—the rich kids only played adventure until they were reminded of how cushy the good life was. "Diggelby, you can't!"

"I have to," he said sadly. "If I just vanish with the rest of you there's no chance these people will come around, is there? But they deserve a chance to see the light, same as anyone, and I'm just the cheeky shepherd to bring them into the fold. After all, I personally witnessed the false Chainites sacrificing the Imperial regiment to summon Jex Toth, and I've been an ambassador between the two wizards who warned us of the danger the Star faces, *and* I'm in deathly need of a hot bath and a new wardrobe. So it's settled, I'm afraid."

"Pasha Diggelby," said Zosia, "even if I didn't have other reasons for telling you that staying in Diadem was a *seriously* bad idea, you wouldn't be able to change anything here. You can't trust those people, and you definitely can't get them to do what you want."

"She's right," said Indsorith, giving her sword a test swing. "Take it from us."

"Well, I certainly won't be winning anyone over with that attitude," said Diggelby. "But I have to try, because if I don't nobody else will. I imagine it will help if I don't approach it as telling them to do what I want, but to do what they know in their heart is right... And I'll stand a watch here by the Gate until whenever Nemi turns up to use it, and then have her pop around to the People's Pack to corroborate my story first. Now that we've got an in with the local elite, who knows, we might be needing you to open another bridge between the Gates, Hoartrap, to take the Diademians to Little Heaven just like the Cobalts!"

"That's where Ji-hyeon and the Cobalts ended up instead of following me here?" asked Zosia.

"To defend the Immaculate Isles from the invading monsters of Jex Toth," said Hoartrap. "But even working together the Cobalt Company and the Immaculate navy weren't able to stop them. They couldn't even slow the tide. Othean is falling, and we are out of time. This is the only way, Zosia, the only way."

"You are right about being out of time," said Diggelby. "Unkie says if I make good on my promise to have you all out of here in the next few minutes without anyone else being hurt, he and I will both be credited with ending this conflict. But if I don't get you all to leave, at once, the rest of the People's Pack will send the troops back in to herd you all into the Gate. Seems they're calling this an escape attempt, though what—"

"It's time, then," said Zosia, saying it but not getting up, still leaning against the foot of the stake where Indsorith had been chained and looking around at the motley crew she had found herself with here, at the edge of a Gate, at the end of her last song, charged with executing a hundred thousand so that millions might live. The fop's makeup had smeared all over his face, making him look like a drowned mime, and blithely popping open a snuff box, he took a pinch of bug dust. Sullen looked down at her with a grimace so pained you'd think his guts were falling out, leaning on his black spear, his raggedy skirt and tunic showing only a few more stitched-up repairs than his naked arms and calves. Hoartrap scowled up into the sky, where the sun was actually burning through the clouds of the Black Cascades for a change. The grotesque warlock idly scratched his wounded arm, which was dripping slow and steady onto the bloody ground. Indsorith glared at the ring of guards that shielded the People's Pack from her gaze, wearing only one of their orange tabards, funerary jewelry, and her black sword. And right there beside Zosia, if only for one final adventure, the dog so dirty no flea would touch him; Choplicker proved his name yet again as he eagerly awaited the command of his mistress.

"All right," said Zosia, picking herself up with a groan at the aching in her arms, the swelling in her knees and knuckles, the stinging in her left tit. A momentary panic gripped her, but patting her belt pouch she felt the intact outline of her new pipe—had to be a good omen that it hadn't been lost or broken in the fight, didn't it? As if she'd ever believed in omens. With a weary sigh she retrieved the hammer that might be crafted from sainted steel but was playing hell with her arthritis.

"All right?" asked Indsorith, all eyes on Cold Zosia as she stretched on the edge of Diadem Gate.

"No, not really, but I'm as ready as I'll ever be. Let's save the Star, stay alive, and get a fucking drink. That order."

CHAPTER
24

Ji-hyeon had heard it said that nothing provoked prayer like being on the bad end of a battle, but in her unfortunately frequent experience curses always seemed closer to her lips. She stood with her witchy sister on the steps of the Temple of Pentacles, surveying the field as the Gate shimmered shut behind them. The last of the Cobalts had crossed over from the other side, but that just meant the Tothans would have to work harder to earn their inevitable victory. For one thing many of Ji-hyeon's soldiers weren't quite human, wildborn from realms beyond the First Dark who had signed on for glory or coin or just the opportunity to see a world beyond their ken, and while they had fought like unbound devils during her campaign through the outer worlds, here on the fields of Othean they seemed to be struggling—the air was too thin, her captains told her, trying to wage war here akin to doing so at the top of a mountain. They were doing their best, though, and it was a poor general who blamed her troops.

No, Ji-hyeon knew the real reason they were so fucked was that she had lied to her people, otherwise they never would have followed her back home to the Star. Long before she had even arrived in the outer lands her father King Jun-hwan had prophesized a weapon that could win any war, the ultimate treasure of the legendary Hell King, and after reuniting with her father and once more taking on the burden of command Ji-hyeon had spent seven long years searching for this enigmatic prize. At the end of the brutal hunt Ji-hyeon and her sisters had stormed the highest citadel of the Hell King, and when she triumphantly returned to her army she informed them that the Forebear of Demons had been impressed by her valor and bequeathed her the mighty relic foretold by her father. This weapon, she had claimed, would utterly destroy their enemies, but at such cost it should not be used unless the odds were otherwise insurmountable.

In reality the final citadel had been little different from the first: overrun with the spectral monsters that had infested the rest of the abandoned estate, and while there was an impressive throne cast from blades and bones and skulls and all the other usual grim heraldry, it was as dusty as the rest of the place, and without anyone or anything that might be mistaken for the Hell King—assuming he had ever been here at all, the godlike beast of legend hadn't been home in quite some time. But she and her sisters had agreed a little deception on this count would be in the best interest of the campaign to return to the Star, for the people needed the prophecy their father had given them. Besides, even without some great and powerful weapon surely their army was strong enough to overcome Tothans and Immaculates alike...

Just not at the same time, apparently, and not with most of her formerly ferocious soldiers panting and wheezing and even collapsing before they'd even been hit. She remembered how sick certain regions of the outer lands had made her and other refugees from the Star, and cursed herself for not having considered this possibility. The irony of it was she'd planned to let the Tothans soften up the Immaculates for her before sweeping in and taking them both out, but all they'd actually accomplished was drawing some of the heat off the Immaculates. Instead of continuing to press into Othean's broken outer wall, the first Tothan army had turned to confront the Cobalts at their rear, and their reinforcements to the north were almost upon them.

Under any normal circumstances Ji-hyeon would have ordered an immediate and hasty retreat before they could be assaulted by both armies at the same time, but Yunjin had expressly warned her that once they came through the Gate there could be no going back. Opening such portals was taxing work, and keeping them open all the more so—even with her coven of battle witches to aid her, Ji-hyeon's sister was too exhausted to facilitate an escape back through the Gate. They were trapped, had nowhere left to run...

On the other, three-fingered hand, it was liberating to have her course decided for her—weighing the merits of half a dozen potential tactics had its time and place, but good command was all about responding swiftly to unexpected developments. Up until now Ji-hyeon had held most of her soldiers back, not wanting to overextend her forces while the steady flow of Cobalts came through the Gate, but now that the last were through they had to act. They couldn't win a two-front battle, but if they drilled straight through the first Tothan army they might be able to slip inside Othean's breached walls before the second regiment arrived.

As fast as the monstrous reinforcements were coming down from the north, such a plan seemed doomed from the start, but they didn't have any alternatives. And hells, if they pushed fast enough and deep enough into the first army they would be so surrounded by enemy soldiers that those in the second regiment wouldn't even be able to reach them. Sort of like covering yourself in ants before raiding a beehive so you'd be insulated from stings.

That was the play, then. Telling Yunjin to get ready to move out, Ji-hyeon left her sister and the rest of the modest coven on the steps of the Temple of Pentacles. The battle witches continued the chanting that would hopefully help with the wildborns' unexpected sickness. Ji-hyeon mounted Shagrath and rode back out into the chaotic mass of Cobalt archers, war machines and their operators, and the increasing number of the wounded who were limping back from the front. From the vantage of her dire pangolin's back she could see that the northern regiment had begun their charge.

"Forward! Forward! Into the Autumn Palace!" She shouted the order over and over until she tasted blood in her throat, and then shouted some more. She was still giving the command when a team of four glowing-eyed horse-things overwhelmed the press of soldiers just in front of her. They dragged an enormous inverted tortoise shell behind them like a chariot, an ebon-plated Tothan soldier standing at the reins and a great grey bladder filling the rest of the vehicle. It bounced wildly through the muck, the heavy shell crushing Cobalts under its bulk and mangling any who were brushed by its jagged sides.

Her black sword held high, Ji-hyeon altered her course to intercept the demonic chariot before it could careen through her archers. The Tothan who steered the vehicle failed to notice her approach on its flank until it was almost too late, but as Shagrath closed the final gap the driver snapped its horned helm in her direction ... and then let go of the reins, falling backward onto the sloshing bladder that filled the rest of the shell.

An explosion. Liquid fire. Driver and horse demons were enveloped in an instant, and Ji-hyeon was thrown from Shagrath's back as the pangolin instinctively went into a roll, drawing itself into a tight bundle of scales.

Darkness devoured light. Silence consumed noise. Stillness arrested motion.

Then the world returned, though it was quieter than Ji-hyeon had left it, and too bright to take in all at once. She heaved herself to her knees, and from her knees to her feet. She was bruised but not broken. She was scorched, but not much worse than a bad sunburn. She was deafened, but the intrusion of a distant ringing told her it was only temporary. Her eye patch had torn free but in the madness of the battlefield her devil-eye became a boon instead of a burden, enabling her to see through the curtains of smoke and rain. Fellwing must be well fed wherever she flapped through the storm, to have kept her mistress in such good stead.

The ringing in her ears became a shriek, and then shrieks. The shimmering brightness of her vision cooled, her watery eyes focusing on a smoking crater. Cobalt soldiers screamed and screamed, running around on fire. She staggered through the chaos and fumes that stank of boiling fat, looking for her pangolin.

A Tothan emerged from out of nowhere, hooked blade coming down, but Ji-hyeon's black steel cut through sword and sword arm alike. The limb dropped but the soldier didn't until Ji-hyeon punched through its faceplate with the tip of her sword. Their armor meant nothing to her black blade.

Another came and another fell, and she felt herself beginning to slip, the way the sword and her devil-eye always wanted her to. To have any hope of survival the Cobalts needed to push deep into the Tothans' ranks, but instead the Tothans were pushing into theirs. The lines were breached and the battle lost, Ji-hyeon knew it, and now all that remained was to take down as many as she could. She fought the rage at her own failure, tried to cast it out of her sword arm by hacking the next Tothan she found nearly in half from the helm down, but that just made it worse. As the lightning crashed and the monstrous army overran the lines of the Cobalt Company here in the barren pumpkin fields where all her adventures had started, Ji-hyeon threw back her head and howled into the black heavens.

———

They came tumbling down the rain-slick steps all in a rush. Hoartrap had initially refused to even consider taking them through the Othean Gate, claiming the whole place was crawling with Tothans, but after obliging to take a peek just to make sure, he had looked up from the Diadem Gate and admitted he'd been wrong. Tothans weren't surrounding the Temple of Pentacles, the Cobalt Company was. Yet as Sullen staggered to a seat on the bottom step, his stomach cramping and his head swimming from the trip through the First Gate, he realized Hoartrap had been wrong on every count.

The place *was* crawling with Tothans—at least, that's who he assumed the formidable black-armored warriors were. And the soldiers they fought in the muddy fields might be *a* Cobalt company but they weren't *the* Cobalt Company—there were more wildborn here than he had ever seen in his life, let alone in one place, and all wore cobalt tabards or other blue heraldry. Hoartrap joined Sullen, carrying Indsorith in his arms, and then set the weakened queen down between them on the step. The stained and dirty militia gear she'd donned before coming through had to be a bit warmer than just the rags she'd had on before, but she still shivered in the rain, her formerly auburn hair now as white as his. Sullen wondered if her injuries were feeling any better than his stomach—Hoartrap had claimed Gate-travel was the best medicine for any ailment, but Sullen's guts throbbed worse than ever. Pulling up the hem of his tunic he saw that the cut Nemi had sewn shut with her own impossibly strong hair had begun to pull back apart after his exertions on the rim of Diadem Gate, lymph oozing along the swollen lip and around the fine stitches.

"Ah, that's too bad," said Hoartrap, leaning around Indsorith to peer into the ragged wound. "I was worried that might happen—you wildborn don't seem to suffer the usual mutative effects of passing through the Gates, so I suppose it's only fair you don't reap the benefits, either. Too much of the First Dark in your blood already for a dip in the primordial pool to make any difference."

"Whatever, I'll be fine," said Sullen, though with his agitated injury and the cold sweat slathering him despite the warm rain he didn't know if that was exactly honest...especially considering he was expected to shake it off and plunge into the insane melee that raged but a short distance away.

"I'm sure you'll be as fine as this beautiful morning—I'm so glad we came!" said the Touch. He used the toe of his sandal to poke the wreckage of a rattan chair that lay crushed and partially buried in the terra-cotta gravel at the base of the stairs. "I mean, really, I know I promised you front row seats to the apocalypse, but this...this...*oh*. No, no no, you old *fool*..."

Hoartrap's face fell and he staggered up from his seat on the temple steps, kicking aside a broken wooden wheel and unearthing a dirty scabbard from the wet gravel. He held up the engraved sheath as though it were the evilest portent he'd ever witnessed in a lifetime of deviltry. It was a strange thing, to see the gruesome witch who found mirth in every misfortune so obviously distraught over a shattered chair, a stray sheath. He looked out into the drizzly battle going down on all sides of this small sanctuary, clutching the scabbard to his chest, and though no sound left his lips it almost looked like Hoartrap said...he was sorry?

Before the awkward silence could die of natural causes they were accosted by a handful of folk who'd been doing some ritual off to the side when Sullen had first fallen out of the Gate.

"Who are you?" demanded a middle-aged Immaculate woman whose conical red hat was taller than any of her fellows'. She shook a rosary of teeth at them. "What are you doing here?"

"Who are *we*?" sneered Hoartrap, flinging the scabbard away and turning to face her. "We're the Cobalt cavalry, come to save the day—the better question is who are you, hedgewitch? I would have noticed your kind skulking around the Company if you'd been with us before."

The woman did not seem to take kindly to the epithet, but before she could respond Sullen asked the all-important question. "Where's Ji-hyeon?"

That got the woman's attention off Hoartrap, if only for the moment. She squinted at Sullen, then Indsorith, and back at the Touch. Then she said, "You're Sullen. And you, you're Hoartrap. And you're Zosia. Yes?"

"Two out of three," said Hoartrap. "Though one Crimson Queen's as good as another these days, I suppose, isn't that right, Indsorith?"

"Get stuffed," said the woman, using Sullen's shoulder to clamber to her feet. Her sword-arm was the only steady part of her. "The fate of the Star's being fought a hundred feet away and the greatest warlock of the age wants to chew the fat and talk the shit."

"She's still sore over a falling out we had, what, eighteen years ago?" said Hoartrap, so quick to gossip with this random old Immaculate woman and her coterie it would have been funny, under less dire circumstances. "We'll join the fracas, Indsorith, just as soon as we determine who our new friends are, and—"

"Blurgh!" The final member of their haggard band came stumbling down the wet stairs with her devilish familiar. Nemi hadn't blown her cover the way Sullen and Diggelby had, but must have stuck around with the mob of spectators on the far side of Diadem Gate when everything went to shit. Just as Hoartrap was working his magic to bring them through the portal to Othean, Sullen had seen Nemi step out of the crowd on the far side, and now she'd followed them through.

Interestingly enough, her brown hair hadn't turned white, nor had the black patches on her cockatrice; the covering had slipped to the side of its cage and Sullen saw that the temperamental little monster looked as content as he'd ever seen it. Nemi, not so much. "Oh dear, I'm going to be sick."

"Who are *you*?" the Immaculate shaman asked the shaky-legged Outlander witch, talking over Hoartrap. "And how many more of you are coming out of there, eh?"

"Nemi's the last, now tell me of Ji-hyeon," said Sullen, rising with a hiss. His guts felt like they were trying to wriggle out of the wound in his belly again, and this time they might succeed. "Where is she?"

"She rode to meet our other sister," said the Immaculate, and as she pointed into the rainy, smoky haze, a howl cut through the air. "Ah, that would be her. She gets that way, sometimes, when—"

But Sullen would find out for himself what way she got, sometimes, already moving off into the field toward the sound. He was so exhausted it hurt to walk, to even breathe, and it hurt worse to hoist Grandfather's spear, but somehow when the first Tothan monster came silently swinging its scythe and Sullen jabbed the blade of his weapon through the creature's helm it didn't hurt at all. Come to think it, that was how it had been back in Diadem, too, fighting the guards—only when the spear was drinking deeply was he able to forget the misery in his stomach.

Soon he barely remembered his pain or his fatigue at all, more and more of the soldiers emerging to be spitted and slashed. He had tried so hard to go easy on those mortal militia members back in Diadem, and felt so bad when he inadvertently mutilated one after another. He felt no such remorse as he cleared his way through the black-shelled warriors that stood between him and the last place he'd heard Ji-hyeon. He darted and weaved as he hunted his beloved through the battle, shrugging off deep cuts and hard blows, dimly aware that one of the stitches in his stomach had popped open, trusting in his gut even as it betrayed him.

An enormous winged monster swooped down just in front of him, trailing spiny tendrils that raked through Cobalts and Tothans alike.

It jerked several soldiers off their feet and carried them away, disappearing into the smoke as quickly as it had appeared. As if following the noxious scent of the flying demon, an even fouler monster writhed through the throng in its wake, something like a serpent composed of countless maggots, or a giant worm composed of writhing snakes. It was dying, Sullen could tell; it had probably been dying ever since it had been unnaturally birthed into this world. Yet in its death throes its component parts slithered in all directions, ensnaring the ankles of both friend and foe, wrapping so tight around everything they touched that armor bent inward and blood welled forth.

Sullen gave the disintegrating worm and its idiot brood of frantically constricting children a wide berth. The smoke was thicker here and he almost stumbled straight into the kicking pikes of some long-legged horror. Its slavering, sideways mouth snapped down to bite off his head but swallowed black steel instead. Then, dodging a Tothan soldier's spear and showing it how a true warrior wielded one, he found her.

Except no, it must be Ji-hyeon's other sister, the one the old woman on the steps had mentioned. While this blood-spattered warrior was the spitting image of his beloved, she was about ten years too old. She fought well, and after she beheaded a Tothan with her black sword they were both momentarily free to catch their breath, and she caught his eyes, and—

It was her. He knew it as soon as their eyes locked through the rain, before his tired head even processed that the hand that held her black blade was indeed missing two fingers. Every night since he'd left her he'd imagined this moment, when they found each other again, and always in his head she gave up nothing more than that secret, fleeting smirk he'd practically overlooked the first few times she'd offered it. Now, though, she smiled wider than he had ever seen, grinning as she came to him, his name on her lips...and then another huge monster reared out of the smoke directly behind her, too swift for even Sullen to stop.

There he was. The handsome Flintlander was exactly as she had remembered him, right down to the sly grin on his face—a grin that turned into a grimace, his spear flying up, and if she hadn't already been holding her sword aloft she never would have brought it across in time to deflect his jab. They both reeled back from the connection of the black steel blades, Shagrath just as confused as Sullen, and likewise inclined to go after the stranger getting too close to his mistress. She called him off, relieved to see that other than some blackened scales her pangolin looked all right—better than Sullen did, anyway, his arms and legs weeping red from a dozen gashes, the front of his tunic leaking through despite there not being a rent in the sweaty cloth.

He wasn't paying any more attention to his wounds than she was to her pangolin, now, the two crossing the last few steps that stood between them...but looking around the whole time to make sure they weren't about to be attacked. The Cobalts had reclaimed this patch of mud for now, all the figures moving through the rain and the smoke wearing blue, and then Sullen planted his spear at her feet and threw his arms around her.

It was the best hug she'd ever experienced, everything that had led to this seeming worth it, at least in the moment, and then the careful, cautious-to-a-fault Flintlander she had missed so much boldly gave her a kiss that was even better. She gave as good as she got, groaning into his mouth from the ache of it—and then pulling away before she got carried away, anxiously scanning for the enemy. Shagrath had protectively curled his tail around the two lovers, but that low fence wouldn't keep out an arrow or spear...

"I missed you," he told her, his fingers brushing her cheek as if he wasn't even sure she was real and needed to keep making sure. She knew how he felt, seeing him for the first time with her devil-eye yet still liking what she saw.

"I've missed you, too, Sullen, more than you can imagine!" The coast clear for now, she stole another rainy kiss...then froze, their lips still touching. "Where...where's Keun-ju? Is he here?"

"No, but Hoartrap says he's safe?" said Sullen, noticing her altered left eye with obvious surprise. "What happened to—no, it can wait, important thing is Keun-ju's okay. I hope. He and Hoartrap were together last I seen him, but that wasn't my fault, us getting separated, and—"

Ji-hyeon shut him up with her mouth, her heart soaring at the news that both of her men still drew breath...and then plummeting as she remembered where they were, how tragic this romance really was. She kissed him harder even as she wished he had never come back, tasting his tongue for what must be the last time. The one bright spot of their looming deaths was that she wouldn't be burdened with untangling the romantic knot she'd gotten them all snarled up in; wherever he was, she hoped Keun-ju was safer than she and Sullen, and that he knew she loved him.

As if sensing that her thoughts had drifted to his rival, Sullen broke the kiss. Brushing away her tears with a blood-sticky hand, he said, "Hate to say it, but we better save any more of that for after the battle, General."

"Oh, Sullen..." She shook her head. "I fear there's not going to be an afterward, not for us. You shouldn't be here. The battle's already lost. We're all going to die."

"Then I got here just in time," he said with another one of his crafty smiles. She knew she had to look away from his rain-slick face, his beautiful blue snow lion eyes, she had to return to the fight...but for just a moment longer she lingered. He'd paid his life to see her one last time, she owed it to him. She owed it to herself.

Shagrath huffed in warning, battering a Tothan soldier with his tail as he uncoiled from his protective posture around his mistress and her lover. The moment was officially ruined. Wars had a way of doing that.

She was just about to tell Sullen their only hope was to break through the Tothan army and storm Othean when she realized the rain had stopped striking them, even as it poured down on all sides. It was the last thing she noticed before being jerked from her feet and slammed into Shagrath's plated flank.

———

The monster had them before Sullen even saw it, hurling them both into Ji-hyeon's steed. The world was batted away, a blur of earth and sky, dull black scales and translucent grey hide. A fat white snake curled around Sullen's arm, its sticky skin burning his flesh. Ji-hyeon falling through the air just beside him, her body limp, more of the twisting white snakes crawling all over them. Pain. Such unbelievable pain.

The speed of the spinning slowed. They had stopped rolling, they were still, but Sullen's skull hadn't caught up with the rest of him yet. He reached for the sliding image of Ji-hyeon, her face too serene, too motionless, but he couldn't find her, the coiling snakes tightening around his limbs, locking him in place.

Not snakes. The tendrils of the giant flying monster he had seen swooping the battlefield before he'd found Ji-hyeon. The thing that snatched soldiers off the ground and carried them away. He tried again to get an arm free, but it was impossible—there was no give whatsoever, and the more he struggled the tighter the corrosive tentacles held him. The titan had them, and when it was high enough it would let them go, dropping them to—

No. The coils of the beast shifted over them, and turning his neck he saw they weren't airborne at all. The flying jellyfish-thing had grabbed them but Ji-hyeon's scaled steed had grabbed it back, dragging it down to the ground. Now the two monsters were locked together in the cratered mud, pale tendrils enveloping the big armadillo even as it bit the flying horror's bat-like wing. The more Ji-hyeon's beast chewed on the grounded horror the tighter it squeezed the coils that enveloped them all, and Sullen moaned despite his efforts to stay quiet. He didn't want to wake Ji-hyeon. Not to this.

Then he saw her. An armored woman, her glistening helm crowned in cascading black quills. She stood atop the convulsing white behemoth, gazing down at the mortals caught in the death struggle between a monster of the sky and a beast of the earth. Then she leaped down from its side, landing lightly in the mud. Ducked under its broken wing. Stood over Sullen, and as the corded tendrils closed off his throat he realized who this must be.

This was Death.

Not his. Ji-Hyeon's. Everyone had their own, after all, and this must be the Death of the Immaculates. Through the slits in her helm he saw cold black eyes watching him, and he gave a final pitiful struggle to reach Ji-hyeon. He didn't want her to go with this cruel emissary, to some foreign afterworld where he couldn't follow her—it wasn't fair, not after they'd died together. Not with Old Black stepping up behind this Immaculate goddess, waiting her turn to collect behind a blurry veil of rain—why not just let them go down together to the Meadhall? Hadn't they earned that?

As if in answer, Old Black raised her arms—in one hand she held Sullen's black spear, and in the other Ji-hyeon's black sword.

The white skull Sullen's ancestor always painted over her face before collecting souls gleamed like ivory in the rain.

His last thought was that in the songs Old Black was always so beautiful, but now that she came into focus through the downpour he saw she was anything but.

CHAPTER
25

Maroto had stuck with Fennec and his guards as they plowed through the press of Tothans, following Fellwing as the devilish owlbat bobbed overhead. As soon as he saw a squid-dragon crash down a short distance ahead, though, he was off like a damn cannonball through the warring mobs of Tothans and Cobalts. Something he'd learned on Jex Toth was that while the Tothan grunts could ride the monsters they didn't have the brains or the proper stink glands or whatever to control their mounts themselves. They needed to have someone from the Vex Assembly aboard or at least in close enough proximity to guide the flocks of squid-dragons, which meant that one of the enemy command might have just crashed into snatching range. He didn't know how exactly he could snatch one of the ancient fuckers, what with their spooky speed and witchy powers, but he'd figure that out once he had it cornered. The fact that he and Fennec had actually made it out of Othean and led their troops across the contested field was proof enough that sometimes mortals could accomplish the impossible, if they were too brave or too stupid to play it safe.

Not that it hadn't been *nearly* impossible to get this far, and this was the easy part—pulling back inside Othean was where the titty got tough. At least now that Fennec's soldiers and Maroto's Chainites had pressed deep enough into the invading army to meet Ji-hyeon's Cobalts in the middle it was possible to take three steps without meeting a Tothan. You might have to take as many as five or six, and even then they were often as not already fighting one of Ji-hyeon's heavies. Even with all the good guys wearing similar shades of blue heraldry it was still easy to tell the new Cobalts from the old, because the soldiers Maroto and Fennec had led out of Othean were mostly human with a few wildborn here and there.

These new Cobalts, though, they were something else. Wilder-born, you might say, with pelts as thick as chainmail and stabbing horns and stomping hooves and great crude clubs that blasted the Tothans' armor into gooey clouds. For all their differences, though, these soldiers bled just as easily as their more human counterparts, the enemy's cruel weaponry cutting them down just as quick. The Tothans' spiny armor packed a nasty sting, if you bumped into their barbs, and their jagged swords and spears were plenty firm until they pierced flesh but broke apart as they were pulled free, filling their victims with bone splinters. Then there were all the horsey things trampling everyone under their spear-legs, and abominations the likes of which he hadn't even glimpsed during his tenure on Jex Toth...

A flash of white through the hordes of inhuman combatants. Maroto ducked under a demonic stallion that had been lassoed by a wildborn, breaking one of the monster's long legs as a courtesy as he came out the other side. The downed squid-dragon was just ahead now, the biggest one he'd ever seen just lying there in the middle of the battlefield, but between him and his quarry half a dozen Tothans had surrounded a ten-foot-tall, ox-faced wildborn laden with iron platemail, blue streamers flying from its horns. Its only weapon was a tower shield it wore like a buckler, smashing back at the ring of hollow soldiers, but there were too many of them...

Until the Mighty Maroto evened up the odds, swinging his mace as hard as he could. He bashed in the back of one Tothan's helm and clipped the top off another, knocking them both to the ground. One of the others brought its barbed blades in his direction but you didn't ever want to turn your back on a bull-headed barbarian, that was just common sense. The wildborn decapitated it with the edge of its rectangular shield, and between the two of them Maroto and the beast took out the rest in a matter of moments.

Moments that drained Maroto of his breath, to be sure, leaving him panting as he struggled to hold his mace aloft after going so hard with it. This whole wading-into-war-without-the-benefit-of-bugs thing was a hell of a lot harder than he remembered. Steaming monster juice and broken bodies at their feet, he and the Cobalt minotaur exchanged nods, and Maroto hoisted his mace at it. He'd only meant it as a gesture of solidarity, but the damn cow either mistook his meaning or was just an arsehole, because with its free hand it wrenched the weapon out of Maroto's grasp and lumbered off with it to find more things to kill. Fucking minotaurs.

Good thing on a battlefield this busy there were plenty of loose weapons lying about. Some of them still had hands attached to them, but no matter, no matter. Striding up behind the fallen squid-dragon he found a spear planted in the earth, and a black-bladed sword just beside it. He settled on the spear, in part because it looked like a Flintlander weapon and in part because the sword's handle had some weird rings built into the hilt that made it look unwieldy as all get-out.

As soon as he seized the spear and started on toward the giant white monster his earlobe stung like an icebee had bit it, but when he clapped his hand to his head there was nothing there. Hurt like a hot coal, though, and the pain gave him a random-arsed surge of nostalgia—it felt just like Da had flicked it, the obnoxious way he was always doing anytime Maroto wasn't paying attention to one of his interminable lectures. The hesitation turned out to be a godsend, though, because just then a Tothan in the craziest armor he'd yet witnessed rose from the back of the beached squid-dragon and jumped down to the ground, its back to Maroto as it went around to the front where the monster's tentacles were all wrapped up in something. With a porcupine helm like that it had to be someone special, obviously one of the Vex Assembly, and Maroto leaned down and snatched up the weird-handled sword after all. Seemed prudent to have as many weapons as he had hands before facing one of the powerful priests—he could always throw the damn sword at it, if nothing else.

Slinking after the Tothan as it ducked under one of the monster's broken wings, Maroto watched it draw a sickle-sword, the gleaming metal crescent only a little less outlandish than the bone weapons of its infantry. Creeping closer still, he saw the Tothan meant to behead the enormous sloth monster that must have grounded its steed. The scaly critter was all tangled up in the squid-dragon's tentacles, reduced to biting its wing since its heavy paws were caught in white coils along with a couple of human corpses. The Tothan raised its blade, and Maroto raised both of his, and—

Fuck, the bastard was fast. Instead of chopping into the scaled sloth the Tothan was about to open up Maroto, sensing his ambush despite how softly he'd been stalking. He parried its slashing sword with his own, already jabbing with his spear. He was going to skewer the Tothan through the belly, armor or no, but somehow the human-shaped monster flew backward a dozen feet before he could connect. Its mane of quills stood erect, a halo of venom-dripping needles, and then it flew straight at Maroto so fast he barely had time to hear his departed Da chastise him for being such a damn fool before its curved sword hacked straight across at his face, severing his—

———

Y'Homa had seen this mortal before. Or rather, her angel had. Down in the underdocks, scraping barnacle-rats off the leviathans. Her holy half shivered with delight at dueling one who had looked upon them with such terror back on Jex Toth, here at last a victim who knew the full extent of his doom. It begged her to take her time, to take the skull-painted mortal apart slowly, but she knew she had to end it quickly if she had any hope of freeing her mount from the monster that had brought it down. Her angel, innocent that it was, simply reveled in all the pain and fear of the current conflict, but Y'Homa was burdened with responsibility and knew unless she quickly removed the threat to their steed it would die, leaving them stranded on the battlefield. First she would kill this mortal man, then she would kill the scaled creature that had attacked their mount, and then they would return to the skies.

It wasn't a fair fight. It wasn't a fight at all. Y'Homa hadn't bothered with martial training in her youth, but since she had been reborn her skill in combat was, like everything else about her, supreme. After dodging the sinner's clumsy spear thrust she fell upon him with her ancient Tothan sword, leaping straight in and hacking off the top of his head. One strike was all it took—her angel was an angel of death.

There wasn't even any resistance as her blade ended this interruption; she might as well have been cutting the air...

Which was about all she had actually accomplished, apparently. He ignored the blow and came at her hard, but the angel in her bones danced her away from his spear and his sword, the man faster than ever. It was as if the tall column of curly hair she'd taken off the top of his head had been slowing him down, that or the minuscule amount of scalp she'd shaved off when he ducked her high attack.

Y'Homa parried spear, parried sword, and when he somehow managed to evade her jab she whipped him with the quilled train of her helm. The needles tattooed half his white face red, popping his left eye like a tiny wineskin. He screamed but didn't falter, his spear tagging her off hand. It only opened a small rent in the living gauntlet but her armored swarm fell off all the way up to her elbow, smoking as they died. Clearly hers weren't the only envenomed weapons, and she dropped back again to let the poison in his face do its work.

She had to wonder if her angel was rebelling against her will, allowing the battle to persist so it might glut itself on the mortal's stinking emotions. Ever since her foe had noticed the pair of sinners and their pet entangled in her mount's tendrils he had been putting off a powerful reek of fury and heartbreak. This must be why her angel had let him live this long, prolonging his suffering. As if the man could read her uncertainty as well as she could read his, he took advantage of her hesitation...and turned his back on her. She did not squander her advantage, the wretch's cowardice costing him his life as she came reaping with her heavenly sword.

———

Sullen. The blueness of his face contrasted the whiteness of the coils enveloping him. Crazy how Maroto hadn't even recognized the boy until this Tothan monster put out his eye, but now his nephew was all he could see even as he faced the greatest opponent he had ever fought. It fell back from his furious onslaught, paused, and in that instant Maroto threw himself into his final gambit.

Sullen was already dead, dead as Maroto would be if he showed his back to this devil-ridden reaver. The squid-dragon had crushed the life from the boy, no doubt about it—he'd probably been dead before Maroto had even arrived. Throwing his own life away couldn't bring his nephew back. Nothing could, short of Old Black's intervention, and the thing about the Old Watchers was they only ever watched, never interceded on behalf of their heirs. Sullen was gone, he was with Da now, down at the Meadhall, and—

Maroto hacked into the tentacles with his sword, with his spear, tears streaming from his right eye, gore from his left. He carved his nephew free, knowing the Tothan's next blow would take off a lot more than just his flattop. Grey slime gouted into the air, the squid-dragon's coils retracting from Sullen and the Immaculate woman beside him as Maroto chopped more and more of the tendrils, only spinning back to look his death in the eye when he'd severed the cord around Sullen's neck.

The Tothan was right on top of him, too close to dodge. All the quills on its helm stood straight up, some oozing white venom and others beaded with blood. Maroto's blood.

The sickle-sword in its clawed gauntlet was laced with blood, too…but not as much as the blade protruding from its chitinous breastplate.

Cracks spread out across the living armor, smoke rising from the fissures. The sword slipped from its hand, it slipped to its knees, and the white-haired woman behind it wrenched her own sword free, then brought it straight across, biting through the back of the Tothan's quilled helm and into its neck. It took several more blows to take the head off entirely, and about that much time for Maroto to recognize the woman who wielded a black blade of her own.

It was the weary smirk she offered Maroto when the dying helm fell free from the severed head that brought recognition to his overtaxed brain—she'd offered him the same look when she had disarmed him in her throne room twenty years before. He would have bowed if he'd thought he could pull it off without falling over, his face on fire with venom, his eye a smoldering pit that burned almost as bright as his broken heart.

"Your Majesty," he managed as a woman carrying a giant birdcage limped up behind Queen Indsorith, leaning heavily on a feathered staff.

"This is bad," this new arrival said. "He'll die if we don't act fast."

"Dying?" That was the best news Maroto had heard all day. He tried to turn back toward Sullen when his shaky legs gave out on him altogether and he fell over in the mud. Weakly pointing at where his nephew, the Immaculate woman, and the giant scaly animal lay in the retracting bed of splattered tentacles, he said, "Help. Help him."

"He's bad, but you're worse," said a familiar voice, the only one that could have given Maroto the strength to raise his head just then, and only because of how badly he wanted to bite the fucker's head off. Hoartrap the stinking Touch knelt down over Sullen and began giving him mouth-to-mouth, Indsorith went to the prone Immaculate, and the woman with the birdcage flopped down in the mud next to Maroto, fiddling with an iron-bound holster on her belt.

"Open your mouth," the girl said, offering Maroto a silver egg. As if he could even think about eating at a time like this, the nettle-stinging agony of his face burning worse and worse, his one eye getting all filmy, his stomach cramping along with the rest of him as the venom did its job. He tried to tell her to sod off and let him die in peace but when he opened his mouth she shoved the egg inside, and as the shell cracked on his teeth he felt a heat as if he'd swallowed the devildamned sun.

Only, like, in a nice way.

He instantly felt better, and was about to say as much when the girl jerked backward onto her feet, snatched another egg from a belt compartment, and hurled it away. A moment later the warmth wasn't just inside his happy mouth or tingling throat but all over his aching body as an explosion shook the mire around his knees, smoke and heat enveloping him in a familiar blanket.

Weird, yes, but it could be a lot worse. This lady could have gotten her eggs mixed up.

———

It all seemed like such a bad dream. Enduring endless torture at the instruments of the Burnished Chain, only to be saved by the last woman Indsorith would have ever expected...

And then the wheel turned again, replacing hope with despair, succor with further torment from the very people the two queens had sought to save. Then a second chance at salvation, there on the cusp of death, on the cusp of Diadem Gate. A journey across the Star, and the surprising truth that the First Dark was no place of horrors and suffering, but a healing balm that restored her strength. Her countless wounds vanished as if she had not recently been tortured twice over... but only so that she might quest forth into this unreal combat against the monsters she had glimpsed in profane visions and the nightmares that followed. Dreams sprang from the First Dark, and feeling vitality coursing through limbs she had barely been able to move on the other side of the Gates, Indsorith recognized that she had fallen into the last one she would ever have.

Liberated by the lucidity, she had plunged into the battle without a second thought, struggling to keep up with Zosia's young Flintlander friend. Indsorith hadn't been able to follow everything they'd said, but had heard enough to recognize that when Hoartrap tried to goad Zosia into unimaginable darkness Sullen had begged her to spare Diadem. Unlike herself the boy obviously hadn't been mended by their sojourn between the Gates, his wound dragging him down, and she wanted to be able to protect him when his strength failed. She wanted to be able to protect someone who deserved it, just once, before the end.

Inhuman warriors surrounded them, separated them, struck at them over and over, but Moonspell struck back harder and faster and crueler. The spatha's edge passed through the rain and armor and flesh with equal ease, the long-missed keening whine of the blade driving Indsorith to swing it harder and harder still. She was nicked and she was pushed and she was almost impaled and she was definitely not dreaming, she realized as a hulking thing gashed open her off hand and she skewered its helm, but that awakening only made her more desperate to find Sullen through the smoke and the storm and the demon horde.

But maybe she was dreaming a little, because in that frantic moment she felt like her mother's sword was guiding her, dragging her forward into the thickest part of the press. She passed through this final crucible of screaming metal and clattering insect armor and scratching blades and barbs, and burst out the other side, straight into the back of yet another nightmarish foe. Moonspell knew the way, and Indsorith followed, and then it was over.

She had spent countless hours imagining this reunion, rehearsing what she might say to her tormentor, if given the chance. Never in her fantasies or her nightmares had she pictured such a scenario as this, Y'Homa dead by her shaking hand before she even realized who she was attacking. It was probably for the best. Had she known who lurked under that monstrous armor she might have hesitated, if only for a moment, and that moment might have meant death for many, many more.

Death. The only courtier who never abandoned the Crimson Queen. The bizarre insect Y'Homa had worn as an armored headdress leaked yellow ichor and grey steam from its mortal wound, spurted its last jets of white venom from its erect quills, the creature's compound eyes as remote and alien to Indsorith as the black orbs of the Black Pope. However familiar the features of this severed head lying in the mud of a smoking battlefield, there was something in those vacant, oily eyes that made Indsorith recognize that her rival from Diadem had died a long time ago. This was a mercy killing… and that withered any satisfaction Indsorith could take before it even fully fruited.

And this was the great riddle of mortality, that which her mother had solved that fatal day in the work camps when Indsorith was but a child: no matter how much we crave it, no matter how much we welcome it, at its heart death is always cruel.

Death was a dream, but at least it was a good one. At the time this scene had been anything but, a grueling nightmare Sullen relived over and over again in his sleep, even years after they had safely made it home. Now, though, the familiar vision brought comfort instead of fear, relief instead of panic. Perhaps it was because in death their roles were reversed, Grandfather carrying him through the snow as Sullen's deep wound dribbled its warmth against the old man's chest. Death didn't cleave families apart. It reunited them.

Grandfather wore Old Black's facepaint, the left half of his skull dyed crimson with blood. The old man had strapped Sullen's spear to his back, the shaft jutting up into the snow like a limbless black tree, and as the thick white flakes landed on Sullen's cheeks they burned instead of cooled. He closed his eyes and let the old man carry him down to the Meadhall Beneath the Iced Earth, content that his song had at last come to an end...and then snapped them open.

"Ji-hyeon," he croaked at his ancestor. "Ji-hyeon. Take her with us. She earned it."

"I don't know if that's how I'd put it, but she's here," said the bloodied skull, but it wasn't Fa, his voice was all wrong. Too nice. He was lifting Sullen farther up, into the air that swirled not with snow but pale ash and crimson cinders.

"Craven," Sullen gasped. "Uncle Craven!"

"Not on your life, pup." The skull winked its only eye at Sullen, the top of its close-shorn head bloody and raw. "Your uncle's the Mighty Maroto, and don't you forget it. Ever."

Then other hands took Sullen, helped steady him on the back of the great scaled beast. Ji-hyeon's hands, on Ji-hyeon's beast. He looked over his shoulder at his girl. She looked just beat to shit. Like, even up this close she looked as if she'd aged a decade in the weeks since he'd seen her last...but then he reckoned he must look a fright, too. A leather belt striped the left side of her face, holding a wad of torn cloth and loose chainmail flush against her skin. He was glad she had scrounged up the makeshift patch; it had frightened him, seeing that second, stranger iris crowding her eye, its wide, curious pupil staring at him with a very different kind of hunger than its twin. It would not be her prettiest song, how she came by that devilish third eye, and what secrets it might show her, but he hoped to live long enough to hear it, and all the rest...

For now she kissed the back of his bruised neck with split lips, her wheeling owlbat as grey as the ash in the air as she helped Sullen settle onto the saddle in front of her.

"I know you said Horned Wolves don't ride but I thought you'd make an exception for me," she rasped in his ear.

"Anytime and every time," he said, his throat feeling as pained as hers sounded. "We...we okay?"

"Not even close," said Fennec, the old Usban standing next to Ji-hyeon's pangolin. He, Maroto, Nemi, and Indsorith were all together, but while the others were looking to the north Fennec only had eyes for Ji-hyeon and Sullen. "No matter what happens, you must get over the wall at the heart of Othean. We'll try to keep up, but if we can't there's nothing you can do. Our only chance is to lead as many of them in after us, and once the Dreaming Priests decide the time is right that will be the end for anyone who isn't safely on the other side. Understand?"

"We understand," Ji-hyeon said before Sullen could protest that he didn't have the slightest fucking idea of what was happening here. Well, so long as she did he'd trust her to see them through... "If you'd be so good as to return our weapons, Maroto, we'll lead the charge into Othean."

"These are yours?" Maroto pulled out the black sword he'd shoved through the belt of his skirt and handed it up to Ji-hyeon, then reached for the spear on his back. Half his fucking face was grotesquely swollen, his left eye a leaking chasm, but at worst he seemed kind of stoned. He held the spear up, but Sullen shook his head.

"You can borrow it, Uncle, until we meet up on the other side."

"Yeah?" Maroto smiled, his ruined face pulsing underneath all the gore. "All right then, it's a deal. Until the other side. Nephew."

The ground rumbled under their feet, and Ji-hyeon's pangolin took that as their cue to get moving. As it took off Sullen gave his uncle a knowing nod...and then his jaw fell open as he saw what the others had been looking at, to the north. A Tothan army massed not a hundred yards away, standing at the ready. Dozens and dozens of the long-legged horse demons pranced in place, and beyond them stretched a black sea of soldiers, massive pale monsters rising here and there from the flood. Over their frontline another of the giant octopus-bats drifted through the rain and the ash, and as he watched a rider on its back seemed to point its spindly arm straight at Sullen. At that, the whole evil army resumed their charge, sweeping down at the scattered Cobalts and Tothans who still struggled against each other on the fields surrounding the Temple of Pentacles.

"Look!" Ji-hyeon shouted as their mount picked up speed, her three-fingered hand turning his head for him when he didn't avert his gaze from the charging horde. He'd assumed that had been what she was talking about, because what else could warrant—oh.

Hoartrap the Touch ran so swiftly he could have outpaced the pangolin, if he'd been of a mind. Instead the naked man leaped from one Tothan soldier to the next, an ivory blur through the ranks, tackling one after another only long enough to crack their helms with his forehead and ram his slime-covered face inside. Sullen had seen the Touch get up to some nasty shit, but this...this was the worst. The old giant's tattoos were pulsing with black light as he landed on another Tothan and bit through its helmet as if it were made of meringue, sucking out a mouthful of runny black gore.

Well. Sullen could have done without seeing that.

The rampaging witch fell from sight as the pangolin galloped around another pack of Tothans. They were making straight for a collapsed portion of Othean's wall, but while their approach was clear for now, Sullen glimpsed more of the black-shelled soldiers amassing on the rooftops beyond. Sullen looked over his shoulder to warn Ji-hyeon that they were about to get back into the shit, but before he could say a word he saw what was swelling out of the battlefield behind them. He could have done without seeing that, too.

Hoartrap rose from the press of Tothans, standing atop a blooming mountain of black insects. Higher and higher the mountain grew, ten feet, then twenty, and then the swarming bugs at his feet began crawling over his flesh, too, consuming the Touch until he resembled an onyx statue, his arms stretched out like the Chainite saint on Diggelby's charm bracelet. The summit of the swarm erupted like the volcano in the Fallen Mother's vision, except instead of liquid fire it shot more and more of the shiny black bugs into the sky. They didn't spread out, either, or fall to earth, but instead whipped around through the air, a tornado of swirling insects that quickly coalesced into a human shape. Somewhere in its center was Hoartrap the Touch, and the last thing Sullen saw before their pangolin scrambled up the ruins of Othean's collapsed outer wall was a fifty-foot-tall construct of living insects striding after them, clearing a path for the Cobalt Company.

———

Fennec had kissed her cheeks with tears streaming down his, had thrust a copy of his map into her hands and made her promise to go on without them, no matter what. Ji-hyeon had agreed, but as she wheeled Shagrath around and steered him back into the Tothan host choking the only entrance to Othean, she figured he didn't have much choice but to forgive her a broken promise or two. He'd been the one to teach her how much fun it was to break oaths, after all. Well, him and Keun-ju.

"Whoa!" Sullen cried, slipping around on the saddle. That seemed to be about the extent of his vocabulary, now that he was riding an animal for the first time in his life. Funny how he knew that command innately, even if Shagrath would only heed it when it came from his mistress. "Whoa!"

"Whoa!" Shagrath obediently came to a stop atop the rubble of the outer wall, mistaking Ji-hyeon's agreement with Sullen's assessment of the field for an order. Which was okay, because it looked like the Cobalt Company wasn't going to have much trouble breaking through into Othean even without her leading the charge.

Ji-hyeon had battled giants in her time beyond the First Dark, but never before had one fought on her side. This headless titan of glistening shell waded through the Tothans behind her, crushing them underfoot and sending dozens flying with each sweep of its heavy arms. Blue rivers rushed after it, filling its footprints in the Tothan horde, both her outer Cobalts and the veterans Fennec had brought to their rescue now following the giant toward the Autumn Palace.

She prayed her sisters were among those who could still flee the folly of her final command, that Sasamaso, Hassan, Din, and Shea were safe and helping shepherd the rest. Witnessing the godlike power of this giant golem she marveled at her hubris, to think she of all people could depose the Empress of the Isles and govern the realm, when she couldn't even govern a simple battle.

Of course, she did have a certain set of skills, she just needed to be willing to use them. Her hands were shaking as she undid the belt wrapped around her head, letting the makeshift blindfold fall away and freeing her devil-eye for the second time that morning. It always tempted her to see more, to look farther, to keep staring until she saw what lurked beyond even the farthest borders of the First Dark... but over the years she had learned to tame her mutation, to make it work for her instead of acting as its slave. Squinting it just so, she cut through the billowing smoke and the swirling embers, through the mobs of mortals and monsters, through flesh and chitin.

Hoartrap was a bright black oil slick sloshing around the heart of the rampaging giant, streamers of spectral light trailing from its swinging arms. She had never seen anything so beautiful, every tiny shell winking a different unnamed color in the scintillating rain. The colossus was almost on top of them when it lurched out of the fragmenting Tothan lists, stepping along the ruined wall and then turning to the north.

Despite the driving rain and stinging fumes Ji-hyeon saw the second Tothan regiment as clearly as if she'd used a hawkglass on a sunny day. The demons came charging down on the retreating Cobalts, and Hoartrap's insectoid simulacrum lumbered back out into the fields to meet them. Now that he was free of the Tothan horde, Ji-hyeon saw that every moment he was shedding hundreds of bugs, their inner light burning out as they fell, the giant diminishing with every heavy footfall. As he reached the galloping horse-things his giant was half as tall as it had started, and while that was still large enough to smash the monsters underfoot and wreck them with its blunt arms his enormous puppet was slowing, growing clumsy.

A hulking elephantine horror reared up out of the charging horde, steady on its rear legs as its six forearms grasped at the giant golem, each limb ending in a mouth so big that Ji-hyeon could see its teeth from here even with her normal eye. They grappled, teetered...and then Hoartrap's pastel-steaming giant sent its Tothan attacker rolling through the ranks, crushing scores of black-plated infantry. The great beast vanquished, Hoartrap again drew strength from his massed victims, his giant no longer disintegrating as the soldiers he touched exploded into clouds of insects that swarmed up his body, swelling him larger than ever. As each soldier fell apart and their components became one with Hoartrap's monstrous puppet, Ji-hyeon's devil-eye also caught a transference of ephemeral light, yellow radiance flowing through the air from each victim to the warlock's pulsing black presence in the center of the giant...and then winking out of existence. While the exact mechanics of the exchange were as mysterious as any of his despicable magics, it was obvious Hoartrap was once more eating his way into obscene power.

There were more of the eight-legged behemoths, though, and they were not content to stand by and watch the giant fatten itself on their army. The four titans stampeded through their own soldiers in their bloodlust to reach Hoartrap, plumes of incandescent intention billowing off their horned backs. The giant strode forward to meet their charge, but before they could clash, another of the flying white monsters that had nearly killed Ji-hyeon, Sullen, and Shagrath came winging down out of the rain. Something on its back shone just as black and brilliant as Hoartrap did inside his titanic armor, and then the winged steed crashed into the chest of his giant.

The two shining ebon presences collided, and everything stopped— the fighting, the furious cries, even the rain, drops hanging in front of Ji-hyeon like crystals from a chandelier. It was only for a moment, but that moment stretched out longer and longer, and as it elongated so, too, did something that not even Ji-hyeon's devil-eye could quite make out, a presence stretching nearer and nearer from somewhere *else*. Her hairs would've stood on end, if only there'd been time, but before she could even register her primal terror the moment reached its breaking point, and as it did a bubble of the First Dark formed in the heart of Hoartrap's giant.

This was what had been coming, and badly as she wanted to look away her devil-eye had been waiting far too long for an unfettered peek into those deepest mysteries to be deterred now. It was as if a miniature Gate had opened right there in the center of Hoartrap's simulacrum, and as she stared the sorcerer and whatever infernal presence had crashed into him tumbled into that infinite vault . . . and out the other side, some place far, far from Othean, but *right there*, a telescopic window hanging over the battlefield. There were *things* on the other side, things like Hoartrap, things like whatever had taken him, but before her ravenous eye could fully see them—and before they could see her—that bubble of the First Dark popped, and everything resumed so abruptly Ji-hyeon nearly fell out of her saddle.

Rain, cries, clanging steel. The flying monster burst out of the giant's back in a spume of countless bugs, spinning out of control into the infantry. Without Hoartrap to hold it together his construct fell apart, a waterfall of insects crashing down on the Tothan army.

"Fuuuuuuck," breathed Sullen, reaching back to give Ji-hyeon a reassuring squeeze. His eyes were still out on the field, which explained why he manhandled her belly through her scalemail. "Good thing we got out when we did."

"We're not out yet," said Ji-hyeon, still trying to recover from the vertiginous vision. She had only intended to look past the obscuring smoke and rain to see how close that second regiment had come before deciding on their plan of action, but as usual her devil-eye had shown her far more than she'd anticipated. It was her own fault for looking behind her instead of ahead, and now she put it to better use scanning the rainy slums between them and the Autumn Palace, her sight passing through buildings as though they were made of stained glass . . . and not much liking what she saw on the far side, she fixed her makeshift eye patch back in place. Trying to stay in the crowded saddle would be hard enough without her devil-eye distracting her. "There are still too many Tothans between us and the inner wall, and we need to thin them out if our people have any chance of getting into Othean before that army overtakes them. Ready to get your hands dirty?"

"I was born in the dirt," said Sullen, worming around on the saddle to give her a quick kiss. "And with you around I can't seem to get dirty enough."

"Too true," said Ji-hyeon, giving him another kiss for good measure and then spurring Shagrath into the contested slums between Othean's walls. They were all going to die, there was no doubt of that, but when she'd been a girl in the Isles her favorite pastime had been make-believe. Some games you never outgrow. "If you're smart enough to live out the day, barbarian, you'll see just how dirty I can get."

"Call me *barbarian* again and I'll spank some manners into you," said Sullen, leaning out on the saddle and grabbing a stray spear that was lodged in the lintel of a passing tenement.

"*Excuse me?*"

He glanced back with a guilty grin, and she smiled at the faint darkening of his cheeks, a blush so subtle she might have missed it entirely if she hadn't been thirstily drinking up his long-missed features. He might have learned a little boldness from his time with Keun-ju, but not nearly enough. Not yet. It felt so good to feel his sweaty back against her chest as they rode together, pretending everything would be all right. Leaning forward, she whispered in his ear, "Barbarian, barbarian, barbarian."

He was just turning back in the saddle to say something smart, or close enough, when Fellwing cheeped on her shoulder and the Tothans who had captured this part of the slums came rushing down the street to greet them, with more dropping from the surrounding rooftops. Ji-hyeon kicked Shagrath into a gallop. These monsters clearly wanted to pay her homage, and it would be rude to ignore them. The Empress of the Immaculate Isles had to be ready to entertain guests at a moment's notice.

CHAPTER
26

In the end the others went through the Diadem Gate first, joining the battle at Othean and leaving Zosia to go for it alone. Well, except for her devil, but that went without saying—he'd been her only companion the last time she'd embarked on an idiotic suicide mission, too, when she'd come for King Kaldruut. A lifetime come and gone, and nothing much had changed.

Well, not quite nothing. Indsorith had wanted to tag along, the long-harried queen probably just as tired of living as her predecessor, but much as Zosia might appreciate the company it wasn't a good idea. Indsorith was already on the verge of collapse and Zosia didn't expect things were going to be getting any easier from here on out. Sullen wasn't doing too much better than Indsorith, ashen and sweaty from some old war wound acting up, he said. While he'd made noises about maybe having an obligation to see this thing through beside her, as soon as he heard Othean was under attack it became very apparent where he wanted to go, even if it was just to die. Hoartrap, on the other hand, didn't even pretend to want anything to do with Zosia's admittedly batshit plan, petulant as a jilted teenager that she hadn't accepted his invitation to sacrifice an entire city.

Everyone had seemed so surprised by her refusal to wake the volcano beneath Diadem, too, which stung a bit, but then Zosia supposed she had something of a reputation. And the truth was she was a little old for idealism, because as soon as Hoartrap took the others through the Gate she'd made Choplicker the offer he seemed so hungry for, with a caveat: *if* she couldn't stop this thing and died trying to win the war on her own terms, he could have his freedom in exchange for ending the invasion on his. You had to take a pragmatic approach, when the fate of the Star depended on you, but she damn sure wasn't letting the Touch overhear that offer in case he got any cute ideas about bumping her off himself.

Standing there in the heart of Diadem, the People's Pack and their twitchy militia watching her every move, Zosia didn't look down into the Gate she was about to enter, but across it. She thought she'd seen someone jump forward into the Gate after Hoartrap and the others, but that had to be her itchy eyes playing tricks on her after a busy, sleepless night. There were still plenty of hooded figures clustered on the opposite bank, those who had come to pay tribute to the passing of the Crimson Queen getting far more of a show than they'd bargained for. They no longer seemed so solemn, nor so faceless under their cowls, the light of morning showing them for what they were— folk plain as any other, who'd come here to try to make a little sense of their dark world, and now stared mystified at what had transpired.

"Well, let's give the people something worth remembering," Zosia told Choplicker, grabbing him harder than was strictly necessary by the back of the neck. "Take me to the leader of Jex Toth."

He looked up at her, his muzzle red and wet from the puddle of blood he'd been lapping, and he gave her another of those hideous smiles she could have done without. Then he pulled her forward and she stepped after him, into the Gate.

As soon as she did, she realized something was wrong. When they had traveled from the Lark's Tongue Gate to Diadem their journey had been terrifying but brief, a single horrific instant, but now the oozing blackness that enveloped her stretched and stretched, thinner and colder, digging into her, through her, filling her. The First Dark was inside her, and even when she was vomited out onto the scratchy wool rug she could still feel its flush permeating her very bones. She gulped the faintly smoky air, unable to move for a spell, the chamber swirling around her as it coalesced…and then familiar fingers brushed away her tears, cocked her chin up to look at him.

Leib.

Her husband smiled sadly down at her, sitting on the floor beside her as he stroked her hair with his callused hand. She tried to speak but only a sob came out, and he gently guided her head into his lap, petting her as she wept and wept, clinging to the sides of the canvas coat he had worn when he'd left that fatal morning, riding down the valley to deliver tribute to the Crimson Empire…

Then her hands balled into fists, and she murdered her grief. Not opening her eyes, she said, "This isn't real. You're not. He's dead."

"He kept me safe," Leib whispered, the sound of his voice demolishing the defenses she'd tried to raise. "Good old Chop kept me safe, just like you wished. He protected me, brought me here. It was the only way. I've been waiting for you for so long, Zee…"

He was crying now, too, his tears warm against her scalp as they soaked through her hair. His voice cracked. "I've missed you so, so much, my love, but now you're home."

"Home," she moaned, burying her face deeper in the thin tunic she'd mended more than once, his slight belly warm against her cheek. She opened her fists and felt his back, reaching up to his broad shoulders, his lithe arms made strong from the raising of their cabin. The cabin where they now held each other, the sound of the aspens and his bone charms clinking in their boughs drifting in through the door that was always open, the smells of brewing kaldi and pipe smoke rich in the air. The cabin she had burned down, after his senseless murder. "Hell, you mean. Is that where you've brought me?"

"Hell?" Fuck, how she had missed his laugh, warm as the crackling fire in the hearth. "I can't pretend to know what this place is, wife, or even *how* this place is, but if you ask me it's just like heaven. It's home. And we aren't alone, either—Kypck's just down the hill, same as ever, and everyone's here, safe as safe can be. Even that cowherd that was always such a thorn in your boot, remember him? I've been teaching him to fish in the lakes over the pass; once he finds out you're back I can't imagine we'll have a moment's peace, the little—"

"Stop." She squeezed her eyes tighter. "Stop it stop it stop it."

"I was confused at first, too," he said, his strong fingers massaging the nape of her neck the way she'd missed so, so much. "But after all the incredible things you've seen, is it so surprising there's more to this world than we'll ever understand? That we don't have to understand life to reap its bounty? Isn't it enough that we're here, together, and we never have to leave?"

His words were fishhooks in her heart. Yes, this was what she wanted. This was all she had ever wanted. What she had burned empires for.

"Isn't this everything you ever wished for, to turn away from all the pain and sorrow of the world and take me to a place where no one could hurt us? This is what you asked for! You've *earned* this, Zosia, after all the sacrifices you've made, after all the trials you've endured to better the lives of others, this is your reward. Just open your eyes and accept it, you obstinate woman!"

That was the worst of all. He'd only ever called her an obstinate woman when they were in bed and she was insisting on making him come first, despite his attempts to hold off, and that fucking tore it right there. Wrenching herself away but keeping her eyes locked shut lest the temptation overwhelm her, even now, she snarled, "Stop it. I don't know why you're doing this, but *stop*. There's only one place I'm going, and that's Jex Toth."

"There's nothing there but death," he said piteously. "Even after all these years, haven't you figured out you can't save everyone? Some battles can't be won, and the only victory is to acknowledge this, to protect yourself, to move on."

"You think I don't know that?" The tears were coming so hot and fast it was a struggle to keep her eyes clamped. "That's what death *is*, giving up on the unwinnable. But I'm not dead yet. Now take me back."

"Time moves differently here, Zosia, it's too late for the Star," he said, no longer sounding like her husband but talking in the voice of Pao Cowherd, the dying boy who'd once begged her to save his life now petitioning her to abandon innumerable others. "In the minutes we've spent here the morning has waned, the battle has been lost, and the Star is falling. It's over, and you have to accept—"

"*You* have to accept *my* orders," she spat. "Now take me back, if only to die with my kind. *Now.*"

The air grew chill around her, and she could hear the wind that haunted the Kutumban reaches come roaring down through the fireplace. Instead of the smells of kaldi and pipe smoke and her husband's sweaty shirt she caught only the tang of charcoal, the stink of wet dog. The comfortable rug melted beneath her rump to a cold hard floor thickly coated in dust, and whatever he said next was lost in a snarling bark.

Zosia fell, the squirming cloying stinking passage through the First Dark no longer so frightening. She welcomed this passage, the breath of time to let her eyes dry. Then she tumbled out across the soft wet ground, her mind continuing to roll even when her body came to a stop, and when she at last opened her eyes it was a place every bit as alien as the spaces between Gates.

She knew she didn't have much time, probably didn't have any, but she seized Choplicker by the scruff of the neck and wrenched his guilty face up to hers.

"We're not finished, you and I," she growled. "Not by a very, very long measure, devil. If I were you I'd work harder than I ever had before to make amends, or else…or else I don't even know what. But it won't be good."

Then she shoved him away and took in the Sunken Kingdom of Jex Toth. Zosia had cleaned enough kills in her day to know at once they weren't just some*where*, they were inside some*thing*, the ribbed arches of the massive hall actual ribs, thirteen living thrones formed of glistening meat and spurred bone rising in a half circle just ahead of her. All of the grotesque chairs were empty save one, where a scrawny man had been mummified in webbing all the way up to his eyes…

Then, through the translucent silk, she recognized the tattoos on the skeletal figure's naked flesh. Only it couldn't be him, it couldn't be—there simply wasn't enough there for it to be him. Yet it could be no other, she was sure of it. In life Hoartrap had been one of the biggest men she'd ever met, sturdy as a bull gorgon, but now his desiccated corpse looked even smaller than her. Only his face looked about the same, his bulky, web-muzzled head sickeningly disproportionate to his wasted body, like a prize-winning pumpkin perched on a rickety scarecrow.

What the devil had happened to him? What was he even doing here? And how long had Zosia been in that other place, that he'd taken the others to Othean, beaten her here, and met a grisly demise before she even turned up?

"Fuck!" Zosia jumped as Hoartrap's watery blue eyes blinked at her. That he was evidently still alive made his condition seem even worse.

Before she could move to free him the rubbery, slightly tacky floor heaved ever so gently beneath her feet, and she had to drop to a crouch to keep from falling over. The devilish mode of travel already threw off her equilibrium, and try as she did to find her sea legs she only succeeded in slipping onto her knees. Hoartrap offered her a series of blinks, but if there was an eyelid-based prisoners' cant she wasn't fluent. The great chamber was dimly lit by glowing veins that flowed through the floors and the walls and even the thrones, revealing that while this plateau was little bigger than Diadem's throne room it rose from the center of a vast grotto. And in the gently pulsing twilight Zosia saw just what a terrible mistake she had made in coming here without an army of her own.

The black-shelled soldiers surrounded her, cutting her off from Hoartrap and the rest of the thrones as they came scuttling up the sides of whatever mesa she had emerged onto. Their stinger-spiked armor looked even more dangerous than their toothed weapons, Choplicker growling low in his throat, and Zosia tightened her grip on her hammer. She would make them work hard if they wanted to grant Hoartrap's wish to sacrifice Diadem... but first she had to try her plan, stupid and hopeless though it surely was.

"Hear me!" she shouted, not even knowing if words were necessary for this psychic army, as Hoartrap had called them, or if they could even understand her, but she didn't know how else to make sure her thoughts went echoing out through the cavernous belly of

Jex Toth. "If I die, you die! If I fall, my devil sends you back to the First Dark!"

If anything, that made them come in faster, Zosia still too dizzy to get off her knees.

"You read minds! Read mine and see if I'm lying!" Her voice broke as they closed the final few meters, not for herself but for the people of Diadem about to be incinerated because she hadn't been smart enough to come up with a better scheme. "Peace for all if I live, death to all if I die! Look in me, damn you, look in me and see if I speak true!"

And they stopped. And even more incredibly, backed away. But Choplicker didn't stop growling, sounding angrier and angrier, and glancing down she saw he'd turned and was staring at something behind them. Clambering up and turning to face the Gate he'd brought her through, she saw what had him so keyed up. This Gate was different from any she'd ever seen, with arched bridges of bone criss-crossing over it, and at each intersection stood a bizarre figure. There were five up there all together, with another five circling the rim at the points where the bone bridges joined, and hanging down from the ceiling over the center of the Gate were the three biggest cocoons she had ever seen. These cultists or whoever they were all stared at Zosia with sunken eyes in grotesque faces—you couldn't even say they were corpselike, for they were so ancient they made mummies seem fresh.

"Your Majesssssssty," hissed the closest figure in High Immaculate, dropping an exaggerated bow. Zosia didn't know what was more unsettling, that the corpulent man's robe was formed of swarming white ants, or that he seemed to be addressing Choplicker instead of her.

CHAPTER
27

Maroto's thighs burned. His Gate-healed knee decided this was as good a time as any to act back up, and now it felt like he was grinding broken glass in there with every step. The stitch in his side hurt as bad as a wound in need of sutures. His spear arm felt ready to fall off, and that was an improvement on the one carrying the witch's birdcage. He was literally sweating blood. His face felt like salt crystals were embedded under the shredded skin. Oh, and he'd really liked that eye, too. Had certainly preferred it to a numb hole, the absence of sensation in that area even more frightening than pain would've been.

Yet for all that, Maroto had never felt better as he led the hundred-odd remaining Chainites back into Othean. Forget bugs, he was a born-again egghead from this day forward! That witch had given him the good shit, no joke. Here at last was a high that didn't deaden his senses from the pain that was his due, but gave him the strength to bear it, and take on even more. Give the creepy-crawlers their credit, though: if he hadn't spent the last couple decades chasing the centipede and building up a lordly tolerance he'd probably already be dead—whatever alien venom that Tothan's quilled helm had injected him with gave him the red sweats and didn't play too nice with the nervous system, either, but his hands were steady enough for killing, and whose heart didn't race during a battle? Obviously the day was young and the witch seemed to think it was only a matter of time before the toxins melted his brain out through his nose, but you could say that about anything, couldn't you? It was all a matter of time, and then you were dead.

Scrambling up the rubble of the inner wall, he paused at the top of the heap. His bloodied volunteers panted past him, dropping down into the street below and continuing their mad flight to the supposed safety of the wall at the middle of Othean. Fennec had hitched a ride with one of Ji-hyeon's sisters on her giant sloth or whatever it was, directing the reunited-but-routed Cobalt Company through the trap-laden western city, but here at the rear of the retreating army Maroto wasn't without new friends. Nemi huffed her way up the debris to join him, Indsorith beside her, and back in the slums Ji-hyeon and Sullen and the rest of the remaining Cobalt cavalry covered their retreat.

It looked like thankless work from up here, with the massive northern regiment pouring into the outer wall after them, and mobs of Tothans from the first force still lurking about the narrow alleys. The only unexpected boon was that most of that first Tothan army was currently swarming the Autumn Palace, overrunning the empty castle complex that was built into the inner wall just south of here. Lupitera's theory must have been right—the Tothans were trying to capture the Immaculate Empress and her court, mistakenly thinking she was here thanks to Maroto's bad but believable intelligence. As he peered at the terraced balconies and exposed stairways teeming with beetle-shelled bastards on their way back down to street level, he imagined they must have figured out the castle was uninhabited. Which meant they were about to come charging back up here at the obvious fleeing targets, and when they reached this breach any Cobalts not safely on the other side would be trapped in the slums between the two walls.

Maroto felt his Charity swell at the prospect of making his last stand, here and now. Watching Hoartrap gird himself in a cockroach colossus and march out to meet the Tothans had shredded some secret chords deep in Maroto's breast—the Touch was the most selfish creature Maroto had ever met, but here at the end he'd sacrificed himself to save his friends, and in truly epic fashion. Whether or not the old warlock had intended it to be his final charge there seemed little doubt he was dead now, dead or worse—the Vex Assembly had endlessly grilled Maroto about Hoartrap, their interest in the wizard unrivaled in its intensity. While none of the creeps had volunteered what exactly it was about the Touch they found so abhorrent it was obvious from their attitude they couldn't wait to get him in their pruny clutches— Maroto had assumed it was just a typical sorcerous rivalry, magic-users being a catty bunch. Watching one of the ancient priests fly its squid-dragon smack into the middle of Hoartrap's titan and bring the giant down, he supposed they had finally caught up with him.

A tough act to follow, that, but Maroto was a consummate professional, the closer's closer, and if Hoartrap the Touch had gone down getting the Cobalts this far, well, Maroto would go down getting them the rest of the way. And within sight of the Temple of Pentacles where Kang-ho had apparently bought it, too. This was the stuff of legends, right here: the Fifth Villain joining the Third and the First in a noble death outside the Autumn Palace. Total fucking classic.

"Come on," Indsorith panted as she passed Maroto, sliding down the mound of debris into the city of West Othean. "They're almost on top of us."

"They *are* on top of us," said Nemi, pointing back at where a massive furry thing with lampreylike mouths on the ends of its many sinuous limbs crested an unbroken section of the outer wall. If the first Tothan army had arrived with giant monsters like that they would have taken the Autumn Palace in hours, not weeks. "Time to run, Captain Maroto—you owe me your life, and etiquette dictates you return the favor."

"I figured as much," he said, euphoric at the prospect of more mortification. "I'll hold this hole as long as I can while you make your getaway. Can you take this spear back to my nephew, though? Not much chance of my delivering it to—"

"Absolutely not!" huffed the witch. "I did not buy your life so that you could simply throw it away again."

"Wait, what?" Maroto couldn't figure this girl out. "You said the poison in my face is going to kill me, right? So why not help everyone get away with a gallant last stand?"

"I said it will *probably* prove terminal," said Nemi, stepping on her tiptoes to examine the oozing pincushion of his face. "But my egg slowed it enough that you have a little time, at least, and you will not squander those priceless minutes on empty dramatics. You *will* carry Zeetatrice to safety, because even after doubling my own dose I'm not fit enough to run with her—if you die she dies, and if she dies I die."

"Ooooooh," said Maroto, nodding his floaty head as he watched one of the enormous mouth-legged monsters leap from the outer wall onto a nearby tenement roof, shattering tiles but not falling through. It moved fast over the rooftops, straight toward them... "Oh! Run!"

Nemi was already moving, though, catching up with Indsorith on the cobblestones below. Maroto slipped his way down after them, the blindfolded cockatrice hissing at him as the cage swung every which way, more Cobalts cresting the stile of rubble behind him and joining the exodus into West Othean. The crowd was fleeing up the eastern boulevard, and crossing a wider avenue that led a mere six blocks down to the Autumn Palace's majestic inner gate he saw the Tothan soldiers come charging out to catch them.

Behind the clacking soldiers, another of the eight-legged monsters dropped over the top of the wall, crashing through the gabled roof of a temple...and then exploding out of its double doors, the fall not having slowed it in the slightest. Rearing on its hind legs, its leathery white bulk stretched as high as the second story of the castle, and from each of its six wavering, ring-mouthed limbs issued discordant, trumpeting wails. Maroto wasn't sure what that might mean, exactly, but he didn't think it was surrendering. After that, he caught up with Nemi and Indsorith in no time.

———

Ji-hyeon whirled her steed around, its tail snapping the legs out from under a horse demon, her sword slicing through a Tothan's helm. Sullen, meanwhile, clung to the saddle horn and tried not to throw up or be thrown off. When they'd been working with the other mounted

Cobalts in the narrow streets between the two walls he'd been able to contribute something, using the spear he'd found to modest success. Now that Ji-hyeon had ordered everyone to flee, however, he was worse than useless, probably blocking her view as he bounced in front of her on the saddle.

After they had galloped up the ruins of the inner wall and dropped down into Othean he had hoped they might be able to slow their pace a little. On the contrary, the wider avenues let them ride faster than ever, and every jostle on the saddle made Sullen feel like he was being stabbed anew in his leaky stomach. With half a Tothan army already overrunning the city around them and a far larger regiment coming in at their heels, their fastest might not be fast enough. They tore through the metropolis that went from completely deserted on one block to choked with enemies on the next, rounding corners so fast their steed slid across the wet cobblestones, bumping into the handsome stone buildings and breaking through the occasional fence. The deeper they penetrated into the sprawling neighborhoods the less frequently they encountered the rest of the Cobalts, though he didn't know whether this was Ji-hyeon's design to lead the enemy away or if they were simply lost in the biggest city on the Star…a place chock-full of deadly traps, apparently.

"Sullen!" They had just overtaken another Tothan throng when Ji-hyeon tapped his thigh with the arm she kept wrapped around his waist. The one holding on to the reins. "Take these—I need to read the map!"

"Uh, sure." Sullen did, fully expecting the animal to throw them both as soon as he touched the leather leads. It didn't, but without Ji-hyeon's arm around him he felt even more likely to slide over its scaled side. When her hand didn't return even as the empty avenue they sped down split into a fork, he said, "Uh, Ji-hyeon?"

"Left? Left!" she said, and Sullen gave the reins a little tug in that direction. The big animal didn't seem to acknowledge it, so he pulled harder…but instead of taking the left-hand path its long head whipped around, yanking the reins out of his hands as it slid to a stop just in front of the intersection. "Sullen!"

"Damn," he said, leaning forward and reaching for the dangling reins as the animal huffed at him. He didn't puke and his guts didn't fall out, though both felt like distinct possibilities as he snatched at them. When he finally caught the straps and straightened back up he that saw that the animal hadn't just taken offense at his inexperienced steering—a huge grey shape came careening down the left-hand path, its many limbs pushing off along both the walls of the alley and the street below. It was maybe a bit like a naked mammoth, only with sharp-toothed trunks instead of legs, and twice as many limbs at that, but Sullen didn't get a really good look since he was already yanking the reins in the other direction and kicking their mount's flanks for all he was worth.

Now it was Ji-hyeon's turn to cling to him as their steed took off down the right-hand street. Terra-cotta tiles rained down around them, and glancing up Sullen saw that the pursuing monster had taken a shortcut over the tops of the buildings separating the two avenues. It kept time with them on the edge of the roofs, its mouths trilling in turn as they loped even faster, overtaking their quarry. Ji-hyeon began tugging at Sullen's hair and desperately scratching at his arms, shouting at him to *stop, stop*, but even if that had seemed like a sane idea he didn't know how.

Up ahead the avenue opened into a plaza, and through the screen of rain he saw the monster leap down to intercept them, its thick limbs tearing up the cobblestones as it landed, spinning around to meet them... and then vanishing as the wide square evaporated into blinding light and blistering heat, a thick fog enveloping them as the rain boiled away.

"Yeah," Sullen said when his ears stopped ringing and he realized Ji-hyeon had been asking if he was all right. Their mount had stopped, the hot avenue still obscured in steam but what he could see of the buildings around them spattered with grey and black daubs of gore. "So... back there I guess you meant my other left, huh?"

Before she could answer, figures began to materialize in the misty ruins of the plaza. Black-shelled figures drawn to the explosion, moving toward them with weapons lowered. Pulling the reins hard to the left to turn them back around, Sullen muttered, "Gonna take that for a yes."

———

Othean's innermost wall towered over the central market district streets, only a dozen blocks away now. Which made it all the more disappointing that when Maroto wheezed around the final bend and came out into the field of stalls between him and safety he found that the Tothans had cut them off. Well, maybe some or even most of the Cobalts had made it to the gatehouse in time, but not all of them, to guess from the torn-up corpses in blue tabards strewn about the market square. As the hundreds of hollow soldiers and their green-eyed cavalry rushed forward to cut down Maroto and the rest of the stragglers, he passed the cockatrice cage back to Nemi and took up his nephew's spear in both hands. No clever words came to mind so he let the silence stand; better no last words at all than something daft. Besides, this Flintland spear would do the talking for both of them.

Somewhere behind them in the city the first explosion went off, punctuating his stoic silence, and now he was grinning despite how much it hurt his face. Or maybe because of it; everything was getting mixed up in his venom-cooked brain. Skip a night's sleep in favor of hours and hours of brutal combat against monsters straight out of a stinghound's nightmare and life begins to feel a little dreamlike. Point was, that blast meant the Immaculates' trap was going off, and every last one of these Tothan freaks was going to die a nasty death. As were Maroto and the rest of the Cobalts here on the wrong side of the central wall, yes, but sometimes that's just how the song ends.

Not always, though.

The rain thickened above the charging Tothans, and then the first three lines were hit with the deluge of arrows that had arced over the wall. Most of them collapsed, especially the infantry, but a bunch of the horsey monstrosities stayed upright despite all the shafts sticking out of them. The volley was a nice gesture, even if it wasn't enough to save them from the rest of the charging legion, but then Maroto saw the unthinkable go down—way over there on the far corner of the market square the portcullis had risen up in the gatehouse, and now rider after rider came streaming out to hit the remaining Tothans from behind. It wasn't just any cavalry, either, but Raniputri dragoons, their lances lowered and shields high.

At the time Maroto had been pretty sore about getting a faceful of Tothan bug juice, especially considering how it was administered, but between this and Nemi's egg he had to fess this was one primo speedball. Indsorith rushing past him with her sword held high reminded him that it was time to make a good day even better—why just gawk at your weird fate when you could hitch up your skirt and dance with it? He glanced back at Nemi to tell her to stay behind him but forgot what he was going to say when he saw she'd sat down on top of her birdcage, tucked in her dress, and planted a saw-toothed sword between her legs. She raised a little bow up into the rain, muttered something, and after snapping the moisture off it, began to play the sword.

It sounded *bad*. Just, like, raw hell. But what better music to go hunting for your own? The pike-limbed demons seemed to like it even less than Maroto, the incoming pack all chattering and rearing back, their flaming green eyes guttering pink and their sideways mouths foaming, and then they wheeled away, stomping back through their own troops. Ill magic, no doubt.

Charging after Indsorith to the sound of possessed cats being exorcised, he had to laugh. When he'd made that pledge all those years ago to never raise weapons against the Crimson Queen he'd hardly expected to one day follow her into battle. Badly as he craved a slow and painful death he knew that was just the Tothan venom talking, and what he *really* wanted was to live out the day so he could tell Indsorith just how closely he'd stuck to his promise, even during the Battle of the Lark's Tongue. Nothing wrong with bragging when you'd earned it.

As Maroto came into the melee after Indsorith he was struck by just how well this spear handled. He'd never been one for pointy weapons, or Flintlander tools at all, truth be told, but this was a bug of another carapace. Probably didn't hurt that the poison in his skull was giving him more of those weird sensory hallucinations; anytime a Tothan came in from his blind side his ear would sting just like it'd been flicked by a mean old bastard, giving him just enough warning to spin around and parry or pike his enemy. Felt so good he had to howl about it, and howling felt so good he had to wonder why he didn't do it more often.

Howl, stab, dodge. Howl, dodge, slash. Trip, howl, spit. Howl howl howl.

Then he was on the other side of the Tothans all of a sudden, staggering out into the milling Raniputri horses and bumping right into the side of a big bay. The rider looked down at him, an old dragoon whose camail-framed face boasted an even woolier lip-weasel than the antennae-mustachioed emperor centipede design of her spiked helm's noseguard. Hey, wait a godsdamned minute...

"Good morning, Captain," said the chevaleresse, offering him the Cobalt salute. "Fancy meeting you here."

"Level with me, Singh," he said suspiciously, all the discordant pieces of this impossible morning finally falling into joint. "I know this time I'm not just crossfaded, I'm really, truly dead—I get that. But is this place some kind of heaven, or some kind of hell?"

"It's just life, you old Villain," she told him, spitting a clod of betel into the blood-tinged puddle at his feet. "Which is to say, a blend of the both. Now let us fall back behind the wall before your bugged-out brain becomes prophetic."

"Trust." Maroto nodded, seeing that Nemi, Indsorith, and the few remaining Cobalts and Chainites were dipping inside the portcullis. He and his fellow Villain were some of the last through the gatehouse before it shut; the final two were his nephew and Ji-hyeon, their beast carrying them under the portcullis even as it began to lower. The riders looked as frazzled as their steed as they burst from the western market into its eastern twin, the animal huffing and puffing around the busy square the way Maroto used to after climbing up a canyon wall, before he'd gotten back into shape.

"Hey, fleet riding, kiddos, how'd—" Maroto began to hail them but Sullen lurched off the side of the animal, losing his lunch before his feet even hit the ground. Ji-hyeon dismounted after him, stroking his back, and that was a bit of bonding Maroto didn't feel like adding his avuncular touch to. Instead he let Singh lead him away through the thronged square where Cobalts shared wineskins with Chainites and Raniputri riders shared beedies with Immaculate archers. There were Flintlanders here, too, but it was clear from their relaxed bearing as much as their studded black leather armor that they hailed from Reh, the Bal-Amon coast, or some other more civilized corner of his homeland. Just about every Arm of the Star was represented in the busy piazza of East Othean, and unlike the desolate city on the other side of the wall, here every window of every building bordering the market was crowded with faces. Frightened ones.

"Did you skip breakfast?" asked Singh as they passed one of the crowded booths that had replaced mundane merchant stalls, and catching the scent of sizzling Immaculate barbecue from the make-shift kitchen, Maroto queued up harder than he had ever queued in his life. The line moved quick enough, since none of the soldiers had to pay for the seaweed-wrapped rolls of rice, burdock, marinated beef, and fermented chili paste, but even still the usually patient chevaleresse was clearly in a rush to be off again. Maroto obliged her by only wolfing down three of the transcendentally delicious food-tubes by the side of the booth, and filled the rest of the way up on a sustained guzzle from a nearby rain barrel—nothing better than a post-fight feast, except maybe a post-fight sit, but Singh was clearly having none of the latter just yet.

"You in some kind of a crazy hurry?" he gasped, that cramp in his side no longer feeling like some welcome reminder of mortality or whatever the fuck he'd been thinking as Singh hustled him out of the market square and through a door in the side of the wall. He whined out loud at seeing another of Othean's infinite staircases awaiting them.

"Yes," she said, not slowing her pace. "We're about to find out if this war can be won, and I do not intend to spend this momentous occasion skulking in a stairway."

"Fiiiine," he said, following after her. "What's about to happen, exactly?"

"Didn't Fennec tell you?" The ornamental yellow stitching on Singh's coat-of-ten-thousand-nails made the armor shine like gold in the torchlight, her mustache even curlier than he remembered. "He told me he had."

"The trap, right, we led the Tothans into a trap." Maroto leaned his head against the cool stone wall. The side that wasn't a puffy mass of crusty bandages. "Fennec's here? He made it?"

"He's waiting for us on the battlement," said the chevaleresse, clomping back down the stairs to help Maroto resume his climb. "We'll have a drink and a smoke and see just what kind of a trap these Immaculate priests have set. It had better be a good one, since you've led an army of monsters straight toward us."

"A smoke and a drink," said Maroto, smacking his lips as he put an arm around Singh and started climbing again. "Decadent. You think we can afford to kick back at a time like this?"

"We cannot afford not to, as this may well be our last opportunity," said Singh. "I believe it is customary for the condemned to have a final smoke, and I have a pipe you can borrow."

"Believe it or not, I got my own for a change," said Maroto, and when they reached the landing at the top of the stairs he took it out to show her. His hands were shaking, so she packed it for him from her pouch, and then filled her own—that heinous briar monstrosity Zosia had carved her way back when. Seeing it made his heart ache for the beautiful tankard-shaped pipe she'd made him, the one he'd lost devils knew where only to have Zosia miraculously return it to him back at the Cobalt camp...where he had lost it a second time, leaving it in his tent during the big battle from which he had never returned. He cursed himself for losing the greatest gift he had ever received, and twice over at that...but then the finest briar in the world is the one in your hand, and wouldn't you know it, this one was Cobalt-carved, too. They got their pipes good and lit before taking them back out into the weather; the rampart was mostly covered, but between the wind and the damp it was better to use the coalstick inside. When their bowls were burning bright and the delicious Oriorentine blend filled the stairwell with the familiar but

long-missed scent of Kang-ho's favorite tubāq, Singh gave the requi-
site knocks and the guards on the other side opened the door, letting
them out onto the top of the wall.

No wonder Singh had been in a hurry to get up here and get lit.
From this vantage he could see clear across West Othean to the hazy
line of the compromised inner wall, the bump of the Autumn Palace.
Between here and there were the miles of city he'd just crossed, some
quarters packed nearly as tight as the outer slums and others expan-
sive estates of the noblesse that sprawled as wide as Raniputri castles.

Good neighborhoods and bad were now equal, however, the
whole fucking place infested with Tothans. Every street looked to
be clogged with black-shelled ranks, bigger monsters jumped from
rooftop to rooftop, and the largest of the lot came crashing through
the buildings themselves, clearing wild paths through the orderly
city. The vanguard would reach this central wall within minutes, and
even from up here Maroto couldn't see far enough back to catch sight
of the army's rear. For all he knew it didn't have one, stretching out to
the Temple of Pentacles and beyond.

"That looks an awful lot like the end of the song to me," confessed
Maroto as they gazed out over the fallen city. The rain had stopped, and
the creamy yet spicy tubāq tickled his tongue as he pulled on Bang's
pipe. There was still an edge of brine to the smoke that made his eyes
water. Well, his eye, anyway. "I'll be honest, Singh, I never expected
you of all people to follow Ji-hyeon through the Lark's Tongue Gate. I
would've put every coin I could borrow on you hightailing it out of the
Witchfinder Plains, no doubt...but I'm glad you're here."

"You should have laid a bet, then, because that is precisely what I
did—I was back in Zygnema just as fast as my pony could carry me."
Singh blew a smoke ring up into the grey sky. "I will risk my life for a
just cause, or a profitable one, but you will not see me risking my soul
by stepping into a Gate."

"Huh?" Maroto looked away from the marching army, cocking
his head at his old friend. "Okay, wait, I thought it was odd Fennec
didn't mention you were here. If you didn't come through the Gate
with the rest of the Cobalts, what're you doing here?"

"I heeded the counsel of one who did, someone who's been awaiting your return for quite some time," said the chevaleresse, taking his arm and leading him down the ramparts. There were soldiers everywhere, the single peacock feathers of the Immaculates' helmets and the double black plumes of the Raniputris' wiggling like worms in the wind, but none of the troopers looked familiar to Maroto. "Granted, when she turned up on my doorstep her proposal was to sack Othean rather than save it, and that was indeed what we set out to do. While I was off enjoying our Cobalt reunion at the Witchfinder Plains my churlish children somehow managed to reunite the Raniputri Dominions, but I knew if I didn't talk them into working together against some outer foe they would soon turn on each other. Near the end of our voyage, however, we were greeted by that same devil vulture who delivered Empress Ryuki's messages to Ji-hyeon back at the Lark's Tongue, and bearing an ironically similar plea: Little Heaven was indeed under attack, the fate of the Star was in peril, and all mortals should surely perish unless we came to Othean's aid... So we did, but only arrived this morning, same as you."

"You sailed clear up here from the Dominions to throw down on the Immaculates, but when you got here decided to help them fight an unbeatable army of monsters instead?" Maroto squinted at the figures gathered on a bastion up ahead. "You must be just as demented as I am."

"Am I to suppose once these demons have had their way with the Isles they will seek no more victories?" Singh shook her head and her pipe in time, her bangles clinking. "I have children, Maroto, and my children have children, and someday their children will have children... but only if the Star persists. Do you understand?"

"Hmmm," said Maroto, recognizing Fennec in the small huddle of Raniputris up ahead. "I understand that the empress offered a handsome reward to whoever came to Othean's defense, and if the city falls your riders can get back down to the docks faster than anyone else on this Isle."

"Well, there is that..." said Singh as they came up to the crowded bastion. "Something tells me your Azgarothian fleet also has practical motivations to complement their noble intentions, as do the seafaring Flintlanders who beat us both here. Othean is where the fate of the Star will be decided...and if we win, well, this adventure's keeping my kids out of trouble for the time being, and I do have an inside connection to make sure my people are especially well compensated."

"And who the devils is that, anyway, the woman who talked you into coming up here?" Maroto asked as Fennec waved them over. "Ji-hyeon? I heard that she jumped into the local Gate and went missing for a while, but did she also pop out down in the Dominions to...to..."

The woman who Fennec had been talking to turned as well, and Maroto saw that despite her Raniputri armor she was not of the Souwest Arm. She was...she was...

He dropped his pipe.

It was her. Not as he'd dreamed her, not exactly, for this vision wore armor instead of her altogether, her fit figure sheathed under brigandine. From her quirk of a smile he supposed Singh's holding back on naming her had been upon request, to preserve the surprise. And that smile! Hard as it was to believe she was actually standing there in front of him, her *smiling* made this seem even more impossible than a dream.

She came to him as he just stood there, slack-limbed, looking into her pretty ruby eyes as more explosions began popping way out in the distance; he felt the same tingling intimacy he'd experienced on Jex Toth when the Vex Assembly had gotten into his head. Only this was a welcome intrusion, and somehow so familiar he wondered if she had spent countless nights dreaming him, just as he had dreamed her...crazy as it sounded, it felt *right*, like this exact moment had played out a hundred times in both their hearts before finally coming to fruition. But he had to wait for the closest explosion yet to fade to give voice to his feelings, because it was so loud there was no way she could—

Choi rolled up on her toes, put her hand on the back of his neck, and gently but firmly pulled him down into a kiss. As his tongue met hers those damnably elusive dreams he could never quite remember upon waking flashed through the back of his mind, in perfect focus at last, but he had no time for them now. She tasted of granted wishes, of coconut water passing over salt-stung lips as he reached out to her across the seas with his aching heart, with some fresh kaldi notes on the end. She tasted alive, and she kissed him all the harder, her fingers exploring his hair but careful not to brush his injured scalp, her other hand finding his arm and running down it to his palm, taking hold of it as if afraid he'd fall away again as she kissed him the way he'd always wanted her to . . .

And then life kneed them both in the crotch, the entire bastion lurching to one side as some terrible force struck the wall. They stumbled apart, and he nicked his tongue on one of her sharp teeth. They both froze, waiting for the wall to buckle beneath their feet and send them tumbling to their deaths, but when there was no immediate catastrophe they straightened up from their panicked crouches. Had any first kiss been greeted with such dark portent?

Well, maybe his and Bang's on that bucolic Tothan hillside just before he'd been captured by monsters, but that had been a fairly chaste peck on the cheek to accompany the wicked spanking. Thinking of Bang now made his heart ache . . . but not out of any irrational guilt, since they'd certainly never talked about exclusivity. No, thinking of the pretty pirate gave Maroto's ticker a wee spasm only because he wished he could kiss her one last time, too, and if that made Maroto a dirty old man, well, he'd never claimed to be anything but.

"Oh," said Choi, noticing something on the wet flagstones and bending down to pick it up. It was the canted bowl of the pipe Maroto had dropped, and the antler stem that had snapped off when it landed. Maybe it actually was for the best Bang wasn't here, if only for the sake of Maroto's buns . . . "This is unfortunate. I broke your pipe."

"Oh hells no, I had the dropsies, and to be honest it was never really mine to begin with," said Maroto, taking the pieces and stowing them back in his pouch. "And I'm beginning to think nothing's so broke it can't be fixed."

"I apologize," she said, "I am trying to stop smiling, but I cannot. You are truly here. This is no dream."

"Never stop smiling, please!" Even looking straight at her adorable gap-toothed grin he couldn't quite believe it was real, either. "I can't...I mean...*you're* the one who talked Singh into sailing on Othean? I hope we live long enough to hear that song!"

"It is brief enough," said Choi in that matter-of-fact way he loved. "When the Tothans attacked I chose to risk entering a hungry mouth alone. I had paid close attention when Fennec first brought us through the Gates to Zygnema, and dared to replicate his method. I was successful. Upon passing over to the Dominions I sought out the chevaleresse, to enlist her in my campaign of vengeance against the empress. I was successful. That is the song...but...there are others I would sing you."

A nearby blast of light lit up the fierce wildborn face he had missed so much, and it was about as good a moment as Maroto could remember having...and then over her shoulder he saw the entire western city go off like a bundle of firecrackers, the explosions rushing in toward the central wall, the horizon going black with smoke as entire estates erupted in blinding flashes, flaming debris already beginning to rain down all around them. Seeing the blasts come closer and closer, and feeling the wind rise, he knew that as tall as this wall was it wasn't tall enough to keep out all the embers blowing in. West Othean was detonating right before his eye, but long before the final bombs went off the eastern city was also going to catch fire. The Dreaming Priests of Othean had a foolproof trap to take out the Tothans, all right—lure in the enemy armies, and then burn the whole damn capital to the ground! Fair play, if a touch shortsighted...or maybe the Immaculates had known all along that theirs was a lost cause, that at best they could deprive their inhuman enemy of a conquest.

So that was that, then. After all this time and blood and doubt Maroto had finally found the girl of his dreams, just in time to die beside her. Wasn't that just always the fucking way?

CHAPTER
28

Purna blinked her gummy eyes, hardly able to believe that here at the end of her exploits this silver fox had strutted back into her song. Zosia wasn't exactly the one that got away, because as much as Purna might've liked to hit that, such a coupling would have brought more drama with it than you could pack in a sky-devil's saddlebags, but it was nevertheless good to see a familiar face. Even if said face was upside down, on account of Purna hanging from the cavern ceiling by her ankles.

Purna tried to call out to Zosia but the webbing they'd wrapped her in was especially tight over her mouth. Hard to assume that was an accident, or the way they'd bundled poor Prince up against her chest like a fluffy baby. That the Vex Assembly had kept her and her chums trussed up like late-blooming butterflies over their Gate even after she'd told the ghouls everything she knew about Hoartrap just went to show that no morally dubious act of betraying the confidence of a creepy old devil-eater went unpunished. Or something. What a lousy day.

The already sour situation had gone off entirely when the Tothan crone they'd originally taken captive had waltzed back onto the ziggurat. It wasn't that Purna expected an evil, immortal witch to cut them some slack on account of how well they had treated her before the tables got turned, because come on now, she wasn't naïve. No, what really burned Purna's biscuits was seeing the smelly old priestess walk on over to the rim of the Gate and take up her position for their mysterious ceremony, easy as you please. They'd hauled her lazy ass all over the damn jungle, assuming she was crippled, but all this time her legs worked just fine!

Annoying a development as this undoubtedly was, things had taken a further turn when another horrible old man suddenly burst out of the Gate below with none other than Hoartrap himself held fast in his spindly arms—at that point the rest of the devil-haunted witches had lost all interest in interrogating Purna or preparing for their ritual in favor of falling upon the subject of their inquiry. Now that they'd laid hold of the Touch they didn't seem much interested in talking, either. Purna had seen some shit in her day, some real *real* shit...but nothing like what they'd done to Hoartrap, and she'd had to close her eyes as he screamed and screamed, lest she find out what happened when you threw up whilst gagged and suspended upside down. The last thing she'd seen was the pack of ancient maniacs tearing away handfuls of Hoartrap's ivory flesh as if he were made of clay or wax, and far more disturbing than the modicum of spattering black blood were the great smelly clouds of pale spores that billowed from his gaping wounds.

After that the Vex Assembly seemed to forget about the three mortals they had bound above their Gate, and neither Best nor Keun-ju nor even brave little Prince seemed inclined to remind their hosts of their presence. There'd been no time to attempt an escape while they were distracted with their former pal, alas, as the ghouls soon tired of tormenting the Touch, restraining what was left of him in one of their thrones. The bony bastard who'd delivered Hoartrap had hopped right back into the Gate, and the other ten hustled back to their posts around the rim and on the bridges that spanned it, eager to resume the ritual that had twice been interrupted by mortal interlopers. Now Zosia appeared, presumably to see if what they said about third attempts was true, and Purna couldn't help but notice the Vex Assembly was giving her a much more civilized welcome than they'd offered her crew or Hoartrap.

The joke was on these jerks, though, because Purna was going to save herself with the very same instrument that had gotten her into this mess: her big fat mouth. While the upside down Vex Assembly was distracted by Zosia's arrival, Purna began gnawing through the garbage-tasting silk. She also tried pumping her bound arms and legs, getting a little sway going so she might alert Best and Keun-ju to the arrival of a potential savior. Prince wiggled for all he was worth against her bosom, but bless his evil heart, neither of them had much to work with in that neighborhood.

Not that she had any idea what they could do even if they did get loose, considering how quickly and absolutely they had been jacked by the Tothan priests, but she knew one thing: heroes didn't dangle, not when glory was to be found. Or the next best thing to glory, anyway. Given that just one of the baddies had obviously overpowered and then abducted Hoartrap, carrying the scary warlock out of the Gate as though he were no more threatening than a sack of tubers, she doubted even Zosia could stand in the way of the Vex Assembly, but that was no excuse to sit idle while the Banshee with a Blade made her last bally stand. Purna just had to get loose without tumbling down into the First Dark below, hanging as they were just above the empty heart of the bone pentagram that bridged the Gate. Chewing a mouthful of fetid web, she figured it shouldn't be too hard…

———

Purna began swinging back and forth like a damn fool, bumping into Best and further tearing the webs that moored her to the ceiling. One more knock like that and she'd come loose entirely, plummeting straight into the First Dark. Unbelievable, especially after how cleverly Best had been cutting her way free from the inside of the tacky net those lobster-devils had spun around her. The living gods of Jex Toth had bested her in combat before she could even finish drawing her sun-knife from its sheath, yes, but in their hubris they had not disarmed her before hanging her up like a haunch to cure in a smokehouse. No doubt the demons wished the sacred weapon to fall into the Gate with her, carrying its holy power out of their infernal realm…

But now it all came to naught, because Purna had indeed persisted in her spastic swinging, and careened into Best even harder than before. The webbing Best had carefully, systematically weakened now gave way entirely, dumping her out like half-digested offal from an oryx's belly. She tumbled through the air, trying to focus on one of the Tothans so she might hurl her sun-knife into it before being consumed by the First Dark, and—

Landed elbow first on one of the bone bridges, her arm breaking with a sharp snap. Purna's pushing must have swung Best to one side, sparing her from falling straight down into the Gate. She would thank the girl later, when they had time to catch their breath down in Old Black's Meadhall. For now she lurched up to a crouch on the sticky spinal causeway, bringing back her unbroken arm to sail her sun-knife into the heart of the robed revenant ahead of her on the bridge.

Before she could throw it, though, some unseen force threw her. Not into the Gate, thank the Fallen Mother, but clear across the top of the ziggurat, smashing into the throne that still housed the soft and shrunken shadow of Hoartrap. She heard something break inside her or her living cushion, she didn't know which, and then Best of the Horned Wolf Clan left the song.

———

Whatever Zosia had expected to emerge from the cocoons hanging over the Gate, it wasn't a Flintlander. The fat Tothan who confronted her didn't even look over to register this interruption, one of his fellows on the edge of the Gate pulling shapes in the air and sending the big woman flying straight into Hoartrap. The sound of her connecting with the bound sorcerer made Zosia wince.

"Zosia!" one of the other cocoons yelped. "Zosia! Help!"

"The fuck is that?" Zosia pointed her hammer at the two dangling blobs of silk as she addressed the corpulent cultist. "Whoever it is, take them down, turn them loose, and start acting civil. That order. Otherwise you're all dead inside of a minute, that's a promise."

"Fooooool!" exclaimed the ant-infested fat man. "Your age ends nooooow!"

And with that he turned his back on Zosia and her devil, waddling back to his position on the side of the Gate as it began to emit a sickly yellow light. The floor started to ooze and melt around their feet, and Zosia cocked her head in disbelief. She had hoped to parley, but failing that had expected a fight. Instead these bug-covered kooks went on with their ritual as if she hadn't just magicked her ass clear across the Star to confront them. Well, if talking was out at least she'd get to use her hammer…

"They're…mad," Hoartrap gasped from behind her. When the Flintlander had crashed into him she'd done even more damage to his shriveled flesh but also torn the webbing around his face, tarry blood seeping down his busted nose and jutting chin as he coughed out the words, along with a cloud of pearlescent powder. "I warned you, Zosia, I did. Nobody listens."

"You said they could see inside my head!" Zosia countered. "I thought that meant they'd know I wasn't bluffing! That unless they called off their plot I'd send them back to the First Dark! That unless they agree to a truce we all die!"

"The oldest, sanest argument against war there is." Hoartrap laughed, ebon bubbles popping in his nostrils. "Pity the Vex Assembly are as crazy…as they are old. You think devils are afraid of the First Dark? You think you can cow them with the promise of going home? You should have listened to me…"

"I'm listening now," said Zosia, the light coming off the Gate growing brighter and brighter as she went to Hoartrap's side, the white-haired Flintland woman sprawled on the softening ground beside him limp and bloody. "You told me they were crazy, and you told me they could look inside my head, inside my heart. You *didn't* say anything about devils—just who are these loonies? You know more than you told me, as fucking usual."

He looked incredulously up at her, wiggled his hands through his webbing and nodded down at his restraints. He'd always had such big soft hands, but now they looked like mean little claws.

"Tell me, Hoartrap, or whatever comes next I leave you here," said Zosia. "I know you love your secrets, you old gossip, but if you don't spill them now you'll take them to your fucking grave!"

He pinched his lips and nodded back and forth as if seriously considering it, and she seriously considered slapping him silly when Choplicker put his paws up on the Touch's lap and growled in his face, finally rattling the truth out of him. "All right, all right. They're the High Priests of Jex Toth—are you happy?"

"Not even close," said Zosia, narrowing her eyes at the scheming old witch but pushing Choplicker back down. "Why'd you call them devils? What's this ritual they're so intent on they don't even care about me sending them back to the First Dark? Just how much do you know about all this shit, anyway?"

"Last question first," said Hoartrap, licking the thick black blood off his lips and frowning like a sommelier asked to give the notes of a bottle of rotgut. "I know *everything*, as usual. As for the ritual, it's the same one they tried pulling five centuries ago—they want to wake the Fallen Mother. I fear they'll find she's not quite what they expected, though she is *definitely* a mother, if you follow my—"

"Devils, Hoartrap, you called them devils," pressed Zosia, a hole in her boot flooding with warm ichor as the whole disgusting meat palace melted around them. "But they're also priests? Which is it?"

"It's the oldest question, isn't it?" said Hoartrap, squinting from the glare of the Gate. "We can bind devils into the flesh of certain animals, into scavengers, but what of the greatest jackal of them all? What of binding a devil into the flesh of a mortal? We had our suspicions, and they were borne out...for those with a strong enough will to master your devil, the rewards are boundless. Powers undreamt, life eternal, all so long as the one who binds the devil to your flesh doesn't set it free—all devils have their masters, after all."

"They...they called devils into *themselves*?" Zosia looked over her shoulder at the ancient figures gathered around the glowing Gate. No wonder they weren't concerned with her arrival—cocky and crazy they might be, but they also had her outdeviled, ten to one.

"Not quite," said Hoartrap. "As it turns out, trying to call a devil into yourself is a very bad idea, so they summoned them into each other. The first sacrificed the second, and the second sacked the third, and so on, forming a circle of devils...a chain, if you will, each priest bound to the next, right back around to the first of equals.

Keeps the Vex Assembly egalitarian, just the way an idealist like you would have things—no priest can ever free the devil they bound or otherwise turn against their fellows, for fear of having the devil inside them set loose in turn. They'll never admit it, of course, but I suspect their antipathy toward yours truly stems less from my actions and more from the fact that I'm my own agent. They're just *sick* with jealousy that I'm not shackled into their demonic circle jerk, and I can—"

"*Wait.*" Illumination made Zosia as lightheaded as if she were on top of the highest peak, or holding her breath at the bottom of the deepest gulf. Of course. Of course of course of course. "You're one of them!"

"Close, close…" Hoartrap leered at her in his bonds. "I was the first. An experiment. My master sat on the Vex Assembly, I but an acolyte to the exalted priests…he tried to sacrifice me, Zosia, to see if a devil could be bound in mortal flesh. I was, as you can imagine, quite the success. But when he went down into the First Dark to take his own devil he proved incapable of handling…the responsibility. He ate himself alive, and bid me help."

Zosia took a step back from the bound horror as he continued.

"The first devil I ever ate was that which dwelled inside my master, and in doing so, I inadvertently chanced into the ideal loophole. You've heard, I'm sure, that devils who aren't set free are condemned to haunt the graves of those who bound them? Lucky me, that I became his tomb!"

Zosia was the baddest of the bad, of that there could be no argument. She'd raised more hell than a dozen diabolists and seen sights that would make a debauched dominatrix blush, but this…this shook her. Hard. She'd always known there was something deeply, deeply wrong with Hoartrap, obviously, but this? Too much. Much, much too much. Choplicker was whining at her, wet nose snuffling her palm to bring her back to this time and place, ill-starred a moment as it surely was, but ultimately it was Hoartrap's familiar trash talk that snapped her out of her shock.

"Why, Zosia, you look like you've been goosed by a ghost!" said the emaciated shade of the hulking man she had known for close to thirty years...thirty years where everyone they'd known had aged but him. "After all you've seen me do, after all you've *asked* me to do, surely a little thing like the truth isn't enough to turn your stomach?"

"You're a devil," she said, barely hearing her own voice over the rising rhythm of an enormous heart that must pulse somewhere deep beneath her feet. "All this time I thought you were a man playing the devil, you've been a devil playing at being a man."

"I. Am. *Not.*" Even in his physically reduced state Hoartrap managed to swell with indignation, straining forward in his bonds as though he might bite her, if given the chance. "I told you, I was stronger than my master. Stronger than any of these lost lunatics. I am *not* like them. I am not like anyone or anything who came before, on either side of the First Dark. I am the Touch."

"Your body..." Zosia laughed softly to herself, ignoring Choplicker's increasing agitation. "That's why you look so different, so much smaller—because your size, your strength, it was never real. Flesh and blood are just another illusion to your kind."

"Flesh and blood are always an illusion, and I hate to break this to you, dearheart, but my kind is *your* kind," said Hoartrap. "And I'm still plenty strong, you'll see that once you cut me loose. It may take my colonies a good long time to grow back to my preferred stature after being so cruelly denuded by my captors, true, but you of all people should know it's what's on the inside that counts."

"Your *colonies?*" Choplicker barked at her, something wriggled against Zosia's ankle in the dissolving flesh cave, and she vigorously shook her head to center herself. "Never mind, never mind, I don't want to know. Edifying as it is to find out you're even older and nastier than you look, Hoartrap, we're running out of time and you haven't told me anything I can use. These Tothans, they're the High Priests of Jex Toth who let themselves be possessed by devils. Great. Gross. But if they're devils who aren't afraid of the First Dark, how come they were stuck out there for so long, and how come they came back?"

"The Chain brought them back, Zosia, at the Lark's Tongue—remember?" A dreamy look passed over his battered face, as though he were reminiscing on a formative sexual encounter or a cherished culinary experience. Maybe both. "As for how they got sent away in the first place, welllll...they were banished as the result of a brilliant strategy on the part of yours truly, with the help of Jex Toth's most hated enemies—Emeritus, back before that empire got forsook. It wasn't a permanent solution, obviously, but it certainly didn't make the Assembly very happy!"

"Why?" said Zosia. "*Why?*"

"Because hard as it is for you sniveling, scrabbling, scheming little scumbags to believe, *I'm* the good guy," said Hoartrap. "I caught wind the Vex Assembly were going to summon their Fallen Mother, and once she returned all the Star would be her sacrifice. I was born and raised in Jex Toth, true—one of the last living Tothans, if you want to split hairs or heirs—but that doesn't mean I'm some crazy cultist who—"

"No no no," said Zosia desperately, Choplicker whining at her heel as the light rising from the Gate behind them began to pulse. "Why did exile in the First Dark make them so unhappy? If they're devils that's just like going home, right? That's what you said!"

"It's *complicated*," said Hoartrap, pulling the obnoxious trick of sounding simultaneously exasperated and patronizing. "When a devil is bound to a lesser animal the flesh becomes its own, lock, stock, and barrel. But we higher creatures aren't so easily overwhelmed, and so there can be a power struggle when appetites don't align. The devils might have been just peachy spending eons in the First Dark, but their human hosts can't have found it to their liking! And of course, as much as devils love fear and hatred and pain and all those other juicy mortal tidbits, they probably didn't care for their bleak exile, either—pity the residents of Jex Toth, trapped in some other, darker realm, with a cadre of devil-possessed priests starving for sensation! Notice that none of the countless Tothan citizens seem to have made it back, only their rulers. So unless you want to find out firsthand what becomes of mortals trapped in hell with only hungry devils for company, I suggest you cut me loose already so I can get us out of here—this world is lost, but there are others, and I can take us there. But we have to leave while there's still time."

"No," said Zosia wearily, feeling all of her many years. She drew the knife she had taken from the Office of Answers. "I'm cutting you free, Hoartrap, because you may be some prehistoric cannibal devil straight from my worst nightmares, but you're also my friend. What you do after is your own business, but I'm not running away with you. I'm not running ever again. I'll give these devils one last chance, and if they don't take it I'll free my own. One way or another, this is the end."

"You're damn right about that," said Hoartrap as Zosia began sawing through the tacky webbing that tied him to the disgusting flesh throne. "If it's any consolation, I almost admire your refusal to concede the moral high ground even in the face of the apocalypse. Almost."

Zosia was still trying to come up with a snappy comeback when Hoartrap's eyes bugged out of his skull at something just behind her and Choplicker's bark of alarm was terminated as abruptly as it began. Some unseen force crashed into Zosia's side, hitting her so hard she was carried off her feet and flew halfway across the raised throne room before splashing down in the disgusting froth of the disintegrating realm. She sloshed upright, all set to free Choplicker and bury Jex Toth at the expense of Diadem when she saw that plan might be a little harder to implement now than it had been a minute before.

The ten Tothan witch-priests still conducted their ritual over the pulsing yellow light of the Gate, but while she'd been trying to free Hoartrap two more of their number had materialized in the throne room. One of them was a lithe crone dressed in shimmering spiders who held Choplicker crushed to her breast, her facsimile of human-ity ending at the distended jaw that had unhinged to accommodate Zosia's devil. The woman staggered in place, poor Chop's entire head somehow disappearing into her drooling mouth, his kicking nails gouging black lines in her throat and belly as her spiders swarmed his furry coat.

So that was bad. But the second priest was even worse. Not because his cadaverous form bristled with spitting cockroaches, nor because the ephemeral, ringed fingers he stretched out toward Zosia gave off a crackling sound like butter burning in a too-hot pan. No, what made this priest even more terrible than the first was simply that he had the drop on her here in the melting throne room of Jex Toth, and she could see the power of the devil protecting him reflected in the deep black depths of his eyes, while hers was halfway down the gullet of his colleague.

Zosia didn't have a fucking chance.

But she did have a big fucking hammer.

There were worse ways to ring in the end of days.

CHAPTER
29

There had been times in Maroto's life where he hadn't much cared if he lived or died, and if anything leaned more toward the latter. This was not one of those times. He didn't just want to live, he *needed* to live, and not just so he and Choi could have something more than the desperate, delicious hump they'd shared in an empty cell they'd found off one of the wall's stairways, blasts echoing in from outside.

Well, okay, so maybe making more time with Choi was the long and the short of Maroto's newfound purpose, but there were worse things to live for than a fit partner who was just as keen as yourself to blow off the big battle for the fate of the world to get rutty in a closet. You might've thought he'd have trouble performing, what with the brutal trauma to his face and all the bugs and drugs coursing through his crazed body, but ultimately those little distractions just helped him stave off a premature nut. It wasn't just good sex, either, it was mystical-like, because the whole time he kept flashing onto all those half-remembered dreams he'd had, the ones he was now dead certain she'd experienced, too. The proof being she knew his body as well as he knew hers; you don't just know the best way to work a wildborn's forked clit by accident, nor the surest means of driving a jaded old barbarian to distraction.

Afterward he told her it was *deja screw*, which she didn't find very clever at all, even after he explained it was a play on a Serpentine expression. As they were fitting their armor back into place she explained the mechanics behind their long-distance courtship, far more bashful about having meditated so hard their dreams somehow joined than she had been about doing that thing he really liked with her horn. What an experience it was, to share this bond with her. If only everyone could get inside each other's heads the Star would be a happier place, as happy as Maroto and Choi...and before he knew it he was back inside somewhere further south, pushing her up against the wall. She had been going real easy on him before, that much quickly became obvious, and when he reeled into his second occasion he felt a great joyous blossom unfurling in his brain...and it wasn't just the egg, either, that was starting to fade, the pain in his face returning even as he shivered out the last of his lust.

"I..." Maroto closed his eye, still inside her. "I really like you, Choi."

"I like you, too," she whispered, her husky voice firming him back up even though there was definitely no time for another round—there really hadn't been time for the first two.

"I mean, I *really* like you," he went on, because with armageddon rattling the walls this was probably his last chance to get something right. "I mean, I might even...do you think you might, too? You know..."

"Maroto," she groaned, moving against him and laying her cool horn against his hot forehead. "Maroto...I do not actually know you very well. And you do not actually know me very well. Not yet. But what I know...I like."

"Yeah?" That right there was better than any fantasy he'd ever harbored, any dream he'd ever clung to, any imagined love he'd ever cherished in his breast, clinging to it in spite of all evidence to the contrary: her beautiful, simple, and ultimately hopeful truth. *Not yet*, she said. Not Yet.

The best part was they wouldn't live long enough for her to figure out what a total fucking catastrophe he was. Romantic advantage: Maroto.

As they rushed back outside onto the battlement and ran south atop the central wall to meet Singh and her dragoons at the southern docks, Choi kept exchanging little mischievous looks with Maroto.

They probably shouldn't have postponed their retreat for a quick-and-dirty rendezvous, but she'd raised the brilliant point that they both might die in the attempt anyway so they might as well make the most of a bad morning. Flush with the afterglow of amazing sex, Maroto felt as good as he could remember, even as the whole bloody western half of the city burned beside them, casting shadows on their fleeing flanks... but then the distant clamor of fighting reached them, and he started feeling like he might throw up again. The old devil that forever haunted him was screaming in his formerly deaf ear that Choi was about to die in front of him, that there was no fucking way an honorable warrior like her would ever back down from a fight. Those industrious damn Tothans seemed to have brought down a section of the wall just ahead, and that meant he was about to see her come apart in bloody pieces... assuming he could even keep up. Why, any moment an arrow or burning bit of debris would come flying in and—

Maroto told that cowardly voice in his mind to stuff it, and somehow this time it listened. He could keep up with her. He would keep up with her. And if she fell, well, it would only be after he went down defending her, and he'd have a horn waiting for her in Old Black's Meadhall whenever she rolled in. Maybe even the one she'd lost part of back when they'd taken on that horned wolf together.

It wasn't that Choi was the love of his life, because really now, how was that for a concept to fuck you all up however the romance panned out. It wasn't even that now that they'd found each other in the flesh he wanted to see where it all went, though he did, he did. What it all came down to was that she was his friend, a good fucking friend, who'd come looking for him when all others had forsaken him, if only in her dreams, and if he had to die he would die defending her the way he hadn't been able to protect Purna, whom he now knew to be dead. He couldn't bring himself to ask Choi to confirm it, but if the feisty little tapai had still been alive she would've been five times as quick as the wildborn to harass Maroto upon his return to the Cobalt fold, and so it was really time to let her go... or join her in the underworld, as the case may be.

They came to the end of the rampart, a hundred-foot section of the central wall collapsed just ahead of them. The sounds of combat drifted up along with the smoke, and looking down they saw a few Immaculate stalwarts still fighting the invading Tothans at the foot of the rubble. With the flames behind the monstrous army it looked like hell itself, and without the slightest hesitation Choi began climbing down the ruined wall to help the last beleaguered defenders of the breach. He was so fucking proud of her, and followed her down in hopes he'd give her something to be proud of, too.

As they dropped down onto the mountainous wreckage of the collapsed wall he saw that they had been too late to help the Immaculate soldiers, the last of them eaten alive by monsters at the base of the ruins. Bad luck for them, and baddest luck for Maroto—the Tothan venom must have finally started stewing his brains, because before his very eye the flames of West Othean went dark, the burning buildings sinking beneath the earth even as their sparks danced upward like swarms of lightning bugs. More disturbing than this obvious hallucination was the very real pack of tall grey horse demons that were nimbly climbing up the ruins of the wall toward him and Choi. Beyond the Tothan horrors the city continued to be engulfed in the smoky blackness that spread across the land, all of West Othean caving in on itself, even its high-flying embers now drawn downward in blazing tornados…

"These horses, their legs are as tusks, and their mouths are worse," said Choi, pointing her long saber at the demons that had spotted them and begun climbing faster.

"Me and Fennec took one out on the other side of the city," he told her, admiring her new sword—looked to be Cocksparian or he was no judge of steel. "And these things are about as close to horses as horned wolves are to goats."

"Whatever we call them, they are as goats before horned wolves," she said, giving him a peck on the lips. "I slew three that attempted to scale the wall just before you arrived, and alone. Between us six should be no significant challenge. We must be swift, however, to flee the hungry mouth that consumes the city."

"Wait, you can see that, too?" he asked, but his question was lost as the nearest demon reared up on its hind legs, its pointed hooves punching the air as its scary sideways mouth split its face down the middle. So many teeth. Hefting his spear, Maroto gave Choi a thumbs-up.

It was kind of like their first date. And while he wasn't a religious barbarian, his need was great, and he offered a prayer to Old Black that it wouldn't be their last.

———

The blasts were shaking the wall beneath their feet as Ji-hyeon scrambled up the final flight of stairs and burst out onto the ramparts. The guards who should have been minding the door were all staring slack-jawed out at the western city, and she couldn't much blame them. Sullen came panting out of the doorway after her, so hot on her heels he almost bumped her over as his eyes were snared by the same hypnotic sight. Terraced roofs and stone pagodas detonated outward, humble stalls and towering warehouses collapsed in on themselves, the greatest city on the Star heaving with explosions, erupting in flames. Inhuman screams echoed inland from the tempestuous sea of fire West Othean had become, but whether it came from Tothan throats or the blistering bones of the city itself none could say.

The heat was already unlike anything she'd ever felt, and Sullen pulled her back, holding her to his sweaty chest as the red snow of cinders began to fall on the ramparts. It wasn't the acrid fumes that flooded her uncovered eye with tears as she watched the capital burn, and she was just about to beg him to flee this place with her, to find their friends and run as fast and as far as they could from this nightmare, when the change that took over his face froze the words on her tongue. He was still looking out at the inferno, but instead of seeing the flames reflected in his leonine eyes she saw only darkness. A chill swam up her sweaty skin as Sullen's shiny black eyes stared past her, and turning back to the west she saw something even worse than half of Othean in flames—she saw that the First Dark she had fought so hard to escape had followed her home.

The forsaken city was still there, but not for long. And the flames still rose from the sinking buildings, but they had turned as black as pitch, casting cold instead of warmth. Even the smoke was drawn down, a black ground fog that couldn't conceal the hungriness beneath it for long. A temple bell cracked loose from its principal post, tolling as it fell, and then going as silent as the rest of West Othean as it vanished into the smoke. Ji-hyeon had to look, had to make sure they weren't about to be pulled in as well, and peering over the side of the rampart she saw that the greasy darkness came right up to the edge of the wall but went no further. Small comfort, that, as she gazed out and saw the distant silhouette of the Autumn Palace slumping down along with the rest of the far wall. She couldn't look away, even when her devil flapped in her face, then landed on her shoulder.

The First Dark had opened underneath West Othean, stretching as far as her mortal eye could see, and while its presence seemed to have put some of the color back in Fellwing's coat, that hardly put Ji-hyeon at ease. She found Sullen's hand with her own, the stumps of her fingers burning against his clammy digits, and together they watched the ancient capital of the Isles twist and warp and cave in on itself as it was pulled down into a Gate the likes of which the Star had never known.

It might have taken all day, or it might have taken minutes. The blizzard of black embers swirling through the air left unctuous smears on everything they touched, freezing flesh and warping metal. Ji-hyeon's devil-eye ached behind its blindfold, punishing her for not letting it watch, but the thought of freeing it now filled her with unspeakable foreboding. The last buildings disappeared into the bottomless, lightless sea that now yawned from here to the remote ring of Othean's outer wall, and no sooner had the final weathervane sunk than the crowds of defenders on the ramparts exhaled as one, more than a few laughing with a nervousness that bordered on the unhinged.

"Those Dreaming Priests who serve the empress, this is their idea of a trap?" Sullen gulped. "They would do this to their own city?"

"I...I don't know," said Ji-hyeon, staring aghast over the vast expanse—even in all her journeys through unbelievable landscapes she had never glimpsed such an enormous Gate. "Even to stop the Tothans, I can't believe they—"

A golden band split open across the center of the Gate, stretching from the base of their wall clear across to the far side, miles long and a hundred meters wide, then two hundred meters, then three, expanding outward in both directions, gold and bright and luminous, there in the First Dark. Except it wasn't quite gold…it was whiter than that. It was the color of the stars on a winter night, and felt just as cold, just as remote.

It flooded Ji-hyeon with a primordial dread, to see that widening path of pale gold through the First Dark—it went against all the laws of nature, for a Gate to be anything but blackest black…And yet it captivated her, drawing her forward to the edge of the rampart, and then stepping up on the edge of the wall, something so entrancingly familiar about the vision, something that made her want to drop down and walk this luminous road, to see where it led with her naked devil-eye, and reaching up to remove her eye patch, she stepped forward to—

Sullen snatched her back from the precipice, wailing, "*Don't look! Don't look…*"

But it was too late, because even with her blindfold still in place, she saw…and *it* saw *her*, the Gate swelling higher and higher, bulging outward, the golden acres of its pupil contracting in the vast blackness of an iris the size of a city. Ji-hyeon screamed, and felt all of the Star screaming with her, a wordless requiem for mortalkind.

CHAPTER
30

Zosia wasn't one to brag of her skill in combat—that she'd made it to her advanced age in spite of waging countless battles, against incredible odds, well, her record spoke for itself. The most important lesson you learn from steel, though, is that it doesn't matter how many fights you win, however glorious your victories. The only fight that counts is the one you lose.

So far, this one was shaping up to be a doozy.

The cockroach-clad ghoul she faced in the liquefying bowels of Jex Toth was faster than fast and meaner than mean—faster than Zosia, in other words, and meaner to boot. She couldn't even catch her breath, let alone her adversary, her hips aching as she splashed backward through the slurry of offal that flooded the organic throne room, batting away his grasping hand with the square hammer she'd inherited from Sister Portolés. Something she'd learned from rolling with Hoartrap was that you never, ever wanted to let a warlock touch you, but from the first time she evaded this Tothan's grasp she knew it wasn't a matter of *if*, it was a matter of *when*. She had never fought an opponent as swift or as relentless, and with each evasion and ineffective counterstrike she could feel the fatigue spreading through her limbs. That vigor she always felt when brawling in Choplicker's presence had deserted her, but she knew better than to look away from her opponent to see if the other Tothan had actually eaten her devil entirely or if they were still struggling. To turn her attention from this fiend for but a moment would be her end.

The only reason she was still alive was that it really, really didn't want to touch her sainted steel hammer, its apparently boneless limbs going through obscene contortions to avoid brushing the black steel weapon. This monster was the greatest foe she had ever faced, but between its commitment to striking her head with its spectrally translucent left hand and aversion to her hammer, their dance persisted far longer than she'd expected, the two of them sloshing around the foul bowl of stew the throne room had become.

It grabbed at her face again but instead of dodging she flung herself forward, hammer aimed at its shriveled nose, and next thing she knew it was a dozen feet back, perched on an empty throne one over from Hoartrap. She didn't have enough time to get her balance back before it flew forward again, but she did have the time to notice her knife floating above Hoartrap's lap, the blade slowly but surely hacking through his sticky bonds even with no hand to physically wield it. *Get it, Hoartrap!*

His escape attempt wasn't much of a distraction. Hardly a distraction at all, really. But it was enough to cost Zosia everything. Devildamn Hoartrap to hell.

Zosia belatedly brought her hammer around to meet the charging priest when its ghostly left hand struck her temple and sank into her skull. Five icy digits stabbed through her brain, the jagged bone rings at its knuckles digging into her scalp. The presumably mortal wound struck, she was it and it was she, their souls as enmeshed as their flesh.

Leib singing to her in the darkness of the aspens, the coals of their campfire illuminating only their discarded boots and a forgotten turnip.

An obscene canticle echoing through the lightless reaches far below the world, a profane orgy taking place among the roots of the tree that had almost reached the heavens before being pruned back by meddling hands.

Pao Cowherd's final wheezing breath in the star-kissed mountains above Kypck.

The final sigh of a thwarted goddess, and her first gasp at a second chance.

Indsorith gasping against Zosia's fingers, begging for release.

Zosia gasping against Maroto in his disturbingly similar fantasies, grinding his skull into these questing fingers.

The cold misery of a friendless widow trying to stoke the embers of hatred in an icy cave.

The blazing furnace of desire propelling She Who Comes up out of the First Dark.

She Who Comes? Better to worry about She Who's Already Here. Maybe this thought-transference crap worked on kids who hadn't spent every ugly day of their ugly lives scowling into the looking glass, but for Zosia it wasn't even a diversion. It was an opportunity. While the Tothan creep was rooting through the panty drawer of her soul, Zosia gritted her teeth and hoisted the hammer that had almost slipped from her grasp at the shock of a psychic invasion.

There's a world of difference between *almost* and *had*.

Like, for example, Zosia *almost* brained the fucking monster with her hammer, but one problem with having your thoughts connected to another is that they see your attack coming even as you launch it. The fiend slipped its ghostly hand out of her skull, slipped just out of range of her swing, and bad as that was the worst was how much she missed it as soon as its fingers fell free of her mind. She fucking *sobbed* at its absence—how was that for fucked up?

"*Do not despair, dearest Zosia,*" it said, its voice as light and warm as its eyes were black and cold. "*Now that I know your wishes I shall grant them.*"

The possessed priest came even faster and sharper the second time, or maybe Zosia was just slow and sloppy, because she didn't have a fucking prayer…but then when was the last time Zosia had taken a knee to old gods or new? Knowing she had no chance she swung her hammer all the same, because that was what heroes did, and it tapped the back of her hand, snapping bones and sending the weapon skipping across the murky surface of its melting lair. Before the pain even registered it tackled her into the warm mire, but she must have landed on some hummock because even lying flat on her back the slushy filth barely reached her ears, not nearly deep enough to cover her mouth. Some blessing, that.

"*Welcome home, Crimson Queen.*" It leered down at her, close enough to kiss but refusing to finish her off, the oily reek of the cockroaches swarming its emaciated flesh almost as bad as its breath. "*You have such sights to show us, don't you, Cold Cobalt? Your crimes are legendary even in hell.*"

"Come a little closer and I'll show you," said Zosia, hoping to punish it for postponing the inevitable by biting off its withered lips. Its smile widened, those burning-cold fingers brushing her brow, and she wondered if it sensed her intentions even now. Before she could make good on her final defiance or it could talk more shit, however, an ivory blur flew in from the side...and then bounced over them, the big cocoon splashing down a short ways off in the pooled gore.

The wizened priest sat back up on its haunches and waggled the more material fingers of its right hand, and just as Hoartrap charged into Zosia's periphery he was sent flying backward. The Touch crashed through the back of the web-strewn throne where he'd been kept prisoner, the living seat snapping with a wet crack and erupting in a fountain of green slime.

Hoartrap hadn't left. He'd cut himself free but he hadn't left. He hadn't been able to save her, true, but he hadn't escaped when he'd had the chance, instead using his sorcery to hurl the heaviest thing he could find at this monster dressed in human skin and a suit of foul black bugs. And that was what made Zosia's eyes fill with tears even as the fiend squatted back over her, even as her unbroken fist futilely battered its grinning face, even as the corporeal fingers of its right hand closed on her neck and the phantasmal fingers of its left resumed toying with her brain. The shifting sleeve of spitting cockroaches scuttled down the arm that held her throat, swarming up her neck and all over her face to form a stinking mask that prodded at her closed lips and eyes, squirming inside her nose and ears.

Zosia tried to shut off her thoughts, to deny it any satisfaction as it kept cutting off her air only to mercilessly let her breathe again, filthy insects crawling into her mouth as she gasped and gagged. She chomped the intruders before they could crawl down her throat, vomiting from the caustic taste, vomiting again as she felt one wriggle under her tongue to hide from her gnashing teeth.

Even in calmer settings meditation had never been her forte, alas, and since thinking of nothing wasn't an option she settled for the next best thing and tried conjuring up all the nonsense songs Maroto used to constantly sing under his breath back when they first met, before he mellowed out with the aid of drink and smoke and the occasional bug; the ceaseless gibberish of a perpetually anxious mind. Even as her every fiber shuddered in revulsion at her torment and her mind twitched at its curious fingers she tried to shut it all down. It would draw neither sorrow nor joy from her memories, no bliss nor heart-break nor even hatred, richly as that last was deserved—this fucker would get only bland nonsense, and it could choke on it the way it choked her on its swarm of cockroaches.

Meanwhile, her left hand had stopped punching her attacker and dumbly groped in the pipe pouch on her belt for something else to choke this devil with, but after giving her appendage the order she focused as hard as she could on anything and everything else. It was like keeping your orgasm at bay even as you kept rhythm atop your obstinate husband, trusting your body to do its fucking job even as your mind studiously avoided acknowledging whatever was happening down there. Stuff and nonsense, Zosia, stuff and nonsense, the broken right hand not knowing what the clever left was up to...

"Brap brap!"

More nonsense, obviously, but as Maroto-ish an exclamation as it was, it came from neither Zosia nor the ancient Tothan who invaded her brain. The bony hand released her throat and the cold fingers slid out from her skull. Batting the insects away from her eyes with her aching right arm, she saw the demoniac looking up, as confused as she was, its fingers beginning to wiggle in some pattern...but before it could complete its spell there was a small bang.

The lower half of its face exploded, fragments of tooth and bone spattering Zosia's face and sending the remaining roaches fleeing into her hair as its chin disappeared in a grisly cloud of red mist. Hard as Zosia had been trying *not* to think about how nice a distraction would be, and what she would do with one if it came along, it took her a moment to act. She hoped that brief hesitation didn't cost Tapai Purna her life, the webbing-draped girl yipping as the mutilated witch-priest levitated her high above them with its convulsing fingers.

Since she had no way of knowing if it was too late for Purna, Zosia had to make sure the girl's sacrifice wouldn't be in vain. Her fingers closed on the tiny lump wedged beside the pipe in her pouch, and still trying as hard as humanly possible not to think abut what she was doing, Zosia sat up and jammed the relic into the bloody wreckage of the Tothan's mouth, feeling for its exposed gullet. It was the strangest thing, because even as she was pressing her cargo past the frayed meat of its tongue she could feel its flesh re-forming around her hand, could see the shards of broken molars prancing back through the air to put themselves back together.

It was all so soft and wet and difficult to see, cold sludgy blood pumping everywhere, that Zosia really had to focus on what she was doing. As soon as she did the demoniac forgot about Purna, letting her drop out of the air as it seized Zosia's wrist and yanked it away from its vulnerable face. The previously docile cockroaches nesting in Zosia's hair began spitting their burning secretions and biting her scalp, and while none had been small enough to penetrate her ear one of the fuckers must've gotten into her nose, the pain as it spat up in her sinuses beyond description.

"*Unwise—*" Its infernal voice lilted out of the jawless ruins of its face, but as soon as it spoke it reflexively gulped on the lump in its throat, and Zosia grinned as wide as a well-fed devil despite her disgust and her agony, even as she knew it was about to break her wrist, and then break everything else…

Except it didn't. The Tothan didn't do anything at all, save make a faint sizzling noise, and then milky orange foam started to bubble out of the ugly red hole where its mouth had been. Maybe the cake the Chainites had hid their payload inside had delayed the response, or maybe Choplicker had been savoring the morsel before swallowing it, but whatever the cause the ensorcelled bone shard they had used to knock out her devil back in Diadem had had an even faster effect on this evil fucker. Shoving its stiff bulk off her, Zosia heaved herself up to her knees in the steaming pool and went absolutely berserk tearing the insects out of her hair, pinching one nostril shut and ejecting a small roach on a bloody snot rocket. Without their patron to control them they'd stopped biting and burning her, but that really wasn't enough of an endorsement to let them stay.

"Fugggg!" Zosia puked again as she felt one she'd missed crawl along the roof of her mouth, but at least that washed out the last of the trespassers. Shuddering on her knees in the warm bath of greasy meat juice, the inside of her nose and most of her scalp on fire with bug venom and her right hand broken and limp, Zosia looked at her prone attacker bobbing facedown in the muck beside her. For a horrible moment she thought he'd begun to move again, but then she realized it was just his suit of roaches squirming all over one another—they'd all migrated onto his back to avoid drowning. Just the same, she had to assume he was only incapacitated for the time being and could bounce back, just as Choplicker had, as soon as one of his buddies pulled the bewitched bone from his gob.

"Fuck," she said again, looking around the too-bright throne room to see if there was anyone left to help her do a better job of disposing of this crippled devil than the Chain had managed with Choplicker...

Choplicker! Wiping bugshit and ichor from her face, she spied the priestess who'd been eating her devil alive last time she'd looked. At first Zosia thought it was some trick of the pulsing yellow light radiating up from the Gate, but no. Her already furious stomach did another debilitating twist as she saw the spider-covered woman sprawled out in one of the thrones, her previously skeletal figure now looking like she was overdue with octuplets. Ropes of drool and clumps of dog fur stuck to her chin and chest, and as if sensing Zosia's gaze she looked over and met her eyes, smiling with satisfaction and patting her obscenely bloated gut. Then she clambered to her feet, smacking her lips as she gave Zosia a look that made her think the demoniac must be contemplating a mortal dessert after her devilish feast. The egg sacs set in her gown of spidersilk sparkled like diamonds, her tiara of interlocked arachnids as regal as the Carnelian Crown as she slowly approached Zosia with stately grace...only to break into a swift waddle as other figures began moving through the flashing brightness of the dissolving throne room.

"Zosia!" The voice sounded familiar but she didn't recognize the white-haired, one-armed Immaculate who tossed her the black hammer he'd pulled out of the bloody muck. She knew better than to try to catch it, especially with one broken hand, but as soon as it splashed in the froth beside her she rooted around and seized the haft. She was too slow, though, the devil-fattened priestess almost on top of her, and—

"Brap brap!" Purna cried again from the other side of Zosia, her pistol punching a hole the size of a fist in the charging Tothan's pendulous gut. The grotesque woman lurched to one side but didn't falter, her taloned fingers stretching for Zosia as her jaw yawned wider and wider, elongating to impossible proportions. She obviously intended to do for the master what she had done for the devil.

Zosia raised back her hammer but even as she did another corpselike figure exploded out of the shallow slime behind the voracious demoniac, and just a little farther back from the main event more reinforcements were rushing forward to join the fray. Long before those black-plated soldiers could reach them, though, the priestess pounced at Zosia, Zosia swung on the priestess, and the skeletal creeper who'd burst from the nauseating flood made a move of his own. He was indeed a reinforcement, just not for the side Zosia had assumed—Hoartrap grabbed the spider-gowned witch from behind, slowing her momentum even as they both slipped forward, and before the Tothan could recover from the sneak attack Zosia hit her dead in the jaw.

Considering how carefully the first priest had avoided her hammer Zosia had hoped for something miraculous to happen when sainted steel met devilish flesh—a crackle of lightning or a blast of divine flames, preferably, but she would've settled for a modest explosion of detonated meat. Instead the only fireworks were what she felt in her arm, painful wobbles arcing down her elbow as if she'd bashed an iron beam, the hammer bouncing back and almost clocking her in the eye. The blow did send both the priestess and Hoartrap skidding backward a few feet in the slimy stew, and as Zosia recovered her wits enough to take a second swing she saw that the attack hadn't been a complete bust—the bloated witch's distended jaw had torn nearly free of her face, but instead of blood countless ivory spiders and streams of smoke poured out of the hideous wound.

Hoartrap released the woman, squealing and slapping at his stick-thin arms as the arachnids swarmed him. Zosia came at the wounded Tothan with everything she had, but without Hoartrap to throw her off her game the priestess was even swifter than her roach-covered colleague. Zosia swung, and Zosia missed, and before she could parry or dodge or swing again the horrible monster that had eaten her devil grabbed Zosia by both wrists and hoisted her off her feet.

Zosia clung to her hammer even as the fiend held her aloft, and kicked the fucker so hard in the distended stomach she broke her toe. Eyes watering and her broken hand going from pretty-fucking-pained to completely-fucking-excruciating as she dangled by her wrists, Zosia glared down at her captor and saw that the deformed jaw she had nearly torn off was beginning to inch its way back into place, the wisps of smoke thinning to nothing. Spiders knit the impossibly wide mouth back together with silk in place of stitches, and from the delighted look on the horror's almost human face Zosia supposed she was in the real shit now. It was obviously too much to hope for a quick death from these devils, otherwise her neck would already be as splintered as her hand.

"Jack move!"

Purna and the one-armed Immaculate came in on either side, both hacking the priestess's stomach with short blades. On a human target it would've been a quick and brutal disembowelment, but on this ancient devil hidden in mortal skin it provided but a momentary distraction. It didn't even drop both of Zosia's wrists, keeping a tight grip on her hammer hand and letting her useless right arm drop free as it slapped aside Purna and then Keun-ju—it was definitely him, after traveling halfway around the Star with the boy Zosia would recognize that yelp anywhere as he went tumbling through the rancid shallows. The lesser mortals out of the way, the priestess looked back up at Zosia with malevolent delight, its monstrous repaired jaw flexing and then widening to take its first bite, and—

A howl split the humid air, and to any other mortal on all the Star such a razor-keen wail would surely chill the blood…but it warmed Zosia's cockles, her roach-stung face splitting in an unholy grin as Choplicker's muzzle wriggled the rest of the way out of the rent in the priestess's heavy stomach. The demoniac sank the talons of her free hand into the side of his drool-slick head, but before she could drop Zosia and add her other limb to the struggle he nosed forward, three feet of eely neck rushing up out of the fleshy prison of her gut and sinking his fangs into her throat. Bones crunched, and Zosia fell.

The sounds, oh, the beautiful sounds! It was like the symphony Kang-ho had dragged them all to that night in Melechesh, a hundred discordant instruments somehow creating an atmosphere of pure emotion in the darkened hall. And what emotion it was. By the time Zosia had splashed out of the runny mire and wiped the warm slime from her eyes the performance was complete, but that lovely sonata echoed in her ears even as she saw the hollowed-out spider-priestess scuttle away over the lip of the throne room. Choplicker helped his mistress get the rest of the gore off her face with his scratchy tongue, and in that instant all was forgiven, Zosia clinging to his tacky coat and shivering with relief that he had survived an ordeal the likes of which she wouldn't wish on even him.

"Woo!" Purna splashed over to them from one direction, Keun-ju from the other. Now that she had time to really pay attention, Zosia noticed that the Ugrakari's hair had gone as white as the Immaculate's, as white as the fur of the familiar lapdog she carried under one arm. It yapped at Choplicker, Chop barked back, wagging his tail, and Zosia wondered just what in the unholy fucking of the false gods was going on around here—she'd seen that little devil boil away to nothing to save Purna after the Battle of the Lark's Tongue, yet here it was in the flesh. "Don't worry, Zosia—I saw where it went!"

"What?" That about covered it, she figured.

"That living fucking god we just triple-teamed!" Purna made it sound like the most obvious thing in the world, her devilish tongue making sloppy noises as she tried to talk and pant at the same time. "We've got that punk running scared now, no doubt."

"Perhaps *some* doubts," said Keun-ju, looking about as rough as Zosia felt. "We may have more important matters to attend to at the moment. Now that we're all free and Zosia and Hoartrap are... are..."

Keun-ju faltered, staring behind Zosia, and bracing herself for the worst she turned to see what fresh hell was bearing down on them. It wasn't what she expected, though, the spiny armored infantry that had seemed poised to attack when she faced the spider-priestess now holding back on the edge of the throne room. No, what Keun-ju was staring agape at was decidedly horrible, yes, but it was the kind of horrible Zosia could roll with, after the kind of day she'd had.

What had captured the boy's attention was good old Hoartrap, and the Tothan that Zosia had paralyzed with that enchanted bone. The Touch was crouched in the warm slush, eating the prone priest alive. He'd already put away most of one arm, his gaunt cheeks painted red with gore, his eyes blazing mirrors that reflected the yellow glare pulsing from the Gate at the far side of the throne room.

"What?" he said, dripping blood from his shiny mouth. "It's the only way to make sure it's really dead."

"Fuck," said Zosia, rubbing her roach-stung temples. "Just make sure you chew, okay? That other witch found out the hard way what comes of wolfing down your food while it's still wriggling."

"You've *got* to try this." Hoartrap held up something black and wet. "Bring it in, friends—you've all earned a place at the table."

"Oh shit, where's Best?" asked Purna, looking around.

"Out cold, but I propped her up on one of the thrones," said Keun-ju.

"I broke the circle," Zosia said to herself, not having any idea what the others were on about and not much caring—now that this small fight was over the immediacy and magnitude of their dilemma returned to her. Louder, now, she said, "Hoartrap, if that fucker's really dead, I broke their circle of devils! Is there some clever way to make the rest of them topple, like blocks in a row?"

"Wouldn't that be nice!" said Hoartrap, which wasn't exactly the answer she'd hoped for. "All you did was make one of the Vex Assembly infinitely more powerful—now that you've taken out the lucky sod's master it's no longer accountable to its cohort and can act with impunity. That *might* make it more inclined to listen to reason, but I wouldn't stake your life on it, let alone mine."

"We can kill them," said Purna, sounding in awe of her own potential. "We killed one—we can kill them all!"

"I wouldn't count on that, either," said Hoartrap, shaking his head and sucking a finger clean. "The five of us, two devils, and the element of surprise, and we barely managed to murder one of them. And I'm still not sure how we even pulled that off! No, no, friends, the only reason we're not all inside out right now is that the rest of the Assembly is holding their Gate of Gates open. As soon as their ritual is over we're as screwed as the rest of the Star, unless we do the sensible thing and nip off into the outer realms before they finish. We're lucky to be alive, and I've never been one to push my good fortune any farther than I can throw a mummified Moocher."

"The ritual..." Zosia swayed on her feet in the slime, squinting at the dazzling glare of the flashing Gate and the ten silhouettes gathered around and atop it. *Lucky to be alive*, Hoartrap said, but luck wasn't everything, was it? Either one of those demoniac priests could have killed Zosia, yet despite having her in their grasp they'd prolonged her suffering. She'd assumed it was just because they were devilish assholes, but now another possibility was niggling at the back of her violated mind...

Then there was the timing of their attack, the Vex Assembly content to ignore her presence entirely until she began to release Hoartrap...

No. It wasn't her freeing Hoartrap that had riled them, but the fact that immediately afterward she had planned to give the Vex Assembly one last chance to stop their ritual before loosing Choplicker to sacrifice Diadem.

Motherlicking mind-reading devils. They hadn't killed her because they weren't *trying* to kill her—because they knew if she died Choplicker would sacrifice Diadem, banishing them back to the First Dark. No, these fuckers were just trying to *stall* her, to keep her busy until their ritual was complete and it was too late to do anything. They hadn't rejected her initial offer because they were unafraid of being exiled a second time, it was that after taking one glance at Zosia these psychic monsters knew she wasn't ready to follow through on her threats. That she wouldn't sacrifice Diadem until she'd begged these devils a dozen times over, giving them chance after chance after chance, because as long as she drew breath she wanted to find another way, a better way.

Well, hell. Now that she knew there *wasn't* a better way, it was time to burn Diadem to the fucking ground and save the Star...assuming there was still time. It couldn't happen to a nicer city. Drawing herself up to her full height as the yellow pulses of the Gate slowed and softened to a constant golden glow, she gave Choplicker a farewell scratch behind the ears and braced herself to make both their wishes come true.

CHAPTER
31

The warrior queen stood proud upon the ramparts, watching the burning world vanish into chaos and ruin. Beside her Nemi of the Bitter Sighs cracked her final egg, but Indsorith only had eyes for the all-seeing orb that filled the void where West Othean had fallen. Would that Sister Portolés had lived to see this, what would that poor conflicted wretch have made of this miracle? It was a funny thing to flit through her fraying mind, but there it went and Indsorith almost laughed as she felt her heart flood with an unspeakable emotion. After all that, Y'Homa had actually been right. The Fallen Mother was real, she loved her children, and now she had returned.

Indsorith stepped forward to join her, when she felt her whole being submerged in a bath of sulfurous ice water.

"Resist the devil, and stay yourself to the very end."

She didn't know where the words came from but she spoke them in tandem with Nemi, and as the final syllable left Indsorith's lips the two women leaned into each other, both exhausted by whatever had passed between them. All around them soldiers were clawing their eyes out or diving over the side of the wall or both, and Indsorith felt that familiar mixture of melancholy and relief at being above and apart from the delusions of the faithful. Instead of staring down into the maddening scope of the golden eye Indsorith looked up into the heavens, and saw that even the rain clouds had been sucked down into that titanic rift in the First Dark.

The pressure in the air swelled around them, and Nemi cried out, but Indsorith kept her eyes fixed on the cobalt sky until the very end.

———

Choi tightened her headlock around Maroto's neck but she couldn't cut off his howls, and he raged against her, desperate to fling himself out over the corpses of the demons they'd killed, down the mountain of rubble. She must think he'd gone as crazy as the soldiers who were leaping into the Gate from the intact sections of the wall to the north and south, but Maroto could tell from their euphoric laughter that the poor broken souls wished to welcome their conqueror, their god. Maroto had other motivations. He recognized a devil when he saw one, and while this titan of the First Dark might be just a little too big to skin, he could damn sure give it the old Cobalt try.

Maroto might not be the sharpest mace on the rack, as Kang-ho used to joke, but he'd finally figured out what had happened here, and the combination of heinous enlightenment and grievous guilt made him howl louder than ever. The Tothans must've found out about the Immaculate trap and perverted it to their advantage, stuffing as many of their troops into Othean as they could before the Court of the Dreaming Priests blew the whole place up. If a humble rat had been sufficient offering for Maroto to summon and bind Crumbsnatcher, what would an entire army of their own soldiers and all their mortal victims call up for the Vex Assembly? The thought-swapping monsters had shown him visions of every corner of the Star besieged by their legions, had ordered him to go and spread the bad word about how doomed everyone was, but now he had to wonder if that had all just been one big ruse designed to draw as many people up here as possible, to really pack in the crowds for Jex Toth's first and final offensive... and to make sure whatever they enticed up to the rim of their colossal Gate saw that it would be well fed on the other side.

And however might the Vex Assembly have hit on such an artful ploy as this, provoking their enemies into an epic battle for the sole purpose of killing off as many of their own loyal soldiers as possible, as quickly as possible, to complete some diabolical ritual? Sad to say but Maroto had a pretty good idea on that score, too—those Tothan freaks had been positively obsessed with extracting every detail they could from him about the Battle of the Lark's Tongue. At the time he hadn't had the foggiest idea what the Burnished Chain had actually pulled out there on the Witchfinder Plains, but the brain-raiding Vex Assembly must have read between the lines, picking up on all the clues his dumb arse had soaked up but overlooked. Did that make this his fault? Like, more than it already was? Should he have somehow seen this coming?

Yes. Of course. What a fool he'd been. All that time caged in with the kooky Vex Assembly it had been *sacrifice this* and *blood offering that*, but instead of hanging on their every screeched word or projected thought he had dismissed them as pure nutters, devil-ridden deviants who wanted to murder the Star for no greater end than evil itself. Maroto of all people should have known that evil is never so simple, and you don't make a sacrifice unless you expect something valuable in return…and the bigger the offering, the greater the reward. The Vex Assembly were *priests*, for fuck's sake, and while he had never figured out exactly what it was they venerated he had a pretty good guess that whatever it was the dread fiend was looking at him right fucking now.

But not for long, because as soon as he got free of Choi he was going to drive his black steel spear straight into that great golden eye. Whatever it was attached to would still rise from the Gate to take this world, *his* world, he knew that…but the fucker would do so blinded, an eye for a fucking eye just like the Chain always said.

Elbowing Choi's ribs and finally slipping out from her grasp, he rolled to his feet and charged down the rubble they had fought so hard to defend. She grabbed at his hair…and grabbed only air, the freshly shorn barbarian howling as he raced out along a spit of broken stone and dove off the side of the ruined wall. The Mighty Maroto rather fancied the eye was focused on him as he fell into it, leading with his spear.

For a dyed-in-the-wig drama queen who had spent countless hours imagining his own death, even he had never imagined going out on such a high note.

CHAPTER
32

Hoartrap continued to feast on the demoniac Zosia had vanquished, a fittingly nasty last meal for a truly nasty man. Purna and Keun-ju offered to back Zosia up but she didn't want any distractions, so they went to check on their unconscious Flintlander friend while Cold Cobalt marched alone to face down a cabal of deathless monsters. Well, not quite alone. Choplicker splashed beside her through the bubbling filth of the disintegrating grotto, toward the golden beacon of the Gate where ten black shadows completed their ritual. It was eerily silent, save for all the dripping. Clearing her throat, Zosia made her second and final appeal to the Vex Assembly.

"Listen up, oh devils of Jex Toth, and listen good, because I'm only giving you one chance to save yourselves!" The threat sounded so flimsy, here in this bizarre realm, and not a one of the swarm-hooded figures turned from their silent ceremony to heed her. This was why they hadn't listened the first time, because she still couldn't believe she was going to do it herself. Taking a deep breath, she looked to Choplicker for strength despite how little she wanted to lean on him. Maybe she should have lingered in his heaven, however hollow it felt... Taking a deep breath, she bellowed, "I've killed one of your number already, and I'm not afraid to cull the rest! I command you to cease your ritual, to cease your war! Immediately! If you do, I offer you peace, here on the Star. If you refuse, you will be banished back to the First Dark. Immediately! Maybe you'll find another way back or maybe this time you won't, but I promise you're going to find out in about five seconds. Look upon me! Look upon my devil! The choice is yours!"

They ignored her. This was it, then. For the Star, maybe. For Diadem, definitely. And for her, most of all. She looked down at where her devil waded in the slime beside her and gave the order before he had to start swimming.

"All right, Chop, you heard the crickets. I hereby grant your freedom in exchange—"

"Your kind has never known peace. You do not desire it. You breed hate and you feed on fear, a cannibal race dedicated to its own extinction."

The prodigious ant-riddled priest had again stepped away from the edge of the Gate, his formerly screechy voice now smooth as butter fresh out of the churn, his bloodshot eyes gone as black as the bottom of a caved-in mine.

"That's putting an awfully fine point on it," said Zosia, though the sentiment was one she herself had shared on occasion, especially when she was a teenager. "I'll allow that peace is hard to hold on to, but that doesn't mean we shouldn't try. And I know you're just trying to stall me long enough to finish your ritual, so you've got to the count of five to take part in the great experiment. One."

"Othean is lost, and your world with it." It smiled sympathetically as it splashed toward her. *"For the second time you mortals have made our sacrifices for us. First with the blood of your kind, to bring us home. Now with the offering of our kind, to bring home She Who Comes. The Gate of Gates yawns and the Black Goddess gazes out upon her tribute. She shall rise to quench your sun, to burn your moon, to—"*

"Don't know what that means, don't give a fuck," said Zosia, sloshing forward to meet this fat piece of shit that was nowhere near as scary as the dog now paddling beside her. "Two. And three, while we're at it—when I hit five, Chop, if their ritual isn't aborted you've got your freedom in exchange for sacrificing Diadem, so long as it banishes Jex Toth and all these devils back to the First Dark."

"Your threats ring as hollow as your heart, Cold Zosia." As she stepped so close she could see the ants marching into one nostril and out the other, the thing inside the priest murmured, *"I scent the*

stink of hope upon you. You have vanquished Sherdenn, and I am duly impressed... but contrary to your desire it brings me no pleasure to lose my master."

"Fuck pleasure," said Zosia. "If that was your master I iced let's talk about opportunity. You're now the only member of the Vex Assembly who never has to worry about losing your power, your immortality. I gave you true freedom, and all I'm asking in exchange is for you to pull rank with your goon squad and call off this clusterfuck. I've been in a summoning circle a time or two myself, big boy, and I know you all have to work together to pull it off, right? And with the one who summoned you out of the song for good you can *choose* to opt out without repercussions, *right*?"

"*You understand nothing of our kind. My resolve is not weakened for having lost my master, and our order is not weakened for having lost a brother. You cannot begin to comprehend what it means, that we now hold open the Gate of Gates, and through it She Who Comes—*"

"Don't know, don't give a fuck," Zosia singsonged. "This is your last chance, *stupid*. Shut this Gate of Gates, call off your armies. *Now.* This isn't a conversation. Either you do as I fucking tell you and we see if mortals and devils can coexist, or you and the rest of your Assembly go back to the First Dark to blabber around your sewing circle about how sweet it would've been to taste the fruits of your harvest, to daydream about what's happening up here. Maybe the demented fanatic you're trapped inside wants an evil goddess to reap all life from the Star, but I'm thinking you educated devils are smarter than that. I'm thinking you realize that working with me gets you a world teeming with mortal passions and pains, instead of banishment back beyond the Gates. Your master's dead and gone, and that means you've got nobody to answer to but yourself—so put your apocalypse back in the bottle and let it cellar for another age or two, or you're going back in the basement yourself. That's four, and if the next word out of your host isn't *surrender* I'm damning us all—look in my heart and see if I'm still bluffing."

It didn't speak, but she could feel an itchy tingling at her temples like the gentle cousin of the first Tothan's intruding fingers, felt a pressure behind her eyes like a mounting migraine. Then it smiled big enough to eat the world, and Choplicker snarled, and Zosia was tired of this bullshit, anyway.

"Five."

So much for diplomacy. Zosia's last thought as Choplicker unfurled beside her was that she wished she had done this from the outset, so that she could have watched Diadem burn from the top of her throne room. That was hindsight for you.

———

As the eye of the First Dark opened upon the world of mortals and everyone up on the wall lost their damn shit, Sullen really, really wished he hadn't talked Zosia out of sacrificing Diadem. It was just like Ma, Fa, and everyone else he'd ever met had always said—he was too damn soft, too damn sweet, the human equivalent of one of those gooey cinnamon breads Diggelby had turned him on to at that breakfast bar back in Thao, what seemed like a lifetime ago. Now he was grappling his girlfriend on the battlements to prevent her from leaping down to greet whatever god of gods or devil of devils was looking out upon them... Served him right for listening to the Faceless Mistress, who was probably laughing her spooky ass off right about now. Don't get mixed up with other people's gods—that was just basic shit, man.

So here at the saga's end it turned out he'd been in a farce from the very beginning. Sullen Soggybrains, who went ahead and listened to a foreign devil queen even when the greatest heroes of his age all told him it was a bad idea, that they knew of an easy way to thwart the First Dark. Hard to think of this dreary, drawn-out quest as anything other than a fable against folly, now that the final chorus was chiming in. What had he expected, really, when every time the action started he was either entirely absent or quick to have his lamp knocked dark? How had he ever thought himself the champion of an epic song when he was fainting dead away as soon as the fights started, when the mightiest foes he'd faced hadn't been monsters or gods but his own damn mom and a ten-year-old boy? And now he was fixing to lose a wrestling match against his girlfriend, who he knew for a *fact* didn't even know the rudimentary moves...

Then Ji-hyeon went still, which Sullen would have taken as a good sign except his whole body locked up, too, what he saw out of the corner of his eye shutting down his ability to even breathe. Whatever was on the other side of that epic Gate hadn't just been watching them, and now it wasn't just on the other side…It gave off the most brilliant golden-white light as it poured up into the sky, a living moon, and as he stared it blossomed outward, a crown of wavering tendrils to cover the world, blotting out the light of sun and stars, a new heaven for the mortals that survived its coming. The warm red tears peeled up off Sullen's cheeks, falling into the sky, up to the hungry god that had come among them…

———

Zosia swung her hammer even as she loosed Choplicker, eager to break this stupid fucker's fat face. Or try to, anyway. With a devil in him he'd obviously be hard to catch…but then Zosia had caught devils before. Not that she expected the sainted steel to do any more permanent damage to him than it had done to his spidery friend, especially without Choplicker around to back her up, but since she had just condemned herself to exile in the First Dark right along with her enemies it was important to get hell off on the right foot.

They must already be on their way, the light from the Gate going out and the warm slurry of liquefied fat and melting meat turning gelid around her calves. As the head of her hammer came down on the smug face of the priest, she felt no fury or heartbreak, only disgust that all beings were as stupid and cruel as she. Then her target was five feet out of range, his devil propelling him backward so fast her eye hadn't been able to track his dodge. Zosia was in for a very long eternity…or a very short one, depending on what exactly the Vex Assembly decided to do to her.

Choplicker whined unhappily beside her, and she saw he hadn't actually gone anywhere, hadn't *done* anything…except from his hangdog expression maybe he had, though it brought him no pleasure.

"*Your time is nothing to She Who Comes; we grant you this reprieve,*" said the thing inside the pudgy priest, offering an unexpectedly petulant shrug. The other nine turned away from their positions around and above the darkened Gate, gathering in around Zosia and her devil. "*A truce is struck.*"

"You were bluffing, too..." Zosia said, marveling that her plan had actually fucking worked. If these monsters hadn't abandoned their ritual at the last possible moment a hundred thousand innocent people would have burned because of her... but if she hadn't been able to pull that trigger then the whole bloody Star would've died, Diadem included. "It's really over? Your black goddess didn't arrive to ruin the Star? Your armies are backing off?"

"*Our legions are in retreat,*" said the ancient devil of Jex Toth. "*Had She Who Comes fully crossed the Gate of Gates you would harbor no doubts, mortal queen—her very coming would have shredded your reality.*"

That sounded okay, sure, but Zosia was never one to let the scent of good news distract her from the vague taste of something rotten. "What's this '*fully* crossed the Gate' mean, exactly? Be specific."

"*Do not fret, O bravest monkey, your realm is safe for now,*" it said with a smile. "*She began to rise, yes, but we resealed the Gate of Gates before she could complete her ascension. What little that passed through was forced to conform to this world, just as your world would have been forced to conform to her. As I say, you are safe. For now. Yet there is a condition to our truce—*"

"You don't get Hoartrap, that's not up for discussion," said Zosia, knowing what the Vex Assembly must want but refusing to give up her gross boy now that she knew what he was really made of. "You wanted to talk terms and make deals, you shouldn't have forced my fucking hand."

"*We will come to our own arrangements with the Betrayer of Jex Toth, but that is none of your concern.*" It might have been her imagination but that snowmead-sweet voice sounded peevish. "*Our condition is, as you say, not up for discussion, for you have forced our hand as much as we have forced yours. It is this: you shall be our advocate. With the Star and its keepers. You are bound to us now, as we are to you, and any peace shall only be as strong and as long as you make it. You will look to our*" *best interests, ensure our needs are met, and see that Jex Toth prospers. You will swear it on your devil's freedom, and swear it now."*

"I will, will I?" Zosia wasn't about to make herself beholden to a pack of devils…except she already was, wasn't she? This was the very reason she had fled her throne in the first place, because winning a war proved so much easier than keeping a peace…but this time she wouldn't run. This time she would do everything she could, no matter how frustrating or impossible it seemed to keep the Star from catching flame, no matter the toll it took on her. "All right, it's a deal…but only on the further condition that this is indeed the end of the war, the end of your efforts to sacrifice this world to some outer god. You must harm no mortals, save in self-defense, and, though I don't know if he counts anymore, you have to let Hoartrap go, too. Whatever *arrangements* you make with him end with the Touch and me leaving Jex Toth together."

This last especially sat poorly with some of the bug-infested old fuckers, those whose eyes were clear shrieking in High Immaculate at her and each other and those with black-filled sockets seeming to communicate even more with just their baleful stares and intricately repulsive odors. In her brief tenure as Crimson Queen she had come to think of bureaucracy as the definition of hell on earth, and that seemed to be borne out down here. Even with a council of devils beholden to one another there seemed to be precious little unity.

"Agreeeeed!" screamed the slimy husk of a crone after an interminable debate, her robe of snails clicking as she waded through the icy gel thickening around their thighs. "Your terrrrrrms! Swear themmmmm!"

"As your spiritual counsel, I strongly suggest you put everything into writing." Hoartrap burped, moseying up with a bloody foot held idly in one hand. He was still desiccated from whatever they'd done to him, but his stomach looked as pregnant as the spider-clad priestess had after eating Choplicker alive. "And let me look over it first."

"That might not be a bad idea…" mused Zosia. "Just so I can have official documentation to take before the people of the Star. You devils may think you know your way around an ironbound contract, but you've never had to treat with merchant guild lawyers."

"Mundane as fuuuuck," called Purna from where she and Keun-ju were splashing ichor onto the passed-out Flintlander's face in an effort to revive her.

"Mundanity is preferable to mendacity," said Keun-ju. "And if you need a scribe for any contracts, I am ambidextrous. Or I was, I should say..."

"We shall draft the pledge at once," said an especially tall and horrifically gaunt woman clothed in baroque wasps' nests. *"You are forewarned. We have grown wiser at reading the human heart and all its deceptions, and we shall be on guard against it. We shall not be misled again, and if you seek to obscure the full truth or lead us false as Maroto did, your devil and your life will be forfeit."*

Choplicker sighed heavily, no doubt disappointed that despite all the excitement he wasn't going to get to incinerate a city after all. Not today, anyway. Giving him a consolatory scritch for being such a plausible threat, Zosia said, "So you've met Maroto, huh? Guess we've got even more to talk about than I thought, but I'll tell you right now, I've been wrong about him before, too. You've got to understand he's not a bad guy, just...complicated, like the rest of us."

"We do not wish to understand Maroto any more than we already doooo!" The fat man's eyes had gone back to being as white as his ants, his voice screeching and his expression as bitter as an unhappy ex-lover.

"Yeah, well, as much as I hear that we're all going to have to try to understand each other a lot more in the days to come," said Zosia, but she wasn't meeting the wild eyes of the lucid priests or the black ones of those whose devils had risen to the forefront. Instead, she was looking down at Choplicker.

CHAPTER
33

The great golden eye of the First Dark burst like a boil, just as Maroto's must have when that Tothan witch queen had whipped his face. Except this wasn't from his spear lancing it, because he was still falling the last few meters toward its glistening surface when it exploded upward. Something hard and hot and horrible slammed into him, but in doing so it also slammed into the spear, and he clung to the shaft as it carried him high into the air. He was pinned flat against it from the speed with which it flew, its glowing bulk crushing into him, boiling blood pooling around the spear and spattering outward to scald his already raw cheek. There was no telling if the deafening howl came from his own lips, the titanic god-monster he'd wounded, or simply the wind as it carried Maroto Devilskinner into the screaming heavens.

Then it stopped so abruptly Maroto was whipped off it, up into the air, his palms blistering as his momentum pulled him all the way up the shaft of the embedded spear, Othean a miniature diorama far below...and then he stopped, doing an impromptu handstand with his haft-burned fingers still clinging to the very butt of the spear. It was something, to hover there for a moment, upside down in the giddiest of giddy heights, but it couldn't last. It didn't. He fell, at least a thousand feet of cold air between him and a rough reunion with the earth...and landed flat on his face back where he'd started, splayed out on the rough white expanse his spear was lodged in. Woof.

He stayed where he lay, heart pounding, a gust of wind buffeting him, and then slowly, slowly took in his surroundings.

He was lying facedown on an enormous tentacle that was frozen in the sky.

All right, that was enough of taking in his surroundings for the moment. He closed his eye, waited for the vertigo to pass...but not looking only made it worse. Taking a deep breath, he dared another look. Laughed out loud, but it was a small, nervous laugh, one the wind was quick to snatch from his lips.

He wasn't lying on a tentacle...or at least he wasn't anymore. He was splayed out on the branch of a tree. The biggest tree in all the Star by a significant margin, no doubt, but a tree nonetheless. A white rowan, to be specific, though he hadn't thought they grew in the Isles. Hardly the most remarkable aspect of the thing, and peeking over the side of the four-foot-wide bough, he felt his body go all boneless again. He had to be a quarter of a mile from the damn trunk of the thing, and from there it was a very, very, very long way down to the surface of the...lake?

Maroto rubbed the bark dust from his eye and looked again, and now his laugh was a lot stronger, even if it was just as confused. East Othean was spread out beneath him, plain as a map, but beyond the central wall where that enormous eye had opened up was nothing but sparkling blue water, with the mountainous rowan sprouting from its center. What the devils had happened?

Well, one obvious possibility was that he'd died, either from the poison that even now was prickling through his face or from jumping off a damn wall. The Crowned Eagle People held that there was a big old tree at the center of all things, so maybe this was it? Of course, anytime things got really weird or bad, Maroto's first assumption was that he'd died and gone to some improbable afterlife...

If he wasn't dead, though, and he'd really jumped face-first onto a giant tree branch as it sprang up out of a city-sized eye, what the hell did *that* mean? Had his sticking it with the spear done something? Or was it just dumb chance that he'd leaped when he had? Did this mean the threat to Othean had passed? Or was this a portent that things were only getting worse? Was that a naval battle going down off the northern coast of the isle, which he could actually see from this ludicrously high vantage?

And, real talk now, the most important question of all: how the fuck was he supposed to get down from up here?

———

"I...can't....believe it," breathed Ji-hyeon, wriggling deeper into Sullen's arms as they stared up at the tree, listened to waves lap against the foot of the wall. "What does it *mean*? What *is it*?"

"It's, uh, a tree?" Sullen supplied, and they both laughed nervously. Sullen squeezed her and sat up on an elbow, as if they were lying in a comfortable bed and not splayed out on a battlement overlooking an impossibility. "I...I've been wrong before, and often, but yeah, I think it's a tree."

"*Sullen.*" She sat all the way up and gave him her most incredulous raised eyebrow. He must have missed receiving it as much as she'd missed giving it because he grinned as he sat up, too, putting his arm back around her and letting Fellwing crawl over his skinned knuckles.

"Well, okay, we agree it's a tree and all, but other than that you've got me. Though..." Sullen pursed his lips thoughtfully, as if scanning through his endless catalogue of songs and folktales. "Yeah, more I think about it the more I think it's an improvement on a great devilish eye. I like that it's growing from a lake instead of a Gate, too."

"A lake?" Ji-hyeon rubbed the ash from her eye and saw that he was right; where West Othean had burned a few minutes before now there was nothing but azure water, the unbelievably massive tree springing from way out in its tranquil depths. Her devil-eye throbbed behind the makeshift patch Sullen must have put back in place as she was recovering from her fit, but she could barely take in what her normal eye was showing her so decided to let it bide for now. "You're right— that is an improvement. And you promise you don't have any idea where it came from, what it means?"

"Huh..." Sullen craned his neck at the sky of white, white

branches and green, green leaves set with clouds of red, red berries. "You know, I think that's a rowan. Hoartrap and Purna swapped all kinds of ghost stories about them, and the spookiest of the lot was one about how they weren't really trees at all. They're fingers of the First Dark that reached up into our world, stretching up to seize the sun, but before they could reach it something magical happened and they were turned into rowans. Devil-haunted trees, always listening..."

Ji-hyeon shivered, the song reminding her of one her first father had sung her as a child about the legendary trees called Gate-ashes that supposedly grew in the highest reaches of the Ugrakari mountains. She couldn't remember many of the details, but considering this thing had sprouted straight up from a Gate, that name couldn't be a coincidence. "We'll do our research once the day is won, but that story...does it feel right to you?"

"Only thing I know for sure is some gods must like us, even if they aren't the ones we were counting on," said Sullen. After thinking it over, he added. "Well, that and I'd really like to kiss you right now."

Their lips brushed, then parted. Tasting the blood and dirt and ash and all the times they'd almost died that morning she kissed him harder, and harder still, until Fellwing politely took wing to give them their privacy. Well, such as it was to be found on the crowded battlement where the rest of the survivors were also coming out of their daze to find that the drizzly, monster-riddled morning had burned off into a hazy and miracle-filled afternoon.

"More of that later, but for now I've got a war to wage, handsome," Ji-hyeon said at last, breaking away. "Care to join me?"

"I would, but it doesn't look like any Tothans survived that... whatever it was." Sullen got up with a groan and offered her his hand. "That, or maybe they got grossed out watching us neck and called it a day?"

"Hey, who taught you how to crack wise?" she said, this day just getting better and better. "And if our kiss did that, just imagine what it'll be like once we get into each other's pants. We might bring about world peace."

"Worth a try, anyway." Sullen grinned, not so bashful about ribald flirting as she'd remembered, either. "Before that, though, we've got some songs to sing each other, no doubt."

"Unless you can sing with your mouth full, songs can wait," said Ji-hyeon, but already her attention was shifting to the other side of the wall. Limping over and looking down, she saw that the streets of East Othean were thick not just with Immaculates but soldiers from all over the Star, mundane men and women bumping shoulders and knuckles with the wildest of her wildborn. More than one pennant looked familiar, too... "So Fennec has whoever's left of my old Cobalts, I've got a serious crew of my own, and those are without a doubt Singh's Raniputri dragoons... this just might work. Do you recognize any of those Flintland flags, and more importantly, do you think they're the sort to flip on their employer for a significant raise? If we—"

"Whoa whoa whoa," said Sullen, holding up his palms. "What happened, now? All I know is Hoartrap said you and the rest of the company were captured, that there was a trap, but the empress offered the Cobalts their freedom if you defended the Autumn Palace. I could tell at a glance that wasn't the full story, given, uh, certain factors..." He was staring at her face, and she blushed, wondering just how old she must look to him now. "Has Hoartrap been telling his wizard-lies again?"

"Some details might have been overlooked," said Ji-hyeon, forcing herself to focus on the practicalities for now. "You were right, Sullen, we do have some songs to sing each other. But first we're moving somewhere more comfortable."

"Yeah, should probably see if there's an open bathhouse around here, get cleaned up," said Sullen, nodding thoughtfully. "You ever been to a bathhouse? I mean, obviously you have, but *damn*. Keun-ju and Diggelby turned me on to them a minute back, and that sounds like just the spot."

"I was thinking more like the Samjok-o Throne Room," she said, taking his hand in hers and lifting it into the air as she made eye contact with her sister Hyori in the crowd below. Time to start rounding the troops back up. "We'll have to move swiftly, before the Immaculates recover from their surprise at this morning's developments. But if we team up with our Cobalt kin we should be able to hit the empress with everything we've got before she even realizes the wolf is in the yard."

"Wait..." Sullen pursed his lips, beetling his brows as he looked out at all the weary warriors and relieved citizenry gathering in the square and streets below. "You wanna have another great big fight, like, right now? This one wasn't bad enough for you?"

"There's a song in it, like I told you," she said. "But yes."

"Damn but I've missed you," he said, and leaned back down for another kiss.

CHAPTER
34

As they settled into the fabulously disgusting flesh-and-bone cabin of the Tothan seabeast that would take them all back to the Star, Best looked so down in the mouth that Purna thought she might actually cry. Purna liked a good clean scrap as much as the next girl, and it *had* been one hell of an epic fight, but being so disappointed about not getting another rematch against the devilish witches who had whipped you good the first two times? Well, it definitely wasn't out of character, but that just went to show that this particular character was out to lunch.

Both Best and Keun-ju remained standing in the wide chamber long after they were under way, seemingly reluctant to touch anything in the pulsating cabin, but Purna had immediately claimed one of the top bunks—it was a long voyage to Othean so why not embrace the vile novelty of sleeping in a nice warm flesh pocket? Keun-ju's upbeat mood was much more in line with Purna's, although the moist and meaty mode of transport seemed to have made him seasick before they'd even left the antediluvian white harbor. Fighting was fun, duh, but it was wasted on war, where everything was terminally serious, and, as Digs would have it, everything serious was terminally dull.

Well, most things—for as hard as he fronted at being the carefree bon vivant, it was common knowledge that the pasha had a sentimental streak seven leagues wide. And looking down at the devil licking the fleshy floor of the cabin, she knew there was one thing he took even more seriously than throwing parties or throwing shade. As if reading her thoughts like a fuzzy little Tothan corpselord, Prince stopped his icky swabbing of the deck and looked up at her with his tiny black eyes.

"Say goodbye to Prince, chums," said Purna, dropping back down from the bunk onto the rubbery floor to give him a final scratch.

"Already?" said Keun-ju, not moving to pet the devil. "I'm not surprised, given who I'm talking to, but you only have one chance to make the right wish. Why rush things, when keeping a devil around is good for your health?"

"Can't get rid of it soon enough," said Best, beginning to pace as the muscly walls of their cabin bowed to one side, the seabeast presumably banking through the deep.

"No wishes," said Purna, scooping up the little bastard to show him that somebody still cared, even if Best and Keun-ju weren't dog lovers. It was like she'd always said, devils were just animals that mortals hadn't figured out yet. "But I need your word, both of you—when we see Pasha Diggelby, none of this ever happened. If it can't be helped you can fess to my having bound a devil dog and then turned it loose, that way nobody's caught in a fib, but the details... the details might upset him."

"Diggelby loved that creature," said Keun-ju. "I heard so many stories involving canine shenanigans I swore I never wanted to see another spaniel. So why not keep him, reunite Prince with his old master? Ji-hyeon's owlbat Fellwing was once her second father's, and I always got the impression some bond remained between them."

Prince looked up at Purna as if to ask, *Yes, why not?* Or maybe she still had some snail salad on her face from lunch, you never could tell with him. "I'm telling you as Digs's best droog, that shit would not fly. He feels bad enough about having kept a bound devil the once, and I show back up to tempt him with his old pup? No and no. Prince wins because he's free, and I win because I don't have to tell Digs nuthin' about how me and his devil had all kinds of adventures together... and how I didn't set him loose immediately, but kept him on hand for emergencies. I mean, obviously that was the smart play, since I'm pretty sure this little guy miraculously kept my black powder dry enough to pop that priestess back in soggy Jex Toth, but even still I know it would sit poorly with the pasha. So swear it—Prince was never here."

"I will not take part in deception," said Best, her rapid pacing making her even more annoying to talk to. "But then I do not intend to speak to your friend Diggelby ever again."

"Diggelby is everyone's friend," said Keun-ju, "but I see your point, Purna, and I swear it. But again, what is your wish?"

"No wishes, I told you," she said, addressing Prince as well as Keun-ju. Remembering Diggelby's ghastly story of the devil melting into a soup when he'd saved her on the battlefield, she set the dog back down. "Prince, I release you from your bond, no payment necessary."

The lapdog-shaped hellspawn cocked his head at Purna in that adorable way he had.

"I don't think it works that way," said Keun-ju. "They want to serve. They *have* to serve. You've got to give him something to work with."

"Oh, you've done this a lot, have you?" said Purna, and putting her hands on her hips and considering the devil, she had herself a wee ponder. "I wish that in exchange for your freedom, you...you go wherever and do whatever *you* wish, free of my bond."

Prince yapped at her, and Keun-ju was just saying something smart when the spaniel exploded. Not, like, into gory pieces, but as a foul cloud of grey smoke that smelled like everything bad that could possibly come out of a dog. They were obliged to flee the windowless cabin, Best and Keun-ju coughing and Purna cackling. They took shelter in the room across the hall, letting the veiny door ooze shut behind them.

"Do you mind?" asked Hoartrap, looking up from the stack of parchment he was sorting. He was sitting on the floor using his wicker pack as a kaldi table, a monocle securely embedded in the too-soft flesh of his face. He was still but a shadow of his former self but growing bulkier by the day—unfortunately, his improving health and increasing mass corresponded to a powerful, pus-like aroma emanating from his baggy robes. Zosia lounged in a bunk a safe distance away, leafing through more of the papers. Choplicker had somehow gotten into an upper berth, yawning at the interlopers.

"They will," said Zosia, her dour face brightening. "You've all just been enlisted by the ambassador to Jex Toth to do some very important work. You can split my stack among you."

"I do not read." Best said it like it was a point of pride.

"Happy day, more for both of you!" said Zosia, waving Purna and Keun-ju over with her documents. "We're looking through these Chainite records for priests and nuns and such who aren't the absolute worst. So far it's a short list."

"Why don't I get any input?" groused Hoartrap. "I retrieved the damn files for you, and put the fear of me into the People's Pack and their tame Chainites to make sure they heed our counsel."

"You don't get any input because you said instead of stacking the new Holy See with our own appointees we should round up every single Chainite and sacrifice them," said Zosia, taking out a supremely cool-looking pipe and tools as Purna and Keun-ju divided the papers between them. "So what you kids are looking for are disciplinary hearings, interesting transgressions on their penance reports, basically anything that marks them as trouble for the old guard— any member of the clergy who has a good report we don't want in power. Got it?"

"Ah, not to sound harsh…" said Keun-ju. "But Hoartrap does raise an interesting point. Why not just execute them all, after what they did?"

"Well, more Chainites rebelled against the Black Pope's madness than you might expect, and we can't very well treat the reformers in Diadem the same as the swine who sailed to Jex Toth," said Zosia. "Besides, indiscriminately massacring everyone is exactly what the old Burnished Chain would do, if they got ahold of their enemies, and in all things we shall endeavor to be unlike the Chain."

"And because she doesn't wish to make martyrs of them," Hoartrap chimed in. "Lest we forget a young lady who told me she *wished* she could execute them all. And meanwhile she has the tool to grant her every desire still languishing at her heel."

"Your way's more gratifying, but my way's better," said Zosia, packing her pipe. "There's always going to be a Burnished Chain, or something like it, so the most we can hope for is to exert our influence on what direction it takes from here. The wildborn clerics and their sympathizers in Diadem seem to have mostly gotten their reformation off on the right hoof, but especially after how they treated me and Indsorith I'm not convinced they wouldn't benefit from a little oversight. What a happy day for the mother church, that I have such learned clerks as you lot to help make the difficult decisions."

"Maybe this is a dumb question..." said Purna, taking out her own pipe as conspicuously as possible so Zosia could see the piece she'd made for Maroto had ended up in steadier hands. "But why would the Burnished Chain defer to our judgment on *anything*, let alone something as important as choosing their new leaders?"

"Lots of reasons," said Zosia, "ranging from the practical to the political to the self-preserving. The abridged version is if they don't make my life easier I'll make theirs a whole lot fucking harder, and they know it. Lucky for them the Stricken Queen is quick to compromise these days, and since anyone I nominate for the Holy See will be pulled from their own ranks they can't cry too loudly."

"Maybe you should just convert," suggested Hoartrap. "Move back to your old place, swap one throne for another?"

"Ugh," said Zosia. "Not funny."

"*I* could convert!" said Purna, imagining the look on Diggelby's face if she nibbled his style after all the times he'd chomped hers.

"You're certainly deranged enough to pass for a Chainite," said Keun-ju, then self-consciously glanced at Best. Perhaps suspecting that their Flintlander friend's ever-deepening frown stemmed from the irreverent tone of the conversation, he added, "No offense intended, Best—we're only joking."

"Conversion is nothing to laugh at," said the holy-minded Horned Wolf.

"I couldn't agree less," said Hoartrap. "There's nothing funnier than the thought that you three scalawags nearly ended up joining the Vex Assembly. It almost would have been worth the end of the world just to see what came of *that* conversion!"

Purna hated to admit it when Hoartrap's cryptic shit went right over her head, so she was relieved when Best didn't let the aside fade away unanswered.

"What insult is this?" demanded the Flintlander. "Every one of us would have chosen death before joining those witches."

"Quite so, quite so!" said Hoartrap, and seeing their confusion, his ugly mug broke into an uglier grin. "Don't tell me you still haven't guessed why the Vex Assembly lured you to their throne room and kept you within snatching distance throughout the ritual!"

"We weren't *lured* anywhere," said Purna, happily accepting the leather tubāq pouch Zosia offered her and returning the woman's knowing nod at her barrel-shaped briar. "We stole a pair of sky-devils and invaded their lair because we are solid brass badasses, like I told you. And they hung us up over the Gate to interrogate us because they recognized we were solid brass badasses and knew we had valuable information, *also* like I told you."

"Oh yes, yes, I'm sure that's all there was to it," said the difficult warlock with a snicker. "It all sounds terribly plausible."

"Hoartrap," groaned Keun-ju. "Have mercy on we feeble mortals who lack both your brilliant intellect and superior sense of humor. Enlighten us, I beg you."

"Very well, but only to put an end to your groveling. Really, I'm embarrassed on your behalf to see you debase yourself so—"

"*Hoartrap*," said Zosia, and at her exasperated tone he finally spilled the kaldi grounds.

"The Vex Assembly drew you to them in case any of their number was lost during the Battle of Othean. Three devil-ridden Tothans were on the field that day, and so the Assembly kept three mortals in reserve, lest the need arise to replace their fallen fellows. The corker is that their newest convert did indeed die that day, so at least one of you would have ended up on the wrong side of a devil summoning ceremony if Zosia hadn't arrived when she did!"

Hoartrap obviously found that scenario pretty funny, but not Purna...and not Keun-ju, or Best, or Zosia, to go on their unified frown front in the face of his ghoulish giggle. Purna wasn't the most devout adherent to the Thirty-Six Chambers of Ugrakar, admittedly, but even she knew the whole moral behind the legend of the Living Saint was that immortality is a curse, not a blessing. And that wasn't even taking into account just how gnarly the Vex Assembly's version of immortality truly was! To be lowered into a Gate as a sacrifice, and have a devil take up residence in your flesh...well, at least now Purna knew what she'd be having nightmares about for the rest of her damn life. Thanks, Hoartrap.

"So here's a question for you," said Keun-ju. "Since you obviously know everything about everything and are generous with your wisdom—who is the Procuress Vex Ferlune?"

Purna perked up at the mention of Diggelby's Jackal Woman contact in Thao—ah, to think of a happier time when the statuesque Procuress was the scariest witch they had encountered! Other than Hoartrap, of course.

"I told you back in the Haunted Forest, I've never had the pleasure," said Hoartrap.

"Yes, but after meeting the Vex Assembly I assumed you were feigning your ignorance," said Keun-ju. "It hardly seems a coincidence that Vex Ferlune would use that same ancient honorific of Jex Toth, and since you and the Assembly obviously have a history I thought—"

"No, you didn't *think*, you just *thought* you thought!" snapped Hoartrap. "If you actually had enough sense in your skull to have a *real* thought you wouldn't always assume the worst about me. I may have massaged the truth a time or two, yes, but only ever for the greater good, and in this matter I am as honest as I am bored. If you want answers about mysterious mummers who flatter themselves with stupid titles like Vex, Y, or Z, I suggest you swim back to the Sunken Kingdom and inquire at the Tothan pity party."

Rather than being hurt by Hoartrap's bullying, Keun-ju only gave Purna a knowing look. He'd definitely poked a nerve, which was *definitely* interesting. Maybe after they met back up with the rest of the Moochers another Thaoan road trip was in order, see if the Procuress could procure them some answers about who she really was... or then again, maybe it was best to let sleeping jackals lie.

"Hey, here's a fun idea," said Zosia as Purna packed her pipe using the complicated Stank Method that Digs had taught her. "Since the kids obviously appreciate just how witty and hilarious you are, Hoartrap, why don't you tell the story you told me earlier? About how a certain glutton didn't think about the fact that by eating one demoniac he was ensuring that a different devil-possessed priest would have to follow him around for all eternity, haunting the living grave of its master. I'm sure they'll have a good laugh at how you got yourself out of that fine mess."

"I'm not happy with the punchline on that one..." grumbled Hoartrap, no longer looking very amused. If anything he seemed a bit queasy, putting a malformed hand on his stomach, and Purna almost felt bad for the ageless abomination who had first betrayed his insane society when her own civilization was in its infancy.

"We could've started calling you Hoartrap the Tomb!" needled Zosia. "Hoartrap the Tomb and his Amazing Ant-boy Assistant—sounds like a pretty good vaudeville act. I bet with Maroto's connections in the industry he could've gotten you plenty of gigs. You'd have been an overnight sensation."

It was Hoartrap's turn to groan. "Did you insist we eschew the convenience of traveling through the Gates because you've genuinely developed an aversion to passing through the First Dark, or was that but a deception so you could torture me at your leisure?"

"I'll admit it's not a bad bonus," said Zosia as she took her pouch back from Purna. "But no, in all seriousness I'm never dipping another toe in the First Dark if I can help it."

"Nor I," said Best.

"Nor I," said Keun-ju.

"Yes, yes, because crawling inside a sea monster that smells remarkably like old ham is somehow less sinister," said Hoartrap, taking out a pouch of his own and popping a salted gumdrop in his mouth.

"I might be convinced to do some more Gate-tripping further down the road..." Purna thought out loud. "But first I need to hook back up with Nemi and feel her out on the subject, see what she thinks about the practice."

"And with that we return to work," said Hoartrap, officiously waving his stack of parchments at them. "Before I am further rewarded for my many gifts by being subjected to lurid tales of Purna feeling up my hideous apprentice."

"Feeling *out*, and *former* apprentice," Purna corrected him, her heart beating faster than the pulsing floor of the cabin at the memory of the cutest girl she'd ever kissed. The girl she might be kissing again, before too much longer, and more besides...All of a sudden Purna had an intense craving for a country-style omelet.

"Hmmm..." Keun-ju scanned the top page of his stack with more interest than Purna would ever be able to fake. "Just to be sure of our obligations, all we need to do is set aside disciplinary documents and the like, so that you might then identify potential candidates? There are not specific individuals we are looking for, merely a general sort of cleric, one who butted horns with the old Chainite establishment?"

"That's what we've been doing so far," said Zosia. "I've also got a list of possible names the current stewards of Diadem graciously shared with Hoartrap, and once we've checked those out we'll blow the ash from the dottle. Oh yeah, and I meant to ask—does your friend Diggelby really have an uncle who's a cardinal, or was that some highbrow humor that went over my head? The Chain has all these crooked requirements where the best jobs require a hereditary connection to the church, and to keep things looking legitimate we'd rather bend the rules than break them."

"He told me he did, though I don't remember if it was a cardinal or a bishop," said Purna, squinting at the crawling Cascadian script on the top page of her stack. "I can't read this either, I thought it'd be in Immaculate."

"Pity that pasha of yours isn't a virgin or we'd have the solution to all our problems," said Hoartrap, making Zosia choke as she was lighting her pipe. "Can you imagine?"

"Um…" said Purna, not wanting to dish on a friend's sex life, or lack thereof…but what if it was in the service of getting him his dream job? He'd told her himself how he admired the cardinals' fashion sense almost as much as their parties.

Hoartrap took off his monocle and Zosia lowered her pipe, both looking at her intently.

"*Um* what?" asked the Touch.

"Welllllllll, funny you should mention it…"

CHAPTER
35

Ji-hyeon had originally thought about going all out, making it a real production, but in the end it was a very understated, tasteful ceremony, with only the necessary officials and a few of their closest friends and family in attendance. The dress code was left to the discretion of the guests, save for the prohibition on wearing white. Othean had mourned enough for five hundred years, and this was a joyous occasion.

The festival boats launched from the new dock under construction on the northern end of the Winter Palace, drifting leisurely across Lake Othean. The waters were so clear they could see the mighty roots winding beneath them like the arms of a kraken, melding with the reflection of the skyscraping boughs overhead. The Gate-ash had taken on especial importance to the Dreaming Priests, who declared it the manifestation of the spirit world's intervention on behalf of mortalkind in their moment of darkest peril. Reading the more sinister legends about rowans and then gazing at it with her devil-eye Ji-hyeon had been less than convinced. Not because of what it showed her, but because of what it didn't—which was anything. From where its trunk disappeared into the lake to where its highest leaves brushed the clouds the entire Gate-ash was pure ebon nothingness, a black silhouette that seemed to tug on Ji-hyeon's altered eye even as it made her sick to her stomach. In all her many exploits throughout strange worlds it was the first thing other than a Gate that her devil-eye couldn't penetrate, at least not at first, but while she felt the familiar itching to keep gazing at the enigma, to come in for a closer look, she denied her eye and slipped her patch back into place. In time she would turn her attention to investigating it further— and no doubt the Court of the Dreaming Priests were already way ahead of her—but at present everyone seemed very confident that any forces that might lurk within the wood were bound tight.

For now, anyway, and it never hurt to treat the unknown with respect. To that end her modest fleet circled its castle-thick trunk three times before continuing on their way, winding another band of warding ribbons around its width on their final pass. It never hurt to take precautions, either.

Under cobalt heavens they passed over the sunken ruins of the inner wall and the Autumn Palace, where Yunjin claimed harpyfish now held court, and then out along the channel in the outer wall. The lake had used the breach in Othean's defenses to escape its enclosure and form a new shore on the distant edges of the former pumpkin fields. It filled Ji-hyeon's eyes to see the little white temple rising from the waters like a buoy in the flood; she remembered how it had reminded her of a lighthouse so many years ago. This was where it had all started—her troubles and her conquests, her heartbreaks and her heroics—and it seemed a fitting place to end that chapter of her life, and begin a new one. How lucky she was that her three closest friends were still with her as she did so.

She looked for them from her bench on the prow where she sat with Hyori and Yunjin, her two sisters debating whether it would be appropriate for Yunjin to chant one of her throat-songs after the ceremony. Choi was easy to spot, as she was standing with the rest of the Samjok-o Guard on the next boat over. Between her new suit of jade-tinged armor and the Imperial cavalry saber on her hip, Ji-hyeon's old Honor Guard looked, well, immaculate, but even from this distance Ji-hyeon could tell her face was even sterner than usual. Maroto's condition must have further declined. Ji-hyeon knew from Sullen's frequent visits to his uncle's sickbed that the man was not long for the world of mortals, and Choi had formed an attachment that was as obvious as it was unexpected.

Almost as unexpected as Maroto clinging to life as long as he had, really—by all accounts he had been poisoned and wounded even before falling the last hundred feet from the Gate-ash, and from that height the waters of the lake must have hit him as hard as steel. Sullen's theory was that the only thing keeping the man alive was his need to get high with his absent friends one more time. If that was true he might perish at any moment, seeing as Zosia had just arrived at the Winter Palace with Purna, Hoartrap, Sullen's mother, and, of course, Keun-ju. If they had been an hour later Ji-hyeon's former Virtue Guard wouldn't have been able to take part in the ceremony, and she craned her neck around to find him as they sailed toward the Temple he had so fervently tried to talk her out of visiting the fateful night of the Equinox Ceremony, when they were both so young...

She finally caught sight of him on the third and final ship, standing at the railing with Sullen. They were holding hands, and she felt her eyes dampen anew at how blissfully they were all enjoying their reunion. Under different circumstances the vision of the handsome men sharing a moment would have dampened something else, but this was a solemn ceremony and she turned her thoughts from such matters... after only a momentary indulgence.

"Your Elegance," said Fennec, stepping up behind her on the deck strewn with gingko leaves and hibiscus blossoms. He still wore his Cobalt uniform despite how much gall it raised in certain sections of the Immaculate military. He'd offered to retire it for her, but she'd told him he could wear anything he damn well pleased, considering the debt all the Isles owed the Cobalt Companies for their defense of the realm... and given how relatively bloodless the coup had been, for that matter. "The Court of the Dreaming Priests have informed me that the condemned declines your benevolent invitation to make a final public address."

"Told you," said Yunjin.

"Good morning, General Fennec," said Hyori, her own parade dress decked with blue swashes and ostentatious medals. Ji-hyeon's formerly younger sister had taken something of a shine to the Usban fox, which Fennec bore with his usual charm (though he'd drunkenly joked to

Ji-hyeon that if Kang-ho had borne a *son*, well then . . . at which point Ji-hyeon had tugged his ponytail—also a little drunkenly, perhaps).

"And a very good morning to you both, General Hyori, Sister Yunjin," he replied, offering a smart salute to the women. "Is there anything you wish me to convey to the Court before we begin?"

"Maybe ask them again why they're so opposed to holding elections if the heavens will ordain the proper ruler and her ministers anyway," said Ji-hyeon.

"We have been through this and through this and through this— the time is not yet right," said Yunjin, sticking up for her new coven the way she always did. Ji-hyeon had initially been pleased when her sister had revealed that their first father had been a member of the somewhat secret society, and that as a result the Bong family had major inroads with the power behind the Samjok-o Throne, but ever since they'd gotten back and Yunjin had joined the Court of the Dreaming Priests it was one damn thing after another with this girl.

"The time is always right to snap the shackles of the oppressor," said Ji-hyeon, at which Hyori snorted and pointed at Ji-hyeon's chunky bracelets.

"I would suggest starting with those, Your Elegance, but I fear you'd break your scrawny fingers in the bargain."

"I'll snap something, don't you fret."

"*Sisters*," said Yunjin in the authoritative tone only eldest siblings can ever master. "We're here."

So they were. Taking a deep breath, Ji-hyeon rose to her sandaled feet from her thronelike bench, and all the guests on the trio of boats stood as well. They bobbed close together at three points of the compass, representing Othean's three intact palaces: the royal craft in the north, the military craft in the east, and the boat that carried only the condemned and her keepers to the south. Their destination occupied the west.

A long gangplank extended from the southern boat, and then a second, and a third, creating a wide bridge from the prow of the small ship to where the lake lapped at the top stair of the Temple of Pentacles. They watched in silence as the deposed empress Ryuki was led out from the cabin, her unicorn devil at her side.

Ji-hyeon's heart beat faster, a part of her hoping the condemned woman would try to fight after all, but then if she'd preferred death to this she could have accepted her conqueror's other offer. Ji-hyeon had thought it more than fair, and more than she deserved, but the woman had still chosen to take her chances with the Gate rather than be exiled to Hwabun. Maybe she was counting on finding her way back for revenge, the way the Bong Sisters had. Or maybe she just knew her chances for survival were better in the First Dark than on the Isle she had ordered scraped of all life, its soil salted and its water poisoned, so that Ji-hyeon's childhood home was no better than a barren spit of rock upon the edge of the Haunted Sea.

They walked down the bridge to the Temple of Pentacles, the lady and the monster. Ji-hyeon really hadn't expected it to come to this, had assumed the former regent would loose her devil and escape long before the sentence could be carried out. Yet each morning the woman was still in her cell with the sardonically smiling fiend. Perhaps after everything that had happened to her family and her city Ryuki had lost the will to fight back... or perhaps the unicorn knew where they were destined, and so declined the freedom she offered it, as certain powerful devils were said to do.

Ji-hyeon felt an unexpected surge of sentimentality as the woman who had stolen her fathers stepped from the gangplank onto the top stair of the Temple of Pentacles. She drew her black sword and pointed it at the woman, just as she had when she'd made a silent promise to the empress at this very spot to one day avenge her people. Yet as much as she wanted Ryuki to turn and see her and remember it, too, the defeated tyrant denied her. She and her devil walked into the Gate without looking back.

Ji-hyeon would soon follow her. She must return to the outer realms for the many noncombatants of the Cobalt Company who had remained behind until the war for the Star was won. On that jubilant day the refugees would parade home through the Temple of Pentacles... but that day was not today. For now silence stretched out over Othean Lake, and taking a final lesson from her predecessor, the Empress Ji-hyeon Bong directed her people home without a backward glance.

CHAPTER
36

It was a *big* tree. They all just stared at it from the gangway for a while, trying to take in its enormity. Utterly failing. It made the Winter Palace look no bigger than a hunting cabin, Othean's walls as low as picket fences. That devil-haunted priest had creeped Zosia out plenty with its talk of She Who Comes leaving a lingering manifestation when the Gate of Gates abruptly closed, and she felt her hackles climb looking at the godly rowan. Of course, both the priest and the devil inside him were obviously insane or worse, so who knew how literally you could take what they said... but wherever it had come from, and whatever it meant—what a fucking *tree*.

Disembarking from the leviathan at Othean Bay attracted quite a crowd. Zosia hated crowds, but then again when was the last time anyone had thrown confetti at her instead of something substantially harder? Eventually they got through the thick of it and saw that most of the revelers had come down not to welcome them in particular but to marvel at the obscene mockery of natural laws that they had sailed down inside.

Most, but not all. Keun-ju was whisked away by uniformed Immaculates before they were a dozen feet out from the mob, and Purna and Best had been all set to cause a scene when they were informed he was needed to take part in a state function, at which point they couldn't wash their hands of him fast enough. They had their own urgent plans, after all: to reunite with any and all old friends they could find and get roaringly drunk to celebrate the end of the war, which Zosia and even Hoartrap agreed was a very good idea. It was right up there with bathing, after being cooped up inside their living vessel for way, way too long.

Yet the next person to greet them on the quay looked even more serious than the Immaculates who had shown up for Keun-ju. She was a young, frail-seeming woman with more stray metal in her face than a blacksmith's apron, and Purna and Best raced to be the first one to accost her—Best with questions, and Purna with embraces. Zosia and Hoartrap hung back a respectful distance, since she looked to be laying bad news on them.

"My apprentice, Nemi," said Hoartrap, blinking like an owl in the morning sunlight as Choplicker stretched and yawned between them.

"The other witch, right," said Zosia, already feeling a headache coming on from the glare off all the terraces. "Purna wouldn't shut up about her. By the six devils I bound, Hoartrap, how's a nice girl like that fall in with a goblin like you?"

"Would you believe I grew her from an *egg*?" Hoartrap dramatically arched his eyebrows and fired up the lavender-and-crotch-rot-reeking pipe Zosia had refused to let him smoke in their confined quarters. He sounded dead serious, which was all part of his supposed humor that she'd had more than enough of over the course of their long journey. Between puffs he said, "It's...actually...an interesting...story."

"One for another boat ride," said Zosia, seeing that the girl had turned back down the quay and Purna and Best were following her off. "Hey-o, where are you ladies headed?"

"Oh, um..." Purna suddenly found something between Choplicker's ears very interesting.

"My brother is hurt, but he asked you both to stay away," said Best, always reliable in a pinch to tell you the truth however much it stung. Especially then.

"Stuff that," said Zosia, moving to follow them anyway. "If I lost a tooth every time Maroto told me to piss off and never come back I'd be better at sucking eggs than Hoartrap's...well."

She was only going to say *mother*, but trailed off as she noticed the squirrely-looking apprentice glaring at her. The girl said, "His injuries are grave, and his bedside has been overbusy enough with welcome visitors."

"Look, you two, I'll sort this out," said Purna, slapping one hand on Zosia's arm and the other on Hoartrap's. She let them linger there for a moment, as if appreciating how few people had ever done such a thing and walked away. "Quick to fight and quick to forgive, that's our boy. Five minutes alone with me and he'll be begging to see the both of you."

"That I don't doubt!" said Hoartrap, but let them go without raising his own stink about being kept from Maroto's bedside. Interesting.

Less interesting but more depressing: how had Zosia grown into the sort of baggage the younger crowd ditched along with Hoartrap? That was a wake-up call if ever there was one... but for now there was nothing to do but make the most of it.

"Well, you old nightmare, what do you say we eat ourselves sick, drink ourselves stupid, and smoke ourselves sane again? That order, and I'm buying."

"Would that I could, but I seem to be indisposed by the Snort of the Creaming Beasts," sighed Hoartrap, pointing his pipe at the flagpole at the end of the quay. An old woman was leaning against it, and Zosia squinted to see who she might be, but then a yellow-robed figure stepped out from behind the pole... and another, and another, until a row of five had emerged from a space that had looked too narrow to conceal even one. In addition to their Immaculate robes they wore golden masks and matching horsehair hats, and each carried a staff with a different animal carved into the head, of similar make to the owl-stick Hoartrap always used to carry. Patting Zosia's shoulder before picking up the pace, he said, "Try to stay out of trouble, and remember that as advocate for the nation of monsters who eradicated half this city you're actually more hated than ever before in your especially hated life. Toodles!"

"Toodles," said Zosia, trying to imitate his lilt, but from Choplicker's snort he didn't think much of her impression.

"Hey," said an Immaculate-dressed Imperial girl at the end of the quay as Zosia almost walked right past her, eager to get out of the sun. Choplicker had stopped for a pet, though, tail wagging like all get-out, and Zosia nearly tripped over her own borrowed boots. With that white hair she'd assumed the woman was a lot older.

"Oh, hey!" It had been a little while, sure, and her hair had been bleached by her ride through the Gates, right, but Zosia couldn't believe how much better Indsorith looked than the last time she'd seen her...or that she was waiting here for her? "You...you're waiting for me?"

"Cobalt Zosia, the Banshee with a Brain," said Indsorith, crossing the arms of her Immaculate coat. "Now why do you think that never caught on?"

"Maybe if we pool our noble minds over a cheeky half or twelve we can get to the bottom of that mystery," said Zosia. "What do you say, Your Majesty?"

A haughty shadow flashed across Indsorith's face. It was cute. Probably a lot cuter than whatever crossed Zosia's as the younger woman smirked and said, "It would be an honor, Your Majesty."

———

It was just a pint.

Well, it was just a bowl of rice liquor, if you wanted to put a fine point on it, but that wasn't the pertinent detail. What mattered was that it was—somehow, in spite of all the reasons it shouldn't be—*normal*. They sat together at the lacquered bar, putting away obscene amounts of food and sipping at their drinks, and chitchatted as if they were a pair of old friends catching one another up on a few weeks of idle gossip.

It was nice. Not dramatic, in spite of the fate of the world nearly slipping into the First Dark and a wicked nemesis bested on a demonic battlefield. Not romantic, either, not really, though Indsorith was beginning to suspect Zosia's flirting might be more than idle habit. It was just...nice. The woman insisted on ordering for her, which was so old-fashioned it went from being annoying clear back around to endearing, and Indsorith had to admit Zosia knew her way around an Immaculate menu. Those sticky fishcakes and octopus in red chili sauce were quite possibly the greatest invention of mortalkind.

Course after course and hour after hour they talked and talked, but neither fallen queen broached the subject of what had happened to them back in Diadem, in the time between their separation in the Upper Chainhouse and their reunion on the lip of Diadem Gate. They would get there eventually, but this afternoon the People's Pack was not invited. Nor did Indsorith's thoughts ever turn to her mother or her father, and not even the ghosts of her brothers put in an appearance, hard as it was to believe after the fact. There were no unwelcome guests at their table at all—as the light faded beyond the open window and the lanterns were turned up they were just a couple of Outlanders making merry in a foreign bar.

They laughed. They laughed at stupid fucking jokes, as if they both hadn't blamed the other for their deepest, rawest wounds at one point or another. As if they hadn't wished the most brutal revenge against the other, and plotted and schemed to bring the other as low as the lowest worm, and then grind them into shit beneath their boot. They laughed at Zosia impetuously signing on to be ambassador to a mysterious land that apparently boasted all of eleven human-shaped entities, tens and tens of thousands of weirdly sentient insects, and stranger monsters still. They laughed at Indsorith's new and inadvertently Immaculate haircut. They laughed at the prospect of the rematch Indsorith had challenged Zosia to, and they laughed at the results of the arm-wrestling bouts that stood in for a sword fight until the barkeep politely asked them to stop making such a ruckus. They laughed at Zosia's good-tempered old devil, wagging his tail under the table as Indsorith slipped him seared pieces of pork belly. And then they laughed at the fact that they were laughing.

And when it was all over Zosia picked up the bill.

As well she fucking should.

CHAPTER
37

Nemi had warned Purna that he was bad, had gone over things with her half a dozen times on the long hike to his chambers in the Winter Palace, so she had been prepared for the extent of his injuries. She had even been prepared to see him dying, because she'd been around the block enough times to pick up what Nemi kept putting down. What she hadn't been ready for was to see Maroto looking so *old*.

That was what choked her up as soon as the screen closed behind her, Best good enough to wait outside with Nemi for now. Part of it was the bed, sure, because everyone looks as ancient as a Tothan witch-priest bundled up on one of those big Immaculate stone beds, but that wasn't it, not by half. His hair might've been the worst of it, that once dark and regal flattop gone, replaced with snowy hair chopped so far down he'd lost some skin in the bargain. It made him look like his hairline had receded all the way back overnight, he'd grown the scraggly beard of a beggar, and in between these bad extremes was a dark bandage covering half his face. Then the ashy skin and new crop of wrinkles weren't doing him any favors, either, the poor old bastard looking like he'd been brined with the pickles and then tossed out to bleach in the sun . . .

"Yeah, I'm crying, too," he said, sitting up on his pillow. "You just can't tell 'cause it's only from the one eye, and I left it somewhere on the other side of Othean."

That right there was what really busted Purna's pipes, because as changed as he looked, as *diminished*, that voice was the same, and she flew to his side so fast her tears must have stained the screens on the windows. Nemi had warned her against holding him too tight, against touching him at all, if she could help it, but Maroto wasn't having any of that nonsense. He dragged her onto the bed with him and hugged her so tight she thought he'd break something of hers, instead of the other way round.

And there they stayed for a very, very long time, neither of them saying a word. Neither being capable of it. Neither needing to.

When he finally let her go, she saw he'd apparently gotten his eyes mixed up, because the one he still had was red and dripping, half her damn hair soaked from it. She looked into his tired, battered face, and took his shaking, callused hand in hers... and then they laughed at their own tears, as only the best of friends can.

"I thought I looked bad..." Maroto finally managed, which just set them both off again. That was how it went, deep into the day, bad jokes culturing worse ones, and when the tales were told they grew all the sillier in the telling, because everyone knows laughter is the only thing that can keep Old Black at bay, when she comes to guide you down... Horned Wolves are overly serious like that, have been from the very beginning.

"Oh shit!" Purna immediately lowered her voice and leaned in close. "Speaking of, your sister is right outside. She wants to see you."

"Ah shit, really?" Maroto rolled his eye. "You *are* trying to kill me, aren't you?"

"You've gotta see her, man," said Purna. "She's family... and she's cool."

"You've always had a sick sense of humor," said Maroto. "We both know I'm the only cool one in my family."

"Hey, Sullen's good, too!" said Purna, and then hesitated, realizing she hadn't gotten more than the barest of bones from Nemi. "I mean, are you guys good? I haven't seen him since back in the Haunted Forest, but Nemi said he's been visiting you a lot so I thought maybe you two..."

"Oh yeah, we're good." Maroto smiled, mostly to himself, it seemed. "And yeah, he's in and out of here like crazy. Says he's making me and his girlfriend matching eye patches, if you can believe it. So we've made up for a lot of lost time, and my nephew's definitely good...but good's not the same as cool."

"No, I suppose it isn't," Purna agreed. "I...I hope you don't mind, I made him a Moocher, while we were on the road looking for you. I mean, don't worry—he earned it!"

"Oh shiiiit!" Maroto tried sitting up but had a coughing fit. When it subsided with the help of some spiked barley tea, he said, "Moochers. My Maroto fucking Moochers. They *had* to have told you who else turned up with Ji-hyeon, didn't they?"

"First of all, the only one of us who's a Maroto-fucker is you, and second, I literally just got off the stinky monster boat, so nobody's told me shit except I needed to get to you with the quickness, since you could croak any minute..." Purna swallowed. "It's not true, is it? Nemi can fix anything...can't she?"

"You miiiiight be surprised as to who else around here is a Maroto-fucker," he said, wagging his eyebrow. That painful and painfully false dodge did not bode well, but he just carried on, trying to change the subject the way he always did when he wasn't up for Hard Truth Theater. "And regarding that other matter, well, if nobody else spoiled Ji-hyeon's surprise I won't do it, either. You're in for one hell of a shock when you see who—"

"Tell me," she said, not able to play along anymore. "Tell me, Maroto. I can handle it."

He sighed, looking at his hands. How shaky they were. Then he looked at her with his only eye, and said, "I know you can, girl. I was never worried about you. I just...I just can't bring myself to say it out loud? So come in real close, and I'll whisper it in your ear."

She did, fully expecting him to give her a wet willy or something. Hoping he would. Instead, he told her the truth.

———

Telling Purna was the hardest part, but now that it was done he could finally relax. He'd told her the whole truth, too, whether or not she thought he was bullshitting her: he really, truly believed they would meet again. Best friends always do, and in the weirdest places.

That would have been a far more fitting note to go out on, but a good actor could draw power from even an overwrought page. And so he went ahead and invited his sister in, after kissing Purna's cheek and sending her off to her unwitting reunion with the inexplicably ancient Duchess Din and Count Hassan. He wasn't kidding, he really wished he could have been there for that...but it was more than he deserved, anyway. For the man who screwed the Star to save his own butt, a painful death in a lonely sickroom was about on point.

Of course, the sickroom could've been lonelier. Best stalked in as if she were on hostile hunting ground, sizing him up like he was a predator that might be too long in the tooth to be worthy of her blades. It'd been many years since he'd seen his sister, but damn she looked *old*.

Well, if she wasn't going to talk first, neither was he...Except after a hot minute of her just staring at him like she was trying out a new method of skinning game with just her eyes, he cleared his throat and said, "Hey, sister."

"The tree out there, they say you *climbed* it?" The first thing she'd said to him in well over a decade. Typical.

"Yeah," said Maroto, then smiled at the memory of his last misadventure. "Well, sort of. I jumped at a giant eye, but it turned into a tree? And tried to climb down, but, uh, slipped. Anyway, it's a long story."

For the first time in his whole damn memory of her, Best smiled. Or tried to, anyway—you could tell she didn't come by it naturally. But she came over and stood by his bed and said, "Tell me, brother."

Maroto considered everything that was odd about this picture. Most pictures were pretty odd, where they concerned his family. "Well, all right. But only because Purna vouches for you."

"She does?" Her words were sharp as her eyes, but how had he never seen how vulnerable they were, too?

"Sounds like you have a song to sing me, too, but the host makes the first boast," said Maroto, not feeling so bad about entertaining his sister anymore. Not so bad at all. Made him wonder about all the other things that might not have been so bad, if he'd had the courage

to face them. All the things he'd run from, or ran out of time for...
and then he stowed that shit back where it belonged, so he could sing
his blood the best damn song she'd ever heard.

———

There would be others. Many of them. He was well-loved. And he owed
a lot of money. There would be more than came to her wake, certainly,
but it's unwise to get competitive about such things. What mattered was
that of all the many who would come, he wanted her to be the first.

Zosia made Choplicker wait outside. She would feed him well in
the days to come, that seemed unavoidable, but he wouldn't have a
single drop of this. The screen clicked shut behind her, and she went
to the stone bed.

Even looking down at him, she couldn't believe it. She found herself feeling his limp flesh for a pulse like a frantic child. Scratching
his cold skin with her fingernail, to see if this was some wax double.
Acting like she had with Choplicker in the Office of Answers, as if he
were some sleeping devil she could rouse if only she found the secret
key. Unable to accept it, because deep down she was sure she would
have felt it when he went, close as they'd been. Unable to believe that
even as bad as they'd hurt each other he really would have deprived
her of a chance to say goodbye. To say she was sorry.

But he had. And there, tucked into his winding sheet, was the
final prick in a lifetime of fencing. A sealed letter bearing the letter Z.

She wanted to ignore it, to deny him the last words he'd denied
her... but she couldn't. Tore it open, crimson wax falling on the silver coin that covered his only eye. Read it quickly in the half-light of
the evening, read it again, then crumpled it into the fist she slowly
ground against his cold chest, as if even in death she could reach that
stupid heart of his.

Hating him in that moment not for what he'd done, but because
he'd been too scared to give her the chance to forgive him.

And hating herself for being the kind of villain who inspired that
fear in her own best friend.

CHAPTER
38

Exhausted though he was after all the fun they'd had breaking in Keun-ju's new lust-harness, Sullen couldn't sleep. He should've just gotten up ages ago instead of fighting it, hoping he'd drift off through force of will, but that just proved no matter how much you learned in this life there were some mistakes you were just going to keep making. Softly and quietly as he could manage, he moved Ji-hyeon's arm off his chest and eased out of the wide stone bed. Sleeping arrangements were another thing the Immaculates knew how to do better than anyone outside of Flintland—usually Sullen never slept so good as on the slab mattress, but not tonight. Stepping over the clothes scattered hither and yon in the enormous room, he went to the screen wall where the moonlight shone through and softly slid it open, stepping out onto the balcony.

He didn't think he could ever get used to this sight, the mountains of moonlit roofs stretching out to the sea. Ji-hyeon told him the Spring Palace was even nicer, but how did you even reckon a thing like that? At a certain point things were as fine as a baby's baby hairs, and you couldn't get finer than that.

There was a time not so long ago that being out under the naked night sky like this didn't feel so nice, and he'd be checking the edge of every cloud to see if the Faceless Mistress was creeping on him. Now that the song was good and sung he figured he wouldn't mind running into her again, so's he could knock her mighty knuckles with his own and tell her that was some good looking out. He still peered over his shoulder on sleepless nights like this, mind, but that was only so he could take in the silhouette of the majestic rowan spreading out high above the city.

It wasn't the same as coming back to a low fire and finding Fa waiting up for him, but it was as close as he'd ever come again in this life, and he was glad for it. Sometimes he wondered if the reason he was being so slow about climbing up and retrieving the black spear Uncle Maroto had left lodged in one of those branches was so that he'd always feel the old man watching over him, no matter where he was in Othean. Well, that, and it would be one dangerous ruddy clamber, and with his luck he reckoned he'd be scouting a lot of cloud-kissed branches before he hit on the right one.

Or maybe Fa would save him the hassle, give a whistle to let him know which bough to scurry up the first try. You never could tell with that old wolf—times you assumed he'd go easy on you turned out to be harder than a diamond nipple, and times you figured he'd make it tough he just offered one of those rare blissed-out smiles and passed you the beedi. Sullen sighed up at the rowan, appreciating how the pale bark shimmered in the moonlight as if it were carved from a glacier, and even from this distance he could dimly make out ephemeral devils dancing down the paths of its stately branches, if he squinted just right. He remembered how as a pup his mom and his grandfather were always arguing over whether his snow lion eyes were a blessing or a curse, whether he was marked by the gods or marked by the devils, but here in the Isles folk didn't seem to think there was any difference—spirits were spirits, and far removed from mortal notions of good and evil, right and wrong. Sullen liked that interpretation, even if he was sure his born-again mother wouldn't.

Feeling the mild ocean breeze ruffle his hair, Sullen wondered how hot it was on the Frozen Savannahs right now, if Ma had been right and they were really melting or if it had just been one of those warm spells everyone always took too seriously. He wondered…

The bedroom screen slid open again and Keun-ju stepped out, the breeze Sullen had found so balmy making the Immaculate shiver in his robe. Of course, that could just be a pretext to have Sullen put his arm around him, but either way the solution was agreeable.

"Is your stomach bothering you again?" whispered Keun-ju as he cuddled against Sullen.

"Nah, it's actually been better—how's the arm?"

"Amputated."

Sullen shook his head. "Does that ever get old?"

"Not really," said Keun-ju, wiggling his shoulder nub into Sullen's armpit. When the bigger man didn't take the rough-housing bait Keun-ju asked, "Is it anything you want to talk about?"

"Nah, I mean, it's just..."

"Family drama?"

"Family drama." Sullen smiled, squeezing his partner. "I guess it's like, I lost Fa, and I handled that. I did. But then I lost Uncle Maroto just as soon as we finally fixed things between us, and that's bad, worse than Fa, even, but I'm handling it, too—but her just cutting out like that? Without even coming to see me *once*? How am I sup-posed to make that right?"

"You're not," said Keun-ju firmly. "You've done all you can for that woman. She is a crazy person."

"Well, yeah, but blood is blood," said Sullen, the same excuse she had always made for him and Fa when the other clanfolk were riled up over something they'd said or done...or not said or not done.

"Sullen, did you ever think maybe she didn't come to see you because *she* didn't know how to make things right, except by leav-ing?" Keun-ju rested his head against Sullen's shoulder. "Your mother is very proud, and very opinionated, and very, very crazy. If she thought there was more to be said—or more likely, more blood to be shed—would she have left? In a hundred years?"

"Nooooo," sighed Sullen. "I know you're right. Her ways are her ways, and if she's finally acknowledged that they'll never be mine we can all sleep better."

A snore from the Empress of the Immaculate Isles made them both smile. In the morning they would tackle all the challenges that came from being the bodyguards of a bloody-handed reaver who had usurped the very throne of Little Heaven, according to the rogue Isles who refused to acknowledge their new sovereign. For a few more hours, at least, though, they could luxuriate in having fulfilled the destiny they had chosen for themselves, and with no veil to slow him down, Sullen kissed Keun-ju on the balcony of the Winter Palace.

Then they went back inside, to the bed they shared with Empress Ji-hyeon Bong.

Horned Wolves did not ride, except when absolutely necessary. Such as when the interior of a vardo is cramped with folk and echoing with chatter for hour after hour, day after day. Purna was a respectable huntress, but *loud*, and her friends were louder. The pair of Outlanders were both very old, and so it was to be expected that they should be outspoken—Best's father, after all, had only grown more irascible with age. These heavily perfumed greypelts also had songs of great and wild hunts, such as Best would have scoffed at had she not lived through such mad days herself, but neither the Duchess Din nor the Count Hassan constrained themselves to tales of glory and battle. If anything, they viewed these things as ancillary to all the feasts they had eaten, the new games of chance they had invented, and the bawdy songs they had learned. It was the songs in particular that had eventually driven Best to ride atop the vardo beside Nemi that last afternoon, and she was pleased to find it not unlike flying above the endless fields of saw grass.

"There it is," said Nemi, slowing Myrkur as they came to the familiar greasy smudge on the earth where nothing would ever grow...a circle not unlike the one Best had stepped inside, back in an empty church in the Haunted Forest. "I could carry you farther—we're taking Purna's friends all the way down to the Serpent's Circle, so adding another few days won't make much difference."

"This is where we met, this is where we part," said Best. "I will walk the rest of the way alone."

"Well, shall I let Purna know so you can say your goodbyes?" asked Nemi of the Bitter Sighs, a far more sentimental sorceress than Best had presumed.

"Farewells are for the dead, and we may yet meet again in this world," said Best, taking her old pack and her new spear and dropping from the wagon. The impact sent a jolt of pain through her still-mending arm, and the pain made her smile—it reminded her she had warred against the very gods and lived to sing the song. Then, for the first time since meeting these strange companions of hers, she reached out and stroked the horned wolf. She found herself barely able to stop, once her fingers were running through Myrkur's pelt, the feeling of a live one so much different... "But I know you put stock in such words, and so I once more say good hunting to you, Nemi of the Bitter Sighs, and to this one as well."

"Good hunting, Best of the Horned Wolf Clan," said the witch, adjusting her pince-nez on her nose. "And if in my sojourns I travel through Flintland perhaps we shall indeed meet again."

"You will not find me there," said Best, shouldering her pack. "I go only to warn my clan they have been deceived by the Burnished Chain, and to meet any in the Honor Circle who would stop me from leaving once I have had my say."

"Well!" said Nemi, no doubt as impressed by Best's candor as Father Turisa, the Poison Oracle, and the council of elders would be. "Where will you go after that?"

"Where else?" said Best, casting her gaze back the way they had come. "Like my father before me, I shall go to dwell with my child until the last of my days."

CHAPTER
39

Zosia walked her dog down the quay, admiring all the damage being diligently repaired by teams of tarshirts, listening to the three-copper opera of lusty shouts and pounding pegs and sawing wood. There was scarcely a ship in Othean Bay that wasn't in a bad way from their run-in with the leviathans of the Tothan navy, but Zosia was headed for one of the few that had escaped unscathed.

Well, almost unscathed, the replacement of the bowsprit nearly complete. They had supposedly lost it when the fearless captain had steered her vessel out from under cover of fog and sailed straight into the back of the greatest sea monster seen at the Battle of Othean, a titan that had risen from the waves to pluck sailors off the Azgarothian ships in its many wavering arms and snapping claws. Now that same captain straddled the new bowsprit, fiddling with the stays... and looking up with obvious alarm as Zosia hailed her.

"That's what I like to see!" called Zosia as Choplicker flopped down to warm his lazy belly on the sunny quay. "A good captain always double-checks everything herself, makes sure there's no loose ends on the yards."

"Why, if it isn't the pipemaker Moor Clell!" said Bang, clambering back toward the prow. "Hold on, I've got your piece right here. Been keeping it safe for you."

"For me or from me, Bad Bang, and are we talking briar or a cross-bow you've got stashed up there?"

"My but you're one suspicious pipemaker," said Bang, and reaching over the lip of the prow, retrieved the pipe Zosia had given up for lost so long ago. "Would you believe this beauty made it clear up to Jex Toth with me? And that I lost it in the wreck, only to have your boy Maroto come swimming out of the Haunted Sea with it clenched in his jaw? How's that for luck?"

"All my pipes have a devil's own," said Zosia, pulling the cabernet-finished masterpiece she'd carved in her cell back at Diadem out from the apron of her dirndl and puffing the caldera back to life; she hadn't wanted to alert the pirate to her arrival, being downwind on the dock. "And Maroto never was my boy. I'll say he tried to do good. Sometimes. But that doesn't cancel out the bad."

"Well," said Bang, "there's bad and then there's—"

"You know what I found on his body?" Zosia asked, her throat closing up all over again, Choplicker's tail beating on the boards. "After he refused to see me on his deathbed, so I only got to say goodbye to his corpse? A letter, from him to me, confessing he was the one who set Imperials on my town. Not a lot of detail how, and certainly not a word of why, but I'll tell you this—I thought I knew him, but reading that... reading that I knew he meant every word he wrote. Oh, and did I mention he betrayed our whole race to the monsters who just tried to sacrifice the Star? So no, he's not my *boy*."

"Well, he was mine, and whatever your trouble with him I'm not ashamed to say it," said Bang, and if she was lying she was a better actor than the departed. "He was clumsy, though. I gave him this pipe, see, since he recognized it was one of yours and was coveting it from the first, but the poltroon broke it. I found the pieces in his pouch when I was up in that same sickroom as you, and seemed a shame to let them go up in the pyre... especially since I knew it weren't really his. It was yours."

"What'd you fix it with?" said Zosia, not really wanting to know but having to ask.

"Well, first I tried whale wax but when it heated up that didn't do, so then I worked in some birch tar, and—"

"Keep it," Zosia decided, letting go of another sliver of her long-broken heart. "I carved that for my husband, Leib Cherno. He was murdered, and it was all I had left of him in the world."

Bang looked genuinely taken aback. "I...I never thought..."

"No, pirates never do," said Zosia, and when Choplicker whined at her she sighed. "Most of us don't, as a matter of habit. But we can choose to start. I'm not chopping off your arms and legs today, Bang Lin, nor putting out your eyes. Remember that the next time the Star seems dark and cruel and hopeless."

"And you're letting me keep the pipe," said Bang, scratching her greasy tattooed brow with the stem carved from the antler of the first buck Zosia had shot on their mountain, when she and Leib had first come to Kypck. *Let it go, old woman, let it all go.*

"And I'm letting you keep the pipe," agreed Zosia. "I lost someone who held it, but so did you. A gift for the grieving."

"Thanks," Bang said as Zosia turned back down the quay. "But hey, don't you want to claim your prize before you go? I promised you a kiss if you ever caught me, and I'll not have it said that Bad Bang don't keep her word."

"You said you'd kiss me anywhere I liked, if memory serves," said Zosia. "So you can go ahead and kiss my ass."

"Ha! Fair enough!" Bang called after her. "And where are you retiring to, then, in case I ever need to commission a new briar from the greatest carver in the Star?"

"I've had my fill of retirement," said Zosia, waving her new pipe over her shoulder in farewell. "It's time to get back to work."

The first order of business was exorcising the ghost of drugged tubāq that Boris had sullied her pipe with...and on its very first bowl, too! Even in the service of busting her out of prison the crime was almost too terrible to be forgiven, but then the last time she'd seen him he hadn't seemed long for this world, and Zosia had too many troubles with the living to waste any more energy harboring grudges against the dead. Besides, her old superstition about the inaugural bowl somehow defining the fate of the pipe was just that, and best discarded.

This beautiful briar had been tainted from its very first flame, true, and for now the cheap aftertaste of whatever pungent all-sorts blend he'd used to cover up the poison impregnated the wood even if its soporific effects didn't, yes...but then she'd barely begun to break the pipe in, and so long as she kept it well fed with the good stuff from here on out that badness would soon fade into nothing. This rhum-kissed twist of the best brown vergins from the far fields of Hoggawith and figgy pu'rique fermented in Saint Pease's Parish would bless the briar with a hard black cake, and even now the lingering funk of Boris's blend only really intruded on the tongue when she let herself notice it...so she tried not to, focusing on the sweet yet tangy tingle of the smoke, smiling to see how the sea breeze carried off her modest clouds to join their grand cousins in the sky. Every true puffer knows there's nothing more important than making the most out of every pipe you're privileged enough to enjoy, in savoring every sip...but every true puffer also appreciates that neither a briar nor a blend are defined by a single smoke, and while not every bowl can be the best one's ever had, well, the one we pack tomorrow just might be...

Lunting can make a philosopher out of most anyone, but the problem with walking and smoking a pipe *and* letting your mind wander on a busy quay is it's awfully easy to let your feet wander, too; Zosia almost strolled right off into Othean Bay before she caught herself. Waving away her fragrant halo and looking clear up the docks, she took in the glory that was the Winter Palace. Towering high above that Star-famous monument to human skill and hard work was the colossal Gate-ash that had sprung up in an instant, a testament that no matter how hard mortals might struggle or how high they might climb, their achievements could never hope to touch the mysterious powers pulsing just beneath their feet. Or at their heel, as the case may be.

Anyway, it was a big fucking tree.

As she dropped her eyes from the inscrutable heavens to where Indsorith sat waiting for her on a bollard in the distance, Zosia's old knees ached anew at the prospect of all the day's activity still ahead of them. Ever since that final battle in Jex Toth she'd been losing the youthful vigor Choplicker had granted her, the twinges and arthritis returning, but if that was another price for peace she was happy to pay it. After all the time she'd spent convincing herself that he wasn't just some animal, here at the end of the song it turned out devils were indeed just like dogs—you couldn't let them get away with eating whatever they wanted all the time or they'd get fat and spoiled. Looking down at the old monster she was saddled with for the First Dark only knew how many more years, she figured it was time to put him back on a diet.

It was a long way back, so Zosia did the only thing she could and picked up her pace.

CHAPTER
40

A yawn. A scratch. A scratch for Prince. A yawn from Prince.

Diggelby rolled over in his velvety den, giving his dog a great big contented sigh—what could be better than waking up every day next to your best friend? Oh wait a tick, Diggelby knew the answer to that puzzler—being able to do that, and be Black Pope! Though really, if he had to choose only one miracle, you could bet your bottom button he'd take his devil over his day job.

Not that Prince was *his* devil anymore...he didn't think? It was all frightfully queer, as befitted a supernatural entity in the guise of an Ugrakari spaniel turning up one morning in your bed, ages after you freed the beggar the first time. He even tried firmly telling Prince to *go home*, just in case there was some confusion about the fact that Pope Diggelby did not keep devils against their will, but the darling had merely whined and licked the papal ring with his stubby little tongue. Status of Diggelby's heart at that moment: melted at such high heat it evaporated into a delicate mist.

He knew he really ought to get out of bed, chockablock day as he had ahead of him, but why be pope if you couldn't sneak a quick mope? Meeting with the Holy See was hard work, half the clowns on there not knowing Chainite scripture from a Trvevian aphorism; why didn't he promote Bishop Boris to cardinal? *Technically* clerics were supposed to have a familial connection to the church to hold such an exalted position, but if that's all it took, well, there was nothing stopping Diggelby from adopting the fellow as his son, was there?

Having someone with such creative interpretations of doctrine sit on the Holy See would be sure to stir up some healthy debate.

And that was what being alive was all about, wasn't it, asking the really difficult questions? That was why the Fallen Mother had given mortals their curiosity—if she had ever even existed at all, of course! If the point of being alive was the great eternal ponder, then the best part was that there were no real right or wrong answers, just a whole lot of wondering, and then *plop*. The joy to life is that there are questions in the first place.

"Here's a serious query for you, Princey," said Diggelby, lifting his lapdog up to hover above his chest. "Should we start our day by promoting that angry little amputee to cardinal, or should we drop graveworms and go looking for holy visions in the stained glass windows again?"

Prince barked twice, which might mean *let's do both* or might just mean *put me down, peasant*, but either way, what a great morning to be alive in the Star! Huzzah for Prince! And huzzah for Pope Diggelby the First!

EPILOGUE

The *Goddess Thief* hugged the western coast of Jex Toth, now a solid week farther out than any craft from the Star had yet ventured. The coast of Jex Toth. Captain Bang shook her head, still scarcely able to wrap it around where she was, and what she was doing. When she, Dong-won, and Niki-hyun had absconded with this boat and a pair of others just before the Battle of Othean it had been with the express purpose of sailing in the opposite direction of this place, but then the gods of wind and sea had apparently had other ideas…

Well, if not the gods of wind and sea, then certainly the gods of fucking Bang Lin sideways: a massive Raniputri fleet had appeared on the southern horizon before her trio of ships were more than a few hours into their getaway. Who knew the Dominions even *had* a fleet? They had done a quick about-face lest the Raniputris try to conscript a few more tubs into their navy, threading east through the Isles to shake them off…and then running smack into more trouble when they hit the Bitter Gulf, this time in the form of a fast-moving Flintlander flotilla. Who knew the Noreast Arm even *had* a flotilla?

Nothing for it then but to try to lose them in the brewing tempest to the north, but the persistent peckers followed them every splash of the way, until the next thing Bang knew they were rounding the upper end of Othean. Niki-hyun had begged her not to sail into that ominous fog, too, arguing they'd be better off slowing down and trying to talk terms with the pursuing Flintlanders, but that just went to show why Bad Bang was the captain: because she was always right. Now admittedly, when they had careened out of the mists and crashed directly into that sea monster Bang had momentarily doubted herself, but in the end that happy accident had earned them the eternal gratitude of several nations who would have otherwise paid to see every member of her crew hanged, so there you had it.

The captain is always right.

It bore repeating, especially in the face of such madness as the verdant seaboard they currently surveyed, Jex Toth was not only back from the briny deep but apparently here to stay. Who would have believed such a thing could not only come to pass in her lifetime, but that a fisher girl from the Cuttlefish Cays would be the first to chart it? Dong-won, ever the pragmatist, had pointed out that cartography probably didn't pay quite as well as piracy, but Bang had her suspicions that the first accurate map of the fabled land would be worth a fortune to every power on the Star. Peace was fine and dandy, but like most dandies she'd met it had a bad habit of slipping into the drink after a few of its own, and when that happened everybody was going to want to know the inlets and outcroppings of the Risen Kingdom.

Except by now they were well past the supposed borders of the Tothans' territories and still the coast kept going and going, and that was really what gave Bang the itch. Anywhere they put in now would be completely unexplored territory, and from the look of it the jungles here were as vast as the sea, and even thicker with potential plunder. That ruined city she and Maroto had discovered on their first foray into the interior had stoked her curiosity, especially since the moon-touched, basement-dwelling Tothans apparently didn't give a toss about their own ancient civilization, or material treasure in general.

She loved the sea so much it flowed in her very veins, albeit stained crimson from all the Azgarothian port she'd put away over the years, but exploring this strangely beautiful and exhilaratingly dangerous land had thrilled her in new and exciting ways...and the high probability that there were forgotten cities from the Age of Wonders ripe for the looting stirred a very familiar thirst in her purse.

But a woman had other thirsts, and other purses for that matter, and turning away from the spires of rock crowning the most recent bay she scanned over the ship, looking for a suitable candidate. As she did she unfurled her tubāq pouch and packed her cutty with a coconut brandy-cased mixture of burly, lemon vergins, and sweet leaf, but then the stupid gum she'd tried to bond the pipe with came loose and the stem popped free. Again. She was still trying to reset it when the handsome new mate they'd taken on in Othean saw what she was doing and offered to help.

"If you can get it on there good this time, you can be part of my party when we go ashore," said Bang, the wildborn holding up the bowl to peer in the shank.

"The stem has broken off inside," said Choi, as though this were some revelation. "You will not be able to bind it like this. First you must remove the broken piece, and then carve a new stem."

"Wonderful," said Bang, scowling at her bad-luck briar.

"Let me see that thing," said her cabin boy, and using one of the nails in his front pocket he began jimmying it around in the shank of the pipe. Even that mild exertion looked to be beyond his ability, his eye watering from the slight shift of his shoulder... Then he gave a triumphant cry as the broken bit of stem that had lodged in the briar came free, a tight cylinder of horn spitted on his nail. "There. Now that this busted tenon's out of the way just wiggle a reed or coral tube up in there. Won't hold forever, but should tide you over till someone good with their hands gives you what you need."

"Uh-huh," said Bang, the old dog's lines not getting any fresher. "I'd sure find that useful. Maybe I should have just invited my old friend Moor Clell along—I bet she could've done it in a trice."

"Don't even joke about letting her on the boat."

"My boat, my jokes," said Bang. "It would've been something to see her face if I'd turned you over to her, after how well that witch-egg laid you out—I mean, I don't fool easy, and up until you sat up in the berth and cracked your head on the top bunk I was *convinced* you'd fucked up and got yourself dead for real."

"Nemi said she used the same trick to escape Hoartrap back in the day," he said peevishly. "Does the Touch seem like he fools easy to you?"

"More the fool than Zosia," said Bang. "But chin up, buckaroo, Hoartrap obviously got over his apprentice playing opossum on 'im, so maybe if some dark and stormy night Cold Cobalt bumps into you at a bar she'll forgive the whole thing!"

"Not bloody likely."

"From the captain's account of their conversation it does not sound like your letter contained the full story as you relayed it to me, and also miscast your encounters on Jex Toth," said Choi. "Why give her a worse impression?"

"Because sometimes the best thing you can do for someone is let them hate you," said Maroto with that effortless charm and optimism that was his hallmark. "If this truce with Jex Toth is going to last, people are going to need a scapegoat, someone to hang the war on *other* than the Vex Assembly. That's me. I as good as told them to attack Othean, so there you go! And as for how I put things in Zosia's letter, well…okay, say I tell her the more complicated version? That I don't have any proof it was my freeing Crumbsnatcher with the wish to see her again what led to everything happening to her town—"

"*You* don't even know that's what happened," said Bang, mentally tallying all the demerits he was accruing for rehashing his sob story. A regular epicurean for discipline. Just the way she liked him. "You know you freed your devil, but you don't know it planted the notion to go after her village in the young colonel's head. No one can ever say for certain, 'cause who knows where dumb ideas even come from?"

"*I* know," said Maroto, scratching under his eye patch. "And now so does Zosia, so she can get on with her fucking life without always wondering who was to blame."

"She might have forgiven you, had you told her," said Choi, the wildborn far more tender with her partner here on the deck than she was in the privacy of the captain's quarters.

"You're right, she might've—and that would have made it worse. A lot worse." He turned the pipe over in his hand and then handed it back to Bang. "I've got to own what I've done."

"Faking your death seems a queer way of doing that," Bang pointed out.

"What can I say?" the Mighty Maroto said with a sad smile. "I learned from the best."

ACKNOWLEDGMENTS

At the end of a long journey there's nothing better than unlacing your boots, packing your bowl, and pouring yourself a powerful snoot of something brown and strong. Before you tuck in, though, there's one last thing that needs doing: thanking those who helped you out along the way. It's been a very long trek since I first set out to the Star, so there are a goodly many names in need of praise, and if you've made it this far you know brevity isn't exactly my strong suit, but I'll do my best to keep it as short and sweet as some well-aged flake smoldering away in a handsome briar volcano...

Thank you to my fearless, formidable agent, Sally Harding, who took a look at the first few chapters I did on a lark and saw the potential for something great, and thank you to everyone else at the Cooke Agency who makes my career possible—I have an amazing team.

Thank you to Jenni Hill, Anne Clarke, and Tim Holman, my editors at Orbit who took a chance on this project, and through patience, hard work, and voluminous input (and more patience!) helped nurture it from a rough stand-alone novel to the epic trilogy you've just finished. Thank you to Ellen Wright and Alex Lencicki and Bradley Englert and everyone else at Orbit for all they do to make me look so damn good. Thanks to Lauren Panepinto and her team for even more dope covers, and thanks to Tim Paul, cartographer par excellence, for turning my middle school dungeon master scribblings into a damn fine map.

Thank you to the staff and owners of Flatiron Coffee, Trve Brewing, Backcountry Pizza, Edwards Tobacco, Barlowe's, Johnny's Cigar Bar, Waterworks, War Horse, All Saints Café, (dearly departed) St. Mike's, Convoy Coffee, Ada's Technical Books and Café, the Pioneer Collective, Stone Way Café, Miir, Fremont Coffee, Fremont Brewing, Caffe Vita, Caffe Ladro, Elm Coffee Roasters, Broadcast Coffee, the Panama Hotel, the Barrel Thief, (especially) Add-a-Ball (and its crew of irregular regulars), my parents' gazebo, and any other venues and taverns I haunted while tapping away on this project. Your patience—and your beverages, pinball, and snacks—have fed this machine of guts and bone and vapors. Thanks to the Brothers of Briar, that not so secret society of worthy gentlepersons, and to the wizardly Mark Tinsky for lending his brain to this project, and his briar to my grateful rack. Thank you to all the musicians I listened to on endless repeat, thank you to the venues where I recharged my vile energies at shows, and thank you to the countless writers, filmmakers, and other artists whose visions I pillaged and plundered to stitch together my own. I've said it before and I'll say it again: I'm standing on the shoulders of frost giants.

Thank you to all my family and friends who inspired me, encouraged me, and, when necessary, put up with me, especially my parents, Bruce and Lisa, my sister Tessa, and my brother Aaron. Huge props to Raechel Dumas for being my first pair of eyes on everything, and all-around bestie. Epic thanks to Caleb Wilson, who beta-read the whole ruddy series and offered brilliant suggestions that I shamelessly appropriated. Many thanks to Molly Tanzer for providing a wealth of aid in the early stages of this project, and thanks to Allison Beckett for beta-reading the grand finale—they all helped transform the project from something with potential to something special. And thanks to John Gove for listening to me endlessly blather about it as the fumes swirled about us, and for always providing a dash of wisdom to go with a splash of scotch.

I owe a great debt to Trevor Marshall, who put me up to this project and lent me his surname, and another to Alex Bryant, who is no doubt waiting down in Old Black's Meadhall to give me a hard time for taking his first—I miss you, homie. Thanks to Selena Chambers and Josh for countless edifying evenings talking about this, that, and the other . . . and the other other. Thanks to Teo Acosta for keeping me cvlt and trve (or trying, anyway). Thanks to Paul Smith for showing me around New York, and stranger realms. Thanks to Jason Heller for being a champion, a frequent sounding board, and for turning me on to Ghost, Year of the Goat, Ides of Gemini, and so much more. Thanks to Anthony Hudson for being so cool about his alter ego Carla Rossi making a cameo in the Star. Thanks to Django and Indra and Huw and Andy and Carol and Wendy and Ian and Amy and all the other writerly folks who welcomed me to the Pacific Northwest. Thanks to Django Wexler, John Gwynne, David Dalglish, and Kameron Hurley for blurbing this series back before anyone knew who the hell I was, and another thank you to Kameron for the interview where we dropped the mask. Thanks to Adrian Collins, Rob Matheny, Phil Overby, and everyone else who reviewed the project, invited me for an interview, and/or generally signal-boosted the project—even the haters! Especially the haters? Well, let's not get carried away...

More thanks? More thanks. Thank you to everyone who saw me through another obligatory European research trip: Robby, Jimmy, and Sean for helping show me the door; Travis, Ari, and Riley for host-with-the-mosting me in Amsterdam; Willem and Joyce for Dordrecht times; Laurent, Valerie, and Hildegaard for seeing me safely through the wolf-haunted hills of Provence; my sister Tessa for offering me Florentine sanctuary (and pizza); Joseph and Sandra for leading us into Etruscan necropolii and monstrous gardens; Lisa and Joshua for braving mountainside hot springs; Jenni, Anne, Jared, Ruth, and Chris for overdosing on garlic with me in London; Ally and Mike and their cats for jaunts through York's living pagan history; and of course my faithful manservant Luke, who missed the once-in-five-lifetimes Hieronymus Bosch exhibition in Den Bosch because I told him we didn't need to book tickets in advance. Don't worry—I eventually made it there myself...and I bought him a mug.

Penultimately, crucially, thanks to Shandra, my patient partner and ideal reader, without whom this project never would have come together as it did...and who, without this project, I never would have met. It's kind of a long story and you're obviously just coming off one of those, but suffice to say we live in a weird and wonderful and sometimes lovely world, and I have a weird and wonderful always lovely partner...

And thanks to you, for reading. I mean it. Head down,

extras

orbit

meet the author

Photo Credit: Molly Tanzer

ALEX MARSHALL is a pseudonym for Jesse Bullington, acclaimed author of several novels in different genres, including *The Sad Tale of the Brothers Grossbart* and *The Enterprise of Death*. He lives in the Pacific Northwest.

if you enjoyed
A WAR IN CRIMSON EMBERS

look out for

THE TWO OF SWORDS: VOLUME ONE

by

K. J. Parker

A soldier with a gift for archery. A woman who kills without care. Two brothers, both unbeatable generals, now fighting for opposing armies. No one in the vast and once glorious United Empire remains untouched by the rift between East and West, and the war has been fought for as long as anyone can remember. Some still survive who know how it was started, but no one knows how it will end. Except, perhaps, the Two of Swords.

World Fantasy Award–winning author K. J. Parker delivers the first volume of his most ambitious work yet—the story of a war on a grand scale, told through the eyes of soldiers, politicians, victims, and heroes.

1

THE CROWN PRINCE

The draw in Rhus is to the corner of the mouth; it says so in the Book, it's the law. In Overend, they draw to the ear; in the South, it's the middle of the lower lip—hence the expression, "archer's kiss." Why Imperial law recognises three different optimum draws, given that the bow and the arrow are supposedly standardised throughout the empire, nobody knows. In Rhus, of course, they'll tell you that the corner of the mouth is the only possible draw if you actually want to hit anything. Drawing to the ear messes up your sightline down the arrow, and the Southerners do the kiss because they're too feeble to draw a hundred pounds that extra inch.

Teucer had a lovely draw, everybody said so. Old men stood him drinks because it was so perfect, and the captain made him stand in front of the beginners and do it over and over again. His loose wasn't quite so good—he had a tendency to snatch, letting go of the string rather than allowing it to slide from his fingers—which cost him valuable points in matches. Today, however, for some reason he wished he could isolate, preserve in vinegar and bottle, he was loosing exactly right. The arrow left the string without any conscious action on his part—a thought, maybe: *round about now would be a good time*, and then the arrow was in the air, bounding off to join its friends in the dead centre of the target, like a happy dog. The marker at the far end of the butts held up a yellow flag: a small one. Eight shots into the string, Teucer suddenly realised he'd shot eight inner golds, and was just two away from a possible.

He froze. In the long and glorious history of the Merebarton butts, only two possibles had ever been shot: one by a legendary figure called Old Shan, who may or may not have existed some time a hundred years ago, and one by Teucer's great-uncle Ree, who'd been a regular and served with Calojan. Nobody had had the heart to pull the arrows out of that target; it had stayed on the far right of the butts for twenty years, until the straw was completely rotten, and the rusty heads had fallen out into the nettles. Every good archer had shot a fifty. One or two in the village had shot fifty with eight or fifty with nine. A possible—fifty with ten, ten shots in the inner circle of the gold—was something completely different.

People were looking at him, and then at his target, and the line had gone quiet. A possible at one hundred yards is—well, possible; but extremely unlikely, because there's only just enough space in the inner ring for ten arrowheads. Usually what happens is that you drop in seven, maybe eight, and then the next one touches the stem of an arrow already in place on its way in and gets deflected; a quarter-inch into the outer gold if you're lucky, all the way out of the target and into the nettles if you're not. In a match, with beer or a chicken riding on it, the latter possibility tends to persuade the realistic competitor to shade his next shot just a little, to drop it safely into the outer gold and avoid the risk of a match-losing score-nought. Nobody in history anywhere had ever shot a possible in a match. But this was practice, nothing to play for except eternal glory, the chance for his name to be remembered a hundred years after his death; he had no option but to try for it. He squinted against the evening light, trying to figure out the lie of his eight shots, but the target was a hundred yards away: all he could see of the arrows was the yellow blaze of the fletchings. He considered calling hold, stopping the shoot while he walked up the range and took a closer look. That was allowed, even in a match, but to do so would be to acknowledge that he was trying for a possible, so that when he failed—

A voice in his head, which he'd never heard before, said quite clearly, *go and look*. No, I can't, he thought, and the voice didn't argue. Quite. Only an idiot argues with himself. Go and look. He took a deep breath and said, "Hold."

It came out loud, high and squeaky, but nobody laughed; instead, they laid their bows down on the grass and took a step back. Dead silence. Men he'd known all his life. Then, as he took his first stride up the range, someone whose voice he couldn't identify said, "Go on, Teuce." It was said like a prayer, as though addressed to a god—please send rain, please let my father get well. They *believed* in him. It made his stomach turn and his face go cold. He walked up the range as if to the gallows.

When he got there: not good. The marker (Pilad's uncle Sen; a quiet man, but they'd always got on well) gave him a look that said *sorry, son*, then turned away. Six arrows were grouped tight in the exact centre of the inner gold, one so close to the others that the shaft was actually flexed; God only knew how it had gone in true. The seventh was out centre-right, just cutting the line. The eighth was in clean, but high left. That meant he had to shoot two arrows into the bottom centre, into a half-moon about the size of his thumb, from a hundred yards away. He stared at it. Can't be done. It was, no pun intended, impossible.

Pilad's uncle Sen gave him a wan smile and said, "Good luck." He nodded, turned away and started back down the range.

Sen's nephew Pilad was his best friend, something he'd never quite been able to understand. Pilad was, beyond question, the glory of Merebarton. Not yet nineteen (he was three weeks older than Teucer) he was already the best stockman, the best reaper and mower, champion ploughman, best thatcher and hedge-layer; six feet tall, black-haired and brown-eyed, the only possible topic of conversation when three girls met, undisputed champion horse-breaker and second-best archer. And now consider Teucer, his best friend; shorter, ordinary-looking, awkward with girls, a good worker but a bit slow, you'd have trouble remembering him ten minutes after you'd met him, and the only man living to have shot a hundred-yard possible on Merebarton range—

He stopped, halfway between butts and firing point, and laughed. The hell with it, he thought.

Pilad was shooting second detail, so he was standing behind the line, in with a bunch of other fellows. As Teucer walked up, he noticed that Pilad was looking away, standing behind someone's shoulder, trying to make himself inconspicuous. Teucer reached the line, turned and faced the target; like the time he'd had to go and bring in the old white bull, and it had stood there glaring at him with mad eyes, daring him to take one more step. Even now he had no idea where the courage had come from that day; he'd opened the gate and gone in, a long stride directly towards certain death; on that day, the bull had come quietly, gentle as a lamb while he put the halter on, walking to heel like a good dog. Maybe, Teucer thought, when I was born Skyfather allotted me a certain number of good moments, five or six, maybe, to last me my whole life. If so, let this be one of them.

Someone handed him his bow. His fingers closed round it, and the feel of it was like coming home. He reached for the ninth arrow, stuck point first into the ground. He wasn't aware of nocking it, but it got on to the string somehow. *Just look at the target*:

that voice again, and he didn't yet know it well enough to decide whether or not it could be trusted. He drew, and he was looking straight down the arrow at a white circle on a black background. Just look at the target. He held on it for three heartbeats, and then the arrow left him.

Dead silence, for the impossibly long time it took for the arrow to get there. Pilad's uncle Sen walked to the target with his armful of flags, picked one out and lifted it. Behind Teucer, someone let out a yell they must've heard back in the village.

Well, he thought, that's forty-five with nine; good score, enough to win most matches. And still one shot in hand. Let's see what we can do.

The draw. He had a lovely draw. This time, he made himself enjoy it. To draw a hundred-pound bow, you first use and then abuse nearly every muscle and every joint in your body. There's a turning point, a hinge, where the force of the arms alone is supplemented by the back and the legs. He felt the tip of his middle finger brush against his lip, travel the length of it, until it found the far corner. Just look at the target. It doesn't matter, he told himself. *It matters*, said the voice. *But that's all right. That helps.*

He'd never thought of it like that before. It matters. And that helps. Yes, he thought, it helps, and the arrow flew.

It lifted, the way an arrow does, swimming in the slight headwind he presumed he'd allowed for, though he had no memory of doing so. It lifted, reaching the apex of its flight, and he thought: however long I live, let a part of me always be in this moment, this split second when I could've shot a hundred-yard possible; this moment at which it's still on, it hasn't missed yet, the chance, the *possibility* is still alive, so that when I'm sixty-six and half blind and a nuisance to my family, I'll still have this, the one thing that could've made me great—

Uncle Sen walked to the target. He wasn't carrying his flags.

He stood for a moment, the only thing that existed in the whole world. Then he raised both his arms and shouted.

Oh, Teucer thought; and then something hit him in the back and sent him flat on his face in the grass, and for a moment he couldn't breathe, and it *hurt*. He was thinking: who'd want to do that to me; they're supposed to be my friends. And then he was grabbed by his arms and yanked upright, and everybody was shouting in his face, and Pilad's grin was so close to his eyes he couldn't see it clearly; and he thought: I did it.

He didn't actually want to go and look, just in case there had been a mistake, but they gave him no choice; he was scooped up and planted on two bony shoulders, so that he had to claw at heads with his fingers to keep from falling off. At the butts they slid him off on to his knees, so that when he saw the target he was in an attitude of worship, like in Temple. Fair enough. Arrows nine and ten were both in, clean, not even touching the line. They looked like a bunch of daffodils, or seedlings badly in need of thinning. A possible. The only man living. And then he thought: they won't let me pull my arrows out, and they're my match set, and I can't afford to buy another one—

And Pilad, who'd been one of the bony shoulders, gave him another murderous slap on the back and said, "Nicely, Teuce, nicely," and with a deep feeling of shame and remorse he realised that Pilad meant it; no resentment, no envy, sheer joy in his friend's extraordinary achievement. (But if Pilad had been the shooter, how would he be feeling now? Don't answer that.) He felt as if he'd just betrayed his friend, stolen from him or told lies about him behind his back. He wanted to say he was sorry, but it would be too complicated to explain.

They let him go eventually. Pilad and Nical walked with him as far as the top of the lane. He explained that he wanted to check on the lambs, so he'd take a short cut across the top meadow. It's possible that they believed him. He walked the rest of the way following the line of the hedge, as though he didn't want to be seen.

It was nearly dark when he got home; there was a thin line of bright yellow light under the door and he could smell roast chicken. He grinned, and lifted the latch.

"Dad, Mum, you're not going to believe—" He stopped. They were sitting at the table, but it wasn't laid for dinner. In the middle of it lay a length of folded yellow cloth. It looked a bit like a scarf.

"This came for you," his father said.

He said it like someone had died. It was just some cloth. Oh, he thought. He took a step forward, picked it up and unfolded it. Not a scarf; a sash.

His mother had been crying. His father looked as though he'd woken up to find all the stock dead, and the wheat burned to the ground and the thatch blown off.

"I shot a possible," he said, but he knew it didn't matter.

His father frowned, as though he didn't understand the words. "That's good," he said, looking away; not at Teucer, not at the sash. "Well?" his father said suddenly. "Tell me about it."

"Later," Teucer said. He was looking at the sash. "When did this come?"

"Just after you went out. Two men, soldiers. Guess they're going round all the farms."

Well, of course. If they were raising the levy, they wouldn't make a special journey just for him. "Did they say when?"

"You got to be at the Long Ash cross, first light, day after tomorrow," his father said. "Kit and three days' rations. They're raising the whole hundred. That's all they'd say."

It went without saying they had records; the census, conducted by the Brothers every five years. They'd know his father was exactly one year overage for call-up, just as they'd known he had a son, nineteen, eligible. It would all be written down somewhere in a book; a sort of immortality, if you cared to look at it that way. Somewhere in the city, the provincial capital, strangers knew their names, knew that they existed, just as people a hundred years hence would know about Teucer from Merebarton, who'd once shot ten with ten at a hundred yards.

He wasn't the least bit hungry now. "What's for dinner?" he said.

if you enjoyed
A WAR IN CRIMSON EMBERS

look out for

SOUL OF THE WORLD

The Ascension Cycle: Book One

by

David Mealing

It is a time of revolution. In the cities, food shortages stir citizens to riots against the crown. In the wilds, new magic threatens the dominance of the tribes. And on the battlefields, even the most brilliant commanders struggle in the shadow of total war. Three lines of magic must be mastered in order to usher in a new age, and three heroes must emerge.

Sarine is an artist on the streets of New Sarresant whose secret familiar helps her uncover bloodlust and madness where she expected only revolutionary fervor.

extras

*Arak'Jur wields the power of beasts to keep his people
safe, but his strength cannot protect them
from war amongst themselves.*

*Erris is a brilliant cavalry officer trying to defend
New Sarresant from an enemy general armed with
magic she barely understands.*

*Each must learn the secrets of their power in time to
guide their people through ruin. But a greater evil
may be trying to stop them.*

1

SARINE

"Throw!" came the command from the green.

A bushel of fresh-cut blossoms sailed into the air, chased by darts and the tittering laughter of lookers-on throughout the gardens.

It took quick work with her charcoals to capture the flowing lines as they moved, all feathers and flares. Ostentatious dress was the fashion this spring; her drab grays and browns would have stood out as quite peculiar had the young nobles taken notice of her as she worked.

Just as well they didn't. Her leyline connection to a source of *Faith* beneath the palace chapel saw to that.

Sarine smirked, imagining the commotion were she to sever her bindings, to appear plain as day sitting in the middle of the green. Rasailles was a short journey southwest of New Sarresant but may as well have been half a world apart. A public park, but no mistaking for whom among the public the green was intended. The guardsmen ringing the receiving ground made clear the requirement for a certain pedigree, or at least a certain display of wealth, and she fell far short of either.

She gave her leyline tethers a quick mental check, pleased to find them holding strong. No sense being careless. It was a risk coming here, but Zi seemed to relish these trips, and sketches of the nobles were among the easiest to sell. Zi had only just materialized in front of her, stretching like a cat. He made a show of it, arching his back, blue and purple iridescent scales glittering as he twisted in the sun.

She paused midway through reaching into her pack for a fresh sheet of paper, offering him a slow clap. Zi snorted and cozied up to her feet.

It's cold. Zi's voice sounded in her head. *I'll take all the sunlight I can get.*

"Yes, but still, quite a show," she said in a hushed voice, satisfied none of the nobles were close enough to hear.

What game is it today?

"The new one. With the flowers and darts. Difficult to follow, but I believe Lord Revellion is winning."

Mmm.

A warm glow radiated through her mind. Zi was pleased. And so for that matter were the young ladies watching Lord Revellion saunter up to take his turn at the line. She returned to a cross-legged pose, beginning a quick sketch of the nobles' repartee, aiming to capture Lord Revellion's simple confidence as he charmed the ladies on the green. He was the picture of an eligible Sarresant noble: crisp-fitting blue cavalry uniform, free-flowing coal-black hair, and neatly chiseled features, enough to remind her that life was not fair. Not that a child raised on the streets of the Maw needed reminding on that point.

He called to a group of young men nearby, the ones holding the flowers. They gathered their baskets, preparing to heave, and Revellion turned, flourishing the darts he held in each hand, earning himself titters and giggles from the fops on the green. She worked to capture the moment, her charcoal pen tracing the lines of his coat as he stepped forward, ready to throw. Quick strokes for his hair, pushed back by the breeze. One simple line to suggest the concentrated poise in his face.

The crowd gasped and cheered as the flowers were tossed. Lord Revellion sprang like a cat, snapping his darts one by one in quick succession. *Thunk. Thunk. Thunk. Thunk.* More cheering. Even at this distance it was clear he had hit more than he missed, a rare enough feat for this game.

You like this one, the voice in her head sounded. Zi uncoiled, his scales flashing a burnished gold before returning to blue and purple. He cocked his head up toward her with an inquisitive look. *You could help him win, you know.*

"Hush. He does fine without my help."

She darted glances back and forth between her sketch paper and the green, trying to include as much detail as she could. The patterns of the blankets spread for the ladies as they reclined on the grass, the carefree way they laughed. Their practiced movements as they sampled fruits and cheeses, and the bowed heads of servants holding the trays on bended knees. The black charcoal medium wouldn't capture the vibrant colors of the flowers, but she could do their forms justice, soft petals scattering to the wind as they were tossed into the air.

It was more detail than was required to sell her sketches. But details made it real, for her as much as her customers. If she hadn't seen and drawn them from life, she might never have believed such abundance possible: dances in the grass, food and wine at a snap of their fingers, a practiced poise in every movement. She gave a bitter laugh, imagining the absurdity of practicing sipping your wine just so, the better to project the perfect image of a highborn lady.

Zi nibbled her toe, startling her. *They live the only lives they know,* he thought to her. His scales had taken on a deep green hue.

She frowned. She was never quite sure whether he could actually read her thoughts.

"Maybe," she said after a moment. "But it wouldn't kill them to share some of those grapes and cheeses once in a while."

She gave the sketch a last look. A decent likeness; it might fetch a half mark, perhaps, from the right buyer. She reached into her pack for a jar of sediment, applying the yellow flakes with care to avoid smudging her work. When it was done she set the paper on the grass, reclining on her hands to watch another round of darts. The next thrower fared poorly, landing only a single *thunk*. Groans from some of the onlookers, but just as many whoops and cheers. It appeared Revellion had won. The young lord pranced forward to take a deep bow, earning polite applause from across the green as servants dashed out to collect the darts and flowers for another round.

She retrieved the sketch, sliding it into her pack and withdrawing a fresh sheet. This time she'd sketch the ladies, perhaps, a show of the latest fashions for—

She froze.

Across the green a trio of men made way toward her, drawing curious eyes from the nobles as they crossed the gardens. The three of them stood out among the nobles' finery as sure as she would have done: two men in the blue and gold leather of the palace guard, one in simple brown robes. A priest.

Not all among the priesthood could touch the leylines, but she wouldn't have wagered a copper against this one having the talent, even if she wasn't close enough to see the scars on the backs of his hands to confirm it. Binder's marks, the by-product of the test administered to every child the crown could get its hands on. If this priest had the gift, he could follow her tethers whether he could see her or no.

She scrambled to return the fresh page and stow her charcoals, slinging the pack on her shoulder and springing to her feet.

Time to go? Zi asked in her thoughts.

She didn't bother to answer. Zi would keep up. At the edge of the green, the guardsmen patrolling the outer gardens turned to watch the priest and his fellows closing in. Damn. Her *Faith* would hold long enough to get her over the wall, but there wouldn't be any stores to draw on once she left the green. She'd been hoping for another hour at least, time for half a dozen more sketches and another round of games. Instead there was a damned priest on watch. She'd be lucky to escape with no more than a chase through the woods, and thank the Gods they didn't seem to have hounds or horses in tow to investigate her errant binding.

Better to move quickly, no?

She slowed mid-stride. "Zi, you know I hate—"

Shh.

Zi appeared a few paces ahead of her, his scales flushed a deep, sour red, the color of bottled wine. Without further warning her heart leapt in her chest, a red haze coloring her vision. Blood seemed to pound in her ears. Her muscles surged with raw energy, carrying her forward with a springing step that left the priest and his guardsmen behind as if they were mired in tar.

Her stomach roiled, but she made for the wall as fast as her feet could carry her. Zi was right, even if his gifts made her want to sick up the bread she'd scrounged for breakfast. The sooner she could get over the wall, the sooner she could drop her *Faith* tether and stop the priest tracking her binding. Maybe he'd think it no more than a curiosity, an errant cloud of ley-energy mistaken for something more.

She reached the vines and propelled herself up the wall in a smooth motion, vaulting the top and landing with a cat's poise on the far side. *Faith* released as soon as she hit the ground, but she kept running until her heartbeat calmed, and the red haze faded from her sight.

The sounds and smells of the city reached her before the trees cleared enough to see it. A minor miracle for there to be trees at all; the northern and southern reaches had been cut to grassland, from the trade roads to the Great Barrier between the colonies and the wildlands beyond. But the Duc-Governor had ordered a wood maintained around the palace at Rasailles, and so the axes looked elsewhere for their fodder. It made for peaceful walks, when she wasn't waiting for priests and guards to swoop down looking for signs she'd been trespassing on the green.

She'd spent the better part of the way back in relative safety. Zi's gifts were strong, and thank the Gods they didn't seem to register on the leylines. The priest gave up the chase with time enough for her to ponder the morning's games: the decadence, a hidden world of wealth and beauty, all of it a stark contrast to the sullen eyes and sunken faces of the cityfolk. Her uncle would tell her it was part of the Gods' plan, all the usual Trithetic dogma. A hard story to swallow, watching the nobles eating, laughing, and playing at their games when half the city couldn't be certain where they'd find tomorrow's meals. This was supposed to be a land of promise, a land of freedom and purpose—a New World. Remembering the opulence of Rasailles palace, it looked a lot like the old one to her. Not that she'd ever been across the sea, or anywhere in the colonies but here in New Sarresant. Still.

There was a certain allure to it, though.

It kept her coming back, and kept her patrons buying sketches whenever she set up shop in the markets. The fashions, the finery, the dream of something otherworldly almost close enough to touch. And Lord Revellion. She had to admit he was handsome, even far away. He seemed so confident, so prepared for the life he lived. What would he think of her? One thing to use her gifts and skulk her way onto the green, but that was a pale shadow of a real invitation. And that was where she fell short. Her gifts set her apart, but underneath it all she was still *her*. Not for the first time she wondered if that was enough. Could it be? Could it be enough to end up somewhere like Rasailles, with someone like Lord Revellion?

Zi pecked at her neck as he settled onto her shoulder, giving her a start. She smiled when she recovered, flicking his head.

We approach.

"Yes. Though I'm not sure I should take you to the market after you shushed me back there."

Don't sulk. It was for your protection.

"Oh, of course," she said. "Still, Uncle could doubtless use my help in the chapel, and it *is* almost midday..."

Zi raised his head sharply, his eyes flaring like a pair of hot pokers, scales flushed to match.

"Okay, okay, the market it is."

Zi cocked his head as if to confirm she was serious, then nestled down for a nap as she walked. She kept a brisk pace, taking care to avoid prying eyes that might be wondering what a lone girl was doing coming in from the woods. Soon she was back among the crowds of Southgate district, making her way toward the markets at the center of the city. Zi flushed a deep blue as she walked past the bustle of city life, weaving through the press.

Back on the cobblestone streets of New Sarresant, the lush greens and floral brightness of the royal gardens seemed like another world, foreign and strange. This was home: the sullen grays, worn wooden and brick buildings, the downcast eyes of the cityfolk as they went about the day's business. Here a gilded coach drew eyes and whispers, and not always from a place as benign as envy. She knew better than to court the attention of that sort—the hot-eyed men who glared at the nobles' backs, so long as no city watch could see.

She held her pack close, shoving past a pair of rough-looking pedestrians who'd stopped in the middle of the crowd. They gave her a dark look, and Zi raised himself up on her shoulders, giving them a snort. She rolled her eyes, as much for his bravado as theirs. Sometimes it was a good thing she was the only one who could see Zi.

As she approached the city center, she had to shove her way past another pocket of lookers-on, then another. Finally the press became too heavy and she came to a halt just outside the central square. A low rumble of whispers rolled through the crowds ahead, enough for her to know what was going on.

An execution.

She retreated a few paces, listening to the exchanges in the crowd. Not just one execution—three. Deserters from the army, which made them traitors, given the crown had declared war on the Gandsmen two seasons past. A glorious affair, meant to check a tyrant's expansion, or so they'd proclaimed in the colonial papers. All it meant in her quarters of the city was food carts diverted southward, when the Gods knew there was little enough to spare.

Voices buzzed behind her as she ducked down an alley, with a glance up and down the street to ensure she was alone. Zi swelled up, his scales pulsing as his head darted about, eyes wide and hungering.

"What do you think?" she whispered to him. "Want to have a look?"

Yes. The thought dripped with anticipation.

Well, that settled that. But this time it was her choice to empower herself, and she'd do it without Zi making her heart beat in her throat.

She took a deep breath, sliding her eyes shut.

In the darkness behind her eyelids, lines of power emanated from the ground in all directions, a grid of interconnecting strands of light. Colors and shapes surrounded the lines, fed by energy from the shops, the houses, the people of the city.

Overwhelmingly she saw the green pods of *Life*, abundant wherever people lived and worked. But at the edge of her vision she saw the red motes of *Body*, a relic of a bar fight or something of that sort. And, in the center of the city square, a shallow pool of *Faith*. Nothing like an execution to bring out belief and hope in the Gods and the unknown.

She opened herself to the leylines, binding strands of light between her body and the sources of the energy she needed.

Her eyes snapped open as *Body* energy surged through her. Her muscles became more responsive, her pack light as a feather. At the same time, she twisted a *Faith* tether around herself, fading from view.

By reflex she checked her stores. Plenty of *Faith*. Not much *Body*. She'd have to be quick. She took a step back, then bounded forward, leaping onto the side of the building. She twisted away as she kicked off the wall, spiraling out toward the roof's overhang. Grabbing hold of the edge, she vaulted herself up onto the top of the tavern in one smooth motion.

Very nice, Zi thought to her. She bowed her head in a flourish, ignoring his sarcasm.

Now, can we go?

Urgency flooded her mind. Best not to keep Zi waiting when he got like this. She let *Body* dissipate but maintained her shroud of *Faith* as she walked along the roof of the tavern. Reaching the edge, she lowered herself to have a seat atop a window's overhang as she looked down into the square. With luck she'd avoid catching the attention of any more priests or other binders in the area, and that meant she'd have the best seat in the house for these grisly proceedings.

She set her pack down beside her and pulled out her sketching materials. Might as well make a few silvers for her time.

orbit

Follow us:

f **/orbitbooksUS**

𝕏 **/orbitbooks**

▶ **/orbitbooks**

Join our mailing list
to receive alerts on our
latest releases and deals.

orbitbooks.net

Enter our monthly
giveaway for the chance
to win some epic prizes.

orbitloot.com